GULLIVER'S TRAVELS

SECOND EDITION

An Authoritative Text
The Correspondence of Swift
Pope's Verses on Gulliver's Travels
Critical Essays

W. W. NORTON & COMPANY, INC.
also publishes

THE NORTON ANTHOLOGY OF AMERICAN LITERATURE
edited by Nina Baym et al.

THE NORTON ANTHOLOGY OF CONTEMPORARY FICTION
edited by R. V. Cassill

THE NORTON ANTHOLOGY OF ENGLISH LITERATURE
edited by M. H. Abrams et al.

THE NORTON ANTHOLOGY OF LITERATURE BY WOMEN
edited by Sandra M. Gilbert and Susan Gubar

THE NORTON ANTHOLOGY OF MODERN POETRY
edited by Richard Ellmann and Robert O'Clair

THE NORTON ANTHOLOGY OF POETRY
edited by Alexander W. Allison et al.

THE NORTON ANTHOLOGY OF SHORT FICTION
edited by R. V. Cassill

THE NORTON ANTHOLOGY OF WORLD MASTERPIECES
edited by Maynard Mack et al.

THE NORTON FACSIMILE OF
THE FIRST FOLIO OF SHAKESPEARE
prepared by Charlton Hinman

THE NORTON INTRODUCTION TO LITERATURE
edited by Carl E. Bain, Jerome Beaty, and J. Paul Hunter

THE NORTON INTRODUCTION TO THE SHORT NOVEL
edited by Jerome Beaty

THE NORTON READER
edited by Arthur M. Eastman et al.

THE NORTON SAMPLER
edited by Thomas Cooley

A NORTON CRITICAL EDITION

JONATHAN SWIFT

GULLIVER'S TRAVELS

AN AUTHORITATIVE TEXT
THE CORRESPONDENCE OF SWIFT
POPE'S VERSES ON *GULLIVER'S TRAVELS*
CRITICAL ESSAYS

SECOND EDITION

Edited by

ROBERT A. GREENBERG

QUEENS COLLEGE

W · W · NORTON & COMPANY

New York · London

W. W. Norton & Company, Inc., 500 Fifth Avenue, New York, NY 10110
W. W. Norton & Company Ltd., 10 Coptic Street London WC1A 1PU

Library of Congress Catalog Card No. 78–116116

Printed in the United States of America

5 6 7 8 9 0

ISBN 0-393-09941-5

CONTENTS

PREFACE TO THE SECOND EDITION

The publishing of a second edition has made it possible to do several things: most importantly, to give representation to the works on Swift and the *Travels* that have appeared during the last decade. These materials are reflected in the seven commentaries added to the critical section, as well as in the bibliography, which has been revised and brought up to date. There is also in this edition a new section consisting of the five poems, "Verses on *Gulliver's Travels*," that were in the front matter of the second edition of the *Travels* in 1727. These poems in various genres from the hand of Pope (guided probably by Gay and Arbuthnot), besides being a delight in themselves, are helpful in suggesting how this most remarkable of volumes was received by Swift's own circle. This motif has been carried into the section of correspondence, which has been enlarged to include more of Swift and to introduce also the voices of Pope, Gay, and Arbuthnot, who record their own and London's reactions. I am indebted to the Clarendon Press for permission to use Harold Williams' monumental edition of the *Correspondence* as the basis of my text of Swift's letters. Finally, I have taken this opportunity to increase somewhat the annotations to the text and to the accompanying background and critical materials.

New York City
February, 1970

Robert A. Greenberg

PREFACE

This volume represents a departure from the usual *Gulliver* in that perhaps a third of it consists of accessory materials of one order or another. The largest and most important of these is a section of critical essays, primarily interpretive, on Swift, his method, and the *Travels* both generally and in part. The essays are supplemented by a selection from Swift's correspondence, made for its relevance as commentary on the *Travels*, and by an annotated bibliography of some fifty important studies. Running throughout is a series of annotations on the text designed to clarify topical references and a variety of minor details. Put most simply, my hope has been to provide a careful and reliable text of *Gulliver's Travels* in an edition that the reader will find both challenging and useful.

Choosing the critical comment presented a number of difficulties, largely because of the diversity and abundance at hand. Thus, the great temptation was to include criticism of this quality:

> . . . as for the moral [of Book IV], I think it horrible, shameful, unmanly, blasphemous; and giant and great as this Dean is, I say we should hoot him. . . . a monster gibbering shrieks, and gnashing imprecations against mankind—tearing down all shreds of modesty, past all sense of manliness and shame; filthy in word, filthy in thought, furious, raging, obscene.

This is Thackeray, and mid-nineteenth century, and so of some historical value; moreover, as an obvious instance of what to avoid, it also has a certain instructive, if cautionary, value. But it and its type were excluded, in the end, on the assumption that the reader would best be served by offering him only such criticism as he could honestly consider and respect (whether he ultimately agrees with a given approach or conclusion is, of course, another matter). This assumption, I trust, has controlled all my choices. Paradoxically, there was, too, a danger from the opposite direction: that the collection as finally constituted might prove a miscellaneous gathering of notable *Gulliver* commentary, without other plan or pattern. The alternative that seemed to answer best was to include criticism that dealt primarily with the major issues of the book, but at the same time interpreted and assessed them from many varying points of view. The final discriminations and judgments would thus rest with the reader. The issues themselves seemed clearly definable: the unity and coherence of the total work; the meaning and method of Book IV, and, relatedly, the question of Swift's misanthropy; Swift's outlook generally; the nature, quality, and function of his satire.

The text I have used is substantially that of Volume III of the Dublin edition of Swift's works, published in 1735 by George Faulkner. It is remarkable for having Swift's approval and incorporating his corrections and revisions of the earlier London editions. His estimate of these last was clear enough: "change of Style, new things foysted in, that are false facts, and I know not what, is very provoking. . . . Besides, the whole Sting is taken out in severall passages, in order to soften them. Thus the Style is debased, the humour quite lost, and the matter insipid." In several instances I have also drawn on the corrections and additions variously compiled by Swift's friend, Charles Ford.

I must state my indebtedness to each of the authors represented in the critical section, and especially to Professor R. S. Crane for permission to include his unpublished essay; to Professor M. H. Abrams, of Cornell University, for his interest and willingness to counsel; and most of all, to my wife, Dolores Greenberg, for supports that exceed my ability to reckon.

Ithaca, New York
February, 1961

Robert A. Greenberg

THE TEXT OF GULLIVER'S TRAVELS

CAPT. LEMUEL GULLIVER
Splendide Mendax. Hor.

VOLUME III.

Of the AUTHOR's

WORKS.

CONTAINING,

TRAVELS

INTO SEVERAL

Remote Nations of the WORLD.

In Four PARTS, *viz.*

I. A Voyage to LILLIPUT.

II. A Voyage to BROBDINGNAG.

III. A Voyage to LAPUTA, BALNIBARBI, LUGGNAGG, GLUBBDUBDRIB and JAPAN.

IV. A Voyage to the COUNTRY of the HOUYHNHNMS.

By *LEMUEL GULLIVER*, first a Surgeon, and then a CAPTAIN of several SHIPS.

——— ——— *Retroq;*
Vulgus abhorret ab his.

In this Impression several Errors in the *London* and *Dublin* Editions are corrected.

DUBLIN:

Printed by and for GEORGE FAULKNER, Printer and Bookseller, in *Essex-Street*, opposite to the Bridge. MDCCXXXV.

A LETTER

from Capt. Gulliver, to his Cousin Sympson

I hope you will be ready to own publickly, whenever you shall be called to it, that by your great and frequent Urgency you prevailed on me to publish a very loose and uncorrect Account of my Travels; with Direction to hire some young Gentlemen of either University to put them in Order, and correct the Style, as my Cousin *Dampier*[1] did by my Advice, in his Book called, A *Voyage round the World*. But I do not remember I gave you Power to consent, that any thing should be omitted, and much less that any thing should be inserted: Therefore, as to the latter, I do here renounce every thing of that Kind; particularly a Paragraph about her Majesty the late Queen *Anne*, of most pious and glorious Memory; although I did reverence and esteem her more than any of human Species. But you, or your Interpolator, ought to have considered, that as it was not my Inclination, so was it not decent to praise any Animal of our Composition before my Master *Houyhnhnm:* And besides, the Fact was altogether false; for to my Knowledge, being in *England* during some Part of her Majesty's Reign, she did govern by a chief Minister; nay, even by two successively; the first whereof was the Lord of *Godolphin*, and the second the Lord of *Oxford;* so that you have made me *say the thing that was not*. Likewise, in the Account of the Academy of Projectors, and several Passages of my Discourse to my Master *Houyhnhnm*, you have either omitted some material Circumstances, or minced or changed them in such a Manner, that I do hardly know mine own Work. When I formerly hinted to you something of this in a Letter, you were pleased to answer, that you were afraid of giving Offence; that People in Power were very watchful over the Press; and apt not only to interpret, but to punish every thing

[1] William Dampier (1652-1715), a noted explorer whose books on travel were widely read. Swift may have patterned some of Gulliver's traits after him.

which looked like an *Inuendo* (as I think you called it.) But pray, how could that which I spoke so many Years ago, and at above five Thousand Leagues distance, in another Reign, be applyed to any of the *Yahoos*, who now are said to govern the Herd; especially, at a time when I little thought on or feared the Unhappiness of living under them. Have not I the most Reason to complain, when I see these very *Yahoos* carried by *Houyhnhnms* in a Vehicle, as if these were Brutes, and those the rational Creatures? And, indeed, to avoid so monstrous and detestable a Sight, was one principal Motive of my Retirement hither.

Thus much I thought proper to tell you in Relation to your self, and to the Trust I reposed in you.

I do in the next Place complain of my own great Want of Judgment, in being prevailed upon by the Intreaties and false Reasonings of you and some others, very much against mine own Opinion, to suffer my Travels to be published. Pray bring to your Mind how often I desired you to consider, when you insisted on the Motive of *publick Good*; that the *Yahoos* were a species of Animals utterly incapable of Amendment by Precepts or Examples: And so it hath proved; for instead of seeing a full Stop put to all Abuses and Corruptions, at least in this little Island, as I had Reason to expect: Behold, after above six Months Warning, I cannot learn that my Book hath produced one single Effect according to mine Intentions: I desired you would let me know by a Letter, when Party and Faction were extinguished; Judges learned and upright; Pleaders honest and modest, with some Tincture of common Sense; and *Smithfield* blazing with Pyramids of Law-Books; the young Nobility's Education entirely changed; the Physicians banished; the Female *Yahoos* abounding in Virtue, Honour, Truth and good Sense; Courts and Levees of great Ministers thoroughly weeded and swept; Wit, Merit and Learning rewarded; all Disgracers of the Press in Prose and Verse, condemned to eat nothing but their own Cotten, and quench their Thirst with their own Ink. These, and a Thousand other Reformations, I firmly counted upon by your Encouragement; as indeed they were plainly deducible from the Precepts delivered in my Book. And, it must be owned that seven Months were a sufficient Time to correct every Vice and Folly to which *Yahoos* are subject; if their Natures had been capable of the least Disposition to Virtue or Wisdom: Yet so far have you been from answering mine Expectation in any of your

Letters; that on the contrary, you are loading our Carrier every Week with Libels, and Keys, and Reflections, and Memoirs, and Second Parts; wherein I see myself accused of reflecting upon great States-Folk; of degrading human Nature, (for so they have still the Confidence to stile it) and of abusing the Female Sex. I find likewise, that the Writers of those Bundles are not agreed among themselves; for some of them will not allow me to be Author of mine own Travels; and others make me Author of Books to which I am wholly a Stranger.[2]

I find likewise, that your Printer hath been so careless as to confound the Times, and mistake the Dates of my several Voyages and Returns; neither assigning the true Year, or the true Month, or Day of the Month: And I hear the original Manuscript is all destroyed, since the Publication of my Book. Neither have I any Copy left; however, I have sent you some Corrections, which you may insert, if ever there should be a second Edition: And yet I cannot stand to them, but shall leave that Matter to my judicious and candid Readers, to adjust it as they please.

I hear some of our Sea-*Yahoos* find Fault with my Sea-Language, as not proper in many Parts, nor now in Use. I cannot help it. In my first Voyages, while I was young, I was instructed by the oldest Mariners, and learned to speak as they did. But I have since found that the Sea-*Yahoos* are apt, like the Land ones, to become new fangled in their Words; which the latter change every Year; insomuch, as I remember upon each Return to mine own Country, their old Dialect was so altered, that I could hardly understand the new. And I observe, when any *Yahoo* comes from *London* out of Curiosity to visit me at mine own House, we neither of us are able to deliver our Conceptions in a Manner intelligible to the other.

If the Censure of *Yahoos* could any Way affect me, I should have great Reason to complain, that some of them are so bold as to think my Book of Travels a meer Fiction out of mine own Brain; and have gone so far as to drop Hints, that the *Houyhnhnms*, and *Yahoos* have no more Existence than the Inhabitants of *Utopia*.

Indeed I must confess, that as to the People of *Lilliput*, *Brobdingrag*, (for so the Word should have been spelt, and not

[2] The immediate success of the *Travels* inspired several publishers to issue keys and continuations; none came from Swift.

erroneously *Brobdingnag*) and *Laputa;* I have never yet heard of any *Yahoo* so presumptuous as to dispute their Being, or the Facts I have related concerning them; because the Truth immediately strikes every Reader with Conviction. And, is there less Probability in my Account of the *Houyhnhnms* or *Yahoos*, when it is manifest as to the latter, there are so many Thousands even in this City, who only differ from their Brother Brutes in *Houyhnhnmland*, because they use a Sort of a *Jabber*, and do not go naked. I wrote for their Amendment, and not their Approbation. The united Praise of the whole Race would be of less Consequence to me, than the neighing of those two degenerate *Houyhnhnms* I keep in my Stable; because, from these, degenerate as they are, I still improve in some Virtues, without any Mixture of Vice.

Do these miserable Animals presume to think that I am so far degenerated as to defend my Veracity; *Yahoo* as I am, it is well known through all *Houyhnhnmland*, that by the Instructions and Example of my illustrious Master, I was able in the Compass of two Years (although I confess with the utmost Difficulty) to remove that infernal Habit of Lying, Shuffling, Deceiving, and Equivocating, so deeply rooted in the very Souls of all my Species; especially the *Europeans*.

I have other Complaints to make upon this vexatious Occasion; but I forbear troubling myself or you any further. I must freely confess, that since my last Return, some Corruptions of my *Yahoo* Nature have revived in me by conversing with a few of your Species, and particularly those of mine own Family, by an unavoidable Necessity; else I should never have attempted so absurd a Project as that of reforming the *Yahoo* Race in this Kingdom; but, I have now done with all such visionary Schemes for ever.

April 2, 1727.

THE PUBLISHER TO THE READER

The author of these Travels, *Mr. Lemuel Gulliver*,[1] is my antient and intimate Friend; there is likewise some Relation between us by the Mother's Side. About three Years ago Mr. *Gulliver* growing weary of the Concourse of curious People coming to him at his House in *Redriff*, made a small Purchase of Land, with a convenient House, near *Newark*, in *Nottinghamshire*, his native Country; where he now lives retired, yet in good Esteem among his Neighbours.

Although Mr. *Gulliver* were born in *Nottinghamshire*, where his Father dwelt, yet I have heard him say, his Family came from *Oxfordshire;* to confirm which, I have observed in the Church-Yard at *Banbury*, in that County, several Tombs and Monuments of the *Gullivers*.

Before he quitted *Redriff*, he left the Custody of the following Papers in my Hands, with the Liberty to dispose of them as I should think fit. I have carefully perused them three Times; The Style is very plain and simple; and the only Fault I find is, that the Author, after the Manner of Travellers, is a little too circumstantial. There is an Air of Truth apparent through the whole; and indeed the Author was so distinguished for his Veracity, that it became a Sort of Proverb among his Neighbors at *Redriff*, when any one affirmed a Thing, to say, it was as true as if Mr. *Gulliver* had spoke it.

By the Advice of several worthy Persons, to whom, with the Author's Permission, I communicated these Papers, I now venture to send them into the World; hoping they may be, at least for some time, a better Entertainment to our young Noblemen, than the common Scribbles of Politicks and Party.

[1] Gulliver's initial name carries perhaps a Biblical resonance: see Proverbs 31 for the wise counsel of King Lemuel.

This Volume would have been at least twice as large, if I had not made bold to strike out innumerable Passages relating to the Winds and Tides, as well as to the Variations and Bearings in the several Voyages; together with the minute Descriptions of the Management of the Ship in Storms, in the Style of Sailors: Likewise the Account of the Longitudes and Latitudes; wherein I have Reason to apprehend that Mr. *Gulliver* may be a little dissatisfied: But I was resolved to fit the Work as much as possible to the general Capacity of Readers. However, if my own Ignorance in Sea-Affairs shall have led me to commit some Mistakes, I alone am answerable for them: And if any Traveller hath a Curiosity to see the whole Work at large, as it came from the Hand of the Author, I will be ready to gratify him.

As for any further Particulars relating to the Author, the Reader will receive Satisfaction from the first Pages of the Book.

RICHARD SYMPSON

CONTENTS

PART I: A *Voyage to Lilliput*

PART IV: *A Voyage to the Country of the Houyhnhnms*

PART I A VOYAGE TO LILLIPUT

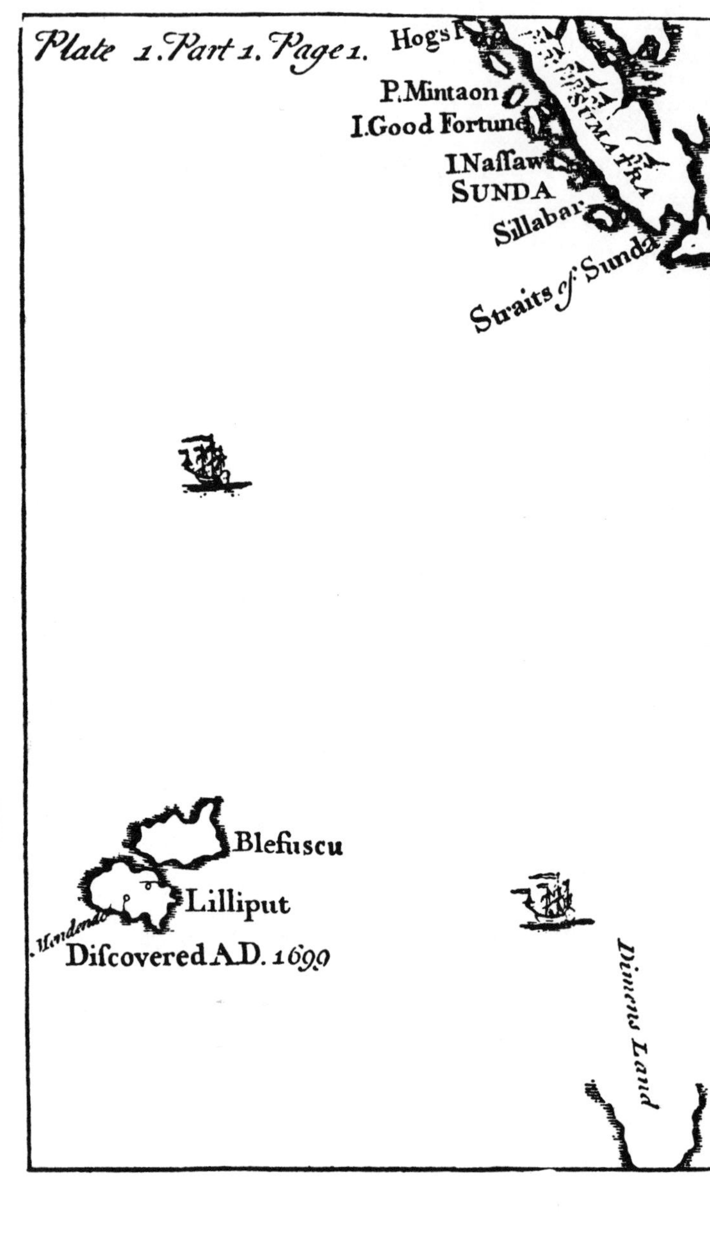
Plate 1. Part 1. Page 1.
Hogs I.
P. Mintaon
I. Good Fortune
I. Nassaw
SUNDA
Sillabar
Straits of Sunda
Blefuscu
Lilliput
Discovered A.D. 1699
Dimens Land

CHAPTER I

The Author giveth some Account of himself and Family; his first Inducements to travel. He is shipwrecked, and swims for his Life; gets safe on shoar in the Country of Lilliput; *is made a Prisoner, and carried up the Country.*

My Father had a small Estate in *Nottinghamshire;* I was the Third of five Sons. He sent me to *Emanuel-College* in *Cambridge,* at Fourteen Years old, where I resided three Years, and applied my self close to my Studies: But the Charge of maintaining me (although I had a very scanty Allowance) being too great for a narrow Fortune; I was bound Apprentice to Mr. *James Bates,* an eminent Surgeon in *London,* with whom I continued four Years; and my Father now and then sending me small Sums of Money, I laid them out in learning Navigation, and other Parts of the Mathematicks, useful to those who intend to travel, as I always believed it would be some time or other my Fortune to do. When I left Mr. *Bates,* I went down to my Father; where, by the Assistance of him and my Uncle *John,* and some other Relations, I got Forty Pounds, and a Promise of Thirty Pounds a Year to maintain me at *Leyden:*[1] There I studied Physick two Years and seven Months, knowing it would be useful in long Voyages.

Soon after my Return from *Leyden,* I was recommended by my good Master Mr. *Bates,* to be Surgeon to the *Swallow,* Captain *Abraham Pannell* Commander; with whom I continued three Years and a half, making a Voyage or two into the *Levant* and some other Parts. When I came back, I resolved to settle in *London,* to which Mr. *Bates,* my Master, encouraged me; and by him I was recommended to several Patients. I took Part of a small House in the *Old Jury;* and being advised to alter my Condition, I married Mrs. *Mary Burton,* second Daughter to Mr. *Edmond Burton,* Hosier, in

[1] The University of Leyden, important as a center for the study of medicine.

Newgate-street, with whom I received four Hundred Pounds for a Portion.

But, my good Master *Bates* dying in two Years after, and I having few Friends, my Business began to fail; for my Conscience would not suffer me to imitate the bad Practice of too many among my Brethren. Having therefore consulted with my Wife, and some of my Acquaintance, I determined to go again to Sea. I was Surgeon successively in two Ships, and made several Voyages, for six Years, to the *East* and *West-Indies*; by which I got some Addition to my Fortune. My Hours of Leisure I spent in reading the best Authors, ancient and modern; being always provided with a good Number of Books; and when I was ashore, in observing the Manners and Dispositions of the People, as well as learning their Language; wherein I had a great Facility by the Strength of my Memory.

The last of these Voyages not proving very fortunate, I grew weary of the Sea, and intended to stay at home with my Wife and Family. I removed from the *Old Jury* to *Fetter Lane,* and from thence to *Wapping,* hoping to get Business among the Sailors; but it would not turn to account. After three Years Expectation that things would mend, I accepted an advantageous Offer from Captain *William Prichard,* Master of the *Antelope,* who was making a Voyage to the *South-Sea.* We set sail from *Bristol, May* 4th, 1699 and our Voyage at first was very prosperous.

It would not be proper for some Reasons, to trouble the Reader with the Particulars of our Adventures in those Seas: Let it suffice to inform him, that in our Passage from thence to the *East-Indies,* we were driven by a violent Storm to the North-west of *Van Diemen's* Land. By an Observation, we found ourselves in the Latitude of 30 Degrees 2 Minutes South. Twelve of our Crew were dead by immoderate Labour, and ill Food; the rest were in a very weak Condition. On the fifth of *November,* which was the beginning of Summer in those Parts, the Weather being very hazy, the Seamen spyed a Rock, within half a Cable's length of the Ship; but the Wind was so strong, that we were driven directly upon it, and immediately split. Six of the Crew, of whom I was one, having let down the Boat into the Sea, made a Shift to get clear of the Ship, and the Rock. We rowed by my Computation, about three Leagues, till we were able to work no longer, being already spent with Labour while we were in the Ship. We therefore trusted ourselves to the Mercy of the Waves; and in about half an Hour the Boat was overset by a sudden Flurry from the North. What became of my Companions in the Boat, as well as of those who escaped on the Rock, or were left in the Vessel, I cannot tell; but conclude they were all lost. For my own Part, I swam as Fortune directed me, and was pushed forward by Wind and Tide. I often let my Legs drop, and could feel no Bottom; But when I was almost gone, and able to struggle no longer, I found myself within my Depth; and by this Time the Storm was much abated. The Declivity was so small, that I walked near a Mile before I got to the Shore, which I conjectured was about Eight o'Clock in the Evening. I then advanced forward near half a Mile, but could not discover any Sign of Houses or Inhabitants; at least I was in so weak a Condition, that I did not observe them. I was extremely tired, and with that, and the Heat of the Weather, and about half a Pint of Brandy that I drank as I left the Ship, I found my self much inclined to sleep. I lay down on the Grass, which was very short and soft; where I slept sounder than ever I remember to have done in my Life, and as I reckoned, above Nine Hours; for when I awaked, it was just Day-light. I attempted to rise, but was not able to stir: For as I happened to lie on my Back, I found my Arms and Legs were strongly fastened on each Side to the Ground; and my Hair, which was long and thick, tied down in the same Manner. I likewise felt several slender Ligatures across my Body, from my Armpits to my Thighs. I could only look upwards; the Sun began to grow hot, and the Light offended my Eyes. I heard a confused Noise about me, but in the Posture I lay, could see nothing except the Sky. In a little time I felt something alive moving on my left Leg, which advancing gently forward over my Breast, came almost up to my Chin; when bending my Eyes downwards as much as I could, I perceived it to be a human Creature not six Inches high,[2] with a Bow and Arrow in his Hands, and a Quiver at his Back. In the mean time, I felt at least Forty more of the same Kind (as I conjectured) following the first. I was in the utmost Astonishment, and roared so loud, that they all ran back in a Fright; and some of them, as I was afterwards told, were hurt with the Falls they got by leaping from my Sides upon the Ground. However, they

[2] The scale of Lilliput to Gulliver's world is generally one to twelve. If this creature is a typical Lilliputian, then Gulliver is somewhat under six feet tall.

soon returned; and one of them, who ventured so far as to get a full Sight of my Face, lifting up his Hands and Eyes by way of Admiration, cryed out in a shrill, but distinct Voice, *Hekinah Degul:* The others repeated the same Words several times, but I then knew not what they meant. I lay all this while, as the Reader may believe, in great Uneasiness; At length, struggling to get loose, I had the Fortune to break the Strings, and wrench out the Pegs that fastened my left Arm to the Ground; for, by lifting it up to my Face, I discovered the Methods they had taken to bind me; and, at the same time, with a violent Pull, which gave me excessive Pain, I a little loosened the Strings that tied down my Hair on the left Side; so that I was just able to turn my Head about two Inches. But the Creatures ran off a second time, before I could seize them; whereupon there was a great Shout in a very shrill Accent; and after it ceased, I heard one of them cry aloud, *Tolgo Phonac;* when in an Instant I felt above an Hundred Arrows discharged on my left Hand, which pricked me like so many Needles; and besides, they shot another Flight into the Air, as we do Bombs in *Europe;* whereof many, I suppose, fell on my Body, (though I felt them not) and some on my Face, which I immediately covered with my left Hand. When this Shower of Arrows was over, I fell a groaning with Grief and Pain; and then striving again to get loose, they discharged another Volly larger than the first; and some of them attempted with Spears to stick me in the Sides; but, by good Luck, I had on me a Buff Jerkin, which they could not pierce. I thought it the most prudent Method to lie still; and my Design was to continue so till Night, when my left Hand being already loose, I could easily free myself: And as for the Inhabitants, I had Reason to believe I might be a Match for the greatest Armies they could bring against me, if they were all of the same Size with him that I saw. But Fortune disposed otherwise of me. When the People observed I was quiet, they discharged no more Arrows: But by the Noise increasing, I knew their Numbers were greater; and about four Yards from me, over-against my right Ear, I heard a Knocking for above an Hour, like People at work; when turning my Head that Way, as well as the Pegs and Strings would permit me, I saw a Stage erected about a Foot and a half from the Ground, capable of holding four of the Inhabitants, with two or three Ladders to mount it: From whence one of them, who seemed to be a Person of Quality, made me a long Speech, whereof I understood not one Syllable. But I should have mentioned, that before the principal Person began his Oration, he cryed out three times *Langro Dehul san*: (these Words and the former were afterwards repeated and explained to me.) Whereupon immediately about fifty of the Inhabitants came, and cut the Strings that fastened the left side of my Head, which gave me the Liberty of turning it to the right, and of observing the Person and Gesture of him who was to speak. He appeared to be of a middle Age, and taller than any of the other three who attended him; whereof one was a Page, who held up his Train, and seemed to be somewhat longer than my middle Finger; the other two stood one on each side to support him. He acted every part of an Orator; and I could observe many Periods of Threatnings, and others of Promises, Pity and Kindness. I answered in a few Words, but in the most submissive Manner, lifting up my left Hand and both my eyes to the Sun, as calling him for a Witness; and being almost famished with Hunger, having not eaten a Morsel for some Hours before I left the Ship, I found the Demands of Nature so strong upon me, that I could not forbear shewing my Impatience (perhaps against the strict Rules of Decency) by putting my Finger frequently on my Mouth, to signify that I wanted Food. The *Hurgo* (for so they call a great Lord, as I afterwards learnt) understood me very well: He descended from the Stage, and commanded that several Ladders should be applied to my Sides, on which above an hundred of the Inhabitants mounted, and walked towards my Mouth, laden with Baskets full of Meat, which had been provided and sent thither by the King's Orders upon the first Intelligence he received of me. I observed there was the Flesh of several Animals, but could not distinguish them by the Taste. There were Shoulders, Legs, and Loins shaped like those of Mutton, and very well dressed, but smaller than the Wings of a Lark. I eat them by two or three at a Mouthful; and took three Loaves at a time, about the bigness of Musket Bullets. They supplyed me as fast as they could, shewing a thousand Marks of Wonder and Astonishment at my Bulk and Appetite. I then made another Sign that I wanted Drink. They found by my eating that a small Quantity would not suffice me; and being a most ingenious People, they slung up with great Dexterity one of their largest Hogsheads; then rolled it towards my Hand, and beat out the Top; I drank it off at a Draught, which I might well do, for it hardly held half a Pint, and tasted like a small Wine of *Burgundy*, but much more delicious. They brought me a second Hogshead, which I drank in the same Manner, and made Signs for more, but they had none to give me. When I had performed these Wonders, they shouted for Joy, and danced upon my Breast, repeating several times as they did at first, *Hekinah Degul*. They made me a Sign that I should throw down the two Hogsheads, but first warned the People below to stand out of the Way, crying aloud, *Borach Mivola*; and when they saw the Vessels in the Air, there was an universal Shout of *Hekinah Degul*. I confess I was often tempted, while they were passing backwards and forwards on my Body, to seize Forty or Fifty of the first that came in my Reach, and dash them against the Ground. But the Remembrance of what I had felt, which probably might not be the worst they could do; and the Promise of Honour I made them, for so I interpreted my submissive Behaviour, soon drove out those Imaginations. Besides, I now considered my self as bound by the Laws of Hospitality to a People who had treated me with so much Expence and Magnificence. However, in my Thoughts I could not sufficiently wonder at the Intrepidity of these diminutive Mortals, who durst venture to mount and walk on my Body, while one of my Hands was at Liberty, without trembling at the very Sight of so prodigious a Creature as I must appear to them. After some time, when they observed that I made no more Demands for Meat, there appeared before me a Person of high Rank from his Imperial Majesty. His Excellency having mounted on the Small of my Right Leg, advanced forwards up to my Face, with about a Dozen of his Retinue; And producing his Credentials under the Signet Royal, which he applied close to my Eyes, spoke about ten Minutes, without any Signs of Anger, but with a kind of determinate Resolution; often pointing forwards, which, as I afterwards found, was towards the Capital City, about half a Mile distant, whither it was agreed by his Majesty in Council that I must be conveyed. I answered in few Words, but to no Purpose, and made a Sign with my Hand that was loose, putting it to the other, (but over his Excellency's Head, for Fear of hurting him or his Train) and then to my own Head and Body, to signify that I desired my Liberty. It appeared that he understood me well enough; for he shook his Head by way of Disapprobation, and held his Hand in a Posture to shew that I must be carried as a Prisoner. However, he made other Signs to let me understand that I should have Meat and Drink enough, and very good Treatment. Whereupon I once more thought of attempting to break my Bonds; but again, when I felt the Smart of their Arrows upon my Face and Hands, which were all in Blisters, and many of the Darts still sticking in them; and observing likewise that the Number of my Enemies encreased; I gave Tokens to let them know that they might do with me what they pleased. Upon this, the *Hurgo* and his Train withdrew, with much Civility and chearful Countenances. Soon after I heard a general Shout, with frequent Repetitions of the Words, *Peplom Selan*, and I felt great Numbers of the People on my Left Side relaxing the Cords to such a Degree, that I was able to turn upon my Right, and to ease my self with making Water; which I very plentifully did, to the great Astonishment of the People, who conjecturing by my Motions what I was going to do, immediately opened to the right and left on that Side, to avoid the Torrent which fell with such Noise and Violence from me. But before this, they had dawbed my Face and both my Hands with a sort of Ointment very pleasant to the Smell, which in a few Minutes removed all the Smart of their Arrows. These Circumstances, added to the Refreshment I had received by their Victuals and Drink, which were very nourishing, disposed me to sleep. I slept about eight Hours as I was afterwards assured; and it was no Wonder; for the Physicians, by the Emperor's Order, had mingled a sleeping Potion in the Hogsheads of Wine.

It seems that upon the first Moment I was discovered sleeping on the Ground after my Landing, the Emperor had early Notice of it by an Express; and determined in Council that I should be tyed in the Manner I have related, (which was done in the Night while I slept) that Plenty of Meat and Drink should be sent me, and a Machine prepared to carry me to the Capital City.

This Resolution perhaps may appear very bold and dangerous, and I am confident would not be imitated by any Prince in *Europe* on the like Occasion; however, in my Opinion it was extremely Prudent as well as Generous. For supposing these People had endeavoured to kill me with their Spears and Arrows while I was asleep; I should certainly have awaked with the first Sense of Smart, which might so far have rouzed my Rage and Strength, as to enable me to break the Strings wherewith I was tyed; after which, as they were not able to make Resistance, so they could expect no Mercy.

These People are most excellent Mathematicians, and arrived to a great Perfection in Mechanicks by the Countenance and Encouragement of the Emperor, who is a renowned Patron of Learning. This Prince hath several Machines fixed on Wheels, for the Carriage of Trees and other great Weights. He often buildeth his largest Men of War, whereof some are Nine Foot long, in the Woods where the Timber grows, and has them carried on these Engines three or four Hundred Yards to the Sea. Five Hundred Carpenters and Engineers were immediately set at work to prepare the greatest Engine they had. It was a Frame of Wood raised three Inches from the Ground, about seven Foot long and four wide, moving upon twenty two Wheels. The Shout I heard, was upon the Arrival of this Engine, which, it seems, set out in four Hours after my Landing. It was brought parallel to me as I lay. But the principal Difficulty was to raise and place me in this Vehicle. Eighty Poles, each of one Foot high, were erected for this Purpose, and very strong Cords of the bigness of Pack thread were fastened by Hooks to many Bandages, which the Workmen had girt round my Neck, my Hands, my Body, and my Legs. Nine Hundred of the strongest Men were employed to draw up these Cords by many Pullies fastned on the Poles; and thus in less than three Hours, I was raised and slung into the Engine, and there tyed fast. All this I was told; for while the whole Operation was performing, I lay in a profound Sleep, by the Force of that soporiferous Medicine infused into my Liquor. Fifteen hundred of the Emperor's largest Horses, each about four Inches and a half high, were employed to draw me towards the Metropolis, which, as I said, was half a Mile distant.

About four Hours after we began our Journey, I awaked by a very ridiculous Accident; for the Carriage being stopt a while to adjust something that was out of Order, two or three of the young Natives had the Curiosity to see how I looked when I was asleep; they climbed up into the Engine, and advancing very softly to my Face, one of them, an Officer in the Guards, put the sharp End of his Half-Pike a good way up into my left Nostril, which tickled my Nose like a Straw, and made me sneeze violently: Whereupon they stole off unperceived; and it was three Weeks before I knew the Cause of my awaking so suddenly. We made a long March the remaining Part of the Day, and rested at Night with Five Hundred Guards on each Side of me, half with Torches, and half with Bows and Arrows, ready to shoot me if I should offer to stir. The next Morning at Sunrise we continued our March, and arrived within two Hundred Yards of the City-Gates about Noon. The Emperor, and all his Court, came out to meet us; but his great Officers would by no Means suffer his Majesty to endanger his Person by mounting on my Body.

At the Place where the Carriage stopt, there stood an ancient Temple, esteemed to be the largest in the whole Kingdom; which having been polluted some Years before by an unnatural Murder, was, according to the Zeal of those People, looked upon as Prophane, and therefore had been applied to common Uses, and all the Ornaments and Furniture carried away. In this Edifice it was determined I should lodge. The great Gate fronting to the North was about four Foot high, and almost two Foot wide, through which I could easily creep. On each Side of the Gate was a small Window not above six Inches from the Ground: Into that on the Left Side, the King's Smiths conveyed fourscore and eleven Chains, like those that hang to a Lady's Watch in *Europe*, and almost as large, which were locked to my Left Leg with six and thirty Padlocks. Over against this Temple, on the other Side of the great Highway, at twenty Foot Distance, there was a Turret at least five Foot high. Here the Emperor ascended with many principal Lords of his Court, to have an Opportunity of viewing me, as I was told, for I could not see them. It was reckoned that above an hundred thousand Inhabitants came out of the Town upon the same Errand; and in spight of my Guards, I believe there could not be fewer than ten thousand, at several Times, who mounted upon my Body by the Help of Ladders. But a Proclamation was soon issued to forbid it, upon Pain of Death. When the Workmen found it was impossible for me to break loose, they cut all the Strings that bound me; whereupon I rose up with as melancholy a Disposition as ever I had in my Life. But the Noise and Astonishment of the People at seeing me rise and walk, are not to be expressed. The Chains that held my left Leg were about two Yards long, and gave me not only the Liberty of walking backwards and forwards in a Semicircle; but being fixed within four Inches of the Gate, allowed me to creep in, and lie at my full Length in the Temple.

CHAPTER II

The Emperor of Lilliput, *attended by several of the Nobility, comes to see the Author in his Confinement. The Emperor's Person and Habit described. Learned Men appointed to teach the Author their Language. He gains Favour by his mild Disposition. His Pockets are searched, and his Sword and Pistols taken from him.*

When I found myself on my Feet, I looked about me, and must confess I never beheld a more entertaining Prospect. The Country round appeared like a continued Garden; and the inclosed Fields, which were generally Forty Foot square, resembled so many Beds of Flowers. These Fields were intermingled with Woods of half a Stang,[1] and the tallest Trees, as I could judge, appeared to be seven Foot high. I viewed the Town on my left Hand, which looked like the painted Scene of a City in a Theatre.

I had been for some Hours extremely pressed by the Necessities of Nature; which was no Wonder, it being almost two Days since I had last disburthened myself. I was under great Difficulties between Urgency and Shame. The best Expedient I could think on, was to creep into my House, which I accordingly did; and shutting the Gate after me, I went as far as the Length of my Chain would suffer; and discharged my Body of that uneasy Load. But this was the only Time I was ever guilty of so uncleanly an Action; for which I cannot but hope the candid Reader will give some Allowance, after he hath maturely and impartially considered my Case, and the Distress I was in. From this Time my constant Practice was, as soon as I rose, to perform that Business in open Air, at the full Extent of my Chain; and due Care was taken every Morning before Company came, that the offensive Matter should be carried off in Wheel-barrows, by two Servants appointed for that Purpose.

[1] A quarter of an acre.

I would not have dwelt so long upon a Circumstance, that perhaps at first Sight may appear not very momentous; if I had not thought it necessary to justify my Character in Point of Cleanliness to the World; which I am told, some of my Maligners have been pleased, upon this and other Occasions, to call in Question.

When this Adventure was at an End, I came back out of my House, having Occasion for fresh Air. The Emperor was already descended from the Tower, and advancing on Horseback towards me, which had like to have cost him dear; for the Beast, although very well trained, yet wholly unused to such a Sight, which appeared as if a Mountain moved before him, reared up on his hinder Feet: But that Prince, who is an excellent Horseman, kept his Seat, until his Attendants ran in, and held the Bridle, while his Majesty had Time to dismount. When he alighted, he surveyed me round with great Admiration, but kept beyond the Length of my Chains. He ordered his Cooks and Butlers, who were already prepared, to give me Victuals and Drink, which they pushed forward in a sort of Vehicles upon Wheels until I could reach them. I took these Vehicles, and soon emptied them all; twenty of them were filled with Meat, and ten with Liquor; each of the former afforded me two or three good Mouthfuls, and I emptied the Liquor of ten Vessels, which was contained in earthen Vials into one Vehicle, drinking it off at a Draught; and so I did with the rest. The Empress, and young Princes of the Blood, of both Sexes, attended by many Ladies, sate at some Distance in their Chairs; but upon the Accident that happened to the Emperor's Horse, they alighted, and came near his Person; which I am now going to describe. He is taller by almost the Breadth of my Nail, than any of his Court; which alone is enough to strike an Awe into the Beholders. His Features are strong and masculine, with an *Austrian* Lip, and arched Nose, his Complexion olive, his Countenance erect, his Body and Limbs well proportioned, all his Motions graceful, and his Deportment majestick.[2] He was was then past his Prime, being twenty-eight Years and three Quarters old, of which he had reigned about seven, in great Felicity, and generally victorious. For the better Convenience of beholding him, I lay on my Side, so that my Face was parallel to his, and he stood but three Yards off: However, I have

[2] Swift intended the Emperor to represent George I, who reigned 1714-1727. Swift's description is a calculated irony since George was gross and unattractive.

had him since many Times in my Hand, and therefore cannot be deceived in the Description. His Dress was very plain and simple, the Fashion of it between the *Asiatick* and the *European*; but he had on his Head a light Helmet of Gold, adorned with Jewels, and a Plume on the Crest. He held his Sword drawn in his Hand, to defend himself, if I should happen to break loose; it was almost three Inches long, the Hilt and Scabbard were Gold enriched with Diamonds. His Voice was shrill, but very clear and articulate, and I could distinctly hear it when I stood up. The Ladies and Courtiers were all most magnificently clad, so that the Spot they stood upon seemed to resemble a Petticoat spread on the Ground, embroidered with Figures of Gold and Silver. His Imperial Majesty spoke often to me, and I returned Answers, but neither of us could understand a Syllable. There were several of his Priests and Lawyers present (as I conjectured by their Habits) who were commanded to address themselves to me, and I spoke to them in as many Languages as I had the least Smattering of, which were *High* and *Low Dutch, Latin, French, Spanish, Italian,* and *Lingua Franca*; but all to no purpose. After about two Hours the Court retired, and I was left with a strong Guard, to prevent the Impertinence, and probably the Malice of the Rabble, who were very impatient to croud about me as near as they durst; and some of them had the Impudence to shoot their Arrows at me as I sate on the Ground by the Door of my House; whereof one very narrowly missed my left Eye. But the Colonel ordered six of the Ringleaders to be seized, and thought no Punishment so proper as to deliver them bound into my Hands, which some of his Soldiers accordingly did, pushing them forwards with the Butt-ends of their Pikes into my Reach: I took them all in my right Hand, put five of them into my Coat-pocket; and as to the sixth, I made a Countenance as if I would eat him alive. The poor Man squalled terribly, and the Colonel and his Officers were in much Pain, especially when they saw me take out my Penknife: But I soon put them out of Fear; for, looking mildly, and immediately cutting the Strings he was bound with, I set him gently on the Ground, and away he ran. I treated the rest in the same Manner, taking them one by one out of my Pocket; and I observed, both the Soldiers and People were highly obliged at this Mark of my Clemency, which was represented very much to my Advantage at Court.

Towards Night I got with some Difficulty into my House, where

I lay on the Ground, and continued to do so about a Fortnight; during which time the Emperor gave Orders to have a Bed prepared for me. Six Hundred Beds of the common Measure were brought in Carriages, and worked up in my House; an Hundred and Fifty of their Beds sown together made up the Breadth and Length, and these were four double, which however kept me but very indifferently from the Hardness of the Floor, that was of smooth Stone. By the same Computation they provided me with Sheets, Blankets, and Coverlets, tolerable enough for one who had been so long enured to Hardships as I.

As the News of my Arrival spread through the kingdom, it brought prodigious Numbers of rich, idle, and curious People to see me; so that the Villages were almost emptied, and great Neglect of Tillage and Houshold Affairs must have ensued, if his Imperial Majesty had not provided by several Proclamations and Orders of State against this Inconveniency. He directed that those, who had already beheld me, should return home, and not presume to come within fifty Yards of my House, without Licence from Court; whereby the Secretaries of State got considerable Fees.

In the mean time, the Emperor held frequent Councils to debate what Course should be taken with me; and I was afterwards assured by a particular Friend, a Person of great Quality, and who was as much in the *Secret* as any; that the Court was under many Difficulties concerning me. They apprehended my breaking loose; that my Diet would be very expensive, and might cause a Famine. Sometimes they determined to starve me, or at least to shoot me in the Face and Hands with poisoned Arrows, which would soon dispatch me: But again they considered, that the Stench of so large a Carcase might produce a Plague in the Metropolis, and probably spread through the whole Kingdom. In the midst of these Consultations, several Officers of the Army went to the Door of the great Council Chamber; and two of them being admitted, gave an Account of my Behaviour to the six Criminals above-mentioned; which made so favourable an Impression in the Breast of his Majesty, and the whole Board, in my Behalf, that an Imperial Commission was issued out, obliging all the Villages nine hundred Yards round the City, to deliver in every Morning six Beeves, forty Sheep, and other Victuals for my Sustenance; together with a proportionable Quantity of Bread and Wine, and other Liquors: For the due Payment of which his Majesty gave Assignments upon his Treasury. For this Prince lives chiefly upon his own Demesnes; seldom, except upon great Occasions raising any Subsidies upon his Subjects, who are bound to attend him in his Wars at their own Expence. An Establishment was also made of Six Hundred Persons to be my Domesticks, who had Board-Wages allowed for their Maintenance, and Tents built for them very conveniently on each side of my Door. It was likewise ordered, that three hundred Taylors should make me a Suit of Cloaths after the Fashion of the Country: That, six of his Majesty's greatest Scholars should be employed to instruct me in their Language: And, lastly, that the Emperor's Horses, and those of the Nobility, and Troops of Guards, should be exercised in my Sight, to accustom themselves to me. All these Orders were duly put in Execution; and in about three Weeks I made a great Progress in Learning their Language; during which Time, the Emperor frequently honoured me with his Visits, and was pleased to assist my Masters in teaching me. We began already to converse together in some Sort; and the first Words I learnt, were to express my Desire, that he would please to give me my Liberty; which I every Day repeated on my Knees. His Answer, as I could apprehend, was, that this must be a Work of Time, not to be thought on without the Advice of his Council; and that first I must *Lumos Kelmin pesso desmar lon Emposo*; that is, *Swear a Peace with him and his Kingdom*. However, that I should be used with all Kindness; and he advised me to acquire by my Patience and discreet Behaviour, the good Opinion of himself and his Subjects. He desired I would not take it ill, if he gave Orders to certain proper Officers to search me; for probably I might carry about me several Weapons, which must needs be dangerous Things, if they answered the Bulk of so prodigious a Person. I said, his Majesty should be satisfied, for I was ready to strip my self, and turn up my Pockets before him. This I delivered, part in Words, and part in Signs. He replied, that by the Laws of the Kingdom, I must be searched by two of his Officers: That he knew this could not be done without my Consent and Assistance; that he had so good an Opinion of my Generosity and Justice, as to trust their Persons in my Hands: That whatever they took from me should be returned when I left the Country, or paid for at the Rate which I would set upon them. I took up the two Officers in my Hands, put them first into my Coat-Pockets, and then into every other Pocket about me, except my two Fobs, and another secret Pocket which I had no Mind should be searched, wherein I had some little Necessaries of no Consequence to any but my self. In one of my Fobs there was a Silver Watch, and in the other a small Quantity of Gold in a Purse. These Gentlemen, having Pen, Ink, and Paper about them, made an exact Inventory of every thing they saw; and when they had done, desired I would set them down, that they might deliver it to the Emperor. This Inventory I afterwards translated into *English*, and is Word for Word as follows.

Imprimis, In the right Coat-Pocket of the *Great Man Mountain* (for so I interpret the Words *Quinbus Flestrin*) after the strictest Search, we found only one great Piece of coarse Cloth, large enough to be a Foot-Cloth for your Majesty's chief Room of State. In the left Pocket, we saw a huge Silver Chest, with a Cover of the same Metal, which we, the Searchers, were not able to lift. We desired it should be opened; and one of us stepping into it, found himself up to the mid Leg in a sort of Dust, some part whereof flying up to our Faces, set us both a sneezing for several Times together. In his right Waistcoat-Pocket, we found a prodigious Bundle of white thin Substances, folded one over another, about the Bigness of three Men, tied with a strong Cable, and marked with black Figures; which we humbly conceive to be Writings; every Letter almost half as large as the Palm of our Hands. In the left there was a sort of Engine, from the Back of which were extended twenty long Poles, resembling the Pallisado's before your Majesty's Court; wherewith we conjecture the *Man Mountain* combs his Head; for we did not always trouble him with Questions, because we found it a great Difficulty to make him understand us. In the large Pocket on the right Side of his middle Cover, (so I translate the Word *Ranfu-Lo*, by which they meant my Breeches) we saw a hollow Pillar of Iron, about the Length of a Man, fastened to a strong Piece of Timber, larger than the Pillar; and upon one side of the Pillar were huge Pieces of Iron sticking out, cut into strange Figures; which we know not what to make of. In the left Pocket, another Engine of the same kind. In the smaller Pocket on the right Side, were several round flat Pieces of white and red Metal, of different Bulk: Some of the white, which seemed to be Silver, were so large and heavy, that my Comrade and I could hardly lift them. In the left Pocket were two black Pillars irregularly shaped: we could not, without Difficulty, reach the Top of them as we stood at the Bottom of his Pocket: One of them was covered, and seemed all of a

Piece; but at the upper End of the other, there appeared a white round Substance, about twice the bigness of our Heads. Within each of these was inclosed a prodigious Plate of Steel; which, by our Orders, we obliged him to shew us, because we apprehended they might be dangerous Engines. He took them out of their Cases, and told us, that in his own Country his Practice was to shave his Beard with one of these, and to cut his Meat with the other. There were two Pockets which we could not enter: These he called his Fobs; they were two large Slits cut into the Top of his middle Cover, but squeezed close by the Pressure of his Belly. Out of the right Fob hung a great Silver Chain, with a wonderful kind of Engine at the Bottom. We directed him to draw out whatever was at the End of that Chain; which appeared to be a Globe, half Silver, and half of some transparent Metal: For on the transparent Side we saw certain strange Figures circularly drawn, and thought we could touch them, until we found our Fingers stopped with that lucid Substance. He put this Engine to our Ears, which made an incessant Noise like that of a Water-Mill. And we conjecture it is either some unknown Animal, or the God that he worships: But we are more inclined to the latter Opinion, because he assured us (if we understood him right, for he expressed himself very imperfectly) that he seldom did any Thing without consulting it. He called it his Oracle, and said it pointed out the Time for every Action of his Life. From the left Fob he took out a Net almost large enough for a Fisherman, but contrived to open and shut like a Purse, and served him for the same Use: We found therein several massy Pieces of yellow Metal, which if they be of real Gold, must be of immense Value.

Having thus, in Obedience to your Majesty's Commands, diligently searched all his Pockets; we observed a Girdle about his Waist made of the Hyde of some prodigious Animal; from which, on the left Side, hung a Sword of the Length of five Men; and on the right, a Bag or Pouch divided into two Cells; each Cell capable of holding three of your Majesty's Subjects. In one of these Cells were several Globes or Balls of a most ponderous Metal, about the Bigness of our Heads, and required a strong Hand to lift them: The other Cell contained a Heap of certain black Grains, but of no great Bulk or Weight, for we could hold about fifty of them in the Palms of our Hands.

This is an exact Inventory of what we found about the Body of the *Man Mountain*; who used us with great Civility, and due

Respect to your Majesty's Commission. Signed and Sealed on the fourth Day of the eighty ninth Moon of your Majesty's auspicious Reign.[3]

Clefren Frelock, Marsi Frelock.

When this Inventory was read over to the Emperor, he directed me to deliver up the several Particulars. He first called for my Scymiter, which I took out, Scabbard and all. In the mean time he ordered three thousand of his choicest Troops, who then attended him, to surround me at a Distance, with their Bows and Arrows just ready to discharge: But I did not observe it; for my Eyes were wholly fixed upon his Majesty. He then desired me to draw my Scymiter, which, although it had got some Rust by the Sea-Water, was in most Parts exceeding bright. I did so, and immediately all the Troops gave a Shout between Terror and Surprize; for the Sun shone clear, and the Reflexion dazzled their Eyes, as I waved the Scymiter to and fro in my Hand. His Majesty, who is a most magnanimous Prince, was less daunted than I could expect; he ordered me to return it into the Scabbard, and cast it on the Ground as gently as I could, about six Foot from the End of my Chain. The next Thing he demanded was one of the hollow Iron Pillars, by which he meant my Pocket-Pistols. I drew it out, and at his Desire, as well as I could, expressed to him the Use of it, and charging it only with Powder, which by the Closeness of my Pouch, happened to escape wetting in the Sea, (an Inconvenience that all prudent Mariners take special Care to provide against) I first cautioned the Emperor not to be afraid; and then I let it off in the Air. The Astonishment here was much greater than at the Sight of my Scymiter. Hundreds fell down as if they had been struck dead; and even the Emperor, although he stood his Ground, could not recover himself in some time. I delivered up both my Pistols in the same Manner as I had done my Scymiter, and then my Pouch of Powder

[3] This search and listing, like many of the details in the first voyage, refer to the conflict between Tories and Whigs in the first quarter of the eighteenth century. Though Swift began as a Whig, he joined with the Tories in 1710, a connection he never abandoned. In a general sense, he is here satirizing Whig suspicions and investigations of their opponents; in particular, he is probably alluding to an investigation in 1715 of the Earl of Oxford and Viscount Bolingbroke. Both were leaders of the Tories, and Swift's close friends. Gulliver in Bk. I often stands for Oxford or Bolingbroke, and occasionally (as here) for both.

and Bullets; begging him that the former might be kept from Fire; for it would kindle with the smallest Spark, and blow up his Imperial Palace into the Air. I likewise delivered up my Watch, which the Emperor was very curious to see; and commanded two of his tallest Yeomen of the Guards to bear it on a Pole upon their Shoulders, as Dray-men in *England* do a Barrel of Ale. He was amazed at the continual Noise it made, and the Motion of the Minute-hand, which he could easily discern; for their Sight is much more acute than ours: He asked the Opinions of his learned Men about him, which were various and remote, as the Reader may well imagine without my repeating; although indeed I could not very perfectly understand them. I then gave up my Silver and Copper Money, my Purse with nine large Pieces of Gold, and some smaller ones; my Knife and Razor, my Comb and Silver Snuff-Box, my Handkerchief and Journal Book. My Scymiter, Pistols, and Pouch, were conveyed in Carriages to his Majesty's Stores; but the rest of my Goods were returned me.

I had, as I before observed, one private Pocket which escaped their Search, wherein there was a Pair of Spectacles (which I sometimes use for the Weakness of my Eyes) a Pocket Perspective, and several other little Conveniences; which being of no Consequence to the Emperor, I did not think my self bound in Honour to discover; and I apprehended they might be lost or spoiled if I ventured them out of my Possession.

CHAPTER III

The Author diverts the Emperor and his Nobility of both Sexes, in a very uncommon Manner. The Diversions of the Court of Lilliput *described. The Author hath his Liberty granted him upon certain Conditions.*

My Gentleness and good Behaviour had gained so far on the Emperor and his Court, and indeed upon the Army and People in general, that I began to conceive Hopes of getting my Liberty in a short Time. I took all possible Methods to cultivate this favourable Disposition. The Natives came by Degrees to be less apprehensive of any Danger from me. I would sometimes lie down, and let five or six of them dance on my Hand. And at last the Boys and Girls would venture to come and play at Hide and Seek in my Hair. I had now made a good Progress in understanding and speaking their Language. The Emperor had a mind one Day to entertain me with several of the Country Shows; wherein they exceed all Nations I have known, both for Dexterity and Magnificence. I was diverted with none so much as that of the Rope-Dancers, performed upon a slender white Thread, extended about two Foot, and twelve Inches from the Ground. Upon which, I shall desire Liberty, with the Reader's Patience, to enlarge a little.

This Diversion is only practised by those Persons, who are Candidates for great Employments, and high Favour, at Court. They are trained in this Art from their Youth, and are not always of noble Birth, or liberal Education. When a great Office is vacant, either by Death or Disgrace, (which often happens) five or six of those Candidates petition the Emperor to entertain his Majesty and the Court with a Dance on the Rope; and whoever jumps the highest without falling, succeeds in the Office. Very often the chief Ministers themselves are commanded to shew their Skill, and to convince the Emperor that they have not lost their Faculty. *Flimnap*, the Treasurer, is allowed to cut a Caper on the strait Rope, at least an Inch higher than any other Lord in the whole Empire. I have seen him do the Summerset several times together, upon a Trencher fixed on the Rope, which is no thicker than a common Packthread in *England*. My Friend *Reldresal*, principal Secretary for private Affairs, is, in my Opinion, if I am not partial, the second after the Treasurer; the rest of the great Officers are much upon a Par.

These Diversions are often attended with fatal Accidents, whereof great Numbers are on Record. I my self have seen two or three Candidates break a Limb. But the Danger is much greater, when the Ministers themselves are commanded to shew their Dexterity: For, by contending to excel themselves and their Fellows, they strain so far, that there is hardly one of them who hath not received a Fall; and some of them two or three. I was assured, that a Year or two before my Arrival, *Flimnap* would have infallibly broke his Neck, if one of the *King's Cushions,* that accidentally lay on the Ground, had not weakened the Force of his Fall.

There is likewise another Diversion, which is only shewn before the Emperor and Empress, and first Minister, upon particular Occasions. The Emperor lays on a Table three fine silken Threads of six Inches long. One is Blue, the other Red, and the third Green. These Threads are proposed as Prizes, for those Persons whom the Emperor hath a mind to distinguish by a peculiar Mark of his Favour. The Ceremony is performed in his Majesty's great Chamber of State; where the Candidates are to undergo a Tryal of Dexterity very different from the former; and such as I have not observed the least Resemblance of in any other Country of the old or the new World. The Emperor holds a Stick in his Hands, both Ends parallel to the Horizon, while the Candidates advancing one by one, sometimes leap over the Stick, sometimes creep under it backwards and forwards several times, according as the Stick is advanced or depressed. Sometimes the Emperor holds one End of the Stick, and his first Minister the other; sometimes the Minister has it entirely to himself. Whoever performs his Part with most Agility, and holds out the longest in *leaping* and *creeping,* is rewarded with the Blue-coloured Silk; the Red is given to the next, and the Green to the third, which they all wear girt twice round about the Middle; and you see few great Persons about this Court, who are not adorned with one of these Girdles.[1]

The Horses of the Army, and those of the Royal Stables, having been daily led before me, were no longer shy, but would come up to my very Feet, without starting. The Riders would leap them over my Hand as I held it on the Ground; and one of the Emperor's Huntsmen, upon a large Courser, took my Foot, Shoe and all; which was indeed a prodigious Leap. I had the good Fortune to divert the Emperor one Day, after a very extraordinary Manner. I desired he would order several Sticks of two Foot high, and the Thickness of an ordinary Cane, to be brought me; whereupon his Majesty commanded the Master of his Woods to give Directions

[1] The previous four paragraphs convey Swift's estimate of the court of George I. Flimnap represents Robert Walpole, the Whig leader; Reldresal, probably Walpole's successor in 1717; the "King's Cushion," the King's mistress who helped Walpole return to office (1721) after his "fall." The colored threads correspond to the Orders of the Garter, the Bath, and the Thistle.

accordingly; and the next Morning six Wood-men arrived with as many Carriages, drawn by eight Horses to each. I took nine of these Sticks, and fixing them firmly in the Ground in a Quadrangular Figure, two Foot and a half square; I took four other Sticks, and tyed them parallel at each Corner, about two Foot from the Ground; and then I fastened my Handkerchief to the nine Sticks that stood erect; and extended it on all Sides, till it was as tight as the Top of a Drum; and the four parallel Sticks rising about five Inches higher than the Handkerchief, served as Ledges on each Side. When I had finished my Work, I desired the Emperor to let a Troop of his best Horse, Twenty-four in Number, come and exercise upon this Plain. His Majesty approved of the Proposal, and I took them up one by one in my Hands, ready mounted and armed, with the proper Officers to exercise them. As soon as they got into Order, they divided into two Parties, performed mock Skirmishes, discharged blunt Arrows, drew their Swords, fled and pursued, attacked and retired; and in short discovered the best military Discipline I ever beheld. The paralled Sticks secured them and their Horses from falling over the Stage; and the Emperor was so much delighted, that he ordered this Entertainment to be repeated several Days; and once was pleased to be lifted up, and give the Word of Command; and, with great Difficulty, persuaded even the Empress her self to let me hold her in her close Chair, within two Yards of the Stage, from whence she was able to take a full View of the whole Performance. It was my good Fortune that no ill Accident happened in these Entertainments; only once a fiery Horse that belonged to one of the Captains, pawing with his Hoof struck a Hole in my Handkerchief, and his Foot slipping, he overthrew his Rider and himself; but I immediately relieved them both: For covering the Hole with one Hand, I set down the Troop with the other, in the same Manner as I took them up. The Horse that fell was strained in the left Shoulder, but the Rider got no Hurt, and I repaired my Handkerchief as well as I could: However, I would not trust to the Strength of it any more in such dangerous Enterprizes.

About two or three Days before I was set at Liberty, as I was entertaining the Court with these Kinds of Feats, there arrived an Express to inform his Majesty, that some of his Subjects riding near the Place where I was first taken up, had seen a great black Substance lying on the Ground, very oddly shaped, extending its

Edges round as wide as his Majesty's Bedchamber, and rising up in the Middle as high as a Man. That it was no living Creature, as they at first apprehended; for it lay on the Grass without Motion, and some of them had walked round it several Times: That by mounting upon each others Shoulders, they had got to the Top, which was flat and even; and, stamping upon it, they found it was hollow within: That they humbly conceived it might be something belonging to the *Man-Mountain*; and if his Majesty pleased, they would undertake to bring it with only five Horses. I presently knew what they meant; and was glad at Heart to receive this Intelligence. It seems, upon my first reaching the Shore, after our Shipwreck, I was in such Confusion, that before I came to the Place where I went to sleep, my Hat, which I had fastened with a String to my Head while I was rowing, and had stuck on all the Time I was swimming, fell off after I came to Land; the String, as I conjecture, breaking by some Accident which I never observed, but thought my Hat had been lost at Sea. I intreated his Imperial Majesty to give Orders it might be brought to me as soon as possible, describing to him the Use and the Nature of it: And the next Day the Waggoners arrived with it, but not in a very good Condition; they had bored two Holes in the Brim, within an Inch and a half of the Edge, and fastened two Hooks in the Holes; these Hooks were tyed by a long Cord to the Harness, and thus my Hat was dragged along for above half an *English* Mile: but the Ground in that Country being extremely smooth and level, it received less Damage than I expected.

Two Days after this Adventure, the Emperor having ordered that Part of his Army, which quarters in and about his Metropolis, to be in a Readiness, took a fancy of diverting himself in a very singular Manner. He desired I would stand like a *Colossus*, with my Legs as far asunder as I conveniently could. He then commanded his General (who was an old experienced Leader, and a great Patron of mine) to draw up the Troops in close Order, and march them under me; the Foot by Twenty-four in a Breast, and the Horse by Sixteen, with Drums beating, Colours flying, and Pikes advanced. This Body consisted of three Thousand Foot, and a Thousand Horse. His Majesty gave Orders, upon Pain of Death, that every Soldier in his March should observe the strictest Decency, with regard to my Person; which, however, could not prevent some of the younger Officers from turning up their Eyes as they passed under me. And, to confess the Truth, my Breeches were at that Time in so ill a Condition, that they afforded some Opportunities for Laughter and Admiration.

I had sent so many Memorials and Petitions for my Liberty, that his Majesty at length mentioned the Matter first in the Cabinet, and then in a full Council; where it was opposed by none, except *Skyresh Bolgolam*, who was pleased, without any Provocation, to be my mortal Enemy. But it was carried against him by the whole Board, and confirmed by the Emperor. That Minister was *Galbet*, or Admiral of the Realm; very much in his Master's Confidence, and a Person well versed in Affairs, but of a morose and sour Complection. However, he was at length persuaded to comply; but prevailed that the Articles and Conditions upon which I should be set free, and to which I must swear, should be drawn up by himself. These Articles were brought to me by *Skyresh Bolgolam* in Person, attended by two under Secretaries, and several Persons of Distinction. After they were read, I was demanded to swear to the Performance of them; first in the Manner of my own Country, and afterwards in the Method prescribed by their Laws; which was to hold my right Foot in my left Hand, to place the middle Finger of my right Hand on the Crown of my Head, and my Thumb on the Tip of my right Ear. But, because the Reader may perhaps be curious to have some Idea of the Style and Manner of Expression peculiar to that People, as well as to know the Articles upon which I recovered my Liberty; I have made a Translation of the Whole Instrument, Word for Word, as near as I was able; which I here offer to the Publick.

GOLBASTO MOMAREN EVLAME GURDILO SHEFIN MULLY ULLY GUE, most Mighty Emperor of *Lilliput*, Delight and Terror of the Universe, whose Dominions extend five Thousand Blustrugs, (about twelve Miles in Circumference) to the Extremities of the Globe: Monarch of all Monarchs: Taller than the Sons of Men; whose Feet press down to the Center, and whose Head strikes against the Sun: At whose Nod the Princes of the Earth shake their Knees; pleasant as the Spring, comfortable as the Summer, fruitful as Autumn, dreadful as Winter. His most sublime Majesty proposeth to the *Man-Mountain*, lately arrived at our Celestial Dominions, the following Articles, which by a solemn Oath he shall be obliged to perform.

First, The *Man-Mountain* shall not depart from our Dominions, without our Licence under our Great Seal.

Secondly, He shall not presume to come into our Metropolis, without our express Order; at which time, the Inhabitants shall have two Hours Warning, to keep within their Doors.

Thirdly, The said *Man-Mountain* shall confine his Walks to our principal high Roads; and not offer to walk or lie down in a Meadow, or Field of Corn.

Fourthly, As he walks the said Roads, he shall take the utmost Care not to trample upon the Bodies of any of our loving Subjects, their Horses, or Carriages; nor take any of our said Subjects into his Hands, without their own Consent.

Fifthly, If an express require extraordinary Dispatch; the *Man-Mountain* shall be obliged to carry in his Pocket the Messenger and Horse, a six Days Journey once in every Moon, and return the said Messenger back (if so required) safe to our Imperial Presence.

Sixthly, He shall be our Ally against our Enemies in the Island of *Blefuscu*, and do his utmost to destroy their Fleet, which is now preparing to invade Us.

Seventhly, That the said *Man-Mountain* shall, at his Times of Leisure, be aiding and assisting to our Workmen, in helping to raise certain great Stones, towards covering the Wall of the principal Park, and other our Royal Buildings.

Eighthly, That the said *Man-Mountain* shall, in two Moons Time, deliver in an exact survey of the Circumference of our Dominions, by a Computation of his own Paces round the Coast.

Lastly, That upon his solemn Oath to observe all the above Articles, the said *Man-Mountain* shall have a daily Allowance of Meat and Drink, sufficient for the Support of 1728 of our Subjects; with free Access to our Royal Person, and other Marks of our Favour. Given at our Palace at *Belfaborac* the Twelfth Day of the Ninety-first Moon of our Reign.

I swore and subscribed to these Articles with great Chearfulness and Content, although some of them were not so honourable as I could have wished; which proceeded wholly from the Malice of *Skyresh Bolgolam* the High Admiral: Whereupon my Chains were immediately unlocked, and I was at full Liberty: The Emperor himself, in Person, did me the Honour to be by at the whole Ceremony. I made my Acknowledgments, by prostrating myself at his Majesty's Feet: But he commanded me to rise; and after many gracious Expressions, which, to avoid the Censure of Vanity, I shall not repeat; he added, that he hoped I should prove a useful Servant, and well deserve all the Favours he had already conferred upon me, or might do for the future.

The Reader may please to observe, that in the last Article for the Recovery of my Liberty, the Emperor stipulates to allow me a Quantity of Meat and Drink, sufficient for the Support of 1728 *Lilliputians*. Some time after, asking a Friend at Court how they came to fix on that determinate Number; he told me, that his Majesty's Mathematicians, having taken the Height of my Body by the Help of a Quadrant, and finding it to exceed theirs in the Proportion of Twelve to One, they concluded from the Similarity of their Bodies, that mine must contain at least 1728 of theirs, and consequently would require as much Food as was necessary to support that Number of *Lilliputians*. By which, the Reader may conceive an Idea of the Ingenuity of that People, as well as the prudent and exact Oeconomy of so great a Prince.

CHAPTER IV

Mildendo, *the Metropolis of* Lilliput, *described, together with the Emperor's Palace. A Conversation between the Author and a principal Secretary, concerning the Affairs of that Empire. The Author's Offers to serve the Emperor in his Wars.*

The first Request I made after I had obtained my Liberty, was, that I might have Licence to see *Mildendo*, the Metropolis;

which the Emperor easily granted me, but with a special Charge to do no Hurt, either to the Inhabitants, or their Houses. The People had Notice by Proclamation of my Design to visit the Town. The Wall which encompassed it, is two Foot and an half high, and at least eleven Inches broad, so that a Coach and Horses may be driven very safely round it; and it is flanked with strong Towers at ten Foot Distance. I stept over the great *Western* Gate, and passed very gently, and sideling through the two principal Streets, only in my short Waistcoat, for fear of damaging the Roofs and Eves of the Houses with the Skirts of my Coat. I walked with the utmost Circumspection, to avoid treading on any Stragglers, who might remain in the Streets, although the Orders were very strict, that all People should keep in their Houses, at their own Peril. The Garret Windows and Tops of Houses were so crowded with Spectators, that I thought in all my Travels I had not seen a more populous Place. The City is an exact Square, each Side of the Wall being five Hundred Foot long. The two great Streets which run cross and divide it into four Quarters, are five Foot wide. The Lanes and Alleys which I could not enter, but only viewed them as I passed, are from Twelve to Eighteen Inches. The Town is capable of holding five Hundred Thousand Souls. The Houses are from three to five Stories. The Shops and Markets well provided.

The Emperor's Palace is in the Center of the City, where the two great Streets meet. It is inclosed by a Wall of two Foot high, and Twenty Foot distant from the Buildings. I had his Majesty's Permission to step over this Wall; and the Space being so wide between that and the Palace, I could easily view it on every Side. The outward Court is a Square of Forty Foot, and includes two other Courts: In the inmost are the Royal Apartments, which I was very desirous to see, but found it extremely difficult; for the great Gates, from one Square into another, were but Eighteen Inches high, and seven Inches wide. Now the Buildings of the outer Court were at least five Foot high; and it was impossible for me to stride over them, without infinite Damage to the Pile, although the Walls were strongly built of hewn Stone, and four Inches thick. At the same time, the Emperor had a great Desire that I should see the Magnificence of his Palace: But this I was not able to do till three Days after, which I spent in cutting down with my Knife some of the largest Trees in the Royal Park, about an Hundred Yards distant from the City. Of these Trees I made two Stools, each about three Foot high, and strong enough to bear my Weight. The People having received Notice a second time, I went again through the City to the Palace, with my two Stools in my Hands. When I came to the Side of the outer Court, I stood upon one Stool, and took the other in my Hand: This I lifted over the Roof, and gently set it down on the Space between the first and second Court, which was eight Foot wide. I then stept over the Buildings very conveniently from one Stool to the other, and drew up the first after me with a hooked Stick. By this Contrivance I got into the inmost Court; and lying down upon my Side, I applied my Face to the Windows of the middle Stories, which were left open on Purpose, and discovered the most splendid Apartments that can be imagined. There I saw the Empress, and the young Princes in their several Lodgings, with their chief Attendants about them. Her Imperial Majesty was pleased to smile very graciously upon me and gave me out of the Window her Hand to kiss.

But I shall not anticipate the Reader with farther Descriptions of this Kind, because I reserve them for a greater Work, which is now almost ready for the Press; containing a general Description of this Empire, from its first Erection, through a long Series of Princes, with a particular Account of their Wars and Politicks, Laws, Learning, and Religion; their Plants and Animals, their peculiar Manners and Customs, with other Matters very curious and useful; my chief Design at present being only to relate such Events and Transactions as happened to the Publick, or to my self, during a Residence of about nine Months in that Empire.

One Morning, about a Fortnight after I had obtained my Liberty, *Reldresal*, Principal Secretary (as they style him) of private Affairs, came to my House, attended only by one Servant. He ordered his Coach to wait at a Distance, and desired I would give him an Hour's Audience; which I readily consented to, on Account of his Quality, and Personal Merits, as well as of the many good Offices he had done me during my Sollicitations at Court. I offered to lie down, that he might the more conveniently reach my Ear; but he chose rather to let me hold him in my Hand during our Conversation. He began with Compliments on my Liberty; said, he might pretend to some Merit in it; but, however, added, that if it had not been for the present Situation of things at Court, perhaps I might not have obtained it so soon. For, *said he*, as flourishing a Condition as we appear to be in to Foreigners, we labour under two mighty Evils; a violent Faction at home, and the Danger of an Invasion by a most potent Enemy from abroad. As to the first, you are to understand, that for above seventy Moons past, there have been two struggling Parties in this Empire, under the Names of *Tramecksan*, and *Slamecksan*, from the high and low Heels on their Shoes, by which they distinguish themselves.

It is alledged indeed, that the high Heels are most agreeable to our ancient Constitution: But however this be, his Majesty hath determined to make use of only low Heels in the Administration of the Government, and all Offices in the Gift of the Crown; as you cannot but observe; and particularly, that his Majesty's Imperial Heels are lower at least by a *Drurr* than any of his Court; (*Drurr* is a Measure about the fourteenth Part of an Inch.) The Animosities between these two Parties run so high, that they will neither eat nor drink, nor talk with each other. We compute the *Tramecksan*, or High-Heels, to exceed us in Number; but the Power is wholly on our Side. We apprehend his Imperial Highness, the Heir to the Crown, to have some Tendency towards the High-Heels; at least we can plainly discover one of his Heels higher than the other; which gives him a Hobble in his Gait.[1] Now, in the midst of these intestine Disquiets, we are threatened with an Invasion from the Island of *Blefuscu*, which is the other great Empire of the Universe, almost as large and powerful as this of his Majesty.[2] For as to what we have heard you affirm, that there are other Kingdoms and States in the World, inhabited by human Creatures as large as your self, our Philosophers are in much Doubt; and would rather conjecture that you dropt from the Moon, or one of the Stars; because it is certain, that an hundred Mortals of your Bulk, would, in a short Time, destroy all the Fruits and Cattle of his Majesty's Dominions. Besides, our Histories of six Thousand Moons make no Mention of any other Regions, than the two great Empires of *Lilliput* and *Blefuscu*. Which two mighty Powers have, as I was going to tell you, been engaged in a most obstinate War for six and thirty Moons

[1] The High-Heels stand for the Tories, or high-church party; the Low-Heels for the Whigs, or low-church party. George I favored the Whigs; the Prince of Wales (afterwards George II) indicated favor to both parties, hence his hobble.

[2] As Lilliput is England, so Blefuscu is France. England and France were the principal opponents in the War of the Spanish Succession (1701-1713), in progress at the time of Gulliver's adventure.

past. It began upon the following Occasion. It is allowed on all Hands, that the primitive Way of breaking Eggs before we eat them, was upon the larger End: But his present Majesty's Grandfather, while he was a Boy, going to eat an Egg, and breaking it according to the ancient Practice, happened to cut one of his Fingers. Whereupon the Emperor his Father, published an Edict, commanding all his Subjects, upon great Penalties, to break the smaller End of their Eggs. The People so highly resented this Law, that our Histories tell us, there have been six Rebellions raised on that Account; wherein one Emperor lost his Life, and another his Crown. These civil Commotions were constantly fomented by the Monarchs of *Blefuscu*; and when they were quelled, the Exiles always fled for Refuge to that Empire. It is computed, that eleven Thousand Persons have, at several Times, suffered Death, rather than submit to break their Eggs at the smaller End. Many hundred large Volumes have been published upon this Controversy: But the Books of the *Big-Endians* have been long forbidden, and the whole Party rendred incapable by Law of holding Employments.[3] During the Course of these Troubles, the Emperors of *Blefuscu* did frequently expostulate by their Ambassadors, accusing us of making a Schism in Religion, by offending against a fundamental Doctrine of our great Prophet *Lustrog*, in the fifty-fourth Chapter of the *Brundrecal*, (which is their *Alcoran*.) This, however, is thought to be a meer Strain upon the Text: For the Words are these; *That all true Believers shall break their Eggs at the convenient End*: and which is the convenient End, seems, in my humble Opinion, to be left to every Man's Conscience, or at least in the Power of the chief Magistrate to determine. Now the *Big-Endian* Exiles have found so much Credit in the Emperor of *Blefuscu's* Court; and so much private Assistance and Encouragement from their Party here at home, that a bloody War hath been carried on between the two Empires for six and thirty Moons with various Success; during which Time we have lost Forty Capital Ships, and a much greater

[3] Swift is referring to three related conflicts: (1) that originally between England and Rome, during which Henry VIII issued an "Edict" denying Papal authority; (2) that within England, between Roman Catholics (Big-Endians) and Protestants (Little-Endians), which resulted in the execution of Charles I, the forced exile of James II, and the imposing of restrictions on native Catholics; and (3) that between Protestant England and Catholic France, during which France harbored Catholic exiles, and was accused of plotting against England.

Number of smaller Vessels, together with thirty thousand of our best Seamen and Soldiers; and the Damage received by the Enemy is reckoned to be somewhat greater than ours. However, they have now equipped a numerous Fleet, and are just preparing to make a Descent upon us: And his Imperial Majesty, placing great Confidence in your Valour and Strength, hath commanded me to lay this Account of his affairs before you.

I desired the Secretary to present my humble Duty to the Emperor, and to let him know, that I thought it would not become me, who was a Foreigner, to interfere with Parties; but I was ready, with the Hazard of my Life, to defend his Person and State against all Invaders.

CHAPTER V

The Author by an extraordinary Stratagem prevents an Invasion. A high Title of Honour is conferred upon him. Ambassadors arrive from the Emperor of Blefuscu, *and sue for Peace. The Empress's Apartment on fire by an Accident; the Author instrumental in saving the Rest of the Palace.*

The Empire of *Blefuscu,* is an Island situated to the North North-East Side of *Lilliput,* from whence it is parted only by a Channel of eight Hundred Yards wide. I had not yet seen it, and upon this Notice of an intended Invasion, I avoided appearing on that Side of the Coast, for fear of being discovered by some of the Enemies' Ships, who had received no Intelligence of me; all intercourse between the two Empires having been strictly forbidden during the War, upon Pain of Death; and an Embargo laid by our Emperor upon all Vessels whatsoever. I communicated to his Majesty a Project I had formed of seizing the Enemies' whole Fleet; which, as our Scouts assured us, lay at Anchor in the Harbour ready to sail with the first fair Wind. I consulted the most experienced Seamen, upon the Depth of the Channel, which they had often plummed; who told me, that in the Middle at high Water it was seventy *Glumgluffs* deep, which is about six Foot of *European* Measure; and the rest of it fifty *Glumgluffs* at most. I walked to the North-East Coast over against *Blefuscu*; where, lying down behind a Hillock, I took out my small Pocket Perspective Glass, and viewed the Enemy's Fleet at Anchor, consisting of about fifty Men of War, and a great Number of Transports: I then came back to my House, and gave Order (for which I had a Warrant) for a great Quantity of the strongest Cable and Bars of Iron. The Cable was about as thick as Packthread, and the Bars of the Length and Size of a Knitting-Needle. I trebled the Cable to make it stronger; and for the same Reason I twisted three of the Iron Bars together, bending the Extremities into a Hook. Having thus fixed fifty Hooks to as many Cables, I went back to the North-East Coast, and putting off my Coat, Shoes, and Stockings, walked into the Sea in my Leathern Jerkin, about half an Hour before high Water. I waded with what Haste I could, and swam in the Middle about thirty Yards until I felt the Ground; I arrived at the Fleet in less than half an Hour. The Enemy was so frighted when they saw me, that they leaped out of their Ships, and swam to Shore; where there could not be fewer than thirty thousand Souls. I then took my Tackling, and fastning a Hook to the Hole at the Prow of each, I tyed all the Cords together at the End. While I was thus employed, the Enemy discharged several Thousand Arrows, many of which stuck in my Hands and Face; and besides the excessive Smart, gave me much Disturbance in my Work. My greatest Apprehension was for my Eyes, which I should have infallibly lost, if I had not suddenly thought of an Expedient. I kept, among other little Necessaries, a Pair of Spectacles in a private Pocket, which, as I observed before, had escaped the Emperor's Searchers. These I took out, and fastened as strongly as I could upon my Nose; and thus armed went on boldly with my Work in spight of the Enemy's Arrows; many of which struck against the Glasses of my Spectacles, but without any other Effect, further than a little to discompose them. I had now fastened all the Hooks, and taking the Knot in my Hand, began to pull; but not a Ship would stir, for they were all too fast held by their Anchors; so that the boldest Part of my Enterprize remained. I therefore let go the Cord, and leaving the Hooks fixed to the Ships, I resolutely cut with my Knife the Cables that fastened the Anchors; receiving above two hundred Shots in my Face and Hands: Then I took up the knotted End of the Cables to which my Hooks were tyed; and with great Ease drew fifty of the Enemy's largest Men of War after me.

The *Blefuscudians*, who had not the least Imagination of what I intended, were at first confounded with Astonishment. They had seen me cut the Cables, and thought my Design was only to let the Ships run a-drift, or fall foul on each other: But when they perceived the whole Fleet moving in Order, and saw me pulling at the End; they set up such a Scream of Grief and Dispair, that it is almost impossible to describe or conceive. When I had got out of Danger, I stopt a while to pick out the Arrows that stuck in my Hands and Face, and rubbed on some of the same Ointment that was given me at my first Arrival, as I have formerly mentioned. I then took off my Spectacles, and waiting about an Hour until the Tyde was a little fallen, I waded through the Middle with my Cargo, and arrived safe at the Royal Port of *Lilliput*.

The Emperor and his whole Court stood on the Shore, expecting the Issue of this great Adventure. They saw the Ships move forward in a large Half-Moon, but could not discern me, who was up to my Breast in Water. When I advanced to the Middle of the Channel, they were yet more in Pain because I was under Water to my Neck. The Emperor concluded me to be drowned, and that the Enemy's Fleet was approaching in a hostile Manner: But he was soon eased of his Fears; for the Channel growing shallower every Step I made, I came in a short Time within Hearing; and holding up the End of the Cable by which the Fleet was fastened, I cryed in a loud Voice, *Long live the most puissant Emperor of Lilliput!* This great Prince received me at my Landing with all possible Encomiums, and created me a *Nardac* upon the Spot, which is the highest Title of Honour among them.

His Majesty desired I would take some other Opportunity of bringing all the rest of his Enemy's Ships into his Ports. And so unmeasurable is the Ambition of Princes, that he seemed to think of nothing less than reducing the whole Empire of *Blefuscu* into a Province, and governing it by a Viceroy; of destroying the *Big-Endian* Exiles, and compelling that People to break the smaller End of their Eggs; by which he would remain sole Monarch of the whole World. But I endeavoured to divert him from this Design, by many Arguments drawn from the Topicks of Policy as well as Justice: And I plainly protested, that I would never be an Instrument of bringing a free and brave People into Slavery: And when the Matter was debated in Council, the wisest Part of the Ministry were of my Opinion.

This open bold Declaration of mine was so opposite to the Schemes and Politicks of his Imperial Majesty, that he could never forgive me: He mentioned it in a very artful Manner at Council, where, I was told, that some of the wisest appeared, at least by their Silence, to be of my Opinion; but others, who were my secret Enemies, could not forbear some Expressions, which by a Side-wind reflected on me. And from this Time began an Intrigue between his Majesty, and a Junta of Ministers maliciously bent against me, which broke out in less than two Months, and had like to have ended in my utter Destruction. Of so little Weight are the greatest Services to Princes, when put into the Balance with a Refusal to gratify their Passions.

About three Weeks after this Exploit, there arrived a solemn Embassy from *Blefuscu*, with humble Offers of a Peace; which was soon concluded upon Conditions very advantageous to our Emperor; wherewith I shall not trouble the Reader. There were six Ambassadors, with a Train of about five Hundred Persons; and their Entry was very magnificent, suitable to the Grandeur of their Master, and the Importance of their Business. When their Treaty was finished, wherein I did them several good Offices by the Credit I now had, or at least appeared to have at Court; their Excellencies, who were privately told how much I had been their Friend, made me a Visit in Form. They began with many Compliments upon my Valour and Generosity; invited me to that Kingdom in the Emperor their Master's Name; and desired me to shew them some Proofs of my prodigious Strength, of which they had heard so many Wonders; wherein I readily obliged them, but shall not interrupt the Reader with the Particulars.

When I had for some time entertained their Excellencies to their infinite Satisfaction and Surprize, I desired they would do me the Honour to present my most humble Respects to the Emperor their Master, the Renown of whose Virtues had so justly filled the whole World with Admiration, and whose Royal Person I resolved to attend before I returned to my own Country. Accordingly, the next time I had the Honour to see our Emperor, I desired his general Licence to wait on the *Blefuscudian* Monarch, which he was pleased to grant me, as I could plainly perceive, in a very cold Manner; but could not guess the Reason, till I had a Whisper from a certain Person, that *Flimnap* and *Bolgolam* had represented my Intercourse with those Ambassadors, as a Mark of Disaffection, from which I am sure my Heart was wholly free. And this was the first time I began to conceive some imperfect Idea of Courts and Ministers.[1]

It is to be observed, that these Ambassadors spoke to me by an Interpreter; the Languages of both Empires differing as much from each other as any two in *Europe*, and each Nation priding itself upon the Antiquity, Beauty, and Energy of their own Tongues, with an avowed Contempt for that of their Neighbour: Yet our Emperor standing upon the Advantage he had got by the Seizure of their Fleet, obliged them to deliver their Credentials, and make their Speech in the *Lilliputian* Tongue. And it must be confessed, that from the great Intercourse of Trade and Commerce between both Realms; from the continual Reception of Exiles, which is mutual among them; and from the Custom in each Empire to send their young Nobility and richer Gentry to the other, in order to polish themselves, by seeing the World, and understanding Men and Manners; there are few Persons of Distinction, or Merchants, or Seamen, who dwell in the Maritime Parts, but what can hold Conversation in both Tongues; as I found some Weeks after, when I went to pay my Respects to the Emperor of *Blefuscu*, which in the Midst of great Misfortunes, through the Malice of my Enemies, proved a very happy Adventure to me, as I shall relate in its proper Place.

The Reader may remember, that when I signed those Articles upon which I recovered my Liberty, there were some which I disliked upon Account of their being too servile, neither could any thing but an extreme Necessity have forced me to submit. But being now a *Nardac*, of the highest Rank in that Empire, such Offices were looked upon as below my Dignity; and the Emperor (to do him Justice) never once mentioned them to me. However, it was not long before I had an Opportunity of doing his Majesty,

[1] Gulliver's capture of the fleet has reference to the Treaty of Utrecht, which, effected by the Tories, ended the war with France. Claims of Gulliver's "disaffection" echo Whig claims that the Treaty was too generous to France, while the fact that Gulliver's was a naval victory reflects the Tory contention that the Treaty preserved England's mastery of the seas. Here again, Gulliver stands for the Tory leaders, Oxford and Bolingbroke.

at least, as I then thought, a most signal Service. I was alarmed at Midnight with the Cries of many Hundred People at my Door; by which being suddenly awaked, I was in some Kind of Terror. I heard the Word *Burglum* repeated incessantly; several of the Emperor's Court making their Way through the Croud, intreated me to come immediately to the Palace, where her Imperial Majesty's Apartment was on fire, by the Carelessness of a Maid of Honour, who fell asleep while she was reading a Romance. I got up in an Instant; and Orders being given to clear the Way before me; and it being likewise a Moonshine Night, I made a shift to get to the Palace without trampling on any of the People. I found they had already applied Ladders to the Walls of the Apartment, and were well provided with Buckets, but the Water was at some Distance. These Buckets were about the Size of a large Thimble, and the poor People supplied me with them as fast as they could; but the Flame was so violent, that they did little Good. I might easily have stifled it with my Coat, which I unfortunately left behind me for haste, and came away only in my Leathern Jerkin. The Case seemed wholly desperate and deplorable; and this magnificent Palace would have infallibly been burnt down to the Ground, if, by a Presence of Mind, unusual to me, I had not suddenly thought of an Expedient. I had the Evening before drank plentifully of a most delicious Wine, called *Glimigrim*, (the *Blefuscudians* call it *Flunec*, but ours is esteemed the better Sort) which is very diuretick. By the luckiest Chance in the World, I had not discharged myself of any Part of it. The Heat I had contracted by coming very near the Flames, and by my labouring to quench them, made the Wine begin to operate by Urine; which I voided in such a Quantity, and applied so well to the proper Places, that in three Minutes the Fire was wholly extinguished; and the rest of that noble Pile, which had cost so many Ages in erecting, preserved from Destruction.

It was now Day-light, and I returned to my House, without waiting to congratulate with the Emperor; because, although I had done a very eminent Piece of Service, yet I could not tell how his Majesty might resent the Manner by which I had performed it: For, by the fundamental Laws of the Realm, it is Capital in any Person, of what Quality soever, to make water within the Precincts of the Palace. But I was a little comforted by a Message from his Majesty, that he would give Orders to the Grand Justiciary for passing my Pardon in Form; which, however, I could not obtain.

And I was privately assured, that the Empress conceiving the greatest Abhorrence of what I had done, removed to the most distant Side of the Court, firmly resolved that those Buildings should never be repaired for her Use; and, in the Presence of her chief Confidents, could not forbear vowing Revenge.[2]

CHAPTER VI

Of the Inhabitants of Lilliput; *their Learning, Laws, and Customs. The Manner of Educating their Children. The Author's Way of living in that Country. His Vindication of a great Lady.*

Although I intend to leave the Description of this Empire to a particular Treatise, yet in the mean time I am content to gratify the curious Reader with some general Ideas. As the common Size of the Natives is somewhat under six Inches, so there is an exact Proportion in all other Animals, as well as Plants and Trees: For Instance, the tallest Horses and Oxen are between four and five Inches in Height, the Sheep an Inch and a half, more or less; their Geese about the Bigness of a Sparrow; and so the several Gradations downwards, till you come to the smallest, which, to my Sight, were almost invisible; but Nature hath adapted the Eyes of the *Lilliputians* to all Objects proper for their View: They see with great Exactness, but at no great Distance. And to show the Sharpness of their Sight towards Objects that are near, I have been much pleased with observing a Cook pulling a Lark, which was not so large as a common Fly; and a young Girl threading an invisible Needle with invisible Silk. Their tallest Trees are about seven Foot high; I mean some of those in the great Royal Park, the Tops whereof I could but just reach with my Fist clinched. The

[2] The Empress here represents Queen Anne, and her response seems to relate to Anne's reaction to Swift's earlier work, A *Tale of a Tub*, which she thought coarse and disrespectful to religion. Her "revenge" was to limit Swift's chances of preferment within the Church of England.

other Vegetables are in the same Proportion: But this I leave to the Reader's Imagination.

I shall say but little at present of their Learning, which for many Ages hath flourished in all its Branches among them: But their Manner of Writing is very peculiar; being neither from the Left to the Right, like the *Europeans*; nor from the Right to the Left, like the *Arabians*; nor from up to down, like the *Chinese*; nor from down to up, like the *Cascagians*; but aslant from one Corner of the Paper to the other, like Ladies in *England*.

They bury their Dead with their Heads directly downwards; because they hold an Opinion, that in eleven Thousand Moons they are all to rise again; in which Period, the Earth (which they conceive to be flat) will turn upside down, and by this Means they shall, at their Resurrection, be found ready standing on their Feet. The Learned among them confess the Absurdity of this Doctrine; but the Practice still continues, in Compliance to the Vulgar.

There are some Laws and Customs in this Empire very peculiar; and if they were not so directly contrary to those of my own dear Country, I should be tempted to say a little in their Justification. It is only to be wished, that they were as well executed. The first I shall mention, relateth to Informers. All Crimes against the State, are punished here with the utmost Severity; but if the Person accused make his Innocence plainly to appear upon his Tryal, the Accuser is immediately put to an ignominious Death; and out of his Goods or Lands, the innocent Person is quadruply recompensed for the Loss of his Time, for the Danger he underwent, for the Hardship of his Imprisonment, and for all the Charges he hath been at in making his Defence. Or, if that Fund be deficient, it is largely supplyed by the Crown. The Emperor doth also confer on him some publick Mark of his Favour; and Proclamation is made of his Innocence through the whole City.

They look upon Fraud as a greater Crime than Theft, and therefore seldom fail to punish it with Death: For they alledge, that Care and Vigilance, with a very common Understanding, may preserve a Man's Goods from Thieves; but Honesty hath nc Fence against superior Cunning: And since it is necessary that there should be a perpetual Intercourse of buying and selling, and dealing upon Credit; where Fraud is permitted or connived at, or hath no Law to punish it, the honest Dealer is always undone, and the Knave gets the Advantage. I remember when I was once interceeding with the King for a Criminal who had wronged his Master of a great Sum of Money, which he had received by Order, and ran away with; and happening to tell his Majesty, by way of Extenuation, that it was only a Breach of Trust; the Emperor thought it monstrous in me to offer, as a Defence, the greatest Aggravation of the Crime: And truly, I had little to say in Return, farther than the common Answer, that different Nations had different Customs; for, I confess, I was heartily ashamed.

Although we usually call Reward and Punishment, the two Hinges upon which all Government turns; yet I could never observe this Maxim to be put in Practice by any Nation, except that of *Lilliput*. Whoever can there bring sufficient Proof that he hath strictly observed the Laws of his Country for Seventy-three Moons, hath a Claim to certain Privileges, according to his Quality and Condition of Life, with a proportionable Sum of Money out of a Fund appropriated for that Use: He likewise acquires the Title of *Snilpall*, or *Legal*, which is added to his Name, but doth not descend to his Posterity. And these People thought it a prodigious Defect of Policy among us, when I told them that our Laws were enforced only by Penalties, without any Mention of Reward. It is upon this account that the Image of Justice, in their Courts of Judicature, is formed with six Eyes, two before, as many behind, and on each Side one, to signify Circumspection; with a Bag of Gold open in her right Hand, and a Sword sheathed in her left, to shew she is more disposed to reward than to punish.

In chusing Persons for all Employments, they have more Regard to good Morals than to great Abilities: For, since Government is necessary to Mankind, they believe that the common Size of human Understandings, is fitted to some Station or other; and that Providence never intended to make the Management of publick Affairs a Mystery, to be comprehended only by a few Persons of sublime Genius, of which there seldom are three born in an Age: But, they suppose Truth, Justice, Temperance, and the like, to be in every Man's Power; the Practice of which Virtues, assisted by Experience and a good Intention, would qualify any Man for the Service of his Country, except where a Course of Study is required. But they thought the Want of Moral Virtues was so far from being supplied by superior Endowments of the Mind, that Employments could never be put into such dangerous Hands as those of Persons so qualified; and at least, that the Mistakes committed by Ignorance in a virtuous Disposition, would never be of such fatal Consequence to the Publick Weal, as the Practices of a Man, whose Inclinations led him to be corrupt, and had great Abilities to manage, to multiply, and defend his Corruptions.

In like Manner, the Disbelief of a Divine Providence renders a Man uncapable of holding any publick Station: For, since Kings avow themselves to be the Deputies of Providence, the *Lilliputians* think nothing can be more absurd than for a Prince to employ such Men as disown the Authority under which he acteth.

In relating these and the following Laws, I would only be understood to mean the original Institutions, and not the most scandalous Corruptions into which these People are fallen by the degenerate Nature of Man. For as to that infamous Practice of acquiring great Employment by dancing on the Ropes, or Badges of Favour and Distinction by leaping over Sticks, and creeping under them; the Reader is to observe, that they were first introduced by the Grandfather of the Emperor now reigning; and grew to the present Height, by the gradual Increase of Party and Faction.

Ingratitude is among them a capital Crime, as we read it to have been in some other Countries: For they reason thus; that whoever makes ill Returns to his Benefactor, must needs be a common Enemy to the rest of Mankind, from whom he hath received no Obligation; and therefore such a Man is not fit to live.

Their Notions relating to the Duties of Parents and Children differ extremely from ours. For, since the Conjunction of Male and Female is founded upon the great Law of Nature, in order to propagate and continue the Species; the *Lilliputians* will needs have it, that Men and Women are joined together like other Animals, by the Motives of Concupiscence; and that their Tenderness towards their Young, proceedeth from the like natural Principle: For which Reason they will never allow, that a Child is under any Obligation to his Father for begetting him, or to his Mother for bringing him into the World; which, considering the Miseries of human Life, was neither a Benefit in itself, nor intended so by his Parents, whose Thoughts in their Love-encounters were otherwise employed. Upon these, and the like Reasonings, their Opinion is, that Parents are the last of all others to be trusted with the Education of their own Children: And therefore they have in every Town publick Nurseries, where all Parents, except Cottagers and Labourers, are obliged to send their Infants of both Sexes to be reared and educated when they come to the Age of twenty Moons; at which Time they are supposed to have some Rudiments of Docility. These Schools are of several Kinds, suited to different Qualities, and to both Sexes. They have certain Professors well skilled in preparing Children for such a Condition of Life as befits the Rank of their Parents, and their own Capacities as well as Inclinations. I shall first say something of the Male Nurseries, and then of the Female.

The Nurseries for Males of Noble or Eminent Birth, are provided with grave and learned Professors, and their several Deputies. The Clothes and Food of the Children are plain and simple. They are bred up in the Principles of Honour, Justice, Courage, Modesty, Clemency, Religion, and Love of their Country: They are always employed in some Business, except in the Times of eating and sleeping, which are very short, and two Hours for Diversions, consisting of bodily Exercises. They are dressed by Men until four Years of Age, and then are obliged to dress themselves, although their Quality be ever so great; and the Women Attendants, who are aged proportionably to ours at fifty, perform only the most menial Offices. They are never suffered to converse with Servants, but go together in small or greater Numbers to take their Diversions, and always in the Presence of a Professor, or one of his Deputies; whereby they avoid those early bad Impressions of Folly and Vice to which our Children are subject. Their Parents are suffered to see them only twice a Year; the Visit is not to last above an Hour; they are allowed to kiss the Child at Meeting and Parting; but a Professor, who always standeth by on those Occasions, will not suffer them to whisper, or use any fondling Expressions, or bring any Presents of Toys, Sweet-meats, and the like.

The Pension from each Family for the Education and Entertainment of a Child, upon Failure of due Payment, is levyed by the Emperor's Officers.

The Nurseries for Children of ordinary Gentlemen, Merchants, Traders, and Handicrafts, are managed proportionably after the same Manner; only those designed for Trades, are put out Apprentices at seven Years old; whereas those of Persons of Quality continue in their Exercises until Fifteen, which answers to One and Twenty with us: But the Confinement is gradually lessened for the last three Years.

In the Female Nurseries, the young Girls of Quality are educated much like the Males, only they are dressed by orderly Servants of their own Sex, but always in the Presence of a Professor or Deputy, until they come to dress themselves, which is at five Years old. And if it be found that these Nurses ever presume to entertain the Girls with frightful or foolish Stories, or the common Follies practised by Chamber-Maids among us; they are publickly whipped thrice about the City, imprisoned for a Year, and banished for Life to the most desolate Parts of the Country. Thus the young Ladies there are as much ashamed of being Cowards and Fools, as the Men; and despise all personal Ornaments beyond Decency and Cleanliness; neither did I perceive any Difference in their Education, made by their Difference of Sex, only that the Exercises of the Females were not altogther so robust; and that some Rules were given them relating to domestick Life, and a smaller Compass of Learning was enjoyned them: For, their Maxim is, that among People of Quality, a Wife should be always a reasonable and agreeable Companion, because she cannot always be young. When the Girls are twelve Years old, which among them is the marriageable Age, their Parents or Guardians take them home, with great Expressions of Gratitude to the Professors, and seldom without Tears of the young Lady and her Companions.

In the Nurseries of Females of the meaner Sort, the Children are instructed in all Kinds of Works proper for their Sex, and their several Degrees: Those intended for Apprentices are dismissed at seven Years old, the rest are kept to eleven.

The meaner Families who have Children at these Nurseries, are obliged, besides their annual Pension, which is as low as possible, to return to the Steward of the Nursery a small Monthly Share of their Gettings, to be a Portion for the Child; and therefore all Parents are limited in their Expences by the Law. For the *Lilliputians* think nothing can be more unjust, than that People, in Subservience to their own Appetites, should bring Children into the World, and leave the Burthen of supporting them on the Publick. As to Persons of Quality, they give Security to appropriate a certain Sum for each Child, suitable to their Condition; and these Funds are always managed with good Husbandry, and the most exact Justice.

The Cottagers and Labourers keep their Children at home, their Business being only to till and cultivate the Earth; and therefore their Education is of little Consequence to the Publick; but the

Old and Diseased among them are supported by Hospitals: For begging is a Trade unknown in this Empire.

And here it may perhaps divert the curious Reader, to give some Account of my Domestick, and my Manner of living in this Country, during a Residence of nine Months and thirteen Days. Having a Head mechanically turned, and being likewise forced by Necessity, I had made for myself a Table and Chair convenient enough, out of the largest Trees in the Royal Park. Two hundred Sempstresses were employed to make me Shirts, and Linnen for my Bed and Table, all of the strongest and coarsest kind they could get; which, however, they were forced to quilt together in several Folds; for the thickest was some Degrees finer than Lawn. Their Linnen is usually three Inches wide, and three Foot make a Piece. The Sempstresses took my Measure as I lay on the Ground, one standing at my Neck, and another at my Mid-Leg, with a strong Cord extended, that each held by the End, while the third measured the Length of the Cord with a Rule of an Inch long. Then they measured my right Thumb, and desired no more; for by a mathematical Computation, that twice round the Thumb is once round the Wrist, and so on to the Neck and the Waist; and by the Help of my old Shirt, which I displayed on the Ground before them for a Pattern, they fitted me exactly. Three hundred Taylors were employed in the same Manner to make me Clothes; but they had another Contrivance for taking my Measure. I kneeled down, and they raised a Ladder from the Ground to my Neck; upon this Ladder one of them mounted, and let fall a Plum-Line from my Collar to the Floor, which just answered the Length of my Coat; but my Waist and Arms I measured myself. When my Cloaths were finished, which was done in my House, (for the largest of theirs would not have been able to hold them) they looked like the Patch-work made by the Ladies in *England*, only that mine were all of a Colour.

I had three hundred Cooks to dress my Victuals, in little convenient Huts built about my House, where they and their Families lived, and prepared me two Dishes a-piece. I took up twenty Waiters in my Hand, and placed them on the Table; an hundred more attended below on the Ground, some with Dishes of Meat, and some with Barrels of Wine, and other Liquors, slung on their Shoulders; all which the Waiters above drew up as I wanted, in a very ingenious Manner, by certain Cords, as we draw the Bucket up a Well in *Europe*. A Dish of their Meat was a good Mouthful, and a Barrel of their Liquor a reasonable Draught. Their Mutton yields to ours, but their Beef is excellent. I have had a Sirloin so large, that I have been forced to make three Bites of it; but this is rare. My Servants were astonished to see me eat it Bones and all, as in our Country we do the Leg of a Lark. Their Geese and Turkeys I usually eat at a Mouthful, and I must confess they far exceed ours. Of their smaller Fowl I could take up twenty or thirty at the End of my Knife.

One day his Imperial Majesty being informed of my Way of living, desired that himself, and his Royal Consort, with the young Princes of the Blood of both Sexes, might have the Happiness (as he was pleased to call it) of dining with me. They came accordingly, and I placed them upon Chairs of State on my Table, just over against me, with their Guards about them. *Flimnap* the Lord High Treasurer attended there likewise, with his white Staff; and I observed he often looked on me with a sour Countenance, which I would not seem to regard, but eat more than usual, in Honour to my dear Country, as well as to fill the Court with Admiration. I have some private Reasons to believe, that this Visit from his Majesty gave *Flimnap* an Opportunity of doing me ill Offices to his Master. That Minister had always been my secret Enemy, although he outwardly caressed me more than was usual to the Moroseness of his Nature. He represented to the Emperor the low Condition of his Treasury; that he was forced to take up Money at great Discount; that Exchequer Bills would not circulate under nine *per Cent.* below Par; that I had cost his Majesty above a Million and a half of *Sprugs,* (their greatest Gold Coin, about the Bigness of a Spangle;) and upon the whole, that it would be advisable in the Emperor to take the first fair Occasion of dismissing me.

I am here obliged to vindicate the Reputation of an excellent Lady, who was an innocent Sufferer upon my Account. The Treasurer took a Fancy to be jealous of his Wife, from the Malice of some evil Tongues, who informed him that her Grace had taken a violent Affection for my Person; and the Court-Scandal ran for some Time that she once came privately to my Lodging. This I solemnly declare to be a most infamous Falshood, without any Grounds, farther than that her Grace was pleased to treat me with all innocent Marks of Freedom and Friendship.[1] I own she came

[1] This affair is another slash at Walpole, who, unlike the over-sensitive Flimnap, was little bothered by his wife's infidelities.

often to my House, but always publickly, nor ever without three more in the Coach, who were usually her Sister, and young Daughter, and some particular Acquaintance; but this was common to many other Ladies of the Court. And I still appeal to my Servants round, whether they at any Time saw a Coach at my Door without knowing what Persons were in it. On those occasions, when a Servant had given me Notice, my Custom was to go immediately to the Door; and after paying my Respects, to take up the Coach and two Horses very carefully in my Hands, (for if there were six Horses, the Postillion always unharnessed four) and place them on a Table, where I had fixed a moveable Rim quite round, of five Inches high, to prevent Accidents. And I have often had four Coaches and Horses at once on my Table full of Company, while I sat in my Chair leaning my Face towards them; and when I was engaged with one Sett, the Coachmen would gently drive the others round my Table. I have passed many an Afternoon very agreeably in these Conversations: But I defy the Treasurer, or his two Informers, (I will name them, and let them make their best of it) *Clustril* and *Drunlo*, to prove that any Person ever came to me *incognito*, except the Secretary *Reldresal*, who was sent by express Command of his Imperial Majesty, as I have before related. I should not have dwelt so long upon this Particular, if it had not been a Point wherein the Reputation of a great Lady is so nearly concerned, to say nothing of my own; although I had the Honour to be a *Nardac*, which the Treasurer himself is not; for all the World knows he is only a *Clumglum*, a Title inferior by one Degree, as that of a Marquess is to a Duke in *England*; yet I allow he preceded me in right of his Post. These false Informations, which I afterwards came to the Knowledge of, by an Accident not proper to mention, made the Treasurer shew his Lady for some Time an ill Countenance, and me a worse: For although he were at last undeceived and reconciled to her, yet I lost all Credit with him; and found my Interest decline very fast with the Emperor himself, who was indeed too much governed by that Favourite.

CHAPTER VII

The Author being informed of a Design to accuse him of High Treason, makes his Escape to Blefuscu. *His Reception there.*

Before I proceed to give an Account of my leaving this Kingdom, it may be proper to inform the Reader of a private Intrigue which had been for two Months forming against me.

I had been hitherto all my Life a Stranger to Courts, for which I was unqualified by the Meanness of my Condition. I had indeed heard and read enough of the Dispositions of great Princes and Ministers; but never expected to have found such terrible Effects of them in so remote a Country, governed, as I thought, by very different Maxims from those in *Europe*.

When I was just preparing to pay my Attendance on the Emperor of *Blefuscu*; a considerable Person at Court (to whom I had been very serviceable at a time when he lay under the highest Displeasure of his Imperial Majesty) came to my House very privately at Night in a close Chair, and without sending his Name, desired Admittance: The Chair-men were dismissed; I put the Chair, with his Lordship in it, into my Coat-Pocket; and giving Orders to a trusty Servant to say I was indisposed and gone to sleep, I fastened the Door of my House, placed the Chair on the Table, according to my usual Custom, and sat down by it. After the common Salutations were over, observing his Lordship's Countenance full of Concern; and enquiring into the Reason, he desired I would hear him with Patience, in a Matter that highly concerned my Honour and my Life. His Speech was to the following Effect, for I took Notes of it as soon as he left me.

You are to know, said he, that several Committees of Council have been lately called in the most private Manner on your Account: And it is but two Days since his Majesty came to a full Resolution.

You are very sensible that *Skyris Bolgolam* (*Galbet*, or High Admiral) hath been your mortal Enemy almost ever since your Arrival. His original Reasons I know not; but his Hatred is much increased since your great Success against *Blefuscu*, by which his Glory, as Admiral, is obscured. This Lord, in Conjunction with *Flimnap* the High Treasurer, whose Enmity against you is notorious on Account of his Lady; *Limtoc* the General, *Lalcon* the Chamberlain, and *Balmuff* the grand Justiciary, have prepared Articles of Impeachment against you, for Treason, and other capital Crimes.

This Preface made me so impatient, being conscious of my own Merits and Innocence, that I was going to interrupt; when he intreated me to be silent; and thus proceeded.

Out of Gratitude for the Favours you have done me, I procured Information of the whole Proceedings, and a Copy of the Articles, wherein I venture my Head for your Service.

Articles of Impeachment against Quinbus Flestrin,

(*the* Man-Mountain).[1]

ARTICLE 1

Whereas, by a Statute made in the Reign of his Imperial Majesty *Calin Deffar Plune*, it is enacted, That whoever shall make water within the Precincts of the Royal Palace, shall be liable to the Pains and Penalties of High Treason: Notwithstanding, the said *Quinbus Flestrin*, in open Breach of the said Law, under Colour of extinguishing the Fire kindled in the Apartment of his Majesty's most dear Imperial Consort, did maliciously, traitorously, and devilishly, by discharge of his Urine, put out the said Fire kindled in the said Apartment, lying and being within the Precincts of the said Royal Palace; against the Statute in that Case provided, &c. against the Duty, &c.

ARTICLE 2

That the said *Quinbus Flestrin* having brought the Imperial Fleet of *Blefuscu* into the Royal Port, and being afterwards commanded by his Imperial Majesty to seize all the other Ships of the said Empire of *Blefuscu*, and reduce that Empire to a

[1] The investigation of Oxford and Bolingbroke in 1715 (see p. 19, n. 3) led to their impeachment for treason; the charges against them Swift satirizes in the articles that follow.

Province, to be governed by a Vice-Roy from hence; and to destroy and put to death not only all the *Big-Endian Exiles*, but likewise all the People of that Empire, who would not immediately forsake the *Big-Endian* Heresy: He the said *Flestrin*, like a false Traitor against his most Auspicious, Serene, Imperial Majesty, did petition to be excused from the said Service, upon Pretence of Unwillingness to force the Consciences, or destroy the Liberties and Lives of an innocent People.

ARTICLE 3

That, whereas certain Embassadors arrived from the Court of *Blefuscu* to sue for Peace in his Majesty's Court:

He the said *Flestrin* did, like a false Traitor, aid, abet, comfort, and divert the said Embassadors; although he knew them to be Servants to a Prince who was lately an open Enemy to his Imperial Majesty, and in open War against his said Majesty.

ARTICLE 4

That the said *Quinbus Flestrin*, contrary to the Duty of a faithful Subject, is now preparing to make a Voyage to the Court and Empire of *Blefuscu*, for which he hath received only verbal Licence from his Imperial Majesty; and under Colour of the said Licence, doth falsely and traitorously intend to take the said Voyage, and thereby to aid, comfort, and abet the Emperor of *Blefuscu*, so late an Enemy, and in open War with his Imperial Majesty aforesaid.

There are some other Articles, but these are the most important, of which I have read you an Abstract.

In the several Debates upon this Impeachment, it must be confessed that his Majesty gave many Marks of his great *Lenity*; often urging the Services you had done him, and endeavouring to extenuate your Crimes. The Treasurer and Admiral insisted that you should be put to the most painful and ignominious Death, by setting Fire on your House at Night; and the General was to attend with Twenty Thousand Men armed with poisoned Arrows, to shoot you on the Face and Hands. Some of your Servants were to have private Orders to strew a poisonous Juice on your Shirts and Sheets, which would soon make you tear your own Flesh, and die in the utmost Torture. The General came into the same Opinion; so that for a long time there was a Majority against you. But his Majesty resolving, if possible, to spare your Life, at last brought off the Chamberlain.

Upon this Incident, *Reldresal*, principal Secretary for private Affairs, who always approved himself your true Friend, was commanded by the Emperor to deliver his Opinion, which he accordingly did; and therein justified the good Thoughts you have of him. He allowed your Crimes to be great; but that still there was room for Mercy, the most commendable Virtue in a Prince, and for which his Majesty was so justly celebrated. He said, the Friendship between you and him was so well known to the World, that perhaps the most honourable Board might think him partial: However, in Obedience to the Command he had received, he would freely offer his Sentiments. That if his Majesty, in Consideration of your Services, and pursuant to his own merciful Disposition, would please to spare your Life, and only give order to put out both your Eyes; he humbly conceived, that by this Expedient, Justice might in some measure be satisfied, and all the World would applaud the *Lenity* of the Emperor, as well as the fair and generous Proceedings of those who have the Honour to be his Counsellors. That the Loss of your Eyes would be no Impediment to your bodily Strength, by which you might still be useful to his Majesty. That Blindness is an Addition to Courage, by concealing Dangers from us; that the Fear you had for your Eyes, was the greatest Difficulty in bringing over the Enemy's Fleet; and it would be sufficient for you to see by the Eyes of the Ministers, since the greatest Princes do no more.

This Proposal was received with the utmost Disapprobation by the whole Board. *Bolgolam*, the Admiral, could not preserve his Temper; but rising up in Fury, said, he wondered how the Secretary durst presume to give his Opinion for preserving the Life of a Traytor: That the Services you had performed, were, by all true Reasons of State, the great Aggravation of your Crimes; that you, who were able to extinguish the Fire, by discharge of Urine in her Majesty's Apartment (which he mentioned with Horror) might, at another time, raise an Inundation by the same Means, to drown the whole Palace; and the same Strength which enabled you to bring over the Enemy's Fleet, might serve, upon the first Discontent, to carry it back; that he had good Reasons to think you were a *Big-Endian* in your Heart; and as Treason begins in the Heart before it appears in Overt-Acts; so he accused you as a Traytor on that Account, and therefore insisted you should be put to death.

The Treasurer was of the same Opinion; he shewed to what Streights his Majesty's Revenue was reduced by the Charge of maintaining you, which would soon grow insupportable: That the Secretary's Expedient of putting out your Eyes, was so far from being a Remedy against this Evil, that it would probably increase it; as it is manifest from the common Practice of blinding some Kind of Fowl, after which they fed the faster, and grew sooner fat: That his sacred Majesty, and the Council, who are your Judges, were in their own Consciences fully convinced of your Guilt; which was a sufficient Argument to condemn you to death, without the *formal Proofs required by the strict Letter of the Law.*

But his Imperial Majesty fully determined against capital Punishment, was graciously pleased to say, that since the Council thought the Loss of your Eyes too easy a Censure, some other may be inflicted hereafter. And your Friend the Secretary humbly desiring to be heard again, in Answer to what the Treasurer had objected concerning the great Charge his Majesty was at in maintaining you; said, that his Excellency, who had the sole Disposal of the Emperor's Revenue, might easily provide against this Evil, by gradually lessening your Establishment; by which, for want of sufficient Food, you would grow weak and faint, and lose your Appetite, and consequently decay and consume in a few Months; neither would the Stench of your Carcass be then so dangerous, when it should become more than half diminished; and immediately upon your Death, five or six Thousand of his Majesty's Subjects might, in two or three Days, cut your Flesh from your Bones, take it away by Cart-loads, and bury it in distant Parts to prevent Infection; leaving the Skeleton as a Monument of Admiration to Posterity.

Thus by the great Friendship of the Secretary, the whole Affair was compromised. It was strictly enjoined, that the Project of starving you by Degrees should be kept a Secret; but the Sentence of putting out your Eyes was entered on the Books; none dissenting except *Bolgolam* the Admiral, who being a Creature of the Empress, was perpetually instigated by her Majesty to insist upon your Death; she having born perpetual Malice against you, on Account of that infamous and illegal Method you took to extinguish the Fire in her Apartment.

In three Days your Friend the Secretary will be directed to come to your House, and read before you the Articles of Impeachment; and then to signify the great *Lenity* and Favour of his Majesty and Council; whereby you are only condemned to the Loss of your Eyes, which his Majesty doth not question you will gratefully and humbly submit to; and Twenty of his Majesty's Surgeons will attend, in order to see the Operation well performed, by discharging very sharp pointed Arrows into the Balls of your Eyes, as you lie on the Ground

I leave to your Prudence what Measures you will take; and to avoid Suspicion, I must immediately return in as private a Manner as I came.

His Lordship did so, and I remained alone, under many Doubts and Perplexities of Mind.

It was a Custom introduced by this Prince and his Ministry, (very different, as I have been assured, from the Practices of former Times) that after the Court had decreed any cruel Execution, either to gratify the Monarch's Resentment, or the Malice of a Favourite; the Emperor always made a Speech to his whole Council, expressing his *great Lenity and Tenderness, as Qualities known and confessed by all the* World. This Speech was immediately published through the Kingdom; nor did any thing terrify the People so much as those Encomiums on his Majesty's Mercy; because it was observed, that the more these Praises were enlarged and insisted on, the more *inhuman* was the Punishment, and the *Sufferer more innocent*. Yet, as to myself, I must confess, having never been designed for a Courtier, either by my Birth or Education, I was so ill a Judge of Things, that I could not discover the *Lenity* and Favour of this Sentence; but conceived it (perhaps erroneously) rather to be rigorous than gentle. I sometimes thought of standing my Tryal; for although I could not deny the Facts alledged in the several Articles, yet I hoped they would admit of some Extenuations. But having in my Life perused many State-Tryals, which I ever observed to terminate as the Judges thought fit to direct; I durst not rely on so dangerous a Decision, in so critical a Juncture, and against such powerful Enemies. Once I was strongly bent upon Resistance: For while I had Liberty, the whole Strength of that Empire could hardly subdue me, and I might easily with Stones pelt the Metropolis to Pieces: But I soon rejected that Project with Horror, by remembering the Oath I had made to the Emperor, the Favours I received from him, and the high Title of *Nardac* he conferred upon me. Neither had I so soon learned the Gratitude of Courtiers, to persuade myself that his Majesty's *present Severities acquitted me of all past Obligations.*

At last I fixed upon a Resolution, for which it is probable I may incur some Censure, and not unjustly; for I confess I owe the preserving my Eyes, and consequently my Liberty, to my own great Rashness and Want of Experience: Because if I had then known the Nature of Princes and Ministers, which I have since observed in many other Courts, and their Methods of treating Criminals less obnoxious than myself; I should with great Alacrity and Readiness have submitted to so *easy* a Punishment. But hurried on by the Precipitancy of Youth; and having his Imperial Majesty's Licence to pay my Attendance upon the Emperor of *Blefuscu;* I took this Opportunity, before the three Days were elapsed, to send a Letter to my Friend the Secretary, signifying my Resolution of setting out that Morning for *Blefuscu,* pursuant to the Leave I had got; and without waiting for an Answer, I went to that Side of the Island where our Fleet lay. I seized a large Man of War, tied a Cable to the Prow, and lifting up the Anchors, I stript myself, put my Cloaths (together with my Coverlet, which I carryed under my Arm) into the Vessel; and drawing it after me, between wading and swimming, arrived at the Royal Port of *Blefuscu,* where the People had long expected me[2]: They lent me two Guides to direct me to the Capital City, which is of the same Name; I held them in my Hands until I came within two Hundred Yards of the Gate; and desired them to signify my Arrival to one of the Secretaries, and let him know, I there waited his Majesty's Commands. I had an Answer in about an Hour, that his Majesty, attended by the Royal Family, and great Officers of the Court, was coming out to receive me. I advanced a Hundred Yards; the Emperor, and his Train, alighted from their Horses, the Empress and Ladies from their Coaches; and I did not perceive they were in any Fright or Concern. I lay on the Ground to kiss his Majesty's and the Empress's Hand. I told his Majesty, that I was come according to my Promise, and with the Licence of the Emperor my Master, to have the Honour of seeing so mighty a Monarch, and to offer him any Service in my Power, consistent with my Duty to my own Prince;

[2] Gulliver's departure corresponds to Bolingbroke's escape to France just prior to the trial. Oxford remained in England, and the charges against him were dropped two years later.

not mentioning a Word of my Disgrace, because I had hitherto no regular Information of it, and might suppose myself wholly ignorant of any such Design; neither could I reasonably conceive that the Emperor would discover the Secret while I was out of his Power: Wherein, however, it soon appeared I was deceived.

I shall not trouble the Reader with the particular Account of my Reception at this Court, which was suitable to the Generosity of so great a Prince; nor of the Difficulties I was in for want of a House and Bed, being forced to lie on the Ground, wrapt up in my Coverlet.

CHAPTER VIII

The Author, by a lucky Accident, finds Means to leave Blefuscu; *and, after some Difficulties, returns safe to his Native Country.*

Three Days after my Arrival, walking out of Curiosity to the North-East Coast of the Island; I observed, about half a League off, in the Sea, somewhat that looked like a Boat overturned: I pulled off my Shoes and Stockings, and wading two or three Hundred Yards, I found the Object to approach nearer by Force of the Tide; and then plainly saw it to be a real Boat, which I supposed might, by some Tempest, have been driven from a Ship. Whereupon I returned immediately towards the City, and desired his Imperial Majesty to lend me Twenty of the tallest Vessels he had left after the Loss of his Fleet, and three Thousand Seamen under the Command of his Vice Admiral. This Fleet sailed round, while I went back the shortest Way to the Coast where I first discovered the Boat; I found the Tide had driven it still nearer; the Seamen were all provided with Cordage, which I had beforehand twisted to a sufficient Strength. When the Ships came up, I stript myself, and waded till I came within an Hundred Yards of the Boat; after which I was forced to swim till I got up to it. The Seamen threw me the End of the Cord, which I fastened to a Hole in the fore-part of the Boat, and the other End to a Man of War: But I found all my Labour to little Purpose; for being out of my Depth, I was not able to work. In this Necessity, I was forced to swim behind, and push the Boat forwards as often as I could, with one of my Hands; and the Tide favouring me, I advanced so far, that I could just hold up my Chin and feel the Ground. I rested two or three Minutes, and then gave the Boat another Shove, and so on till the Sea was no higher than my Arm-pits. And now the most laborious Part being over, I took out my other Cables which were stowed in one of the Ships, and fastening them first to the Boat, and then to nine of the Vessels which attended me; the Wind being favourable, the Seamen towed, and I shoved till we arrived within forty Yards of the Shore; and waiting till the Tide was out, I got dry to the Boat, and by the Assistance of two Thousand Men, with Ropes and Engines, I made a shift to turn it on its Bottom, and found it was but little damaged.

I shall not trouble the Reader with the Difficulties I was under by the Help of certain Paddles, which cost me ten Days making, to get my Boat to the Royal Port of *Blefuscu*; where a mighty Concourse of People appeared upon my Arrival, full of Wonder at the Sight of so prodigious a Vessel. I told the Emperor, that my good Fortune had thrown this Boat in my Way, to carry me to some Place from whence I might return into my native Country; and begged his Majesty's Orders for getting Materials to fit it up; together with his Licence to depart; which, after some kind Expostulations, he was pleased to grant.

I did very much wonder, in all this Time, not to have heard of any Express relating to me from our Emperor to the Court of *Blefuscu*. But I was afterwards given privately to understand, that his Imperial Majesty, never imagining I had the least Notice of his Designs, believed I was only gone to *Blefuscu* in Performance of my Promise, according to the Licence he had given me, which was well known at our Court; and would return in a few Days when that Ceremony was ended. But he was at last in pain at my long absence; and, after consulting with the Treasurer, and the rest of that Cabal; a Person of Quality was dispatched with the Copy of the Articles against me. This Envoy had Instructions to represent to the Monarch of *Blefuscu*, the great *Lenity* of his Master, who was content to punish me no further than with the Loss of my Eyes: That I had fled from Justice, and if I did not return in two Hours, I should be deprived of my Title of *Nardac*, and declared a Traitor. The Envoy further added; that in order to maintain the Peace and Amity between both Empires, his Master expected, that his Brother of *Blefuscu* would give Orders to have me sent back to *Lilliput*, bound Hand and Foot, to be punished as a Traitor.

The Emperor of *Blefuscu* having taken three Days to consult, returned an Answer consisting of many Civilities and Excuses. He said, that as for sending me bound, his Brother knew it was impossible; that although I had deprived him of his Fleet, yet he owed great Obligations to me for many good Offices I had done him in making the Peace. That however, both their Majesties would soon be made easy; for I had found a prodigious Vessel on the Shore, able to carry me on the Sea, which he had given order to fit up with my own Assistance and Direction; and he hoped in a few Weeks both Empires would be freed from so insupportable an Incumbrance.

With this Answer the Envoy returned to *Lilliput*, and the Monarch of *Blefuscu* related to me all that had past; offering me at the same time (but under the strictest Confidence) his gracious Protection, if I would continue in his Service; wherein although I believed him sincere, yet I resolved never more to put any Confidence in Princes or Ministers, where I could possibly avoid it; and therefore, with all due Acknowledgments for his favourable Intentions, I humbly begged to be excused. I told him, that since Fortune, whether good or evil, had thrown a Vessel in my Way; I was resolved to venture myself in the Ocean, rather than be an Occasion of Difference between two such mighty Monarchs. Neither did I find the Emperor at all displeased; and I discovered by a certain Accident, that he was very glad of my Resolution, and so were most of his Ministers.

These Considerations moved me to hasten my Departure somewhat sooner than I intended; to which the Court, impatient to have me gone, very readily contributed. Five hundred Workmen were employed to make two Sails to my Boat, according to my Directions, by quilting thirteen fold of their strongest Linnen together. I was at the Pains of making Ropes and Cables, by twisting ten, twenty or thirty of the thickest and strongest of theirs. A great Stone that I happened to find, after a long Search by the Seashore, served me for an Anchor. I had the Tallow of three hundred Cows for greasing my Boat, and other Uses. I was at incredible Pains in cutting down some of the largest Timber Trees for Oars and Masts, wherein I was, however, much assisted by his Majesty's Ship-Carpenters, who helped me in smoothing them, after I had done the rough Work.

In about a Month, when all was prepared, I sent to receive his Majesty's Commands, and to take my leave. The Emperor and Royal Family came out of the Palace; I lay down on my Face to kiss his Hand, which he very graciously gave me; so did the Empress, and young Princes of the Blood. His Majesty presented me with fifty Purses of two hundred *Sprugs* a-piece, together with his Picture at full length, which I put immediately into one of my Gloves, to keep it from being hurt. The Ceremonies at my Departure were too many to trouble the Reader with at this time.

I stored the Boat with the Carcasses of an hundred Oxen, and three hundred Sheep, with Bread and Drink proportionable, and as much Meat ready dressed as four hundred Cooks could provide. I took with me six Cows and two Bulls alive, with as many Yews and Rams, intending to carry them into my own Country and propagate the Breed. And to feed them on board, I had a good Bundle of Hay, and a Bag of Corn. I would gladly have taken a Dozen of the Natives; but this was a thing the Emperor would by no Means permit; and besides a diligent Search into my Pockets, his Majesty engaged my Honour not to carry away any of his Subjects, although with their own Consent and Desire.

Having thus prepared all things as well as I was able; I set sail on the Twenty-fourth Day of *September* 1701, at six in the Morning; and when I had gone about four Leagues to the Northward, the Wind being at South-East; at six in the Evening, I descryed a small Island about half a League to the North-West. I advanced forward, and cast Anchor on the Lee-side of the Island, which seemed to be uninhabited. I then took some Refreshment, and went to my Rest. I slept well, and as I conjecture at least six Hours; for I found the Day broke in two Hours after I awaked. It was a clear Night; I eat my Breakfast before the Sun was up; and heaving Anchor, the Wind being favourable, I steered the same Course that I had done the Day before, wherein I was directed by my Pocket-Compass. My Intention was to reach, if possible, one of those Islands, which I had reason to believe lay to the North-East of *Van Diemen's* Land. I discovered nothing all that Day; but upon the next, about three in the Afternoon, when I had by my Computation made Twenty-four Leagues from *Blefuscu,* I descryed a Sail steering to the South-East; my Course was due East. I hailed her, but could get no Answer; yet I found I gained upon her, for the Wind slackened. I made all the Sail I could, and in half an Hour she spyed me, then hung out her Antient,[1] and discharged a Gun. It is not easy to express the Joy I was in upon the unexpected Hope of once more seeing my beloved Country, and the dear Pledges I had left in it. The Ship slackned her Sails, and I came up with her between five and six in the Evening, *September* 26; but my Heart leapt within me to see her *English* Colours. I put my Cows and Sheep into my Coat-Pockets, and got on board with all my Cargo of Provisions. The Vessel was an *English* Merchant-man, returning from *Japan* by the *North* and *South Seas;* the Captain, Mr. *John Biddel* of *Deptford,* a very civil Man, and an excellent Sailor. We were now in the Latitude of 30 Degrees South; there were about fifty Men in the Ship; and here I met an old Comrade of mine, one *Peter Williams,* who gave me a good Character to the Captain. This Gentleman treated me with Kindness, and desired I would let him know what Place I came from last, and whither I was bound; which I did in few Words; but he thought I was raving, and that the Dangers I underwent had disturbed my Head; whereupon I took my black Cattle and Sheep out of my Pocket, which, after great Astonishment, clearly convinced him of my Veracity. I then shewed him the Gold given me by the Emperor of *Blefuscu,* together with his Majesty's Picture at full Length, and some other Rarities of that Country. I gave him two Purses of two Hundred *Sprugs* each, and promised, when we arrived in *England,* to make him a Present of a Cow and a Sheep big with Young.

I shall not trouble the Reader with a particular Account of this Voyage; which was very prosperous for the most Part. We arrived in the *Downs*[2] on the 13th of *April* 1702. I had only one Misfortune, that the Rats on board carried away one of my Sheep; I found her Bones in a Hole, picked clean from the Flesh. The rest of my Cattle I got safe on Shore, and set them a grazing in a Bowling-Green at *Greenwich,* where the Fineness of the Grass made them feed very heartily, although I had always feared the

[1] Hung out her flag.
[2] A roadstead on the coast of southeastern England.

contrary: Neither could I possibly have preserved them in so long a Voyage, if the Captain had not allowed me some of his best Bisket, which rubbed to Powder, and mingled with Water, was their constant Food. The short Time I continued in *England*, I made a considerable Profit by shewing my Cattle to many Persons of Quality, and others: And before I began my second Voyage, I sold them for six Hundred Pounds. Since my last Return, I find the Breed is considerably increased, especially the Sheep; which I hope will prove much to the Advantage of the Woollen Manufacture, by the Fineness of the Fleeces.

I stayed but two Months with my Wife and Family; for my insatiable Desire of seeing foreign Countries would suffer me to continue no longer. I left fifteen Hundred Pounds with my Wife, and fixed her in a good House at *Redriff*. My remaining Stock I carried with me, Part in Money, and Part in Goods, in Hopes to improve my Fortunes. My eldest Uncle, *John*, had left me an Estate in Land, near *Epping*, of about Thirty Pounds a Year; and I had a long Lease of the *Black-Bull* in *Fetter-Lane*, which yielded me as much more: So that I was not in any Danger of leaving my Family upon the Parish. My Son *Johnny*, named so after his Uncle, was at the Grammar School, and a towardly Child. My Daughter *Betty* (who is now well married, and has Children) was then at her Needle-Work. I took Leave of my Wife, and Boy and Girl, with Tears on both Sides; and went on board the *Adventure*, a Merchant-Ship of Three Hundred Tons, bound for *Surat*, Captain *John Nicholas* of *Liverpool*, Commander. But my Account of this Voyage must be referred to the second Part of my Travels.

The End of the First Part

PART II A VOYAGE TO BROBDINGNAG

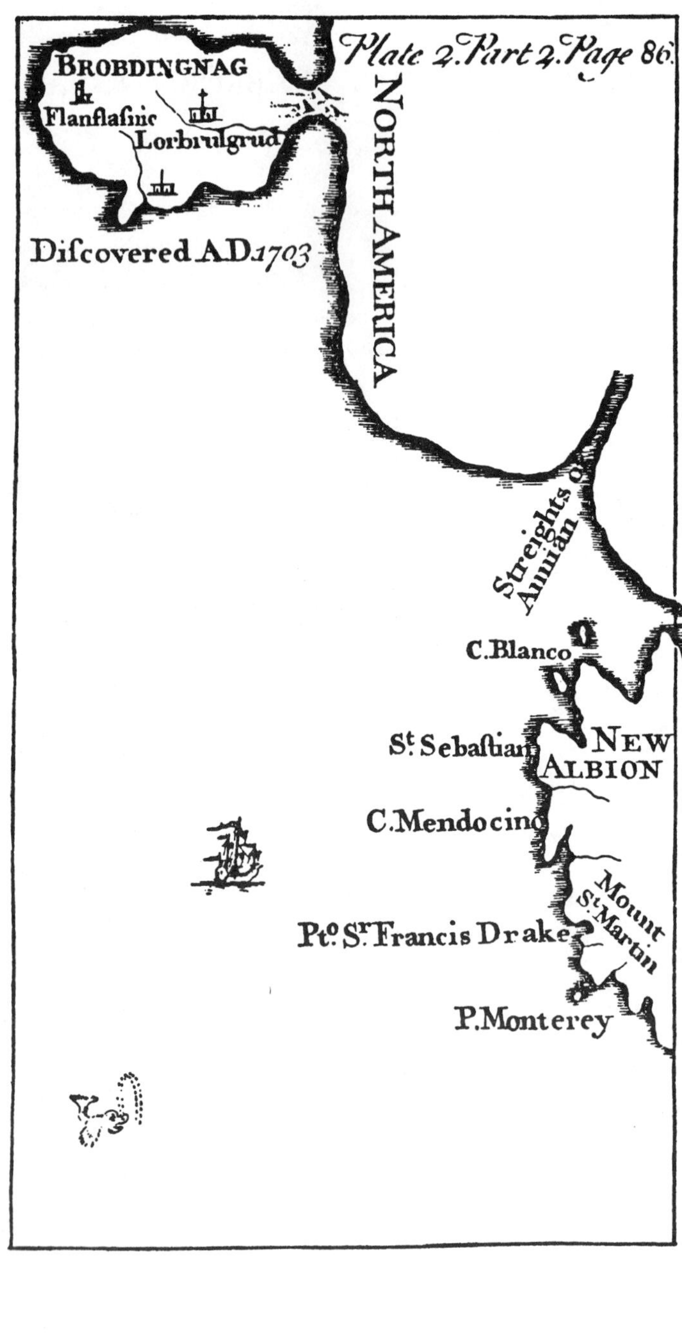
Plate 2. Part 2. Page 86.
BROBDINGNAG
Flanflasnic
Lorbrulgrud
Discovered A.D. 1703
NORTH AMERICA
Streights of Anian
C. Blanco
St. Sebastian
NEW ALBION
C. Mendocino
Mount St. Martin
Pto. Sr. Francis Drake
P. Monterey

CHAPTER I

A great Storm described. The long Boat sent to fetch Water, the Author goes with it to discover the Country. He is left on Shoar, is seized by one of the Natives, and carried to a Farmer's House. His Reception there, with several Accidents that happened there. A Description of the Inhabitants.

Having been condemned by Nature and Fortune to an active and restless Life; in two Months after my Return, I again left my native Country, and took Shipping in the *Downs* on the 20th Day of *June* 1702, in the *Adventure*, Capt. *John Nicholas*, a *Cornish* Man, Commander, bound for *Surat*. We had a very prosperous Gale till we arrived at the *Cape* of *Good-hope*, where we landed for fresh Water; but discovering a Leak we unshipped our Goods, and wintered there; for the Captain falling sick of an Ague, we could not leave the *Cape* till the End of *March*. We then set sail, and had a good Voyage till we passed the *Streights* of *Madagascar*; but having got Northward of that Island, and to about five Degrees South Latitude, the Winds, which in those Seas are observed to blow a constant equal Gale between the North and West, from the Beginning of *December* to the Beginning of *May*, on the 19th of *April* began to blow with much greater Violence, and more Westerly than usual; continuing so for twenty Days together, during which time we were driven a little to the East of the *Molucca* Islands, and about three Degrees Northward of the Line, as our Captain found by an Observation he took the 2d of *May*, at which time the Wind ceased, and it was a perfect Calm, whereat I was not a little rejoyced. But he being a Man well experienced in the Navigation of those Seas, bid us all prepare against a Storm, which accordingly happened the Day following: For a Southern Wind, called the Southern *Monsoon*, began to set in.

Finding it was like to overblow, we took in our Spritsail, and stood by to hand the Fore-sail; but making foul Weather, we looked the Guns were all fast, and handed the Missen. The Ship lay very broad off, so we thought it better spooning before the Sea, than trying or hulling. We reeft the Foresail and set him, we hawled aft the Foresheet; the Helm was hard a Weather. The Ship wore bravely. We belay'd the Foredown-hall; but the Sail was split, and we hawl'd down the Yard, and got the Sail into the Ship, and unbound all the things clear of it. It was a very fierce Storm; the Sea broke strange and dangerous. We hawl'd off upon the Lanniard of the Wipstaff, and helped the Man at Helm. We would not get down our Top-Mast, but let all stand, because she scudded before the Sea very well, and we knew that the Top-Mast being aloft, the Ship was the wholesomer, and made better way through the Sea, seeing we had Sea room. When the Storm was over, we set Fore-sail and Main-sail, and brought the Ship to. Then we set the Missen, Maintop-Sail and the Foretop-Sail. Our Course was East North-east, the Wind was at South-west. We got the Star-board tacks aboard, we cast off our Weather-braces and Lifts; we set in the Lee-braces, and hawl'd forward by the Weather-bowlings, and hawl'd them tight, and belayed them, and hawl'd over the Missen Tack to Windward, and kept her full and by as near as she would lye.[1]

During this Storm, which was followed by a strong Wind West South-west, we were carried by my Computation about five hundred Leagues to the East, so that the oldest Sailor on Board could not tell in what part of the World we were. Our Provisions held out well, our Ship was staunch, and our Crew all in good Health; but we lay in the utmost Distress for Water. We thought it best to hold on the same Course rather than turn more Northerly, which might have brought us to the North-west Parts of great *Tartary*, and into the frozen Sea.

On the 16*th* Day of *June* 1703, a Boy on the Top-mast discovered Land. On the 17*th* we came in full View of a great Island or Continent, (for we knew not whether) on the South-side whereof was a small Neck of Land jutting out into the Sea, and a Creek too shallow to hold a Ship of above one hundred Tuns. We cast Anchor

[1] Gulliver, the "experienced" sailor, has fallen into the worst nautical jargon. The paragraph, taken almost verbatim from Samuel Sturmy's *Mariners Magazine* (1669), is, of course, Swift's hit at specialist language. See p. 142 for another such parody.

within a League of this Creek, and our Captain sent a dozen of his Men well armed in the Long Boat, with Vessels for Water if any could be found. I desired his leave to go with them, that I might see the Country, and make what Discoveries I could. When we came to Land we saw no River or Spring, nor any Sign of Inhabitants. Our Men therefore wandered on the Shore to find out some fresh Water near the Sea, and I walked alone about a Mile on the other Side, where I observed the Country all barren and rocky. I now began to be weary, and seeing nothing to entertain my Curiosity, I returned gently down towards the Creek; and the Sea being full in my View, I saw our Men already got into the Boat, and rowing for Life to the Ship. I was going to hollow after them, although it had been to little purpose, when I observed a huge Creature walking after them in the Sea, as fast as he could: He walked not much deeper than his Knees, and took prodigious strides: But our Men had the start of him half a League, and the Sea thereabouts being full of sharp pointed Rocks, the Monster was not able to overtake the Boat. This I was afterwards told, for I durst not stay to see the Issue of that Adventure; but run as fast as I could the Way I first went; and then climbed up a steep Hill, which gave me some Prospect of the Country. I found it fully cultivated; but that which first surprized me was the Length of the Grass, which in those Grounds that seemed to be kept for Hay, was above twenty Foot high.

I fell into a high Road, for so I took it to be, although it served to the Inhabitants only as a foot Path through a Field of Barley. Here I walked on for sometime, but could see little on either Side, it being now near Harvest, and the Corn rising at least forty Foot. I was an Hour walking to the end of this Field; which was fenced in with a Hedge of at least one hundred and twenty Foot high, and the Trees so lofty that I could make no Computation of their Altitude. There was a Stile to pass from this Field into the next: It had four Steps, and a Stone to cross over when you came to the uppermost. It was impossible for me to climb this Stile, because every Step was six Foot high, and the upper Stone above twenty. I was endeavouring to find some Gap in the Hedge; when I discovered one of the Inhabitants in the next Field advancing towards the Stile, of the same Size with him whom I saw in the Sea pursuing our Boat. He appeared as Tall as an ordinary Spire-steeple; and took about ten Yards at every Stride, as near as I could guess. I was struck with the utmost Fear and Astonishment, and ran to hide my self in the Corn, from whence I saw him at the Top of the Stile, looking back into the next Field on the right Hand; and heard him call in a Voice many Degrees louder than a speaking Trumpet; but the Noise was so High in the Air, that at first I certainly thought it was Thunder. Whereupon seven Monsters like himself came towards him with Reaping-Hooks in their Hands, each Hook about the largeness of six Scythes. These People were not so well clad as the first, whose Servants or Labourers they seemed to be. For, upon some Words he spoke, they went to reap the Corn in the Field where I lay. I kept from them at as great a Distance as I could, but was forced to move with extream Difficulty; for the Stalks of the Corn were sometimes not above a Foot distant, so that I could hardly squeeze my Body betwixt them. However, I made a shift to go forward till I came to a part of the Field where the Corn had been laid by the Rain and Wind: Here it was impossible for me to advance a step; for the Stalks were so interwoven that I could not creep through, and the Beards of the fallen Ears so strong and pointed, that they pierced through my Cloaths into my Flesh. At the same time I heard the Reapers not above an hundred Yards behind me. Being quite dispirited with Toil, and wholly overcome by Grief and Despair, I lay down between two Ridges, and heartily wished I might there end my Days. I bemoaned my desolate Widow, and Fatherless Children: I lamented my own Folly and Wilfulness in attempting a second Voyage against the Advice of all my Friends and Relations. In this terrible Agitation of Mind I could not forbear thinking of *Lilliput*, whose Inhabitants looked upon me as the greatest Prodigy that ever appeared in the World; where I was able to draw an Imperial Fleet in my Hand, and perform those other Actions which will be recorded for ever in the Chronicles of that Empire, while Posterity shall hardly believe them, although attested by Millions. I reflected what a Mortification it must prove to me to appear as inconsiderable in this Nation, as one single *Lilliputian* would be among us. But, this I conceived was to be the least of my Misfortunes: For, as human Creatures are observed to be more Savage and cruel in Proportion to their Bulk; what could I expect but to be a Morsel in the Mouth of the first among these enormous Barbarians who should happen to seize me? Undoubtedly Philosophers are in the Right when they tell us, that nothing is great or little otherwise than by Comparison: It might have pleased Fortune to let the *Lilliputians* find some Nation, where the People were as diminutive with respect to them, as they were to me. And who knows but that even this prodigious Race of Mortals might be equally overmatched in some distant Part of the World, whereof we have yet no Discovery?

Scared and confounded as I was, I could not forbear going on with these Reflections; when one of the Reapers approaching within ten Yards of the Ridge where I lay, made me apprehend that with the next Step I should be squashed to Death under his Foot, or cut in two with his Reaping Hook. And therefore when he was again about to move, I screamed as loud as Fear could make me. Whereupon the huge Creature trod short, and looking round about under him for some time, at last espied me as I lay on the Ground. He considered a while with the Caution of one who endeavours to lay hold on a small dangerous Animal in such a Manner that it shall not be able either to scratch or to bite him; as I my self have sometimes done with a *Weasel* in *England*. At length he ventured to take me up behind by the middle between his Fore-finger and Thumb, and brought me within three Yards of his Eyes, that he might behold my Shape more perfectly. I guessed his Meaning; and my good Fortune gave me so much Presence of Mind, that I resolved not to struggle in the least as he held me in the Air above sixty Foot from the Ground; although he grievously pinched my Sides, for fear I should slip through his Fingers. All I ventured was to raise my Eyes towards the Sun, and place my Hands together in a supplicating Posture, and to speak some Words in an humble melancholy Tone, suitable to the Condition I then was in. For, I apprehended every Moment that he would dash me against the Ground, as we usually do any little hateful Animal which we have a Mind to destroy. But my good Star would have it, that he appeared pleased with my Voice and Gestures, and began to look upon me as a Curiosity; much wondering to hear me pronounce articulate Words, although he could not understand them. In the mean time I was not able to forbear Groaning and shedding Tears, and turning my Head towards my Sides; letting him know, as well as I could, how cruelly I was hurt by the Pressure of his Thumb and Finger. He seemed to apprehend my Meaning; for, lifting up the Lappet of his Coat, he put me gently into it, and immediately ran along with me to his Master, who was a substantial Farmer, and the same Person I had first seen in the Field.

The Farmer having (as I supposed by their Talk) received such an Account of me as his Servant could give him, took a piece of a small Straw, about the Size of a walking Staff, and therewith lifted up the Lappets of my Coat; which it seems he thought to be some kind of Covering that Nature had given me. He blew my Hairs aside to take a better View of my Face. He called his Hinds about him, and asked them (as I afterwards learned) whether they had ever seen in the Fields any little Creature that resembled me. He then placed me softly on the Ground upon all four; but I got immediately up, and walked slowly backwards and forwards, to let those People see I had no Intent to run away. They all sate down in a Circle about me, the better to observe my Motions. I pulled off my Hat, and made a low Bow towards the Farmer: I fell on my Knees, and lifted up my Hands and Eyes, and spoke several Words as loud as I could: I took a Purse of Gold out of my Pocket, and humbly presented it to him. He received it on the Palm of his Hand, then applied it close to his Eye, to see what it was, and afterwards turned it several times with the Point of a Pin, (which he took out of his Sleeve,) but could make nothing of it. Whereupon I made a Sign that he should place his Hand on the Ground: I then took the Purse, and opening it, poured all the Gold into his Palm. There were six *Spanish*-Pieces of four Pistoles each, besides twenty or thirty smaller Coins. I saw him wet the Tip of his little Finger upon his Tongue, and take up one of my largest Pieces, and then another; but he seemed to be wholly ignorant what they were. He made me a Sign to put them again into my Purse, and the Purse again into my Pocket; which after offering to him several times, I thought it best to do.

The Farmer by this time was convinced I must be a rational Creature. He spoke often to me, but the Sound of his Voice pierced my Ears like that of a Water-Mill; yet his Words were articulate enough. I answered as loud as I could in several Languages; and he often laid his Ear within two Yards of me, but all in vain, for we were wholly unintelligible to each other. He then sent his Servants to their Work, and taking his Handkerchief out of his Pocket, he doubled and spread it on his Hand, which he placed flat on the Ground with the Palm upwards, making me a Sign to step into it, as I could easily do, for it was not above a Foot in thickness. I thought it my part to obey; and for fear of falling, laid my self at full Length upon the Handkerchief, with the Remainder of which he lapped me up to the Head for further Security; and in this Manner carried me home to his House. There he called his Wife, and shewed me to her; but she screamed and ran back as Women in *England* do at the Sight of a Toad or a Spider. However, when she had a while seen my Behaviour, and how well I observed the Signs her Husband made, she was soon reconciled, and by Degrees grew extreamly tender of me.

It was about twelve at Noon, and a Servant brought in Dinner. It was only one substantial Dish of Meat (fit for the plain Condition of an Husband-Man) in a Dish of about four and twenty Foot Diameter. The Company were the Farmer and Wife, three Children, and an old Grandmother: When they were sat down, the Farmer placed me at some Distance from him on the Table, which was thirty Foot high from the Floor. I was in a terrible Fright, and kept as far as I could from the Edge, for fear of falling. The Wife minced a bit of Meat, then crumbled some Bread on a Trencher, and placed it before me. I made her a low Bow, took out my Knife and Fork, and fell to eat; which gave them exceeding Delight. The Mistress sent her Maid for a small Dram-cup, which held about two Gallons; and filled it with Drink: I took up the Vessel with much difficulty in both Hands, and in a most respectful Manner drank to her Lady-ship's Health, expressing the Words as loud as I could in *English*; which made the Company laugh so heartily, that I was almost deafened with the Noise. This Liquour tasted like a small Cyder, and was not unpleasant. Then the Master made me a Sign to come to his Trencher side; but as I walked on the Table, being in great surprize all the time, as the indulgent Reader will easily conceive and excuse, I happened to stumble against a Crust, and fell flat on my Face, but received no hurt. I got up immediately, and observing the good People to be in much Concern, I took my Hat (which I held under my Arm out of good Manners) and waving it over my Head, made three Huzza's, to shew I had got no Mischief by the Fall. But advancing forwards toward my Master (as I shall henceforth call him) his youngest Son who sate next him, an arch Boy of about ten Years old, took me up by the Legs, and held me so high in the Air, that I trembled every Limb; but his Father snatched me from him; and at the same time gave him such a Box on the left Ear, as would have felled an *European* Troop of Horse to the Earth; ordering him to be taken from the Table. But, being afraid the Boy might owe me a Spight; and well remembring how mischievous all Children among us naturally are to Sparrows, Rabbits, young Kittens, and Puppy-Dogs; I fell on my Knees, and pointing to the Boy, made my Master understand, as well as I could, that I desired his Son might be pardoned. The Father complied, and the Lad took his Seat again; whereupon I went to him and kissed his Hand, which my Master took, and made him stroak me gently with it.

In the Midst of Dinner my Mistress's favourite Cat leapt into her Lap. I heard a Noise behind me like that of a Dozen Stocking-Weavers at work; and turning my Head, I found it proceeded from the Purring of this Animal, who seemed to be three Times larger than an Ox, as I computed by the View of her Head, and one of her Paws, while her Mistress was feeding and stroaking her. The Fierceness of this Creature's Countenance altogether discomposed me; although I stood at the further End of the Table, above fifty Foot off; and although my Mistress held her fast for fear she might give a Spring, and seize me in her Talons. But it happened there was no Danger; for the Cat took not the least Notice of me when my Master placed me within three Yards of her. And as I have been always told, and found true by Experience in my Travels, that flying, or discovering Fear before a fierce Animal, is a certain Way to make it pursue or attack you; so I resolved in this dangerous Juncture to shew no Manner of Concern. I walked with Intrepidity five or six Times before the very Head of the Cat, and came within half a Yard of her; whereupon she drew her self back, as if she were more afraid of me: I had less Apprehension concerning the Dogs, whereof three or four came into the Room, as it is usual in Farmers Houses; one of which was a Mastiff equal in Bulk to four Elephants, and a Grey-hound somewhat taller than the Mastiff, but not so large.

When Dinner was almost done, the Nurse came in with a Child of a Year old in her Arms; who immediately spyed me, and began a Squall that you might have heard from *London-Bridge* to *Chelsea*; after the usual Oratory of Infants, to get me for a Play-thing. The Mother out of pure Indulgence took me up, and put me towards the Child, who presently seized me by the Middle, and got my Head in his Mouth, where I roared so loud that the Urchin was frighted, and let me drop; and I should infallibly have broke my

Neck, if the Mother had not held her Apron under me. The Nurse to quiet her Babe made use of a Rattle, which was a Kind of hollow Vessel filled with great Stones, and fastned by a Cable to the Child's Waist: But all in vain, so that she was forced to apply the last Remedy by giving it suck. I must confess no Object ever disgusted me so much as the Sight of her monstrous Breast, which I cannot tell what to compare with, so as to give the curious Reader an Idea of its Bulk, Shape and Colour. It stood prominent six Foot, and could not be less than sixteen in Circumference. The Nipple was about half the Bigness of my Head, and the Hue both of that and the Dug so varified with Spots, Pimples and Freckles, that nothing could appear more nauseous: For I had a near Sight of her, she sitting down the more conveniently to give Suck, and I standing on the Table. This made me reflect upon the fair Skins of our *English* Ladies, who appear so beautiful to us, only because they are of our own Size, and their Defects not to be seen but through a magnifying Glass, where we find by Experiment that the smoothest and whitest Skins look rough and coarse, and ill coloured.

I remember when I was at *Lilliput*, the Complexions of those diminutive People appeared to me the fairest in the World: And talking upon this Subject with a Person of Learning there, who was an intimate Friend of mine; he said, that my Face appeared much fairer and smoother when he looked on me from the Ground, than it did upon a nearer View when I took him up in my Hand, and brought him close; which he confessed was at first a very shocking Sight. He said, he could discover great Holes in my Skin; that the Stumps of my Beard were ten Times stronger than the Bristles of a Boar; and my Complexion made up of several Colours altogether disagreeable: Although I must beg Leave to say for my self, that I am as fair as most of my Sex and Country, and very little Sunburnt by all my Travels. On the other Side, discoursing of the Ladies in that Emperor's Court, he used to tell me, one had Freckles, another too wide a Mouth, a third too large a Nose; nothing of which I was able to distinguish. I confess this Reflection was obvious enough; which, however, I could not forbear, lest the Reader might think those vast Creatures were actually deformed: For I must do them Justice to say they are a comely Race of People; and particularly the Features of my Master's Countenance, although he were but a Farmer, when I beheld him from the Height of sixty Foot, appeared very well proportioned.

When Dinner was done, my Master went out to his Labourers; and as I could discover by his Voice and Gesture, gave his Wife a strict Charge to take Care of me. I was very much tired and disposed to sleep, which my Mistress perceiving, she put me on her own Bed, and covered me with a clean white Handkerchief, but larger and coarser than the Main Sail of a Man of War.

I slept about two Hours, and dreamed I was at home with my Wife and Children, which aggravated my Sorrows when I awaked and found my self alone in a vast Room, between two and three Hundred Foot wide, and above two Hundred high; lying in a Bed twenty Yards wide. My Mistress was gone about her houshold Affairs, and had locked me in. The Bed was eight Yards from the Floor. Some natural Necessities required me to get down: I durst not presume to call, and if I had, it would have been in vain with such a Voice as mine at so great a Distance from the Room where I lay, to the Kitchen where the Family kept. While I was under these Circumstances, two Rats crept up the Curtains, and ran smelling backwards and forwards on the Bed: One of them came up almost to my Face; whereupon I rose in a Fright, and drew out my Hanger[2] to defend my self. These horrible Animals had the Boldness to attack me on both Sides, and one of them held his Fore-feet at my Collar; but I had the good Fortune to rip up his Belly before he could do me any Mischief. He fell down at my Feet; and the other seeing the Fate of his Comrade, made his Escape, but not without one good Wound on the Back, which I gave him as he fled, and made the Blood run trickling from him. After this Exploit I walked gently to and fro on the Bed, to recover my Breath and Loss of Spirits. These Creatures were of the Size of a large Mastiff, but infinitely more nimble and fierce; so that if I had taken off my Belt before I went to sleep, I must have infallibly been torn to Pieces and devoured. I measured the Tail of the dead Rat, and found it to be two Yards long, wanting an Inch; but it went against my Stomach to drag the Carcass off the Bed, where it lay still bleeding; I observed it had yet some Life, but with a strong Slash cross the Neck, I thoroughly dispatched it.

Soon after, my Mistress came into the Room, who seeing me all bloody, ran and took me up in her Hand. I pointed to the dead *Rat*, smiling and making other Signs to shew I was not hurt; whereat she was extremely rejoyced, calling the Maid to take up

[2] A short sword attached to his belt.

the dead *Rat* with a Pair of Tongs, and throw it out of the Window. Then she set me on a Table, where I shewed her my Hanger all bloody, and wiping it on the Lappet of my Coat, returned it to the Scabbard. I was pressed to do more than one Thing, which another could not do for me; and therefore endeavoured to make my Mistress understand that I desired to be set down on the Floor; which after she had done, my Bashfulness would not suffer me to express my self farther than by pointing to the Door, and bowing several Times. The good Woman with much Difficulty at last perceived what I would be at; and taking me up again in her Hand, walked into the Garden where she set me down. I went on one Side about two Hundred Yards; and beckoning to her not to look or follow me, I hid my self between two Leaves of Sorrel, and there discharged the Necessities of Nature.

I hope, the gentle Reader will excuse me for dwelling on these and the like Particulars; which however insignificant they may appear to grovelling vulgar Minds, yet will certainly help a Philosopher to enlarge his Thoughts and Imagination, and apply them to the Benefit of publick as well as private Life; which was my sole Design in presenting this and other Accounts of my Travels to the World; wherein I have been chiefly studious of Truth, without affecting any Ornaments of Learning, or of Style. But the whole Scene of this Voyage made so strong an Impression on my Mind, and is so deeply fixed in my Memory, that in committing it to Paper, I did not omit one material Circumstance: However, upon a strict Review, I blotted out several Passages of less Moment which were in my first Copy, for fear of being censured as tedious and trifling, whereof Travellers are often, perhaps not without Justice, accused.

CHAPTER II

A Description of the Farmer's Daughter. The Author carried to a Market-Town, and then to the Metropolis. The Particulars of his Journey.

My Mistress had a Daughter of nine Years old, a Child of towardly Parts for her Age, very dextrous at her Needle, and skilful in dressing her Baby.[1] Her Mother and she contrived to fit up the Baby's Cradle for me against Night: The Cradle was put into a small Drawer of a Cabinet, and the Drawer placed upon a hanging Shelf for fear of the *Rats*. This was my Bed all the Time I stayed with those People, although made more convenient by Degrees, as I began to learn their Language, and make my Wants known. This young Girl was so handy, that after I had once or twice pulled off my Cloaths before her, she was able to dress and undress me, although I never gave her that Trouble when she would let me do either my self. She made me seven Shirts, and some other Linnen of as fine Cloth as could be got, which indeed was coarser than Sackcloth; and these she constantly washed for me with her own Hands. She was likewise my School-Mistress to teach me the Language: When I pointed to any thing, she told me the Name of it in her own Tongue, so that in a few Days I was able to call for whatever I had a mind to. She was very good natured, and not above forty Foot high, being little for her Age. She gave me the Name of *Grildrig*, which the Family took up, and afterwards the whole Kingdom. The Word imports what the *Latins* call *Nanunculus*, the *Italians Homunceletino*,[2] and the *English Mannikin*. To her I chiefly owe my Preservation in that Country: We never parted

[1] Her doll.

[2] No such Latin or Italian words exist. Swift may be undercutting his hero's pretenses as a linguist (see p. 135, n. 5 for a more elaborate instance of this).

while I was there; I called her my *Glumdalclitch*, or little Nurse: And I should be guilty of great Ingratitude if I omitted this honourable Mention of her Care and Affection towards me, which I heartily wish it lay in my Power to requite as she deserves, instead of being the innocent but unhappy Instrument of her Disgrace, as I have too much Reason to fear.

It now began to be known and talked of in the Neighbourhood, that my Master had found a strange Animal in the Fields, about the Bigness of a *Splacknuck*, but exactly shaped in every Part like a human Creature; which it likewise imitated in all its Actions; seemed to speak in a little Language of its own, had already learned several Words of theirs, went erect upon two Legs, was tame and gentle, would come when it was called, do whatever it was bid, had the finest Limbs in the World, and a Complexion fairer than a Nobleman's Daughter of three Years old. Another Farmer who lived hard by, and was a particular Friend of my Master, came on a Visit on Purpose to enquire into the Truth of this Story. I was immediately produced, and placed upon a Table; where I walked as I was commanded, drew my Hanger, put it up again, made my Reverence to my Master's Guest, asked him in his own Language how he did, and told him he was welcome; just as my little Nurse had instructed me. This Man, who was old and dimsighted, put on his Spectacles to behold me better, at which I could not forbear laughing very heartily; for his Eyes appeared like the Full-Moon shining into a Chamber at two Windows. Our People, who discovered the Cause of my Mirth, bore me Company in Laughing; at which the old Fellow was Fool enough to be angry and out of Countenance. He had the Character of a great Miser; and to my Misfortune he well deserved it by the cursed Advice he gave my Master, to shew me as a Sight upon a Market-Day in the next Town, which was half an Hour's Riding, about two and twenty Miles from our House. I guessed there was some Mischief contriving, when I observed my Master and his Friend whispering long together, sometimes pointing at me; and my Fears made me fancy that I overheard and understood some of their Words. But, the next Morning *Glumdalclitch* my little Nurse told me the whole Matter, which she had cunningly picked out from her Mother. The poor Girl laid me on her Bosom, and fell a weeping with Shame and Grief. She apprehended some Mischief would happen to me from rude vulgar Folks, who might squeeze me to Death, or break one of my Limbs by taking me in their Hands. She had also observed how modest I was in my Nature, how nicely I regarded my Honour; and what an Indignity I should conceive it to be exposed for Money as a publick Spectacle to the meanest of the People.[3] She said, her *Papa* and *Mamma* had promised that *Grildrig* should be hers; but now she found they meant to serve her as they did last Year, when they pretended to give her a Lamb; and yet, as soon as it was fat, sold it to a Butcher. For my own Part, I may truly affirm that I was less concerned than my Nurse. I had a strong Hope which never left me, that I should one Day recover my Liberty; and as to the Ignominy of being carried about for a Monster, I considered my self to be a perfect Stranger in the Country; and that such a Misfortune could never be charged upon me as a Reproach if ever I should return to *England*; since the King of *Great Britain* himself, in my Condition, must have undergone the same Distress.

My Master, pursuant to the Advice of his Friend, carried me in a Box the next Market-Day to the neighbouring Town; and took along with him his little Daughter my Nurse upon a Pillion behind me. The Box was close on every Side, with a little Door for me to go in and out, and a few Gimlet-holes to let in Air. The Girl had been so careful to put the Quilt of her Baby's Bed into it, for me to lye down on. However, I was terribly shaken and discomposed in this Journey, although it were but of half an Hour. For the Horse went about forty Foot at every Step; and trotted so high, that the Agitation was equal to the rising and falling of a Ship in a great Storm, but much more frequent: Our Journey was somewhat further than from *London* to St. *Albans*. My Master alighted at an Inn which he used to frequent; and after consulting a while with the Inn-keeper, and making some necessary Preparations, he hired the *Grultrud*, or Cryer, to give Notice through the Town, of a strange Creature to be seen at the Sign of the Green *Eagle*, not so big as a *Splacknuck*, (an Animal in that Country very finely shaped, about six Foot long) and in every Part of the Body resembling an human Creature; could speak several Words, and perform an Hundred diverting Tricks.

I was placed upon a Table in the largest Room of the Inn,

[3] In Swift's time, it was quite common to display abnormal creatures, both human and animal, "for Money as a publick Spectacle." Gulliver's hardships are thus firmly rooted in an eighteenth-century diversion.

which might be near three Hundred Foot square. My little Nurse stood on a low Stool close to the Table, to take care of me, and direct what I should do. My Master, to avoid a Croud, would suffer only Thirty People at a Time to see me. I walked about on the Table as the Girl commanded; she asked me Questions as far as she knew my Understanding of the Language reached, and I answered them as loud as I could. I turned about several Times to the Company, paid my humble Respects, said they were welcome; and used some other Speeches I had been taught. I took up a Thimble filled with Liquor, which *Glumdalclitch* had given me for a Cup, and drank their Health. I drew out my Hanger, and flourished with it after the Manner of Fencers in *England.* My Nurse gave me Part of a Straw, which I exercised as a Pike, having learned the Art in my Youth. I was that Day shewn to twelve Sets of Company; and as often forced to go over again with the same Fopperies, till I was half dead with Weariness and Vexation. For, those who had seen me, made such wonderful Reports, that the People were ready to break down the Doors to come in. My Master for his own Interest would not suffer any one to touch me, except my Nurse; and, to prevent Danger, Benches were set round the Table at such a Distance, as put me out of every Body's Reach. However, an unlucky School-Boy aimed a Hazel-Nut directly at my Head, which very narrowly missed me; otherwise, it came with so much Violence, that it would have infallibly knocked out my Brains; for it was almost as large as a small Pumpion[4]: But I had the Satisfaction to see the young Rogue well beaten, and turned out of the Room.

My Master gave publick Notice, that he would shew me again the next Market-Day: And in the mean time, he prepared a more convenient Vehicle for me, which he had Reason enough to do; for I was so tired with my first Journey, and with entertaining Company eight Hours together, that I could hardly stand upon my Legs, or speak a Word. It was at least three Days before I recovered my Strength; and that I might have no rest at home, all the neighbouring Gentlemen from an Hundred Miles round, hearing of my Fame, came to see me at my Master's own House. There could not be fewer than thirty Persons with their Wives and Children; (for the Country is very populous;) and my Master demanded the Rate

[4] Pumpkin.

of a full Room whenever he shewed me at Home although it were only to a single Family. So that for some time I had but little Ease every Day of the Week, (except *Wednesday*, which is their Sabbath) although I were not carried to the Town.

My Master finding how profitable I was like to be, resolved to carry me to the most considerable Cities of the Kingdom. Having therefore provided himself with all things necessary for a long Journey, and settled his Affairs at Home; he took Leave of his Wife; and upon the 17*th* of *August* 1703, about two Months after my Arrival, we set out for the Metropolis, situated near the Middle of that Empire, and about three Thousand Miles distance from our House: My Master made his Daughter *Glumdalclitch* ride behind him. She carried me on her Lap in a Box tied about her Waist. The Girl had lined it on all Sides with the softest Cloth she could get, well quilted underneath; furnished it with her Baby's Bed, provided me with Linnen and other Necessaries; and made every thing as convenient as she could. We had no other Company but a Boy of the House, who rode after us with the Luggage.

My Master's Design was to shew me in all the Towns by the Way, and to step out of the Road for Fifty or an Hundred Miles, to any Village or Person of Quality's House where he might expect Custom. We made easy Journies of not above seven or eight Score Miles a Day: For *Glumdalclitch*, on Purpose to spare me, complained she was tired with the trotting of the Horse. She often took me out of my Box at my own Desire, to give me Air, and shew me the Country; but always held me fast by Leading-strings. We passed over five or six Rivers many Degrees broader and deeper than the *Nile* or the *Ganges*; and there was hardly a Rivulet so small as the *Thames* at *London-Bridge*. We were ten Weeks in our Journey; and I was shewn in Eighteen large Towns, besides many Villages and private Families.

On the 26th Day of *October*, we arrived at the Metropolis, called in their Language *Lorbrulgrud*, or *Pride of the Universe*. My Master took a Lodging in the principal Street of the City, not far from the Royal Palace; and put out Bills in the usual Form, containing an exact Description of my Person and Parts. He hired a large Room between three and four Hundred Foot wide. He provided a Table sixty Foot in Diameter, upon which I was to act my Part; and palisadoed it round three Foot from the Edge, and as many high, to prevent my falling over. I was shewn ten Times a Day to the Wonder and Satisfaction of all People. I could now speak the Language tolerably well; and perfectly understood every Word that was spoken to me. Besides, I had learned their Alphabet, and could make a shift to explain a Sentence here and there; for *Glumdalclitch* had been my Instructer while we were at home, and at leisure Hours during our Journey. She carried a little Book in her Pocket, not much larger than a *Sanson's Atlas*; it was a common Treatise for the use of young Girls, giving a short Account of their Religion; out of this she taught me my Letters, and interpreted the Words.

CHAPTER III

The Author sent for to Court. The Queen buys him of his Master the Farmer, and presents him to the King. He disputes with his Majesty's great Scholars. An Apartment at Court provided for the Author. He is in high Favour with the Queen. He stands up for the Honour of his own Country. His Quarrels with the Queen's Dwarf.

The frequent Labours I underwent every Day, made in a few Weeks a very considerable Change in my Health: The more my Master got by me, the more unsatiable he grew. I had quite lost my Stomach, and was almost reduced to a Skeleton. The Farmer observed it; and concluding I soon must die, resolved to make as good a Hand of me as he could. While he was thus reasoning and resolving with himself; a *Slardral*, or Gentleman Usher, came from Court, commanding my Master to bring me immediately thither for the Diversion of the Queen and her Ladies. Some of the latter had already been to see me; and reported strange Things of my Beauty, Behaviour, and good Sense. Her Majesty and those who attended her, were beyond Measure delighted with my Demeanor. I fell on my Knees, and begged the Honour of kissing her Imperial Foot; but this Gracious Princess held out her little Finger towards me (after I was set on a table) which I embraced in both my Arms, and put the Tip of it, with the utmost Respect, to my Lip. She made me some general Questions about my Country and my Travels, which I answered as distinctly and in as few Words as I could. She asked, whether I would be content to live at Court. I bowed down to the Board of the Table, and humbly answered, that I was my Master's Slave; but if I were at my own Disposal, I should be proud to devote my Life to her Majesty's Service. She then asked my Master whether he were willing to sell me at a good Price. He, who apprehended I could not live a Month, was ready enough to part with me; and demanded a Thousand Pieces of Gold; which were ordered him on the Spot, each Piece being about the Bigness of eight Hundred Moydores: But, allowing for the Proportion of all Things between that Country and *Europe*, and the high Price of Gold among them; was hardly so great a Sum as a Thousand Guineas would be in *England*. I then said to the Queen; since I was now her Majesty's most humble Creature and Vassal, I must beg the Favour, that *Glumdalclitch*, who had always tended me with so much Care and Kindness, and understood to do it so well, might be admitted into her Service, and continue to be my Nurse and Instructor. Her Majesty agreed to my Petition; and easily got the Farmer's Consent, who was glad enough to have his Daughter preferred at Court: And the poor Girl herself was not able to hide her Joy. My late Master withdrew, bidding me farewell, and saying he had left me in a good Service; to which I replyed not a Word, only making him a slight Bow.

The Queen observed my Coldness; and when the Farmer was gone out of the Apartment, asked me the Reason. I made bold to tell her Majesty, that I owed no other Obligation to my late Master, than his not dashing out the Brains of a poor harmless Creature found by Chance in his Field; which Obligation was amply recompenced by the Gain he had made in shewing me through half the Kingdom, and the Price he had now sold me for. That the Life I had since led, was laborious enough to kill an Animal of ten Times my Strength. That my Health was much impaired by the continual Drudgery of entertaining the Rabble every Hour of the Day; and that if my Master had not thought my Life in Danger, her Majesty perhaps would not have got so cheap a Bargain. But as I was out of all fear of being ill treated under the Protection of so great and good an Empress, the Ornament of Nature, the Darling of the World, the Delight of her Subjects, the Phoenix of the Creation; so, I hoped my late Master's Apprehensions would appear to be groundless; for I already found my Spirits to revive by the Influence of her most August Presence.

This was the Sum of my Speech, delivered with great Improprieties and Hesitation; the latter Part was altogether framed in the Style peculiar to that People, whereof I learned some Phrases from *Glumdalclitch,* while she was carrying me to Court.

The Queen giving great Allowance for my Defectiveness in speaking, was however surprised at so much Wit and good Sense in so diminutive an Animal. She took me in her own Hand, and carried me to the King, who was then retired to his Cabinet. His Majesty, a Prince of much Gravity, and austere Countenance, not well observing my Shape at first View, asked the Queen after a cold Manner, how long it was since she grew fond of a *Splacknuck;* for such it seems he took me to be, as I lay upon my Breast in her Majesty's right Hand. But this Princess, who hath an infinite deal of Wit and Humour, set me gently on my Feet upon the Scrutore; and commanded me to give His Majesty an Account of my self, which I did in a very few Words; and *Glumdalclitch,* who attended at the Cabinet Door, and could not endure I should be out of her Sight, being admitted; confirmed all that had passed from my Arrival at her Father's House.

The King, although he be as learned a Person as any in his Dominions; and had been educated in the Study of Philosophy, and particularly Mathematicks; yet when he observed my Shape exactly, and saw me walk erect, before I began to speak, conceived I might be a piece of Clockwork, (which is in that Country arrived to a very great Perfection) contrived by some ingenious Artist. But, when he heard my Voice, and found what I delivered to be regular and rational, he could not conceal his Astonishment. He was by no means satisfied with the Relation I gave him of the Manner I came into his Kingdom; but thought it a Story concerted between *Glumdalclitch* and her Father, who had taught me a Sett of Words to make me sell at a higher Price. Upon this Imagination he put several other Questions to me, and still received rational Answers, no otherwise defective than by a Foreign Accent, and an imperfect Knowledge in the Language; with some rustick Phrases which I had learned at the Farmer's House, and did not suit the polite Style of a Court.

His Majesty sent for three great Scholars who were then in their weekly waiting (according to the Custom in that Country.) These Gentlemen, after they had a while examined my Shape with much Nicety, were of different Opinion concerning me. They all agreed that I could not be produced according to the regular Laws of Nature; because I was not framed with a Capacity of preserving my Life, either by Swiftness, or climbing of Trees, or digging Holes in the Earth. They observed by my Teeth, which they viewed with great Exactness, that I was a carnivorous Animal; yet most Quadrupeds being an Overmatch for me; and Field-Mice, with some others, too nimble, they could not imagine how I should be able to support my self, unless I fed upon Snails and other Insects; which they offered by many learned Arguments to evince that I could not possibly do. One of them seemed to think that I might be an Embrio, or abortive Birth. But this Opinion was rejected by the other two, who observed my Limbs to be perfect and finished; and that I had lived several Years, as it was manifested from my Beard; the Stumps whereof they plainly discovered through a Magnifying-Glass. They would not allow me to be a Dwarf, because my Littleness was beyond all Degrees of Comparison; for the Queen's favourite Dwarf, the smallest ever known in that Kingdom, was near thirty Foot high. After much Debate, they concluded unanimously that I was only *Relplum Scalcath*, which is interpreted literally *Lusus Naturae*,[1] a Determination exactly agreeable to the Modern Philosophy of *Europe*: whose Professors, disdaining the old Evasion of *occult Causes*, whereby the Followers of *Aristotle* endeavour in vain to disguise their Ignorance; have invented this wonderful Solution of all Difficulties, to the unspeakable Advancement of human Knowledge.

After this decisive Conclusion, I entreated to be heard a Word or two. I applied my self to the King, and assured His Majesty, that I came from a Country which abounded with several Millions of both Sexes, and of my own Stature; where the Animals, Trees, and Houses were all in Proportion; and where by Consequence I might be as able to defend my self, and to find Sustenance, as any of his Majesty's Subjects could do here; which I took for a full Answer to those Gentlemen's Arguments. To this they only replied with a Smile of Contempt; saying, that the Farmer had instructed me very well in my Lesson. The King, who had a much better

[1] A freak of nature.

Understanding, dismissing his learned Men, sent for the Farmer, who by good Fortune was not yet gone out of Town: Having therefore first examined him privately, and then confronted him with me and the young Girl; his Majesty began to think that what we told him might possibly be true. He desired the Queen to order, that a particular Care should be taken of me; and was of Opinion, that *Glumdalclitch* should still continue in her Office of tending me, because he observed we had a great Affection for each other. A convenient Apartment was provided for her at Court; she had a sort of Governess appointed to take care of her Education, a Maid to dress her, and two other Servants for menial Offices; but, the Care of me was wholly appropriated to her self. The Queen commanded her own Cabinet-maker to contrive a Box that might serve me for a Bed-chamber, after the Model that *Glumdalclitch* and I should agree upon. This Man was a most ingenious Artist; and according to my Directions, in three Weeks finished for me a wooden Chamber of sixteen Foot square, and twelve High; with Sash Windows, a Door, and two Closets, like a *London* Bed-chamber. The Board that made the Cieling was to be lifted up and down by two Hinges, to put in a Bed ready furnished by her Majesty's Upholsterer; which *Glumdalclitch* took out every Day to air, made it with her own Hands, and letting it down at Night, locked up the Roof over me. A Nice Workman, who was famous for little Curiosities, undertook to make me two Chairs, with Backs and Frames, of a Substance not unlike Ivory; and two Tables, with a Cabinet to put my Things in. The Room was quilted on all Sides, as well as the Floor and the Cieling, to prevent any Accident from the Carelessness of those who carried me; and to break the Force of a Jolt when I went in a Coach. I desired a Lock for my Door to prevent Rats and Mice from coming in: The Smith after several Attempts made the smallest that was ever seen among them; for I have known a larger at the Gate of a Gentleman's House in *England*. I made a shift to keep the Key in a Pocket of my own, fearing *Glumdalclitch* might lose it. The Queen likewise ordered the thinnest Silks that could be gotten, to make me Cloaths; not much thicker than an *English* Blanket, very cumbersome till I was accustomed to them. They were after the Fashion of the Kingdom, partly resembling the *Persian*, and partly the *Chinese*; and are a very grave decent Habit.

The Queen became so fond of my Company, that she could not

dine without me. I had a Table placed upon the same at which her Majesty eat, just at her left Elbow; and a Chair to sit on. *Glumdalclitch* stood upon a Stool on the Floor, near my Table, to assist and take Care of me. I had an entire set of Silver Dishes and Plates, and other Necessaries, which in Proportion to those of the Queen, were not much bigger than what I have seen in a *London* Toy-shop, for the Furniture of a Baby-house: These my little Nurse kept in her Pocket, in a Silver Box, and gave me at Meals as I wanted them; always cleaning them her self. No Person dined with the Queen but the two Princesses Royal; the elder sixteen Years old, and the younger at that time thirteen and a Month. Her Majesty used to put a Bit of Meat upon one of my Dishes, out of which I carved for my self; and her Diversion was to see me eat in Miniature. For the Queen (who had indeed but a weak Stomach) took up at one Mouthful, as much as a dozen *English* Farmers could eat at a Meal, which to me was for some time a very nauseous Sight. She would craunch the Wing of a Lark, Bones and all, between her Teeth, although it were nine Times as large as that of a full grown Turkey; and put a Bit of Bread in her Mouth, as big as two twelve-penny Loaves. She drank out of a Golden Cup, above a Hogshead at a Draught. Her Knives were twice as long as a Scythe set strait upon the Handle. The Spoons, Forks, and other Instruments were all in the same Proportion. I remember when *Glumdalclitch* carried me out of Curiosity to see some of the Tables at Court, where ten or a dozen of these enormous Knives and Forks were lifted up together; I thought I had never till then beheld so terrible a Sight.

It is the Custom, that every *Wednesday*, (which as I have before observed, was their Sabbath) the King and Queen, with the Royal Issue of both Sexes, dine together in the Apartment of his Majesty; to whom I was now become a Favourite; and at these Times my little Chair and Table were placed at his left Hand before one of the Salt-sellers. This Prince took a Pleasure in conversing with me; enquiring into the Manners, Religion, Laws, Government, and Learning of *Europe*, wherein I gave him the best Account I was able. His Apprehension was so clear, and his Judgment so exact, that he made very wise Reflexions and Observations upon all I said. But, I confess, that after I had been a little too copious in talking of my own beloved Country; of our Trade, and Wars by Sea and Land, of our Schisms in Religion, and Parties in the State; the Prejudices of his Education prevailed so far, that he could not forbear taking me up in his right Hand, and stroaking me gently with the other; after an hearty Fit of laughing, asked me whether I were a *Whig* or a *Tory*. Then turning to his first Minister, who waited behind him with a white Staff, near as tall as the Main-mast of the Royal *Sovereign*; he observed, how contemptible a Thing was human Grandeur, which could be mimicked by such diminutive Insects as I: And yet, said he, I dare engage, those Creatures have their Titles and Distinctions of Honour; they contrive little Nests and Burrows, that they call Houses and Cities; they make a Figure in Dress and Equipage; they love, they fight, they dispute, they cheat, they betray. And thus he continued on, while my Colour came and went several Times, with Indignation to hear our noble Country, the Mistress of Arts and Arms, the Scourge of *France*, the Arbitress of *Europe*, the Seat of Virtue, Piety, Honour and Truth, the Pride and Envy of the World, so contemptously treated.

But, as I was not in a Condition to resent Injuries, so, upon mature Thoughts, I began to doubt whether I were injured or no. For, after having been accustomed several Months to the Sight and Converse of this People, and observed every Object upon which I cast my Eyes, to be of proportionable Magnitude; the Horror I had first conceived from their Bulk and Aspect was so far worn off, that if I then beheld a Company of *English* Lords and Ladies in their Finery and Birth-day Cloaths, acting their several Parts in the most courtly Manner of Strutting, and Bowing and Prating; to say the Truth, I should have been strongly tempted to laugh as much at them as this King and his Grandees did at me. Neither indeed could I forbear smiling at my self, when the Queen used to place me upon her Hand towards a Looking-Glass, by which both our Persons appeared before me in full View together; and there could nothing be more ridiculous than the Comparison: So that I really began to imagine my self dwindled many Degrees below my usual Size.

Nothing angred and mortified me so much as the Queen's Dwarf, who being of the lowest Stature that was ever in that Country, (for I verily think he was not full Thirty Foot high) became so insolent at seeing a Creature so much beneath him, that he would always affect to swagger and look big as he passed by me in the Queen's Antichamber, while I was standing on some Table talking with the Lords or Ladies of the Court; and he seldom failed of a smart Word or two upon my Littleness; against which I could only revenge my self by calling him *Brother*, challenging him to wrestle; and such Repartees as are usual in the Mouths of *Court Pages*. One Day at Dinner, this malicious little Cubb was so nettled with something I had said to him, that raising himself upon the Frame of her Majesty's Chair, he took me up by the Middle, as I was sitting down, not thinking any Harm, and let me drop into a large Silver Bowl of Cream; and then ran away as fast as he could. I fell over Head and Ears, and if I had not been a good Swimmer, it might have gone very hard with me; for *Glumdalclitch* in that Instant happened to be at the other End of the Room; and the Queen was in such a Fright, that she wanted Presence of Mind to assist me. But my little Nurse ran to my Relief; and took me out, after I had swallowed above a Quart of Cream. I was put to Bed; however I received no other Damage than the Loss of a Suit of Cloaths, which was utterly spoiled. The Dwarf was soundly whipped, and as a further Punishment, forced to drink up the Bowl of Cream, into which he had thrown me; neither was he ever restored to Favour: For, soon after the Queen bestowed him to a Lady of high Quality; so that I saw him no more, to my very great Satisfaction; for I could not tell to what Extremitys such a malicious Urchin might have carried his Resentment.

He had before served me a scurvy Trick, which set the Queen a laughing, although at the same time she were heartily vexed, and would have immediately cashiered him, if I had not been so generous as to intercede. Her Majesty had taken a Marrow-bone upon her Plate; and after knocking out the Marrow, placed the Bone again in the Dish erect as it stood before; the Dwarf watching his Opportunity, while *Glumdalclitch* was gone to the Side-board, mounted the Stool that she stood on to take care of me at Meals; took me up in both Hands, and squeezing my Legs together, wedged them into the Marrow-bone above my Waist; where I stuck for some time, and made a very ridiculous Figure. I believe it was near a Minute before any one knew what was become of me; for I thought it below me to cry out. But, as Princes seldom get their Meat hot, my Legs were not scalded, only my Stockings and Breeches in a sad Condition. The Dwarf at my Entreaty had no other Punishment than a sound whipping.

I was frequently raillied by the Queen upon Account of my Fearfulness; and she used to ask me whether the People of my Country were as great Cowards as my self. The Occasion was this. The Kingdom is much pestered with Flies in Summer; and these odious Insects, each of them as big as a *Dunstable* Lark, hardly gave me any Rest while I sat at Dinner, with their continual Humming and Buzzing about my Ears. They would sometimes alight upon my Victuals, and leave their loathsome Excrement or Spawn behind, which to me was very visible, although not to the Natives of that Country, whose large Opticks were not so acute as mine in viewing smaller Objects. Sometimes they would fix upon my Nose or Forehead, where they stung me to the Quick, smelling very offensively; and I could easily trace that viscous Matter, which our Naturalists tell us enables those Creatures to walk with their Feet upwards upon a Cieling. I had much ado to defend my self against these detestable Animals, and could not forbear starting when they came on my Face. It was the common Practice of the Dwarf to catch a Number of these Insects in his Hand, as Schoolboys do among us, and let them out suddenly under my Nose, on Purpose to frighten me, and divert the Queen. My Remedy was to cut them in Pieces with my Knife as they flew in the Air; wherein my Dexterity was much admired.

I remember one Morning when *Glumdalclitch* had set me in my Box upon a Window, as she usually did in fair Days to give me Air, (for I durst not venture to let the Box be hung on a Nail out of the Window, as we do with Cages in *England*) after I had lifted up one of my Sashes, and sat down at my Table to eat a Piece of Sweet-Cake for my Breakfast; above twenty Wasps, allured by the Smell, came flying into the Room, humming louder than the Drones of as many Bagpipes. Some of them seized my Cake, and carried it piecemeal away; others flew about my Head and Face, confounding me with the Noise, and putting me in the utmost Terror of their Stings. However I had the Courage to rise and draw my Hanger, and attack them in the Air. I dispatched four of them, but the rest got away; and I presently shut my Window. These Insects were as large as Partridges; I took out their Stings, found them an Inch and a half long, and as sharp as Needles. I carefully preserved them all, and having since shewn them with some other Curiosities in several Parts of *Europe*;

upon my Return to *England* I gave three of them to *Gresham College*,[2] and kept the fourth for my self.

CHAPTER IV

The Country described. A Proposal for correcting modern Maps. The King's Palace, and some Account of the Metropolis. The Author's Way of travelling. The chief Temple described.

I now intend to give the Reader a short Description of this Country, as far as I travelled in it, which was not above two thousand Miles round *Lorbrulgrud* the Metropolis. For, the Queen, whom I always attended, never went further when she accompanied the King in his Progresses; and there staid till his Majesty returned from viewing his Frontiers. The whole Extent of this Prince's Dominions reacheth about six thousand Miles in Length, and from three to five in Breadth. From whence I cannot but conclude, that our Geographers of *Europe* are in a great Error, by supposing nothing but Sea between *Japan* and *California*: For it was ever my Opinion, that there must be a Balance of Earth to counterpoise the great Continent of *Tartary*; and therefore they ought to correct their Maps and Charts, by joining this vast Tract of Land to the North-west Parts of *America*; wherein I shall be ready to lend them my Assistance.

The Kingdom is a Peninsula, terminated to the North-east by a Ridge of Mountains thirty Miles high which are altogether impassable by Reason of the Volcanoes upon the Tops. Neither do the most Learned know what sort of Mortals inhabit beyond those Mountains, or whether they be inhabited at all. On the three other Sides it is bounded by the Ocean. There is not one Sea-port in the whole Kingdom; and those Parts of the Coasts into which the

[2] The official quarters of the Royal Society of London for Improving Natural Knowledge, that is, of scientific investigation in England.

Rivers issue, are so full of pointed Rocks, and the Sea generally so rough, that there is no venturing with the smallest of their Boats; so that these People are wholly excluded from any Commerce with the rest of the World. But the large Rivers are full of Vessels, and abound with excellent Fish; for they seldom get any from the Sea, because the Sea-fish are of the same Size with those in *Europe*, and consequently not worth catching; whereby it is manifest, that Nature in the Production of Plants and Animals of so extraordinary a Bulk, is wholly confined to this Continent; of which I leave the Reasons to be determined by Philosophers. However, now and then they take a Whale that happens to be dashed against the Rocks, which the common People feed on heartily. These Whales I have known so large that a Man could hardly carry one upon his Shoulders; and sometimes for Curiosity they are brought in Hampers to *Lobrulgrud*: I saw one of them in a Dish at the King's Table, which passed for a Rarity; but I did not observe he was fond of it; for I think indeed the Bigness disgusted him, although I have seen one somewhat larger in *Greenland*.

The Country is well inhabited, for it contains fifty one Cities, near an hundred walled Towns, and a great Number of Villages. To satisfy my curious Reader, it may be sufficient to describe *Lobrulgrud*. This City stands upon almost two equal Parts on each Side the River that passes through. It contains above eighty thousand Houses. It is in Length three *Glonglungs* (which make about fifty four English Miles) and two and a half in Breadth, as I measured it myself in the Royal Map made by the King's Order, which was laid on the Ground on purpose for me, and extended an hundred Feet; I paced the Diameter and Circumference several times Bare-foot, and computing by the Scale, measured it pretty exactly.

The King's Palace is no regular Edifice, but an Heap of Buildings about seven Miles round: The chief Rooms are generally two hundred and forty Foot high, and broad and long in Proportion. A Coach was allowed to *Glumdalclitch* and me, wherein her Governess frequently took her out to see the Town, or go among the Shops; and I was always of the Party, carried in my Box; although the Girl at my own Desire would often take me out, and hold me in her Hand, that I might more conveniently view the Houses and the People as we passed along the Streets. I reckoned our Coach to be about a Square of *Westminster-Hall*, but not altogether so high, however, I cannot be very exact. One Day the Governess ordered our Coachman to stop at several Shops; where the Beggars watching their Opportunity, crouded to the Sides of the Coach, and gave me the most horrible Spectacles that ever an *European* Eye beheld. There was a Woman with a Cancer in her Breast, swelled to a monstrous Size, full of Holes, in two or three of which I could have easily crept, and covered my whole Body. There was a Fellow with a Wen in his Neck, larger than five Wool-packs; and another with a couple of wooden Legs, each about twenty Foot high. But, the most hateful Sight of all was the Lice crawling on their Cloaths: I could see distinctly the Limbs of these Vermin with my naked Eye, much better than those of an *European* Louse through a Microscope; and their Snouts with which they rooted like Swine. They were the first I ever beheld; and I should have been curious enough to dissect one of them, if I had proper Instruments (which I unluckily left behind me in the Ship) although indeed the Sight was so nauseous, that it perfectly turned my Stomach.

Beside the large Box in which I was usually carried, the Queen ordered a smaller one to be made for me, of about twelve Foot Square, and ten high, for the Convenience of Travelling; because the other was somewhat too large for *Glumdalclitch's* Lap, and cumbersom in the Coach; it was made by the same Artist, whom I directed in the whole Contrivance. This travelling Closet was an exact Square with a Window in the Middle of three of the Squares, and each Window was latticed with Iron Wire on the outside, to prevent Accidents in long Journeys. On the fourth Side, which had no Window, two strong Staples were fixed, through which the Person that carried me, when I had a Mind to be on Horseback, put in a Leathern Belt, and buckled it about his Waist. This was always the Office of some grave trusty Servant in whom I could confide, whether I attended the King and Queen in their Progresses, or were disposed to see the Gardens, or pay a Visit to some great Lady or Minister of State in the Court, when *Glumdalclitch* happened to be out of Order: For I soon began to be known and esteemed among the greatest Officers, I suppose more upon Account of their Majesty's Favour, than any Merit of my own. In Journeys, when I was weary of the Coach, a Servant on Horseback would buckle my Box, and place it on a Cushion before him; and there I had a full Prospect of the Country on three Sides from my three

Windows. I had in this Closet a Field-Bed and a Hammock hung from the Cieling, two Chairs and a Table, neatly screwed to the Floor, to prevent being tossed about by the Agitation of the Horse or the Coach. And having been long used to Sea-Voyages, those Motions, although sometimes very violent, did not much discompose me.

Whenever I had a Mind to see the Town, it was always in my Travelling-Closet; which *Glumdalclitch* held in her Lap in a kind of open Sedan, after the Fashion of the Country, borne by four Men, and attended by two others in the Queen's Livery. The People who had often heard of me, were very curious to croud about the Sedan; and the Girl was complaisant enough to make the Bearers stop, and to take me in her Hand that I might be more conveniently seen.

I was very desirious to see the chief Temple, and particularly the Tower belonging to it, which is reckoned the highest in the Kingdom. Accordingly one Day my Nurse carried me thither, but I may truly say I came back disappointed; for, the Height is not above three thousand Foot, reckoning from the Ground to the highest Pinnacle top; which allowing for the Difference between the Size of those People, and us in *Europe*, is no great matter for Admiration, nor at all equal in Proportion, (if I rightly remember) to *Salisbury* Steeple. But, not to detract from a Nation to which during my Life I shall acknowledge myself extremely obliged; it must be allowed, that whatever this famous Tower wants in Height, is amply made up in Beauty and Strength. For the Walls are near an hundred Foot thick, built of hewn Stone, whereof each is about forty Foot square, and adorned on all Sides with Statues of Gods and Emperors cut in Marble larger than the Life, placed in their several Niches. I measured a little Finger which had fallen down from one of these Statues, and lay unperceived among some Rubbish; and found it exactly four Foot and an Inch in Length. *Glumdalclitch* wrapped it up in a Handkerchief, and carried it home in her Pocket to keep among other Trinkets, of which the Girl was very fond, as Children at her Age usually are.

The King's Kitchen is indeed a noble Building, vaulted at Top, and about six hundred Foot high. The great Oven is not so wide by ten Paces as the Cupola at St. *Paul's*: For I measured the latter on purpose after my Return. But if I should describe the Kitchen-grate, the prodigious Pots and Kettles, the Joints of Meat turning on the Spits, with many other Particulars; perhaps I should be hardly believed; at least a severe Critick would be apt to think I enlarged a little, as Travellers are often suspected to do. To avoid which Censure, I fear I have run too much into the other Extream; and that if this Treatise should happen to be translated into the Language of *Brobdingnag,* (which is the general Name of that Kingdom) and transmitted thither; the King and his People would have Reason to complain; that I had done them an Injury by a false and diminutive Representation.

His Majesty seldom keeps above six hundred Horses in his Stables: They are generally from fifty four to sixty Foot high. But, when he goes abroad on solemn Days, he is attended for State by a Militia Guard of five hundred Horse, which indeed I thought was the most splendid Sight that could be ever beheld, till I saw part of his Army in Battalia; whereof I shall find another Occasion to speak.

CHAPTER V

Several Adventures that happened to the Author. The Execution of a Criminal. The Author shews his Skill in Navigation.

I should have lived happy enough in that Country, if my Littleness had not exposed me to several ridiculous and troublesome Accidents; some of which I shall venture to relate. *Glumdalclitch* often carried me into the Gardens of the Court in my smaller Box, and would sometimes take me out of it and hold me in her Hand, or set me down to walk. I remember, before the Dwarf left the Queen, he followed us one Day into those Gardens; and my Nurse having set me down, he and I being close together, near some Dwarf Apple-trees, I must need shew my Wit by a silly Allusion between him and the Trees, which happens to hold in their Language as it doth in ours. Whereupon, the malicious Rogue watching his Opportunity, when I was walking under one of them, shook it directly over my Head, by which a dozen Apples, each of them near as large as a *Bristol* Barrel, came tumbling about my Ears; one of them hit me on the Back as I chanced to stoop, and knocked me down flat on my Face, but I received no other Hurt; and the Dwarf was pardoned at my Desire, because I had given the Provocation.

Another Day, *Glumdalclitch* left me on a smooth Grassplot to divert my self while she walked at some Distance with her Governess. In the mean time, there suddenly fell such a violent Shower of Hail, that I was immediately by the Force of it struck to the Ground: And when I was down, the Hail-stones gave me such cruel Bangs all over the Body, as if I had been pelted with Tennis-Balls; however I made a Shift to creep on all four, and shelter my self by lying flat on my Face on the Lee-side of a Border of Lemmon Thyme; but so bruised from Head to Foot, that I could not go abroad in ten Days. Neither is this at all to be wondered at; because Nature in that Country observing the same Proportion through all her Operations, a Hail-stone is near Eighteen Hundred Times as large as one in *Europe*; which I can assert upon Experience, having been so curious to weigh and measure them.

But, a more dangerous Accident happened to me in the same Garden, when my little Nurse, believing she had put me in a secure Place, which I often entreated her to do, that I might enjoy my own Thoughts; and having left my Box at home to avoid the Trouble of carrying it, went to another Part of the Gardens with her Governess and some Ladies of her Acquaintance. While she was absent and out of hearing, a small white Spaniel belonging to one of the chief Gardiners, having got by Accident into the Garden, happened to range near the Place where I lay. The Dog following the Scent, came directly up, and taking me in his Mouth, ran strait to his Master, wagging his Tail, and set me gently on the Ground. By good Fortune he had been so well taught, that I was carried between his Teeth without the least Hurt, or even tearing my Cloaths. But, the poor Gardiner, who knew me well, and had a great Kindness for me, was in a terrible Fright. He gently took me up in both his Hands, and asked me how I did; but I was so amazed and out of Breath, that I could not speak a Word. In a few Minutes I came to my self, and he carried me safe to my little Nurse, who by this time had returned to the Place where she left me, and was in cruel Agonies when I did not appear, nor answer when she called; she severely reprimanded the Gardiner on Account of his Dog. But, the Thing was hushed up, and never known at Court; for the Girl was afraid of the Queen's Anger; and truly as to my self, I thought it would not be for my Reputation that such a Story should go about.

This Accident absolutely determined *Glumdalclitch* never to trust me abroad for the future out of her Sight. I had been long afraid of this Resolution; and therefore concealed from her some little unlucky Adventures that happened in those Times when I was left by my self. Once a Kite hovering over the Garden, made a Stoop at me, and if I had not resolutely drawn my Hanger, and run under a thick Espalier, he would have certainly carried me away in his Talons. Another time, walking to the Top of a fresh Molehill, I fell to my Neck, in the Hole through which that Animal had cast up the Earth; and coined some Lye not worth remembring, to excuse my self for spoiling my Cloaths. I likewise broke my right Shin against the Shell of a Snail, which I happened to stumble over, as I was walking alone, and thinking on poor *England*.

I cannot tell whether I were more pleased or mortified to observe in those solitary Walks, that the smaller Birds did not appear to be at all afraid of me; but would hop about within a Yard Distance, looking for Worms, and other Food, with as much Indifference and Security as if no Creature at all were near them. I remember, a Thrush had the Confidence to snatch out of my Hand with his Bill, a Piece of Cake that *Glumdalclitch* had just given me for my Breakfast. When I attempted to catch any of these Birds, they would boldly turn against me, endeavouring to pick my Fingers, which I durst not venture within their Reach; and then they would hop back unconcerned to hunt for Worms or Snails, as they did before. But, one Day I tool a thick Cudgel, and threw it with all my Strength so luckily at a Linnet, that I knocked him down, and seizing him by the Neck with both my Hands, ran with him in Triumph to my Nurse. However, the Bird who had only been stunned, recovering himself, gave me so many Boxes with his Wings on both Sides of my Head and Body, although I held him at Arms Length, and was out of the Reach of his Claws, that I was twenty Times thinking to let him go. But I was soon relieved by one of our Servants, who wrung off the Bird's Neck; and I had him next Day for Dinner by the Queen's Command. This

Linnet, as near as I can remember, seemed to be somewhat larger than an English Swan.

The Maids of Honor often invited *Glumdalclitch* to their Apartments, and desired she would bring me along with her, on Purpose to have the Pleasure of seeing and touching me. They would often strip me naked from Top to Toe, and lay me at full Length in their Bosoms; wherewith I was much disgusted; because, to say the Truth, a very offensive Smell came from their Skins; which I do not mention or intend to the Disadvantage of those excellent Ladies, for whom I have all Manner of Respect: But, I conceive, that my Sense was more acute in Proportion to my Littleness; and that those illustrious Persons were no more disagreeable to their Lovers, or to each other, than People of the same Quality are with us in *England*. And, after all, I found their natural Smell was much more supportable than when they used Perfumes, under which I immediately swooned away. I cannot forget, that an intimate Friend of mine in *Lilliput* took the Freedom in a warm Day, when I had used a good deal of Exercise, to complain of a strong Smell about me; although I am as little faulty that way as most of my Sex: But I suppose, his Faculty of Smelling was as nice with regard to me, as mine was to that of this People. Upon this Point, I cannot forbear doing Justice to the Queen my Mistress, and *Glumdalclitch* my Nurse; whose Persons were as sweet as those of any Lady in *England*.

That which gave me most Uneasiness among these Maids of Honour, when my Nurse carried me to visit them, was to see them use me without any Manner of Ceremony, like a Creature who had no Sort of Consequence. For, they would strip themselves to the Skin, and put on their Smocks in my Presence, while I was placed on their Toylet directly before their naked Bodies; which, I am sure, to me was very far from being a tempting Sight, or from giving me any other Motions than those of Horror and Disgust. Their Skins appeared so coarse and uneven, so variously coloured when I saw them near, with a Mole here and there as broad as a Trencher, and Hairs hanging from it thicker than Pack-threads; to say nothing further concerning the rest of their Persons. Neither did they at all scruple while I was by, to discharge what they had drunk, to the Quantity of at least two Hogsheads, in a Vessel that held above three Tuns. The handsomest among these Maids of

Honour, a pleasant frolicksome Girl of sixteen, would sometimes set me astride upon one of her Nipples; with many other Tricks, wherein the Reader will excuse me for not being over particular. But, I was so much displeased, that I entreated *Glumdalclitch* to contrive some Excuse for not seeing that young Lady any more.

One Day, a young Gentleman who was Nephew to my Nurse's Governess, came and pressed them both to see an Execution. It was of a Man who had murdered one of that Gentleman's intimate Acquaintance. *Glumdalclitch* was prevailed on to be of the Company, very much against her Inclination, for she was naturally tender hearted: And, as for my self, although I abhorred such Kind of Spectacles; yet my Curiosity tempted me to see something that I thought must be extraordinary. The Malefactor was fixed in a Chair upon a Scaffold erected for the Purpose; and his Head cut off at one Blow with a Sword of about forty Foot long. The Veins and Arteries spouted up such a prodigious Quantity of Blood, and so high in the Air, that the great *Jet d'Eau* at *Versailles* was not equal for the Time it lasted; and the Head when it fell on the Scaffold Floor, gave such a Bounce, as made me start, although I were at least an *English* Mile distant.

The Queen, who often used to hear me talk of my Sea-Voyages, and took all Occasions to divert me when I was melancholy, asked me whether I understood how to handle a Sail or an Oar; and whether a little Exercise of Rowing might not be convenient for my Health. I answered, that I understood both very well. For although my proper Employment had been to be Surgeon or Doctor to the Ship; yet often upon a Pinch, I was forced to work like a common Mariner. But, I could not see how this could be done in their Country, where the smallest Wherry was equal to a first Rate Man of War among us; and such a Boat as I could manage, would never live in any of their Rivers: Her Majesty said, if I would contrive a Boat, her own Joyner should make it, and she would provide a Place for me to sail in. The Fellow was an ingenious Workman, and by my Instructions in ten Days finished a Pleasure-Boat with all its Tackling, able conveniently to hold eight *Europeans*. When it was finished, the Queen was so delighted, that she ran with it in her Lap to the King, who ordered it to be put in a Cistern full of Water, with me in it, by way of Tryal; where I could not manage my two Sculls or little Oars for want of Room. But, the Queen had before contrived another Project. She ordered the Joyner to make a wooden Trough of three Hundred Foot long, fifty broad, and eight deep; which being well pitched to prevent leaking, was placed on the Floor along the Wall, in an outer Room of the Palace. It had a Cock near the Bottom, to let out the Water when it began to grow stale; and two Servants could easily fill it in half an Hour. Here I often used to row for my Diversion, as well as that of the Queen and her Ladies, who thought themselves agreeably entertained with my Skill and Agility. Sometimes I would put up my Sail, and then my Business was only to steer, while the Ladies gave me a Gale with their Fans; and when they were weary, some of the Pages would blow my Sail forward with their Breath, while I shewed my Art by steering Starboard or Larboard as I pleased. When I had done, *Glumdalclitch* always carried back my Boat into her Closet, and hung it on a Nail to dry.

In this Exercise I once met an Accident which had like to have cost me my Life. For, one of the Pages having put my Boat into the Trough; the Governess who attended *Glumdalclitch*, very officiously lifted me up to place me in the Boat; but I happened to slip through her Fingers, and should have infallibly fallen down forty Foot upon the Floor, if by the luckiest Chance in the World, I had not been stop'd by a Corking-pin that stuck in the good Gentlewoman's Stomacher; the Head of the Pin passed between my Shirt and the Waistband of my Breeches; and thus I was held by the Middle in the Air, till *Glumdalclitch* ran to my Relief.

Another time, one of the Servants, whose Office it was to fill my Trough every third Day with fresh Water; was so careless to let a huge Frog (not perceiving it) slip out of his Pail. The Frog lay concealed till I was put into my Boat, but then seeing a resting Place, climbed up, and made it lean so much on one Side, that I was forced to balance it with all my Weight on the other, to prevent overturning. When the Frog was got in, it hopped at once half the Length of the Boat, and then over my Head, backwards and forwards, dawbing my Face and Cloaths with its odious Slime. The Largeness of its Features made it appear the most deformed Animal that can be conceived. However, I desired *Glumdalclitch* to let me deal with it alone. I banged it a good while with one of my Sculls, and at last forced it to leap out of the Boat.

But, the greatest Danger I ever underwent in that Kingdom, was from a Monkey, who belonged to one of the Clerks of the Kitchen. *Glumdalclitch* had locked me up in her Closet,[1] while she went somewhere upon Business, or a Visit. The Weather being very warm, the Closet Window was left open, as well as the Windows and the Door of my bigger Box, in which I usually lived, because of its Largeness and Conveniency. As I sat quietly meditating at my Table, I heard something bounce in at the Closet Window, and skip about from one Side to the other; whereat, although I were much alarmed, yet I ventured to look out, but not stirring from my Seat; and then I saw this frolicksome Animal, frisking and leaping up and down, till at last he came to my Box, which he seemed to view with great Pleasure and Curiosity, peeping in at the Door and every Window. I retreated to the farther Corner of my Room, or Box; but the Monkey looking in at every Side, put me into such a Fright, that I wanted Presence of Mind to conceal my self under the Bed, as I might easily have done. After some time spent in peeping, grinning, and chattering, he at last espyed me; and reaching one of his Paws in at the Door, as a Cat does when she plays with a Mouse, although I often shifted Place to avoid him; he at length seized the Lappet of my Coat (which being made of that Country Silk, was very thick and strong) and dragged me out. He took me up in his right Fore-foot, and held me as a Nurse doth a Child she is going to suckle; just as I have seen the same Sort of Creature do with a Kitten in *Europe*: And when I offered to struggle, he squeezed me so hard, that I thought it more prudent to submit. I have good Reason to believe that he took me for a young one of his own Species, by his often stroaking my Face very gently with his other Paw. In these Diversions he was interrupted by a Noise at the Closet Door, as if some Body were opening it; whereupon he suddenly leaped up to the Window at which he had come in, and thence upon the Leads and Gutters, walking upon three Legs, and holding me in the fourth, till he clambered up to a Roof that was next to ours. I heard *Glumdalclitch* give a Shriek at the Moment he was carrying me out. The poor Girl was almost distracted: That Quarter of the Palace was all in an Uproar; the Servants ran for Ladders; the Monkey was seen by Hundreds in the Court, sitting upon the Ridge of a Building, holding me like a Baby in one of his Fore-Paws, and feeding me with the other, by cramming into my Mouth some Victuals he had squeezed out of

[1] A small private room.

the Bag on one Side of his Chaps, and patting me when I would not eat; whereat many of the Rabble below could not forbear laughing; neither do I think they justly ought to be blamed; for without Question, the Sight was ridiculous enough to every Body but my self. Some of the People threw up Stones, hoping to drive the Monkey down; but this was strictly forbidden, or else very probably my Brains had been dashed out.

The Ladders were now applied, and mounted by several Men; which the Monkey observing, and finding himself almost encompassed; not being able to make Speed enough with his three Legs, let me drop on a Ridge-Tyle, and made his Escape. Here I sat for some time five Hundred Yards from the Ground, expecting every Moment to be blown down by the Wind, or to fall by my own Giddiness, and come tumbling over and over from the Ridge to the Eves. But an honest Lad, one of my Nurse's Footmen, climbed up, and putting me into his Breeches Pocket, brought me down safe.

I was almost choaked with the filthy Stuff the Monkey had crammed down my Throat; but, my dear little Nurse picked it out of my Mouth with a small Needle; and then I fell a vomiting, which gave me great Relief. Yet I was so weak and bruised in the Sides with the Squeezes given me by this odious Animal, that I was forced to keep my Bed a Fortnight. The King, Queen, and all the Court, sent every Day to enquire after my Health; and her Majesty made me several Visits during my Sickness. The Monkey was killed, and an Order made that no such Animal should be kept about the Palace.

When I attended the King after my Recovery, to return him Thanks for his Favours, he was pleased to railly me a good deal upon this Adventure. He asked me what my Thoughts and Speculations were while I lay in the Monkey's Paw; how I liked the Victuals he gave me, his Manner of Feeding; and whether the fresh Air on the Roof had sharpened my Stomach. He desired to know what I would have done upon such an Occasion in my own Country. I told his Majesty, that in *Europe* we had no Monkies, except such as were brought for Curiosities from other Places, and so small, that I could deal with a Dozen of them together, if they presumed to attack me. And as for that monstrous Animal with whom I was so lately engaged, (it was indeed as large as an Elephant) if my Fears had suffered me to think so far as to make

Use of my Hanger (looking fiercely, and clapping my Hand upon the Hilt as I spoke) when he poked his Paw into my Chamber, perhaps I should have given him such a Wound, as would have made him glad to withdraw it with more Haste than he put it in. This I delivered in a firm Tone, like a Person who was jealous lest his Courage should be called in Question. However, my Speech produced nothing else besides a loud Laughter; which all the Respect due to his Majesty from those about him, could not make them contain. This made me reflect, how vain an Attempt it is for a Man to endeavour doing himself Honour among those who are out of all Degree of Equality or Comparison with him. And yet I have seen the Moral of my own Behaviour very frequent in *England* since my Return; where a little contemptible Varlet, without the least Title to Birth, Person, Wit, or common Sense, shall presume to look with Importance, and put himself upon a Foot with the greatest Persons of the Kingdom.

I was every Day furnishing the Court with some ridiculous Story; and *Glumdalclitch*, although she loved me to Excess, yet was arch enough to inform the Queen, whenever I committed any Folly that she thought would be diverting to her Majesty. The Girl who had been out of Order, was carried by her Governess to take the Air about an Hour's Distance, or thirty Miles from Town. They alighted out of the Coach near a small Foot-path in a Field; and *Glumdalclitch* setting down my travelling Box, I went out of it to walk. There was a Cow-dung in the Path, and I must needs try my Activity by attempting to leap over it. I took a Run, but unfortunately jumped short, and found my self just in the Middle up to my Knees. I waded through with some Difficulty, and one of the Footmen wiped me as clean as he could with his Handkerchief; for I was filthily bemired, and my Nurse confined me to my Box until we returned home; where the Queen was soon informed of what had passed, and the Footmen spread it about the Court; so that all the Mirth, for some Days, was at my Expence.

CHAPTER VI

Several Contrivances of the Author to please the King and Queen. He shews his Skill in Musick. The King enquires into the State of Europe, *which the Author relates to him. The King's Observations thereon.*

I used to attend the King's Levee once or twice a Week, and had often seen him under the Barber's Hand, which indeed was at first very terrible to behold. For, the Razor was almost twice as long as an ordinary Scythe. His Majesty, according to the Custom of the Country, was only shaved twice a Week. I once prevailed on the Barber to give me some of the Suds or Lather, out of which I picked Forty or Fifty of the strongest Stumps of Hair, I then took a Piece of fine Wood, and cut it like the Back of a Comb, making several Holes in it at equal Distance, with as small a Needle as I could get from *Glumdalclitch*. I fixed in the Stumps so artificially, scraping and sloping them with my Knife towards the Points, that I made a very tolerable Comb; which was a seasonable Supply, my own being so much broken in the Teeth, that it was almost useless: Neither did I know any Artist in that Country so nice and exact, as would undertake to make me another.

And this puts me in mind of an Amusement wherein I spent many of my leisure Hours. I desired the Queen's Woman to save for me the Combings of her Majesty's Hair, whereof in time I got a good Quantity; and consulting with my Friend the Cabinet-maker, who had received general Orders to do little Jobbs for me; I directed him to make two Chair-frames, no larger than those I had in my Box, and then to bore little Holes with a fine Awl round those Parts where I designed the Backs and Seats; through these Holes I wove the strongest Hairs I could pick out, just after the Manner of Cane-chairs in *England*. When they were finished, I made a Present of them to her Majesty, who kept them in her Cabinet, and used to shew them for Curiosities; as indeed they were the Wonder of every one who beheld them. The Queen would have had me sit upon one of these Chairs, but I absolutely refused to obey her; protesting I would rather dye a Thousand Deaths than place a dishonourable Part of my Body on those precious Hairs that once adorned her Majesty's Head. Of these Hairs (as I had always a Mechanical Genius) I likewise made a neat little Purse about five Foot long, with her Majesty's Name decyphered in Gold Letters; which I gave to *Glumdalclitch*, by the Queen's Consent. To say the Truth, it was more for Shew than Use, being not of Strength to bear the Weight of the larger Coins; and therefore she kept nothing in it, but some little Toys that Girls are fond of.

The King, who delighted in Musick, had frequent Consorts[1] at Court, to which I was sometimes carried, and set in my Box on a Table to hear them: But, the Noise was so great, that I could hardly distinguish the Tunes. I am confident, that all the Drums and Trumpets of a Royal Army, beating and sounding together just at your Ears, could not equal it. My Practice was to have my Box removed from the Places where the Performers sat, as far as I could; then to shut the Doors and Windows of it, and draw the Window-Curtains; after which I found their Musick not disagreeable.

I had learned in my Youth to play a little upon the Spinet; *Glumdalclitch* kept one in her Chamber, and a Master attended twice a Week to teach her: I call it a Spinet, because it somewhat resembled that Instrument, and was play'd upon in the same Manner. A Fancy came into my Head, that I would entertain the King and Queen with an *English* Tune upon this Instrument. But this appeared extremely difficult: For, the Spinet was near sixty Foot long, each Key being almost a Foot wide; so that, with my Arms extended, I could not reach to above five Keys; and to press them down required a good smart stroak with my Fist, which would be too great a Labour, and to no purpose. The Method I contrived was this. I prepared two round Sticks about the Bigness of common Cudgels; they were thicker at one End than the other; and I covered the thicker End with a Piece of a Mouse's Skin, that by rapping on them, I might neither Damage the Tops of the Keys, nor interrupt the Sound. Before the Spinet,

[1] Concerts.

a Bench was placed about four Foot below the Keys, and I was put upon the Bench. I ran sideling upon it that way and this, as fast as I could, banging the proper Keys with my two Sticks; and made a shift to play a Jigg to the great Satisfaction of both their Majesties: But, it was the most violent Exercise I ever underwent, and yet I could not strike above sixteen Keys, nor, consequently, play the Bass and Treble together, as other Artists do; which was a great Disadvantage to my Performance.

The King, who as I before observed, was a Prince of excellent Understanding, would frequently order that I should be brought in my Box, and set upon the Table in his Closet. He would then command me to bring one of my Chairs out of the Box, and sit down within three Yards Distance upon the Top of the Cabinet; which brought me almost to a Level with his Face. In this Manner I had several Conversations with him. I one Day took the Freedom to tell his Majesty, that the Contempt he discovered towards *Europe*, and the rest of the World, did not seem answerable to those excellent Qualities of Mind, that he was Master of. That, Reason did not extend itself with the Bulk of the Body: On the contrary, we observed in our Country, that the tallest Persons were usually least provided with it. That among other Animals, Bees and Ants had the Reputation of more Industry, Art, and Sagacity than many of the larger Kinds. And that, as inconsiderable as he took me to be, I hoped I might live to do his Majesty some signal Service. The King heard me with Attention; and began to conceive a much better Opinion of me than he had ever before. He desired I would give him as exact an Account of the Government of *England* as I possibly could; because, as fond as Princes commonly are of their own Customs (for so he conjectured of other Monarchs by my former Discourses) he should be glad to hear of any thing that might deserve Imitation.

Imagine with thy self, courteous Reader, how often I then wished for the Tongue of *Demosthenes* or *Cicero*, that might have enabled me to celebrate the Praise of my own dear native Country in a Style equal to its Merits and Felicity.

I began my Discourse by informing his Majesty, that our Dominions consisted of two Islands, which composed three mighty Kingdoms under one Sovereign, besides our Plantations[2] in *America*. I dwelt long upon the Fertility of our Soil, and the Temperature

[2] Colonies.

of our Climate. I then spoke at large upon the Constitution of an *English* Parliament, partly made up of an illustrious Body called the House of Peers, Persons of the noblest Blood, and of the most ancient and ample Patrimonies. I described that extraordinary Care always taken of their Education in Arts and Arms, to qualify them for being Counsellors born to the King and Kingdom; to have a Share in the Legislature, to be Members of the highest Court of Judicature from whence there could be no Appeal; and to be Champions always ready for the Defence of their Prince and Country by their Valour, Conduct and Fidelity. That these were the Ornament and Bulwark of the Kingdom; worthy Followers of their most renowned Ancestors, whose Honour had been the Reward of their Virtue; from which their Posterity were never once known to degenerate. To these were joined several holy Persons, as part of that Assembly, under the Title of Bishops; whose peculiar Business it is, to take care of Religion, and of those who instruct the People therein. These were searched and sought out through the whole Nation, by the Prince and wisest Counsellors, among such of the Priesthood, as were most deservedly distinguished by the Sanctity of their Lives, and the Depth of their Erudition; who were indeed the spiritual Fathers of the Clergy and the People.

That, the other Part of the Parliament consisted of an Assembly called the House of Commons; who were all principal Gentlemen, *freely* picked and culled out by the People themselves, for their great Abilities, and Love of their Country, to represent the Wisdom of the whole Nation. And, these two Bodies make up the most august Assembly in *Europe*; to whom, in Conjunction with the Prince, the whole Legislature is committed.

I then descended to the Courts of Justice, over which the Judges, those venerable Sages and Interpreters of the Law, presided, for determining the disputed Rights and Properties of Men, as well as for the Punishment of Vice, and Protection of Innocence. I mentioned the prudent Management of our Treasury; the Valour and Atchievements of our Forces by Sea and Land. I computed the Number of our People, by reckoning how many Millions there might be of each Religious Sect, or Political Party among us. I did not omit even our Sports and Pastimes, or any other Particular which I thought might redound to the Honour of my Country. And, I finished all with a brief historical Account of Affairs and Events in *England* for about an hundred Years past.

This Conversation was not ended under five Audiences, each of several Hours; and the King heard the whole with great Attention; frequently taking Notes of what I spoke, as well as Memorandums of what Questions he intended to ask me.

When I had put an End to these long Discourses, his Majesty in a sixth Audience consulting his Notes, proposed many Doubts, Queries, and Objections, upon every Article. He asked, what Methods were used to cultivate the Minds and Bodies of our young Nobility; and in what kind of Business they commonly spent the first and teachable Part of their Lives. What Course was taken to supply that Assembly, when any noble Family became extinct. What Qualifications were necessary in those who are to be created new Lords: Whether the Humour of the Prince, a Sum of Money to a Court-Lady, or a Prime Minister; or a Design of strengthening a Party opposite to the publick Interest, ever happened to be Motives in those Advancements. What Share of Knowledge these Lords had in the Laws of their Country, and how they came by it, so as to enable them to decide the Properties of their Fellow-Subjects in the last Resort. Whether they were always so free from Avarice, Partialities, or Want, that a Bribe, or some other sinister View, could have no Place among them. Whether those holy Lords I spoke of, were constantly promoted to that Rank upon Account of their Knowledge in religious Matters, and the Sanctity of their Lives; had never been compliers with the Times, while they were common Priests; or slavish prostitute Chaplains to some Nobleman, whose Opinions they continued servilely to follow after they were admitted into that Assembly.

He then desired to know, what Arts were practised in electing those whom I called Commoners. Whether, a Stranger with a strong Purse might not influence the vulgar Voters to chuse him before their own Landlords, or the most considerable Gentleman in the Neighbourhood. How it came to pass, that People were so violently bent upon getting into this Assembly, which I allowed to be a great Trouble and Expence, often to the Ruin of their Families, without any Salary or Pension: Because this appeared such an exalted Strain of Virtue and publick Spirit, that his Majesty seemed to doubt it might possibly not be always sincere: And he desired to know, whether such zealous Gentlemen could have any Views of refunding themselves for the Charges and Trouble they were at, by sacrificing the publick Good to the Designs of a weak and vicious Prince, in Conjunction with a corrupted Ministry. He multiplied his Questions, and sifted me thoroughly upon every Part of this Head; proposing numberless Enquiries and Objections, which I think it not prudent or convenient to repeat.

Upon what I said in relation to our Courts of Justice, his Majesty desired to be satisfied in several Points: And, this I was the better able to do, having been formerly almost ruined by a long Suit in Chancery, which was decreed for me with Costs. He asked, what Time was usually spent in determining between Right and Wrong; and what Degree of Expence. Whether Advocates and Orators had Liberty to plead in Causes manifestly known to be unjust, vexatious, or oppressive. Whether Party in Religion or Politicks were observed to be of any Weight in the Scale of Justice. Whether those pleading Orators were Persons educated in the general Knowledge of Equity; or only in provincial, national, and other local Customs. Whether they or their Judges had any Part in penning those Laws, which they assumed the Liberty of interpreting and glossing upon at their Pleasure. Whether they had ever at different Times pleaded for and against the same Cause, and cited Precedents to prove contrary Opinions. Whether they were a rich or a poor Corporation. Whether they received any pecuniary Reward for pleading or delivering their Opinions. And particularly whether they were ever admitted as Members in the lower Senate.

He fell next upon the Management of our Treasury; and said, he thought my Memory had failed me, because I computed our Taxes at about five or six Millions a Year; and when I came to mention the Issues, he found they sometimes amounted to more than double; for, the Notes he had taken were very particular in this Point; because he hoped, as he told me, that the Knowledge of our Conduct might be useful to him; and he could not be deceived in his Calculations. But, if what I told him were true, he was still at a Loss how a Kingdom could run out of its Estate like a private Person. He asked me, who were our Creditors? and, where we found Money to pay them? He wondered to hear me talk of such chargeable and extensive Wars; that, certainly we must be a quarrelsome People, or live among very bad Neighbours; and that our Generals must needs be richer than our Kings. He asked, what Business we had out of our own Islands, unless upon the Score of Trade or Treaty, or to defend the Coasts with our Fleet. Above all, he was amazed to hear me talk of a mercenary standing

Army in the Midst of Peace, and among a free People. He said, if we were governed by our own Consent in the Persons of our Representatives, he could not imagine of whom we were afraid, or against whom we were to fight; and would hear my Opinion, whether a private Man's House might not better be defended by himself, his Children, and Family; than by half a Dozen Rascals picked up at a Venture in the Streets, for small Wages, who might get an Hundred Times more by cutting their Throats.

He laughed at my odd Kind of Arithmetick (as he was pleased to call it) in reckoning the Numbers of our People by a Computation drawn from the several Sects among us in Religion and Politicks. He said, he knew no Reason, why those who entertain Opinions prejudicial to the Publick, should be obliged to change, or should not be obliged to conceal them. And, as it was Tyranny in any Government to require the first, so it was Weakness not to enforce the second: For, a Man may be allowed to keep Poisons in his Closet, but not to vend them about as Cordials.

He observed, that among the Diversions of our Nobility and Gentry, I had mentioned Gaming. He desired to know at what Age this Entertainment was usually taken up, and when it was laid down. How much of their Time it employed; whether it ever went so high as to affect their Fortunes. Whether mean vicious People, by their Dexterity in that Art, might not arrive at great Riches, and sometimes keep our very Nobles in Dependance, as well as habituate them to vile Companions; wholly take them from the Improvement of their Minds, and force them by the Losses they received, to learn and practice that infamous Dexterity upon others.

He was perfectly astonished with the historical Account I gave him of our Affairs during the last Century; protesting it was only an Heap of Conspiracies, Rebellions, Murders, Massacres, Revolutions, Banishments; the very worst Effects that Avarice, Faction, Hypocrisy, Perfidiousness, Cruelty, Rage, Madness, Hatred, Envy, Lust, Malice, and Ambition could produce.

His Majesty in another Audience, was at the Pains to recapitulate the Sum of all I had spoken; compared the Questions he made, with the Answers I had given; then taking me into his Hands, and stroaking me gently, delivered himself in these Words, which I shall never forget, nor the Manner he spoke them in. My little Friend *Grildrig*; you have made a most admirable Panegyrick upon your Country. You have clearly proved that Ignorance, Idleness, and Vice are the proper Ingredients for qualifying a Legislator. That Laws are best explained, interpreted, and applied by those whose Interest and Abilities lie in perverting, confounding, and eluding them. I observe among you some Lines of an Institution, which in its Original might have been tolerable; but these half erased, and the rest wholly blurred and blotted by Corruptions. It doth not appear from all you have said, how any one Perfection is required towards the Procurement of any one Station among you; much less that Men are ennobled on Account of their Virtue, that Priests are advanced for their Piety or Learning, Soldiers for their Conduct or Valour, Judges for their Integrity, Senators for the Love of their Country, or Counsellors for their Wisdom. As for yourself (continued the King) who have spent the greatest Part of your Life in travelling; I am well disposed to hope you may hitherto have escaped many Vices of your Country. But, by what I have gathered from your own Relation, and the Answers I have with much Pains wringed and extorted from you; I cannot but conclude the Bulk of your Natives, to be the most pernicious Race of little odious Vermin that Nature ever suffered to crawl upon the Surface of the Earth.

CHAPTER VII

The Author's Love of his Country. He makes a Proposal of much Advantage to the King; which is rejected. The King's great Ignorance in Politicks. The Learning of that Country very imperfect and confined. Their Laws, and military Affairs, and parties in the state.

Nothing but an extreme Love of Truth could have hindered me from concealing this Part of my Story. It was in vain to discover my Resentments, which were always turned into Ridicule: And I was forced to rest with Patience, while my noble and most beloved Country was so injuriously treated. I am heartily sorry as any of my Readers can possibly be, that such an Occasion was given: But this Prince happened to be so curious and inquisitive upon every Particular, that it could not consist either with Gratitude or good Manners to refuse giving him what Satisfaction I was able. Yet thus much I may be allowed to say in my own Vindication; that I artfully eluded many of his Questions; and gave to every Point a more favourable turn by many Degrees than the strictness of Truth would allow. For, I have always born that laudable Partiality to my own Country, which *Dionysius Halicarnassensis* with so much Justice recommends to an Historian.[1] I would hide the Frailties and Deformities of my Political Mother, and place her Virtues and Beauties in the most advantageous Light. This was my sincere Endeavour in those many Discourses I had with that mighty Monarch, although it unfortunately failed of success.

But, great Allowances should be given to a King who lives wholly secluded from the rest of the World, and must therefore be altogether unacquainted with the Manners and Customs that most prevail in other Nations: The want of which Knowledge will ever produce many *Prejudices*, and a certain *Narrowness of Thinking*; from which we and the politer Countries of *Europe* are wholly exempted. And it would be hard indeed, if so remote a Prince's Notions of Virtue and Vice were to be offered as a Standard for all Mankind.

To confirm what I have now said, and further to shew the miserable Effects of a *confined Education*; I shall here insert a Passage which will hardly obtain Belief. In hopes to ingratiate my self farther into his Majesty's Favour, I told him of an Invention discovered between three and four hundred Years ago, to make a certain Powder; into an heap of which the smallest Spark of Fire falling, would kindle the whole in a Moment, although it were as big as a Mountain; and make it all fly up in the Air together, with a Noise and Agitation greater than Thunder. That, a proper Quantity of this Powder rammed into an hollow Tube of Brass or Iron, according to its Bigness, would drive a Ball of Iron or Lead with such Violence and Speed, as nothing was able

[1] Swift is here ironic at Gulliver's expense. Dionysius, a Greek writer who lived in Rome under Augustus, celebrated the Romans in order to persuade the conquered Greeks to submit to this superior people.

to sustain its Force. That, the largest Balls thus discharged, would not only Destroy whole Ranks of an Army at once; but batter the strongest Walls to the Ground; sink down Ships with a thousand Men in each, to the Bottom of the Sea; and when linked together by a Chain, would cut through Masts and Rigging; divide Hundreds of Bodies in the Middle, and lay all Waste before them. That we often put this Powder into large hollow Balls of Iron, and discharged them by an Engine into some City we were besieging; which would rip up the Pavement, tear the Houses to Pieces, burst and throw Splinters on every Side, dashing out the Brains of all who came near. That I knew the Ingredients very well, which were Cheap, and common; I understood the Manner of compounding them, and could direct his Workmen how to make those Tubes of a Size proportionable to all other Things in his Majesty's Kingdom; and the largest need not be above two hundred Foot long; twenty or thirty of which Tubes, charged with the proper Quantity of Powder and Balls, would batter down the Walls of the strongest Town in his Dominions in a few Hours; or destroy the whole Metropolis, if ever it should pretend to dispute his absolute Commands. This I humbly offered to his Majesty, as a small Tribute of Acknowledgment in return of so many Marks that I had received of his Royal Favour and Protection.

The King was struck with Horror at the Description I had given of those terrible Engines, and the Proposal I had made. He was amazed how so impotent and groveling an Insect as I (these were his Expressions) could entertain such inhuman Ideas, and in so familiar a Manner as to appear wholly unmoved at all the Scenes of Blood and Desolation, which I had painted as the common Effects of those destructive Machines; whereof he said, some evil Genius, Enemy to Mankind, must have been the first Contriver. As for himself, he protested, that although few Things delighted him so much as new Discoveries in Art or in Nature; yet he would rather lose Half his Kingdom than be privy to such a Secret; which he commanded me, as I valued my Life, never to mention any more.

A strange Effect of *narrow Principles* and *short Views*! that a Prince possessed of every Quality which procures Veneration, Love and Esteem; of strong Parts, great Wisdom and profound Learning; endued with admirable Talents for Government, and almost adored by his Subjects; should from a *nice unnecessary Scruple*, whereof in *Europe* we can have no Conception, let slip an Opportunity put into his Hands, that would have made him absolute Master of the Lives, the Liberties, and the Fortunes of his People. Neither do I say this with the least Intention to detract from the many Virtues of that excellent King; whose Character I am sensible will on this Account be very much lessened in the Opinion of an *English* Reader: But, I take this Defect among them to have risen from their Ignorance; by not having hitherto reduced *Politicks* into a *Science*, as the more acute Wits of *Europe* have done. For, I remember very well, in a Discourse one Day with the King; when I happened to say, there were several thousand Books among us written upon the *Art of Government*; it gave him (directly contrary to my Intention) a very mean Opinion of our Understandings. He professed both to abominate and despise all *Mystery*, *Refinement*, and *Intrigue*, either in a Prince or a Minister. He could not tell what I meant by *Secrets of State*, where an Enemy or some Rival Nation were not in the Case. He confined the Knowledge of governing within very *narrow Bounds*; to common Sense and Reason, to Justice and Lenity, to the Speedy Determination of Civil and criminal Causes; with some other obvious Topicks which are not worth considering. And, he gave it for his Opinion; that whoever could make two Ears of Corn, or two Blades of Grass to grow upon a Spot of Ground where only one grew before; would deserve better of Mankind, and do more essential Service to his Country, than the whole Race of Politicians put together.

The Learning of this People is very defective; consisting only in Morality, History, Poetry and Mathematicks; wherein they must be allowed to excel. But, the last of these is wholly applied to what may be useful in Life; to the Improvement of Agriculture and all mechanical Arts; so that among us it would be little esteemed. And as to Ideas, Entities, Abstractions and Transcendentals, I could never drive the least Conception into their Heads.

No Law of that Country must exceed in Words the Number of Letters in their Alphabet; which consists only of two and twenty. But indeed, few of them extend even to that Length. They are expressed in the most plain and simple Terms, wherein those People are not Mercurial enough to discover above one Interpretation. And, to write a Comment upon any Law, is a capital Crime. As to the Decision of civil Causes, or Proceedings against Criminals, their Precedents are so few, that they have little Reason to boast of any extraordinary Skill in either.

They have had the Art of Printing, as well as the *Chinese*, Time out of Mind. But their Libraries are not very large; for that of the King's, which is reckoned the largest, doth not amount to above a thousand Volumes; placed in a Gallery of twelve hundred Foot long; from whence I had Liberty to borrow what Books I pleased. The Queen's Joyner had contrived in one of *Glumdalclitch's* Rooms a Kind of wooden Machine five and twenty Foot high, formed like a standing Ladder; the Steps were each fifty Foot long: it was indeed a movable Pair of Stairs, the lowest End placed at ten Foot Distance from the Wall of the Chamber. The Book I had a Mind to read was put up leaning against the Wall. I first mounted to the upper Step of the Ladder, and turning my Face towards the Book, began at the Top of the Page, and so walking to the Right and Left about eight or ten Paces according to the Length of the Lines, till I had gotten a little below the Level of my Eyes; and then descending gradually till I came to the Bottom: After which I mounted again, and began the other Page in the same Manner, and so turned over the Leaf, which I could easily do with both my Hands, for it was as thick and stiff as a Paste-board, and in the largest Folios not above eighteen or twenty Foot long.

Their Stile is clear, masculine, and smooth, but not Florid; for they avoid nothing more than multiplying unnecessary Words, or using various Expressions. I have perused many of their Books, especially those in History and Morality. Among the latter I was much diverted with a little old Treatise, which always lay in *Glumdalclitch's* Bed-chamber, and belonged to her Governess, a grave elderly Gentlewoman, who dealt in Writings of Morality and Devotion. The Book treats of the Weakness of Human kind; and is in little Esteem except among Women and the Vulgar. However, I was curious to see what an Author of that Country could say upon such a Subject. This Writer went through all the usual Topicks of *European* Moralists; shewing how diminutive, contemptible, and helpless an Animal was Man in his own Nature; how unable to defend himself from the Inclemencies of the Air, or the Fury of wild Beasts: How much he was excelled by one Creature in Strength, by another in Speed, by a third in Foresight, by a fourth in Industry. He added, that Nature was degenerated in these latter declining Ages of the World, and could now produce only small abortive Births in Comparison of those in ancient Times. He said, it was very reasonable to think, not only that the Species of Men were originally much larger, but also that there must have been Giants in former Ages; which, as it is asserted by History and Tradition, so it hath been confirmed by huge Bones and Sculls casually dug up in several Parts of the Kingdom, far exceeding the common dwindled Race of Man in our Days. He argued, that the very Laws of Nature absolutely required we should have been made in the Beginning, of a Size more large and robust, not so liable to Destruction from every little Accident of a Tile falling from an House, or a Stone cast from the Hand of a Boy, or of being drowned in a little Brook. From this Way of Reasoning the Author drew several moral Applications useful in the Conduct of Life, but needless here to repeat. For my own Part, I could not avoid reflecting, how universally this Talent was spread of drawing Lectures in Morality, or indeed rather Matter of Discontent and repining, from the Quarrels we raise with Nature. And, I believe upon a strict Enquiry, those Quarrels might be shewn as ill-grounded among us, as they are among that People.

As to their military Affairs; they boast that the King's Army consists of an hundred and seventy six thousand Foot, and thirty two thousand Horse: If that may be called an Army, which is made up of Tradesmen in the several Cities, and Farmers in the Country, whose Commanders are only the Nobility and Gentry, without Pay or Reward. They are indeed perfect enough in their Exercises; and under very good Discipline, wherein I saw no great Merit: For, how should it be otherwise, where every Farmer is under the Command of his own Landlord, and every Citizen under that of the principal Men in his own City, chosen after the Manner of *Venice* by *Ballot*?

I have often seen the Militia of *Lorbrulgrud* drawn out to Exercise in a great Field near the City, of twenty Miles Square. They were in all not above twenty five thousand Foot, and six thousand Horse; but it was impossible for me to compute their Number, considering the Space of Ground they took up. A *Cavalier* mounted on a large Steed might be about Ninety Foot high. I have seen this Whole Body of Horse upon the Word of Command draw their Swords at once, and brandish them in the Air. Imagination can Figure nothing so Grand, so surprising and so astonishing. It looked as if ten thousand Flashes of Lightning were darting at the same time from every Quarter of the Sky.

I was curious to know how this Prince, to whose Dominions there is no Access from any other Country, came to think of Armies, or to teach his People the Practice of military Discipline. But I was soon informed, both by Conversation, and Reading their Histories. For, in the Course of many Ages they have been troubled with the same Disease, to which the whole Race of Mankind is Subject; the Nobility often contending for Power, the People for Liberty, and the King for absolute Dominion. All which, however happily tempered by the Laws of that Kingdom, have been sometimes violated by each of the three Parties; and have more than once occasioned Civil Wars, the last whereof was happily put an End to by this Prince's Grandfather in a general Composition; and the Militia then settled with common Consent hath been ever since kept in the strictest Duty.

CHAPTER VIII

The King and Queen make a Progress to the Frontiers. The Author attends them. The Manner in which he leaves the Country very particularly related. He returns to England.

I had always a strong Impulse that I should some time recover my Liberty, although it were impossible to conjecture by what Means, or to form any Project with the least Hope of succeeding. The Ship in which I sailed was the first known to be driven within Sight of that Coast; and the King had given strict Orders, that if at any Time another appeared, it should be taken ashore, and with all its Crew and Passengers brought in a Tumbril [1] to *Lorbrulgrud*. He was strongly bent to get me a Woman of my own Size, by whom I might propagate the Breed: But I think I should rather have died than undergone the Disgrace of leaving a Posterity to be kept in Cages like tame Canary Birds; and perhaps in time sold about the Kingdom to Persons of Quality for Curiosi-

[1] A cart.

ties. I was indeed treated with much Kindness; I was the Favourite of a great King and Queen, and the Delight of the whole Court; but it was upon such a Foot as ill became the Dignity of human Kind. I could never forget those domestick Pledges I had left behind me. I wanted to be among People with whom I could converse upon even Terms; and walk about the Streets and Fields without Fear of being trod to Death like a Frog or young Puppy. But, my Deliverance came sooner than I expected, and in a Manner not very common: The whole Story and Circumstances of which I shall faithfully relate.

I had now been two Years in this Country; and, about the Beginning of the third, *Glumdalclitch* and I attended the King and Queen in Progress to the South Coast of the Kingdom. I was carried as usual in my Travelling-Box, which, as I have already described, was a very convenient Closet of twelve Foot wide. I had ordered a Hammock to be fixed by silken Ropes from the four Corners at the Top; to break the Jolts, when a Servant carried me before him on Horseback, as I sometimes desired; and would often sleep in my Hammock while we were upon the Road. On the Roof of my Closet, set not directly over the Middle of the Hammock, I ordered the Joyner to cut out a Hole of a Foot square to give me Air in hot Weather as I slept; which Hole I shut at pleasure with a Board that drew backwards and forwards through a Groove.

When we came to our Journey's End, the King thought proper to pass a few Days at a Palace he hath near *Flanflasnic*, a City within eighteen *English* Miles of the Sea-side. *Glumdalclitch* and I were much fatigued: I had gotten a small Cold; but the poor Girl was so ill as to be confined to her Chamber. I longed to see the Ocean, which must be the only Scene of my Escape, if ever it should happen. I pretended to be worse than I really was; and desired leave to take the fresh Air of the Sea, with a Page whom I was very fond of, and who had sometimes been trusted with me. I shall never forget with what Unwillingness *Glumdalclitch* consented; nor the strict Charge she gave the Page to be careful of me; bursting at the same time into a Flood of Tears, as if she had some Foreboding of what was to happen. The Boy took me out in my Box about Half an Hour's walk from the Palace, towards the Rocks on the Sea-shore. I ordered him to set me down; and lifting up one of my Sashes, cast many a wistful melancholy Look towards the Sea. I found myself not very well; and told the Page that I had a Mind to take a Nap in my Hammock, which I hoped would do me good. I got in, and the Boy shut the Window close down, to keep out the Cold. I soon fell asleep: And all I can conjecture is, that while I slept, the Page, thinking no Danger could happen, went among the Rocks to look for Birds Eggs; having before observed him from my Window searching about, and picking up one or two in the Clefts. Be that as it will; I found my self suddenly awaked with a violent Pull upon the Ring which was fastned at the Top of my Box for the Conveniency of Carriage. I felt the Box raised very high in the Air, and then born forward with prodigious Speed. The first Jolt had like to have shaken me out of my Hammock; but afterwards the Motion was easy enough. I called out several times as loud as I could raise my Voice, but all to no purpose. I looked towards my Windows, and could see nothing but the Clouds and Sky. I heard a Noise just over my Head like the clapping of Wings; and then began to perceive the woful Condition I was in; that some Eagle had got the Ring of my Box in his Beak, with an Intent to let it fall on a Rock, like a Tortoise in a Shell, and then pick out my Body and devour it. For the Sagacity and Smell of this Bird enable him to discover his Quarry at a great Distance, although better concealed than I could be within a two Inch Board.

In a little time I observed the Noise and flutter of Wings to encrease very fast; and my Box was tossed up and down like a Sign-post in a windy Day. I heard several Bangs or Buffets, as I thought, given to the Eagle (for such I am certain it must have been that held the Ring of my Box in his Beak) and then all on a sudden felt my self falling perpendicularly down for above a Minute; but with such incredible Swiftness that I almost lost my Breath. My Fall was stopped by a terrible Squash, that sounded louder to my Ears than the Cataract of *Niagara*; after which I was quite in the Dark for another Minute, and then my Box began to rise so high that I could see Light from the Tops of my Windows. I now perceived that I was fallen into the Sea. My Box, by the Weight of my Body, the Goods that were in, and the broad Plates of Iron fixed for Strength at the four Corners of the Top and Bottom, floated about five Foot deep in Water. I did then, and do now suppose, that the Eagle which flew away with my Box was pursued by two or three others, and forced to let me drop while he was defending himself against the Rest, who hoped to share in the Prey. The Plates of Iron fastned at the Bottom of the Box, (for those were the strongest) preserved the Balance while it fell; and hindred it from being broken on the Surface of the Water. Every Joint of it was well grooved, and the Door did not move on Hinges, but up and down like a Sash; which kept my Closet so tight that very little Water came in. I got with much Difficulty out of my Hammock, having first ventured to draw back the Slip board on the Roof already mentioned, contrived on purpose to let in Air; for want of which I found my self almost stifled.

How often did I then wish my self with my dear *Glumdalclitch*, from whom one single Hour had so far divided me! And I may say with Truth, that in the midst of my own Misfortune, I could not forbear lamenting my poor Nurse, the Grief she would suffer for my Loss, the Displeasure of the Queen, and the Ruin of her Fortune. Perhaps many Travellers have not been under greater Difficulties and Distress than I was at this Juncture; expecting every Moment to see my Box dashed in Pieces, or at least overset by the first violent Blast, or a rising Wave. A Breach in one single Pane of Glass would have been immediate Death: Nor could any thing have preserved the Windows but the strong Lattice Wires placed on the outside against Accidents in Travelling. I saw the Water ooze in at several Crannies, although the Leaks were not considerable; and I endeavoured to stop them as well as I could. I was not able to lift up the Roof of my Closet, which otherwise I certainly should have done, and sat on the Top of it, where I might at least preserve myself from being shut up, as I may call it, in the Hold. Or, if I escaped these Dangers for a Day or two, what could I expect but a miserable Death of Cold and Hunger! I was four Hours under these Circumstances, expecting and indeed wishing every Moment to be my last.

I have already told the Reader, that there were two strong Staples fixed upon the Side of my Box which had no Window, and into which the Servant, who used to carry me on Horseback, would put a Leathern Belt, and buckle it about his Waist. Being in this disconsolate State, I heard, or at least thought I heard some kind of grating Noise on that Side of my Box where the Staples were fixed; and soon after I began to fancy that the Box was pulled, or towed along in the Sea; for I now and then felt a sort of tugging, which made the Waves rise near the Tops of my Windows, leaving me almost in the Dark. This gave me some faint Hopes of Relief, although I were not able to imagine how it could be brought about.

I ventured to unscrew one of my Chairs, which were always fastned to the Floor; and having made a hard shift to screw it down again directly under the Slipping-board that I had lately opened; I mounted on the Chair, and putting my Mouth as near as I could to the Hole, I called for Help in a loud Voice, and in all the Languages I understood. I then fastned my Handkerchief to a Stick I usually carried, and thrusting it up the Hole, waved it several times in the Air; that if any Boat or Ship were near, the Seamen might conjecture some unhappy Mortal to be shut up in the Box.

I found no Effect from all I could do, but plainly perceived my Closet to be moved along; and in the Space of an Hour, or better, that Side of the Box where the Staples were, and had no Window, struck against something that was hard. I apprehended it to be a Rock, and found my self tossed more than ever. I plainly heard a Noise upon the Cover of my Closet, like that of a Cable, and the grating of it as it passed through the Ring. I then found my self hoisted up by Degrees at least three Foot higher than I was before. Whereupon, I again thrust up my Stick and Handkerchief, calling for Help till I was almost hoarse. In return to which, I heard a great Shout repeated three times, giving me such Transports of Joy as are not to be conceived but by those who feel them. I now heard a trampling over my Head; and somebody calling through the Hole with a loud Voice in the *English* Tongue: *If there be any Body below, let them speak.* I answered, I was an *Englishman*, drawn by ill Fortune into the greatest Calamity that ever any Creature underwent; and begged, by all that was moving, to be delivered out of the Dungeon I was in. The Voice replied, I was safe, for my Box was fastned to their Ship; and the Carpenter should immediately come, and saw an Hole in the Cover, large enough to pull me out. I answered, that was needless, and would take up too much Time; for there was no more to be done, but let one of the Crew put his Finger into the Ring, and take the Box out of the Sea into the Ship, and so into the Captain's Cabbin. Some of them upon hearing me talk so wildly, thought I was mad; others laughed; for indeed it never came into my Head, that I was now got among People of my own Stature and Strength. The Carpenter came, and in a few Minutes sawed a Passage about four Foot square; then let down a small Ladder, upon which I mounted, and from thence was taken into the Ship in a very weak Condition.

The Sailors were all in Amazement, and asked me a thousand

Questions, which I had no Inclination to answer. I was equally confounded at the Sight of so many Pigmies; for such I took them to be, after having so long accustomed my Eyes to the monstrous Objects I had left. But the Captain, Mr. *Thomas Wilcocks*, an honest worthy *Shropshire* Man, observing I was ready to faint, took me into his Cabbin, gave me a Cordial to comfort me, and made me *turn in* upon his own Bed; advising me to take a little Rest, of which I had great need. Before I went to sleep I gave him to understand, that I had some valuable Furniture in my Box too good to be lost; a fine Hammock, an handsome Field-Bed, two Chairs, a Table and a Cabinet: That my Closet was hung on all Sides, or rather quilted with Silk and Cotton: That if he would let one of the Crew bring my Closet into his Cabbin, I would open it before him, and shew him my Goods. The Captain hearing me utter these Absurdities, concluded I was raving: However, (I suppose to pacify me) he promised to give Order as I desired; and going upon Deck, sent some of his Men down into my Closet, from whence (as I afterwards found) they drew up all my Goods, and stripped off the Quilting; but the Chairs, Cabinet and Bed-sted being screwed to the Floor, were much damaged by the Ignorance of the Seamen, who tore them up by Force. Then they knocked off some of the Boards for the Use of the Ship; and when they had got all they had a Mind for, let the Hulk drop into the Sea, which by Reason of many Breaches made in the Bottom and Sides, sunk *to rights*. And indeed I was glad not to have been a Spectator of the Havock they made; because I am confident it would have sensibly touched me, by bringing former Passages into my Mind, which I had rather forget.

I slept some Hours, but perpetually disturbed with Dreams of the Place I had left, and the Dangers I had escaped. However, upon waking I found my self much recovered. It was now about eight a Clock at Night, and the Captain ordered Supper immediately, thinking I had already fasted too long. He entertained me with great Kindness, observing me not to look wildly, or talk inconsistently; and when we were left alone, desired I would give him a Relation of my Travels, and by what Accident I came to be set adrift in that monstrous wooden Chest. He said, that about twelve a Clock at Noon, as he was looking through his Glass, he spied it at a Distance, and thought it was a Sail, which he had a Mind to make; being not much out of his Course, in hopes of buying some Biscuit, his own beginning to fall short. That, upon coming nearer, and finding his Error, he sent out his Long-boat to discover what I was; that his Men came back in a Fright, swearing they had seen a swimming House. That he laughed at their Folly, and went himself in the Boat, ordering his Men to take a strong Cable along with them. That the Weather being calm, he rowed round me several times, observed my Windows, and the Wire Lattices that defended them. That he discovered two Staples upon one Side, which was all of Boards, without any Passage for Light. He then commanded his Men to row up to that Side; and fastning a Cable to one of the Staples, ordered his Men to tow my Chest (as he called it) towards the Ship. When it was there, he gave Directions to fasten another Cable to the Ring fixed in the Cover, and to raise up my Chest with Pullies, which all the Sailors were not able to do above two or three Foot. He said, they saw my Stick and Handkerchief thrust out of the Hole, and concluded, that some unhappy Man must be shut up in the Cavity. I asked whether he or the Crew had seen any prodigious Birds in the Air about the Time he first discovered me: To which he answered, that discoursing this Matter with the Sailors while I was asleep, one of them said he had *observed* three Eagles flying towards the North; but remarked nothing of their being larger than the usual Size; which I suppose must be imputed to the great Height they were at: And he could not guess the Reason of my Question. I then asked the Captain how far he reckoned we might be from Land; he said, by the best Computation he could make, we were at least an hundred Leagues. I assured him, that he must be mistaken by almost half; for I had not left the Country from whence I came, above two Hours before I dropt into the Sea. Whereupon he began again to think that my Brain was disturbed, of which he gave me a Hint, and advised me to go to Bed in a Cabin he had provided. I assured him I was well refreshed with his good Entertainment and Company, and as much in my Senses as ever I was in my Life. He then grew serious, and desired to ask me freely whether I were not troubled in Mind by the Consciousness of some enormous Crime, for which I was punished at the Command of some Prince, by exposing me in that Chest; as great Criminals in other Countries have been forced to Sea in a leaky Vessel without Provisions: For, although he should be sorry to have taken so ill a Man into his Ship, yet he would engage his Word to set me safe on Shore in the first Port where we arrived. He added, that his

Suspicions were much increased by some very absurd Speeches I had delivered at first to the Sailors, and afterwards to himself, in relation to my Closet or Chest, as well as by my odd Looks and Behaviour while I was at Supper.

I begged his Patience to hear me tell my Story; which I faithfully did from the last Time I left *England*, to the Moment he first discovered me. And, as Truth always forceth its Way into rational Minds; so, this honest worthy Gentleman, who had some Tincture of Learning, and very good Sense, was immediately convinced of my Candor and Veracity. But, further to confirm all I had said, I entreated him to give Order that my Cabinet should be brought, of which I kept the Key in my Pocket, (for he had already informed me how the Seamen disposed of my Closet) I opened it in his Presence, and shewed him the small Collection of Rarities I made in the Country from whence I had been so strangely delivered. There was the Comb I had contrived out of the Stumps of the King's Beard; and another of the same Materials, but fixed into a paring of her Majesty's Thumb-nail, which served for the Back. There was a Collection of Needles and Pins from a Foot to half a Yard long. Four Wasp-Stings, like Joyners Tacks: Some Combings of the Queen's Hair: A Gold Ring which one Day she made me a Present of in a most obliging Manner, taking it from her little Finger, and throwing it over my Head like a Collar. I desired the Captain would please to accept this Ring in Return of his Civilities; which he absolutely refused. I shewed him a Corn that I had cut off with my own Hand from a Maid of Honour's Toe; it was about the Bigness of a *Kentish* Pippin, and grown so hard, that when I returned to *England*, I got it hollowed into a Cup and set in Silver. Lastly, I desired him to see the Breeches I had then on, which were made of a Mouse's Skin.

I could force nothing on him but a Footman's Tooth, which I observed him to examine with great Curiosity, and found he had a Fancy for it. He received it with abundance of Thanks, more than such a Trifle could deserve. It was drawn by an unskilful Surgeon in a Mistake from one of *Glumdalclitch's* Men, who was afflicted with the Tooth-ach; but it was as sound as any in his Head. I got it cleaned, and put it into my Cabinet. It was about a Foot long, and four Inches in Diameter.

The Captain was very well satisfied with this plain Relation I had given him; and said, he hoped when we returned to *England*, I would oblige the World by putting it in Paper, and making it publick. My Answer was, that I thought we were already over-stocked with Books of Travels: That nothing could now pass which was not extraordinary; wherein I doubted, some Authors less consulted Truth than their own Vanity or Interest, or the Diversion of ignorant Readers. That my Story could contain little besides common Events, without those ornamental Descriptions of strange Plants, Trees, Birds, and other Animals; or the barbarous Customs and Idolatry of savage People, with which most Writers abound. However, I thanked him for his good Opinion, and promised to take the Matter into my Thoughts.

He said, he wondered at one Thing very much; which was, to hear me speak so loud; asking me whether the King or Queen of that Country were thick of Hearing. I told him it was what I had been used to for above two Years past; and that I admired as much at the Voices of him and his Men, who seemed to me only to whisper, and yet I could hear them well enough. But, when I spoke in that Country, it was like a Man talking in the Street to another looking out from the Top of a Steeple, unless when I was placed on a Table, or held in any Person's Hand. I told him, I had likewise observed another Thing; that when I first got into the Ship, and the Sailors stood all about me, I thought they were the most little contemptible Creatures I had ever beheld. For, indeed, while I was in that Prince's Country, I could never endure to look in a Glass after my Eyes had been accustomed to such prodigious Objects; because the Comparison gave me so despicable a Conceit of my self. The Captain said, that while we were at Supper, he observed me to look at every thing with a Sort of Wonder; and that I often seemed hardly able to contain my Laughter; which he knew not well how to take, but imputed it to some Disorder in my Brain. I answered, it was very true; and I wondered how I could forbear, when I saw his Dishes of the Size of a Silver Three-pence, a Leg of Pork hardly a Mouthful, a Cup not so big as a Nutshell: And so I went on, describing the rest of his Houshold stuff and Provisions after the same Manner. For although the Queen had ordered a little Equipage of all Things necessary for me while I was in her Service; yet my Ideas were wholly taken up with what I saw on every Side of me; and I winked at my own Littleness, as People do at their own Faults. The Captain understood my Raillery very well, and merrily replied with the old *English* Proverb, that he doubted, my Eyes were bigger than my Belly; for he did not observe my Stomach so good, although I had fasted all Day: And continuing in his Mirth, protested he would have gladly given an Hundred Pounds to have seen my Closet in the Eagle's Bill, and afterwards in its Fall from so great an Height into the Sea; which would certainly have been a most astonishing Object, worthy to have the Description of it transmitted to future Ages: And the Comparison of *Phaeton* was so obvious, that he could not forbear applying it, although I did not much admire the Conceit.[2]

The Captain having been at *Tonquin*, was in his Return to *England* driven North Eastward to the Latitude of 44 Degrees, and of Longitude 143. But meeting a Trade Wind two Days after I came on board him, we sailed Southward a long Time, and coasting *New-Holland*,[3] kept our Course West-south-west, and then South-south-west till we doubled the *Cape of Good-hope*. Our Voyage was very prosperous, but I shall not trouble the Reader with a Journal of it. The Captain called in at one or two Ports, and sent in his Long-boat for Provisions and fresh Water; but I never went out of the Ship till we came into the *Downs*, which was on the 3d Day of *June* 1706, about nine Months after my Escape. I offered to leave my Goods in Security for Payment of my Freight; but the Captain protested he would not receive one Farthing. We took kind Leave of each other; and I made him promise he would come to see me at my House in *Redriff*. I hired a Horse and Guide for five Shillings, which I borrowed of the Captain.

As I was on the Road; observing the Littleness of the Houses, the Trees, the Cattle and the People, I began to think my self in *Lilliput*. I was afraid of trampling on every Traveller I met; and often called aloud to have them stand out of the Way; so that I had like to have gotten one or two broken Heads for my Impertinence.

When I came to my own House, for which I was forced to enquire, one of the Servants opening the Door, I bent down to go in (like a Goose under a Gate) for fear of striking my Head. My Wife ran out to embrace me, but I stooped lower than her Knees, thinking she could otherwise never be able to reach my Mouth. My Daughter kneeled to ask me Blessing, but I could not see her till she

[2] A witty turn of thought.

[3] "Tonquin": Tongking, a port in French Indo-China; "coasting New Holland": following the coast line of Australia.

arose; having been so long used to stand with my Head and Eyes erect to above Sixty Foot; and then I went to take her up with one Hand, by the Waist. I looked down upon the Servants, and one or two Friends who were in the House, as if they had been Pigmies, and I a Giant. I told my Wife, she had been too thrifty; for I found she had starved herself and her Daughter to nothing. In short, I behaved my self so unaccountably, that they were all of the Captain's Opinion when he first saw me; and concluded I had lost my Wits. This I mention as an Instance of the great Power of Habit and Prejudice.

In a little Time I and my Family and Friends came to a right Understanding: But my Wife protested I should never go to Sea any more; although my evil Destiny so ordered, that she had not Power to hinder me; as the Reader may know hereafter. In the mean Time, I here conclude the second Part of my unfortunate Voyages.

The End of the Second Part

PART III A VOYAGE TO LAPUTA, BALNIBARBI, GLUBBDUBDRIB, LUGGNAGG, AND JAPAN

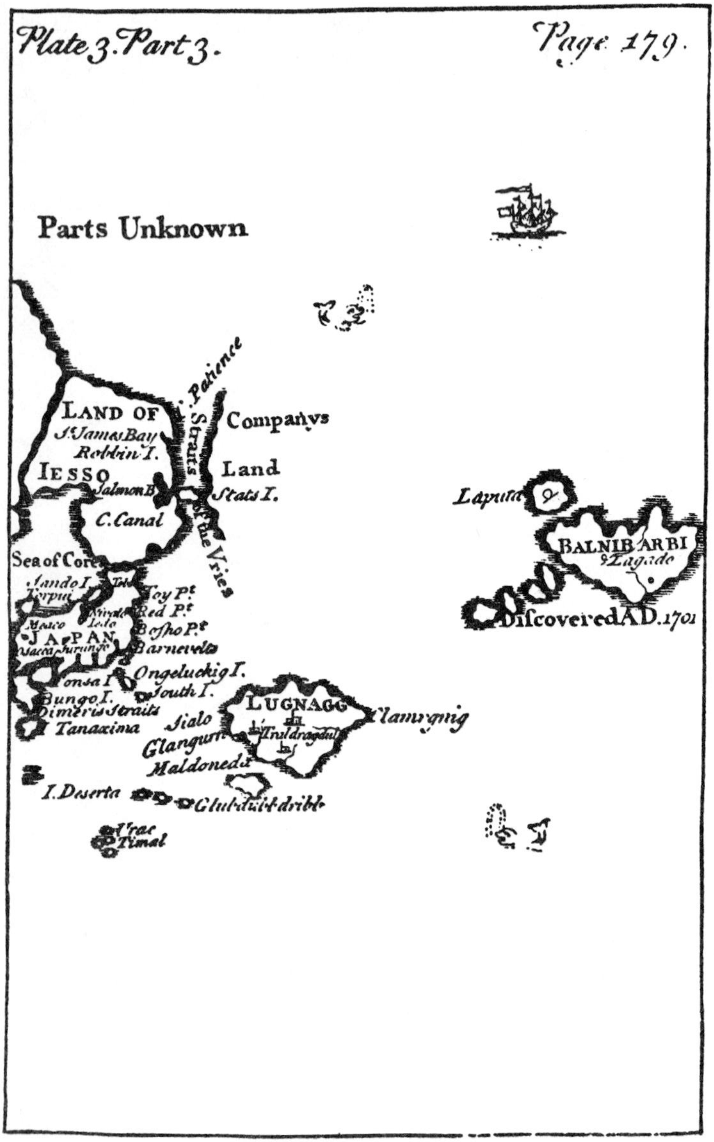

Parts Unknown

Land of
St. James Bay
Robbin I.
Iesso
Salmon B.
C. Canal
Patience
Straits
Companys
Land
Stats I.
of the Vries
Sea of Core
Iando I.
Toy Pt.
Red Pt.
Bosho Pt.
Japan
Barnevelts
Tonsa I.
Ongeluckig I.
South I.
Bungo I.
Dimeris Straits
Tanaxima
Lugnagg
Traldragdubh
Sialo
Glanguen
Maldonada
Clamegnig
I. Deserta
Glubdubdrib
Vrac
Timal
Laputa
Balnibarbi
Lagado
Discovered A.D. 1701

CHAPTER I

The Author sets out on his Third Voyage. Is taken by Pyrates. The Malice of a Dutchman. *His Arrival at an Island. He is received into* Laputa.

I had not been at home above ten Days, when Captain *William Robinson,* a *Cornish* Man, Commander of the *Hopewell,* a stout Ship of three Hundred Tuns, came to my House. I had formerly been Surgeon of another Ship where he was Master, and a fourth Part Owner, in a Voyage to the *Levant.* He had always treated me more like a Brother than an inferior Officer; and hearing of my Arrival made me a Visit, as I apprehended only out of Friendship, for nothing passed more than what is usual after long Absence. But repeating his Visits often, expressing his Joy to find me in good Health, asking whether I were now settled for Life, adding that he intended a Voyage to the *East-Indies,* in two Months, at last he plainly invited me, although with some Apologies, to be Surgeon of the Ship. That I should have another Surgeon under me, besides our two Mates; that my Sallary should be double to the usual Pay; and that having experienced my Knowledge in Sea-Affairs to be at least equal to his, he would enter into any Engagement to follow my Advice, as much as if I had Share in the Command.

He said so many other obliging things, and I knew him to be so honest a Man, that I could not reject his Proposal; the Thirst I had of seeing the World, notwithstanding my past Misfortunes, continuing as violent as ever. The only Difficulty that remained, was to persuade my Wife, whose Consent however I at last obtained, by the Prospect of Advantage she proposed to her Children.

We set out the 5th Day of *August,* 1706, and arrived at Fort St. *George,*[1] the 11th of *April* 1707. We stayed there three Weeks to refresh our Crew, many of whom were sick. From thence we went to *Tonquin,* where the Captain resolved to continue some time;

[1] Madras, in southeastern India.

because many of the Goods he intended to buy were not ready, nor could he expect to be dispatched in several Months. Therefore in hopes to defray some of the Charges he must be at, he bought a Sloop, loaded it with several Sorts of Goods, wherewith the *Tonquinese* usually trade to the neighbouring Islands; and putting Fourteen Men on Board, whereof three were of the Country, he appointed me Master of the Sloop, and gave me Power to traffick, while he transacted his Affairs at *Tonquin*.

We had not sailed above three Days, when a great Storm arising, we were driven five Days to the North-North-East, and then to the East; after which we had fair Weather, but still with a pretty strong Gale from the West. Upon the tenth Day we were chased by two Pyrates, who soon overtook us; for my Sloop was so deep loaden, that she sailed very slow; neither were we in a Condition to defend our selves.

We were boarded about the same Time by both the Pyrates, who entered furiously at the Head of their Men; but finding us all prostrate upon our Faces, (for so I gave Order), they pinioned us with strong Ropes, and setting a Guard upon us, went to search the Sloop.

I observed among them a *Dutchman*, who seemed to be of some Authority, although he were not Commander of either Ship. He knew us by our Countenances to be *Englishmen*, and jabbering to us in his own Language, swore we should be tyed Back to Back, and thrown into the Sea. I spoke *Dutch* tolerably well; I told him who we were, and begged him in Consideration of our being Christians and Protestants, of neighbouring Countries, in strict Alliance, that he would move the Captains to take some Pity on us. This inflamed his Rage; he repeated his Threatnings, and turning to his Companions, spoke with great Vehemence, in the *Japanese* Language, as I suppose; often using the Word *Christianos*.[2]

The largest of the two Pyrate Ships was commanded by a *Japanese* Captain, who spoke a little *Dutch*, but very imperfectly. He came up to me, and after several Questions, which I answered in

[2] Though allied militarily against France in 1707 (the year of Gulliver's voyage), Holland and England remained vigorous commercial rivals. Moreover, Swift detested the Dutch policy of religious tolerance, which undermined the concept of a national church. Hence, Swift's attitude to the Dutch, and the combination here of Dutch–pirate–antiChristian (see also pp. 185-187).

great Humility, he said we should not die. I made the Captain a very low Bow, and then turning to the *Dutchman*, said, I was sorry to find more Mercy in a Heathen, than in a Brother Christian. But I had soon Reason to repent those foolish Words; for that malicious Reprobate, having often endeavoured in vain to persuade both the Captains that I might be thrown into the Sea, (which they would not yield to after the Promise made me, that I should not die) however prevailed so far as to have a Punishment inflicted on me, worse in all human Appearance than Death it self. My Men were sent by an equal Division into both the Pyrate-Ships, and my Sloop new manned. As to my self, it was determined that I should be set a-drift, in a small Canoe, with Paddles and a Sail, and four Days Provisions; which last the *Japanese* Captain was so kind to double out of his own Stores, and would permit no Man to search me. I got down into the Canoe, while the *Dutchman* standing upon the Deck, loaded me with all the Curses and injurious Terms his Language could afford.

About an Hour before we saw the Pyrates, I had taken an Observation, and found we were in the Latitude of 46 N. and of Longitude 183. When I was at some Distance from the Pyrates, I discovered by my Pocket-Glass several Islands to the South-East. I set up my Sail, the Wind being fair, with a Design to reach the nearest of those Islands, which I made a Shift to do in about three Hours. It was all rocky; however I got many Birds Eggs; and striking Fire, I kindled some Heath and dry Sea Weed, by which I roasted my Eggs. I eat no other Supper, being resolved to spare my Provisions as much as I could. I passed the Night under the Shelter of a Rock, strowing some Heath under me, and slept pretty well.

The next Day I sailed to another Island, and thence to a third and fourth, sometimes using my Sail, and sometimes my Paddles. But not to trouble the Reader with a particular Account of my Distresses; let it suffice, that on the 5th Day, I arrived at the last Island in my Sight, which lay South-South-East to the former.

This Island was at a greater Distance than I expected, and I did not reach it in less than five Hours. I encompassed it almost round before I could find a convenient Place to land in, which was a small Creek, about three Times the Wideness of my Canoe. I found the Island to be all rocky, only a little intermingled with Tufts of Grass, and sweet smelling Herbs. I took out my small Provisions, and after having refreshed myself, I secured the Remainder in a Cave, whereof there were great Numbers. I gathered Plenty of Eggs upon the Rocks, and got a Quantity of dry Sea-weed, and parched Grass, which I designed to kindle the next Day, and roast my Eggs as well as I could. (For I had about me my Flint, Steel, Match, and Burning-glass.) I lay all Night in the Cave where I had lodged my Provisions. My Bed was the same dry Grass and Sea-weed which I intended for Fewel. I slept very little; for the Disquiets of my Mind prevailed over my Wearyness, and kept me awake. I considered how impossible it was to preserve my Life, in so desolate a Place; and how miserable my End must be. Yet I found my self so listless and desponding, that I had not the Heart to rise; and before I could get Spirits enough to creep out of my Cave, the Day was far advanced. I walked a while among the Rocks, the Sky was perfectly clear, and the Sun so hot, that I was forced to turn my Face from it: When all on a Sudden it became obscured, as I thought, in a Manner very different from what happens by the Interposition of a Cloud. I turned back, and perceived a vast Opake Body between me and the Sun, moving forwards towards the Island: It seemed to be about two Miles high, and hid the Sun six or seven Minutes, but I did not observe the Air to be much colder, or the Sky more darkned, than if I had stood under the Shade of a Mountain. As it approached nearer over the Place where I was, it appeared to be a firm Substance, the Bottom flat, smooth, and shining very bright from the Reflexion of the Sea below. I stood upon a Height about two Hundred Yards from the Shoar, and saw this vast Body descending almost to a Parallel with me, at less than an *English* Mile Distance. I took out my Pocket-Perspective, and could plainly discover Numbers of People moving up and down the Sides of it, which appeared to be sloping, but what those People were doing, I was not able to distinguish.

The natural Love of Life gave me some inward Motions of Joy; and I was ready to entertain a Hope, that this Adventure might some Way or other help to deliver me from the desolate Place and Condition I was in. But, at the same Time, the Reader can hardly conceive my Astonishment, to behold an Island in the Air, inhabited by Men, who were able (as it should seem) to raise, or sink, or put it into a progressive Motion, as they pleased.[3] But not being,

[3] The conception of a flying island was not original with Swift; for some of his sources, see the Bibliography, below: Eddy, *Gulliver's Travels*, and Nicolson and Mohler, "Swift's Flying Island . . ."

at that Time, in a Disposition to philosophise upon this Phaenomenon, I rather chose to observe what Course the Island would take; because it seemed for a while to stand still. Yet soon after it advanced nearer; and I could see the Sides of it, encompassed with several Gradations of Galleries and Stairs, at certain Intervals, to descend from one to the other. In the lowest Gallery, I beheld some People fishing with long Angling Rods, and others looking on. I waved my Cap, (for my Hat was long since worn out), and my Handkerchief towards the Island; and upon its nearer Approach, I called and shouted with the utmost Strength of my Voice; and then looking circumspectly, I beheld a Crowd gathered to that Side which was most in my View. I found by their pointing towards me and to each other, that they plainly discovered me, although they made no Return to my Shouting: But I could see four or five Men running in great Haste up the Stairs to the Top of the Island, who then disappeared. I happened rightly to conjecture, that these were sent for Orders to some Person in Authority upon this Occasion.

The Number of People increased; and in less than Half an Hour, the Island was moved and raised in such a Manner, that the lowest Gallery appeared in a Parallel of less than an Hundred Yards Distance from the Height where I stood. I then put my self into the most supplicating Postures, and spoke in the humblest Accent, but received no Answer. Those who stood nearest over-against me, seemed to be Persons of Distinction, as I supposed by their Habit. They conferred earnestly with each other, looking often upon me. At length one of them called out in a clear, polite, smooth Dialect, not unlike in Sound to the *Italian*; and therefore I returned an Answer in that Language, hoping at least that the Cadence might be more agreeable to his Ears. Although neither of us understood the other, yet my Meaning was easily known, for the People saw the Distress I was in.

They made Signs for me to come down from the Rock, and go towards the Shoar, which I accordingly did; and the flying Island being raised to a convenient Height, the Verge directly over me, a Chain was let down from the lowest Gallery, with a Seat fastned to the Bottom, to which I fixed my self, and was drawn up by Pullies.

CHAPTER II

The Humours and Dispositions of the Laputians *described. An Account of their Learning. Of the King and his Court. The Author's Reception there. The Inhabitants subject to Fears and Disquietudes. An Account of the Women.*

At my alighting I was surrounded by a Crowd of People, but those who stood nearest seemed to be of better Quality. They beheld me with all the Marks and Circumstances of Wonder; neither indeed was I much in their Debt; having never till then seen a Race of Mortals so singular in their Shapes, Habits, and Countenances. Their Heads were all reclined to the Right, or the Left; one of their Eyes turned inward, and the other directly up to the Zenith.[1] Their outward Garments were adorned with the Figures of Suns, Moons, and Stars, interwoven with those of Fiddles, Flutes, Harps, Trumpets, Harpsicords, and many more Instruments of Musick, unknown to us in *Europe*. I observed here and there many in the Habit of Servants, with a blown Bladder fastned like a Flail to the End of a short Stick, which they carried in their Hands. In each Bladder was a small Quantity of dried Pease, or little Pebbles, (as I was afterwards informed.) With these Bladders they now and then flapped the Mouths and Ears of those who stood near them, of which Practice I could not then conceive the Meaning. It seems, the Minds of these People are so taken up with intense Speculations, that they neither can speak, or attend to the Discourses of others, without being rouzed by some external Taction upon the Organs of Speech and Hearing; for which Reason, those Persons

[1] Swift intended the Laputians to represent those of his contemporaries who had given themselves to abstract science, mathematics, and musical theory, disciplines he considered wildly impractical and irrelevant to man's proper concern, ethics.

who are able to afford it, always keep a *Flapper*, (the Original is *Climenole*) in their Family, as one of their Domesticks; nor ever walk abroad or make Visits without him. And the Business of this Officer is, when two or more Persons are in Company, gently to strike with his Bladder the Mouth of him who is to speak, and the Right Ear of him or them to whom the Speaker addresseth himself. This *Flapper* is likewise employed diligently to attend his Master in his Walks, and upon Occasion to give him a soft Flap on his Eyes; because he is always so wrapped up in Cogitation, that he is in manifest Danger of falling down every Precipice, and bouncing his Head against every Post; and in the Streets, of jostling others, or being jostled himself into the Kennel.[2]

It was necessary to give the Reader this Information, without which he would be at the same Loss with me, to understand the Proceedings of these People, as they conducted me up the Stairs to the Top of the Island, and from thence to the Royal Palace. While we were ascending, they forgot several Times what they were about, and left me to my self, till their Memories were again rouzed by their *Flappers*; for they appeared altogether unmoved by the Sight of my foreign Habit and Countenance, and by the Shouts of the Vulgar, whose Thoughts and Minds were more disengaged.

At last we entered the Palace, and proceeded into the Chamber of Presence; where I saw the King[3] seated on his Throne, attended on each Side by Persons of prime Quality. Before the Throne, was a large Table filled with Globes and Spheres, and Mathematical Instruments of all Kinds. His Majesty took not the least Notice of us, although our Entrance were not without sufficient Noise, by the Concourse of all Persons belonging to the Court. But, he was then deep in a Problem, and we attended at least an Hour, before he could solve it. There stood by him on each Side, a young Page, with Flaps in their Hands; and when they saw he was at Leisure, one of them gently struck his Mouth, and the other his Right Ear; at which he started like one awaked on the sudden, and looking towards me, and the Company I was in, recollected the Occasion of our coming, whereof he had been informed before. He spoke some Words; whereupon immediately a young Man with a Flap came up to my Side, and flapt me gently on the Right Ear; but I

[2] The gutter.

[3] Swift's target is again George I, who, though a patron of music and science, had no real knowledge of either.

made Signs as well as I could, that I had no Occasion for such an Instrument; which as I afterwards found, gave his Majesty and the whole Court a very mean Opinion of my Understanding. The King, as far as I could conjecture, asked me several Questions, and I addressed my self to him in all the Languages I had. When it was found, that I could neither understand nor be understood, I was conducted by his Order to an Apartment in his Palace, (this Prince being distinguished above all his Predecessors for his Hospitality to Strangers,) where two Servants were appointed to attend me. My Dinner was brought, and four Persons of Quality, whom I remembered to have seen very near the King's Person, did me the Honour to dine with me. We had two Courses, of three Dishes each. In the first Course, there was a Shoulder of Mutton, cut into an Æquilateral Triangle; a Piece of Beef into a Rhomboides; and a Pudding into a Cycloid. The second Course was two Ducks, trussed up into the Form of Fiddles; Sausages and Puddings resembling Flutes and Haut-boys,[4] and a Breast of Veal in the Shape of a Harp. The Servants cut our Bread into Cones, Cylinders, Parallelograms, and several other Mathematical Figures.

While we were at Dinner, I made bold to ask the Names of several Things in their Language; and those noble Persons, by the Assistance of their *Flappers*, delighted to give me Answers, hoping to raise my Admiration of their great Abilities, if I could be brought to converse with them. I was soon able to call for Bread, and Drink, or whatever else I wanted.

After Dinner my Company withdrew, and a Person was sent to me by the King's Order, attended by a *Flapper*. He brought with him Pen, Ink, and Paper, and three or four Books; giving me to understand by Signs, that he was sent to teach me the Language. We sat together four Hours, in which Time I wrote down a great Number of Words in Columns, with the Translations over against them. I likewise made a Shift to learn several short Sentences. For my Tutor would order one of my Servants to fetch something, to turn about, to make a Bow, to sit, or stand, or walk, and the like. Then I took down the Sentence in Writing. He shewed me also in one of his Books, the Figures of the Sun, Moon, and Stars, the Zodiack, the Tropics and Polar Circles, together with the Denominations of many Figures of Planes and Solids. He gave me the

[4] Oboes.

Names and Descriptions of all the Musical Instruments, and the general Terms of Art in playing on each of them. After he had left me, I placed all my Words with their Interpretations in alphabetical Order. And thus in a few Days, by the Help of a very faithful Memory, I got some Insight into their Language.

The Word, which I interpret the *Flying* or *Floating Island*, is in the Original *Laputa*; whereof I could never learn the true Etymology. *Lap* in the old obsolete Language signifieth *High*, and *Untuh* a *Governor*; from which they say by Corruption was derived *Laputa* from *Lapuntuh*. But I do not approve of this Derivation, which seems to be a little strained. I ventured to offer to the Learned among them a Conjecture of my own, that *Laputa* was *quasi Lap outed*; *Lap* signifying properly the dancing of the Sun Beams in the Sea; and *outed* a Wing, which however I shall not obtrude, but submit to the judicious Reader.[5]

Those to whom the King had entrusted me, observing how ill I was clad, ordered a Taylor to come next Morning, and take my Measure for a Suit of Cloths. This Operator did his Office after a different Manner from those of his Trade in *Europe*. He first took my Altitude by a Quadrant, and then with Rule and Compasses, described the Dimensions and Out-Lines of my whole Body; all which he entred upon Paper, and in six Days brought my Cloths very ill made, and quite out of Shape, by happening to mistake a Figure in the Calculation. But my Comfort was, that I observed such Accidents very frequent, and little regarded.

During my Confinement for want of Cloaths, and by an Indisposition that held me some Days longer, I much enlarged my Dictionary; and when I went next to Court, was able to understand many Things the King spoke, and to return him some Kind of Answers. His Majesty had given Orders, that the Island should move North-East and by East, to the vertical Point over *Lagado*, the Metropolis of the whole Kingdom, below upon the firm Earth. It was about Ninety Leagues distant, and our Voyage lasted four Days and an Half. I was not in the least sensible of the progressive Motion made in the Air by the Island. On the second Morning, about Eleven o'Clock, the King himself in Person, attended by his Nobil-

[5] Another Swift parody, this time of the philology of his day. Gulliver misses the likely derivation, the Spanish *la puta*, "the whore," an apt, if ironic, name for a people that has dealt so unnaturally with its physical nature.

ity, Courtiers, and Officers, having prepared all their Musical Instruments, played on them for three Hours without Intermission; so that I was quite stunned with the Noise; neither could I possibly guess the Meaning, till my Tutor informed me. He said, that the People of their Island had their Ears adapted to hear the Musick of the Spheres, which always played at certain Periods; and the Court was now prepared to bear their Part in whatever Instrument they most excelled.

In our Journey towards *Lagado* the Capital City, his Majesty ordered that the Island should stop over certain Towns and Villages, from whence he might receive the Petitions of his Subjects. And to this Purpose, several Packthreads were let down with small Weights at the Bottom. On these Packthreads the People strung their Petitions, which mounted up directly like the Scraps of Paper fastned by School-boys at the End of the String that holds their Kite. Sometimes we received Wine and Victuals from below, which were drawn up by Pullies.

The Knowledge I had in Mathematicks gave me great Assistance in acquiring their Phraseology, which depended much upon that Science and Musick; and in the latter I was not unskilled. Their Ideas are perpetually conversant in Lines and Figures. If they would, for Example, praise the Beauty of a Woman, or any other Animal, they describe it by Rhombs, Circles, Parallelograms, Ellipses, and other Geometrical Terms; or else by Words of Art drawn from Musick, needless here to repeat. I observed in the King's Kitchen all Sorts of Mathematical and Musical Instruments, after the Figures of which they cut up the Joynts that were served to his Majesty's Table.

Their Houses are very ill built, the Walls bevil, without one right Angle in any Apartment; and this Defect ariseth from the Contempt they bear for practical Geometry; which they despise as vulgar and mechanick, those Instructions they give being too refined for the Intellectuals of their Workmen; which occasions perpetual Mistakes. And although they are dextrous enough upon a Piece of Paper, in the Management of the Rule, the Pencil, and the Divider, yet in the common Actions and Behaviour of Life, I have not seen a more clumsy, awkward, and unhandy People, nor so slow and perplexed in their Conceptions upon all other Subjects, except those of Mathematicks and Musick. They are very bad Reasoners, and vehemently given to Opposition, unless when they happen to be of the right Opinion, which is seldom their Case. Imagination, Fancy, and Invention, they are wholly Strangers to, nor have any Words in their Language by which those Ideas can be expressed; the whole Compass of their Thoughts and Mind, being shut up within the two forementioned Sciences.

Most of them, and especially those who deal in the Astronomical Part, have great Faith in judicial Astrology, although they are ashamed to own it publickly. But, what I chiefly admired, and thought altogether unaccountable, was the strong Disposition I observed in them towards News and Politicks; perpetually enquiring into publick Affairs, giving their Judgments in Matters of State; and passionately disputing every Inch of a Party Opinion. I have indeed observed the same Disposition among most of the Mathematicians I have known in *Europe*; although I could never discover the least Analogy between the two Sciences; unless those People suppose, that because the smallest Circle hath as many Degrees as the largest, therefore the Regulation and Management of the World require no more Abilities than the handling and turning of a Globe. But, I rather take this Quality to spring from a very common Infirmity of human Nature, inclining us to be more curious and conceited in Matters where we have least Concern, and for which we are least adapted either by Study or Nature.

These People are under continual Disquietudes, never enjoying a Minute's Peace of Mind; and their Disturbances proceed from Causes which very little affect the rest of Mortals. Their Apprehensions[6] arise from several Changes they dread in the Celestial Bodies. For instance; that the Earth by the continual Approaches of the Sun towards it, must in Course of Time be absorbed or swallowed up. That the Face of the Sun will by Degrees be encrusted with its own Effluvia, and give no more Light to the World. That, the Earth very narrowly escaped a Brush from the Tail of the last Comet, which would have infallibly reduced it to Ashes; and that the next, which they have calculated for One and Thirty Years hence, will probably destroy us. For, if in its Perihelion it should approach within a certain Degree of the Sun, (as by their Calculations they have Reason to dread) it will conceive a Degree of Heat ten Thousand Times more intense than that of red hot glowing

[6] The catalogue of fears that follows is based on actual speculations by the scientists of Swift's time (see in the Bibliography, Nicolson and Mohler, "The Scientific Background of Swift's *Voyage to Laputa*").

Iron; and in its Absence from the Sun, carry a blazing Tail Ten Hundred Thousand and Fourteen Miles long; through which if the Earth should pass at the Distance of one Hundred Thousand Miles from the *Nucleus*, or main Body of the Comet, it must in its Passage be set on Fire, and reduced to Ashes. That the Sun daily spending its Rays without any Nutriment to supply them, will at last be wholly consumed and annihilated; which must be attended with the Destruction of this Earth, and of all the Planets that receive their Light from it.

They are so perpetually alarmed with the Apprehensions of these and the like impending Dangers, that they can neither sleep quietly in their Beds, nor have any Relish for the common Pleasures or Amusements of Life. When they meet an Acquaintance in the Morning, the first Question is about the Sun's Health; how he looked at his Setting and Rising, and what Hopes they have to avoid the Stroak of the approaching Comet. This Conversation they are apt to run into with the same Temper that Boys discover, in delighting to hear terrible Stories of Sprites and Hobgoblins, which they greedily listen to, and dare not go to Bed for fear.

The Women of the Island have Abundance of Vivacity; they contemn their Husbands, and are exceedingly fond of Strangers, whereof there is always a considerable Number from the Continent below, attending at Court, either upon Affairs of the several Towns and Corporations, or their own particular Occasions; but are much despised, because they want the same Endowments. Among these the Ladies chuse their Gallants: But the Vexation is, that they act with too much Ease and Security; for the Husband is always so rapt in Speculation, that the Mistress and Lover may proceed to the greatest Familiarities before his Face, if he be but provided with Paper and Implements, and without his *Flapper* at his Side.

The Wives and Daughters lament their Confinement to the Island, although I think it the most delicious Spot of Ground in the World; and although they live here in the greatest Plenty and Magnificence, and are allowed to do whatever they please: They long to see the World, and take the Diversions of the Metropolis, which they are not allowed to do without a particular Licence from the King; and this is not easy to be obtained, because the People of Quality have found by frequent Experience, how hard it is to persuade their Women to return from below. I was told, that a great

Court Lady, who had several Children, is married to the prime Minister, the richest Subject in the Kingdom, a very graceful Person, extremely fond of her, and lives in the finest Palace of the Island; went down to *Lagado*, on the Pretence of Health, there hid her self for several Months, till the King sent a Warrant to search for her; and she was found in an obscure Eating-House all in Rags, having pawned her Cloths to maintain an old deformed Footman, who beat her every Day, and in whose Company she was taken much against her Will. And although her Husband received her with all possible Kindness, and without the least Reproach; she soon after contrived to steal down again with all her Jewels, to the same Gallant, and hath not been heard of since.

This may perhaps pass with the Reader rather for an *European* or *English Story*, than for one of a Country so remote. But he may please to consider, that the Caprices of Womankind are not limited by any Climate or Nation; and that they are much more uniform than can be easily imagined.

In about a Month's Time I had made a tolerable Proficiency in their Language, and was able to answer most of the King's Questions, when I had the Honour to attend him. His Majesty discovered not the least Curiosity to enquire into the Laws, Government, History, Religion, or Manners of the Countries where I had been; but confined his Questions to the State of Mathematicks, and received the Account I gave him, with great Contempt and Indifference, though often rouzed by his *Flapper* on each Side.

CHAPTER III

A Phænomenon solved by modern Philosophy and Astronomy. The Laputians *great Improvements in the latter. The King's Method of suppressing Insurrections.*

I desired Leave of this Prince to see the Curiosities of the Island; which he was graciously pleased to grant, and ordered my

Tutor to attend me. I chiefly wanted to know to what Cause in Art or in Nature, it owed its several Motions; whereof I will now give a philosophical Account to the Reader.[1]

The flying or floating Island is exactly circular; its Diameter 7837 Yards, or about four Miles and an Half, and consequently contains ten Thousand Acres. It is three Hundred Yards thick. The Bottom, or under Surface, which appears to those who view it from below, is one even regular Plate of Adamant, shooting up to the Height of about two Hundred Yards. Above it lye the several Minerals in their usual Order; and over all is a Coat of rich Mould ten or twelve Foot deep. The Declivity of the upper Surface, from the Circumference to the Center, is the natural Cause why all the Dews and Rains which fall upon the Island, are conveyed in small Rivulets towards the Middle, where they are emptyed into four large Basons, each of about Half a Mile in Circuit, and two Hundred Yards distant from the Center. From these Basons the Water is continually exhaled by the Sun in the Day-time, which effectually prevents their overflowing. Besides, as it is in the Power of the Monarch to raise the Island above the Region of Clouds and Vapours, he can prevent the falling of Dews and Rains whenever he pleases. For the highest Clouds cannot rise above two Miles, as Naturalists agree, at least they were never known to do so in that Country.

At the Center of the *Island* there is a Chasm about fifty Yards in Diameter, from whence the Astronomers descend into a large Dome, which is therefore called *Flandona Gagnole*, or the *Astronomers Cave*; situated at the Depth of an Hundred Yards beneath the upper Surface of the Adamant. In this Cave are Twenty Lamps continually burning, which from the Reflection of the Adamant cast a strong Light into every Part. The Place is stored with great Variety of Sextants, Quadrants, Telescopes, Astrolabes, and other Astronomical Instruments. But the greatest Curiosity, upon which the Fate of the Island depends, is a Load-stone of a prodigious Size, in Shape resembling a Weaver's Shuttle. It is in Length six Yards, and in the thickest Part at least three Yards over. This Magnet is sustained by a very strong Axle of Adamant, passing through its Middle, upon which it plays, and is poized so exactly that the weakest Hand can turn it. It is hooped round with an hollow

[1] The "philosophical account" in the next several paragraphs is Swift's parody of the typical scientific paper published in the *Transactions* of the Royal Society.

Plate 4. Part 3. Page 205

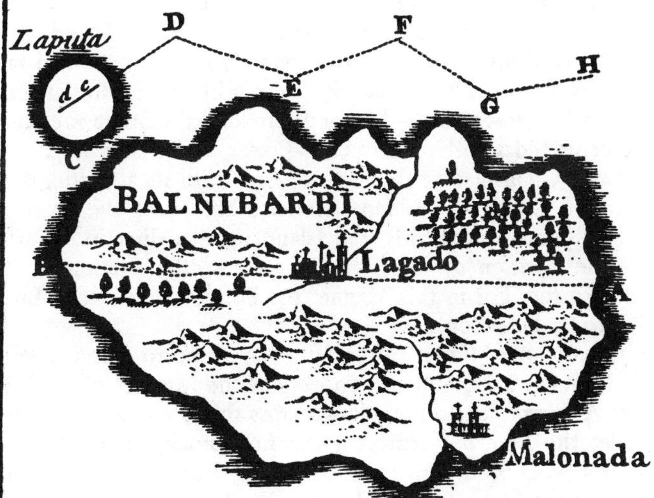

Cylinder of Adamant, four Foot deep, as many thick, and twelve Yards in Diameter, placed horizontally, and supported by Eight Adamantine Feet, each Six Yards high. In the Middle of the Concave Side there is a Groove Twelve Inches deep, in which the Extremities of the Axle are lodged, and turned round as there is Occasion.

This Stone cannot be moved from its Place by any Force, because the Hoop and its Feet are one continued Piece with that Body of Adamant which constitutes the Bottom of the Island.

By Means of his Load-stone, the Island is made to rise and fall, and move from one Place to another. For, with respect to that Part of the Earth over which the Monarch presides, the Stone is endued at one of its Sides with an attractive Power, and at the other with a repulsive. Upon placing the Magnet erect with its attracting End towards the Earth, the Island descends; but when the repelling Extremity points downwards, the Island mounts directly upwards. When the Position of the Stone is oblique, the Motion of the Island is so too. For in this Magnet the Forces always act in Lines parallel to its Direction.

By this oblique Motion the Island is conveyed to different Parts of the Monarch's Dominions. To explain the Manner of its Progress, let *A B* represent a Line drawn cross the Dominions of *Balnibarbi*; let the Line *c d* represent the Load-stone, of which let *d* be the repelling End, and *c* the attracting End, the Island being over C; let the Stone be placed in the Position *c d* with its repelling End downwards; then the Island will be driven upwards obliquely towards *D*. When it is arrived at *D*, let the Stone be turned upon its Axle till its attracting End points towards E, and then the Island will be carried obliquely towards *E*; where if the Stone be again turned upon its Axle till it stands in the Position *E F*, with its repelling Point downwards, the Island will rise obliquely towards *F*, where by directing the attracting End towards G, the Island may be carried to G, and from G to *H*, by turning the Stone, so as to make its repelling Extremity point directly downwards. And thus by changing the Situation of the Stone as often as there is Occasion, the Island is made to rise and fall by Turns in an oblique Direction; and by those alternate Risings and Fallings (the Obliquity being not considerable) is conveyed from one Part of the Dominions to the other.

But it must be observed, that this Island cannot move beyond the Extent of the Dominions below; nor can it rise above the Height of four Miles. For which the Astronomers (who have written large Systems concerning the Stone) assign the following Reason: That the Magnetick Virtue does not extend beyond the Distance of four Miles, and that the Mineral which acts upon the Stone in the Bowels of the Earth, and in the Sea about six Leagues distant from the Shoar, is not diffused through the whole Globe, but terminated with the Limits of the King's Dominions: And it was easy from the great Advantage of such a superior Situation, for a Prince to bring under his Obedience whatever Country lay within the Attraction of that Magnet.

When the Stone is put parallel to the Plane of the Horizon, the Island standeth still; for in that Case, the Extremities of it being at equal Distance from the Earth, act with equal Force, the one in drawing downwards, the other in pushing upwards; and consequently no Motion can ensue.

This Load-stone is under the Care of certain Astronomers, who from Time to Time give it such Positions as the Monarch directs. They spend the greatest Part of their Lives in observing the celestial Bodies, which they do by the Assistance of Glasses, far excelling ours in Goodness. For, although their largest Telescopes do not exceed three Feet, they magnify much more than those of a Hundred with us, and shew the Stars with greater Clearness. This Advantage hath enabled them to extend their Discoveries much farther than our Astronomers in *Europe*. They have made a Catalogue of ten Thousand fixed Stars, whereas the largest of ours do not contain above one third Part of that Number. They have likewise discovered two lesser Stars, or *Satellites*, which revolve about *Mars*; whereof the innermost is distant from the Center of the primary Planet exactly three of his Diameters, and the outermost five; the former revolves in the Space of ten Hours, and the latter in Twenty-one and an Half; so that the Squares of their periodical Times, are very near in the same Proportion with the Cubes of their Distance from the Center of *Mars*; which evidently shews them to be governed by the same Law of Gravitation, that influences the other heavenly Bodies.

They have observed Ninety-three different Comets, and settled their Periods with great Exactness. If this be true, (and they affirm it with great Confidence) it is much to be wished that their Observations were made publick; whereby the Theory of Comets, which at present is very lame and defective, might be brought to the same Perfection with other Parts of Astronomy.

The King would be the most absolute Prince in the Universe, if he could but prevail on a Ministry to join with him; but these having their Estates below on the Continent, and considering that the Office of a Favourite hath a very uncertain Tenure, would never consent to the enslaving their Country.

If any Town should engage in Rebellion or Mutiny, fall into violent Factions, or refuse to pay the usual Tribute; the King hath two Methods of reducing them to Obedience. The first and the mildest Course is by keeping the Island hovering over such a Town, and the Lands about it; whereby he can deprive them of the Benefit of the Sun and the Rain, and consequently afflict the Inhabitants with Dearth and Diseases. And if the Crime deserve it, they are at the same time pelted from above with great Stones, against which they have no Defence, but by creeping into Cellars or Caves, while the Roofs of their Houses are beaten to Pieces. But if they still continue obstinate, or offer to raise Insurrections; he proceeds to the last Remedy, by letting the Island drop directly upon their Heads, which makes a universal Destruction both of Houses and Men. However, this is an Extremity to which the Prince is seldom driven, neither indeed is he willing to put it in Execution; nor dare his Ministers advise him to an Action, which as it would render them odious to the People, so it would be a great Damage to their own Estates that lie all below; for the Island is the King's Demesn.

But there is still indeed a more weighty Reason, why the Kings of this Country have been always averse from executing so terrible an Action, unless upon the utmost Necessity. For if the Town intended to be destroyed should have in it any tall Rocks, as it generally falls out in the larger Cities; a Situation probably chosen at first with a View to prevent such a Catastrophe: Or if it abound in high Spires or Pillars of Stone, a sudden Fall might endanger the Bottom or under Surface of the Island, which although it consist as I have said, of one entire Adamant two hundred Yards thick, might happen to crack by too great a Choque, or burst by approaching too near the Fires from the Houses below; as the Backs both of Iron and Stone will often do in our Chimneys. Of all this the People are well apprized, and understand how far to carry their Obstinacy, where their Liberty or Property is concerned.

And the King, when he is highest provoked, and most determined to press a City to Rubbish, orders the Island to descend with great Gentleness, out of a Pretence of Tenderness to his People, but indeed for fear of breaking the Adamantine Bottom; in which Case it is the Opinion of all their Philosophers, that the Load-stone could no longer hold it up, and the whole Mass would fall to the Ground.

About three Years before my Arrival among them,[2] while the King was in his Progress over his Dominions there happened an extraordinary Accident which had like to have put a Period to the Fate of that Monarchy, at least as it is now instituted. Lindalino the second City in the Kingdom was the first his Majesty visited in his Progress. Three Days after his Departure, the Inhabitants who had often complained of great Oppressions, shut the Town Gates, seized on the Governor, and with incredible Speed and Labour erected four large Towers, one at every Corner of the City (which is an exact Square) equal in Height to a strong pointed Rock that stands directly in the Center of the City. Upon the Top of each Tower, as well as upon the Rock, they fixed a great Loadstone, and in case their Design should fail, they had provided a vast Quantity of the most combustible Fewel, hoping to burst therewith the adamantine Bottom of the Island, if the Loadstone Project should miscarry.

It was eight Months before the King had perfect Notice that the Lindalinians were in Rebellion. He then commanded that the Island should be wafted over the City. The People were unanimous, and had laid in Store of Provisions, and a great River runs through the middle of the Town. The King hovered over them several Days to deprive them of the Sun and the Rain. He ordered many Packthreads to be let down, yet not a Person offered to send up a

[2] This paragraph, and the next four, were omitted from all editions (including the first) until introduced in 1899. The first publishers of *Gulliver*, fearing government reprisals, found them too dangerous to include; others omitted them most likely through ignorance of their existence. Allegorically, they tell of Ireland's campaign against the introduction of a debased currency manufactured by an ironmonger named Wood who had purchased the privilege from a mistress of George I. Swift sided with the Irish, pressing the cause in a series of letters (1724) under the name of M. B., Drapier. These letters (alluded to in the allegory as a "most combustible Fewel") were influential in forcing England to cancel the project. Dublin is here disguised as Lindalino.

Petition, but instead thereof, very bold Demands, the Redress of all their Grievances, great Immunitys, the Choice of their own Governor, and other the like Exorbitances. Upon which his Majesty commanded all the Inhabitants of the Island to cast great Stones from the lower gallery into the Town; but the Citizens had provided against this Mischief by conveying their Persons and Effects into the four Towers, and other strong Buildings, and Vaults under Ground.

The King being now determined to reduce this proud People, ordered that the Island should descend gently within fourty Yards of the Top of the Towers and Rock. This was accordingly done; but the Officers employed in that Work found the Descent much speedier than usual, and by turning the Loadstone could not without great Difficulty keep it in a firm position, but found the Island inclining to fall. They sent the King immediate Intelligence of this astonishing Event and begged his Majesty's Permission to raise the Island higher; the King consented, a general Council was called, and the Officers of the Loadstone ordered to attend. One of the oldest and expertest among them obtained leave to try an Experiment. He took a strong Line of an Hundred Yards, and the Island being raised over the Town above the attracting Power they had felt, He fastened a Piece of Adamant to the End of his Line which had in it a Mixture of Iron mineral, of the same Nature with that whereof the Bottom or lower Surface of the Island is composed, and from the lower Gallery let it down slowly towards the Top of the Towers. The Adamant was not descended four Yards, before the Officer felt it drawn so strongly downwards, that he could hardly pull it back. He then threw down several small Pieces of Adamant, and observed that they were all violently attracted by the Top of the Tower. The same Experiment was made on the other three Towers, and on the Rock with the same Effect.

This Incident broke entirely the King's Measures and (to dwell no longer on other Circumstances) he was forced to give the Town their own Conditions.

I was assured by a great Minister, that if the Island had descended so near the Town, as not to be able to raise it self, the Citizens were determined to fix it for ever, to kill the King and all his Servants, and entirely change the Government.

By a fundamental Law of this Realm, neither the King nor either of his two elder Sons, are permitted to leave the Island; nor the Queen till she is past Child-bearing.

CHAPTER IV

The Author leaves Laputa, *is conveyed to* Balnibarbi, *arrives at the Metropolis. A Description of the Metropolis, and the Country adjoining. The Author hospitably received by a great Lord. His Conversation with that Lord.*

Although I cannot say that I was ill treated in this Island, yet I must confess I thought my self too much neglected, not without some Degree of Contempt. For neither Prince nor People appeared to be curious in any Part of Knowledge, except Mathematicks and Musick, wherein I was far their inferior, and upon that Account very little regarded.

On the other Side, after having seen all the Curiosities of the Island, I was very desirous to leave it, being heartily weary of those People. They were indeed excellent in two Sciences for which I have great Esteem, and wherein I am not unversed; but at the same time so abstracted and involved in Speculation, that I never met with such disagreeable Companions. I conversed only with Women, Tradesmen, *Flappers*, and Court-Pages, during two Months of my Abode there; by which at last I rendered my self extremely contemptible; yet these were the only People from whom I could ever receive a reasonable Answer.

I had obtained by hard Study a good Degree of Knowledge in their Language: I was weary of being confined to an Island where I received so little Countenance; and resolved to leave it with the first Opportunity.

There was a great Lord at Court, nearly related to the King, and for that Reason alone used with Respect. He was universally reckoned the most ignorant and stupid Person among them. He had performed many eminent Services for the Crown, had great natural and acquired Parts, adorned with Integrity and Honour; but so ill an Ear for Musick, that his Detractors reported he had been often known to beat Time in the wrong Place; neither could his Tutors without extreme Difficulty teach him to demonstrate the most easy Proposition in the Mathematicks. He was pleased to shew me many Marks of Favour, often did me the Honour of a Visit, desired to be informed in the Affairs of *Europe*, the Laws and Customs, the Manners and Learning of the several Countries where I had travelled. He listened to me with great Attention, and made very wise Observations on all I spoke. He had two *Flappers* attending him for State, but never made use of them except at Court, and in Visits of Ceremony; and would always command them to withdraw when we were alone together.

I intreated this illustrious Person to intercede in my Behalf with his Majesty for Leave to depart; which he accordingly did, as he was pleased to tell me, with Regret: For, indeed he had made me several Offers very advantageous, which however I refused with Expressions of the highest Acknowledgment.

On the 16th Day of *February*, I took Leave of his Majesty and the Court. The King made me a Present to the Value of about two Hundred Pounds *English*; and my Protector his Kinsman as much more, together with a Letter of Recommendation to a Friend of his in *Lagado*, the Metropolis: The Island being then hovering over a Mountain about two Miles from it, I was let down from the lowest Gallery, in the same Manner as I had been taken up.

The Continent, as far as it is subject to the Monarch of the *Flying Island*, passeth under the general Name of *Balnibarbi*; and the Metropolis, as I said before, is called *Lagado*. I felt some little Satisfaction in finding my self on firm Ground. I walked to the City without any Concern, being clad like one of the Natives, and sufficiently instructed to converse with them. I soon found out the Person's House to whom I was recommended; presented my Letter from his Friend the Grandee in the Island, and was received with much Kindness. This great Lord, whose Name was *Munodi*,[1] ordered me an Apartment in his own House, where I continued during my Stay, and was entertained in a most hospitable Manner.

[1] One scholar has suggested that "Munodi" may be derived from *mundum odi* ("I hate the world"). Lord Munodi may be either Bolingbroke or Oxford, perhaps a composite of both.

The next Morning after my Arrival he took me in his Chariot to see the Town, which is about half the Bigness of *London*; but the Houses very strangely built, and most of them out of Repair. The People in the Streets walked fast, looked wild, their Eyes fixed, and were generally in Rags. We passed through one of the Town Gates, and went about three Miles into the Country, where I saw many Labourers working with several Sorts of Tools in the Ground, but was not able to conjecture what they were about; neither did I observe any Expectation either of Corn or Grass, although the Soil appeared to be excellent. I could not forbear admiring at these odd Appearances both in Town and Country; and I made bold to desire my Conductor, that he would be pleased to explain to me what could be meant by so many busy Heads, Hands and Faces, both in the Streets and the Fields, because I did not discover any good Effects they produced; but on the contrary, I never knew a Soil so unhappily cultivated, Houses so ill contrived and so ruinous, or a People whose Countenances and Habit expressed so much Misery and Want.

This Lord *Munodi* was a Person of the first Rank, and had been some Years Governor of *Lagado*; but by a Cabal of Ministers was discharged for Insufficiency. However the King treated him with Tenderness, as a well-meaning Man, but of a low contemptible Understanding.

When I gave that free Censure of the Country and its Inhabitants, he made no further Answer than by telling me, that I had not been long enough among them to form a Judgment; and that the different Nations of the World had different Customs; with other common Topicks to the same Purpose. But when we returned to his Palace, he asked me how I liked the Building, what Absurdities I observed, and what Quarrel I had with the Dress or Looks of his Domesticks. This he might safely do; because every Thing about him was magnificent, regular and polite. I answered, that his Excellency's Prudence, Quality, and Fortune, had exempted him from those Defects which Folly and Beggary had produced in others. He said, if I would go with him to his Country House about Twenty Miles distant, where his Estate lay, there would be more Leisure for this Kind of Conversation. I told his Excellency, that I was entirely at his Disposal; and accordingly we set out next Morning.

During our Journey, he made me observe the several Methods

used by Farmers in managing their Lands; which to me were wholly unaccountable: For except in some very few Places, I could not discover one Ear of Corn, or Blade of Grass. But, in three Hours travelling, the Scene was wholly altered; we came into a most beautiful Country; Farmers Houses at small Distances, neatly built, the Fields enclosed, containing Vineyards, Corn-grounds and Meadows. Neither do I remember to have seen a more delightful Prospect. His Excellency observed my Countenance to clear up; he told me with a Sigh, that there his Estate began, and would continue the same till we should come to his House. That his Countrymen ridiculed and despised him for managing his Affairs no better, and for setting so ill an Example to the Kingdom; which however was followed by very few, such as were old and wilful, and weak like himself.

We came at length to the House, which was indeed a noble Structure, built according to the best Rules of ancient Architecture. The Fountains, Gardens, Walks, Avenues, and Groves were all disposed with exact Judgment and Taste. I gave due Praises to every Thing I saw, whereof his Excellency took not the least Notice till after Supper; when, there being no third Companion, he told me with a very melancholy Air, that he doubted he must throw down his Houses in Town and Country, to rebuild them after the present Mode; destroy all his Plantations, and cast others into such a Form as modern Usage required; and give the same Directions to all his Tenants, unless he would submit to incur the Censure of Pride, Singularity, Affectation, Ignorance, Caprice; and perhaps encrease his Majesty's Displeasure.

That the Admiration I appeared to be under, would cease or diminish when he had informed me of some Particulars, which probably I never heard of at Court, the People there being too much taken up in their own Speculations, to have Regard to what passed here below.

The Sum of his Discourse was to this Effect. That about Forty Years ago, certain Persons went up to *Laputa,* either upon Business or Diversion; and after five Months Continuance, came back with a very little Smattering in Mathematicks, but full of Volatile Spirits acquired in that Airy Region. That these Persons upon their Return, began to dislike the Management of every Thing below; and fell into Schemes of putting all Arts, Sciences, Languages, and Mechanics upon a new Foot. To this End they procured a Royal

Patent for erecting an Academy of PROJECTORS in *Lagado*:[2] And the Humour prevailed so strongly among the People, that there is not a Town of any Consequence in the Kingdom without such an Academy. In these Colleges, the Professors contrive new Rules and Methods of Agriculture and Building, and new Instruments and Tools for all Trades and Manufactures, whereby, as they undertake, one Man shall do the Work of Ten; a Palace may be built in a Week, of Materials so durable as to last for ever without repairing. All the Fruits of the Earth shall come to Maturity at whatever Season we think fit to chuse, and increase an Hundred Fold more than they do at present; with innumerable other happy Proposals. The only Inconvenience is, that none of these Projects are yet brought to Perfection; and in the mean time, the whole Country lies miserably waste, the Houses in Ruins, and the People without Food or Cloaths. By all which, instead of being discouraged, they are Fifty Times more violently bent upon prosecuting their Schemes, driven equally on by Hope and Despair: That, as for himself, being not of an enterprizing Spirit, he was content to go on in the old Forms; to live in the Houses his Ancestors had built, and act as they did in every Part of Life without Innovation. That, some few other Persons of Quality and Gentry had done the same; but were looked on with an Eye of Contempt and ill Will, as Enemies to Art, ignorant, and ill Commonwealthsmen, preferring their own Ease and Sloth before the general Improvement of their Country.

His Lordship added, that he would not by any further Particulars prevent the Pleasure I should certainly take in viewing the grand Academy, whither he was resolved I should go. He only desired me to observe a ruined Building upon the Side of a Mountain about three Miles distant, of which he gave me this Account. That he had a very convenient Mill within Half a Mile of his House, turned by a Current from a large River, and sufficient for his own Family as well as a great Number of his Tenants. That, about seven Years ago, a Club of those Projectors came to him with Proposals to destroy this Mill, and build another on the Side of that Mountain, on the long Ridge whereof a long Canal must be cut for a Repository of Water, to be conveyed up by Pipes and Engines to supply the Mill: Because the Wind and Air upon a

[2] Swift intended the Academy of Lagado to correspond to the Royal Society, while by a "Projector" he meant anyone given to impractical or visionary schemes and activities.

Height agitated the Water, and thereby made it fitter for Motion: And because the Water descending down a Declivity would turn the Mill with half the Current of a River whose Course is more upon a Level. He said, that being then not very well with the Court, and pressed by many of his Friends, he complyed with the Proposal; and after employing an Hundred Men for two Years, the Work miscarryed, the Projectors went off, laying the Blame intirely upon him; railing at him ever since, and putting others upon the same Experiment, with equal Assurance of Success, as well as equal Disappointment.

In a few Days we came back to Town; and his Excellency, considering the bad Character he had in the Academy, would not go with me himself, but recommended me to a Friend of his to bear me Company thither. My Lord was pleased to represent me as a great Admirer of Projects, and a Person of much Curiosity and easy Belief; which indeed was not without Truth; for I had my self been a Sort of Projector in my younger Days.

CHAPTER V

The Author permitted to see the grand Academy of Lagado. *The Academy largely described. The Arts wherein the Professors employ themselves.*

This Academy is not an entire single Building, but a Continuation of several Houses on both Sides of a Street; which growing waste, was purchased and applyed to that Use.

I was received very kindly by the Warden, and went for many Days to the Academy. Every Room hath in it one or more Projectors; and I believe I could not be in fewer than five Hundred Rooms.

The first Man I saw was of a meagre Aspect, with sooty Hands and Face, his Hair and Beard long, ragged and singed in several Places. His Clothes, Shirt, and Skin were all of the same Colour. He had been Eight Years upon a Project for extracting Sun-Beams out of Cucumbers, which were to be put into Vials hermetically sealed, and let out to warm the Air in raw inclement Summers.[1] He told me, he did not doubt in Eight Years more, that he should be able to supply Governors Gardens with Sun-shine at a reasonable Rate; but he complained that his Stock was low, and intreated me to give him something as an Encouragement to Ingenuity, especially since this had been a very dear Season for Cucumbers. I made him a small Present, for my Lord had furnished me with Money on purpose, because he knew their Practice of begging from all who go to see them.

I went into another Chamber, but was ready to hasten back, being almost overcome with a horrible Stink. My Conductor pressed me forward, conjuring me in a Whisper to give no Offence, which would be highly resented; and therefore I durst not so much as stop my Nose. The Projector of this Cell was the most ancient Student of the Academy. His Face and Beard were of a pale Yellow; his Hands and Clothes dawbed over with Filth. When I was presented to him, he gave me a very close Embrace, (a Compliment I could well have excused). His Employment from his first coming into the Academy, was an Operation to reduce human Excrement to its original Food, by separating the several Parts, removing the Tincture which it receives from the Gall, making the Odour exhale, and scumming off the Saliva. He had a weekly Allowance from the Society, of a Vessel filled with human Ordure, about the Bigness of a *Bristol* Barrel.

I saw another at work to calcine Ice into Gunpowder; who likewise shewed me a Treatise he had written concerning the Malleability of Fire, which he intended to publish.

There was a most ingenious Architect who had contrived a new Method for building Houses, by beginning at the Roof, and working downwards to the Foundation; which he justified to me by the like Practice of those two prudent Insects the Bee and the Spider.

There was a Man born blind, who had several Apprentices in his own Condition: Their Employment was to mix Colours for Painters, which their Master taught them to distinguish by feeling and smelling. It was indeed my Misfortune to find them at that Time not very perfect in their Lessons; and the Professor himself

[1] The experiments described in this chapter are based on actual experiments undertaken or proposed by Swift's contemporaries.

happened to be generally mistaken: This Artist is much encouraged and esteemed by the whole Fraternity.

In another Apartment I was highly pleased with a Projector, who had found a Device of plowing the Ground with Hogs, to save the Charges of Plows, Cattle, and Labour. The Method is this: In an Acre of Ground you bury at six Inches Distance, and eight deep, a Quantity of Acorns, Dates, Chestnuts, and other Maste or Vegetables whereof these Animals are fondest; then you drive six Hundred or more of them into the Field, where in a few Days they will root up the whole Ground in search of their Food, and make it fit for sowing, at the same time manuring it with their Dung. It is true, upon Experiment they found the Charge and Trouble very great, and they had little or no Crop. However, it is not doubted that this Invention may be capable of great Improvement.

I went into another Room, where the Walls and Ceiling were all hung round with Cobwebs, except a narrow Passage for the Artist to go in and out. At my Entrance he called aloud to me not to disturb his Webs. He lamented the fatal Mistake the World had been so long in of using Silk-Worms, while we had such plenty of domestick Insects, who infinitely excelled the former, because they understood how to weave as well as spin. And he proposed farther, that by employing Spiders, the Charge of dying Silks would be wholly saved; whereof I was fully convinced when he shewed me a vast Number of Flies most beautifully coloured, wherewith he fed his Spiders; assuring us, that the Webs would take a Tincture from them; and as he had them of all Hues, he hoped to fit every Body's Fancy, as soon as he could find proper Food for the Flies, of certain Gums, Oyls, and other glutinous Matter, to give a Strength and Consistence to the Threads.

There was an Astronomer who had undertaken to place a Sun-Dial upon the great Weather-Cock on the Town-House, by adjusting the annual and diurnal Motions of the Earth and Sun, so as to answer and coincide with all accidental Turnings of the Wind.

I was complaining of a small Fit of the Cholick; upon which my Conductor led me into a Room, where a great Physician resided, who was famous for curing that Disease by contrary Operations from the same Instrument. He had a large Pair of Bellows, with a long slender Muzzle of Ivory. This he conveyed eight Inches up the Anus, and drawing in the Wind, he affirmed he could make the Guts as lank as a dried Bladder. But when the Disease was more stubborn and violent, he let in the Muzzle while the Bellows was full of Wind, which he discharged into the Body of the Patient; then withdrew the Instrument to replenish it, clapping his Thumb strongly against the Orifice of the Fundament; and this being repeated three or four Times, the adventitious Wind would rush out, bringing the noxious along with it (like Water put into a Pump) and the Patient recovers. I saw him try both Experiments upon a Dog, but could not discern any Effect from the former. After the latter, the Animal was ready to burst, and made so violent a Discharge, as was very offensive to me and my Companions. The Dog died on the Spot, and we left the Doctor endeavouring to recover him by the same Operation.

I visited many other Apartments, but shall not trouble my Reader with all the Curiosities I observed, being studious of Brevity.

I had hitherto seen only one Side of the Academy, the other being appropriated to the Advancers of speculative Learning; of whom I shall say something when I have mentioned one illustrious Person more, who is called among them *the universal Artist.* He told us, he had been Thirty Years employing his Thoughts for the Improvement of human Life. He had two large Rooms full of wonderful Curiosities, and Fifty Men at work. Some were condensing Air into a dry tangible Substance, by extracting the Nitre, and letting the aqueous or fluid Particles percolate: Others softening Marble for Pillows and Pin-cushions; others petrifying the Hoofs of a living Horse to preserve them from foundring. The Artist himself was at that Time busy upon two great Designs: The first, to sow Land with Chaff, wherein he affirmed the true seminal Virtue to be contained, as he demonstrated by several Experiments which I was not skilful enough to comprehend. The other was, by a certain Composition of Gums, Minerals, and Vegetables outwardly applied, to prevent the Growth of Wool upon two young Lambs; and he hoped in a reasonable Time to propagate the Breed of naked Sheep all over the Kingdom.

We crossed a Walk to the other Part of the Academy, where, as I have already said, the Projectors in speculative Learning resided.

The first Professor I saw was in a very large Room, with Forty Pupils about him. After Salutation, observing me to look earnestly upon a Frame, which took up the greatest Part of both the Length and Breadth of the Room; he said, perhaps I might wonder to see him employed in a Project for improving speculative Knowledge by practical and mechanical Operations. But the World would soon be sensible of its Usefulness; and he flattered himself, that a more noble exalted Thought never sprang in any other Man's Head. Every one knew how laborious the usual Method is of attaining to Arts and Sciences; whereas by his Contrivance, the most ignorant Person at a reasonable Charge, and with a little bodily Labour, may write Books in Philosophy, Poetry, Politicks, Law, Mathematicks and Theology, without the least Assistance from Genius or Study. He then led me to the Frame, about the Sides whereof all his Pupils stood in Ranks. It was Twenty Foot square, placed in the Middle of the Room. The Superficies was composed of several Bits of Wood, about the Bigness of a Dye, but some larger than others. They were all linked together by slender Wires. These Bits of Wood were covered on every Square with Papers pasted on them; and on these Papers were written all the Words of their Language in their several Moods, Tenses, and Declensions, but without any Order. The Professor then desired me to observe, for he was going to set his Engine at work. The Pupils at his Command took each of them hold of an Iron Handle, whereof there were Forty fixed round the Edges of the Frame; and giving them a sudden Turn, the whole Disposition of the Words was entirely changed. He then commanded Six and Thirty of the Lads to read the several Lines softly as they appeared upon the Frame; and where they found three or four Words together that might make Part of a Sentence, they dictated to the four remaining Boys who were Scribes. This Work was repeated three or four Times, and at every Turn the Engine was so contrived, that the Words shifted into new Places, as the square Bits of Wood moved upside down.

Six Hours a-Day the young Students were employed in this Labour; and the Professor shewed me several Volumes in large Folio already collected, of broken Sentences, which he intended to piece together; and out of those rich Materials to give the World a compleat Body of all Arts and Sciences; which however might be still improved, and much expedited, if the Publick would raise a Fund for making and employing five Hundred such Frames in *Lagado*, and oblige the Managers to contribute in common their several Collections.

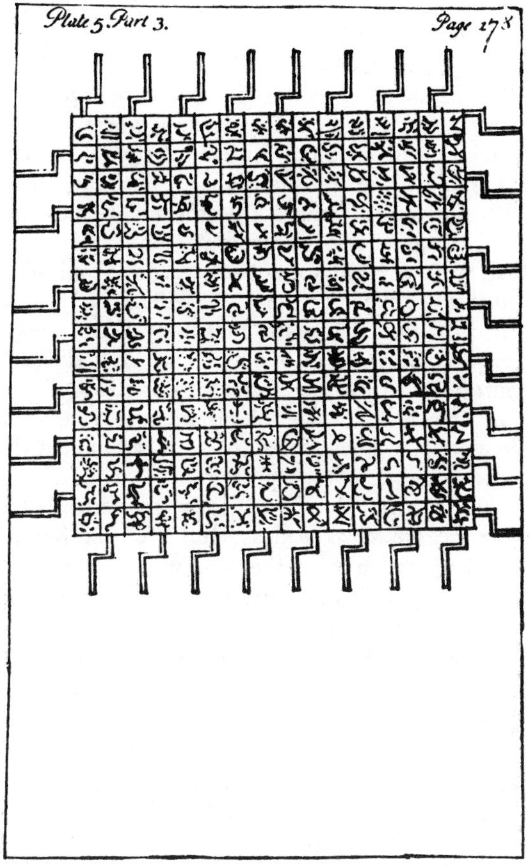

He assured me, that this Invention had employed all his Thoughts from his Youth; that he had emptyed the whole Vocabulary into his Frame, and made the strictest Computation of the general Proportion there is in Books between the Numbers of Particles, Nouns, and Verbs, and other Parts of Speech.

I made my humblest Acknowledgments to this illustrious Person for his great Communicativeness; and promised if ever I had the good Fortune to return to my native Country, that I would do him Justice, as the sole Inventor of this wonderful Machine; the Form and Contrivance of which I desired Leave to delineate upon Paper as in the Figure here annexed. I told him, although it were the Custom of our Learned in *Europe* to steal Inventions from each other, who had thereby at least this Advantage, that it became a Controversy which was the right Owner; yet I would take such Caution, that he should have the Honour entire without a Rival.

We next went to the School of Languages, where three Professors sat in Consultation upon improving that of their own Country.

The first Project was to shorten Discourse by cutting Polysyllables into one, and leaving out Verbs and Participles; because in Reality all things imaginable are but Nouns.

The other, was a Scheme for entirely abolishing all Words whatsoever: And this was urged as a great Advantage in Point of Health as well as Brevity. For, it is plain, that every Word we speak is in some Degree a Diminution of our Lungs by Corrosion; and consequently contributes to the shortening of our Lives. An Expedient was therefore offered, that since Words are only Names for *Things*, it would be more convenient for all Men to carry about them, such *Things* as were necessary to express the particular Business they are to discourse on. And this Invention would certainly have taken Place, to the great Ease as well as Health of the Subject, if the Women in Conjunction with the Vulgar and Illiterate had not threatned to raise a Rebellion, unless they might be allowed the Liberty to speak with their Tongues, after the Manner of their Forefathers: Such constant irreconcileable Enemies to Science are the common People. However, many of the most Learned and Wise adhere to the new Scheme of expressing themselves by *Things*; which hath only this Inconvenience attending it; that if a Man's Business be very great, and of various Kinds, he must be obliged in Proportion to carry a greater Bundle of *Things* upon his Back, unless he can afford one or two strong Servants to attend him. I have often beheld two of those Sages almost sinking under the Weight of their Packs, like Pedlars among us, who when they met in the Streets, would lay down their Loads, open their Sacks, and hold Conversation for an Hour together; then put up their Implements, help each other to resume their Burthens, and take their Leave.

But, for short Conversations a Man may carry Implements in his Pockets and under his Arms, enough to supply him, and in his House he cannot be at a Loss; therefore the Room where Company meet who practice this Art, is full of all *Things* ready at Hand, requisite to furnish Matter for this Kind of artificial Converse.

Another great Advantage proposed by this Invention, was, that it would serve as an universal Language to be understood in all civilized Nations, whose Goods and Utensils are generally of the same Kind, or nearly resembling, so that their Uses might easily be comprehended. And thus, Embassadors would be qualified to treat with foreign Princes or Ministers of State, to whose Tongues they were utter Strangers.

I was at the Mathematical School, where the Master taught his Pupils after a Method scarce imaginable to us in *Europe*. The Proposition and Demonstration were fairly written on a thin Wafer, with Ink composed of a Cephalick Tincture. This the Student was to swallow upon a fasting Stomach, and for three Days following eat nothing but Bread and Water. As the Wafer digested, the Tincture mounted to his Brain, bearing the Proposition along with it. But the Success hath not hitherto been answerable, partly by some Error in the *Quantum* or Composition, and partly by the Perverseness of Lads; to whom this Bolus is so nauseous, that they generally steal aside, and discharge it upwards before it can operate neither have they been yet persuaded to use so long an Abstinence as the Prescription requires.

CHAPTER VI

A further Account of the Academy. The Author proposeth some Improvements, which are honourably received.

In the School of political Projectors I was but ill entertained; the Professors appearing in my Judgment wholly out of their Senses; which is a Scene that never fails to make me melancholy. These unhappy People were proposing Schemes for persuading Monarchs to chuse Favourites upon the Score of their Wisdom,

Capacity and Virtue; of teaching Ministers to consult the publick Good; of rewarding Merit, great Abilities, and eminent Services; of instructing Princes to know their true Interest, by placing it on the same Foundation with that of their People: Of chusing for Employments Persons qualified to exercise them; with many other wild impossible Chimæras, that never entered before into the Heart of Man to conceive; and confirmed in me the old Observation, that there is nothing so extravagant and irrational which some Philosophers have not maintained for Truth.

But, however I shall so far do Justice to this Part of the Academy, as to acknowledge that all of them were not so visionary. There was a most ingenious Doctor who seemed to be perfectly versed in the whole Nature and System of Government. This illustrious Person had very usefully employed his Studies in finding out effectual Remedies for all Diseases and Corruptions, to which the several Kinds of publick Administration are subject by the Vices or Infirmities of those who govern, as well as by the Licentiousness of those who are to obey. For Instance: Whereas all Writers and Reasoners have agreed, that there is a strict universal Resemblance between the natural and the political Body; can there be any thing more evident, than that the Health of both must be preserved, and the Diseases cured by the same Prescriptions? It is allowed, that Senates and great Councils are often troubled with redundant, ebullient, and other peccant Humours; with many Diseases of the Head, and more of the Heart; with strong Convulsions, with grievous Contractions of the Nerves and Sinews in both Hands, but especially the Right: With Spleen, Flatus, Vertigoes and Deliriums; with scrophulous Tumours full of fœtid purulent Matter; with sower frothy Ructations; with Canine Appetites and Crudeness of Digestion; besides many others needless to mention. This Doctor therefore proposed, that upon the meeting of a Senate, certain Physicians should attend at the three first Days of their sitting, and at the Close of each Day's Debate, feel the Pulses of every Senator; after which having maturely considered, and consulted upon the Nature of the several Maladies, and the Methods of Cure; they should on the fourth Day return to the Senate-House, attended by their Apothecaries stored with proper Medicines; and before the Members sat, administer to each of them Lenitives, Aperitives, Abstersives, Corrosives, Restringents, Palliatives, Laxatives, Cephalalgicks, Ictericks, Apophlegmaticks, Acousticks, as their several Cases required; and according as these Medicines should operate, repeat, alter, or omit them at the next Meeting.

This Project could not be of any great Expence to the Publick; and might in my poor Opinion, be of much Use for the Dispatch of Business in those Countries where Senates have any Share in the legislative Power; beget Unanimity, shorten Debates, open a few Mouths which are now closed, and close many more which are now open; curb the Petulancy of the Young, and correct the positiveness of the Old; rouze the Stupid, and damp the Pert.

Again; Because it is a general Complaint that the Favourites of Princes are troubled with short and weak Memories; the same Doctor proposed, that whoever attended a first Minister, after having told his Business with the utmost Brevity, and in the plainest Words; should at his Departure give the said Minister a Tweak by the Nose, or a Kick in the Belly, or tread on his Corns, or lug him thrice by both Ears, or run a Pin into his Breech, or pinch his Arm black and blue; to prevent Forgetfulness: And at every Levee Day repeat the same Operation, till the Business were done or absolutely refused.

He likewise directed, that every Senator in the great Council of a Nation, after he had delivered his Opinion, and argued in the Defence of it, should be obliged to give his Vote directly contrary; because if that were done, the Result would infallibly terminate in the Good of the Publick.

When Parties in a State are violent, he offered a wonderful Contrivance to reconcile them. The Method is this. You take an Hundred Leaders of each Party; you dispose them into Couples of such whose Heads are nearest of a Size; then let two nice Operators saw off the *Occiput* of each Couple at the same Time, in such a Manner that the Brain may be equally divided. Let the *Occiputs* thus cut off be interchanged, applying each to the Head of his opposite Party-man. It seems indeed to be a Work that requireth some Exactness; but the Professor assured us, that if it were dextrously performed, the Cure would be infallible. For he argued thus; that the two half Brains being left to debate the Matter between themselves within the Space of one Scull, would soon come to a good Understanding, and produce that Moderation as well as Regularity of Thinking, so much to be wished for in the Heads of those, who imagine they came into the World only to watch and govern its Motion: And as to the Difference of Brains in Quantity or Quality, among those who are Directors in Faction; the Doctor assured us from his own Knowledge, that it was a perfect Trifle.

I heard a very warm Debate between two Professors, about the most commodious and effectual Ways and Means of raising Money without grieving the Subject. The first affirmed, the justest Method would be to lay a certain Tax upon Vices and Folly; and the Sum fixed upon every Man, to be rated after the fairest Manner by a Jury of his Neighbours. The second was of an Opinion directly contrary; to tax those Qualities of Body and Mind for which Men chiefly value themselves; the Rate to be more or less according to the Degrees of excelling; the Decision whereof should be left entirely to their own Breast. The highest Tax was upon Men, who are the greatest Favourites of the other Sex; and the Assessments according to the Number and Natures of the Favours they have received; for which they are allowed to be their own Vouchers. Wit, Valour, and Politeness were likewise proposed to be largely taxed, and collected in the same Manner, by every Person giving his own Word for the Quantum of what he possessed. But, as to Honour, Justice, Wisdom and Learning, they should not be taxed at all; because, they are Qualifications of so singular a Kind, that no Man will either allow them in his Neighbour, or value them in himself.

The Women were proposed to be taxed according to their Beauty and Skill in Dressing; wherein they had the same Privilege with the Men, to be determined by their own Judgment. But Constancy, Chastity, good Sense, and good Nature were not rated, because they would not bear the Charge of Collecting.

To keep Senators in the Interest of the Crown, it was proposed that the Members should raffle for Employments; every Man first taking an Oath, and giving Security that he would vote for the Court, whether he won or no; after which the Losers had in their Turn the Liberty of raffling upon the next Vacancy. Thus, Hope and Expectation would be kept alive; none would complain of broken Promises, but impute their Disappointments wholly to Fortune, whose Shoulders are broader and stronger than those of a Ministry.

Another Professor shewed me a large Paper of Instructions for discovering Plots and Conspiracies against the Government. He advised great Statesmen to examine into the Dyet of all suspected Persons; their Times of eating; upon which Side they lay in Bed; with which Hand they wiped their Posteriors; to take a strict View of their Excrements, and from the Colour, the Odour, the Taste, the Consistence, the Crudeness, or Maturity of Digestion, form a Judgment of their Thoughts and Designs: Because Men are never so serious, thoughtful, and intent, as when they are at Stool; which he found by frequent Experiment: For in such Conjunctures, when he used merely as a Trial to consider which was the best Way of murdering the King, his Ordure would have a Tincture of Green; but quite different when he thought only of raising an Insurrection, or burning the Metropolis.

The whole Discourse was written with great Acuteness, containing many Observations both curious and useful for Politicians, but as I conceived not altogether compleat. This I ventured to tell the Author, and offered if he pleased to supply him with some Additions. He received my Proposition with more Compliance than is usual among Writers, especially those of the Projecting Species; professing he would be glad to receive farther Information.

I told him, that in the Kingdom of *Tribnia*, by the Natives called *Langden*,[1] where I had long sojourned, the Bulk of the People consisted wholly of Discoverers, Witnesses, Informers, Accusers, Prosecutors, Evidences, Swearers; together with their several subservient and subaltern Instruments; all under the Colours, the Conduct, and pay of Ministers and their Deputies. The Plots in that Kingdom are usually the Workmanship of those Persons who desire to raise their own Characters of profound Politicians; to restore new Vigour to a crazy Administration; to stifle or divert general Discontents; to fill their Coffers with Forfeitures; and raise or sink the Opinion of publick Credit, as either shall best answer their private Advantage. It is first agreed and settled among them, what suspected Persons shall be accused of a Plot: Then, effectual Care is taken to secure all their Letters and other Papers, and put the Owners in Chains. These Papers are delivered to a Set of Artists very dextrous in finding out the mysterious Meanings of Words, Syllables and Letters. For Instance, they can decypher a Close-stool to signify a Privy-Council; a Flock of Geese, a Senate; a lame Dog, an Invader; the Plague, a standing Army; a Buzard, a Minister; the Gout, a High Priest; a Gibbet, a Secretary of State; a Chamber pot, a Committee of Grandees; a Sieve, a Court Lady; a Broom, a Revolution; a Mouse-trap, an Employment; a bottomless Pit, the Treasury; a Sink, a C[our]t; a Cap and Bells, a Favourite; a broken

[1] Anagrams of "Britain" and "England."

Reed, a Court of Justice; an empty Tun, a General; a running Sore, the Administration.

When this Method fails, they have two others more effectual; which the Learned among them call Acrosticks, and Anagrams. *First,* they can decypher all initial Letters into political Meanings: Thus, *N,* shall signify a Plot; *B,* a Regiment of Horse; *L,* a Fleet at Sea. Or, *secondly,* by transposing the Letters of the Alphabet, in any suspected Paper, they can lay open the deepest Designs of a discontented Party. So for Example, if I should say in a Letter to a Friend, *Our Brother* Tom *hath just got the Piles;* a Man of Skill in this Art would discover how the same Letters which compose that Sentence, may be analysed into the following Words; *Resist,* ——a *Plot is brought home——The Tour.* And this is the Anagrammatick Method.[2]

The Professor made me great Acknowledgments for communicating these Observations, and promised to make honourable mention of me in his Treatise.

I saw nothing in this Country that could invite me to a longer Continuance; and began to think of returning home to *England.*

CHAPTER VII

The Author leaves Lagado, *arrives at* Maldonada. *No Ship ready. He takes a short* Voyage *to* Glubbdubdrib. *His Reception by the Governor.*

The Continent of which this Kingdom is a part, extends itself, as I have Reason to believe, Eastward to that unknown Tract of *America,* Westward of *California,* and North to the Pacifick Ocean, which is not above an hundred and fifty Miles from *Lagado;* where there is a good Port and much Commerce with the great Island of *Luggnagg;* situated to the North-West about 29 Degrees

[2] Swift seems doubly allusive in these paragraphs: to the kind of evidence he thought fabricated by the government in the trial (1723) of his friend Bishop Atterbury; to the earlier proceedings against another friend, Bolingbroke, who had used the pseudonym "La Tour" (see p. 19, n.3; p. 53, n. 2).

North Latitude, and 140 Longitude. This Island of *Luggnagg* stands South Eastwards of *Japan*, about an hundred Leagues distant. There is a strict Alliance between the *Japanese* Emperor and the King of *Luggnagg*, which affords frequent Opportunities of sailing from one Island to the other. I determined therefore to direct my Course this Way, in order to my Return to *Europe*. I hired two Mules with a Guide to shew me the Way, and carry my small Baggage. I took leave of my noble Protector, who had shewn me so much Favour, and made me a generous Present at my Departure.

My Journey was without any Accident or Adventure worth relating. When I arrived at the Port of *Maldonada*, (for so it is called) there was no Ship in the Harbour bound for *Luggnagg*, nor like to be in some Time. The Town is about as large as *Portsmouth*. I soon fell into some Acquaintance, and was very hospitably received. A Gentleman of Distinction said to me, that since the Ships bound for *Luggnagg* could not be ready in less than a Month, it might be no disagreeable Amusement for me to take a Trip to the little Island of *Glubbdubdrib*, about five Leagues off to the South-West. He offered himself and a Friend to accompany me, and that I should be provided with a small convenient Barque for the Voyage.

GLUBBDUBDRIB, as nearly as I can interpret the Word, signifies the Island of *Sorcerers or Magicians*. It is about one third as large as the Isle of *Wight*, and extreamly fruitful: It is governed by the Head of a certain Tribe, who are all Magicians. This Tribe marries only among each other; and the eldest in Succession is Prince or Governor. He hath a noble Palace, and a Park of about three thousand Acres, surrounded by a Wall of hewn Stone twenty Foot high. In this Park are several small Inclosures for Cattle, Corn and Gardening.

The Governor and his Family are served and attended by Domesticks of a Kind somewhat unusual. By his Skill in Necromancy, he hath Power of calling whom he pleaseth from the Dead, and commanding their Service for twenty four Hours, but no longer; nor can he call the same Persons up again in less than three Months, except upon very extraordinary Occasions.

When we arrived at the Island, which was about Eleven in the Morning, one of the Gentlemen who accompanied me, went to the Governor, and desired Admittance for a Stranger, who came on purpose to have the Honour of attending on his Highness. This was immediately granted, and we all three entered the Gate of the

Palace between two Rows of Guards, armed and dressed after a very antick Manner. and something in their Countenances that made my Flesh creep with a Horror I cannot express. We passed through several Apartments between Servants of the same Sort, ranked on each Side as before, till we came to the Chamber of Presence, where after three profound Obeysances, and a few general Questions, we were permitted to sit on three Stools near the lowest Step of his Highness's Throne. He understood the Language of *Balnibarbi*, although it were different from that of his Island. He desired me to give him some Account of my Travels; and to let me see that I should be treated without Ceremony, he dismissed all his Attendants with a Turn of his Finger, at which to my great Astonishment they vanished in an Instant, like Visions in a Dream, when we awake on a sudden. I could not recover myself in some Time, till the Governor assured me that I should receive no Hurt; and observing my two Companions to be under no Concern, who had been often entertained in the same Manner, I began to take Courage; and related to his Highness a short History of my several Adventures, yet not without some Hesitation, and frequently looking behind me to the Place where I had seen those domestick Spectres. I had the Honour to dine with the Governor, where a new Set of Ghosts served up the Meat, and waited at Table. I now observed myself to be less terrified than I had been in the Morning. I stayed till Sun-set, but humbly desired his Highness to excuse me for not accepting his Invitation of lodging in the Palace. My two Friends and I lay at a private House in the Town adjoining, which is the Capital of this little Island; and the next Morning we returned to pay our Duty to the Governor, as he was pleased to command us.

After this Manner we continued in the Island for ten Days, most Part of every Day with the Governor, and at Night in our Lodging. I soon grew so familiarized to the Sight of Spirits, that after the third or fourth Time they gave me no Emotion at all; or if I had any Apprehensions left, my Curiosity prevailed over them. For his Highness the Governor ordered me to call up whatever Persons I would chuse to name, and in whatever Numbers among all the Dead from the Beginning of the World to the present Time, and command them to answer any Questions I should think fit to ask; with this Condition, that my Questions must be confined within the Compass of the Times they lived in.

And one Thing I might depend upon, that they would certainly tell me Truth; for Lying was a Talent of no Use in the lower World.

I made my humble Acknowledgments to his Highness for so great a Favour. We were in a Chamber, from whence there was a fair Prospect into the Park. And because my first Inclination was to be entertained with Scenes of Pomp and Magnificence, I desired to see *Alexander* the Great, at the Head of his Army just after the Battle of *Arbela*; which upon a Motion of the Governor's Finger immediately appeared in a large Field under the Window, where we stood. *Alexander* was called up into the Room: It was with great Difficulty that I understood his *Greek*, and had but little of my own. He assured me upon his Honour that he was not poisoned, but dyed of a Fever by excessive Drinking.

Next I saw *Hannibal* passing the *Alps*, who told me he had not a Drop of Vinegar in his Camp.[1]

I saw *Cæsar* and *Pompey* at the Head of their Troops just ready to engage. I saw the former in his last great Triumph. I desired that the Senate of *Rome* might appear before me in one large Chamber, and a modern Representative, in Counterview, in another. The first seemed to be an Assembly of Heroes and Demy-Gods; the other a Knot of Pedlars, Pick-pockets, Highwaymen and Bullies. The Governor at my Request gave the Sign for *Cæsar* and *Brutus* to advance towards us. I was struck with a profound Veneration at the Sight of *Brutus*; and could easily discover the most consummate Virtue, the greatest Intrepidity, and Firmness of Mind, the truest Love of his Country, and general Benevolence for Mankind in every Lineament of his Countenance. I observed with much Pleasure, that these two Persons were in good Intelligence with each other; and *Cæsar* freely confessed to me, that the greatest Actions of his own Life were not equal by many Degrees to the Glory of taking it away. I had the Honour to have much Conversation with *Brutus*; and was told that his Ancestor *Junius*, *Socrates*, *Epaminondas*, *Cato* the Younger, Sir *Thomas More* and himself, were perpetually together: A *Sextumvirate* to which all the Ages of the World cannot add a Seventh.

It would be tedious to trouble the Reader with relating what

[1] A large rock supposedly prevented Hannibal's army from crossing the Alps; his solution was to heat it and then wet it with vinegar, whereupon it cut easily.

vast Numbers of illustrious Persons were called up, to gratify that insatiable Desire I had to see the World in every Period of Antiquity placed before me. I chiefly fed my Eyes with beholding the Destroyers of Tyrants and Usurpers, and the Restorers of Liberty to oppressed and injured Nations. But it is impossible to express the Satisfaction I received in my own Mind, after such a Manner as to make it a suitable Entertainment to the Reader.

CHAPTER VIII

A further Account of Glubbdubdrib. *Antient and Modern History corrected.*

Having a Desire to see those Antients, who were most renowned for Wit and Learning, I set apart one Day on purpose. I proposed that *Homer* and *Aristotle* might appear at the Head of all their Commentators; but these were so numerous, that some Hundreds were forced to attend in the Court and outward Rooms of the Palace. I knew and could distinguish those two Heroes at first Sight, not only from the Croud, but from each other. *Homer* was the taller and comelier Person of the two, walked very erect for one of his Age, and his Eyes were the most quick and piercing I ever beheld.[1] *Aristotle* stooped much, and made use of a Staff. His Visage was meager, his Hair lank and thin, and his Voice hollow. I soon discovered, that both of them were perfect Strangers to the rest of the Company, and had never seen or heard of them before. And I had a Whisper from a Ghost, who shall be nameless, that these Commentators always kept in the most distant Quarters from their Principals in the lower World, through a Consciousness of Shame and Guilt, because they had so horribly misrepresented the Meaning of those Authors to Posterity. I introduced *Didymus* and *Eustathius* to *Homer*, and prevailed on him to treat them

[1] Swift has Gulliver correct the traditionally accepted view that Homer was blind.

better than perhaps they deserved; for he soon found they wanted a Genius to enter into the Spirit of a Poet. But *Aristotle* was out of all Patience with the Account I gave him of *Scotus* and *Ramus*, as I presented them to him; and he asked them whether the rest of the Tribe were as great Dunces as themselves.[2]

I then desired the Governor to call up *Descartes* and *Gassendi*, with whom I prevailed to explain their Systems to *Aristotle*. This great Philosopher freely acknowledged his own Mistakes in Natural Philosophy, because he proceeded in many things upon Conjecture, as all Men must do; and he found, that *Gassendi*, who had made the Doctrine of *Epicurus* as palatable as he could, and the *Vortices* of *Descartes*, were equally exploded.[3] He predicted the same Fate to *Attraction*,[4] whereof the present Learned are such zealous Asserters. He said, that new Systems of Nature were but new Fashions, which would vary in every Age; and even those who pretend to demonstrate them from Mathematical Principles, would flourish but a short Period of Time, and be out of Vogue when that was determined.

I spent five Days in conversing with many others of the antient Learned. I saw most of the first *Roman* Emperors. I prevailed on the Governor to call up *Eliogabalus's* Cooks[5] to dress us a Dinner; but they could not shew us much of their Skill, for want of Materials. A *Helot* of *Agesilaus* made us a Dish of *Spartan* Broth, but I was not able to get down a second Spoonful.

The two Gentlemen who conducted me to the Island were pressed by their private Affairs to return in three Days, which I employed in seeing some of the modern Dead, who had made the greatest Figure for two or three Hundred Years past in our own and other Countries of *Europe*; and having been always a great Admirer of old illustrious Families, I desired the Governor would call up a Dozen or two of Kings with their Ancestors in order, for

[2] Didymus and Eustathius: commentators on Homer. Duns Scotus: a thirteenth-century proponent of Aristotle; Pierre de la Ramée: a sixteenth-century humanist, critical of Aristotle.

[3] René Descartes: seventeenth-century philosopher and mathematician whose theory that all motions are circular Swift thought preposterous. Pierre Gassendi: a contemporary of Descartes and proponent of the Epicurean system of physics—hence an opponent of both Aristotle and Descartes.

[4] Newton's theory of gravitation.

[5] Heliogabalus, a Roman Emperor noted for over-eating.

eight or nine Generations. But my Disappointment was grievous and unexpected. For, instead of a long Train with Royal Diadems, I saw in one Family two Fidlers, three spruce Courtiers, and an *Italian* Prelate. In another, a Barber, an Abbot, and two Cardinals. I have too great a Veneration for crowned Heads to dwell any longer on so nice a Subject: But as to Counts, Marquesses, Dukes, Earls, and the like, I was not so scrupulous. And I confess it was not without some Pleasure that I found my self able to trace the particular Features, by which certain Families are distinguished up to their Originals. I could plainly discover from whence one Family derives a long Chin; why a second hath abounded with Knaves for two Generations, and Fools for two more; why a third happened to be crack-brained, and a fourth to be Sharpers. Whence it came, what *Polydore Virgil* says of a certain great House, *Nec Vir fortis, nec Fœmina Casta.*[6] How Cruelty, Falshood, and Cowardice grew to be Characteristicks by which certain Families are distinguished as much as by their Coat of Arms. Who first brought the Pox into a noble House, which hath lineally descended in scrophulous Tumours to their Posterity. Neither could I wonder at all this, when I saw such an Interruption of Lineages by Pages, Lacqueys, Valets, Coachmen, Gamesters, Fidlers, Players, Captains, and Pickpockets.

I was chiefly disgusted with modern History. For having strictly examined all the Persons of greatest Name in the Courts of Princes for an Hundred Years past, I found how the World had been misled by prostitute Writers, to ascribe the greatest Exploits in War to Cowards, the wisest Counsel to Fools, Sincerity to Flatterers, *Roman* Virtue to Betrayers of their Country, Piety to Atheists, Chastity to Sodomites, Truth to Informers. How many innocent and excellent Persons had been condemned to Death or Banishment, by the practising of great Ministers upon the Corruption of Judges, and the Malice of Factions. How many Villains had been exalted to the highest Places of Trust, Power, Dignity, and Profit: How great a Share in the Motions and Events of Courts, Councils, and Senates might be challenged by Bawds, Whores, Pimps, Parasites, and Buffoons: How low an Opinion I had of human Wisdom and Integrity, when I was truly informed of the Springs and Motives of great Enterprizes and Revolutions

[6] "Not a man of them brave, not a woman pure." Polydore Virgil was a sixteenth-century Italian clergyman who composed a history of England in Latin.

in the World, and of the contemptible Accidents to which they owed their Success.

Here I discovered the Roguery and Ignorance of those who pretend to write *Anecdotes*, or secret History; who send so many Kings to their Graves with a Cup of Poison; will repeat the Discourse between a Prince and chief Minister, where no Witness was by; unlock the Thoughts and Cabinets of Embassadors and Secretaries of State; and have the perpetual Misfortune to be mistaken. Here I discovered the true Causes of many great events that have surprized the World: How a Whore can govern the Back-stairs, the Back-stairs a Council, and the Council a Senate. A General confessed in my Presence that he got a Victory purely by the Force of Cowardice and ill Conduct: And an Admiral, that for want of proper Intelligence, he beat the Enemy to whom he intended to betray the Fleet. Three Kings protested to me, that in their whole Reigns they did never once prefer any Person of Merit, unless by Mistake or Treachery of some Minister in whom they confided: Neither would they do it if they were to live again; and they shewed with great Strength of Reason, that the Royal Throne could not be supported without Corruption; because, that positive, confident, restive Temper, which Virtue infused into Man, was a perpetual Clog to publick Business.

I had the Curiosity to enquire in a particular Manner, by what Method great Numbers had procured to themselves high Titles of Honour, and prodigious Estates; and I confined my Enquiry to a very modern Period: However, without grating upon present Times, because I would be sure to give no Offence even to Foreigners (for I hope the Reader need not be told that I do not in the least intend my own Country in what I say upon this Occasion) a great Number of Persons concerned were called up, and upon a very slight Examination, discovered such a Scene of Infamy, that I cannot reflect upon it without some Seriousness. Perjury, Oppression, Subornation, Fraud, Pandarism, and the like *Infirmities* were amongst the most excusable Arts they had to mention; and for these I gave, as it was reasonable, due Allowance. But when some confessed, they owed their Greatness and Wealth to Sodomy or Incest; others to the prostituting of their own Wives and Daughters; others to the betraying their Country or their Prince; some to poisoning, more to the perverting of Justice in order to destroy the Innocent: I hope I may be pardoned if these Discoveries inclined me a little to abate of that profound Veneration which I am naturally apt to pay to Persons of high Rank, who ought to be treated with the utmost Respect due to their sublime Dignity, by us their Inferiors.

I had often read of some great Services done to Princes and States, and desired to see the Persons by whom those Services were performed. Upon Enquiry I was told, that their Names were to be found on no Record, except a few of them whom History hath represented as the vilest Rogues and Traitors. As to the rest, I had never once heard of them. They all appeared with dejected Looks, and in the meanest Habit; most of them telling me they died in Poverty and Disgrace, and the rest on a Scaffold or a Gibbet.

Among others there was one Person whose Case appeared a little singular. He had a Youth about Eighteen Years old standing by his Side. He told me, he had for many Years been Commander of a Ship; and in the Sea Fight at *Actium*, had the good Fortune to break through the Enemy's great Line of Battle, sink three of their Capital Ships, and take a fourth, which was the sole Cause of *Antony's* Flight, and of the Victory that ensued: That the Youth standing by him, his only Son, was killed in the Action. He added, that upon the Confidence of some Merit, the War being at an End, he went to *Rome*, and solicited at the Court of *Augustus* to be preferred to a greater Ship, whose Commander had been killed; but without any regard to his Pretensions, it was given to a Boy who had never seen the Sea, the Son of a *Libertina*, who waited on one of the Emperor's Mistresses. Returning back to his own Vessel, he was charged with Neglect of Duty, and the Ship given to a favourite Page of *Publicola* the Vice-Admiral; whereupon he retired to a poor Farm, at a great Distance from *Rome*, and there ended his Life. I was so curious to know the Truth of this Story, that I desired *Agrippa* might be called, who was Admiral in that Fight. He appeared, and confirmed the whole Account, but with much more Advantage to the Captain; whose Modesty had extenuated or concealed a great Part of his Merit.

I was surprized to find Corruption grown so high and so quick in that Empire, by the Force of Luxury so lately introduced; which made me less wonder at many parallel Cases in other Countries, where Vices of all Kinds have reigned so much longer, and where the whole Praise as well as Pillage hath been engrossed by the chief Commander, who perhaps had the least Title to either.

As every Person called up made exactly the same Appearance he had done in the World, it gave me melancholy Reflections to observe how much the Race of human Kind was degenerate among us, within these Hundred Years past. How the Pox under all its Consequences and Denominations had altered every Lineament of an *English* Countenance; shortened the Size of Bodies, unbraced the Nerves, relaxed the Sinews and Muscles, introduced a sallow Complexion, and rendered the Flesh loose and *rancid.*

I descended so low as to desire that some *English* Yeomen of the old Stamp, might be summoned to appear; once so famous for the Simplicity of their Manners, Dyet and Dress; for Justice in their Dealings; for their true Spirit of Liberty; for their Valour and Love of their Country. Neither could I be wholly unmoved after comparing the Living with the Dead, when I considered how all these pure native Virtues were prostituted for a Piece of Money by their Grand-children; who in selling their Votes, and managing at Elections have acquired every Vice and Corruption that can possibly be learned in a Court.

CHAPTER IX

The Author's return to Maldonada. *Sails to the Kingdom of* Luggnagg. *The Author confined. He is sent for to Court. The Manner of his Admittance. The King's great Lenity to his Subjects.*

The Day of our Departure being come, I took leave of his Highness the Governor of *Glubbdubdrib,* and returned with my two Companions to *Maldonada,* where after a Fortnight's waiting, a Ship was ready to sail for *Luggnagg.* The two Gentlemen and some others were so generous and kind as to furnish me with Provisions, and see me on Board. I was a Month in Voyage. We had one violent Storm, and were under a Necessity of steering Westward to get into the Trade-Wind, which holds for above sixty Leagues. On the 21st of *April,* 1708, we sailed in the River of *Clumegnig,* which is a Sea-port Town, at the South-East Point of *Luggnagg*. We cast Anchor within a League of the Town, and made a Signal for a Pilot. Two of them came on Board in less than half an Hour, by whom we were guided between certain Shoals and Rocks, which are very dangerous in the Passage, to a large Basin, where a Fleet may ride in Safety within a Cable's Length of the Town-Wall.

Some of our Sailors, whether out of Treachery or Inadvertence, had informed the Pilots that I was a Stranger and a great Traveller, whereof these gave Notice to a Custom-House Officer, by whom I was examined very strictly upon my landing. This Officer spoke to me in the Language of *Balnibarbi*, which by the Force of much Commerce is generally understood in that Town, especially by Seamen, and those employed in the Customs. I gave him a short Account of some Particulars, and made my Story as plausible and consistent as I could; but I thought it necessary to disguise my Country, and call my self a *Hollander*; because my Intentions were for *Japan*, and I knew the *Dutch* were the only *Europeans* permitted to enter into that Kingdom.[1] I therefore told the Officer, that having been shipwrecked on the Coast of *Balnibarbi*, and cast on a Rock, I was received up into *Laputa*, or the flying Island (of which he had often heard) and was now endeavouring to get to *Japan*, from whence I might find a Convenience of returning to my own Country. The Officer said, I must be confined till he could receive Orders from Court, for which he would write immediately, and hoped to receive an Answer in a Fortnight. I was carried to a convenient Lodging, with a Centry placed at the Door; however I had the Liberty of a large Garden, and was treated with Humanity enough, being maintained all the Time at the King's Charge. I was visited by several Persons, chiefly out of Curiosity, because it was reported I came from Countries very remote, of which they had never heard.

I hired a young Man who came in the same Ship to be an Interpreter; he was a Native of *Luggnagg*, but had lived some Years at *Maldonada*, and was a perfect Master of both Languages. By his Assistance I was able to hold a Conversation with those that came to visit me; but this consisted only of their Questions and my Answers.

[1] Japan was closed to all, except the Dutch and Chinese, after the anti-Christian rebellions of 1637.

The Dispatch came from Court about the Time we expected. It contained a Warrant for conducting me and my Retinue to *Traldragdubh* or *Trildrogdrib*, (for it is pronounced both Ways as near as I can remember) by a Party of Ten Horse. All my Retinue was that poor Lad for an Interpreter, whom I persuaded into my Service. At my humble Request we had each of us a Mule to ride on. A Messenger was dispatched half a Day's Journey before us, to give the King Notice of my Approach, and to desire that his Majesty would please to appoint a Day and Hour, when it would be his gracious Pleasure that I might have the Honour to *lick the Dust before his Footstool*. This is the Court Style, and I found it to be more than Matter of Form: For upon my Admittance two Days after my Arrival, I was commanded to crawl upon my Belly, and lick the Floor as I advanced; but on account of my being a Stranger, Care was taken to have it so clean that the Dust was not offensive. However, this was a peculiar Grace, not allowed to any but Persons of the highest Rank, when they desire an Admittance: Nay, sometimes the Floor is strewed with Dust on purpose, when the Person to be admitted happens to have powerful Enemies at Court: And I have seen a great Lord with his Mouth so crammed, that when he had crept to the proper Distance from the Throne, he was not able to speak a Word. Neither is there any Remedy, because it is capital for those who receive an Audience to spit or wipe their Mouths in his Majesty's Presence. There is indeed another Custom, which I cannot altogether approve of. When the King hath a Mind to put any of his Nobles to Death in a gentle indulgent Manner; he commands to have the Floor strowed with a certain brown Powder, of a deadly Composition, which being licked up infallibly kills him in twenty-four Hours. But in Justice to this Prince's great Clemency, and the Care he hath of his Subjects Lives (wherein it were much to be wished that the Monarchs of *Europe* would imitate him) it must be mentioned for his Honour, that strict Orders are given to have the infected Parts of the Floor well washed after every such Execution; which if his Domesticks neglect, they are in Danger of incurring his Royal Displeasure. I my self heard him give Directions, that one of his Pages should be whipt, whose Turn it was to give Notice about washing the Floor after an Execution, but maliciously had omitted it; by which Neglect a young Lord of great Hopes coming to an Audience, was unfortunately poisoned, although the

King at that Time had no Design against his Life. But this good Prince was so gracious, as to forgive the Page his Whipping, upon Promise that he would do so no more, without special Orders.

To return from this Digression; when I had crept within four Yards of the Throne, I raised my self gently upon my Knees, and then striking my Forehead seven Times against the Ground, I pronounced the following Words, as they had been taught me the Night before, *Ickpling Gloffthrobb Squutserumm blhiop Mlashnalt Zwin tnodbalkguffh Slhiophad Gurdlubh Asht.* This is the Compliment established by the Laws of the Land for all Persons admitted to the King's Presence. It may be rendered into *English* thus: *May your cœlestial Majesty out-live the Sun, eleven Moons and an half.* To this the King returned some Answer, which although I could not understand, yet I replied as I had been directed; *Fluft drin Yalerick Dwuldum prastrad mirplush,* which properly signifies, *My Tongue is in the Mouth of my Friend*; and by this Expression was meant that I desired leave to bring my Interpreter; whereupon the young Man already mentioned was accordingly introduced; by whose Intervention I answered as many Questions as his Majesty could put in above an Hour. I spoke in the *Balnibarbian* Tongue, and my Interpreter delivered my Meaning in that of *Luggnagg.*

The King was much delighted with my Company, and ordered his *Bliffmarklub* or High Chamberlain to appoint a Lodging in the Court for me and my Interpreter, with a daily Allowance for my Table, and a large Purse of Gold for my common Expences.

I stayed three Months in this Country out of perfect Obedience to his Majesty, who was pleased highly to favour me, and made me very honourable Offers. But I thought it more consistent with Prudence and Justice to pass the Remainder of my Days with my Wife and Family.

CHAPTER X

The Luggnuggians *commended. A particular Description of the* Struldbruggs, *with many Conversations between the Author and some eminent Persons upon that Subject.*

The *Luggnuggians* are a polite and generous People, and although they are not without some Share of that Pride which is peculiar to all *Eastern* Countries, yet they shew themselves courteous to Strangers, especially such who are countenanced by the Court. I had many Acquaintance among Persons of the best Fashion, and being always attended by my Interpreter, the Conversation we had was not disagreeable.

One Day in much good Company, I was asked by a Person of Quality, whether I had seen any of their *Struldbruggs* or *Immortals*. I said I had not; and desired he would explain to me what he meant by such an Appellation, applyed to a mortal Creature. He told me, that sometimes, although very rarely, a Child happened to be born in a Family with a red circular Spot in the Forehead, directly over the left Eye-brow, which was an infallible Mark that it should never dye. The Spot, as he described it, was about the Compass of a Silver Threepence, but in the Course of Time grew larger, and changed its Colour; for at Twelve Years old it became green, so continued till Five and Twenty, then turned to a deep blue; at Five and Forty it grew coal black, and as large as an *English* Shilling; but never admitted any farther Alteration. He said these Births were so rare, that he did not believe there could be above Eleven Hundred *Struldbruggs* of both Sexes in the whole Kingdom, of which he computed about Fifty in the Metropolis, and among the rest a young Girl born about three Years ago. That, these Productions were not peculiar to any Family, but a meer Effect of Chance; and the Children of the *Struldbruggs* themselves, were equally mortal with the rest of the People.

I freely own myself to have been struck with inexpressible Delight upon hearing this Account: And the Person who gave it me happening to understand the *Balnibarbian* Language, which I spoke very well, I could not forbear breaking out into Expressions perhaps a little too extravagant. I cryed out as in a Rapture; Happy Nation, where every Child hath at least a Chance for being immortal! Happy People who enjoy so many living Examples of antient Virtue, and have Masters ready to instruct them in the Wisdom of all former Ages! But, happiest beyond all Comparison are those excellent *Struldbruggs*, who being born exempt from that universal Calamity of human Nature, have their Minds free and disingaged, without the Weight and Depression of Spirits caused by the continual Apprehension of Death. I discovered my Admiration that I had not observed any of these illustrious Persons at Court; the black Spot on the Fore-head, being so remarkable a Distinction, that I could not have easily overlooked it: And it was impossible that his Majesty, a most judicious Prince, should not provide himself with a good Number of such wise and able Counsellors. Yet perhaps the Virtue of those Reverend Sages was too strict for the corrupt and libertine Manners of a Court. And we often find by Experience, that young Men are too opinionative and volatile to be guided by the sober Dictates of their Seniors. However, since the King was pleased to allow me Access to his Royal Person, I was resolved upon the very first Occasion to deliver my Opinion to him on this Matter freely, and at large by the Help of my Interpreter; and whether he would please to take my Advice or no, yet in one Thing I was determined, that his Majesty having frequently offered me an Establishment in this Country, I would with great Thankfulness accept the Favour, and pass my Life here in the Conversation of those superiour Beings the *Struldbruggs*, if they would please to admit me.

The Gentleman to whom I addressed my Discourse, because (as I have already observed) he spoke the Language of *Balnibarbi*, said to me with a Sort of a Smile, which usually ariseth from Pity to the Ignorant, that he was glad of any Occasion to keep me among them, and desired my Permission to explain to the Company what I had spoke. He did so; and they talked together for some time in their own Language, whereof I understood not a Syllable, neither could I observe by their Countenances what Impression my Discourse had made on them. After a short Silence, the same Person told me, that his Friends and mine (so he thought fit to express himself) were very much pleased with the judicious Remarks I had made on the great Happiness and Advantages of immortal Life; and they were desirous to know in a particular Manner, what Scheme of Living I should have formed to myself, if it had fallen to my Lot to have been born a *Struldbrugg.*

I answered, it was easy to be eloquent on so copious and delightful a Subject, especially to me who have been often apt to amuse myself with Visions of what I should do if I were a King, a General, or a great Lord: And upon this very Case I had frequently run over the whole System how I should employ myself, and pass the Time if I were sure to live for ever.

That, if it had been my good Fortune to come into the World a *Struldbrugg;* as soon as I could discover my own Happiness by understanding the Difference between Life and Death, I would first resolve by all Arts and Methods whatsoever to procure myself Riches: In the Pursuit of which, by Thrift and Management, I might reasonably expect in about two Hundred Years, to be the wealthiest Man in the Kingdom. In the second Place, I would from my earliest Youth apply myself to the Study of Arts and Sciences, by which I should arrive in time to excel all others in Learning. Lastly, I would carefully record every Action and Event of Consequence that happened in the Publick, impartially draw the Characters of the several Successions of Princes, and great Ministers of State; with my own Observations on every Point. I would exactly set down the several Changes in Customs, Languages, Fashions of Dress, Dyet and Diversions. By all which Acquirements, I should be a living Treasury of Knowledge and Wisdom, and certainly become the Oracle of the Nation.

I would never marry after Threescore, but live in an hospitable Manner, yet still on the saving Side. I would entertain myself in forming and directing the Minds of hopeful young Men, by convincing them from my own Remembrance, Experience and Observation, fortified by numerous Examples, of the Usefulness of Virtue in publick and private Life. But, my choise and constant Companions should be a Sett of my own immortal Brotherhood, among whom I would elect a Dozen from the most ancient down to my own Contemporaries. Where any of these wanted Fortunes, I would provide them with convenient Lodges round my own Estate, and have some of them always at my Table, only mingling a few of the most valuable among you Mortals, whom Length of Time would harden me to lose with little or no Reluctance, and treat your Posterity after the same Manner; just as a Man diverts himself with the annual Succession of Pinks and Tulips in his Garden, without regretting the Loss of those which withered the preceding Year.

These *Struldbruggs* and I would mutually communicate our Observations and Memorials through the Course of Time; remark the several Gradations by which Corruption steals into the World, and oppose it in every Step, by giving perpetual Warning and Instruction to Mankind; which, added to the strong Influence of our own Example, would probably prevent that continual Degeneracy of human Nature, so justly complained of in all Ages.

Add to all this, the Pleasure of seeing the various Revolutions of States and Empires; the Changes in the lower and upper World; antient Cities in Ruins, and obscure Villages become the Seats of Kings. Famous Rivers lessening into shallow Brooks; the Ocean leaving one Coast dry, and overwhelming another: The Discovery of many Countries yet unknown. Barbarity over-running the politest Nations, and the most barbarous becoming civilized. I should then see the Discovery of the *Longitude*, the *perpetual Motion*, the *universal Medicine*, and many other great Inventions brought to the utmost Perfection.

What wonderful Discoveries should we make in Astronomy, by outliving and confirming our own Predictions, by observing the Progress and Returns of Comets, with the Changes of Motion in the Sun, Moon and Stars.

I enlarged upon many other Topicks, which the natural Desire of endless Life and sublunary Happiness could easily furnish me with. When I had ended, and the Sum of my Discourse had been interpreted as before, to the rest of the Company, there was a good Deal of Talk among them in the Language of the Country, not without some Laughter at my Expence. At last the same Gentleman who had been my Interpreter, said, he was desired by the rest to set me right in a few Mistakes, which I had fallen into through the common Imbecility of human Nature, and upon that Allowance was less answerable for them. That, this Breed of *Struldbruggs* was peculiar to their Country, for there were no such People either in *Balnibarbi* or *Japan*, where he had the Honour to be Embassador from his Majesty, and found the Natives in both those Kingdoms very hard to believe that the Fact was possible; and it appeared from my Astonishment when he first mentioned the Matter to me, that I received it as a Thing wholly new, and scarcely to be credited. That in the two Kingdoms above-mentioned, where during his Residence he had conversed very much, he observed long Life to be the universal Desire and Wish of Mankind. That, whoever had one Foot in the Grave, was sure to hold back the other as strongly as he could. That the oldest had still Hopes of living one Day longer, and looked on Death as the greatest Evil, from which Nature always prompted him to retreat; only in this Island of *Luggnagg*, the Appetite for living was not so eager, from the continual Example of the *Struldbruggs* before their Eyes.

That the System of Living contrived by me was unreasonable and unjust, because it supposed a Perpetuity of Youth, Health, and Vigour, which no Man could be so foolish to hope, however extravagant he might be in his Wishes. That, the Question therefore was not whether a Man would chuse to be always in the Prime of Youth, attended with Prosperity and Health; but how he would pass a perpetual Life under all the usual Disadvantages which old Age brings along with it. For although few Men will avow their Desires of being immortal upon such hard Conditions, yet in the two Kingdoms before mentioned of *Balnibarbi* and *Japan*, he observed that every Man desired to put off Death for sometime longer, let it approach ever so late; and he rarely heard of any Man who died willingly, except he were incited by the Extremity of Grief or Torture. And he appealed to me whether in those Countries I had travelled as well as my own, I had not observed the same general Disposition.

After this Preface, he gave me a particular account of the *Struldbruggs* among them. He said they commonly acted like Mortals, till about Thirty Years old, after which by Degrees they grew melancholy and dejected, increasing in both till they came to Fourscore. This he learned from their own Confession; for otherwise there not being above two or three of that Species born in an Age, they were too few to form a general Observation by. When they came to Fourscore Years, which is reckoned the Extremity of living in this Country, they had not only all the Follies and Infirmities of other old Men, but many more which arose from the dreadful Prospect of never dying. They were not only opinionative, peevish, covetous, morose, vain, talkative; but uncapable of Friendship, and dead to all natural Affection, which never descended below their Grand-children. Envy and impotent Desires, are their prevailing Passions. But those Objects against which their Envy seems principally directed, are the Vices of the younger Sort, and the Deaths of the old. By reflecting on the former, they find themselves cut off from all Possibility of Pleasure; and whenever they see a Funeral, they lament and repine that others are gone to an Harbour of Rest, to which they themselves never can hope to arrive. They have no Remembrance of any thing but what they learned and observed in their Youth and middle Age, and even that is very imperfect: And for the Truth or Particulars of any Fact, it is safer to depend on common Traditions than upon their best Recollections. The least miserable among them, appear to be those who turn to Dotage, and entirely lose their Memories; these meet with more Pity and Assistance, because they want many bad Qualities which abound in others.

If a *Struldbrugg* happen to marry one of his own Kind, the Marriage is dissolved of Course by the Courtesy of the Kingdom, as soon as the younger of the two comes to be Fourscore. For the Law thinks it a reasonable Indulgence, that those who are condemned without any Fault of their own to a perpetual Continuance in the World, should not have their Misery doubled by the Load of a Wife.

As soon as they have compleated the Term of Eighty Years, they are looked on as dead in Law; their Heirs immediately succeed to their Estates, only a small Pittance is reserved for their Support; and the poor ones are maintained at the publick Charge. After that Period they are held incapable of any Employement of Trust or Profit; they cannot purchase Lands, or take Leases, neither are they allowed to be Witnesses in any Cause, either Civil or Criminal, not even for the Decision of Meers and Bounds.

At Ninety they lose their Teeth and Hair; they have at that Age no Distinction of Taste, but eat and drink whatever they can get, without Relish or Appetite. The Diseases they were subject to, still continue without encreasing or diminishing. In talking they forget the common Appellation of Things, and the Names of Persons, even of those who are their nearest Friends and Relations. For the same Reason they never can amuse themselves with reading, because their Memory will not serve to carry them from the Beginning of a Sentence to the End; and by this Defect they are deprived of the only Entertainment whereof they might otherwise be capable.

The Language of this Country being always upon the Flux, the *Struldbruggs* of one Age do not understand those of another; neither are they able after two Hundred Years to hold any Conversation (farther than by a few general Words) with their Neighbours the Mortals; and thus they lye under the Disadvantage of living like Foreigners in their own Country.

This was the Account given me of the *Struldbruggs*, as near as I can remember. I afterwards saw five or six of different Ages, the youngest not above two Hundred Years old, who were brought to me at several Times by some of my Friends; but although they were told that I was a great Traveller, and had seen all the World, they had not the least Curiosity to ask me a Question; only desired I would give them *Slumskudask*, or a Token of Remembrance; which is a modest Way of begging, to avoid the Law that strictly forbids it, because they are provided for by the Publick, although indeed with a very scanty Allowance.

They are despised and hated by all Sorts of People: When one of them is born, it is reckoned ominous, and their Birth is recorded very particularly; so that you may know their Age by consulting the Registry, which however hath not been kept above a Thousand Years past, or at least hath been destroyed by Time or publick Disturbances. But the usual Way of computing how old they are, is, by asking them what Kings or great Persons they can remember, and then consulting History; for infallibly the last Prince in their Mind did not begin his Reign after they were Fourscore Years old.

They were the most mortifying Sight I ever beheld; and the Women more horrible than the Men. Besides the usual Deformities in extreme old Age, they acquired an additional Ghastliness in Proportion to their Number of Years, which is not to be described; and among half a Dozen I soon distinguished which was the oldest, although there were not above a Century or two between them.

The Reader will easily believe, that from what I had heard and seen, my keen Appetite for Perpetuity of Life was much abated. I grew heartily ashamed of the pleasing Visions I had formed; and thought no Tyrant could invent a Death into which I would not run with Pleasure from such a Life. The King heard of all that had passed between me and my Friends upon this Occasion, and raillied me very pleasantly; wishing I would send a Couple of *Struldbruggs* to my own Country, to arm our People against the Fear of Death; but this it seems is forbidden by the fundamental Laws of the Kingdom; or else I should have been well content with the Trouble and Expence of transporting them.

I could not but agree, that the Laws of this Kingdom relating to the *Struldbruggs*, were founded upon the strongest Reasons, and such as any other Country would be under the Necessity of enacting in the like Circumstances. Otherwise, as Avarice is the necessary Consequent of old Age, those Immortals would in time become Proprietors of the whole Nation, and engross the Civil Power; which, for want of Abilities to manage, must end in the Ruin of the Publick.

CHAPTER XI

The Author leaves Luggnagg *and sails to* Japan. *From thence he returns in a* Dutch *Ship to* Amsterdam, *and from* Amsterdam *to* England.

I thought this Account of the *Struldbruggs* might be some Entertainment to the Reader, because it seems to be a little out of the common Way; at least, I do not remember to have met the like in any Book of Travels that hath come to my Hands: And if I am deceived, my Excuse must be, that it is necessary for Travellers, who describe the same Country, very often to agree in dwelling on the same Particulars, without deserving the Censure of having borrowed or transcribed from those who wrote before them.

There is indeed a perpetual Commerce between this Kingdom and the great Empire of *Japan*; and it is very probable that the *Japanese* Authors may have given some Account of the *Struldbruggs*; but my Stay in *Japan* was so short, and I was so entirely a Stranger to the Language, that I was not qualified to make any Enquiries. But I hope the *Dutch* upon this Notice will be curious and able enough to supply my Defects.

His Majesty having often pressed me to accept some Employment in his Court, and finding me absolutely determined to return to my Native Country; was pleased to give me his Licence to depart; and honoured me with a Letter of Recommendation under his own Hand to the Emperor of *Japan*. He likewise presented me with four Hundred forty-four large Pieces of Gold (this Nation delighting in even Numbers) and a red Diamond which I sold in *England* for Eleven Hundred Pounds.

On the 6th Day of *May*, 1709, I took a solemn Leave of his Majesty, and all my Friends. This Prince was so gracious as to order a Guard to conduct me to *Glanguenstald*, which is a Royal Port to the *South-West* Part of the Island. In six Days I found a Vessel ready to carry me to *Japan*; and spent fifteen Days in the Voyage. We landed at a small Port-Town called *Xamoschi*, situated on the *South-East* Part of *Japan*. The Town lies on the *Western* Part, where there is a narrow Streight, leading *Northward* into a long Arm of the Sea, upon the *North-West* Part of which *Yedo* the Metropolis stands. At landing I shewed the Custom-House Officers my Letter from the King of *Luggnagg* to his Imperial Majesty: They knew the Seal perfectly well; it was as broad as the Palm of my Hand. The Impression was, *A King lifting up a lame Beggar from the Earth*. The Magistrates of the Town hearing of my Letter, received me as a publick Minister; they provided me with Carriages and Servants, and bore my Charges to *Yedo*, where I was admitted to an Audience, and delivered my Letter; which was opened with great Ceremony, and explained to the Emperor by an Interpreter, who gave me Notice of his Majesty's Order, that I should signify my Request; and whatever it were, it should be granted for the sake of his Royal Brother of *Luggnagg*. This Interpreter was a Person employed to transact Affairs with the *Hollanders*: He soon conjectured by my Countenance that I was an European, and therefore repeated his Majesty's Commands in *Low-Dutch*, which he spoke perfectly well. I answered, (as I had before determined) that I was a *Dutch* Merchant, shipwrecked in a very remote Country, from whence I travelled by Sea and Land to *Luggnagg*, and then took Shipping for *Japan*, where I knew my Countrymen often traded, and with some of these I hoped to get an Opportunity of returning into *Europe*: I therefore most humbly entreated his Royal Favour to give Order, that I should be conducted in Safety to *Nangasac*. To this I added another Petition, that for the sake of my Patron the King of *Luggnagg*, his Majesty would condescend to excuse my performing the Ceremony imposed on my Countrymen, of *trampling upon the Crucifix*; because I had been thrown into his Kingdom by my Misfortunes, without any Intention of trading. When this latter Petition was interpreted to the Emperor, he seemed a little surprised; and said, he believed I was the first of my Countrymen who ever made any Scruple in this Point; and that he began to doubt whether I were a real *Hollander* or no; but rather suspected I must be a Christian. However, for the Reasons I had offered, but chiefly to gratify the King of *Luggnagg*, by an uncommon Mark of his Favour, he would comply with the *singularity* of my Humour; but the Affair must be managed with Dexterity, and his Officers should be commanded to let me pass as it were by Forgetfulness. For he assured me, that if the Secret should be discovered by my Countrymen, the *Dutch*, they would cut my Throat in the Voyage. I returned my Thanks by the Interpreter for so unusual a Favour; and some Troops being at that Time on their March to *Nangasac*, the Commanding Officer had Orders to convey me safe thither, with particular Instructions about the Business of the *Crucifix*.

On the 9th Day of *June*, 1709, I arrived at *Nangasac*, after a very long and troublesome Journey. I soon fell into Company of some *Dutch* Sailors belonging to the *Amboyna* of *Amsterdam*, a stout Ship of 450 Tuns. I have lived long in *Holland*, pursuing my Studies at *Leyden*, and I spoke *Dutch* well: The Seamen soon knew from whence I came last; they were curious to enquire into my Voyages and Course of Life. I made up a Story as short and probable as I could, but concealed the greatest Part. I knew many Persons in *Holland*; I was able to invent Names for my Parents, whom I pretended to be obscure People in the Province of *Guelderland*. I would have given the Captain (one *Theodorus Vangrult*) what he pleased to ask for my Voyage to *Holland*; but, understanding I was a Surgeon, he was contented to take half the usual Rate, on Condition that I would serve him in the Way of my Calling. Before we took Shipping, I was often asked by some of the Crew, whether I had performed the Ceremony above-mentioned? I evaded the Question by general Answers, that I had satisfied the Emperor and Court in all Particulars. However, a malicious Rogue of a Skipper[1]

[1] A common seaman.

went to an Officer, and pointing to me, told him, I had not yet *trampled on the Crucifix*: But the other, who had received Instructions to let me pass, gave the Rascal twenty Strokes on the Shoulders with a Bamboo; after which I was no more troubled with such Questions.

Nothing happened worth mentioning in this Voyage. We sailed with a fair Wind to the *Cape of Good Hope,* where we staid only to take in fresh Water. On the 6th of *April* we arrived safe at *Amsterdam,* having lost only three Men by Sickness in the Voyage, and a fourth who fell from the Fore-mast into the Sea, not far from the Coast of *Guinea.* From *Amsterdam* I soon after set sail for *England* in a small Vessel belonging to that City.

On the 10th of *April,* 1710, we put in at the *Downs.* I landed the next Morning, and saw once more my Native Country after an Absence of five Years and six Months compleat. I went strait to *Redriff,* whither I arrived the same Day at two in the Afternoon, and found my Wife and Family in good Health.

The End of the Third Part

PART IV A VOYAGE TO THE COUNTRY OF THE HOUYHNHNMS

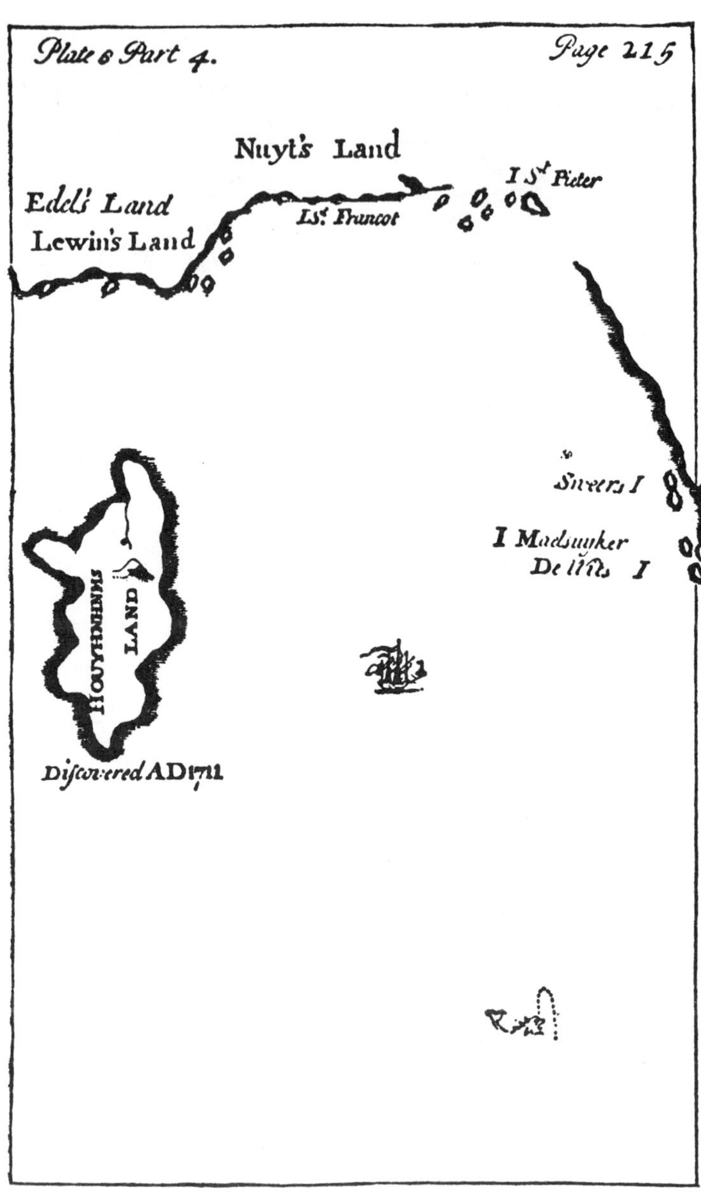
Plate 6 Part 4.
Page 215
Nuyt's Land
Edels Land
Lewin's Land
I St. Francot
I St. Pieter
Sweers I
I Madsuyker
De Wits I
HOUYHNHNMS LAND
Discovered AD1711

CHAPTER I

The Author sets out as Captain of a Ship. His Men conspire against him, confine him a long Time to his Cabbin, set him on Shore in an unknown Land. He travels up into the Country. The Yahoos, *a strange Sort of Animal, described. The Author meets two* Houyhnhnms.

I continued at home with my Wife and Children about five Months in a very happy Condition, if I could have learned the Lesson of knowing when I was well. I left my poor Wife big with Child, and accepted an advantageous Offer made me to be Captain of the *Adventure,* a stout Merchant-man of 350 Tuns: For I understood Navigation well, and being grown weary of a Surgeon's Employment at Sea, which however I could exercise upon Occasion, I took a skilful young Man of that Calling, one *Robert Purefoy,* into my Ship. We set sail from *Portsmouth* upon the 7th Day of *September,* 1710; on the 14th we met with Captain *Pocock* of *Bristol,* at *Tenariff,* who was going to the Bay of *Campeachy,* to cut Logwood. On the 16th he was parted from us by a Storm: I heard since my Return, that his Ship foundered, and none escaped, but one Cabbin-Boy. He was an honest Man, and a good Sailor, but a little too positive in his own Opinions, which was the Cause of his Destruction, as it hath been of several others. For if he had followed my Advice, he might at this Time have been safe at home with his Family as well as my self.

I had several Men died in my Ship of Calentures,[1] so that I was forced to get Recruits out of *Barbadoes,* and the *Leeward Islands,* where I touched by the Direction of the Merchants who employed me; which I had soon too much Cause to repent; for I found afterwards that most of them had been Buccaneers. I had fifty Hands on Board; and my Orders were, that I should trade with the *Indians* in the *South-Sea,* and make what Discoveries I could. These

[1] Tropical fever, accompanied by delirium: a foretelling (perhaps) of Gulliver's future enraptures.

Rogues whom I had picked up, debauched my other Men, and they all formed a Conspiracy to seize the Ship and secure me; which they did one Morning, rushing into my Cabbin, and binding me Hand and Foot, threatening to throw me overboard, if I offered to stir. I told them, I was their Prisoner, and would submit. This they made me swear to do, and then unbound me, only fastening one of my Legs with a Chain near my Bed; and placed a Centry at my Door with his Piece charged, who was commanded to shoot me dead if I attempted my Liberty. They sent me down Victuals and Drink, and took the Government of the Ship to themselves. Their Design was to turn Pirates, and plunder the *Spaniards,* which they could not do, till they got more Men. But first they resolved to sell the Goods in the Ship, and then go to *Madagascar* for Recruits, several among them having died since my Confinement. They sailed many Weeks, and traded with the *Indians*; but I knew not what Course they took, being kept close Prisoner in my Cabbin, and expecting nothing less than to be murdered, as they often threatened me.

Upon the 9th Day of *May,* 1711, one *James Welch* came down to my Cabbin; and said he had Orders from the Captain to set me ashore. I expostulated with him, but in vain; neither would he so much as tell me who their new Captain was. They forced me into the Long-boat, letting me put on my best Suit of Cloaths, which were as good as new, and a small Bundle of Linnen, but no Arms except my Hanger; and they were so civil as not to search my Pockets, into which I conveyed what Money I had, with some other little Necessaries. They rowed about a League; and then set me down on a Strand. I desired them to tell me what Country it was: They all swore, they knew no more than my self, but said, that the Captain (as they called him) was resolved, after they had sold the Lading, to get rid of me in the first Place where they discovered Land. They pushed off immediately, advising me to make haste, for fear of being overtaken by the Tide; and bade me farewell.

In this desolate Condition I advanced forward, and soon got upon firm Ground, where I sat down on a Bank to rest my self, and consider what I had best to do. When I was a little refreshed, I went up into the Country, resolving to deliver my self to the first Savages I should meet; and purchase my Life from them by some Bracelets, Glass Rings, and other Toys, which Sailors usually provide themselves with in those Voyages, and whereof I had some about me:

The Land was divided by long Rows of Trees, not regularly planted, but naturally growing; there was great Plenty of Grass, and several Fields of Oats. I walked very circumspectly for fear of being surprised, or suddenly shot with an Arrow from behind, or on either Side. I fell into a beaten Road, where I saw many Tracks of human Feet, and some of Cows, but most of Horses. At last I beheld several Animals in a Field, and one or two of the same Kind sitting in Trees. Their Shape was very singular, and deformed, which a little discomposed me, so that I lay down behind a Thicket to observe them better. Some of them coming forward near the Place where I lay, gave me an Opportunity of distinctly marking their Form. Their Heads and Breasts were covered with a thick Hair, some frizzled and others lank; they had Beards like Goats, and a long Ridge of Hair down their Backs, and the fore Parts of their Legs and Feet; but the rest of their Bodies were bare, so that I might see their Skins, which were of a brown Buff Colour. They had no Tails, nor any Hair at all on their Buttocks, except about the *Anus*; which, I presume Nature had placed there to defend them as they sat on the Ground; for this Posture they used, as well as lying down, and often stood on their hind Feet. They climbed high Trees, as nimbly as a Squirrel, for they had strong extended Claws before and behind, terminating in sharp Points, and hooked. They would often spring, and bound, and leap with prodigious Agility. The Females were not so large as the Males; they had long lank Hair on their Heads, and only a Sort of Down on the rest of their Bodies, except about the *Anus*, and *Pudenda*. Their Dugs hung between their fore Feet, and often reached almost to the Ground as they walked. The Hair of both Sexes was of several Colours, brown, red, black and yellow. Upon the whole, I never beheld in all my Travels so disagreeable an Animal, or one against which I naturally conceived so strong an Antipathy. So that thinking I had seen enough, full of Contempt and Aversion, I got up and pursued the beaten Road, hoping it might direct me to the Cabbin of some *Indian*. I had not gone far when I met one of these Creatures full in my Way, and coming up directly to me. The ugly Monster, when he saw me, distorted several Ways every Feature of his Visage, and stared as at an Object he had never seen before; then approaching nearer, lifted up his fore Paw, whether out of Curiosity or Mischief, I could not tell: But I drew my Hanger, and gave him a good Blow with the flat Side of it; for I durst not strike him with the Edge, fearing the Inhabitants might be provoked against me, if they should come to know, that I had killed or maimed any of their Cattle. When the Beast felt the Smart, he drew back, and roared so loud, that a Herd of at least forty came flocking about me from the next Field, howling and making odious Faces; but I ran to the Body of a Tree, and leaning my Back against it, kept them off, by waving my Hanger. Several of this cursed Brood getting hold of the Branches behind, leaped up into the Tree, from whence they began to discharge their Excrements on my Head: However, I escaped pretty well, by sticking close to the Stem of the Tree, but was almost stifled with the Filth, which fell about me on every Side.

In the Midst of this Distress, I observed them all to run away on a sudden as fast as they could; at which I ventured to leave the Tree, and pursue the Road, wondering what it was that could put them into this Fright. But looking on my Left-Hand, I saw a Horse walking softly in the Field; which my Persecutors having sooner discovered, was the Cause of their Flight. The Horse started a little when he came near me, but soon recovering himself, looked full in my Face with manifest Tokens of Wonder: He viewed my Hands and Feet, walking round me several times. I would have pursued my Journey, but he placed himself directly in the Way, yet looking with a very mild Aspect, never offering the least Violence. We stood gazing at each other for some time; at last I took the Boldness, to reach my Hand towards his Neck, with a Design to stroak it; using the common Style and Whistle of Jockies when they are going to handle a strange Horse. But, this Animal seeming to receive my Civilities with Disdain, shook his Head, and bent his Brows, softly raising up his Left Fore-Foot to remove my Hand. Then he neighed three or four times, but in so different a Cadence, that I almost began to think he was speaking to himself in some Language of his own.

While He and I were thus employed, another Horse came up; who applying himself to the first in a very formal Manner, they gently struck each others Right Hoof before, neighing several times by Turns, and varying the Sound, which seemed to be almost articulate. They went some Paces off, as if it were to confer together, walking Side by Side, backward and forward, like Persons deliberating upon some Affair of Weight; but often turning their Eyes towards me, as it were to watch that I might not escape. I was amazed to see such Actions and Behaviour in Brute Beasts; and concluded with myself, that if the Inhabitants of this Country were endued with a proportionable Degree of Reason, they must needs be the wisest People upon Earth. This Thought gave me so much Comfort, that I resolved to go forward untill I could discover some House or Village, or meet with any of the Natives; leaving the two Horses to discourse together as they pleased. But the first, who was a Dapple-Grey, observing me to steal off, neighed after me in so expressive a Tone, that I fancied myself to understand what he meant; whereupon I turned back, and came near him, to expect his farther Commands; but concealing my Fear as much as I could; for I began to be in some Pain, how this Adventure might terminate; and the Reader will easily believe I did not much like my present Situation.

The two Horses came up close to me, looking with great Earnestness upon my Face and Hands. The grey Steed rubbed my Hat all round with his Right Fore-hoof, and discomposed it so much, that I was forced to adjust it better, by taking it off, and settling it again; whereat both he and his Companion (who was a brown Bay) appeared to be much surprized; the latter felt the Lappet of my Coat, and finding it to hang loose about me, they both looked with new Signs of Wonder. He stroaked my Right Hand, seeming to admire the Softness, and Colour; but he squeezed it so hard between his Hoof and his Pastern, that I was forced to roar; after which they both touched me with all possible Tenderness. They were under great Perplexity about my Shoes and Stockings, which they felt very often, neighing to each other, and using various Gestures, not unlike those of a Philosopher, when he would attempt to solve some new and difficult Phænomenon.

Upon the whole, the Behaviour of these Animals was so orderly and rational, so acute and judicious, that I at last concluded, they must needs be Magicians, who had thus metamorphosed themselves upon some Design; and seeing a Stranger in the Way, were resolved to divert themselves with him; or perhaps were really amazed at the Sight of a Man so very different in Habit, Feature and Complexion from those who might probably live in so remote a Climate. Upon the Strength of this Reasoning, I ventured to address them in the following Manner: Gentlemen, if you be Conjurers, as I have good Cause to believe, you can understand any Language; therefore I make bold to let your Worships know, that

I am a poor distressed *Englishman*, driven by his Misfortunes upon your Coast; and I entreat one of you, to let me ride upon his Back, as if he were a real Horse, to some House or Village, where I can be relieved. In return of which Favour, I will make you a Present of this Knife and Bracelet, (taking them out of my Pocket.) The two Creatures stood silent while I spoke, seeming to listen with great Attention; and when I had ended, they neighed frequently towards each other, as if they were engaged in serious Conversation. I plainly observed, that their Language expressed the Passions very well, and the Words might with little Pains be resolved into an Alphabet more easily than the *Chinese*.

I could frequently distinguish the Word *Yahoo*, which was repeated by each of them several times; and although it were impossible for me to conjecture what it meant, yet while the two Horses were busy in Conversation, I endeavoured to practice this word upon my Tongue; and as soon as they were silent, I boldly pronounced *Yahoo* in a loud Voice, imitating, at the same time, as near as I could, the Neighing of a Horse; at which they were both visibly surprized, and the Grey repeated the same Word twice, as if he meant to teach me the right Accent, wherein I spoke after him as well as I could, and found myself perceivably to improve every time, although very far from any Degree of Perfection. Then the Bay tried me with a second Word, much harder to be pronounced; but reducing it to the *English Orthography*, may be spelt thus, *Houyhnhnm*.[2] I did not succeed in this so well as the former, but after two or three farther Trials, I had better Fortune; and they both appeared amazed at my Capacity.

After some farther Discourse, which I then conjectured might relate to me, the two Friends took their Leaves, with the same Compliment of striking each other's Hoof; and the Grey made me Signs that I should walk before him; wherein I thought it prudent to comply, till I could find a better Director. When I offered to slacken my Pace, he would cry *Hhuun, Hhuun*; I guessed his Meaning, and gave him to understand, as well as I could, that I was weary, and not able to walk faster; upon which, he would stand a while to let me rest.

[2] The whinny of a horse; perhaps best pronounced, *Whin-num*.

CHAPTER II

The Author conducted by a Houyhnhnm *to his house. The House described. The Author's Reception. The Food of the* Houyhnhnms. *The Author in Distress for Want of Meat, is at last relieved. His Manner of feeding in that Country.*

Having travelled about three Miles, we came to a long Kind of Building, made of Timber, stuck in the Ground, and wattled a-cross; the Roof was low, and covered with Straw. I now began to be a little comforted; and took out some Toys, which Travellers usually carry for Presents to the Savage *Indians* of *America* and other Parts, in hopes the People of the House would be thereby encouraged to receive me kindly. The Horse made me a Sign to go in first; it was a large Room with a smooth Clay Floor, and a Rack and Manger extending the whole Length on one Side. There were three Nags, and two Mares, not eating, but some of them sitting down upon their Hams, which I very much wondered at; but wondered more to see the rest employed in domestick Business: The last seemed but ordinary Cattle; however this confirmed my first Opinion, that a People who could so far civilize brute Animals, must needs excel in Wisdom all the Nations of the World. The Grey came in just after, and thereby prevented any ill Treatment, which the others might have given me. He neighed to them several times in a Style of Authority, and received Answers.

Beyond this Room there were three others, reaching the Length of the House, to which you passed through three Doors, opposite to each other, in the Manner of a Vista: We went through the second Room towards the third; here the Grey walked in first, beckoning me to attend: I waited in the second Room, and got ready my Presents, for the Master and Mistress of the House: They were two Knives, three Bracelets of false Pearl, a small Looking

Glass and a Bead Necklace. The Horse neighed three or four Times, and I waited to hear some answers in a human Voice, but I heard no other Returns than in the same Dialect, only one or two a little shriller than his. I began to think that this House must belong to some Person of great Note among them, because there appeared so much Ceremony before I could gain Admittance. But, that a Man of Quality should be served all by Horses, was Beyond my Comprehension. I feared my Brain was disturbed by my Sufferings and Misfortunes: I roused my self, and looked about me in the Room where I was left alone; this was furnished as the first, only after a more elegant Manner. I rubbed my Eyes often, but the same Objects still occurred. I pinched my Arms and Sides, to awake my self, hoping I might be in a Dream. I then absolutely concluded, that all these Appearances could be nothing else but Necromancy and Magick. But I had no Time to pursue these Reflections; for the Grey Horse came to the Door, and made me a Sign to follow him into the third Room; where I saw a very comely Mare, together with a Colt and Fole, sitting on their Haunches, upon Mats of Straw, not unartfully made, and perfectly neat and clean.

The Mare soon after my Entrance, rose from her Mat, and coming up close, after having nicely observed my Hands and Face, gave me a most contemptuous Look; then turning to the Horse, I heard the Word *Yahoo* often repeated betwixt them; the meaning of which Word I could not then comprehend, although it were the first I had learned to pronounce; but I was soon better informed, to my everlasting Mortification: For the Horse beckoning to me with his Head, and repeating the Word *Hhuun, Hhuun*, as he did upon the Road, which I understood was to attend him, led me out into a kind of Court, where was another Building at some Distance from the House. Here we entered, and I saw three of those detestable Creatures, which I first met after my landing, feeding upon Roots, and the Flesh of some Animals, which I afterwards found to be that of Asses and Dogs, and now and then a Cow dead by Accident or Disease. They were all tied by the Neck with strong Wyths, fastened to a Beam; they held their Food between the Claws of their fore Feet, and tore it with their Teeth.

The Master Horse ordered a Sorrel Nag, one of his Servants, to untie the largest of these Animals, and take him into a Yard. The Beast and I were brought close together; and our Countenances diligently compared, both by Master and Servant, who thereupon repeated several Times the Word *Yahoo*. My Horror and Astonishment are not to be described, when I observed, in this abominable Animal, a perfect human Figure; the Face of it indeed was flat and broad, the Nose depressed, the Lips large, and the Mouth wide: But these Differences are common to all savage Nations, where the Lineaments of the Countenance are distorted by the Natives suffering their Infants to lie grovelling on the Earth, or by carrying them on their Backs, nuzzling with their Face against the Mother's Shoulders. The Fore-feet of the *Yahoo* differed from my Hands in nothing else, but the Length of the Nails, the Coarseness and Brownness of the Palms, and the Hairiness on the Backs. There was the same Resemblance between our Feet, with the same Differences, which I knew very well, although the Horses did not, because of my Shoes and Stockings; the same in every Part of our Bodies, except as to Hairiness and Colour, which I have already described.

The great Difficulty that seemed to stick with the two Horses, was, to see the rest of my Body so very different from that of a *Yahoo*, for which I was obliged to my Cloaths, whereof they had no Conception: The Sorrel Nag offered me a Root, which he held (after their Manner, as we shall describe in its proper Place) between his Hoof and Pastern; I took it in my Hand, and having smelt it, returned it to him again as civilly as I could. He brought out of the *Yahoo's* Kennel a Piece of Ass's Flesh, but it smelt so offensively that I turned from it with loathing; he then threw it to the *Yahoo*, by whom it was greedily devoured. He afterwards shewed me a Wisp of Hay, and a Fettlock full of Oats; but I shook my Head, to signify that neither of these were Food for me. And indeed, I now apprehended, that I must absolutely starve, if I did not get to some of my own Species: For as to those filthy *Yahoos*, although there were few greater Lovers of Mankind, at that time, than myself; yet I confess I never saw any sensitive Being so detestable on all Accounts; and the more I came near them, the more hateful they grew, while I stayed in that Country. This the Master Horse observed by my Behaviour, and therefore sent the *Yahoo* back to his Kennel. He then put his Fore-hoof to his Mouth, at which I was much surprized, although he did it with Ease, and with a Motion that appear'd perfectly natural; and made other Signs to know what I would eat; but I could not return him such an Answer as he was able to apprehend; and if he had understood me, I did not see how it was possible to contrive any way for finding myself Nourishment. While we were thus engaged, I observed a Cow passing by; whereupon I pointed to her, and expressed a Desire to let me go and milk her. This had its Effect; for he led me back into the House, and ordered a Mare-servant to open a Room, where a good Store of Milk lay in Earthen and Wooden Vessels, after a very orderly and cleanly Manner. She gave me a large Bowl full, of which I drank very heartily, and found myself well refreshed.

About Noon I saw coming towards the House a Kind of Vehicle, drawn like a Sledge by four *Yahoos*. There was in it an old Steed, who seemed to be of Quality; he alighted with his Hind-feet forward, having by Accident got a Hurt in his Left Fore-foot. He came to dine with our Horse, who received him with great Civility. They dined in the best Room, and had Oats boiled in Milk for the second Course, which the old Horse eat warm, but the rest cold. Their Mangers were placed circular in the Middle of the Room, and divided into several Partitions, round which they sat on their Haunches upon Bosses of Straw. In the Middle was a large Rack with Angles answering to every Partition of the Manger. So that each Horse and Mare eat their own Hay, and their own Mash of Oats and Milk, with much Decency and Regularity. The Behaviour of the young Colt and Fole appeared very modest; and that of the Master and Mistress extremely chearful and complaisant to their Guest. The Grey ordered me to stand by him; and much Discourse passed between him and his Friend concerning me, as I found by the Stranger's often looking on me, and the frequent Repetition of the Word *Yahoo*.

I happened to wear my Gloves; which the Master Grey observing, seemed perplexed; discovering Signs of Wonder what I had done to my Fore-feet; he put his Hoof three or four times to them, as if he would signify, that I should reduce them to their former Shape, which I presently did, pulling off both my Gloves, and putting them into my Pocket. This occasioned farther Talk, and I saw the Company was pleased with my Behaviour, whereof I soon found the good Effects. I was ordered to speak the few Words I understood; and while they were at Dinner, the Master taught me the Names for Oats, Milk, Fire, Water, and some others; which I could readily pronounce after him; having from my Youth a great Facility in learning Languages.

When Dinner was done, the Master Horse took me aside, and by Signs and Words made me understand the Concern he was in, that

I had nothing to eat. Oats in their Tongue are called *Hlunnh.* This Word I pronounced two or three times; for although I had refused them at first, yet upon second Thoughts, I considered that I could contrive to make a Kind of Bread, which might be sufficient with Milk to keep me alive, till I could make my Escape to some other Country, and to Creatures of my own Species. The Horse immediately ordered a white Mare-servant of his Family to bring me a good Quantity of Oats in a Sort of wooden Tray. These I heated before the Fire as well as I could, and rubbed them till the Husks came off, which I made a shift to winnow from the Grain; I ground and beat them between two Stones, then took Water, and made them into a Paste or Cake, which I toasted at the Fire, and eat warm with Milk. It was at first a very insipid Diet, although common enough in many Parts of *Europe,* but grew tolerable by Time; and having been often reduced to hard Fare in my Life, this was not the first Experiment I had made how easily Nature is satisfied. And I cannot but observe, that I never had one Hour's Sickness, while I staid in this Island. It is true, I sometimes made a shift to catch a Rabbet, or Bird, by Springes made of *Yahoos* Hairs; and I often gathered wholesome Herbs, which I boiled, or eat as Salades with my Bread; and now and then, for a Rarity, I made a little Butter, and drank the Whey. I was at first at a great Loss for Salt; but Custom soon reconciled the Want of it; and I am confident that the frequent Use of Salt among us is an Effect of Luxury, and was first introduced only as a Provocative to Drink; except where it is necessary for preserving of Flesh in long Voyages, or in Places remote from great Markets. For we observe no Animal to be fond of it but Man:[1] And as to myself, when I left this Country, it was a great while before I could endure the Taste of it in any thing that I eat.

This is enough to say upon the Subject of my Dyet, wherewith other Travellers fill their Books, as if the Readers were personally concerned, whether we fare well or ill. However, it was necessary to mention this Matter, lest the World should think it impossible that I could find Sustenance for three Years in such a Country, and among such Inhabitants.

When it grew towards Evening, the Master Horse ordered a Place for me to lodge in; it was but Six Yards from the House, and

[1] Gulliver's (not necessarily Swift's) error: many animals are very fond of salt.

separated from the Stable of the *Yahoos*. Here I got some Straw, and covering myself with my own Cloaths, slept very sound. But I was in a short time better accommodated, as the Reader shall know hereafter, when I come to treat more particularly about my Way of living.

CHAPTER III

The Author studious to learn the Language, the Houyhnhnm *his Master assists in teaching him. The Language described. Several* Houyhnhnms *of Quality come out of Curiosity to see the Author. He gives his Master a short Account of his* Voyage.

My principal Endeavour was to learn the Language, which my Master (for so I shall henceforth call him) and his Children, and every Servant of his House were desirous to teach me. For they looked upon it as a Prodigy, that a brute Animal should discover such Marks of a rational Creature. I pointed to every thing, and enquired the Name of it, which I wrote down in my *Journal Book* when I was alone, and corrected my bad Accent, by desiring those of the Family to pronounce it often. In this Employment, a Sorrel Nag, one of the under Servants, was very ready to assist me.

In speaking, they pronounce through the Nose and Throat, and their Language approaches nearest to the *High Dutch* or *German*, of any I know in *Europe*; but is much more graceful and significant. The Emperor *Charles* V. made almost the same Observation, when he said, That if he were to speak to his Horse, it should be in *High Dutch*.[1]

The Curiosity and Impatience of my Master were so great, that he spent many Hours of his Leisure to instruct me. He was convinced (as he afterwards told me) that I must be a *Yahoo*, but my

[1] Charles was reputed to have said he would address his God in Spanish, his mistress in Italian, and his horse in German.

Teachableness, Civility and Cleanliness astonished him; which were Qualities altogether so opposite to those Animals. He was most perplexed about my Cloaths, reasoning sometimes with himself, whether they were a Part of my Body; for I never pulled them off till the Family were asleep, and got them on before they waked in the Morning. My Master was eager to learn from whence I came; how I acquired those Appearances of Reason, which I discovered in all my Actions; and to know my Story from my own Mouth, which he hoped he should soon do by the great Proficiency I made in learning and pronouncing their Words and Sentences. To help my Memory, I formed all I learned into the *English* Alphabet, and writ the Words down with the Translations. This last, after some time, I ventured to do in my Master's Presence. It cost me much Trouble to explain to him what I was doing; for the Inhabitants have not the least Idea of Books or Literature.

In about ten Weeks time I was able to understand most of his Questions; and in three Months could give him some tolerable Answers. He was extremely curious to know from what Part of the Country I came, and how I was taught to imitate a rational Creature; because the *Yahoos*, (whom he saw I exactly resembled in my Head, Hands and Face, that were only visible,) with some Appearance of Cunning, and the strongest Disposition to Mischief, were observed to be the most unteachable of all Brutes. I answered; that I came over the Sea, from a far Place, with many others of my own Kind, in a great hollow Vessel made of the Bodies of Trees: That, my Companions forced me to land on this Coast, and then left me to shift for myself. It was with some Difficulty, and by the Help of many Signs, that I brought him to understand me. He replied, That I must needs be mistaken, or that I *said the thing which was not*. (For they have no Word in their Language to express Lying or Falshood.) He knew it was impossible that there could be a Country beyond the Sea, or that a Parcel of Brutes could move a wooden Vessel whither they pleased upon Water. He was sure no *Houyhnhnm* alive could make such a Vessel, or would trust *Yahoos* to manage it.

The Word *Houyhnhnm*, in their Tongue, signifies a *Horse*; and in its Etymology, *the Perfection of Nature*. I told my Master, that I was at a Loss for Expression, but would improve as fast as I could; and hoped in a short time I should be able to tell him Wonders: He was pleased to direct his own Mare, his Colt and Fole, and the

Servants of the Family to take all Opportunities of instructing me; and every Day for two or three Hours, he was at the same Pains himself: Several Horses and Mares of Quality in the Neighbourhood came often to our House, upon the Report spread of a wonderful *Yahoo*, that could speak like a *Houyhnhnm*, and seemed in his Words and Actions to discover some Glimmerings of Reason. These delighted to converse with me; they put many Questions, and received such Answers, as I was able to return. By all which Advantages, I made so great a Progress, that in five Months from my Arrival, I understood whatever was spoke, and could express myself tolerably well.

The *Houyhnhnms* who came to visit my Master, out of a Design of seeing and talking with me, could hardly believe me to be a right *Yahoo*, because my Body had a different Covering from others of my Kind. They were astonished to observe me without the usual Hair or Skin, except on my Head, Face and Hands: but I discovered that Secret to my Master, upon an Accident, which happened about a Fortnight before.

I have already told the Reader, that every Night when the Family were gone to Bed, it was my Custom to strip and cover myself with my Cloaths: It happened one Morning early, that my Master sent for me, by the Sorrel Nag, who was his Valet; when he came, I was fast asleep, my Cloaths fallen off on one Side, and my Shirt above my Waste. I awaked at the Noise he made, and observed him to deliver his Message in some Disorder; after which he went to my Master, and in a great Fright gave him a very confused Account of what he had seen: This I presently discovered; for going as soon as I was dressed, to pay my Attendance upon his Honour, he asked me the Meaning of what his Servant had reported; that I was not the same Thing when I slept as I appeared to be at other times; that his Valet assured him, some Part of me was white, some yellow, at least not so white, and some brown.

I had hitherto concealed the Secret of my Dress, in order to distinguish myself as much as possible, from that cursed Race of *Yahoos*; but now I found it in vain to do so any longer. Besides, I considered that my Cloaths and Shoes would soon wear out, which already were in a declining Condition, and must be supplied by some Contrivance from the Hides of *Yahoos*, or other Brutes; whereby the whole Secret would be known. I therefore told my Master, that in the Country from whence I came, those of my

Kind always covered their Bodies with the Hairs of certain Animals prepared by Art, as well for Decency, as to avoid Inclemencies of Air both hot and cold; of which, as to my own Person I would give him immediate Conviction, if he pleased to command me; only desiring his Excuse, if I did not expose those Parts that Nature taught us to conceal. He said, my Discourse was all very strange, but especially the last Part; for he could not understand why Nature should teach us to conceal what Nature had given. That neither himself nor Family were ashamed of any Parts of their Bodies; but however I might do as I pleased. Whereupon, I first unbuttoned my Coat, and pulled it off. I did the same with my Waste-coat; I drew off my Shoes, Stockings and Breeches. I let my Shirt down to my Waste, and drew up the Bottom, fastening it like a Girdle about my Middle to hide my Nakedness.

My Master observed the whole Performance with great Signs of Curiosity and Admiration. He took up all my Cloaths in his Pastern, one Piece after another, and examined them diligently; he then stroaked my Body very gently, and looked round me several Times; after which he said, it was plain I must be a perfect *Yahoo*; but that I differed very much from the rest of my Species, in the Whiteness, and Smoothness of my Skin, my want of Hair in several Parts of my Body, the Shape and Shortness of my Claws behind and before, and my Affectation of walking continually on my two hinder Feet. He desired to see no more; and gave me leave to put on my Cloaths again, for I was shuddering with Cold.

I expressed my Uneasiness at his giving me so often the Appellation of *Yahoo*, an odious Animal, for which I had so utter an Hatred and Contempt. I begged he would forbear applying that Word to me, and take the same Order in his Family, and among his Friends whom he suffered to see me. I requested likewise, that the Secret of my having a false Covering to my Body might be known to none but himself, at least as long as my present Cloathing should last: For as to what the Sorrel Nag his Valet had observed, his Honour might command him to conceal it.

All this my Master very graciously consented to; and thus the Secret was kept till my Cloaths began to wear out, which I was forced to supply by several Contrivances, that shall hereafter be mentioned. In the mean Time, he desired I would go on with my utmost Diligence to learn their Language, because he was more astonished at my Capacity for Speech and Reason, than at the

Figure of my Body, whether it were covered or no; adding, that he waited with some Impatience to hear the Wonders which I promised to tell him.

From thenceforward he doubled the Pains he had been at to instruct me; he brought me into all Company, and made them treat me with Civility, because, as he told them privately, this would put me into good Humour, and make me more diverting.

Every Day when I waited on him, beside the Trouble he was at in teaching, he would ask me several Questions concerning my self, which I answered as well as I could; and by those Means he had already received some general Ideas, although very imperfect. It would be tedious to relate the several Steps, by which I advanced to a more regular Conversation: But the first Account I gave of my self in any Order and Length, was to this Purpose:

That, I came from a very far Country, as I already had attempted to tell him, with about fifty more of my own Species; that we travelled upon the Seas, in a great hollow Vessel made of Wood, and larger than his Honour's House. I described the Ship to him in the best Terms I could; and explained by the Help of my Handkerchief displayed, how it was driven forward by the Wind. That, upon a Quarrel among us, I was set on Shoar on this Coast, where I walked forward without knowing whither, till he delivered me from the Persecution of those execrable *Yahoos*. He asked me, Who made the Ship, and how it was possible that the *Houyhnhnms* of my Country would leave it to the Management of Brutes? My Answer was, that I durst proceed no farther in my Relation, unless he would give me his Word and Honour that he would not be offended; and then I would tell him the Wonders I had so often promised. He agreed; and I went on by assuring him, that the Ship was made by Creatures like myself, who in all the Countries I had travelled, as well as in my own, were the only governing, rational Animals; and that upon my Arrival hither, I was as much astonished to see the *Houyhnhnms* act like rational Beings, as he or his Friends could be in finding some Marks of Reason in a Creature he was pleased to call a *Yahoo*; to which I owned my Resemblance in every Part, but could not account for their degenerate and brutal Nature. I said farther, That if good Fortune ever restored me to my native Country, to relate my Travels hither, as I resolved to do; every Body would believe that I *said the Thing which was not*: that I invented the Story out of my own Head:

And with all possible Respect to Himself, his Family, and Friends, and under his Promise of not being offended, our Countrymen would hardly think it probable, that a *Houyhnhnm* should be the presiding Creature of a Nation, and a *Yahoo* the Brute.

CHAPTER IV

The Houyhnhnms *Notion of Truth and Falsehood. The Author's Discourse disapproved by his Master. The Author gives a more particular* Account *of himself, and the Accidents of his* Voyage.

My Master heard me with great Appearances of Uneasiness in his Countenance; because *Doubting* or *not believing*, are so little known in this Country, that the Inhabitants cannot tell how to behave themselves under such Circumstances. And I remember in frequent Discourses with my Master concerning the Nature of Manhood, in other Parts of the World; having Occasion to talk of *Lying*, and *false Representation*, it was with much Difficulty that he comprehended what I meant; although he had otherwise a most acute Judgment. For he argued thus; That the Use of Speech was to make us understand one another, and to receive Information of Facts; now if any one *said the Thing which was not*, these Ends were defeated; because I cannot properly be said to understand him; and I am so far from receiving Information, that he leaves me worse than in Ignorance; for I am led to believe a Thing *Black* when it is *White*, and *Short* when it is *Long*. And these were all the Notions he had concerning that Faculty of *Lying*, so perfectly well understood, and so universally practised among human Creatures.

To return from this Digression; when I asserted that the *Yahoos* were the only governing Animals in my Country, which my Master said was altogether past his Conception, he desired to know, whether we had *Houyhnhnms* among us, and what was their Employment: I told him, we had great Numbers; that in Summer they grazed in the Fields, and in Winter were kept in Houses, with Hay and Oats, where *Yahoo* Servants were employed to rub their Skins smooth, comb their Manes, pick their Feet, serve them with Food, and make their Beds. I understand you well, said my Master; it is now very plain from all you have spoken, that whatever Share of Reason the *Yahoos* pretend to, the *Houyhnhnms* are your Masters; I heartily wish our *Yahoos* would be so tractable. I begged his Honour would please to excuse me from proceeding any farther, because I was very certain that the Account he expected from me would be highly displeasing. But he insisted in commanding me to let him know the best and the worst: I told him he should be obeyed. I owned, that the *Houyhnhnms* among us, whom we called *Horses*, were the most generous and comely Animal we had; that they excelled in Strength and Swiftness; and when they belonged to Persons of Quality, employed in Travelling, Racing, and drawing Chariots, they were treated with much Kindness and Care, till they fell into Diseases, or became foundered in the Feet; but then they were sold, and used to all kind of Drudgery till they died; after which their Skins were stripped and sold for what they were worth, and their Bodies left to be devoured by Dogs and Birds of Prey. But the common Race of Horses had not so good Fortune, being kept by Farmers and Carriers, and other mean People, who put them to greater Labour, and feed them worse. I described as well as I could, our Way of Riding; the Shape and Use of a Bridle, a Saddle, a Spur, and a Whip; of Harness and Wheels. I added, that we fastened Plates of a certain hard Substance called *Iron* at the Bottom of their Feet, to preserve their Hoofs from being broken by the Stony Ways on which we often travelled.

My Master, after some Expressions of great Indignation, wondered how we dared to venture upon a *Houyhnhnm's* Back; for he was sure, that the weakest Servant in his House would be able to shake off the strongest *Yahoo*; or by lying down, and rouling upon his Back, squeeze the Brute to Death. I answered, That our Horses were trained up from three or four Years old to the several Uses we intended them for; That if any of them proved intolerably vicious, they were employed for Carriages; that they were severely beaten while they were young for any mischievous Tricks: That the Males, designed for the common Use of Riding or Draught, were generally *castrated* about two Years after their Birth, to take down their Spirits, and make them more tame and gentle: That they were indeed sensible of Rewards and Punishments; but his Honour would please to consider, that they had not the least Tincture of Reason any more than the *Yahoos* in this Country.

It put me to the Pains of many Circumlocutions to give my Master a right Idea of what I spoke; for their Language doth not abound in Variety of Words, because their Wants and Passions are fewer than among us. But it is impossible to express his noble Resentment at our savage Treatment of the *Houyhnhnm* Race; particularly after I had explained the Manner and Use of *Castrating* Horses among us, to hinder them from propagating their Kind, and to render them more servile. He said, if it were possible there could be any Country where *Yahoos* alone were endued with Reason, they certainly must be the governing Animal, because Reason will in Time always prevail against Brutal Strength. But, considering the Frame of our Bodies, and especially of mine, he thought no Creature of equal Bulk was so ill-contrived, for employing that Reason in the common Offices of Life; whereupon he desired to know whether those among whom I lived, resembled me or the *Yahoos* of his Country. I assured him, that I was as well shaped as most of my Age; but the younger and the Females were much more soft and tender, and the Skins of the latter generally as white as Milk. He said, I differed indeed from other *Yahoos*, being much more cleanly, and not altogether so deformed; but in point of real Advantage, he thought I differed for the worse. That my Nails were of no Use either to my fore or hinder Feet: As to my fore Feet, he could not properly call them by that Name, for he never observed me to walk upon them; that they were too soft to bear the Ground; that I generally went with them uncovered, neither was the Covering I sometimes wore on them, of the same Shape, or so strong as that on my Feet behind. That I could not walk with any Security; for if either of my hinder Feet slipped, I must inevitably fall. He then began to find fault with other Parts of my Body; the Flatness of my Face, the Prominence of my Nose, my Eyes placed directly in Front, so that I could not look on either Side without turning my Head: That I was not able to feed my self, without lifting one of my fore Feet to my Mouth: And therefore Nature had placed those Joints to answer that Necessity. He knew not what could be the Use of those several Clefts and Divisions in my Feet behind; that these were too soft to bear the

Hardness and Sharpness of Stones without a Covering made from the Skin of some other Brute; that my whole Body wanted a Fence against Heat and Cold, which I was forced to put on and off every Day with Tediousness and Trouble. And lastly, that he observed every Animal in this Country naturally to abhor the *Yahoos*, whom the Weaker avoided, and the Stronger drove from them. So that supposing us to have the Gift of Reason, he could not see how it were possible to cure that natural Antipathy which every Creature discovered against us; nor consequently, how we could tame and render them serviceable. However, he would (as he said) debate the Matter no farther, because he was more desirous to know my own Story, the Country where I was born, and the several Actions and Events of my Life before I came hither.

I assured him, how extreamly desirous I was that he should be satisfied in every Point; but I doubted much, whether it would be possible for me to explain my self on several Subjects whereof his Honour could have no Conception, because I saw nothing in his Country to which I could resemble them. That however, I would do my best, and strive to express my self by Similitudes, humbly desiring his Assistance when I wanted proper Words; which he was pleased to promise me.

I said, my Birth was of honest Parents, in an Island called *England*, which was remote from this Country, as many Days Journey as the strongest of his Honour's Servants could travel in the Annual Course of the Sun. That I was bred a Surgeon, whose Trade it is to cure Wounds and Hurts in the body, got by Accident or Violence. That my Country was governed by a Female Man, whom we called a *Queen*. That I left it to get Riches, whereby I might maintain my self and Family when I should return. That in my last Voyage, I was Commander of the Ship and had about fifty *Yahoos* under me, many of which died at Sea, and I was forced to supply them by others picked out from several Nations. That our Ship was twice in Danger of being sunk; the first Time by a great Storm, and the second, by striking against a Rock. Here my Master interposed, by asking me, How I could persuade Strangers out of different Countries to venture with me, after the Losses I had sustained, and the Hazards I had run. I said, they were Fellows of desperate Fortunes, forced to fly from the Places of their Birth, on Account of their Poverty or their Crimes. Some were undone by Law-suits; others spent all they had in Drinking, Whoring and Gaming; others fled for Treason; many for Murder, Theft, Poysoning, Robbery, Perjury, Forgery, Coining false Money; for committing Rapes or Sodomy; for flying from their Colours, or deserting to the enemy; and most of them had broken Prison. None of these durst return to their native Countries for fear of being hanged, or of starving in a Jail; and therefore were under a Necessity of seeking a Livelihood in other Places.

During this Discourse, my Master was pleased often to interrupt me. I had made Use of many Circumlocutions in describing to him the Nature of the several Crimes, for which most of our Crew had been forced to fly their Country. This Labour took up several Days Conversation before he was able to comprehend me. He was wholly at a Loss to know what could be the Use or Necessity of practising those Vices. To clear up which I endeavoured to give him some Ideas of the Desire of Power and Riches; of the terrible Effects of Lust, Intemperance, Malice, and Envy. All this I was forced to define and describe by putting of Cases, and making Suppositions. After which, like one whose Imagination was struck with something never seen or heard of before, he would lift up his Eyes with Amazement and Indignation. Power, Government, War, Law, Punishment, and a Thousand other Things had no Terms, wherein that Language could express them; which made the Difficulty almost insuperable to give my Master any Conception of what I meant: But being of an excellent Understanding, much improved by Contemplation and Converse, he at last arrived at a competent Knowledge of what human Nature in our Parts of the World is capable to perform; and desired I would give him some particular Account of that Land, which we call *Europe*, especially, of my own Country.

CHAPTER V

The Author, at his Master's Commands informs him of the State of England. *The Causes of War among the Princes of* Europe. *The Author begins to explain the English Constitution.*

The Reader may please to observe, that the following Extract of many Conversations I had with my Master, contains a Summary of the most material Points, which were discoursed at several times for above two Years; his Honour often desiring fuller Satisfaction as I farther improved in the *Houyhnhnm* Tongue. I laid before him, as well as I could, the whole State of *Europe*; I discoursed of Trade and Manufactures, of Arts and Sciences; and the Answers I gave to all the Questions he made, as they arose upon several Subjects, were a Fund of Conversation not to be exhausted. But I shall here only set down the Substance of what passed between us concerning my own Country, reducing it into Order as well as I can, without any Regard to Time or other Circumstances, while I strictly adhere to Truth. My only Concern is, that I shall hardly be able to do Justice to my Master's Arguments and Expressions; which must needs suffer by my Want of Capacity, as well as by a Translation into our barbarous *English*.

In Obedience therefore to his Honour's Commands, I related to him the *Revolution* under the Prince of *Orange*; the long War with *France* entered into by the said Prince, and renewed by his Successor the present Queen; wherein the greatest Powers of *Christendom* were engaged, and which still continued:[1] I computed at his Request, that about a Million of *Yahoos* might have been killed in the whole Progress of it; and perhaps a Hundred or more Cities taken, and five times as many Ships burnt or sunk.

[1] Gulliver refers to the revolution that put William and Mary on the throne in 1689, and to the War of the Spanish Succession.

He asked me what were the usual Causes or Motives that made one Country go to War with another. I answered, they were innumerable; but I should only mention a few of the chief. Sometimes the Ambition of Princes, who never think they have Land or People enough to govern: Sometimes the Corruption of Ministers, who engage their Master in a War in order to stifle or divert the Clamour of the Subjects against their evil Administration. Difference in Opinions hath cost many Millions of Lives: For Instance, whether *Flesh* be *Bread*, or *Bread* be *Flesh*: Whether the Juice of a certain *Berry* be *Blood* or *Wine*: Whether *Whistling* be a Vice or a Virtue: Whether it be better to *kiss a Post*, or throw it into the Fire: What is the best Colour for a *Coat*, whether *Black*, *White*, *Red* or *Grey*; and whether it should be *long* or *short*, *narrow* or *wide*, *dirty* or *clean*;[2] with many more. Neither are any Wars so furious and bloody, or of so long Continuance, as those occasioned by Difference in Opinion, especially if it be in things indifferent.

Sometimes the Quarrel between two Princes is to decide which of them shall dispossess a Third of his Dominions, where neither of them pretend to any Right. Sometimes one Prince quarrelleth with another, for fear the other should quarrel with him. Sometimes a War is entered upon, because the Enemy is too *strong*, and sometimes because he is too *weak*. Sometimes our Neighbours *want* the *Things* which we *have*, or *have* the *Things* which we want; and we both fight, till they take ours or give us theirs. It is a very justifiable Cause of War to invade a Country after the People have been wasted by Famine, destroyed by Pestilence, or embroiled by Factions amongst themselves. It is justifiable to enter into a War against our nearest Ally, when one of his Towns lies convenient for us, or a Territory of Land, that would render our Dominions round and compact. If a Prince send Forces into a Nation, where the People are poor and ignorant, he may lawfully put half of them to Death, and make Slaves of the rest, in order to civilize and reduce them from their barbarous Way of Living. It is a very kingly, honourable, and frequent Practice, when one Prince desires the Assistance of another to secure him against an Invasion, that the Assistant, when he hath driven out the

[2] Religious differences relating to the reality of transubstantiation, the use of music in church services, the importance of the crucifix as symbol, and the color, cut, and propriety of ecclesiastical vestments.

Invader, should seize on the Dominions himself, and kill, imprison or banish the Prince he came to relieve. Allyance by Blood or Marriage, is a sufficient Cause of War between Princes; and the nearer the Kindred is, the greater is their Disposition to quarrel: *Poor* Nations are *hungry,* and *rich* Nations are *proud;* and Pride and Hunger will ever be at Variance. For these Reasons, the Trade of a *Soldier* is held the most honourable of all others: Because a *Soldier* is a *Yahoo* hired to kill in cold Blood as many of his own Species, who have never offended him, as possibly he can.

There is likewise a Kind of beggarly Princes in *Europe,* not able to make War by themselves, who hire out their Troops to richer Nations for so much a Day to each Man; of which they keep three Fourths to themselves, and it is the best Part of their Maintenance; such are those in many *Northern* Parts of *Europe.*

What you have told me, (said my Master) upon the Subject of War, doth indeed discover most admirably the Effects of that Reason you pretend to: However, it is happy that the *Shame* is greater than the *Danger;* and that Nature hath left you utterly uncapable of doing much Mischief: For your Mouths lying flat with your Faces, you can hardly bite each other to any Purpose, unless by Consent. Then, as to the Claws upon your Feet before and behind, they are so short and tender, that one of our *Yahoos* would drive a Dozen of yours before him. And therefore in recounting the Numbers of those who have been killed in Battle, I cannot but think that you have *said the Thing which is not.*

I could not forbear shaking my Head and smiling a little at his Ignorance. And, being no Stranger to the Art of War, I gave him a Description of Cannons, Culverins, Muskets, Carabines, Pistols, Bullets, Powder, Swords, Bayonets, Battles, Sieges, Retreats, Attacks, Undermines, Countermines, Bombardments, Sea-fights; Ships sunk with a Thousand Men; twenty Thousand killed on each Side; dying Groans, Limbs flying in the Air: Smoak, Noise, Confusion, trampling to Death under Horses Feet: Flight, Pursuit, Victory; Fields strewed with Carcases left for Food to Dogs, and Wolves, and Birds of Prey; Plundering, Stripping, Ravishing, Burning and Destroying. And, to set forth the Valour of my own dear Countrymen, I assured him, that I had seen them blow up a Hundred Enemies at once in a Siege, and as many in a Ship; and beheld the dead Bodies drop down in Pieces from the Clouds, to the great Diversion of all the Spectators.

I was going on to more Particulars, when my Master commanded me Silence. He said, whoever understood the Nature of *Yahoos* might easily believe it possible for so vile an Animal, to be capable of every Action I had named, if their Strength and Cunning equalled their Malice. But, as my Discourse had increased his Abhorrence of the whole Species, so he found it gave him a Disturbance in his Mind, to which he was wholly a Stranger before. He thought his Ears being used to such abominable Words, might by Degrees admit them with less Detestation. That, although he hated the *Yahoos* of this Country, yet he no more blamed them for their odious Qualities, than he did a *Gnnayh* (a Bird of Prey) for its Cruelty, or a sharp Stone for cutting his Hoof. But, when a Creature pretending to Reason, could be capable of such Enormities, he dreaded lest the Corruption of that Faculty might be worse than Brutality itself. He seemed therefore confident, that instead of Reason, we were only possessed of some Quality fitted to increase our natural Vices; as the Reflection from a troubled Stream returns the Image of an ill-shapen Body, not only *larger*, but more *distorted*.

He added, That he had heard too much upon the Subject of War, both in this, and some former Discourses. There was another Point which a little perplexed him at present. I had said, that some of our Crew left their Country on Account of being ruined by *Law*: That I had already explained the Meaning of the Word; but he was at a Loss how it should come to pass, that the *Law* which was intended for *every* Man's Preservation, should be any Man's Ruin. Therefore he desired to be farther satisfied what I meant by *Law*, and the Dispensers thereof, according to the present Practice in my own Country: Because he thought, Nature and Reason were sufficient Guides for a reasonable Animal, as we pretended to be, in shewing us what we ought to do, and what to avoid.

I assured his Honour, that *Law* was a Science wherein I had not much conversed, further than by employing Advocates, in vain, upon some Injustices that had been done me. However, I would give him all the Satisfaction I was able.

I said there was a Society of Men among us, bred up from their Youth in the Art of proving by Words multiplied for the Purpose, that *White* is *Black*, and *Black* is *White*, according as they are paid. To this Society all the rest of the People are Slaves.

For Example. If my Neighbour hath a mind to my *Cow*, he

hires a Lawyer to prove that he ought to have my *Cow* from me. I must then hire another to defend my Right; it being against all Rules of *Law* that any Man should be allowed to speak for himself. Now in this Case, I who am the true Owner lie under two great Disadvantages. First, my Lawyer being practiced almost from his Cradle in defending Falshood; is quite out of his Element when he would be an Advocate for Justice, which as an Office unnatural, he always attempts with great Awkwardness, if not with Ill-will. The second Disadvantage is, that my Lawyer must proceed with great Caution: Or else he will be reprimanded by the Judges, and abhorred by his Brethren, as one who would lessen the Practice of the Law. And therefore I have but two Methods to preserve my *Cow*. The first is, to gain over my Adversary's Lawyer with a double Fee; who will then betray his Client, by insinuating that he hath Justice on his Side. The second Way is for my Lawyer to make my Cause appear as unjust as he can; by allowing the *Cow* to belong to my Adversary; and this if it be skilfully done, will certainly bespeak the Favour of the Bench.

Now, your Honour is to know, that these Judges are Persons appointed to decide all Controversies of Property, as well as for the Tryal of Criminals; and picked out from the most dextrous Lawyers who are grown old or lazy: And having been byassed all their Lives against Truth and Equity, lie under such a fatal Necessity of favouring Fraud, Perjury and Oppression; that I have known some of them to have refused a large Bribe from the Side where Justice lay, rather than injure the *Faculty*,[3] by doing any thing unbecoming their Nature or their Office.

It is a Maxim among these Lawyers, that whatever hath been done before, may legally be done again: And therefore they take special Care to record all the Decisions formerly made against common Justice and the general Reason of Mankind. These, under the Name of *Precedents*, they produce as Authorities to justify the most iniquitous Opinions; and the Judges never fail of directing accordingly.

In pleading, they studiously avoid entering into the *Merits* of the Cause; but are loud, violent and tedious in dwelling upon all *Circumstances* which are not to the Purpose. For Instance, in the Case already mentioned: They never desire to know what Claim or

[3] The profession.

Title my Adversary hath to my *Cow*; but whether the said *Cow* were Red or Black; her Horns long or short; whether the Field I graze her in be round or square; whether she were milked at home or abroad; what Diseases she is subject to, and the like. After which they consult *Precedents*, adjourn the Cause, from Time to Time, and in Ten, Twenty, or Thirty Years come to an Issue.

It is likewise to be observed, that this Society hath a peculiar Cant and Jargon of their own, that no other Mortal can understand, and wherein all their Laws are written, which they take special Care to multiply; whereby they have wholly confounded the very Essence of Truth and Falshood, of Right and Wrong; so that it will take Thirty Years to decide whether the Field, left me by my Ancestors for six Generations, belong to me, or to a Stranger three Hundred Miles off.

In the Tryal of Persons accused for Crimes against the State, the Method is much more short and commendable: The Judge first sends to sound the Disposition of those in Power; after which he can easily hang or save the Criminal, strictly preserving all the Forms of Law.

Here my Master interposing, said it was a Pity, that Creatures endowed with such prodigious Abilities of Mind as these Lawyers, by the Description I gave of them must certainly be, were not rather encouraged to be Instructors of others in Wisdom and Knowledge. In Answer to which, I assured his Honour, that in all Points out of their own Trade, they were usually the most ignorant and stupid Generation among us, the most despicable in common Conversation, avowed Enemies to all Knowledge and Learning; and equally disposed to pervert the general Reason of Mankind, in every other Subject of Discourse as in that of their own Profession.

CHAPTER VI

A Continuation of the State of England, *under* Queen Anne. *The Character of a first Minister in the Courts of* Europe.

My Master was yet wholly at a Loss to understand what Motives could incite this Race of Lawyers to perplex, disquiet, and weary themselves by engaging in a Confederacy of Injustice, merely for the Sake of injuring their Fellow-Animals; neither could he comprehend what I meant in saying they did it for *Hire*. Whereupon I was at much Pains to describe to him the Use of *Money*, the Materials it was made of, and the Value of the Metals: That when a *Yahoo* had got a great Store of this precious Substance, he was able to purchase whatever he had a mind to; the finest Cloathing, the noblest Houses, great Tracts of Land, the most costly Meats and Drinks; and have his Choice of the most beautiful Females. Therefore since *Money* alone, was able to perform all these Feats, our *Yahoos* thought, they could never have enough of it to spend or to save, as they found themselves inclined from their natural Bent either to Profusion or Avarice. That, the rich Man enjoyed the Fruit of the poor Man's Labour, and the latter were a Thousand to One in Proportion to the former. That the Bulk of our People was forced to live miserably, by labouring every Day for small Wages to make a few live plentifully. I enlarged myself much on these and many other Particulars to the same Purpose: But his Honour was still to seek: For he went upon a Supposition that all Animals had a Title to their Share in the Productions of the Earth; and especially those who presided over the rest. Therefore he desired I would let him know, what these costly Meats were, and how any of us happened to want them. Whereupon I enumerated as many Sorts as came into my Head, with the various Methods of dressing them, which could not be done without sending Vessels by Sea to everv Part of the World, as well for Liquors to drink, as for Sauces, and innumerable other Conveniencies. I assured him, that this whole Globe of Earth must be at least three Times gone round, before one of our better Female *Yahoos* could get her Breakfast, or a Cup to put it in. He said, That must needs be a miserable Country which cannot furnish Food for its own Inhabitants. But what he chiefly wondered at, was how such vast Tracts of Ground as I described, should be wholly without *Fresh-water*, and the People put to the Necessity of sending over the Sea for Drink. I replied, that *England* (the dear Place of my Nativity) was computed to produce three Times the Quantity of Food, more than its Inhabitants are able to consume, as well as Liquors extracted from Grain, or pressed out of the Fruit of certain Trees, which made excellent Drink; and the same Proportion in every other Convenience of Life. But, in order to feed the Luxury and Intemperance of the Males, and the Vanity of the Females, we sent away the greatest Part of our necessary Things to other Countries, from whence in Return we brought the Materials of Diseases, Folly, and Vice, to spend among ourselves. Hence it follows of Necessity, that vast Numbers of our People are compelled to seek their Livelihood by Begging, Robbing, Stealing, Cheating, Pimping, Forswearing, Flattering, Suborning, Forging, Gaming, Lying, Fawning, Hectoring, Voting, Scribling, Stargazing, Poysoning, Whoring, Canting, Libelling, Free-thinking, and the like Occupations: Every one of which Terms, I was at much Pains to make him understand.

That, *Wine* was not imported among us from foreign Countries, to supply the Want of Water or other Drinks, but because it was a Sort of Liquid which made us merry, by putting us out of our Senses; diverted all melancholy Thoughts, begat wild extravagant Imaginations in the Brain, raised our Hopes, and banished our Fears; suspended every Office of Reason for a Time, and deprived us of the Use of our Limbs, until we fell into a profound Sleep; although it must be confessed, that we always awaked sick and dispirited; and that the Use of this Liquor filled us with Diseases, which made our Lives uncomfortable and short.

But beside all this, the Bulk of our People supported themselves by furnishing the Necessities or Conveniencies of Life to the Rich, and to each other. For Instance, when I am at home and dressed as I ought to be, I carry on my Body the Workmanship of an Hundred Tradesmen; the Building and Furniture of my House employ as many more; and Five Times the Number to adorn my Wife.

I was going on to tell him of another Sort of People, who get their Livelihood by attending the Sick; having upon some Occasions informed his Honour that many of my Crew had died of Diseases. But here it was with the utmost Difficulty, that I brought him to apprehend what I meant. He could easily conceive, that a *Houyhnhnm* grew weak and heavy a few Days before his Death; or by some Accident might hurt a Limb. But that Nature, who worketh all things to Perfection, should suffer any Pains to breed in our Bodies, he thought impossible; and desired to know the Reason of so unaccountable an Evil. I told him, we fed on a Thousand Things which operated contrary to each other; that we eat when we were not hungry, and drank without the Provocation of Thirst: That we sat whole Nights drinking strong Liquors without eating a Bit; which disposed us to Sloth, enflamed our Bodies, and precipitated or prevented Digestion. That, prostitute Female *Yahoos* acquired a certain Malady, which bred Rottenness in the Bones of those, who fell into their Embraces: That this and many other Diseases, were propagated from Father to Son; so that great Numbers come into the World with complicated Maladies upon them: That, it would be endless to give him a Catalogue of all Diseases incident to human Bodies; for they could not be fewer than five or six Hundred, spread over every Limb, and Joynt: In short, every Part, external and intestine, having Diseases appropriated to each. To remedy which, there was a Sort of People bred up among us, in the Profession or Pretence of curing the Sick. And because I had some Skill in the Faculty, I would in Gratitude to his Honour, let him know the whole Mystery and Method by which they proceed.

Their Fundamental is, that all Diseases arise from *Repletion*; from whence they conclude, that a great *Evacuation* of the Body is necessary, either through the natural Passage, or upwards at the Mouth. Their next Business is, from Herbs, Minerals, Gums, Oyls, Shells, Salts, Juices, Seaweed, Excrements, Barks of Trees, Serpents, Toads, Frogs, Spiders, dead Mens Flesh and Bones, Birds, Beasts and Fishes, to form a Composition for Smell and Taste the most abominable, nauseous and detestable, that they can possibly contrive, which the Stomach immediately rejects with Loathing: And this they call a *Vomit*. Or else from the same Store-house, with some other poysonous Additions, they command us to take in at the Orifice *above* or *below*, (just as the Physician then happens to be disposed) a Medicine equally annoying and disgustful to the Bowels; which relaxing the Belly, drives down all before it: And this they call a *Purge*, or a *Clyster*. For Nature (as the Physicians alledge) having intended the superior anterior Orifice only for the *Intromission* of Solids and Liquids, and the inferior Posterior for Ejection; these Artists ingeniously considering that in all Diseases Nature is forced out of her Seat; therefore to replace her in it, the Body must be treated in a Manner directly contrary, by interchanging the Use of each Orifice; forcing Solids and Liquids in at the *Anus*, and making Evacuations at the Mouth.

But, besides real Diseases, we are subject to many that are only imaginary, for which the Physicians have invented imaginary Cures; these have their several Names, and so have the Drugs that are proper for them; and with these our Female *Yahoos* are always infested.

One great Excellency in this Tribe is their Skill at *Prognosticks*, wherein they seldom fail; their Predictions in real Diseases, when they rise to any Degree of Malignity, generally portending *Death*, which is always in their Power, when Recovery is not: And therefore, upon any unexpected Signs of Amendment, after they have pronounced their Sentence, rather than be accused as false Prophets, they know how to approve their Sagacity to the World by a seasonable Dose.

They are likewise of special Use to Husbands and Wives, who are grown weary of their Mates; to eldest Sons, to great Ministers of State, and often to Princes.

I had formerly upon Occasion discoursed with my Master upon the Nature of *Government* in general, and particularly of our own *excellent Constitution*, deservedly the Wonder and Envy of the whole World. But having here accidentally mentioned a *Minister of State*; he commanded me some Time after to inform him, what Species of *Yahoo* I particularly meant by that Appellation.

I told him, that a *First* or *Chief Minister of State*, whom I intended to describe, was a Creature wholly exempt from Joy and Grief, Love and Hatred, Pity and Anger; at least makes use of no other Passions but a violent Desire of Wealth, Power, and Titles: That he applies his Words to all Uses, except to the Indication of his Mind; That he never tells a *Truth*, but with an Intent that you should take it for a *Lye*; nor a *Lye*, but with a Design that you should take it for a *Truth*; That those he speaks worst of behind their Backs, are in the surest way to Preferment; and whenever he begins to praise you to others or to your self, you are from that Day forlorn. The worst Mark you can receive is a Promise, especially when it is confirmed with an Oath; after which every wise Man retires, and gives over all Hopes.

There are three Methods by which a Man may rise to be Chief Minister: The first is, by knowing how with Prudence to dispose of a Wife, a Daughter, or a Sister: The second, by betraying or undermining his Predecessor: And the third is, by a *furious Zeal* in publick Assemblies against the Corruptions of the Court. But a wise Prince would rather chuse to employ those who practise the last of these Methods; because such Zealots prove always the most obsequious and subservient to the Will and Passions of their Master. That, these *Ministers* having all Employments at their Disposal, preserve themselves in Power by bribing the Majority of a Senate or great Council; and at last by an Expedient called an *Act of Indemnity* (whereof I described the Nature to him) they secure themselves from After-reckonings, and retire from the Publick, laden with the Spoils of the Nation.

The Palace of a *Chief Minister*, is a Seminary to breed up others in his own Trade: The Pages, Lacquies, and Porter, by imitating their Master, become *Ministers of State* in their several Districts, and learn to excel in the three principal *Ingredients*, of *Insolence, Lying*, and *Bribery*. Accordingly, they have a *Subaltern* Court paid to them by Persons of the best Rank; and sometimes by the Force of Dexterity and Impudence, arrive through several Gradations to be Successors to their Lord.

He is usually governed by a decayed Wench, or favourite Footman, who are the Tunnels through which all Graces are conveyed, and may properly be called, *in the last Resort*, the Governors of the Kingdom.

One Day, my Master, having heard me mention the *Nobility* of my Country, was pleased to make me a Compliment which I could not pretend to deserve: That, he was sure, I must have been born of some Noble Family, because I far exceeded in Shape, Colour, and Cleanliness, all the *Yahoos* of his Nation, although I seemed to fail in Strength, and Agility, which must be imputed to my different Way of Living from those other Brutes; and besides, I was not only endowed with the Faculty of Speech, but likewise with some Rudiments of Reason, to a Degree, that with all his Acquaintance I passed for a Prodigy.

He made me observe, that among the *Houyhnhnms*, the *White*, the *Sorrel*, and the *Iron-grey*, were not so exactly shaped as the *Bay*, the *Dapple-grey*, and the *Black*; nor born with equal Talents of Mind, or a Capacity to improve them; and therefore continued always in the Condition of Servants, without ever aspiring to match out of their own Race, which in that Country would be reckoned monstrous and unnatural.

I made his Honour my most humble Acknowledgements for the good Opinion he was pleased to conceive of me; but assured him at the same Time, that my Birth was of the lower Sort, having been born of plain, honest Parents, who were just able to give me a tolerable Education: That, *Nobility* among us was altogether a different Thing from the Idea he had of it; That, our young *Noblemen* are bred from their Childhood in Idleness and Luxury; that, as soon as Years will permit, they consume their Vigour, and contract odious Diseases among lewd Females; and when their Fortunes are almost ruined, they marry some Woman of mean Birth, disagreeable Person, and unsound Constitution, merely for the sake of Money, whom they hate and despise. That, the Productions of such Marriages are generally scrophulous, rickety or deformed Children; by which Means the Family seldom continues above three Generations, unless the Wife take Care to provide a healthy Father among her Neighbours, or Domesticks, in order to improve and continue the Breed. That, a weak diseased Body, a meager Countenance, and sallow Complexion, are the true Marks of *noble Blood*; and a healthy robust Appearance is so disgraceful in a Man of Quality, that the World concludes his real Father to have been a Groom or a Coachman. The Imperfections of his Mind run parallel with those of his Body; being a Composition of Spleen, Dulness, Ignorance, Caprice, Sensuality and Pride.

Without the Consent of this illustrious Body, no Law can be enacted, repealed, or altered: And these Nobles have likewise the Decision of all our Possessions without Appeal.

CHAPTER VII

The Author's great Love of his Native Country. His Master's Observations upon the Constitution and Administration of England, *as described by the Author, with parallel Cases and Comparisons. His Master's Observations upon human Nature.*

The Reader may be disposed to wonder how I could prevail on my self to give so free a Representation of my own Species, among a Race of Mortals who were already too apt to conceive the vilest Opinion of Human Kind, from that entire Congruity betwixt me and their *Yahoos*. But I must freely confess, that the many Virtues of those excellent *Quadrupeds* placed in opposite View to human Corruptions, had so far opened my Eyes, and enlarged my Understanding, that I began to view the Actions and Passions of Man in a very different Light; and to think the Honour of my own kind not worth managing; which, besides, it was impossible for me to do before a Person of so acute a Judgment as my Master, who daily convinced me of a thousand Faults in my self, whereof I had not the least Perception before, and which with us would never be numbered even among human Infirmities. I had likewise learned from his Example an utter Detestation of all Falsehood or Disguise; and *Truth* appeared so amiable to me, that I determined upon sacrificing every thing to it.

Let me deal so candidly with the Reader, as to confess, that there was yet a much stronger Motive for the Freedom I took in my Representation of Things. I had not been a Year in this Country, before I contracted such a Love and Veneration for the Inhabitants, that I entered on a firm Resolution never to return to human Kind, but to pass the rest of my Life among these admirable *Houyhnhnms* in the Contemplation and Practice of every Virtue; where I could have no Example or Incitement to Vice. But it was decreed by Fortune, my perpetual Enemy, that so great a Felicity should not fall to my Share. However, it is now some Comfort to reflect, that in what I said of my Countrymen, I *extenuated* their Faults as much as I durst before so strict an Examiner; and upon every Article, gave as *favourable* a Turn as the Matter would bear. For, indeed, who is there alive that will not be swayed by his Byass and Partiality to the Place of his Birth?

I have related the Substance of several Conversations I had with my Master, during the greatest Part of the Time I had the Honour to be in his Service; but have indeed for Brevity sake omitted much more than is here set down.

When I had answered all his Questions, and his Curiosity seemed to be fully satisfied; he sent for me one Morning early, and commanding me to sit down at some Distance, (an Honour which he had never before conferred upon me) He said, he had been very seriously considering my whole Story, as far as it related both to my self and my Country: That, he looked upon us as a Sort of Animals to whose Share, by what Accident he could not conjecture, some small Pittance of *Reason* had fallen, whereof we made no other Use than by its Assistance to aggravate our *natural* Corruptions, and to acquire new ones which Nature had not given us. That, we disarmed our selves of the few Abilities she had bestowed; had been very successful in multiplying our original Wants, and seemed to spend our whole Lives in vain Endeavours to supply them by our own Inventions. That, as to my self, it was manifest I had neither the Strength or Agility of a common *Yahoo*; that I walked infirmly on my hinder Feet; had found out a Contrivance to make my Claws of no Use or Defence, and to remove the Hair from my Chin, which was intended as a Shelter from the Sun and the Weather. Lastly, That I could neither run with Speed, nor climb Trees like my *Brethren* (as he called them) the *Yahoos* in this Country.

That, our Institutions of *Government* and *Law* were plainly owing to our gross Defects in *Reason*, and by consequence, in *Virtue*; because *Reason* alone is sufficient to govern a *Rational* Creature; which was therefore a Character we had no Pretence to challenge, even from the Account I had given of my own People; although he manifestly perceived, that in order to favour them, I had concealed many Particulars, and often *said the Thing which was not.*

He was the more confirmed in this Opinion, because he observed, that as I agreed in every Feature of my Body with other *Yahoos,* except where it was to my real Disadvantage in point of Strength, Speed and Activity, the Shortness of my Claws, and some other Particulars where Nature had no Part; so, from the Representation I had given him of our Lives, our Manners, and our Actions, he found as near a Resemblance in the Disposition of our Minds. He said, the *Yahoos* were known to hate one another more than they did any different Species of Animals; and the Reason usually assigned, was, the Odiousness of their own Shapes, which all could see in the rest, but not in themselves. He had therefore begun to think it not unwise in us to *cover* our Bodies, and by that Invention, conceal many of our Deformities from each other, which would else be hardly supportable. But, he now found he had been mistaken; and that the Dissentions of those Brutes in his Country were owing to the same Cause with ours, as I had described them. For, if (said he) you throw among five *Yahoos* as much Food as would be sufficient for fifty, they will, instead of eating peaceably, fall together by the Ears, each single one impatient to *have all to it self*; and therefore a Servant was usually employed to stand by while they were feeding abroad, and those kept at home were tied at a Distance from each other. That, if a Cow died of Age or Accident, before a *Houyhnhnm* could secure it for his own *Yahoos,* those in the Neighbourhood would come in Herds to seize it, and then would ensue such a Battle as I had described, with terrible Wounds made by their Claws on both Sides, although they seldom were able to kill one another, for want of such convenient Instruments of Death as we had invented. At other Times the like Battles have been fought between the *Yahoos* of several Neighbourhoods without any visible Cause: Those of one District watching all Opportunities to surprise the next before they are prepared. But if they find their Project hath miscarried, they return home, and for want of Enemies, engage in what I call a *Civil War* among themselves.

That, in some Fields of his Country, there are certain *shining Stones* of several Colours, whereof the *Yahoos* are violently fond; and when Part of these *Stones* are fixed in the Earth, as it sometimes happeneth, they will dig with their Claws for whole Days to get them out, and carry them away, and hide them by Heaps in their Kennels; but still looking round with great Caution, for fear their Comrades should find out their Treasure. My Master said, he could never discover the Reason of this unnatural Appetite, or how these *Stones* could be of any Use to a *Yahoo*; but now he believed it might proceed from the same Principle of *Avarice*, which I had ascribed to Mankind. That he had once, by way of Experiment, privately removed a Heap of these *Stones* from the Place where one of his *Yahoos* had buried it: Whereupon, the sordid Animal missing his Treasure, by his loud lamenting brought the whole Herd to the Place, there miserably howled, then fell to biting and tearing the rest; began to pine away, would neither eat nor sleep, nor work, till he ordered a Servant privately to convey the *Stones* into the same Hole, and hide them as before; which when his *Yahoo* had found, he presently recovered his Spirits and good Humour; but took Care to remove them to a better hiding Place; and hath ever since been a very serviceable Brute.

My Master farther assured me, which I also observed my self; That in the Fields where these *shining Stones* abound, the fiercest and most frequent Battles are fought, occasioned by perpetual Inroads of the neighbouring *Yahoos*.

He said, it was common when two *Yahoos* discovered such a *Stone* in a Field, and were contending which of them should be the Proprietor, a third would take the Advantage, and carry it away from them both; which my Master would needs contend to have some Resemblance with our *Suits at Law*; wherein I thought it for our Credit not to undeceive him; since the Decision he mentioned was much more equitable than many Decrees among us: Because the Plaintiff and Defendant there lost nothing beside the *Stone* they contended for; whereas our *Courts of Equity*, would never have dismissed the Cause while either of them had any thing left.

My Master continuing his Discourse, said, There was nothing that rendered the *Yahoos* more odious, than their undistinguished Appetite to devour every thing that came in their Way, whether Herbs, Roots, Berries, corrupted Flesh of Animals, or all mingled together: And it was peculiar in their Temper, that they were fonder of what they could get by Rapine or Stealth at a greater Distance, than much better Food provided for them at home. If their Prey held out, they would eat till they were ready to burst, after which Nature had pointed out to them a certain *Root* that gave them a general Evacuation.

There was also another Kind of *Root* very *juicy*, but something rare and difficult to be found, which the *Yahoos* fought for with much Eagerness, and would suck it with great Delight: It produced the same Effects that Wine hath upon us. It would make them sometimes hug, and sometimes tear one another; they would howl and grin, and chatter, and reel, and tumble, and then fall asleep in the Mud.

I did indeed observe, that the *Yahoos* were the only Animals in this Country subject to any Diseases; which however, were much fewer than Horses have among us, and contracted not by any ill Treatment they meet with, but by the Nastiness and Greediness of that sordid Brute. Neither has their Language any more than a general Appellation for those Maladies; which is borrowed from the Name of the Beast, and called *Hnea Yahoo*, or the *Yahoo's-Evil*; and the Cure prescribed is a Mixture of *their own Dung* and *Urine*, forcibly put down the *Yahoo's* Throat. This I have since often known to have been taken with Success: And do here freely recommend it to my Countrymen, for the publick Good, as an admirable Specifick against all Diseases produced by Repletion.

As to Learning, Government, Arts, Manufactures, and the like; my Master confessed he could find little or no Resemblance between the *Yahoos* of that Country and those in ours. For, he only meant to observe what Parity there was in our Natures. He had heard indeed some curious *Houyhnhnms* observe, that in most Herds there was a Sort of ruling *Yahoo*, (as among us there is generally some leading or principal Stag in a Park) who was always more *deformed* in Body, and *mischievous in Disposition*, than any of the rest. That, this *Leader* had usually a Favourite as *like himself* as he could get, whose Employment was to *lick his Master's Feet and Posteriors, and drive the Female* Yahoos to *his Kennel*; for which he was now and then rewarded with a Piece of Ass's Flesh. This *Favourite* is hated by the whole Herd; and therefore to protect himself, keeps always *near the Person of his Leader*. He usually continues in Office till a worse can be found; but the very Moment he is discarded, his Successor, at the Head of all the *Yahoos* in that District, Young and Old, Male and Female, come in a Body, and discharge their excrements upon him from Head to Foot. But how far this might be applicable to our *Courts* and *Favourites,* and *Ministers of State,* my Master said I could best determine.

I durst make no Return to this malicious Insinuation, which debased human Understanding below the Sagacity of a common *Hound,* who hath Judgment enough to distinguish and follow the Cry of the *ablest Dog in the Pack,* without being ever mistaken.

My Master told me, there were some Qualities remarkable in the *Yahoos,* which he had not observed me to mention, or at least very slightly, in the Accounts I had given him of human Kind. He said, those Animals, like other Brutes, had their Females in common; but in this they differed, that the She-*Yahoo* would admit the Male, while she was pregnant; and that the Hees would quarrel and fight with the Females as fiercely as with each other. Both which Practices were such Degrees of infamous Brutality, that no other sensitive Creature ever arrived at.

Another Thing he wondered at in the *Yahoos,* was their strange Disposition to Nastiness and Dirt; whereas there appears to be a natural Love of Cleanliness in all other Animals. As to the two former Accusations, I was glad to let them pass without any Reply, because I had not a Word to offer upon them in Defence of my Species, which otherwise I certainly had done from my own Inclinations. But I could have easily vindicated human Kind from the Imputation of Singularity upon the last Article, if there had been any *Swine* in that Country, (as unluckily for me there were not) which although it may be a *sweeter Quadruped* than a *Yahoo,* cannot I humbly conceive in Justice pretend to more Cleanliness; and so his Honour himself must have owned, if he had seen their filthy Way of feeding, and their Custom of wallowing and sleeping in the Mud.

My Master likewise mentioned another Quality, which his Servants had discovered in several *Yahoos,* and to him was wholly unaccountable. He said, a Fancy would sometimes take a *Yahoo,* to retire into a Corner, to lie down and howl, and groan, and spurn away all that came near him, although he were young and fat, and wanted neither Food nor Water; nor did the Servants imagine what could possibly ail him. And the only Remedy they found was to set him to hard Work, after which he would infallibly come to himself. To this I was silent out of Partiality to my own Kind;

yet here I could plainly discover the true Seeds of *Spleen*,[1] which only seizeth on the *Lazy*, the *Luxurious*, and the *Rich*; who, if they were forced to undergo the *same Regimen*, I would undertake for the Cure.

His Honour had farther observed, that a Female-*Yahoo* would often stand behind a Bank or a Bush, to gaze on the young Males passing by, and then appear, and hide, using many antick Gestures and Grimaces; at which time it was observed, that she had a most *offensive Smell*; and when any of the Males advanced, would slowly retire, looking often back, and with a counterfeit Shew of Fear, run off into some convenient Place where she knew the Male would follow her.

At other times, if a Female Stranger came among them, three or four of her own Sex would get about her, and stare and chatter, and grin, and smell her all over; and then turn off with Gestures that seemed to express Contempt and Disdain.

Perhaps my Master might refine a little in these Speculations, which he had drawn from what he observed himself, or had been told by others; However, I could not reflect without some Amazement, and much Sorrow, that the Rudiments of *Lewdness*, *Coquetry*, *Censure*, and *Scandal*, should have Place by Instinct in Womankind.

I expected every Moment, that my Master would accuse the *Yahoos* of those unnatural Appetites in both Sexes, so common among us. But Nature it seems hath not been so expert a Schoolmistress; and these politer Pleasures are entirely the Productions of Art and Reason, on our Side of the Globe.

[1] Hypochondria, languor—a fashionable illness, much affected in Swift's day.

CHAPTER VIII

The Author relateth several Particulars of the Yahoos. *The great Virtues of the* Houyhnhnms. *The Education and Exercises of their Youth. Their general Assembly.*

As I ought to have understood human Nature much better than I supposed it possible for my Master to do, so it was easy to apply the Character he gave of the *Yahoos* to myself and my Countrymen; and I believed I could yet make farther Discoveries from my own Observation. I therefore often begged his Honour to let me go among the Herds of *Yahoos* in the Neighbourhood; to which he always very graciously consented, being perfectly convinced that the Hatred I bore those Brutes would never suffer me to be corrupted by them; and his Honour ordered one of his Servants, a strong Sorrel Nag, very honest and good-natured, to be my Guard; without whose Protection I durst not undertake such Adventures. For I have already told the Reader how much I was pestered by those odious Animals upon my first Arrival. I afterwards failed very narrowly three or four times of falling into their Clutches, when I happened to stray at any Distance without my Hanger. And I have Reason to believe, they had some Imagination that I was of their own Species, which I often assisted myself, by stripping up my Sleeves, and shewing my naked Arms and Breast in their Sight, when my Protector was with me: At which times they would approach as near as they durst, and imitate my Actions after the Manner of Monkeys, but ever with great Signs of Hatred; as a tame *Jack Daw* with Cap and Stockings, is always persecuted by the wild ones, when he happens to be got among them.

They are prodigiously nimble from their Infancy; however, I once caught a young Male of three Years old, and endeavoured by all Marks of Tenderness to make it quiet; but the little Imp fell a squalling, and scratching, and biting with such Violence, that I was forced to let it go; and it was high time, for a whole Troop of old ones came about us at the Noise; but finding the Cub was safe, (for away it ran) and my Sorrel Nag being by, they durst not venture near us. I observed the young Animal's Flesh to smell very rank, and the Stink was somewhat between a *Weasel* and a *Fox*, but much more disagreeable. I forgot another Circumstance, (and perhaps I might have the Reader's Pardon, if it were wholly omitted) that while I held the odious Vermin in my Hands, it voided its filthy Excrements of a yellow liquid Substance, all over my Cloaths; but by good Fortune there was a small Brook hard by, where I washed myself as clean as I could; although I durst not come into my Master's Presence, until I were sufficiently aired.

By what I could discover, the *Yahoos* appear to be the most unteachable of all Animals, their Capacities never reaching higher than to draw or carry Burthens. Yet I am of Opinion, this Defect ariseth chiefly from a perverse, restive Disposition. For they are cunning, malicious, treacherous and revengeful. They are strong and hardy, but of a cowardly Spirit, and by Consequence insolent, abject, and cruel. It is observed, that the *Red-haired* of both Sexes are more libidinous and mischievous than the rest, whom yet they much exceed in Strength and Activity.

The *Houyhnhnms* keep the *Yahoos* for present Use in Huts not far from the House; but the rest are sent abroad to certain Fields, where they dig up Roots, eat several Kinds of Herbs, and search about for Carrion, or sometimes catch *Weasels* and *Luhimuhs* (a Sort of *wild Rat*) which they greedily devour. Nature hath taught them to dig deep Holes with their Nails on the Side of a rising Ground, wherein they lie by themselves; only the Kennels of the Females are larger, sufficient to hold two or three Cubs.

They swim from their Infancy like Frogs, and are able to continue long under Water, where they often take Fish, which the Females carry home to their Young. And upon this Occasion, I hope the Reader will pardon my relating an odd Adventure.

Being one Day abroad with my Protector the Sorrel Nag, and the Weather exceeding hot, I entreated him to let me bathe in a River that was near. He consented, and I immediately stripped myself stark naked, and went down softly into the Stream. It happened that a young Female *Yahoo* standing behind a Bank, saw the whole Proceeding; and inflamed by Desire, as the Nag and I conjectured, came running with all Speed, and leaped into the Water within five Yards of the Place where I bathed. I was never in my Life so terribly frighted; the Nag was grazing at some Distance, not suspecting any Harm: She embraced me after a most fulsome Manner; I roared as loud as I could, and the Nag came galloping towards me, whereupon she quitted her Grasp, with the utmost Reluctancy, and leaped upon the opposite Bank, where she stood gazing and howling all the time I was putting on my Cloaths.

This was Matter of Diversion to my Master and his Family, as well as of Mortification to my self. For now I could no longer deny, that I was a real *Yahoo*, in every Limb and Feature, since the Females had a natural Propensity to me as one of their own Species: Neither was the Hair of this Brute of a Red Colour, (which might have been some Excuse for an Appetite a little irregular) but black as a Sloe, and her Countenance did not make an Appearance altogether so hideous as the rest of the Kind; for, I think, she could not be above Eleven Years old.

Having already lived three Years in this Country, the Reader I suppose will expect, that I should, like other Travellers, give him some Account of the Manners and Customs of its Inhabitants, which it was indeed my principal Study to learn.

As these noble *Houyhnhnms* are endowed by Nature with a general Disposition to all Virtues, and have no Conceptions or Ideas of what is evil in a rational Creature; so their grand Maxim is, to cultivate *Reason*, and to be wholly governed by it. Neither is *Reason* among them a Point problematical as with us, where Men can argue with Plausibility on both Sides of a Question; but strikes you with immediate Conviction; as it must needs do where it is not mingled, obscured, or discoloured by Passion and Interest. I remember it was with extreme Difficulty that I could bring my Master to understand the Meaning of the Word *Opinion*, or how a Point could be disputable; because *Reason* taught us to affirm or deny only where we are certain; and beyond our Knowledge we cannot do either. So that Controversies, Wranglings, Disputes, and Positiveness in false or dubious Propositions, are Evils unknown among the *Houyhnhnms*. In the like Manner when I used to explain to him our several Systems of *Natural Philosophy*, he would laugh that a Creature pretending to *Reason*, should value itself upon the Knowledge of other Peoples Conjectures, and in Things, where that Knowledge, if it were certain, could be of no Use. Wherein he agreed entirely with the

Sentiments of *Socrates*, as *Plato* delivers them; which I mention as the highest Honour I can do that Prince of Philosophers. I have often since reflected what Destruction such a Doctrine would make in the Libraries of *Europe*; and how many Paths to Fame would be then shut up in the Learned World.

Friendship and *Benevolence* are the two principal Virtues among the *Houyhnhnms*; and these not confined to particular Objects, but universal to the whole Race. For, a Stranger from the remotest Part, is equally treated with the nearest Neighbour, and where-ever he goes, looks upon himself as at home. They preserve *Decency* and *Civility* in the highest Degrees, but are altogether ignorant of *Ceremony*. They have no Fondness[1] for their Colts or Foles; but the Care they take in educating them proceedeth entirely from the Dictates of *Reason*. And, I observed my Master to shew the same Affection to his Neighbour's Issue that he had for his own. They will have it that *Nature* teaches them to love the whole Species, and it is *Reason* only that maketh a Distinction of Persons, where there is a superior Degree of Virtue.

When the Matron *Houyhnhnms* have produced one of each Sex, they no longer accompany with their Consorts, except they lose one of their Issue by some Casualty, which very seldom happens: But in such a Case they meet again; or when the like Accident befalls a Person, whose Wife is past bearing, some other Couple bestows on him one of their own Colts, and then go together a second Time, until the Mother be pregnant. This Caution is necessary to prevent the Country from being overburthened with Numbers. But the Race of inferior *Houyhnhnms* bred up to be Servants is not so strictly limited upon this Article; these are allowed to produce three of each Sex, to be Domesticks in the Noble Families.

In their Marriages they are exactly careful to chuse such Colours as will not make any disagreeable Mixture in the Breed. *Strength* is chiefly valued in the Male, and *Comeliness* in the Female; not upon the Account of *Love*, but to preserve the Race from degenerating: For, where a Female happens to excel in *Strength*, a Consort is chosen with regard to *Comeliness*. Courtship, Love, Presents, Joyntures, Settlements, have no Place in their Thoughts; or Terms whereby to express them in their Language. The young Couple meet and are joined, merely because it is the Determination of their Parents and Friends: It is what they see done every

[1] Excessive doting.

Day; and they look upon it as one of the necessary Actions in a reasonable Being. But the Violation of Marriage, or any other Unchastity, was never heard of: And the married Pair pass their Lives with the same Friendship, and mutual Benevolence that they bear to all others of the same Species, who come in their Way; without Jealousy, Fondness, Quarrelling, or Discontent.

In educating the Youth of both Sexes, their Method is admirable, and highly deserveth our Imitation. These are not suffered to taste a Grain of *Oats*, except upon certain Days, till Eighteen Years old; nor *Milk*, but very rarely; and in Summer they graze two Hours in the Morning, and as many in the Evening, which their Parents likewise observe; but the Servants are not allowed above half that Time; and a great Part of the Grass is brought home, which they eat at the most convenient Hours, when they can be best spared from Work.

Temperance, Industry, Exercise and *Cleanliness*, are the Lessons equally enjoyned to the young ones of both Sexes: And my Master thought it monstrous in us to give the Females a different Kind of Education from the Males, except in some Articles of Domestick Management; whereby, as he truly observed, one Half of our Natives were good for nothing but bringing Children into the World: And to trust the Care of their Children to such useless Animals, he said was yet a greater Instance of Brutality.

But the *Houyhnhnms* train up their Youth to Strength, Speed, and Hardiness, by exercising them in running Races up and down steep Hills, or over hard stony Grounds; and when they are all in a Sweat, they are ordered to leap over Head and Ears into a Pond or a River. Four times a Year the Youth of certain Districts meet to shew their Proficiency in Running, and Leaping, and other Feats of Strength or Agility; where the Victor is rewarded with a Song made in his or her Praise. On this Festival the Servants drive a Herd of *Yahoos* into the Field, laden with Hay, and Oats, and Milk for a Repast to the *Houyhnhnms*; after which, these Brutes are immediately driven back again, for fear of being noisome to the Assembly.

Every fourth Year, at the *Vernal Equinox*, there is a Representative Council of the whole Nation, which meets in a Plain about twenty Miles from our House, and continueth about five or six Days. Here they inquire into the State and Condition of the several Districts; whether they abound or be deficient in Hay or Oats, or Cows or *Yahoos*? And where-ever there is any Want (which is but seldom) it is immediately supplied by unanimous Consent and Contribution. Here likewise the Regulation of Children is settled: As for instance, if a *Houyhnhnm* hath two Males, he changeth one of them with another who hath two Females: And when a Child hath been lost by any Casualty, where the Mother is past Breeding, it is determined what Family in the District shall breed another to supply the Loss.

CHAPTER IX

A grand Debate at the General Assembly of the Houyhnhnms, *and how it was determined. The Learning of the* Houyhnhnms. *Their Buildings. Their Manner of Burials. The Defectiveness of their Language.*

One of these Grand Assemblies was held in my time, about three Months before my Departure, whither my Master went as the Representative of our District. In this Council was resumed their old Debate, and indeed, the only Debate that ever happened in their Country; whereof my Master after his Return gave me a very particular Account.

The Question to be debated, was, Whether the *Yahoos* should be exterminated from the Face of the Earth. One of the *Members* for the Affirmative offered several Arguments of great Strength and Weight; alledging, That, as the *Yahoos* were the most filthy, noisome, and deformed Animal which Nature ever produced, so they were the most restive and indocible, mischievous and malicious: They would privately suck the Teats of the *Houyhnhnms* Cows; kill and devour their Cats, trample down their Oats and Grass, if they were not continually watched; and commit a Thousand other Extravagancies. He took Notice of a general Tradition, that *Yahoos* had not been always in their Country: But, that many Ages ago, two of these Brutes appeared together upon a Mountain;

whether produced by the Heat of the Sun upon corrupted Mud and Slime, or from the Ooze and Froth of the Sea, was never known. That these *Yahoos* engendered, and their Brood in a short time grew so numerous as to over-run and infest the whole Nation. That the *Houyhnhnms* to get rid of this Evil, made a general Hunting, and at last inclosed the whole Herd; and destroying the Older, every *Houyhnhnm* kept two young Ones in a Kennel, and brought them to such a Degree of Tameness, as an Animal so savage by Nature can be capable of acquiring; using them for Draught and Carriage. That, there seemed to be much Truth in this Tradition, and that those Creatures could not be *Ylnhniamshy* (or *Aborigines* of the Land) because of the violent Hatred the *Houyhnhnms* as well as all other Animals, bore them; which although their evil Disposition sufficiently deserved, could never have arrived at so high a Degree, if they had been *Aborigines*, or else they would have long since been rooted out. That, the Inhabitants taking a Fancy to use the Service of the *Yahoos*, had very imprudently neglected to cultivate the Breed of *Asses*, which were a comely Animal, easily kept, more tame and orderly, without any offensive Smell, strong enough for Labour, although they yield to the other in Agility of Body; and if their Braying be no agreeable Sound, it is far preferable to the horrible Howlings of the *Yahoos*.

Several others declared their Sentiments to the same Purpose; when my Master proposed an Expedient to the Assembly, whereof he had indeed borrowed the Hint from me. He approved of the Tradition, mentioned by the *Honourable Member*, who spoke before; and affirmed, that the two *Yahoos* said to be first seen among them, had been driven thither over the Sea; that coming to Land, and being forsaken by their Companions, they retired to the Mountains, and degenerating by Degrees, became in Process of Time, much more savage than those of their own Species in the Country from whence these two Originals came. The Reason of his Assertion was, that he had now in his Possession, a certain wonderful *Yahoo*, (meaning myself) which most of them had heard of, and many of them had seen. He then related to them, how he first found me; that, my Body was all covered with an artificial Composure of the Skins and Hairs of other Animals: That, I spoke in a Language of my own; and had thoroughly learned theirs: That, I had related to him the Accidents which brought me thither: That, when he saw me without my Covering, I was an exact *Yahoo* in every Part, only of a whiter Colour, less hairy, and with shorter Claws. He added, how I had endeavoured to persuade him, that in my own and other Countries the *Yahoos* acted as the governing, rational Animal, and held the *Houyhnhnms* in Servitude: That, he observed in me all the Qualities of a *Yahoo*, only a little more civilized by some Tincture of Reason; which however was in a Degree as far inferior to the *Houyhnhnm* Race, as the *Yahoos* of their Country were to me: That, among other things, I mentioned a Custom we had of *castrating Houyhnhnms* when they were young, in order to render them tame; that the Operation was easy and safe; that it was no Shame to learn Wisdom from Brutes, as Industry is taught by the Ant, and Building by the Swallow. (For so I translate the Word *Lyhannh*, although it be a much larger Fowl.) That, this Invention might be practiced upon the younger *Yahoos* here, which, besides rendering them tractable and fitter for Use, would in an Age put an End to the whole Species without destroying Life. That, in the mean time the *Houyhnhnms* should be *exhorted* to cultivate the Breed of Asses, which, as they are in all respects more valuable Brutes; so they have this Advantage, to be fit for Service at five Years old, which the others are not till Twelve.

This was all my Master thought fit to tell me at that Time, of what passed in the Grand Council. But he was pleased to conceal one Particular, which related personally to myself, whereof I soon felt the unhappy Effect, as the Reader will know in its proper Place, and from whence I date all the succeeding Misfortunes of my Life.

The *Houyhnhnms* have no Letters, and consequently, their Knowledge is all traditional. But there happening few Events of any Moment among a People so well united, naturally disposed to every Virtue, wholly governed by Reason, and cut off from all Commerce with other Nations; the historical Part is easily preserved without burthening their Memories. I have already observed, that they are subject to no Diseases, and therefore can have no Need of Physicians. However, they have excellent Medicines composed of Herbs, to cure accidental Bruises and Cuts in the Pastern or Frog of the Foot by sharp Stones, as well as other Maims and Hurts in the several Parts of the Body.

They calculate the Year by the Revolution of the Sun and the Moon, but use no Subdivisions into Weeks. They are well enough acquainted with the Motions of those two Luminaries, and understand the Nature of *Eclipses*; and this is the utmost Progress of their *Astronomy*.

In *Poetry* they must be allowed to excel all other Mortals; wherein the Justness of their Similes, and the Minuteness, as well as Exactness of their Descriptions, are indeed inimitable. Their Verses abound very much in both of these; and usually contain either some exalted Notions of Friendship and Benevolence, or the Praises of those who were Victors in Races, and other bodily Exercises. Their Buildings, although very rude and simple, are not inconvenient, but well contrived to defend them from all Injuries of Cold and Heat. They have a Kind of Tree, which at Forty Years old loosens in the Root, and falls with the first Storm; it grows very strait, and being pointed like Stakes with a sharp Stone, (for the *Houyhnhnms* know not the Use of Iron) they stick them erect in the Ground about ten Inches asunder, and then weave in Oat-straw, or sometimes Wattles betwixt them. The Roof is made after the same Manner, and so are the Doors.

The *Houyhnhnms* use the hollow Part between the Pastern and the Hoof of their Fore-feet, as we do our Hands, and this with greater Dexterity, than I could at first imagine. I have seen a white Mare of our Family thread a Needle (which I lent her on Purpose) with that Joynt. They milk their Cows, reap their Oats, and do all the Work which requires Hands, in the same Manner. They have a Kind of hard Flints, which by grinding against other Stones, they form into Instruments, that serve instead of Wedges, Axes, and Hammers. With Tools made of these Flints, they likewise cut their Hay, and reap their Oats, which there groweth naturally in several Fields: The *Yahoos* draw home the Sheaves in Carriages, and the Servants tread them in certain covered Hutts, to get out the Grain, which is kept in Stores. They make a rude Kind of earthen and wooden Vessels, and bake the former in the Sun.

If they can avoid Casualties, they die only of old Age, and are buried in the obscurest Places that can be found, their Friends and Relations expressing neither Joy nor Grief at their Departure; nor does the dying Person discover the least Regret that he is leaving the World, any more than if he were upon returning home from a Visit to one of his Neighbours: I remember, my Master having once made an Appointment with a Friend and his Family to come to his House upon some Affair of Importance; on the Day fixed, the Mistress and her two Children came very late; she made two Excuses, first for her Husband, who, as she said, happened that very Morning to *Lhnuwnh*. The Word is strongly expressive in their Language, but not easily rendered into *English*; it signifies, *to retire to his first Mother*. Her Excuse for not coming sooner, was, that her Husband dying late in the Morning, she was a good while consulting her Servants about a convenient Place where his Body should be laid; and I observed she behaved herself at our House, as chearfully as the rest: She died about three Months after.

They live generally to Seventy or Seventy-five Years, very seldom to Fourscore: Some Weeks before their Death they feel a gradual Decay, but without Pain. During this time they are much visited by their Friends, because they cannot go abroad with their usual Ease and Satisfaction. However, about ten Days before their Death, which they seldom fail in computing, they return the Visits that have been made by those who are nearest in the Neighbourhood, being carried in a convenient Sledge drawn by *Yahoos*; which Vehicle they use, not only upon this Occasion, but when they grow old, upon long Journeys, or when they are lamed by any Accident. And therefore when the dying *Houyhnhnms* return those Visits, they take a solemn Leave of their Friends, as if they were going to some remote Part of the Country, where they designed to pass the rest of their Lives.

I know not whether it may be worth observing, that the *Houyhnhnms* have no Word in their Language to express any thing that is *evil*, except what they borrow from the Deformities or ill Qualities of the *Yahoos*. Thus they denote the Folly of a Servant, an Omission of a Child, a Stone that cuts their Feet, a Continuance of foul or unseasonable Weather, and the like, by adding to each the Epithet of *Yahoo*. For Instance, *Hhnm Yahoo, Whnaholm Yahoo, Ynlhmndwihlma Yahoo,* and an ill contrived House, *Ynholmhnmrohlnw Yahoo.*

I could with great Pleasure enlarge farther upon the Manners and Virtues of this excellent People; but intending in a short time to publish a Volume by itself expressly upon that Subject, I refer the Reader thither. And in the mean time, proceed to relate my own sad Catastrophe.

CHAPTER X

The Author's Oeconomy, and happy Life among the Houyhnhnms. *His great Improvement in Virtue, by conversing with them. Their Conversations. The Author hath Notice given him by his Master that he must depart from the Country. He falls into a Swoon for Grief, but submits. He contrives and finishes a Canoo, by the Help of a Fellow-Servant, and puts to Sea at a Venture.*

I had settled my little Oeconomy to my own Heart's Content. My Master had ordered a Room to be made for me after their Manner, about six Yards from the House; the Sides and Floors of which I plaistered with Clay, and covered with Rush-mats of my own contriving; I had beaten Hemp, which there grows wild, and made of it a Sort of Ticking: This I filled with the Feathers of several Birds I had taken with Springes made of *Yahoos* Hairs; and were excellent Food. I had worked two Chairs with my Knife, the Sorrel Nag helping me in the grosser and more laborious Part. When my Cloaths were worn to Rags, I made my self others with the Skins of Rabbets, and of a certain beautiful Animal about the same Size, called *Nnuhnoh*, the Skin of which is covered with a fine Down. Of these I likewise made very tolerable Stockings. I soaled my Shoes with Wood which I cut from a Tree, and fitted to the upper Leather, and when this was worn out, I supplied it with the Skins of *Yahoos*, dried in the Sun. I often got Honey out of hollow Trees, which I mingled with Water, or eat it with my Bread. No Man could more verify the Truth of these two Maxims, *That, Nature is very easily satisfied*; and, *That, Necessity is the Mother of Invention.* I enjoyed perfect Health of Body, and Tranquility of Mind; I did not feel the Treachery or Inconstancy of a Friend, nor the Injuries of a secret or open Enemy. I had no Occasion of bribing, flattering or pimping, to procure the Favour of any great Man, or of his Minion. I wanted no Fence against Fraud or Oppression: Here was neither Physician to destroy my Body, nor Lawyer to ruin my Fortune: No Informer to watch my Words and Actions, or forge Accusations against me for Hire: Here were no Gibers, Censurers, Backbiters, Pick-pockets, Highwaymen, House-breakers, Attorneys, Bawds, Buffoons, Gamesters, Politicians, Wits, Spleneticks, tedious Talkers, Controvertists, Ravishers, Murderers, Robbers, Virtuosos; no Leaders or Followers of Party and Faction; no Encouragers to Vice, by Seducement or Examples: No Dungeon, Axes, Gibbets, Whipping posts, or Pillories; no cheating Shop-keepers or Mechanicks: No Pride, Vanity or Affectation: No Fops, Bullies, Drunkards, strolling Whores, or Poxes: No ranting, lewd, expensive Wives: No stupid, proud Pedants: No importunate, over-bearing, quarrelsome, noisy, roaring, empty, conceited, swearing Companions: No Scoundrels raised from the Dust upon the Merit of their Vices; or Nobility thrown into it on account of their Virtues: No Lords, Fidlers, Judges or Dancing-Masters.

I had the Favour of being admitted to several *Houyhnhnms*, who came to visit or dine with my Master; where his Honour graciously suffered me to wait in the Room, and listen to their Discourse. Both he and his Company would often descend to ask me Questions, and receive my Answers. I had also sometimes the Honour of attending my Master in his Visits to others. I never presumed to speak, except in answer to a Question; and then I did it with inward Regret, because it was a Loss of so much Time for improving my self: But I was infinitely delighted with the Station of an humble Auditor in such Conversations, where nothing passed but what was useful, expressed in the fewest and most significant Words: Where (as I have already said) the greatest *Decency* was observed, without the least Degree of Ceremony; where no Person spoke without being pleased himself, and pleasing his Companions: Where there was no Interruption, Tediousness, Heat, or Difference of Sentiments. They have a Notion, That when People are met together, a short Silence doth much improve Conversation: This I found to be true; for during those little Intermissions of Talk, new Ideas would arise in their Minds, which very much enlivened the Discourse. Their Subjects are generally on Friendship and Benevolence; on Order and Oeconomy; sometimes upon the visible Operations of Nature, or ancient Traditions; upon the Bounds and Limits of Virtue; upon the unerring Rules of Reason; or upon some

Determinations, to be taken at the next great Assembly; and often upon the various Excellencies of *Poetry*. I may add, without Vanity, that my Presence often gave them sufficient Matter for Discourse, because it afforded my Master an Occasion of letting his Friends into the History of me and my Country, upon which they were all pleased to discant in a Manner not very advantageous to human Kind; and for that Reason I shall not repeat what they said: Only I may be allowed to observe, That his Honour, to my great Admiration, appeared to understand the Nature of *Yahoos* much better than my self. He went through all our Vices and Follies, and discovered many which I had never mentioned to him; by only supposing what Qualities a *Yahoo* of their Country, with a small Proportion of Reason, might be capable of exerting: And concluded, with too much Probability, how vile as well as miserable such a Creature must be.

I freely confess, that all the little Knowledge I have of any Value, was acquired by the Lectures I received from my Master, and from hearing the Discourses of him and his Friends; to which I should be prouder to listen, than to dictate to the greatest and wisest Assembly in *Europe*. I admired the Strength, Comeliness and Speed of the Inhabitants; and such a Constellation of Virtues in such amiable Persons produced in me the highest Veneration. At first, indeed, I did not feel that natural Awe which the *Yahoos* and all other Animals bear towards them; but it grew upon me by Degress, much sooner than I imagined, and was mingled with a respectful Love and Gratitude, that they would condescend to distinguish me from the rest of my Species.

When I thought of my Family, my Friends, my Countrymen, or human Race in general, I considered them as they really were, *Yahoos* in Shape and Disposition, perhaps a little more civilized, and qualified with the Gift of Speech; but making no other Use of Reason, than to improve and multiply those Vices, whereof their Brethren in this Country had only the Share that Nature allotted them. When I happened to behold the Reflection of my own Form in a Lake or Fountain, I turned away my Face in Horror and detestation of my self; and could better endure the Sight of a common *Yahoo*, than of my own Person. By conversing with the *Houyhnhnms*, and looking upon them with Delight, I fell to imitate their Gait and Gesture, which is now grown into a Habit; and my Friends often tell me in a blunt Way, that *I trot like a*

Horse; which, however, I take for a great Compliment: Neither shall I disown, that in speaking I am apt to fall into the Voice and manner of the *Houyhnhnms,* and hear my self ridiculed on that Account without the least Mortification.

In the Midst of this Happiness, when I looked upon my self to be fully settled for Life, my Master sent for me one Morning a little earlier than his usual Hour. I observed by his Countenance that he was in some Perplexity, and at a Loss how to begin what he had to speak. After a short Silence, he told me, he did not know how I would take what he was going to say: That, in the last general Assembly, when the Affair of the *Yahoos* was entered upon, the Representatives had taken Offence at his keeping a *Yahoo* (meaning my self) in his Family more like a *Houyhnhnm* than a Brute Animal. That, he was known frequently to converse with me, as if he could receive some Advantage or Pleasure in my Company: That, such a Practice was not agreeable to Reason or Nature, or a thing ever heard of before among them. The Assembly did therefore *exhort* him, either to employ me like the rest of my Species, or command me to swim back to the Place from whence I came. That, the first of these Expedients was utterly rejected by all the *Houyhnhnms,* who had ever seen me at his House or their own: For, they alledged, That because I had some Rudiments of Reason, added to the natural Pravity of those Animals, it was to be feared, I might be able to seduce them into the woody and mountainous Parts of the Country, and bring them in Troops by Night to destroy the *Houyhnhnms* Cattle, as being naturally of the ravenous Kind, and averse from Labour.

My Master added, That he was daily pressed by the *Houyhnhnms* of the Neighbourhood to have the Assembly's *Exhortation* executed, which he could not put off much longer. He doubted, it would be impossible for me to swim to another Country; and therefore wished I would contrive some Sort of Vehicle resembling those I had described to him, that might carry me on the Sea; in which Work I should have the Assistance of his own Servants, as well as those of his Neighbours. He concluded, that for his own Part he could have been content to keep me in his Service as long as I lived; because he found I had cured myself of some bad Habits and Dispositions, by endeavouring, as far as my inferior Nature was capable, to imitate the *Houyhnhnms.*

I should here observe to the Reader, that a Decree of the general

Assembly in this Country, is expressed by the Word *Hnhloayn*, which signifies an *Exhortation*; as near as I can render it: For they have no Conception how a rational Creature can be *compelled*, but only advised, or *exhorted*; because no Person can disobey Reason, without giving up his Claim to be a rational Creature.

I was struck with the utmost Grief and Despair at my Master's Discourse; and being unable to support the Agonies I was under, I fell into a Swoon at his Feet: When I came to myself, he told me, that he concluded I had been dead. (For these People are subject to no such Imbecillities of Nature) I answered, in a faint Voice, that Death would have been too great an Happiness; that although I could not blame the Assembly's *Exhortation*, or the Urgency of his Friends; yet in my weak and corrupt Judgment, I thought it might consist with Reason to have been less rigorous. That, I could not swim a League, and probably the nearest Land to theirs might be distant above an Hundred: That, many Materials, necessary for making a small Vessel to carry me off, were wholly wanting in this Country, which however, I would attempt in Obedience and Gratitude to his Honour, although I concluded the thing to be impossible, and therefore looked on myself as already devoted to Destruction. That, the certain Prospect of an unnatural Death, was the least of my Evils: For, supposing I should escape with Life by some strange Adventure, how could I think with Temper,[1] of passing my Days among *Yahoos*, and relapsing into my old Corruptions, for want of Examples to lead and keep me within the Paths of Virtue. That, I knew too well upon what solid Reasons all the Determinations of the wise *Houyhnhnms* were founded, not to be shaken by Arguments of mine, a miserable *Yahoo*; and therefore after presenting him with my humble Thanks for the Offer of his Servants Assistance in making a Vessel, and desiring a reasonable Time for so difficult a Work, I told him, I would endeavour to preserve a wretched Being; and, if ever I returned to *England*, was not without Hopes of being useful to my own Species, by celebrating the Praises of the renowned *Houyhnhnms*, and proposing their Virtues to the Imitation of Mankind.

My Master in a few Words made me a very gracious Reply, allowed me the Space of two *Months* to finish my Boat; and ordered the Sorrel Nag, my Fellow-Servant, (for so at this Distance I may presume to call him) to follow my Instructions, because I told my

[1] Temperateness, tranquility.

Master, that his Help would be sufficient, and I knew he had a Tenderness for me.

In his Company my first Business was to go to that Part of the Coast, where my rebellious Crew had ordered me to be set on Shore. I got upon a Height, and looking on every Side into the Sea, fancied I saw a small Island, towards the *North-East*: I took out my Pocket-glass, and could then clearly distinguish it about five Leagues off, as I computed; but it appeared to the Sorrel Nag to be only a blue Cloud: For, as he had no Conception of any Country beside his own, so he could not be as expert in distinguishing remote Objects at Sea, as we who so much converse in that Element.

After I had discovered this Island, I considered no farther; but resolved, it should, if possible, be the first Place of my Banishment, leaving the Consequence to Fortune.

I returned home, and consulting with the Sorrel Nag, we went into a Copse at some Distance, where I with my Knife, and he with a sharp Flint fastened very artificially,[2] after their Manner, to a wooden Handle, cut down several Oak Wattles about the Thickness of a Walking-staff, and some larger Pieces. But I shall not trouble the Reader with a particular Description of my own Mechanicks: Let it suffice to say, that in six Weeks time, with the Help of the Sorrel Nag, who performed the Parts that required most Labour, I finished a Sort of *Indian* Canoo; but much larger, covering it with the Skins of *Yahoos*, well stitched together, with hempen Threads of my own making. My Sail was likewise composed of the Skins of the same Animal; but I made use of the youngest I could get; the older being too tough and thick; and I likewise provided myself with four Paddles. I laid in a Stock of boiled Flesh, of Rabbets and Fowls; and took with me two Vessels, one filled with Milk, and the other with Water.

I tried my Canoo in a large Pond near my Master's House, and then corrected in it what was amiss; stopping all the Chinks with *Yahoos* Tallow, till I found it stanch, and able to bear me, and my Freight. And when it was as compleat as I could possibly make it, I had it drawn on a Carriage very gently by *Yahoos*, to the Sea-side, under the Conduct of the Sorrel Nag, and another Servant.

When all was ready, and the Day came for my Departure, I took Leave of my Master and Lady, and the whole Family, my Eyes flowing with Tears, and my Heart quite sunk with Grief. But his

[2] Adroitly.

Honour, out of Curiosity, and perhaps (if I may speak it without Vanity) partly out of Kindness, was determined to see me in my Canoo; and got several of his neighbouring Friends to accompany him. I was forced to wait above an Hour for the Tide, and then observing the Wind very fortunately bearing towards the Island, to which I intended to steer my Course, I took a second Leave of my Master: But as I was going to prostrate myself to kiss his Hoof, he did me the Honour to raise it gently to my Mouth. I am not ignorant how much I have been censured for mentioning this last Particular. Detractors are pleased to think it improbable, that so illustrious a Person should descend to give so great a Mark of Distinction to a Creature so inferior as I. Neither have I forgot, how apt some Travellers are to boast of extraordinary Favours they have received. But, if these Censurers were better acquainted with the noble and courteous Disposition of the *Houyhnhnms,* they would soon change their Opinion. I paid my Respects to the rest of the *Houyhnhnms* in his Honour's Company; then getting into my Canoo, I pushed off from Shore.

CHAPTER XI

The Author's dangerous Voyage. He arrives at New-Holland, *hoping to settle there. Is wounded with an Arrow by one of the Natives. Is seized and carried by Force into a* Portugueze *Ship. The great Civilities of the Captain. The Author arrives at* England.

I began this desperate Voyage on *February* 15, 1714/5,[1] at 9 o'Clock in the Morning. The Wind was very favourable; however, I made use at first only of my Paddles; but considering I should soon be weary, and that the Wind might probably chop about, I ventured to set up my little Sail; and thus, with the Help

[1] 1715, according to our calendar. In Swift's time, the new year dated from March 25.

of the Tide, I went at the Rate of a League and a Half an Hour, as near as I could guess. My Master and his Friends continued on the Shoar, till I was almost out of Sight; and I often heard the Sorrel Nag (who always loved me) crying out, *Hnuy illa nyha maiah Yahoo,* Take Care of thy self, gentle *Yahoo.*

My Design was, if possible, to discover some small Island uninhabited, yet sufficient by my Labour to furnish me with Necessaries of Life, which I would have thought a greater Happiness than to be first Minister in the politest Court of *Europe*; so horrible was the Idea I conceived of returning to live in the Society and under the Government of *Yahoos.* For in such a Solitude as I desired, I could at least enjoy my own Thoughts, and reflect with Delight on the Virtues of those inimitable *Houyhnhnms,* without any Opportunity of degenerating into the Vices and Corruptions of my own Species.

The Reader may remember what I related when my Crew conspired against me, and confined me to my Cabbin. How I continued there several Weeks, without knowing what Course we took; and when I was put ashore in the Longboat, how the Sailors told me with Oaths, whether true or false, that they knew not in what Part of the World we were. However, I did then believe us to be about ten Degrees *Southward* of the *Cape of Good Hope,* or about 45 Degrees *Southern* Latitude, as I gathered from some general Words I overheard among them, being I supposed to the *South-East* in their intended Voyage to *Madagascar.* And although this were but little better than Conjecture, yet I resolved to steer my Course *Eastward,* hoping to reach the *South-West* Coast of *New-Holland,* and perhaps some such Island as I desired, lying *Westward* of it. The Wind was full West, and by six in the Evening I computed I had gone *Eastward* at least eighteen Leagues; when I spied a very small Island about half a League off, which I soon reached. It was nothing but a Rock with one Creek, naturally arched by the Force of Tempests. Here I put in my Canoo, and climbing a Part of the Rock, I could plainly discover Land to the *East,* extending from *South* to *North.* I lay all Night in my Canoo; and repeating my Voyage early in the Morning, I arrived in seven Hours to the *South-East* Point of *New-Holland.* This confirmed me in the Opinion I have long entertained, that the *Maps* and *Charts* place this Country at least three Degrees more to the *East* than it really is; which Thought I communicated many Years ago to my worthy Friend Mr. *Herman Moll*,[2] and gave him my Reasons for it, although he hath rather chosen to follow other Authors.

I saw no Inhabitants in the Place where I landed; and being unarmed, I was afraid of venturing far into the Country. I found some Shell-Fish on the Shore, and eat them raw, not daring to kindle a Fire, for fear of being discovered by the Natives. I continued three Days feeding on Oysters and Limpits, to save my own Provisions; and I fortunately found a Brook of excellent Water, which gave me great Relief.

On the fourth Day, venturing out early a little too far, I saw twenty or thirty Natives upon a Height, not above five hundred Yards from me. They were stark naked, Men, Women and Children round a Fire, as I could discover by the Smoke. One of them spied me, and gave Notice to the rest; five of them advanced towards me, leaving the Women and Children at the Fire. I made what haste I could to the Shore, and getting into my Canoo, shoved off: The Savages observing me retreat, ran after me; and before I could get far enough into the Sea, discharged an Arrow, which wounded me deeply on the Inside of my left Knee (I shall carry the Mark to my Grave.) I apprehended the Arrow might be poisoned; and paddling out of the Reach of their Darts (being a calm Day) I made a shift to suck the Wound, and dress it as well as I could.

I was at a Loss what to do, for I durst not return to the same Landing-place, but stood to the *North*, and was forced to paddle; for the Wind, although very gentle, was against me, blowing *North-West*. As I was looking about for a secure Landing-place, I saw a Sail to the *North North-East*, which appearing every Minute more visible, I was in some Doubt, whether I should wait for them or no; but at last my Detestation of the *Yahoo* Race prevailed; and turning my Canoo, I sailed and paddled together to the *South*, and got into the same Creek from whence I set out in the Morning; choosing rather to trust my self among these *Barbarians* than live with *European Yahoos*. I drew up my Canoo as close as I could to the Shore, and hid my self behind a Stone by the little Brook, which, as I have already said, was excellent Water.

The Ship came within half a League of this Creek, and sent out

[2] Of Dutch origins, Moll was a noted map-maker who had settled in London.

her Long-Boat with Vessels to take in fresh Water (for the Place it seems was very well known) but I did not observe it until the Boat was almost on Shore; and it was too late to seek another Hiding-Place. The Seamen at their landing observed my Canoo, and rummaging it all over, easily conjectured that the Owner could not be far off. Four of them well armed searched every Cranny and Lurking-hole, till at last they found me flat on my Face behind the Stone. They gazed a while in Admiration at my strange uncouth Dress; my Coat made of Skins, my wooden-soaled Shoes, and my furred Stockings; from whence, however, they concluded I was not a Native of the Place, who all go naked. One of the Seamen in *Portugueze* bid me rise, and asked who I was. I understood that Language very well, and getting upon my Feet, said, I was a poor *Yahoo,* banished from the *Houyhnhnms,* and desired they would please to let me depart. They admired to hear me answer them in their own Tongue, and saw by my Complection I must be an *European*; but were at a Loss to know what I meant by *Yahoos* and *Houyhnhnms,* and at the same Time fell a laughing at my strange Tone in speaking, which resembled the Neighing of a Horse. I trembled all the while betwixt Fear and Hatred: I again desired Leave to depart, and was gently moving to my Canoo; but they laid hold on me, desiring to know what Country I was of? whence I came? with many other Questions. I told them, I was born in *England,* from whence I came about five Years ago, and then their Country and ours was at Peace. I therefore hoped they would not treat me as an Enemy, since I meant them no Harm, but was a poor *Yahoo,* seeking some desolate Place where to pass the Remainder of his unfortunate Life.

When they began to talk, I thought I never heard or saw any thing so unnatural; for it appeared to me as monstrous as if a Dog or a Cow should speak in *England,* or a *Yahoo* in *Houyhnhnm-Land.* The honest *Portugueze* were equally amazed at my strange Dress, and the odd Manner of delivering my Words, which however they understood very well. They spoke to me with great Humanity, and said they were sure their Captain would carry me *gratis* to *Lisbon,* from whence I might return to my own Country; that two of the Seamen would go back to the Ship, to inform the Captain of what they had seen, and receive his Orders; in the mean Time, unless I would give my solemn Oath not to fly, they would secure me by Force. I thought it best to comply with their Proposal.

They were very curious to know my Story, but I gave them very little Satisfaction; and they all conjectured, that my Misfortunes had impaired my Reason. In two Hours the Boat, which went loaden with Vessels of Water, returned with the Captain's Commands to fetch me on Board. I fell on my Knees to preserve my Liberty; but all was in vain, and the Men having tied me with Cords, heaved me into the Boat, from whence I was taken into the Ship, and from thence into the Captain's Cabbin.

His Name was *Pedro de Mendez;* he was a very courteous and generous Person; he entreated me to give some Account of my self, and desired to know what I would eat or drink; said, I should be used as well as himself, and spoke so many obliging Things, that I wondered to find such Civilities from a *Yahoo.* However, I remained silent and sullen; I was ready to faint at the very Smell of him and his Men. At last I desired something to eat out of my own Canoo; but he ordered me a Chicken and some excellent Wine, and then directed that I should be put to Bed in a very clean Cabbin. I would not undress my self, but lay on the Bed-cloaths; and in half an Hour stole out, when I thought the Crew was at Dinner; and getting to the Side of the Ship, was going to leap into the Sea, and swim for my Life, rather than continue among *Yahoos.* But one of the Seamen prevented me, and having informed the Captain, I was chained to my Cabbin.

After Dinner *Don Pedro* came to me, and desired to know my Reason for so desperate an Attempt; assured me he only meant to do me all the Service he was able; and spoke so very movingly, that at last I descended to treat him like an Animal which had some little Portion of Reason. I gave him a very short Relation of my Voyage; of the Conspiracy against me by my own Men; of the Country where they set me on Shore, and of my five Years Residence there. All which he looked upon as if it were a Dream or a Vision; whereat I took great Offence: For I had quite forget the Faculty of Lying, so peculiar to *Yahoos* in all Countries where they preside, and consequently the Disposition of suspecting Truth in others of their own Species. I asked him, Whether it were the Custom of his Country to *say the Thing that was not?* I assured him I had almost forgot what he meant by Falshood; and if I had lived a thousand Years in *Houyhnhnmland,* I should never have heard a Lie from the meanest Servant. That I was altogether indifferent whether he believed me or no; but however, in return for his Favours, I would give so much Allowance to the Corruption of his Nature, as to answer any Objection he would please to make; and he might easily discover the Truth.

The Captain, a wise Man, after many Endeavours to catch me tripping in some Part of my Story, at last began to have a better Opinion of my Veracity. But he added, that since I professed so inviolable an Attachment to Truth, I must give him my Word of Honour to bear him Company in this Voyage without attempting any thing against my Life; or else he would continue me a Prisoner till we arrived at *Lisbon*. I gave him the Promise he required; but at the same time protested that I would suffer the greatest Hardships rather than return to live among *Yahoos*.

Our Voyage passed without any considerable Accident. In Gratitude to the Captain I sometimes sate with him at his earnest Request, and strove to conceal my Antipathy against human Kind, although it often broke out; which he suffered to pass without Observation. But the greatest Part of the Day, I confined myself to my Cabbin, to avoid seeing any of the Crew. The Captain had often intreated me to strip myself of my savage Dress, and offered to lend me the best Suit of Cloaths he had. This I would not be prevailed on to accept, abhorring to cover myself with any thing that had been on the Back of a *Yahoo*. I only desired he would lend me two clean Shirts, which having been washed since he wore them, I believed would not so much defile me. These I changed every second Day, and washed them myself.

We arrived at *Lisbon, Nov.* 5, 1715. At our landing, the Captain forced me to cover myself with his Cloak, to prevent the Rabble from crouding about me. I was conveyed to his own House; and at my earnest Request, he led me up to the highest Room backwards.[3] I conjured him to conceal from all Persons what I had told him of the *Houyhnhnms*; because the least Hint of such a Story would not only draw Numbers of People to see me, but probably put me in Danger of being imprisoned, or burnt by the *Inquisition*. The Captain persuaded me to accept a Suit of Cloaths newly made; but I would not suffer the Taylor to take my Measure; however, Don *Pedro* being almost of my Size, they fitted me well enough. He accoutred me with other Necessaries all new, which I aired for Twenty-four Hours before I would use them.

The Captain had no Wife, nor above three Servants, none of

[3] At the rear.

which were suffered to attend at Meals; and his whole Deportment was so obliging, added to very good *human* Understanding, that I really began to tolerate his Company. He gained so far upon me, that I ventured to look out of the back Window. By Degrees I was brought into another Room, from whence I peeped into the Street, but drew my Head back in a Fright. In a Week's Time he seduced me down to the Door. I found my Terror gradually lessened, but my Hatred and Contempt seemed to increase. I was at last bold enough to walk the Street in his Company, but kept my Nose well stopped with Rue, or sometimes with Tobacco.

In ten Days, Don *Pedro*, to whom I had given some Account of my domestick Affairs, put it upon me as a Point of Honour and Conscience, that I ought to return to my native Country, and live at home with my Wife and Children. He told me, there was an *English* Ship in the Port just ready to sail, and he would furnish me with all things necessary. It would be tedious to repeat his Arguments, and my Contradictions. He said, it was altogether impossible to find such a solitary Island as I had desired to live in; but I might command in my own House, and pass my time in a Manner as recluse as I pleased.

I complied at last, finding I could not do better. I left *Lisbon* the 24th Day of *November*, in an *English* Merchant-man, but who was the Master I never inquired. Don *Pedro* accompanied me to the Ship, and lent me Twenty Pounds. He took kind Leave of me, and embraced me at parting; which I bore as well as I could. During this last Voyage I had no Commerce with the Master, or any of his Men; but pretending I was sick kept close in my Cabbin. On the Fifth of *December*, 1715, we cast Anchor in the *Downs* about Nine in the Morning, and at Three in the Afternoon I got safe to my House at *Redriff*.

My Wife and Family received me with great Surprize and Joy, because they concluded me certainly dead; but I must freely confess, the Sight of them filled me only with Hatred, Disgust and Contempt; and the more, by reflecting on the near Alliance I had to them. For, although since my unfortunate Exile from the *Houyhnhnm* Country, I had compelled myself to tolerate the Sight of *Yahoos*, and to converse with Don *Pedro de Mendez*; yet my Memory and Imaginations were perpetually filled with the Virtues and Ideas of those exalted *Houyhnhnms*. And when I began to consider, that by copulating with one of the *Yahoo*-Species, I had become a Parent of more; it struck me with the utmost Shame, Confusion and Horror.

As soon as I entered the House, my Wife took me in her Arms, and kissed me; at which, having not been used to the Touch of that odious Animal for so many Years, I fell in a Swoon for almost an Hour. At the Time I am writing, it is five Years since my last Return to *England*: During the first Year I could not endure my Wife or Children in my Presence, the very Smell of them was intolerable; much less could I suffer them to eat in the same Room. To this Hour they dare not presume to touch my Bread, or drink out of the same Cup; neither was I ever able to let one of them take me by the Hand. The first Money I laid out was to buy two young Stone-Horses,[4] which I keep in a good Stable, and next to them the Groom is my greatest Favourite; for I feel my Spirits revived by the Smell he contracts in the Stable. My Horses understand me tolerably well; I converse with them at least four Hours every Day. They are Strangers to Bridle or Saddle; they live in great Amity with me, and Friendship to each other.

[4] Stallions.

CHAPTER XII

The Author's Veracity. His Design in publishing this Work. His Censure of those Travellers who swerve from the Truth. The Author clears himself from any sinister Ends in writing. An Objection answered. The Method of planting Colonies. His Native Country commended. The Right of the Crown to those Countries described by the Author, is justified. The Difficulty of conquering them. The Author takes his last Leave of the Reader; proposeth his Manner of Living for the future; gives good Advice, and concludeth.

Thus, gentle Reader, I have given thee a faithful History of my Travels for Sixteen Years, and above Seven Months; wherein I have not been so studious of Ornament as of Truth. I could perhaps like others have astonished thee with strange improbable Tales; but I rather chose to relate plain Matter of Fact in the simplest Manner and Style; because my principal Design was to inform, and not to amuse thee.

It is easy for us who travel into remote Countries, which are seldom visited by *Englishmen* or other *Europeans*, to form Descriptions of wonderful Animals both at Sea and Land. Whereas, a Traveller's chief Aim should be to make Men wiser and better, and to improve their Minds by the bad, as well as good Example of what they deliver concerning foreign Places.

I could heartily wish a Law were enacted, that every Traveller, before he were permitted to publish his Voyages, should be obliged to make Oath before the *Lord High Chancellor*, that all he intended to print was absolutely true to the best of his Knowledge; for then the World would no longer be deceived as it usually is, while some Writers, to make their Works pass the better upon the Publick, impose the grossest Falsities on the unwary Reader. I have perused several Books of Travels with great Delight in my younger Days; but, having since gone over most Parts of the Globe, and been able to contradict many fabulous Accounts from my own Observation; it hath given me a great Disgust against this Part of Reading, and some Indignation to see the Credulity of Mankind so impudently abused. Therefore, since my Acquaintance were pleased to think my poor Endeavours might not be unacceptable to my Country; I imposed on myself as a Maxim, never to be swerved from, that I would *strictly adhere to Truth*; neither indeed can I be ever under the least Temptation to vary from it, while I retain in my Mind the Lectures and Example of my noble Master, and the other illustrious *Houyhnhnms,* of whom I had so long the Honour to be an humble Hearer.

——Nec si miserum Fortuna Sinonem
Finxit, vanum etiam, mendacemque improba finget.[1]

I know very well, how little Reputation is to be got by Writings which require neither Genius nor Learning, nor indeed any other Talent, except a good Memory, or an exact *Journal.* I know likewise, that Writers of Travels, like *Dictionary*-Makers, are sunk into Oblivion by the Weight and Bulk of those who come last, and therefore lie uppermost. And it is highly probable, that such Travellers who shall hereafter visit the Countries described in this Work of mine, may by detecting my Errors, (if there be any) and adding many new Discoveries of their own, jostle me out of Vogue, and stand in my Place; making the World forget that ever I was an Author. This indeed would be too great a Mortification if I wrote for Fame: But, as my sole Intention was the PUBLICK GOOD, I cannot be altogether disappointed. For, who can read the Virtues I have mentioned in the glorious *Houyhnhnms,* without being ashamed of his own Vices, when he considers himself as the reasoning, governing Animal of his Country? I shall say nothing of those remote Nations where *Yahoos* preside; amongst which the least corrupted are the *Brobdingnagians,* whose wise Maxims in

[1] "Though Fortune has made Sinon wretched, she has not made him untrue and a liar" (*Aeneid,* II, 79-80). Gulliver's quotation is accurate, but he has mistaken the context. These are Sinon's words, belied by the very speech in which they occur.

Morality and Government, it would be our Happiness to observe. But I forbear descanting further, and rather leave the judicious Reader to his own Remarks and Applications.

I am not a little pleased that this Work of mine can possibly meet with no Censurers: For what Objections can be made against a Writer who relates only plain Facts that happened in such distant Countries, where we have not the least Interest with respect either to Trade or Negotiations? I have carefully avoided every Fault with which common Writers of Travels are often too justly charged. Besides, I meddle not the least with any *Party*, but write without Passion, Prejudice, or Ill-will against any Man or Number of Men whatsoever. I write for the noblest End, to inform and instruct Mankind, over whom I may, without Breach of Modesty, pretend to some Superiority, from the Advantages I received by conversing so long among the most accomplished *Houyhnhnms*. I write without any View towards Profit or Praise. I never suffer a Word to pass that may look like Reflection, or possibly give the least Offence even to those who are most ready to take it. So that, I hope, I may with Justice pronounce myself an Author perfectly blameless; against whom the Tribes of Answerers, Considerers, Observers, Reflectors, Detecters, Remarkers, will never be able to find Matter for exercising their Talents.

I confess, it was whispered to me, that I was bound in Duty as a Subject of *England*, to have given in a Memorial to a Secretary of State, at my first coming over; because, whatever Lands are discovered by a Subject, belong to the Crown. But I doubt, whether our Conquests in the Countries I treat of, would be as easy as those of *Ferdinando Cortez* over the naked *Americans*. The *Lilliputians* I think, are hardly worth the Charge of a Fleet and Army to reduce them; and I question whether it might be prudent or safe to attempt the *Brobdingnagians*: Or, whether an *English* Army would be much at their Ease with the Flying Island over their Heads. The *Houyhnhnms*, indeed, appear not to be so well prepared for War, a Science to which they are perfect Strangers, and especially against missive Weapons. However, supposing myself to be a Minister of State, I could never give my Advice for invading them. Their Prudence, Unanimity, Unacquaintedness with Fear, and their Love of their Country would amply supply all Defects in the military Art. Imagine twenty Thousand of them breaking into the Midst of an *European* Army, confounding the Ranks, overturning the Carriages, battering the Warriors Faces into Mummy,[2] by terrible Yerks from their hinder Hoofs: For they would well deserve the Character given to *Augustus; Recalcitrat undique tutus.*[3] But instead of Proposals for conquering that magnanimous Nation, I rather wish they were in a Capacity or Disposition to send a sufficient Number of their Inhabitants for civilizing *Europe*; by teaching us the first Principles of Honour, Justice, Truth, Temperance, publick Spirit, Fortitude, Chastity, Friendship, Benevolence, and Fidelity. The *Names* of all which Virtues are still retained among us in most Languages, and are to be met with in modern as well as ancient Authors; which I am able to assert from my own small Reading.

But, I had another Reason which made me less forward to enlarge his Majesty's Dominions by my Discoveries: To say the Truth, I had conceived a few Scruples with relation to the distributive Justice of Princes upon those Occasions. For Instance, A Crew of Pyrates are driven by a Storm they know not whither; at length a Boy discovers Land from the Top-mast; they go on Shore to rob and plunder; they see an harmless People, are entertained with Kindness, they give the Country a new Name, they take formal Possession of it for the King, they set up a rotton Plank or a Stone for a Memorial, they murder two or three Dozen of the Natives, bring away a Couple more by Force for a Sample, return home, and get their Pardon. Here commences a new Dominion acquired with a Title by *Divine Right*. Ships are sent with the first Opportunity; the Natives driven out or destroyed, their Princes tortured to discover their Gold; a free Licence given to all Acts of Inhumanity and Lust; the Earth reeking with the Blood of its Inhabitants: And this execrable Crew of Butchers employed in so pious an Expedition, is a *modern Colony* sent to convert and civilize an idolatrous and barbarous People.

But this Description, I confess, doth by no means affect the *British* Nation, who may be an Example to the whole World for their Wisdom, Care, and Justice in planting Colonies; their liberal Endowments for the Advancement of Religion and Learning; their Choice of devout and able Pastors to propagate *Christianity*; their

[2] Pulp.

[3] "He kicks backwards, protected on each side" (Horace, *Satires*, II, i, 20.)

Caution in stocking their Provinces with People of sober Lives and Conversations from this the Mother Kingdom; their strict Regard to the Distribution of Justice, in supplying the Civil Administration through all their Colonies with Officers of the greatest Abilities, utter Strangers to Corruption: And to crown all, by sending the most vigilant and virtuous Governors, who have no other Views than the Happiness of the People over whom they preside, and the Honour of the King their Master.

But, as those Countries which I have described do not appear to have any Desire of being conquered, and enslaved, murdered or driven out by Colonies; nor abound either in Gold, Silver, Sugar or Tobacco; I did humbly conceive they were by no Means proper Objects of our Zeal, our Valour, or our Interest. However, if those whom it may concern, think fit to be of another Opinion, I am ready to depose, when I shall be lawfully called, That no *European* did ever visit these Countries before me. I mean, if the Inhabitants ought to be believed.

But, as to the Formality of taking Possession in my Sovereign's Name, it never came once into my Thoughts; and if it had, yet as my Affairs then stood, I should perhaps in point of Prudence and Self-Preservation, have put it off to a better Opportunity.

Having thus answered the *only* Objection that can be raised against me as a Traveller; I here take a final Leave of my Courteous Readers, and return to enjoy my own Speculations in my little Garden at *Redriff*; to apply those excellent Lessons of Virtue which I learned among the *Houyhnhnms*; to instruct the *Yahoos* of my own Family as far as I shall find them docible Animals; to behold my Figure often in a Glass, and thus if possible habituate my self by Time to tolerate the Sight of a human Creature: To lament the Brutality of *Houyhnhnms* in my own Country, but always treat their Persons with Respect, for the Sake of my noble Master, his Family, his Friends, and the whole *Houyhnhnm* Race, whom these of ours have the Honour to resemble in all their Lineaments, however their Intellectuals came to degenerate.

I began last Week to permit my Wife to sit at Dinner with me, at the farthest End of a long Table; and to answer (but with the utmost Brevity) the few Questions I ask her. Yet the Smell of a *Yahoo* continuing very offensive, I always keep my Nose well stopt with Rue, Lavender, or Tobacco-Leaves. And although it be hard for a Man late in Life to remove old Habits; I am not altogether out of Hopes in some Time to suffer a Neighbour *Yahoo* in my Company, without the Apprehensions I am yet under of his Teeth or his Claws.

My Reconcilement to the *Yahoo*-kind in general might not be so difficult, if they would be content with those Vices and Follies only which Nature hath entitled them to. I am not in the least provoked at the Sight of a Lawyer, a Pick-pocket, a Colonel, a Fool, a Lord, a Gamster, a Politician, a Whoremunger, a Physician, an Evidence, a Suborner, an Attorney, a Traytor, or the like: This is all according to the due Course of Things: But, when I behold a Lump of Deformity, and Diseases both in Body and Mind, smitten with *Pride,* it immediately breaks all the Measures of my Patience; neither shall I be ever able to comprehend how such an Animal and such a Vice could tally together. The wise and virtuous *Houyhnhnms,* who abound in all Excellencies that can adorn a rational Creature, have no Name for this Vice in their Language, which hath no Terms to express any thing that is evil, except those whereby they describe the detestable Qualities of their *Yahoos;* among which they were not able to distinguish this of Pride, for want of thoroughly understanding Human Nature, as it sheweth it self in other Countries, where that Animal presides. But I, who had more Experience, could plainly observe some Rudiments of it among the wild *Yahoos.*

But the *Houyhnhnms,* who live under the Government of Reason, are no more proud of the good Qualities they possess, than I should be for not wanting a Leg or an Arm, which no Man in his Wits would boast of, although he must be miserable without them. I dwell the longer upon this Subject from the Desire I have to make the Society of an *English Yahoo* by any Means not insupportable; and therefore I here intreat those who have any Tincture of this absurd Vice, that they will not presume to appear in my Sight.

FINIS

EXTRACTS FROM THE CORRESPONDENCE OF SWIFT, POPE, GAY, AND ARBUTHNOT

SWIFT TO CHARLES FORD

Jan 19th, 1724

My greatest want here[1] is of somebody qualifyed to censure and correct what I write, I know not above two or three whose Judgment I would value, and they are lazy, negligent, and without any Opinion of my Abilityes. I have left the Country of Horses, and am in the flying Island, where I shall not stay long, and my two last Journyes will be soon over; so that if you come here this Summer you will find me returnd—adieu—

Aug 14th, 1725

I have finished my Travells, and I am now transcribing them; they are admirable Things, and will wonderfully mend the World.

SWIFT TO THE REV. THOMAS SHERIDAN

Sept, 11, 1725.[2]

If you are indeed a discarded Courtier, you have reason to complain, but none at all to wonder; you are too young for many Experiences to fall in your way, yet you have read enough to make

The correspondence of Swift in this section is reprinted from *The Correspondence of Jonathan Swift,* Vol. III. Oxford, England: The Clarendon Press. Reprinted by permission of the publisher.

[1] Dublin, where, as Dean of St. Patrick's Cathedral, Swift had been in residence since 1714.

[2] Swift's friend, Sheridan, through an indiscretion, had lost favor with the authorities in Ireland, and had lamented that loss to Swift, who here responds.

you know the Nature of Man. It is safer for a Man's Interest to blaspheme God, than to be of a Party out of Power, or even to be thought so. And since the last was the Case, how could you imagine that all Mouths would not be open when you were received, and in some manner prefer'd by the Government, tho' in a poor way? I tell you there is hardly a Whig in *Ireland* who would allow a Potato and Butter-milk to a reputed Tory. . . . Therefore sit down and be quiet, and mind your Business as you should do, and contract your Friendships, and expect no more from Man than such an Animal is capable of, and you will every day find my Description of Yahoes more resembling.

SWIFT TO ALEXANDER POPE

Sep. 29. 1725

I have employd my time (besides ditching) in finishing correcting, amending, and Transcribing my Travells, in four parts Compleat newly Augmented, and intended for the press when the world shall deserve them, or rather when a Printer shall be found brave enough to venture his Eares. . . . the chief end I propose to my self in all my labors is to vex the world rather then divert it, and if I could compass that designe without hurting my own person or Fortune I would be the most Indefatigable writer you have ever seen without reading I am exceedingly pleased that you have done with Translations Lord Treasurer Oxford often lamented that a rascaly World should lay you under a Necessity of Misemploying your Genius for so long a time.[3] But since you will now be so much better employd when you think of the World give it one lash the more at my Request. I have ever hated all Nations professions and Communityes and all my love is towards individualls for instance I hate the tribe of Lawyers, but I love Councellor such a one, Judge such a one for so with Physicians (I will not Speak of my own Trade) Soldiers, English, Scotch, French; and the rest but principally I hate and detest that animal called man, although I hartily love John,

[3] Pope had been occupied on and off for a decade with his translations of Homer.

Peter, Thomas and so forth. this is the system upon which I have governed my self many years (but do not tell) and so I shall go on till I have done with them I have got Materials Towards a Treatis proving the falsity of that Definition *animal rationale*; and to show it should be only *rationis capax*. Upon this great foundation of Misanthropy (though not Timons manner) The whole building of my Travells is erected: And I never will have peace of mind till all honest men are of my Opinion: by Consequence you are to embrace it immediately and procure that all who deserve my Esteem may do so too. The matter is so clear that it will admit little dispute. nay I will hold a hundred pounds that you and I agree in the Point. . . .

Mr Lewis sent me an Account of Dr Arbuthnett's Illness which is a very sensible Affliction to me, who by living so long out of the World have lost that hardness of Heart contracted by years and generall Conversation. I am daily loosing Friends, and neither seeking nor getting others. O, if the World had but a dozen Arbuthnetts in it I would burn my Travells but however he is not without Fault. There is a passage in Bede highly commending the Piety and learning of the Irish in that Age, where after abundance of praises he overthrows them all by lamenting that, Alas, they kept Easter at a wrong time of the Year. So our Doctor has every Quality and virtue that can make a man amiable or usefull, but alas he hath a sort of Slouch in his Walk. I pray god protect him for he is an excellant Christian tho not a Catholick and as fit a man either to dy or Live as ever I knew.

Novr 26, 1725

Drown the World, I am not content with despising it, but I would anger it if I could with safety. I wish there were an Hospital built for it's despisers, where one might act with safety and it need not be a large Building, only I would have it well endowed. . . .

To hear Boys like you talk of Millimums and Tranquility I am older by thirty years. Lord Bol—by Twenty and you but by Ten then when we last were together and we should differ more then ever. You coquetting a Maid of Honour. My Lord looking on to see how the Gamesters play and I railing at you both. I desire you and all my Friends will take a special care that my Affection to the World may not be imputed to my Age, for I have Credible witnesses ready to depose that it hath never varyed from the Twenty First to the f—ty-eighth year of my Life, (pray fill that Blank Charitably) I tell you after all that I do not hate Mankind, it is vous autres who hate them because you would have them reasonable Animals, and are Angry for being disappointed. I have always rejected that Definition and made another of my own. I am no more angry with —— Then I was with the Kite that last week flew away with one of my Chickins and yet I was pleas'd when one of my Servants Shot him two days after, This I say, because you are so hardy as to tell me of your Intentions to write Maxims in Opposition to Rochfoucault who is my Favorite because I found my whole character in him, however I will read him again because it is possible I may have since undergone some alterations.

JOHN ARBUTHNOT TO SWIFT

5 November 1726

I will make over all my profits to you, for the property of Gulliver's Travells, which I believe, will have as great a Run as John Bunian. Gulliver is a happy man that at his age can write such a merry work.

I made my Lord ArchBishop's compliment to her R Highness who returns his Grace her thanks. . . . when I had the honor to see her She was Reading Gulliver, & was just come to the passage of the Hobbling prince, which she laughed at. I tell yow freely the part of the projectors is the least Brilliant. Lewis Grumbles a little at it & says he wants the Key to it. . . .

Gulliver is in every body's Hands Lord Scarborow who is no inventor of Storys told me that he fell in company with a Master of a ship, who told him that he was very well acquainted with Gulliver, but that the printer had Mistaken, that he livd in Wapping,

& not in Rotherhith. I lent the Book to an old Gentleman, who went immediately to his Map to search for Lilly putt.

ALEXANDER POPE TO SWIFT

16 November 1726

I congratulate you first upon what you call your Couzen's wonderful Book, which is *publica trita manu* at present, and I prophecy will be in future the admiration of all men. That countenance with which it is received by some statesmen, is delightful; I wish I could tell you how every single man looks upon it, to observe which has been my whole diversion this fortnight. I've never been a night in London since you left me, till now for this very end, and indeed it has fully answered my expectations.

I find no considerable man very angry at the book: some indeed think it rather too bold, and too general a Satire: but none that I hear of accuse it of particular reflections (I mean no persons of consequence, or good judgment; the mob of Criticks, you know, always are desirous to apply Satire to those that they envy for being above them) so that you needed not to have been so secret upon this head. Motte receiv'd the copy (he tells me) he knew not from whence, nor from whom, dropp'd at his house in the dark, from a Hackney-coach: by computing the time, I found it was after you left England, so for my part, I suspend my judgment.[4]

JOHN GAY TO SWIFT

Nov. 17. 1726.

About ten days ago a Book was publish'd here of the Travels of one Gulliver, which hath been the conversation of the whole town

[4] Benjamin Motte, the publisher in 1726 of *Gulliver's Travels.* Pope wittily alludes to the efforts made to conceal Swift's authorship.

ever since: The whole impression sold in a week; and nothing is more diverting than to hear the different opinions people give of it, though all agree in liking it extreamly. 'Tis generally said that you are the Author, but I am told, the Bookseller declares he knows not from what hand it came. From the highest to the lowest it is universally read, from the Cabinet-council to the Nursery. The Politicians to a man agree, that it is free from particular reflections, but that the Satire on general societies of men is too severe. Not but we now and then meet with people of greater perspicuity, who are in search for particular applications in every leaf; and it is highly probable we shall have keys published to give light into Gulliver's design. Your Lord [Bolingbroke] is the person who least approves it, blaming it as a design of evil consequence to depreciate human nature, at which it cannot be wondered that he takes most offence, being himself the most accomplish'd of his species, and so losing more than any other of that praise which is due both to the dignity and virtue of a man. Your friend, my Lord Harcourt, commends it very much, though he thinks in some places the matter too far carried. The Duchess Dowager of Marlborough is in raptures at it; she says she can dream of nothing else since she read it; she declares, that she hath now found out, that her whole life hath been lost in caressing the worst part of mankind, and treating the best as her foes; and that if she knew Gulliver, tho' he had been the worst enemy she ever had, she would give up all her present acquaintance for his friendship. You may see by this, that you are not much injur'd by being suppos'd the Author of this piece. If you are, you have disoblig'd us, and two or three of your best friends, in not giving us the least hint of it while you were with us; and in particular Dr. Arbuthnot, who says it is ten thousand pitys he had not known it, he could have added such abundance of things upon every subject. Among Lady-critics, some have found out that Mr. Gulliver had a particular malice to maids of honour. Those of them who frequent the Church, say, his design is impious, and that it is an insult on Providence, by depreciating the works of the Creator. Notwithstanding I am told the Princess hath read it with great pleasure. As to other Critics, they think the flying island is the least entertaining; and so great an opinion the town have of the impossibility of Gulliver's writing at all below himself, that 'tis agreed that Part was not writ by the same Hand, tho' this hath its defenders too. It hath pass'd Lords and Commons, *nemine contradicente*; and the whole town, men, women, and children are quite full of it.

Perhaps I may all this time be talking to you of a Book you have never seen, and which hath not yet reach'd Ireland; if it hath not, I believe what we have said will be sufficient to recommend it to your reading, and that you order me to send it to you.

But it will be much better to come over your self, and read it here, where you will have the pleasure of variety of commentators, to explain the difficult passages to you.

SWIFT TO MRS. HOWARD

Novr 27th 1726[5]

When I received your Letter I thought it the most unaccountable one I ever saw in my Life, and was not able to comprehend three words of it together. The Perverseness of your lines astonished me, which tended downwards to the right on one Page, and upward in the two others. This I thought impossible to be done by any Person who did not squint with both Eyes; an Infirmity I never observed in you. However, one thing I was pleased with, that after you had writ me *down*; you repented, and writ me *up*. But I continued four days at a loss for your meaning, till a Bookseller sent me the Travells of one Cap^{tn} Gulliver, who proved a very good Explainer, although at the same time, I thought it hard to be forced to read a Book of seven hundred Pages in order to understand a Letter of fifty lines; especially since those of our Faculty are already but too much pestered with Commentators. The Stuffs you require are making, because the Weaver piques himself upon having them in perfection, but he has read Gulliver's Book, and has no Conception of what you mean by returning Money, for he is become a Proselyte of the Houyhnhnms, whose great Principle (if I rightly remember) is Benevolence. And as to my self, I am

[5] Henrietta Howard, Countess of Suffolk, was officially Bedchamber Woman to the Princess of Wales, and unofficially mistress to the Prince of Wales. She and Swift had a delightful exchange of letters in late 1726, full of playful allusions to the *Travels;* this is an excerpt from one of these.

rightly affronted with such a base Proposall, that I am determined to complain of you to her Royal Highness, that you are a mercenary Yahoo fond of shining Pebbles. What have I to do with you or your Court further than to show the Esteem I have for your Person, because you happen to deserve it, and my Gratitude to Her Royall Highness, who was pleased, a little to distinguish me; which, by the way is the greatest Compliment I ever made, and may probably be the last. For I am not such a prostitute Flatterer as Gulliver; whose chief Study is to extenuate the Vices, and magnify the Virtues, of Mankind, and perpetually dins our Ears with the Praises of his Country, in the midst of Corruptions, and for that Reason alone, hath found so many readers; and probably will have a Pension, which, I suppose, was his chief design in writing: As for his Compliments to the Ladyes, I can easily forgive him as a naturall Effect of that Devotion which our Sex always ought to pay to Yours.

SWIFT TO ALEXANDER POPE

Nov. [27] 1726

I am just come from answering a Letter of Mrs. Howard's writ in such mystical terms, that I should never have found out the meaning, if a Book had not been sent me called *Gulliver's Travellers*, of which you say so much in yours. I read the Book over, and in the second volume observe several passages which appear to be patched and altered, and the style of a different sort (unless I am much mistaken) Dr. Arbuthnot likes the Projectors least, others you tell me, the Flying island; some think it wrong to be so hard upon whole Bodies or Corporations, yet the general opinion is, that reflections on particular persons are most to be blamed: so that in these cases, I think the best method is to let censure and opinion take their course. A Bishop here said, that Book was full of improbable lies, and for his part, he hardly believed a word of it; and so much for Gulliver.

SWIFT TO L'ABBÉ DES FONTAINES

July 1727[6]

We may concede that the taste of nations is not always the same. But we are inclined to believe that good taste is the same everywhere that there are people of wit, of judgment, and of learning. If, then, the writings of Gulliver were intended only for the British Isles, that traveller must be considered a very contemptible author. The same vices and the same follies reign everywhere; at least, in all the civilized countries of Europe: and the author who writes only for a city, a province, a kingdom, or even an age, warrants so little to be translated, that he deserves not even to be read.

The partisans of Gulliver—they number a good many amongst us—maintain that his book will endure as long as our language, because it draws its merit not from certain modes or manners of thought and speaking, but from a series of observations on the imperfections, the follies, and the vices of man. . . . you will no doubt be surprised to learn that [some] consider this ship's surgeon a solemn author, who never departs from seriousness, who never assumes a role, who never prides himself on possessing wit, and who is content to communicate to the public, in a simple and artless narrative, the adventures that have befallen him and the things that he has seen or heard during his voyages.

[6] The Abbé des Fontaines had translated the *Travels* into French, dropping passages he thought inappropriate to France. What follows—Swift's reply to the omissions—is a translation of the French original.

POPE'S VERSES
ON *GULLIVER'S TRAVELS*

VERSES ON *GULLIVER'S TRAVELS**

I. *To Quinbus Flestrin, the Man-Mountain*

a Lilliputian Ode

In Amaze
Lost, I gaze!
Can our Eyes
Reach thy Size?
May my Lays
Swell with Praise
Worthy thee!
Worthy me!
Muse inspire,
All thy Fire!
Bards of old
Of him told,
When they said
Atlas Head
Propt the Skies:
See! and believe your Eyes!

*The five poems that follow date from late 1726, early 1727, and appeared in the latter year as the opening matter of the second edition of the *Travels*. Though they are substantially Pope's work, it is likely that Gay and Arbuthnot collaborated in part. The manner is comic and parodic: as each poem evokes a different context and expresses a different point of view, so each also is awarded its appropriate literary genre. It is significant, perhaps, that all but the third of Gulliver's journeys proved inspirational to the poet.

See him stride
Vallies wide:
Over Woods,
Over Floods.
When he treads,
Mountains Heads
Groan and shake;
Armies quake,
Lest his Spurn
Overturn
Man and Steed:
Troops take Heed!
Left and Right,
Speed your Flight!
Lest an Host
Beneath his Foot be lost.

Turn'd aside
From his Hide,
Safe from Wound
Darts rebound.
From his Nose
Clouds he blows;
When he speaks,
Thunder breaks!
When he eats,
Famine threats;
When he drinks,
Neptune shrinks!
Nigh thy Ear,
In Mid Air,
On thy Hand
Let me stand,
So shall I,
Lofty Poet! touch the Sky.

II. *The Lamentation of Glumdalclitch, for the Loss of Grildrig*

a Pastoral

Soon as *Glumdalclitch* mist her pleasing Care,
She wept, she blubber'd, and she tore her Hair.
No *British* Miss sincerer Grief has known,
Her Squirrel missing, or her Sparrow flown.
She furl'd her Sampler, and hawl'd in her Thread,
And stuck her Needle into *Grildrig's* Bed;
Then spread her Hands, and with a Bounce let fall
Her Baby, like the Giant in *Guild-hall.*
In Peals of Thunder now she roars, and now
She gently whimpers like a lowing Cow.
Yet lovely in her Sorrow still appears:
Her Locks dishevell'd, and her Flood of Tears
Seem like the lofty Barn of some rich Swain,
When from the Thatch drips fast a Show'r of Rain.

In vain she search'd each Cranny of the House,
Each gaping Chink impervious to a Mouse.
'Was it for this (she cry'd) with daily Care
Within thy Reach I set the Vinegar?
And fill'd the Cruet with the Acid Tide,
While Pepper-Water-Worms thy Bait supply'd;
Where twin'd the Silver Eel around thy Hook,
And all the little Monsters of the Brook.
Sure in that Lake he dropt—My *Grilly's* drown'd'—
She dragg'd the Cruet, but no *Grildrig* found.
'Vain is thy Courage, *Grilly*, vain thy Boast;
But little Creatures enterprise the most.
Trembling, I've seen thee dare the Kitten's Paw;
Nay, mix with Children, as they play'd at Taw;
Nor fear the Marbles, as they bounding flew:
Marbles to them, but rolling Rocks to you.

'Why did I trust thee with that giddy Youth?
Who from a *Page* can ever learn the Truth?
Vers'd in Court Tricks, that Money-loving Boy
To some Lord's Daughter sold the living Toy;
Or rent him Limb from Limb in cruel Play,
As Children tear the Wings of Flies away;
From Place to Place o'er *Brobdingnag* I'll roam,
And never will return, or bring thee home.
But who hath Eyes to trace the passing Wind,
How then thy fairy Footsteps can I find?
Dost thou bewilder'd wander all alone,
In the green Thicket of a Mossy Stone,
Or tumbled from the Toadstool's slipp'ry Round,
Perhaps all maim'd, lie grov'ling on the Ground?
Dost thou, inbosom'd in the lovely Rose,
Or sunk within the Peach's Down, repose?
Within the King-Cup if thy Limbs are spread,
Or in the golden Cowslip's Velvet Head;
O show me, *Flora,* 'midst those Sweets, the Flow'r
Where sleeps my *Grildrig* in his fragrant Bow'r!
'But ah! I fear thy little Fancy roves
On little Females, and on little Loves;
Thy Pigmy Children, and thy tiny Spouse,
The Baby Play-things that adorn thy House,
Doors, Windows, Chimnies, and the spacious Rooms,
Equal in Size to Cells of Honeycombs.
Hast thou for these now ventur'd from the Shore,
Thy Bark a Bean-shell, and a Straw thy Oar?
Or in thy Box, now bounding on the Main?
Shall I ne'er bear thy self and House again?
And shall I set thee on my Hand no more,
To see thee leap the Lines, and traverse o'er
My spacious Palm? Of Stature scarce a Span,
Mimick the Actions of a real Man?
No more behold thee turn my Watches Key,
As Seamen at a Capstern Anchors weigh?
How wert thou wont to walk with cautious Tread,
A Dish of Tea like Milk-Pail on thy Head?
How chase the Mite that bore thy Cheese away,
And keep the rolling Maggot at a Bay?'

She said, but broken Accents stopt her Voice,
Soft as the Speaking Trumpet's mellow Noise:
She sobb'd a Storm, and wip'd her flowing Eyes,
Which seem'd like two broad Suns in misty Skies:
O squander not thy Grief, those Tears command
To weep upon our Cod in *Newfound-land*:
The plenteous Pickle shall preserve the Fish,
And *Europe* taste thy Sorrows in a Dish.

III. *To Mr. Lemuel Gulliver, the Grateful Address of the Unhappy Houyhnhnms, Now in Slavery and Bondage In England*

To thee, we Wretches of the *Houyhnhnm* Band,
Condemn'd to labour in a barb'rous Land,
Return our Thanks. Accept our humble Lays,
And let each grateful *Houyhnhnm* neigh thy Praise.

O happy *Yahoo*, purg'd from human Crimes,
By thy sweet Sojourn in those virtuous Climes,
Where reign our Sires! There, to thy Countrey's Shame,
Reason, you found, and Virtue were the same.
Their Precepts raz'd the Prejudice of Youth,
And even a *Yahoo* learn'd the Love of Truth.

Art thou the first who did the Coast explore;
Did never *Yahoo* tread that Ground before?
Yes, Thousands. But in Pity to their Kind,
Or sway'd by Envy, or through Pride of Mind,
They hid their Knowledge of a nobler Race,
Which own'd, would all their Sires and Sons disgrace.

You, like the *Samian*, visit Lands unknown,
And by their wiser Morals mend your own.
Thus *Orpheus* travell'd to reform his Kind,
Came back, and tam'd the Brutes he left behind.

You went, you saw, you heard: With Virtue fraught,
Then spread those Morals which the *Houyhnhnms* taught.
Our Labours here must touch thy gen'rous Heart,
To see us strain before the Coach and Cart;
Compell'd to run each knavish Jockey's Heat!
Subservient to *New-market's* annual cheat!
With what Reluctance do we Lawyers bear,
To fleece their Countrey Clients twice a Year?
Or manag'd in your Schools, for Fops to ride,
How foam, how fret beneath a Load of Pride!
Yes, we are slaves—but yet, by Reason's Force,
Have learnt to bear Misfortune, like a Horse.

O would the Stars, to ease my Bonds, ordain,
That gentle *Gulliver* might guide my Rein!
Safe would I bear him to his Journey's End,
For 'tis a Pleasure to support a Friend.
But if my Life be doom'd to serve the Bad,
O! may'st thou never want an easy Pad!

Houyhnhnm.

IV. *Mary Gulliver to Captain Lemuel Gulliver*

ARGUMENT. *The Captain, some Time after his Return, being retired to Mr.* Sympson's *in the Country, Mrs. Gulliver, apprehending from his late Behaviour some Estrangement of his Affections, writes him the following expostulating, soothing, and tenderly-complaining Epistle.*

Welcome, thrice welcome to thy native Place!
—What, touch me not? what, shun a Wife's Embrace?
Have I for this thy tedious Absence born,
And wak'd and wish'd whole Nights for thy Return?
In five long Years I took no second Spouse;
What *Redriff* Wife so long hath kept her Vows?
Your Eyes, your Nose, Inconstancy betray;
Your Nose you stop, your Eyes you turn away.
'Tis said, that thou shouldst cleave unto thy Wife;
Once *thou* didst cleave, and *I* could cleave for Life.
Hear and relent! hark, how thy Children moan;
Be kind at least to these, they are thy own:
Behold, and count them all; secure to find
The honest Number that you left behind.
See how they pat thee with their pretty Paws:
Why start you? are they Snakes? or have they Claws?
Thy Christian Seed, our mutual Flesh and Bone:
Be kind at least to these, they are thy own.

Biddel, like thee, might farthest *India* rove;
He chang'd his Country, but retain'd his Love.
There's Captain *Pennel*, absent half his Life,
Comes back, and is the kinder to his Wife.
Yet *Pennel's* Wife is brown, compar'd to me;
And Mistress *Biddel* sure is Fifty three.

Not touch me! never Neighbour call'd me Slut!
Was *Flimnap*'s Dame more sweet in *Lilliput*?
I've no red Hair to breathe an odious Fume;
At least thy Consort's cleaner than thy *Groom*.
Why then that dirty Stable-boy thy Care?
What mean those Visits to the *Sorrel Mare*?
Say, by what Witchcraft, or what Daemon led,
Preferr'st thou *Litter* to the Marriage Bed?

Some say the Dev'l himself is in that *Mare*:
If so, our *Dean* shall drive him forth by Pray'r.
Some think you mad, some think you are possest
That *Bedlam* and clean Straw will suit you best:
Vain Means, alas, this Frenzy to appease!
That *Straw*, that *Straw* would heighten the Disease.

My Bed, (the Scene of all our former Joys,
Witness two lovely Girls, two lovely Boys)
Alone I press; in Dreams I call my Dear,
I stretch my Hand, no *Gulliver* is there!
I wake, I rise, and shiv'ring with the Frost,
Search all the House; my *Gulliver* is lost!
Forth in the Street I rush with frantick Cries:
The Windows open; all the Neighbours rise:
Where sleeps my Gulliver? *O tell me where?*
The Neighbours answer, *With the Sorrel Mare.*

At early Morn, I to the Market haste,
(Studious in ev'ry Thing to please thy Taste)
A curious *Fowl* and *Sparagrass* I chose,
(For I remember you were fond of those,)
Three Shillings cost the first, the last sev'n Groats;
Sullen you turn from both, and call for *Oats*.

Others bring Goods and Treasure to their Houses,
Something to deck their pretty Babes and Spouses;
My *only* Token was a Cup like Horn,
That's made of nothing but a Lady's *Corn*.
'Tis not for that I grieve; no, 'tis to see
The *Groom* and *Sorrel Mare* preferr'd to me!

These, for some Monuments when you deign to quit,
And (at due distance) sweet Discourse admit,
'Tis all my Pleasure thy past Toil to know,
For pleas'd Remembrance builds Delight on Woe.
At ev'ry Danger pants thy Consort's Breast,
And gaping Infants squawle to hear the rest.
How did I tremble, when by thousands bound
I saw thee stretch'd on *Lilliputian* Ground;
When scaling Armies climb'd up ev'ry Part,
Each Step they trod, I felt upon my Heart.
But when thy Torrent quench'd the dreadful Blaze,

King, Queen and Nation, staring with Amaze,
Full in my View how all my Husband came,
And what extinguish'd theirs, encreas'd my Flame.
Those *Spectacles*, ordain'd thine Eyes to save,
Were once my Present; *Love* that Armour gave.
How did I mourn at *Bolgolam's* Decree!
For when he sign'd thy Death, he sentenc'd me.

When folks might see thee all the Country round
For Six-pence, I'd have giv'n a thousand Pound.
Lord! when the *Giant-Babe* that Head of thine
Got in his Mouth, my Heart was up in mine!
When in the *Marrow-Bone* I see thee ramm'd;
Or on the House-top by the *Monkey* cramm'd;
The Piteous Images renew my Pain,
And all thy Dangers I weep o'er again!
But on the *Maiden's Nipple* when you rid,
Pray Heav'n, 'twas all a wanton Maiden did!
Glumdalclitch too!—with thee I mourn her Case.
Heav'n guard the gentle Girl from all Disgrace!
O may the King that one Neglect forgive,
And pardon her the Fault by which I live!
Was there no other Way to set him free?
My Life, alas! I fear prov'd Death to Thee!

O teach me, Dear, new Words to speak my Flame;
Teach me to wooe thee by thy best-lov'd Name!
Whether the Style of *Grildrig* please thee most,
So call'd on *Brobdingnag's* stupendous Coast,
When on the Monarch's ample Hand you sate,
And hollow'd in his Ear Intrigues of State:
Or *Quinbus Flestrin* more Endearment brings,
When like a Mountain you look'd down on Kings:
If Ducal *Nardac, Lilliputian* Peer,
Or *Glumglum's* humbler Title sooth thy Ear:
Nay, wou'd kind *Jove* my Organs so dispose,
To hymn harmonious *Houyhnhnm* thro' the Nose,
I'd call thee *Houyhnhnm,* that high sounding Name,
Thy Children's Noses all should twang the same.
So might I find my loving Spouse of course
Endu'd with all the *Virtues* of a *Horse.*

v. *The Words of the King of Brobdingnag, as He Held Captain Gulliver between His Finger and Thumb for the Inspection of the Sages and Learned Men of the Court*

In Miniature see *Nature's* Power appear;
Which wings the Sun-born Insects of the Air,
Which frames the Harvest-bug, too small for Sight,
And forms the Bones and Muscles of the Mite!
Here view him stretch'd. The Microscope explains,
That the Blood, circling, flows in human Veins;
See, in the Tube he pants, and sprawling lies,
Stretches his little Hands, and rolls his Eyes!

Smit with his Countrey's Love, I've heard him prate
Of Laws and Manners in his Pigmy State.
By Travel, generous Souls enlarge the Mind,
Which home-bred Prepossession had confin'd;
Yet will he boast of many Regions known,
But still, with partial Love, extol his own.
He talks of Senates, and of Courtly Tribes,
Admires their Ardour, but forgets their Bribes;
Of hireling Lawyers tells the just Decrees,
Applauds their Eloquence, but sinks their Fees.
Yet who his Countrey's partial Love can blame?
'Tis sure some Virtue to conceal its Shame.

The World's the native City of the Wise;
He sees his *Britain* with a Mother's Eyes;
Softens Defects, and heightens all its Charms,
Calls it the Seat of Empire, Arts and Arms!
Fond of his Hillock Isle, his narrow Mind
Thinks Worth, Wit, Learning, to that Spot confin'd;
Thus Ants, who for a Grain employ their Cares,
Think all the Business of the Earth is theirs.
Thus Honey-combs seem Palaces to Bees;
And Mites imagine all the World a Cheese.

When Pride in such contemptuous Beings lies,
In Beetles, Britons, Bugs and Butterflies,
Shall we, like Reptiles, glory in Conceit?
Humility's the Virtue of the Great.

CRITICAL ESSAYS

I wondered to hear him say of *Gulliver's Travels*, 'When once you have thought of big men and little men, it is very easy to do all the rest.' I endeavoured to make a stand for Swift, and tried to rouse those who were much more able to defend him . . .

Boswell, *Life of Johnson*

Though a different arrangement was possible, it seemed wisest to separate the criticisms that follow into the two parts indicated here by the numerals I and II. The first consists of full-length essays that either treat in detail, or else clearly suggest, most of the major concerns likely to result from a considered reading of the *Travels*; the second offers briefer commentaries which support or qualify the estimates given earlier, and which in several instances look to other aspects of Swift and the *Travels*. The ordering within each part is thematic rather than chronological.

I

LOUIS A. LANDA

Jonathan Swift

It is rare indeed that a commentator appraises any work of Jonathan Swift without reference to biographical fact. If one of Swift's minor efforts is under discussion, as the poem "The Lady's Dressing Room," we may expect the critical judgment to rest upon some such basis as that presented by Sir Walter Scott, who wished the poem to be interpreted in the light of the author's peculiar habits and state of mind. If Part III of *Gulliver's Travels*, where Swift attacks the corruptions of learning, is the object of consideration, the commentator is certain to make an excursion back to Swift's student days at Trinity College, Dublin, to explain that here began his life-long hatred of science and philosophy. And so with the other works, to the point that the criticism of Swift is a sustained endeavor to interpret the writings in the light of the man, although anyone who reads the critics of Swift will be aware too of a simultaneous and converse process—attempts to interpret the man in the light of the works.

With respect to Swift we are often confronted not only with the critical significance of biographical evidence but as well with the biographical significance of critical evidence. It is easy to find commentators who will have it both ways, commentators, for example, who assume a morbid state of mind in Swift as an explanation of his scatological verse, then use the scatological verse to prove that the author undoubtedly was morbid. Traditionally the criticism of Swift's works is so inextricably mingled with biography that one looks almost in vain for critical judgments based upon merely aesthetic assumptions.

The persistent tendency of the commentators has been to assume a direct and fairly simple reflection in the works of the nature

From *English Institute Essays*, 1946 (1947), pp. 20-35. New York. Reprinted by permission of Columbia University Press.

and personality of Swift; and such a work as *Gulliver's Travels* has as often as not been viewed as both a strange and puzzling psychological case history and a representation of its author's objective experiences. No one can doubt for a moment the validity and the fruitfulness of the biographical approach to *Gulliver's Travels* in particular or to Swift's works in general. Considering the character of his writings—their personal, intimate, and topical nature—this approach is the natural one. Yet I think that the interpretation of Swift has at times suffered somewhat from this tendency, this unwillingness of the commentator to detach the work from the man. But the overemphasis upon this approach is rather less disturbing than its misapplication or its loose and incautious use. Commentators who would doubtless feel some hesitation in equating Fielding with Tom Jones or Sterne with Tristram Shandy can accept with apparent ease as a premise of their criticism that Swift is Gulliver. In what follows I wish, first of all, to comment on certain recurring biographical considerations which have played a part—a not very happy part—in the criticism of Swift's works for a period of two centuries, and, secondly, to present some instances in which other biographical considerations of value for criticism have not been explored sufficiently.

The problem which has most preoccupied Swift's critics has been the pessimism and misanthropy of *Gulliver's Travels* and the endeavor to explain these qualities in the work by searching for exactly corresponding qualities in Swift himself. Part IV of *Gulliver's Travels,* with its contrasting picture of Yahoo and Houyhnhnm, has been the focal point of the discussions, and ordinarily the commentators have acted on the assumption, though not always consciously, that here in Part IV is the real key to Swift. It is maintained or implied that in Part IV are the possibilities of a final comprehension and the basis of a final judgment. The image of Swift—the rather horrendous image—which has been transmitted from generation to generation is chiefly the image deduced from Part IV, enforced by a careful selection of biographical fact or myth appropriately chosen to stress the severe lineaments of his character. Only occasionally is the image, a monochrome, softened by reference to the playful Swift, to Swift the author of delightful light verse, the punster, the genial companion of Queen Anne's Lord Treasurer and her Secretary of State, or to the Swift who was a charming guest at great houses and who had a genius for friendship among both sexes.

Perhaps for purposes of discussion we may ignore the volume and range of Swift's works and grant the unwarranted assumption that the masterpiece is somehow the man, and that a particular portion of the masterpiece—Part IV of *Gulliver*—is of such fundamental significance as to outweigh various other considerations. If we trace the progress of the criticism of *Gulliver's Travels* from Swift's earliest biographer, the Earl of Orrery, to the twentieth century, we find preponderantly and repetitiously a set of severe judgments passed on Part IV, judgments referable back to Swift the man. In his *Remarks on the Life and Writings of Dr. Jonathan Swift* (1752), Orrery climaxes his comments with the statement that "no man [was] better acquainted [than Swift] with human nature, both in the highest, and in the lowest scenes of life" (p. 338). Yet, contradictorily, in discussing Part IV of *Gulliver* he observes that Swift's misanthropy is "intolerable," adding that "the representation which he has given us of human nature, must terrify, and even debase the mind of the reader who views it" (p. 184). Orrery then proceeds to a lengthy vindication of mankind mingled with violent charges against Swift, among them that in painting the Yahoos Swift became one himself and that the "voyage to the Houyhnhnms is a real insult upon mankind" (p. 190). Orrery is significant because with few exceptions his is the tone and pretty much the method of criticism of the Fourth Voyage for a century and a half. The fundamental points raised are concerned with the motives or the personality of the author who would present this particular conception of human nature; and Orrery's explanation of Part IV in terms of injured pride, personal disappointments, and a soured temper becomes as time goes on the traditional one.

Even an occasional defender of Swift, as his good friend Patrick Delany, who answers Orrery point by point, is unwilling to undertake the defense of the last book of *Gulliver*; and he too lets fall such phrases as "moral deformity" and "defiled imagination." The eighteenth-century commentators, taking a high moral line, maintained that Swift's misanthropy had led him to write, as James Beattie phrased it, "a monstrous fiction." It was variously and characteristically stated; the gloomy and perverse Dean had talents that tended toward the wicked rather than the sublime; he was motivated by a malignant wish to degrade and brutalize the human race; he had written a libel on human nature. Though generally these commentators prefer to denounce the moral aspects of the Voyage to Houyhnhnmland and the degraded nature of the author, they leave no doubt that they think Part IV an artistic failure as well. In their eyes moral culpability and artistic failure have a necessary connection. The premise seems to be that a person of unsound views concerning human nature or of false moral views cannot write an artistically sound work. It is as though a Buddhist should deny literary value to Dante's *Divine Comedy* or Milton's *Paradise Lost* because these works are ethically and religiously unsound.

Yet it ought to be said to the honor of the eighteenth-century commentators that they generally paid the author of *Gulliver* the compliment of believing him a sane man. It remained for certain nineteenth-century critics to take a new tack and to elaborate a less defensible charge. Though they accepted the view that the Fourth Voyage could be explained in terms of a depraved author, they *added* that it might well be explained in terms of a mad author. The charge of madness was usually presented with a certain caution. Two commentators in the middle of the century may be taken as examples of the willingness to accuse Swift of insanity and the unwillingness, at the same time, to come out unreservedly. In the *North British Review* of 1849 a reviewer writes of Swift's work that it is "*more* or *less* symptomatic of mental disease" (italics mine); and in the following year, in the London *Times*, a writer says that Swift was "more or less mad." It is possible that Sir Walter Scott is responsible for this wavering between outright and qualified assertion. In his edition of Swift's *Works* (1814) he writes that we cannot justify, by saying that it has a moral purpose, "the nakedness with which Swift has sketched this horrible outline of mankind degraded to a bestial state" (1883 ed., I, 315). He prefers to explain the misanthropy of *Gulliver* as the result of "the *first* impressions of . . . *incipient* mental disease" (italics mine). There are nineteenth-century commentators who felt that the Fourth Voyage should not be read. Thackeray gave such advice to the audience who listened to his lectures on the English humorists of the eighteenth century in 1851; and, later, Edmund Gosse—using such phrases as "the horrible satisfaction of disease" and a brain "not wholly under control"—declared that the "horrible foulness of this satire on the Yahoo . . . banishes from decent households a fourth part of one of the most brilliant and delightful of English books." It is somewhat more surprising to find W. E. H. Lecky, who usually showed a well-balanced and sympathetic understanding of Swift, falling into the jargon. He can see Swift's misanthropy as a constitutional melancholy "mainly due to a physical malady which had long acted upon his brain." It is not surprising, however, that in the twentieth century the psychoanalysts have seized on so attractive a subject as Swift; and now we find *Gulliver* explained in terms of neuroses and complexes. The following quotation is taken from the *Psychoanalytic Review* of 1942: *Gulliver's Travels* "may be viewed as a neurotic phantasy with coprophilia as its main content." It furnishes

> abundant evidence of the neurotic makeup of the author and discloses in him a number of perverse trends indicative of fixation at the anal sadistic stage of libidinal development. Most conspicuous among those perverse trends is that of coprophilia, although the work furnishes evidence of numerous other related neurotic characteristics accompanying the general picture of psychosexual infantilism and emotional immaturity.

By a diligent search this psychoanalyst was able to discover in *Gulliver's Travels* strains of misogyny, misanthropy, mysophilia, mysophobia, voyeurism, exhibitionism, and compensatory potency reactions. If this psychoanalytic approach seems to have in it an element of absurdity, we should recognize that it is only a logical development of the disordered-intellect theory of the nineteenth-century critics, the chief difference being that the terminology has changed and that the psychoanalyst frankly sees *Gulliver's Travels* as case history, whereas the critics were presumably making a literary appraisal. Perhaps these crude and amateur attempts deserve little attention, yet they are a phenomenon that the serious student of Swift can hardly ignore in the light of their recurrence and their effectiveness in perpetuating myths. And they sometimes come with great persuasiveness and literary flavor, as witness Mr. Aldous Huxley's essay in which, by virtue of ignoring nine tenths of Swift's works, he can arrive at an amazingly oversimplified explanation of Swift's greatness: "Swift's greatness," Mr. Huxley writes, "lies in the intensity, the almost insane violence, of that 'hatred of bowels' which is the essence of his misanthropy and which underlies the whole of his work" (*Do What You Will*, 1930, p. 105).

I suggest that the commentators who have relied on a theory of insanity or disordered intellect to explain Swift's works have weakened their case, if they have not vitiated it entirely, by resorting to ex post facto reasoning. The failure of Swift's mental faculties toward the end of his life—some fifteen or sixteen years after the publication of *Gulliver's Travels*—was seized upon to explain something the critics did not like and frequently did not understand. It seemed to them valid to push his insanity back in time, to look retrospectively at the intolerable fourth book of *Gulliver's Travels*, and to infer that Swift's insanity must have been at least incipient when he wrote it. One recent commentator, rather more zealous than others, hints that the madness can be traced as far back as *A Tale of a Tub*. Commentators who observe manifestations of a disordered intellect in the Fourth Voyage have not thought to question the intellect behind the Third Voyage, yet we know now that the third was composed in point of time after the fourth. And these commentators have nothing but praise for the vigor, the keenness, the sanity, and the humanity of the mind that produced the *Drapier's Letters*, yet we have reasonable assurance that Swift completed the draft of Part IV of *Gulliver* in January of 1724 and was at work on the first of the *Drapier's Letters* in February.

Another procedure of which the critics of Swift are fond deserves to be scanned: the habit of taking an isolated statement or an isolated incident and giving it undue significance to support their prepossessions. In a recent study of Swift, in many respects of more than ordinary perceptiveness, the author considers Part IV of *Gulliver* as an embodiment of the tragic view of life. In so doing he passes from the work to the facts or presumed facts of Swift's life to enforce his interpretation, adducing as evidence the report of Swift's manner, in his later years, of bidding friends good-by: "Good night, I hope I shall never see you again." If Swift really used this remark, if he used it seriously, some weight may be attached to it; but I should want to know to whom he used it and in what tone or spirit. It sounds very much like his usual banter, his manner of friendly insult and quite genial vituperation which so often distinguishes his letters to friends who understood his ironic turn and his liking for the inverted compliment. How can we rely on such casual remarks or possibly know what weight to give them? But such a remark is related to Swift's habit of reading certain parts of the Book of Job to prove that he hated life, and is made to seem of a piece with the Fourth Voyage of *Gulliver's Travels.* This is typical of the commentators who have culled from Swift's letters, from the biographies, and from other documents all the presumed evidence of gloom and misanthropy in order to uncover what they have a strong prepossession to uncover, the essential misery of his existence. This is the way to prove, in support of the interpretation of the Fourth Voyage, that "Swift's life was a long disease, with its disappointments, its self-torture, its morbid recriminations."

But a matter of statistical balance is involved here: the facts listed and weighted heavily have been too much of one complexion. Too much has been made of the last years of Swift's life, when he bothered less to conceal his moods and his irritations—and when he seemed to get a certain satisfaction in talking about his ailments. I should like to see some biographer counter the gloomy approach by emphasizing Swift's zest for life, his vitality, and the playfulness of his mind. There is ample evidence in his letters—and in what we know of his activities—of high spirits, good humor, and daily satisfactions. Such a study might very well, without distortion, evidence an unexpected mathematical balance between happiness and unhappiness.

I should not want to be put into the position of denying Swift a considerable pessimism and a fair share of misanthropy. These qualities, however, were not so raw or so unassimilated or so crudely operative in his daily existence as has been often represented. The manner in which these personal qualities have been used to explain *Gulliver* deserves to be questioned. It has been an overly simple process of equating biographical fact and artistic statement, of viewing the work as a transcription of the author's experiences or as a precise and complete representation of his personal philosophy—or as a final explanation of his personality. There is an obvious danger in seeing an artistic or imaginative construction as mere duplication. *Gulliver's Travels* is a work of mingled fantasy and satire; it is Utopian literature, highly allusive and symbolic, charged with hidden meanings and projected to a level several removes from the real world of its author.

To leaven the biographical approach other questions deserve attention. What are the artistic necessities of a work of this type? What are the aesthetic principles, quite apart from other considerations, that shape the work? To what extent is there a compromise between these principles and the conscious or the undeliberate tendency of the author to reflect his experiences and his personality?

If the biographical approach to Swift has been crudely used or overemphasized in certain respects, there are other respects in which biographical considerations of critical value have been left almost wholly unexplored. The most significant of these seems to me to be Swift's profession as a Christian divine. Is there in this some clue to an explanation of Part IV of *Gulliver?* If a reading of the sermons can be trusted, the eighteenth-century divine relished his duty to expatiate on the evils and corruptions of this world and the inadequacies of this life. He seemed to enjoy measuring the imperfections before him against a higher set of values. Swift, I think, would have held an optimistic divine to be a contradiction in terms; and his own pessimism is quite consonant with the pessimism at the heart of Christianity. One of Swift's sermons begins as follows:

> The holy Scripture is full of expressions to set forth the miserable condition of man during the whole progress of his life; his weakness, pride, and vanity, his unmeasurable desires, and perpetual disappointments; the prevalency of his passions, and the corruptions of his reason, his deluding hopes, and his real, as well as imaginary, fears . . . his cares and anxieties, the diseases of his body, and the diseases of his mind. . . . And the wise men of all ages have made the same reflections.[1]

If Swift had written his own comment on *Gulliver's Travels,* he might very well have used the words of this sermon. *Gulliver's Travels* certainly is full of expressions to set forth the miserable condition of man—his weakness, pride, and vanity, his unmeasurable desires, the prevalency of his passions and the corruptions of his reason—and so on through the catalogue. Indeed, Swift's few sermons and those of other eighteenth-century divines could easily be used to annotate *Gulliver's Travels.* It is difficult for me to believe that a contemporary could fail to see the affinity between the Fourth Voyage—or the whole of *Gulliver*—and many of the conventional sermons on human nature and the evils of this life. Swift's emphasis on depraved human nature and his evaluation of man's behavior are certainly *not* at odds with Christian tradition. There is no need to ascribe such views solely to personal bitterness or frustrations or

[1] *On The Poor Man's Contentment.*

melancholia. His thinking and status as a divine had an effect much more profound than is generally recognized. A good case can be made for Part IV of *Gulliver* as being in its implications Christian apologetics, though of course in nontheological terms; in a sense it is an allegory which veils human nature and society as a Christian divine views them. It is by indirection a defense of the doctrine of redemption and man's need of grace.

Only an occasional commentator has recognized and stressed the essentially Christian philosophy of the Fourth Voyage. The first was Swift's relative, Deane Swift, who declared that the Christian conception of the evil nature of man is the "groundwork of the whole satyre contained in the voyage to the Houyhnhnms." Then this cousin of Jonathan Swift, this lesser Swift, delivers himself of a catalogue of vices worthy of his great cousin:

> Ought a preacher of righteousness [he asks], ought a watchman of the Christian faith . . . to hold his peace . . . when avarice, fraud, cheating, violence, rapine, extortion, cruelty, oppression, tyranny, rancour, envy, malice, detraction, hatred, revenge, murder, whoredom, adultery, lasciviousness, bribery, corruption, pimping, lying, perjury, subornation, treachery, ingratitude, gaming, flattery, drunkenness, gluttony, luxury, vanity, effeminacy, cowardice, pride, impudence, hypocrisy, infidelity, blasphemy, idolatry, sodomy, and innumerable other vices are as epidemical as the pox, and many of them the notorious characteristicks of the bulk of mankind? [2]

"Dr. Swift," he adds, "was not the first preacher, whose writings import this kind of philosophy." Surely those clergymen who week after week exposed the deceitfulness of the human heart would have agreed with Deane Swift.

It seems to be true, as T. O. Wedel has pointed out,[3] that Swift's view of human nature was opposed to certain contemporary attitudes in which the passions of men were looked on kindly and in which the dignity of human nature was defended in such a way that the doctrine of original sin lost its efficacy. In his *Reasonableness of Christianity* (1695) John Locke could deny, without raising much

[2] *Essay upon the Life, Writings, and Character of Dr. Swift* (1755), pp. 219-20.

[3] For the relationship between Swift and Wesley stated in this paragraph see an article to which I am much indebted, T. O. Wedel, "On the Philosophical Background of *Gulliver's Travels*," *Studies in Philology*, XXIII (1926), 434-50

serious protest, that the fall of Adam implies the corruption of human nature in Adam's posterity. It is this same current of thought that later in the century disturbed John Wesley who complains in one of his sermons (No. XXXVIII, "Original Sin") that "not a few persons of strong understanding, as well as extensive learning, have employed their utmost abilities to show, what they termed, 'the fair side of human nature in Adam's posterity.'" "So that," Wesley continues, "it is now quite unfashionable to say anything to the disparagement of human nature; which is generally allowed, notwithstanding a few infirmities, to be very innocent, and wise, and virtuous." Is it not significant, when Wesley comes to write his treatise on *The Doctrine of Original Sin* (1756), that he should turn to Swift, to Part IV of *Gulliver* for quotations? In this treatise Wesley refers scornfully to those "who gravely talk of the dignity of our nature," and then quotes several times from what he calls "a late eminent hand." The "late eminent hand" is Swift's, whose words from Part IV of *Gulliver* describing man as "a lump of deformity and disease, both in body and mind, smitten with pride" Wesley has seized on. Wesley refers again and again to the "many laboured panegyrics . . . we now read and hear on the dignity of human nature"; and he raises a question which is, I think, a clue to Swift. If men are generally virtuous, what is the need of the doctrine of Redemption? This is pretty much the point of two sermons by Swift, where he is obviously in reaction to the panegyrics on human nature which came from Shaftesbury and the benevolists, from the defenders of the Stoic wise man, and from proponents of the concept of a man of honor. Swift sensed the danger to orthodox Christianity from an ethical system or any view of human nature stressing man's goodness or strongly asserting man's capacity for virtue. He had no faith in the existence of the benevolent man of Shaftesbury and the anti-Hobbists, the proud, magnanimous man of the Stoics, or the rational man of the deists; his man is a creature of the passions, of pride and self-love, a frail and sinful being in need of redemption. The very simple and wholly unoriginal strain of apologetics in Swift's sermons is based upon an attitude common in traditional Christian thought; and to my way of thinking Swift the clergyman repeats himself in *Gulliver's Travels*. . . .

ALLAN BLOOM

An Outline of *Gulliver's Travels*

Gulliver's Travels is an amazing rhetorical achievement. It is the classic children's story and it is a rather obscene tale. Swift was able to charm innocence and amuse corruption, and this is a measure of his talent. I can think of no parallel: Hans Christian Andersen for children, Boccaccio for adults. But, most of all, it is a philosophic book presented in images of overwhelming power. Swift had not only the judgment with which to arrive at a reasoned view of the world, but the fancy by means of which he could recreate that world in a form which teaches where argument fails and which satisfies all while misleading none.

Gulliver's travel memoirs make abundantly clear that he is a Yahoo in the decisive sense. He says "the thing which is not," or, to put it into Yahoo language, he is a liar. This does not mean that I do not believe he underwent the adventures he relates; but he does have something to hide. A small bit of evidence can be gleaned from his own defense of his conduct with a great Lilliputian lady, who had conceived a passion for his person. Gulliver grounds his apology on the alleged fact that no one ever came to see him secretly. But immediately afterward he tells of the secret visit of a minister. We can only suppose the worst in the affair between the lady and Gulliver. And we may further suppose that Gulliver has certain hidden thoughts and intentions which are only to be revealed by closely cross-examining him. He indicates this himself at the close of his travels when he swears to his veracity. He uses for this solemn occasion Sinon's treacherous oath to the Trojans, by means of which that worthy managed to gain admittance for the horse and its concealed burden of Greeks.[1]

I should like to suggest that this book is also such a container, filled with Greeks who are, once introduced, destined to conquer a

From "An Outline of Gulliver's Travels" by Allan Bloom in *Ancients and Moderns*, edited by Joseph Cropsey. New York. © 1964 by Basic Books, Inc., Publishers, and reprinted with their permission.

[1] Bk. IV, Ch. 12; cf. Vergil, *Aeneid*, II. 79–80.

new Troy, or, translated into "the little language," destined to conquer Lilliput. In other words, I wish to contend that *Gulliver's Travels* is one of the last explicit statements in the famous Quarrel between the Ancients and Moderns and perhaps the greatest intervention in that notorious argument. By means of the appeal of its myth, it keeps alive the classical vision in ages when even the importance of the quarrel is denied, not to speak of the importance of that classical viewpoint, which appears to have been swamped by history. The laughter evoked by *Gulliver's Travels* is authorized by a standard drawn from Homer and Plato. . . .

Gulliver's Travels is a discussion of human nature, particularly of political man, in the light of the great split. In general, the plan of the book is as follows: Book I, modern political practice, especially the politics of Britain and France; Book II, ancient political practice on something of a Roman or Spartan model; Book III, modern philosophy in its effect on political practice; Book IV, ancient utopian politics used as a standard for judging man understood as the moderns wished to understand him. By "ancient" Swift means belonging to Greece and Rome—Greece for philosophy and poetry, republican Rome for politics. For Swift, Thomas Aquinas is a modern.

There are many indications of both a substantial and a formal kind, which indicate the order of the parts. For example, Gulliver takes the same ship, the Adventure, to both Brobdingnag and the land of the Houyhnhnms. Books I and III are the only ones which are directly susceptible of an analysis appropriate to a *roman à cléf*: Lilliput is full of characters clearly identifiable as personages in British politics, and Laputa is peopled largely by modern philosophers and members of the Royal Academy. The only clearly identifiable modern elements in Brobdingnag or the land of the Houyhnhnms are those in England referred to by the travelling Gulliver. When he is in Lilliput and Laputa (notice the similarity of the names), he tells nothing of his world or native country. He need not, for the reader should recognize it; Gulliver is alien, and the interesting thing is the world seen through his eyes. His perspective is that of a man totally outside England; with the Brobdingnagians and the Houyhnhnms, he is all English, and they are usually foils used to bring out the weaknesses in his nature. In the former case, he is used as the standard for strictures against modern

England; in the latter, the Houyhnhnms and Brobdingnagians are used as a standard in criticizing him in the role of a modern Englishman. In one sense the book is all about England, in another, it is all about antiquity. The formula is simply this: when he is good, the others are bad; when he is bad, they are good. The bad others are found in books I and III, which treat of the recognizably modern. The good others are in books II and IV, which are, at the least, removed from modernity. Parallel to this movement is Gulliver's sense of shame; in Book I he is shameless—he defecates in a temple and urinates on the palace; and in Lilliput, the people care. In Brobdingnag, where they could not care less, he is full of shame, will not allow himself to be seen performing these functions, and hides behind sorrel leaves. We can say that Gulliver is somehow in between—superior to the inferior and inferior to the superior, but never equal. He lacks something of perfection, but from a certain point of view he is superior to his contemporaries.

Gulliver informs us on his return from Brobdingnag that it was not necessary for him to visit Lilliput in order for him to see Englishmen as Lilliputians; it was only necessary for him to have been to Brobdingnag, for when he landed, he thought himself to be the size of a Brobdingnagian. This was not the case; but having shared their perspective, he could forget his real self and see his likes as he was seen by the giants. The English are truly pygmies. The lesson is that one must study Brobdingnag. Gulliver is as a giant in Lilliput because of what he has learned in Brobdingnag; when he is with the Brobdingnagians, however, he returns to his awareness of himself as a real Lilliputian. He recognizes his weaknesses, but he is great because of his self-consciousness or self-knowledge. He learns "how vain an attempt it is for a man to endeavor to do himself honor among those who are out of all degree of equality or comparison with him."

Swift's device in Lilliput and Brobdingnag is to take moral and intellectual differences and project them in physical dimensions. From this simple change everything else follows. In working this transformation, he pursues Aristotle's suggestion that nature intends the differences in men's souls to be reflected in their bodies and that men whose bodies are greatly superior, resembling the statues of gods, would readily be accepted as masters.[2] As a literary device, Swift's transformation works wonders; for literature lives on

[2] Aristotle, *Politics* 1254^{b} 27–39.

images and sensations, appealing to fancy and imagination, but there is no way that philosophy can make a direct appeal by means of the arts. When the imperceptible differences so suddenly become powerful sensual images, however, all becomes clear. Gulliver's attempts to take the physical beauty of the Lilliputians seriously, or the king of Brobdingnag's holding Gulliver in his hand and asking him if he is a Whig or a Tory, resume hundreds of pages of argument in an instant. And, moreover, the great majority of men cannot, for lack of experience, understand the great superiority of soul which is humanly possible. But when that power is seen in terms of size, all men, if only momentarily, know what superiority is and recognize the difficulties it produces for its possessor and those in its immediate vicinity. To tell men of the vanity of human pretensions may be edifying, but what sermon has the force of the absurd claim that Lilliput is "the terror of the universe"?

Gulliver's adventures in Lilliput are largely an exposition of the problems faced by him and the Lilliputians because of his bigness. With the best of will, neither side can understand the concerns of the other. They do not belong together, but they are forced together, if only by their common humanity—a humanity stretched to its limits. He is imprisoned by them and needs them for his maintenance; they do not know how to get rid of him (if they were to kill him, the stench of his decaying body might sicken the atmosphere) and are torn between fear and distrust, on the one hand, and dazzling hopes for using him, on the other. Their problem is aggravated by their vision: The Lilliputians "see with great exactness but at no great distance." They suffer from a loss of perspective. It is not their fault; that is the way they are built.

What this entails is best revealed when we see giants through the eyes of our Cicerone: nothing could be more revolting than the description of the woman's breast. He sees things which are really there, but he no longer sees the object as a whole; a thing that from the human point of view should be beautiful and attractive becomes in his vision ugly and repulsive. Odors and tastes are distorted; Gulliver in Brobdingnag experiences the literally dirty underside of life. And thus we learn that the Lilliputians experienced him as he did the Brobdingnagians. One Lilliputian even had the audacity to complain of his smell on a hot day, although he was renowned for his cleanliness. They can never grasp him as he really is; the different parts seem ugly; the ugliness of nature, which disappears in the light of its unity, is their overwhelming impression. In them one can understand the maxim "no man is a hero to his valet; not because he is not a hero but because the valet is a valet." I think there can be little doubt that Swift believes the giant's perspective is ultimately proportionate to the true purpose of things; there is not a simple relativity. . . .

Gulliver's disaster in Lilliput occurs because he is too big for the Lilliputians; the specific charges against him are only corollaries of that fact. The outcome was inevitable. Civil society cannot endure such disproportionate greatness; it must either submit itself to the one best man or ostracize him. The condemnation of this comic Socrates is not to be blamed on the prejudices of the Lilliputians; it is a necessity that no amount of talk or education will do away with. The four major charges against Gulliver are as follows. (1) He urinated on the royal palace, even though there was a law against urinating within its confines. (2) He refused to subdue Blefuscu, to utterly destroy the Big-Endian exiles, to force the Blefuscudians to confess the Lilliputian religion, and to accept the Lilliputian monarch. (3) He was friendly to the Blefuscudian ambassadors who came to treat for peace and helped them in their mission. (4) He had the intention of paying a visit to Blefuscu.

If we generalize these charges, they would read as follows. (1) He does not accept the judgments of the Lilliputians about what is noble and what is base. He does what is necessary to preserve the palace, using means indifferent in themselves but repulsive to the queen; from her point of view, of course, what was done was pretty disagreeable. Swift's humor in defense of the crown, which displeased Queen Anne, has been compared to the acts cited in this charge. It is also reminiscent of Aristophanes' Dung-beetle, who, because he goes low, can go high. But the chief thing to underline is the fact that, because of their different situations, Gulliver cannot have the same sentiments as the Lilliputians about what is fair and what is ugly. He identifies the fair or noble with the useful—a rational procedure, but one which can hardly be accepted by civil society which lives on the distinction between the two. (2) He does not share the religious prejudices of the nation and is unwilling to be inhuman for the sake of what can only appear as senseless dogma to him. He cannot see the importance of the faith or of the ambition of the king. Big end, small end—they all appear human to him. (3) He does not accept the distinction between friend and enemy defined by the limits of the nation. Once again, common humanity is what he sees. At the same time, from the Lilliputian standpoint, how can a foreigner who consorts with the enemy be trusted—especially a foreigner of such exceptional power? They can only attribute to him the motivations which they already know; they cannot see the interior workings of his soul, and, if they could, they would not understand them. By any canons, Gulliver's behavior is suspicious, no matter how innocent it may actually be. How can the Lilliputians see he has no ambition to subdue both kingdoms and make himself ruler of the known world? How could they believe that what seems so important to them is too petty to be even considered by Gulliver? (4) Gulliver is not satisfied in his new home; he thinks there is much to be learned elsewhere. He may find what pleases him more in another land. His loyalty is questionable; he has the dubious taste for being away from home.

Gulliver is condemned because the Lilliputians discovered in the palace fire that his moral taste was not the same as theirs. He did not behave as a good citizen; he did not identify what is good with what is Lilliputian. The court jealousies and hatreds were only predisposing factors in the ultimate crisis. Given the uses which could be made of him, he was bound to be an object of flattery and conspiracy, as he appeared to incline to one side or another. The proposal for resolving the Gulliver crisis is the standard for civil society's use of genius: he is to be blinded, for thus he would retain his power but could be used more easily by the civil authority. He is to be a blind giant—blind to the ends which he serves, adding only might to the means which are to achieve them. This is an intolerable solution for him, but the alternative would be for the Lilliputians to alter themselves to fit him. The disproportion is too great. Finally, the high hopes deceived, the kings of both Lilliput and Blefuscu are heartily glad to be rid of him. This is Swift's description of his own situation and that of other great men.

This interpretation of Lilliput depends, of course, on the information supplied by the voyage to Brobdingnag. Gulliver's superiority to the Lilliputians is as the Brobdingnagians' superiority to him. Against the background of Brobdingnag, Gulliver's moral perspective comes into focus. The Brobdingnagians are great because they are virtuous; they are, particularly, temperate. Political life is not a plaything of their lusts. There is neither faction nor Christian controversy (they are polytheists). Hence there is no war, for they have no neighbors and no civil strife—not because of the victory of one part of the body politic over the others, but because of the judicious blending of all three parts. They maintain themselves in a state of constant preparedness, simply for the sake of preserving the advantages stemming from military virtue. Theirs is entirely a citizen army. Their concentration is on obedience to law, not interpretation of it. Law is powerful so long as it is respected, and respect implies assent. The mind should not be used to reason away the clear bases of duty. No commentaries are allowed on the laws. There is no political science. Their learning is only such as will produce good citizens, or, put otherwise, their studies are made to produce not learning, but virtue. They know morality, history, poetry, and mathematics, and that is all.

The vices that Gulliver finds in the common people are at worst summed up in an excess of thrift, and most are simply a result of his peculiar perspective; he assumes ill-intention where there is probably only indifference or inattention. The Brobdingnagians are a simple, decent people whose state exists, not for the pursuit of knowledge or the cultivation of diversity, but for the sake of well-known, common-sense virtues. Brobdingnag is a sort of cross between Sparta and republican Rome; it concurs in almost all respects with the principles of Aristotle's *Ethics*. Swift was an enemy of the Enlightenment, its learning and its politics.

We can make only a short visit to Laputa.[3] Gulliver goes there, after having seen modern politics, to see modern science and its effects on life. He finds a theoretical preoccupation, which is

[3] For the interpretation of the details of the voyages to Laputa and Lagado, cf. Marjorie Nicolson, *Science and Imagination* (Ithaca: Cornell University Press, 1956), pp. 110–154; *Voyages to the Moon* (New York: Macmillan, 1948); with Nora Mohler, "The Scientific Background of Swift's Voyage to Laputa," *Annals of Science*, II (1937), 299–334; "Swift's Flying Island in the Voyage to Laputa," *ibid.*, pp. 405–430.

The unifying theme of all of Swift's criticism of the new science is not the external absurdity of its propositions, or its impious character, or its newness, but its partialness and abstraction from what is known about human things. Modern science represented a complete break with classical principles and methods, and Swift believed that there was a whole range of phenomena it could not grasp but which it would distort. The commitment to it, if absolutized, would destroy the human orientation. This contention remains to be refuted.

abstracted from all human concerns and which did not start from the human dimension. On the flying island the men have one eye turned inward, the other toward the zenith; they are perfect Cartesians—one egotistical eye contemplating the self, one cosmological eye surveying the most distant things. The intermediate range, which previously was the center of concentration and which defined both the ego and the pattern for the study of the stars, is not within the Laputian purview. The only studies are astronomy and music, and the world is reduced to these two sciences. The men have no contact with objects of sensation; this is what permits them to remain content with their science. Communication with others is unnecessary, and the people require a beating to respond to them. Rather than making their mathematics follow the natural shapes of things, they change things so as to fit their mathematics; the food is cut into all sorts of geometrical figures. Their admiration for women, such as it is, is due to the resemblance of women's various parts to specific figures. Jealousy is unknown to them; their wives can commit adultery before their eyes without being noticed. Above all, they lack a sense for poetry. This is a touchstone for Gulliver; no mention is made of poetry in Lilliput and Laputa, although both the Brobdingnagians and the Houyhnhnms have excellent poetry, of a Homeric kind. Poetry expresses the rhythm of life, and its images capture the color of reality. Men without poetry are without a grasp of humanity, for the poetic is the human supplement to philosophy—not poetry in our more modern sense, but in that of the great epics which depict the heroes who are our models for emulation. Modern science cannot understand poetry, and hence it can never be a science of man.

Another peculiarity of these men is described by Gulliver as follows. "What I chiefly admired, and thought altogether unaccountable, was the strong disposition I observed in them towards news and politics, perpetually inquiring into public affairs, giving their judgments in matters of state, and passionately disputing every inch of a party opinion. I have indeed observed the same disposition among most of the mathematicians I have known in Europe, although I could never discover the least analogy between the two sciences." Gulliver, we see, has recovered his old superiority. On this theme of science and politics, so important today, Swift's perspicacity is astonishing. He not only recognizes the scientists' professional incapacity to understand politics, but also their eagerness to manipulate it, as well as their sense of special right to do so. The Laputians' political power rests on the new science. Their flying island is built on the principles of the new physics founded by Gilbert and Newton. Swift saw the possibility of great inventions that would open new avenues to political endeavor. This island allows the king and the nobles to live free from conspiracies by the people—in fact free from contact with them—while still making use of them and receiving the tribute which is necessary to the maintenance and leisure of the rulers. They can crush the terrestrial cities; their power is almost unlimited and their responsibilities nil. Power is concentrated in the hands of the rulers; hence they are not forced even by fear to develop a truly political intelligence. They require no virtue; everything runs itself, so there is no danger that their incompetence, indifference, or vice will harm them. Their island allows their characteristic deformity to grow to the point of monstrosity. Science, in freeing men, destroys the natural conditions which make them human. Here, for the first time in history, is the possibility of tyranny grounded not on ignorance, but on science. Science is no longer theoretical, but serves the wishes and hence the passions of men.

Gulliver is disgusted by this world; he represents common sense, and he is despised for it. This he finds disagreeable, and he seeks to return to earth, where he can be respected. But in Lagado he finds things even worse; everything is topsy-turvy because what works has been abandoned in favor of projects. Here Gulliver's critique, although funny, impresses us less than it does elsewhere. He seems to have seriously underestimated the possible success of the projects. But perhaps some of the reasons supporting this posture are still intelligible to us. The transformations planned by the projectors are direct deductions from the principles used in Laputa; they are willing to give up the old life and the virtues it engendered for the sake of a new life based only on wishes. If the new life succeeded it might produce some comforts; but they do not know what that way of life will do to them. This transformation and this incertitude induce Gulliver to be conservative. He distrusts the motives of the projectors and wonders if they do not represent a debasement of the noble purposes of contemplation. If Gulliver is not right in ridiculing the possibilities of applied science, he may nevertheless be right in doubting its desirability. At any rate, there is today in America a school of social criticism which is heavy-handedly saying the same thing. And as for education and politics, Gulliver looks as sound as ever when he ridicules substitutes for intelligence and study, or when he outlines Harold Lasswell's anal science of politics. Gulliver's attack on modern science and projecting foresaw the problem which has only recently struck the popular consciousness: what does the conquest of nature do to the conquerors?

The visit to Glubdubdribb allows Gulliver to see modern historical science as it really is, because he is able to evoke the shades of those with whom it deals. History is of particular importance, because from it one can understand what has been lost or gained and the direction in which one is going. We learn that this science is most inaccurate. It has embellished modern men and misunderstood the ancients; even our knowledge of the Greek language has decayed to the point of incomprehensibility. Gulliver most admires Homer, Aristotle, and the heroes who opposed tyranny. There is only one modern—Sir Thomas More—among these latter. All the later interpreters of the poets and the philosophers misunderstood and denatured them. An effort to recover them must be made; and the result of that study will be the recognition of the unqualified superiority of classical antiquity. "I desired that the senate of Rome might appear before me in one large chamber, and a modern representative, in counterview, in another. The first seemed an assembly of heroes and demigods; the other, a knot of pedlars, pick-pockets, highwaymen and bullies."

The fourth and last stop which we must make in the voyage to Laputa is Luggnag. Here Gulliver has his interlude on immortality. Death is feared in all other nations, but not in Luggnag, where immortality is constantly present in the form of the Struldbrugs. The desire for immortality, or the fear of death, leads men to all kinds of vain hopes and wishes. Gulliver is to some extent released from this anxiety by his experience with the Struldbrugs, who never die but grow ever older. They are repulsive and have no human traits. "They were not only opinionative, peevish, covetous, morose, and talkative, but incapable of friendship and dead to all natural affection. . . . Envy and impotent desires are their prevailing passions." They hate all that is young. No doubt, most men would prefer to be dead than to live this living death. However, it has often been remarked that to the extent one can imagine immortality, one can imagine perpetual youth. Gulliver himself imagines perpetual youth when he discovers the existence of the Struldbrugs and learns that they are not advisers at court, but are banished. He is surprised. These particular immortals grow old and decrepit; the criticism of man's desire for immortality applies only to those which do not include perpetual youth.

Now, why has Swift presented his case in this way? One might suggest that he was reflecting on the only example in our world of an institution that claims immortality, namely, the Church. I gather this from Gulliver's concluding remark about the Struldbrugs, who are not allowed to hold employment of public trust or to purchase lands:

> I could not but agree that the laws of this kingdom relative to the Struldbrugs were founded upon the strongest reasons and such as any other country would be under necessity of enacting in the like circumstances. Otherwise, as avarice is the necessary consequent of old age, those immortals would in time become proprietors of the whole nation, and engross the civil power, which, for want of abilities to manage, must end in the ruin of the public.[4]

This merely echoes the views prevailing in England after the Reformation on the importance of limiting church lands, especially those of the Roman Catholic Church. Modern times are characterized by an immortal body inhabiting, but not truly part of, civil society—a decrepit body with a dangerous tendency to aggrandize itself. Death is preferable to the extension of life the Church offers; and civil society is safe only so long as that body is contained by law.

The voyage to the Houyhnhnms is of particular significance in our cross-examination of Lemuel Gulliver, for this was his last trip and the one that most affected him; it is under the influence of seeing Houyhnhnms contrasted with Yahoos that he wrote this book, which had as its explicit end the reform of all human vices. In Lilliput and Laputa he learned nothing and found nothing to admire; in Brobdingnag he admired; but among the Houyhnhnms he imitated. Any reform must be in the direction of their practices.

[4] *Gulliver's Travels,* Bk. III, Ch. 10. Although Swift defended the property of the Church of Ireland, he did it only within severe limits and for the sake of preserving an important civil institution. He well knew the dangers of the higher clergy's possible avarice, and he also was perfectly aware of the political difficulties caused by the property and influence of the Roman Church prior to the Reformation.

The Houyhnhnms are not human beings; man's standard is now a nonhuman one. What Swift has done in the land of the Houyhnhnms is to elaborate a utopia, a utopia based on Plato's *Republic*; but it is a super *Republic*, for the problem which made the construction of the best city so difficult for Socrates has disappeared—the Houyhnhnms lack the passionate part of the soul. The whole difficulty in the *Republic* is to make the three orders take their proper role in relation to one another. Punishment and rhetoric are necessary; the book is full of the struggle between the rational and the appetitive; and the irascible or spirited, intended as reason's ally, shows a constant tendency to turn against it. The passionate and the spirited are in perfect natural harmony with the rational in the Houyhnhnms. Swift has taken everything that was connected with the passionate or erotic nature and made a kind of trash heap from it, which he calls the Yahoos. Or, in another and more adequate formulation, Swift has extrapolated the Houyhnhnms from man as depicted by Plato, and the Yahoos from man as depicted by Hobbes.

It is not correct to say that this section is a depreciation of man in general in favor of animals, for the animals are very particular animals, possessing certain human characteristics of a Platonic order, and the men are a very particular kind of passionate men. Man has a dual nature—part god, part beast; Swift has separated the two parts. In reality they are in tension with one another, and one must decide which is in the service of the other. Are the passions directed to the service of reason, or is reason the handmaiden of the passions? If the latter, then the Yahoo is the real man; if the former, then the Houyhnhnms represent man as he really is. The separation effected by Swift leads to clarity about the ends.

Nature is the standard, and the Houyhnhnms are "the perfection of nature," which is what the name means. Nature is Parmenidean; being *is*; the changeable has no meaning. The Houyhnhnms speak and speculate only about what is, for only what is can be said. There is not even a word for opinion, nor do the Houyhnhnms have those passions which partake of nonbeing. There is nothing in them that can take account of what is not or can partake of what is not; hence they cannot say what is not. They need not lie, for like Plato's gods, they need not deceive, nor do they have friends who need to be deceived. Virtue for them is knowledge. They see what must be done and do it; there is no need of moral habituation. They always reason like philosophers; when they recognize what a phenomenon is, they say so—otherwise they say nothing. This is why Gulliver is such a problem: is he a Yahoo or is he not? He is and he is not. This, by the way, perhaps indicates a weakness in the Houyhnhnms' understanding; they cannot adequately grasp this composite being.

Gulliver, who in the first stages of his relationship with his master tried to obscure his Yahoo nature, is finally forced to undress himself. He makes a sort of girdle "to hide my nakedness," echoing Adam before the Lord. Gulliver again feels shame, as he did in Brobdingnag. The Houyhnhnms are shameless; no part of the body is any more or less beautiful than another. Gulliver feels shame because he is a lustful being and cannot control desires which he understands to be bad. He is a sinner and a repenter, whereas the Houyhnhnms are like Aristotle's gentleman who never blushes because he has nothing to be ashamed of. This is the indication which allows us to see the Yahoos as peculiarly modern man. They are a sort of cross between man as Augustine describes him and as Hobbes describes him. They have the uncontrollably corrupted nature of Augustinian man, with particular concentration on sexual lust. And the relation of Yahoos to one another is one of Hobbesean war. The Yahoos have infinite desires, and most of all they hate to see anyone else taking possession of anything at all. They are needy beings with a constant sense of scarcity. They hoard and have an unlimited desire for gold without any idea of what they want to use it for. They know of no natural limits, so they are never satisfied. They are strong, but fearful; and they set a leader over themselves to govern them. If one conceives of the real life of man as in the passions, this is the kind of picture one must have of him. There is absolutely no suggestion in Swift's view of the Houyhnhnms that a being who senses his own corruption and tries to improve himself, or who yearns for salvation, is desirable.

There can be little doubt that the land of the Houyhnhnms is a perfection of the *Republic*. A glance at the list of similarities is convincing; the changes are all based on the Houyhnhnms' superiority. There is hardly any need for politics, because the citizens are so orderly and accept their roles. The needs that cause war are absent. The rulers are free to converse. They are philosophers; in one example of their reasoning—the explanation of the origin of Yahoos—they reason exactly like pre-Socratic philosophers. At all events, this is a land ruled by philosophers.

The Houyhnhnms live simply, and their wants are provided by the community. There is no money. Because they live simply and naturally, there is no need for the arts of medicine or of forensic rhetoric. There is a class system, but one based entirely on natural differences. They do not fear death nor do they mourn those who depart. They regard the land as their first mother. They belong to the land as a whole and have no special, private interests.

To come to the paradoxes treated in Book V of the *Republic*, there is also among the Houyhnhnms equality of women and virtual community of wives and children. Marriages are arranged on grounds of reason; *eros* does not play a role. They separate into couples and have private houses, but when necessary they break up families, service one another, and switch children—all this in the name of the community as a whole. Friendship and benevolence are their virtues and the themes of their conversation. Their poetry, which has all the power of Homeric epics, supports their character. There is, therefore, no need for any of the elaborate devices mentioned in the *Republic* for the censorship of poetry or the destruction of the family interests. There is no distinction between public and private, between the good and one's own. They do not love their children; they take care of them for the sake of the common good.[5]

The contrast in Book IV is between Plato and Hobbes, between the perfected political animal and man in the state of nature. The Yahoos have tyrants; the Houyhnhnms are republicans who need no subordination because they have sufficient virtue to govern themselves. Swift took refuge in animals because nothing in the conception of man indicated the possibility of such a regime in state or soul. He conceived a hatred of the Yahoos; for only by this self-contempt could he cultivate that in himself which was akin to the Houyhnhnms.

It has been asked, Why, with all their virtues, do the Houyhnhnms have no god? But this clearly follows from their principle. They cannot say the thing which is not. They can see only the permanent, eternal, unchanging being. In England, Yahoos

[5] *Ibid.*, Bk. IV, Ch. 8. Note the reference to Socrates and Plato at the beginning of this passage.

have a religion; their sacred issues cannot even be rendered in the Houyhnhnm language. These Trojan horses contain more than they appear to.

Gulliver's Travels has often been called a misanthropic book. Indeed, it does not present a very flattering picture of man. But we should ask ourselves what a misanthrope is. If anything, he is a hater of humanity—one who had great expectations of others and has been deceived. Above all—if we can believe Molière—he is a man who tries to live according to the highest standards of virtue and finds they are unacceptable in human society; he is a man who always tells the truth and acts according to principle. Rousseau, who left society to return to nature, was a misanthrope; and Kant taught the absolute morality of the misanthrope. Gulliver, in his letter to Sympson, doubtlessly speaks in the tones of a misanthrope. He has renounced all hopes of human reform, because he gave his countrymen six months since the publication of his book, which is surely more than sufficient, to improve—and they have not improved a bit.

But we also know that Gulliver is a liar and admires successful liars like Sinon. A liar can hardly be a misanthrope; he cares enough about his fellow men to respect their prejudices; noble lies are acts of generosity. They are based on the truth of becoming and the existence of opinion; they prove an understanding of this world, an understanding not possessed by Houyhnhnms. Finally, and above all, misanthropes are not funny; this world and morality are too serious for that. I do not know about Gulliver, but Swift is surely one of the funniest men who ever lived. His misanthropy is a joke; it is the greatest folly in the world to attempt to improve humanity. That is what it means to understand man. And, after all, perhaps we are not serious beings. In the jest, there is a truth; we glimpse the necessity of the distinction between what we are and what we ought to be. But this leaves us with a final impression of fond sympathy for poor mortals. To understand is to accept; *Gulliver's Travels* makes misanthropy ridiculous by showing us the complexity of our *nature* and thereby teaching us what we must accept.

SAMUEL HOLT MONK

*The Pride of Lemuel Gulliver**

Gulliver's Travels is a complex book. It is, of course, a satire on four aspects of man: the physical, the political, the intellectual, and the moral. The last three are inseparable, and when Swift writes of one he always has in view the others. It is also a brilliant parody of travel literature; and it is at once science fiction and a witty parody of science fiction. It expresses savage indignation at the follies, vices, and stupidities of men, and everywhere implicit in the book as a whole is an awareness of man's tragic insufficiency. But at the same time it is a great comic masterpiece, a fact that solemn and too-sensitive readers often miss.

A friend once wrote me of having shocked an associate by remarking that he had laughed often on rereading *Gulliver's Travels.* 'What should I have done?' he asked me. 'Blown out my brains?' I am sure that Swift would have approved my friend's laughter. To conclude that *Gulliver's Travels* expresses despair or that its import is nihilistic is radically to misread the book. All of Swift's satire was written in anger, contempt, or disgust, but it was written to promote self-knowledge in the faith that self-knowledge will lead to right action. Nothing would have bewildered him more than to learn that he had led a reader to the desperate remedy of blowing out his brains. But the book is so often called morbid, so frequently have readers concluded that it is the work of an incipient madman, that I think it worth while to emphasize the gayety and comedy of the voyages as an indication of their author's essential intellectual and

From *The Sewanee Review,* LXIII (1955), pp. 48-71. Sewanee, Tenn.

* Students of Swift will recognize my very great indebtedness to the work of other critics and scholars. It would be pedantic to acknowledge borrowings so numerous and so self-evident. I hope that it is sufficient here to acknowledge this general indebtedness and to express my gratitude to those who, over a period of twenty-five years, have helped me to better understand Jonathan Swift.

spiritual health. True, seventeen years after finishing *Gulliver's Travels*, Swift was officially declared *non compos mentis*. But his masterpiece was written at the height of his powers, and the comic animation of the book as a whole rules out the suspicion of morbidity and mental illness.

We laugh and were meant to laugh at the toy kingdom of the Lilliputians; at the acrobatic skill of the politicians and courtiers; at the absurd jealousy of the diminutive minister who suspects an adulterous relationship between his wife and the giant Gulliver. We laugh at the plight of Gulliver in Brobdingnag: one of the lords of creation, frightened by a puppy, rendered ludicrous by the tricks of a mischievous monkey, in awe of a dwarf; embarrassed by the lascivious antics of the maids of honor; and at last content to be tended like a baby by his girl-nurse. We laugh at the abstractness of the philosophers of Laputa, at the mad experimenters of Balnibarbi. And I am sure that we are right in at least smiling at the preposterous horses, the Houyhnhnms, so limited and so positive in their knowledge and opinions, so skilled in such improbable tasks as threading needles or carrying trays, so complacent in their assurance that they are 'the Perfection of Nature.' Much of the delight that we take in *Gulliver's Travels* is due to this gay, comic, fanciful inventiveness. Swift might well say in the words of Hamlet: 'Lay not that flattering unction to your soul/That not your trespass but my madness speaks.' Swift did not wish us to blow out our brains; he did wish us to laugh. But beyond the mirth and liveliness are gravity, anger, anxiety, frustration—and he meant us to experience them fully.

For there is an abyss below this fantastic world—the dizzying abyss of corrupt human nature. Swift is the great master of shock. With perfect control of tone and pace, with perfect timing, he startles us into an awareness of this abyss and its implications. We are forced to gaze into the stupid, evil, brutal heart of humanity, and when we do, the laughter that Swift has evoked is abruptly silenced. The surface of the book is comic, but at its center is tragedy, transformed through style and tone into icy irony. Soft minds have found Swift's irony unnerving and depressing and, in self-protection, have dismissed him as a repellent misanthrope. Stronger minds that prefer unpalatable truths to euphoric illusions have found this irony bracing and healthful.

Before I discuss the book itself it is necessary to speak of certain ideas and tendencies that were current in Swift's world. *Gulliver's Travels* was written at the height of that phase of European civilization which we know as the Enlightenment, and the Enlightenment was the first clearly defined manifestation of modernity—the modernity of which our age may be the catastrophic conclusion. Swift wrote always in opposition to the Enlightenment and as an enemy of 'modernism.' He detected with uncanny prescience the implications of such characteristic ideas as the following: (1) Rationalism, especially Cartesianism, with its radical tendency to abstract truth into purely intellectual concepts and its bold rejection of the experience and wisdom of the past. Swift doubted the capacity of human reason to attain metaphysical and theological truth. A safer guide in this life seemed to him to be what he called 'common forms,' the *consensus gentium*, the time-approved wisdom of the race. (2) Experimental and theoretical science, fathered by Bacon and Galileo, vindicated by Newton, and propagandized and nourished by the Royal Society. The science of Swift's day was predominantly concerned with physics and astronomy. Swift, I think, could not imaginatively relate to the moral—*i.e.*, the totally human—life of man the efforts of an astronomer to plot the trajectory of a comet or of a physicist to comprehend a universe that is 'really' no more than abstract mass, extension, and motion. Moreover science gave sanction to the idea of progress, deluding men with the promise of an ever-expanding and improving future, which to Swift seemed necessarily chimerical, man being limited as he is. And finally science unwittingly fostered the secularization of society and of human values, promising men mastery of nature and the abolition of all mysteries, and, by implication at least, of religion. Swift was a religious man. (3) The new conception of man, which was the result of both rationalism and science. It taught the essential goodness of human nature in a sentimental and optimistic tone of voice that irritated Swift and compelled him to reply with all his powers in *Gulliver's Travels*. (4) The new moneyed wealth of England, based upon trade and speculation and bolstering up the national importance of the middle class. Swift regarded this wealth and its owners as irresponsible and dangerous to the state. Divorced from land and the responsibilities implied in the ownership of land, it seemed to him abstract and at the same time frighteningly ambitious; and he had to look only to London and the Court to be assured that this new, vulgar, wealthy class was corrupting both the individual and the social and political institutions of England. (5) The increasing power of centralized government—in Swift's day a few ministers, the Crown, and the court. To Swift, such power seemed necessarily evil since it was divorced from concrete human needs.

Why was Swift inimical to these tendencies—all of which are familiar aspects of our world today? Very simply, I think, because he was a Christian and a humanist. As a Christian he believed that man's fallen nature could never transcend its own limitations and so fulfil the hopes of that optimistic age; as a humanist he was concerned for the preservation of those moral and spiritual qualities which distinguish men from beasts and for the health and continuity of fruitful tradition in church, state, and the sphere of the mind. As both Christian and humanist, he knew that men must be better than they are and that, though our institutions can never be perfect, they need not be corrupt. The 'savage indignation' which motivates all of Swift's satires arises from his anger at the difference between what men are and what they might be if they only would rise to the full height of their humanity. If he indulged no Utopian hopes, he also never gave way to cheap cynicism.

Two famous letters, written in the fall of 1725, the year before *Gulliver's Travels* was published, tell us much about Swift's state of mind at this time. In the first, to Pope, he writes:

> . . . when you think of the world, give it one lash the more at my Request. I have ever hated all Nations, Professions, and Communities; and all my love is towards Individuals; for Instance, I hate the Tribe of Lawyers, Physicians . . . Soldiers, English, Scotch, French, and the rest. But principally I hate and detest that animal called Man, although I heartily love John, Peter, Thomas, and so forth. This is the system upon which I have governed myself many Years . . . and so I shall go on until I have done with them. I have got Materials toward a Treatise, proving the falsity of that Definition, *Animal rationale* and to show that it should be only *rationis capax*. Upon this great foundation of Misanthropy (although not in Timon's Manner) the whole building of my travels is erected; and I will never have Peace of Mind until all honest Men are of my Opinion. . . .

This letter makes three important points.

(1) Swift's life and letters support his assertion that he could and did love individuals. His hatred was directed against abstract

man, against men existing and acting within semi-human or dehumanized racial or professional groups. Apparently he felt that when men submerge their individual judgments and moral beings in such groups, they necessarily further corrupt their already corrupted natures. When for example an individual thinks or acts or feels not as a free moral agent responsible to God, but as a politician, a lawyer, a bishop, he abrogates to some degree his humanity. He becomes the instrument of a force that is larger than himself, but not so large as the moral law: and in so doing he becomes at least potentially evil. We hear a great deal today of group dynamics, group psychology, and mass communication. Swift would oppose these forces on the ground that they abridge the freedom which is necessary to the completely moral and responsible life.

(2) Swift dissociates his 'misanthropy' from that of Plutarch's Timon of Athens, the hero of Shakespeare's play, who withdrew in bitter disillusionment merely to rail in solitude against mankind. Swift knew how sterile such an attitude is. His own satire is seldom merely invective. It is not paradoxical to say that it arises from philanthropy, not misanthropy, from idealism as to what man might be, not from despair at what he is.

(3) Swift rejects the definition of man as *animal rationale* in favor of the definition *animal capax rationis*. I think that he has Descartes in mind here, Descartes, who apparently had forgotten that God made man a little lower than the angels (pure intelligences) and consequently capable of only enough reason to order his world here and to find his way, with God's grace, to the next. The second letter, to Pope and Bolingbroke, amplifies this point.

> I tell you after all I do not hate Mankind, it is *vous autres* who hate them, because you would have them reasonable Animals, and are angry at being disappointed: I have always rejected that Definition, and made another of my own. I am no more angry with ——— than I was with the Kite that last Week flew away with one of my Chickens; and yet I was pleased when one of my servants shot him two days after.

Swift argues that the man really in danger of becoming a misanthrope is he who holds an unrealistic view of the potentialities of human nature and who expects that men can somehow transcend their limitations and become, shall we say, angels. In the phrase *vous autres,* Swift includes all the secular, scientific, deistic, optimistic—in a word, liberal—thinkers of the Enlightenment; and he turns in anger from them. The philanthropist will not be angry when he has to recognize the corruptions and limitations of human nature; he will settle for a creature who is *capable* of reason and will do the best he can with him. The word *capable* is a positive concept, not a negative one. It imposes a sort of moral imperative on man to exploit his capability to its fullest. As Swift makes plain in *Gulliver's Travels,* this task is large enough to occupy the whole attention of man. It is fallacious and stupid to attribute to our race qualities that it can never possess. To do so is pride, the besetting sin of men and angels, the sin that disrupts the natural and supernatural order of God's creation. The theme of pride looms large in all four voyages.

Seven years after the publication of *Gulliver's Travels,* Pope published his well-known comment on the tragic duality of man:

> Placed on this isthmus of a middle state,
> A being darkly wise, and rudely great:
> With too much knowledge for the Sceptic side,
> With too much weakness for the Stoic's pride,
> He hangs between; in doubt to act, or rest;
> In doubt to deem himself a God, or Beast;
> In doubt his Mind or Body to prefer;
> Born but to die, and reas'ning but to err;
> Alike in ignorance, his reason such,
> Whether he thinks too little, or too much:
> Chaos of Thought and Passion, all confused:
> Still by himself abused, or disabused;
> Created half to rise, and half to fall;
> Great lord of all things, yet a prey to all;
> Sole judge of Truth, in endless Error hurl'd:
> The glory, jest, and riddle of the world!

The idea that man occupies an anomalous, a middle, state in creation was a familiar one in Swift's day. The whole of living creation was conceived to be carefully ordered and subtly graded in one vast 'chain of being,' descending from God, through an almost infinite number of pure intelligences, to man, and thence through the lower animals to microscopic forms of life, which finally end in nothing. Man occupies the most uncomfortable position in this chain, since to a limited degree he shares the intelligence of higher creatures, and to an unlimited degree the sensuality of animals. He is the middle link because he is the transitional point between the purely intelligent and the purely sensual. With Pope, with Addison, and a number of other writers this image, for reasons which we shall not inquire into, became one of the chief supports of the optimism of the Enlightenment—optimism concerning God, nature, and man. To Pascal, in his moving 72nd *Pensée*, it had suggested tragic thoughts about the disproportion of man. Swift used it as an instrument of comedy, of irony, and of satire. In three of the four voyages, it plays an important role.

So much for background. Let us turn to the book. The first character to demand our attention is Gulliver himself. He is the narrator, the principal actor. We see through his eyes, feel his feelings, share his thoughts. We are in his company from first to last, and it is important that we come to know him as quickly as possible. What is he like and what is his role in the book? He is first of all a bit of a bore, for his mind is irritatingly circumstantial and unimaginative: observe the numerous insignificant biographical details which he gives us in the first pages of the book. Gradually, however, we come to like him and to enjoy his company. In all respects he is an average good man. He has had some university education both at Cambridge and at Leyden, where he studied medicine. He is observant (and we eventually come to be grateful for his gift of close observation and circumstantial reporting, once he has something worth observing and reporting), reasonably intelligent, thoroughly capable in an emergency, and both brave and hopeful. If he lacks imagination and inventiveness, so much the better; for we can be sure that what he tells us, no matter how strange, is true. He is simple, direct, uncomplicated. At the outset he is full of naive good will, and, though he grows less naive and more critical as a result of his voyaging among remote nations, he retains his benevolence throughout the first three voyages. It is a pity that so fine an example of the bluff, good-natured, honest Englishman should at last grow sick and morbid and should be driven mad—but that, I am afraid, is what befalls him.

All of this Gulliver is; but let us notice carefully what he is NOT. He is NOT Jonathan Swift. The meaning of the book is wholly distorted if we identify the Gulliver of the last voyage with his creator, and lay Gulliver's misanthropy at Swift's door. He is a fully rendered, objective, dramatic character, no more to be identified with Swift than Shylock is to be identified with Shakespeare. This character acts and is acted upon; he changes, he grows in the course of his adventures. Like King Lear, he begins in simplicity, grows into sophistication, and ends in madness. Unlike King Lear he is never cured.

The four voyages 'into several remote nations of the world' are so arranged as to attain a climactic intensification of tone as we travel through increasing darkness into the black heart of humanity. But the forward movement is interrupted by the third voyage, a macabre scherzo on science, politics, economics as they are practiced by madmen—Swift's term for those who misuse and abuse human reason. Observe that the tone of each voyage is established by the nature of the event that brings about the adventure: in the first voyage (the most benign and the gayest) accident, or at worst, the carelessness of the lookout, accounts for the shipwreck; in the second, much more savage in tone, Gulliver is left alone in a strange land, through the cowardice of his shipmates; in the third, he is captured and later abandoned by pirates (evil in action); in the fourth, his crew of cutthroats mutinies, seizes the ship, and leaves him to starve on a near-by island. Gulliver thus describes this crew to his Houyhnhnm master:

> I said they were Fellows of desperate Fortunes, forced to fly from the Places of their Birth, on Account of their Poverty and their Crimes. Some were undone by Lawsuits; others spent all they had in Drinking, Whoring, and gaming; others fled for Treason; many for Murder, Theft, Poisoning, Robbery, Perjury, Forgery, Coining false Money; for committing Rapes and Sodomy; for flying from their Colours, or deserting to the Enemy; and most of them had broken Prison. . . .

The good ship *Adventure* was a little world which housed the whole of unregenerate human nature.

It is best to consider the first two voyages together and to notice how effectively Swift uses the idea of the great chain of being. Pascal, writing of man's disproportion, had asked: 'For in fact, what is man in nature? A nothing in comparison with the Infinite, an All in comparison with the Nothing, a mean between nothing and everything.' Swift transposes this theme into another key, and makes it the major instrument of his satire. In the first two voyages, Gulliver is made aware of his disproportion; placed on this isthmus of a middle state, in the voyage to Lilliput he looks down the chain of being and knows himself an awkward, if kindly, giant in that delicate kingdom; in the voyage to Brobdingnag he looks up the chain and discovers a race of 'superior beings,' among whom his pride shrivels through the humiliating knowledge of his own physical insignificance. The emphasis here is upon size, the physical; but it is none the less notable that Lilliputia calls into operation Gulliver's engaging kindliness and gentleness, and that Brobdingnag brings out his moral and physical courage. Though comically and tragically disproportioned, man has moral virtues which he can and does exercise.

But Swift's satire is a two-edged sword. What of the inhabitants of these strange lands? They too are disproportioned. From the start the Lilliputians win our interest and liking: these pigmies ingeniously capture the Hercules whom chance has cast on their shore; they humanely solve the problem of feeding him; their pretty land and their fascinating little city take our fancy. But in the end what do they prove to be? prideful, envious, rapacious, treacherous, cruel, vengeful, jealous, and hypocritical. Their primitive social and political systems have been corrupted; they are governed by an Emperor who is ambitious totally to destroy the neighboring kingdom, and by courtiers and ministers who are chosen not for their fitness for office, but for their skill in walking the tightrope, leaping over sticks or creeping under them. 'Climbing,' Swift once remarked, 'is performed in the same Posture with Creeping.' These little people, like Gulliver himself, are an instance of the disproportion of man. Their vices, their appetites, their ambitions, their passions are not commensurate with their tiny stature. They appear to Gulliver as he and his kind must appear to the higher orders of beings—as venomous and contemptibly petty.

In Brobdingnag we meet creatures ten times the size of Europeans, and we share Gulliver's anxiety lest their moral natures be as brutish as their bodies. But the reverse is true; and through a violent and effective shift of symbol, tone, and point of view, Gulliver, who seemed lovable and humane among the Lilliputians, appears an ignominious and morally insensitive being in contrast to the enlightened and benevolent Brobdingnagians. Since Gulliver represents us, his shame, insufficiency, and ludicrousness are ours.

When the peasants discover him, they feel both curiosity and repulsion: the farmer picks him up 'with the Caution of one who endeavours to lay hold on a small dangerous Animal in such a Manner that it shall not be able either to scratch or to bite him, . . .' Gulliver fears that his captor may dash him to the ground, 'as we usually do any little hateful Animal which we have a Mind to destroy.' The change in tone and intent is obvious.

Gulliver is submitted to one humiliation after another, but he is still capable of a fatuous blindness to the defects of European society, and when the King questions him about England he describes with uncritical enthusiasm its class system, its constitution, its laws, its military glory, and its history. In the questions which the king asks and which Gulliver meets with only an embarrassed silence, the voice of morality is heard condemning the institutions of the modern world. And the verdict of a moral being on European man is given in words as icy as controlled contempt can make them: 'But, by what I have gathered from your own Relation, and the Answers I have with much Pains wringed and extorted from you; I cannot but conclude the Bulk of your Natives to be the most pernicious Race of little odious Vermin that Nature ever suffered to crawl upon the Surface of the Earth.'

Such a conclusion is inevitable, for the King is high-minded, benevolent, and, in Swift's sense of the word, rational: i.e., he and his people think practically, not theoretically; concretely, not metaphysically; simply, not intricately. Brobdingnag is a Swiftian Utopia of common good sense and morality; and Gulliver, conditioned by the corrupt society from which he comes, appears naive, blind, and insensitive to moral values. His account of the history of England in the seventeenth century evokes the King's crushing retort:

> . . . it was only an Heap of Conspiracies, Rebellions, Murders, Massacres, Revolutions, Banishments; the very worst Effects that Avarice, Faction, Hypocracy, Perfidiousness, Cruelty, Rage, Madness, Hatred, Envy, Lust, Malice and Ambition could produce.

Notice the carefully arranged disorder of that list, the calculated avoidance of climax. This is a favorite device of Swift: the irrational, the appetitive, the evil nature of man *is* disorder.

The King is horrified when Gulliver offers him a way to complete dominion over his subjects by teaching him to make gunpowder. And Gulliver, speaking as a European, feels contemptuous surprise. 'A strange Effect of *narrow Principles* and *short Views!*' The King is baffled by the concept of political *science*—how can the *art* of government be reduced to a science?

He confined the knowledge of governing within very *narrow Bounds*; to common Sense and Reason, to Justice and Lenity, to the Speedy Determination of Civil and criminal Causes; with some other obvious Topicks which are not worth considering. And he gave it for his Opinion; that whoever could make two Ears of Corn, or two Blades of Grass to grow upon a Spot of Ground where only one grew before would deserve better of Mankind, and do more essential Service to his Country, than the whole Race of Politicians put together.

The learning of the Brobdingnagians is simple and practical, 'consisting only in Morality, History, Poetry, and Mathematicks.' Observe that Swift omits metaphysics, theoretical science, and theology from the category of useful knowledge.

Swift's attack on pride in the first two voyages is made more powerful because of his brilliant use of the chain of being. In so far as we recognize ourselves in the Lilliputians or in Gulliver in Brobdingnag, we become aware of our pettiness—of the disproportion of our race and of the shocking difference between what we profess and what we are. But Swift uses the good giants to strike an unexpected blow at human vanity and to introduce a motif which he employed with deadly effect in the last voyage. That motif is disgust, of which, as T. S. Eliot has remarked, he is the great master. Philosophers of the century were never tired of admiring the beautiful perfection of the human body, its intricateness, its perfect articulation, its happy appropriateness to the particular place that men occupy in the scheme of things. But how does this glorious body appear to lesser creatures—say to an insect? Swift forces us to answer by making us share Gulliver's disgust at the cancerous breasts and lousy bodies of the beggars; at the blotched color, the huge pores, the coarse hairs, and the nauseous odors of the maids of honor. Such is the skin, presumably, that the Brobdingnagians love to touch. Our beauty is only apparent; our disproportion is real.

The third voyage has always been considered the least successful; that may well be, but it is none the less interesting. Structurally it is loosely episodic, lacking unity of action and tone. Into it Swift seems to have put all the material that he could not work into the other three voyages. It is a fantasia on two themes which Swift treats under a single metaphor: the metaphor is science, the themes are politics and the abuse of reason. In short, the voyage is a digression on madness, on the divorce of man and good sense in the modern world.

At this point, I fear, it is necessary to defend Swift, since he will seem merely stupid and prejudiced to a generation that enjoys the blessings of television, the common cold, and the hydrogen bomb. Moreover, to liberals he will appear an unenlightened political reactionary. I have said earlier that in my opinion Swift distrusted science because it seemed irrelevant to the moral life of man. Though no scientist, he was not an ignoramus. He had read contemporary science—Descartes, Newton, and the yearly *Transactions of the Royal Society*. The Flying Island is conceived on sound scientific principles; some of the mad experiments of the scientists of Balnibarbi are grotesque distortions of ideas actually advanced by members of the Royal Society. The philosophers of the Flying Island are lost in the abstractions of mathematics, music, and astronomy to the great neglect of all practical reality, including their wives. The very tailors measure Gulliver for clothes by abstruse mathematical processes and contrive a suit which fits him not at all. Swift lived before the age of applied science, but I do not think that he would be surprised to learn that modern citizens of his Flying Island contrived the most significant event of the twentieth century—Hiroshima.

It is also necessary to apologize for Swift's political views. He was a Tory, a conservative—opprobrious terms today. In economics he was an agrarian; in politics a royalist; in religion a high churchman. He disapproved the founding of the National Bank; could make no sense of a national debt, a gadget invented in his time; he distrusted the new moneyed wealth, the ancestor of modern capitalism, which increased the political power and importance of the merchant class, and he found his distrust justified in 1720 by the disastrous collapse of South Sea stocks. Innovation and experimentation in politics he detested and fought. He would have hated the improvisations of the New Deal; he would have deplored the vast powers of our Federal Government; he would have loathed the whole program of the Labor Party in Britain. And were he alive, he would fight the abstract state of this century with every weapon within reach.

Too many liberals are unaware of the fact that a man may be a non-liberal without being illiberal; that he may distrust the abstract power of government, the theoretical formulae of economists, politicians, and social scientists and the like without ceasing to be actively and effectively concerned for human welfare. Swift was a Tory who fought valiantly and at times successfully for the oppressed. Living in Ireland, contemptuous of the Irish, detesting their Catholicism, he none the less became their champion against the oppression and exploitation of his adopted country by the English Court and Parliament. He is one of the heroes of modern Ireland because he first gave effective expression to Irish nationalism. He earned the right to the last sentence of the epitaph which he composed for his own tombstone: *Abi Viator/ et imitare, si poteris/ Strenuum pro virili/ Libertatis Vindicatorem.*

The Flying Island is not only a trope for science; it is also a mordant image of the concentration of political power in the hands of a clique remote from human needs, motivated by pure theory, and given to experiment and improvisation. Laputa (perhaps, as has been suggested, Spanish *La Puta*, 'the whore') is a symbol of such government: it is controlled by madmen who govern scientifically, not morally; it is a *flying* island, and hence out of touch with subject territories, which it exploits and tyrannizes over by means of what we call today air power; it can withhold sun and rain as a punitive device, or can harass through bombing raids, or even tyrannously crush all opposition by settling its great weight upon the land below. One contrasts this form of government with that of the wise and good King of Brobdingnag.

When Gulliver visits the subject land of Balnibarbi, which is of course England, he sees the result of statism.

> The People in the Streets walked fast, looked wild, their Eyes fixed, and were generally in Rags. We passed through one of the Town Gates, and went about three Miles into the Country, where I saw many Labourers working with several Sorts of Tools in the Ground, but was not able to conjecture what they were about; neither did I observe any Expectation either of Corn or Grass, although the Soil appeared to be excellent.

This is what comes of experimentation in government and of financial speculation. It strongly suggests the memories that some of us have of the great depression. A modern Tory used it effectively as the basis of an attack on the post-war Labor Government.

But there are other ills consequent to the abstract state. Too great a concentration of power leads to tyranny, tyranny breeds fear; fear breeds the obnoxious race of spies and informers. The abstract state becomes the police state.

I told him that in the Kingdom of *Tribnia* [Britain], by the Natives called *Langden* [England], where I had sojourned some time in my Travels, the Bulk of the People consist in a manner wholly of Discoverers, Witnesses, Informers, Accusers, Prosecutors, Evidences, Swearers; together with their several subservient and subaltern Intruments; all under Deputies. The Plots in that Kingdom are usually the Workmanship of those Persons who desire to raise their own Character of profound Politicians; to restore new Vigour to a crazy Administration; to stifle or divert general Discontents; to fill their Pockets with Forfeitures; and raise or sink the Opinion of publick Credit, as either shall best answer their private Advantage. It is first agreed and settled among them, what suspected Persons shall be accused of a Plot: then, effectual Care is taken to secure all their Letters and Papers, and put the Criminals in Chains. These Papers are delivered to a Set of Artists, very dexterous in finding out the mysterious Meanings of Words, Syllables, and Letters. For Instance, they can decypher a Close-stool to signify a Privy-Council; a Flock of Geese, a Senate; a lame Dog, an Invader; a Codshead, a [King]; the Plague, a Standing Army; a Buzzard, a Prime Minister; the Gout, a High Priest; a Gibbet, a Secretary of State; a Chamber Pot, a Committee of Grandees; a Sieve, a Court Lady; a Broom, a Revolution; a Mouse-trap, an Employment; a bottomless Pit, The Treasury; a Sink, the C[our]t; a Cap and Bells, a Favourite; a broken Reed, a Court of Justice; an empty Tun, a General; a running Sore, the Administration.

One cannot read that passage without thinking of certain testimony given of late years in Washington.

Such are the fruits of madness—of that pride which impels us to trust our reason beyond its proper scope and which suggests that we can build a heavenly city on earth on principles divorced from humanity and morality.

The climactic fourth voyage is the great section of *Gulliver's Travels*. It has provoked violent attacks on Swift and his book, entirely, I think, because it has been misunderstood. It has offended the unreflective and pious Christian, the sentimentalist, and the optimist. Thackeray, lecturing to the ladies in London in 1851, the year in which the Great Exhibition seemed to give the lie to every opinion that Swift held, may serve as an example, by no means unique, of the capacity of this voyage to shock. He advised his ladies not to read the last voyage, and to hoot the Dean. And the meaning that he found in it was 'that man is utterly wicked, desperate, and imbecile, and his passions are monstrous, and his boasted power mean, that he is and deserves to be the shame of brutes, and ignorance is better than his vaunted reason.' 'It is Yahoo language,' he continues, 'a monster gibbering shrieks and gnashing imprecations against mankind . . . filthy in word, filthy in thought, furious, raging, obscene.'

The legend of Swift as a savage, mad, embittered misanthrope largely rests upon this wrong-headed, sensational reading of the last voyage. In my opinion the work is that of a Christian-humanist and a moralist who no more blasphemes against the dignity of human nature than do St. Paul and some of the angrier prophets of the Old Testament. Swift has been misunderstood for several reasons.

1. The sheer intensity and violent rhetoric of the voyage are overwhelming and may well numb the critical sense of certain readers.

2. Gulliver in the frenzy of his mad misanthropy has been too facilely identified with Swift. Gulliver speaks for Gulliver and not for his creator in the final pages of the book, and careful reading should reveal the plain fact that he becomes the victim of Swift's irony as he grows to hate the human race. The final pages of the book are grimly comic.

3. The primary symbols of the voyage have been totally misunderstood. The Houyhnhnms have been regarded as Swift's ideal for man, and the Yahoos have been identified as his representation of what men are. Neither of these opinions, I believe, is correct.

Let us begin with the Houyhnhnms and the Yahoos. In the first two voyages Gulliver is shown uncomfortably situated on the isthmus of a middle state between the very large and the very small. In this voyage he also stands on the isthmus, but now it is between the purely rational and the purely sensual—between Houyhnhnm and Yahoo. Neither of these symbols can stand for man, since Gulliver himself is the symbol of humanity. Unfortunately for poor Gulliver, he shares somehow in the nature of both extremes. Swift simply isolates the two elements that combine in the duality of man, the middle link, in order to allow Gulliver to contemplate each in its essence.

Does Swift recommend that Gulliver should strive to become a Houyhnhnm? We discover that in every sense Houyhnhnmland is a rationalistic Utopia. The Houyhnhnms are the embodiment of pure reason. They know neither love nor grief nor lust nor ambition. They cannot lie; indeed they have no word for lying and are hard put to it to understand the meaning of *opinion*. Their society is an aristocracy, resting upon the slave labor of the Yahoos and the work of an especially-bred servant class. With icy, stoical calm they face the processes of life—marriage, childbirth, accident, death. Their society is a planned society that has achieved the mild anarchy that many Utopian dreamers have aspired to. They practice eugenics, and since they know no lust, they control the size of their population; children are educated by the state; their agrarian economy is supervised by a democratic council; government is entirely conducted by periodic assemblies. The Houyhnhnms feel natural human affection for each other, but they love every one equally. It is all very admirable, but it is remote from the possibilities of human life.

Does Swift intend us to accept this as his ideal way of life? He who loved and hated and fought and bled internally through *saeva indignatio?* I think not. The Houyhnhnms resemble Cartesians and are clearly stoics. 'Neither is *Reason* among them a Point problematical as with us,' reports Gulliver, 'where Men can argue with Plausibility on both Sides of a Question; but strikes you with immediate Conviction; . . .' This is the Houyhnhnm version of Descartes' rational intuition of clear and distinct ideas. Now Swift was anti-Cartesian from his first published satire, for the simple reason that he held that Descartes was self-deluded and that man's reason was incapable of the feats that Descartes attributed to it. The Houyhnhnms are stoics, and Swift recorded his view of stoicism in *Thoughts on Various Subjects*: 'The Stoical Scheme of supplying our Wants, by lopping off our Desires, is like cutting off our Feet when we want Shoes.' It is Gulliver, not Swift, who is dazzled by the Houyhnhnms and who aspires to rise above the human condition and to become pure intelligence as these horses and the angels are.

The most powerful single symbol in all Swift is the Yahoos. They do not represent Swift's view of man, but rather of the bestial element in man—the unenlightened, unregenerate, irrational element in human nature. Hence the Houyhnhnms classify Gulliver with them; hence the female Yahoo wishes to couple with him; hence despite his instinctive recoiling from them, Gulliver has to admit with shame and horror that he is more like them than he is like the Houyhnhnms. This I think is clear. Because of his neglect or misuse of human reason, European man has sunk nearer to the Yahoo pole of his nature than he has risen toward the Houyhnhnm pole. The seeds of human society and of human depravity, as they exist in Europe, are clearly discerned in the society and conduct of the Yahoos. Gulliver looks into the obscene abyss of human nature unlighted by the frail light of reason and of morality, and the sight drives him mad.

Repelled by what he sees, he, not Swift, identifies the Yahoos with man; and he, not Swift, turns misanthrope. Since he will not be a Yahoo, he seeks to become, as nearly as possible, a Houyhnhnm. But he can do so only by denying his place in and responsibility to humanity, by aspiring above the middle link, which is man, to the next higher link, that of the purely rational. The wise Houyhnhnm, to whom he gives his terrifying account of European man and society, concludes that 'the corruption of reason' is worse than brutality itself, and that man is more dangerous than the Yahoo. This is profoundly true. But its effect on Gulliver is to awaken loathing of all that is human.

Lear, gazing on the naked, shivering Edgar, disguised as a Tom o' Bedlam, cries: 'Thou art the thing itself; unaccommodated man is no more but such a poor, bare, forked animal as thou art.' And in that intense moment, he goes mad. Something of the same thing befalls Gulliver. He thinks he has seen the thing itself. Though the Houyhnhnms never acknowledge that he is more than an unusually gifted Yahoo, he aspires to their rationality, stoicism, and simple wisdom; and persuaded that he has attained them, he feeds his growing misanthropy on pride, which alienates him not only from his remote kinsmen, the Yahoos, but eventually from his brothers, the human race. Looking back with nostalgia on his lost happiness in Houyhnhnmland, he recalls:

I enjoyed perfect Health of Body, and Tranquility of Mind; I did not feel the Treachery or Inconstancy of a Friend, nor the Injuries of a secret or open Enemy. I had no Occasion of bribing, flattering, or pimping, to procure the Favour of any great Man, or of his Minion. I wanted no Fence against Fraud or Oppression: Here was neither physician to destroy my Body, nor Lawyer to ruin my Fortune: No Informer to Watch my Words and Actions, or forge Accusations against me for Hire: Here were no Gibers, Censurers, Backbiters, Pickpockets, Highwaymen, Housebreakers, Attorneys, Bawds, Buffoons, Gamesters, Politicians, Wits, Spleneticks, Tedious Talkers, Controvertists, Ravishers, Murderers, Robbers, Virtuoso's; no Leaders or Followers of Party and Faction; no Encouragers to Vice, by Seducement or Examples: no Dungeon, Axes, Gibbets, Whippingposts, or Pillories; No cheating Shopkeepers or Mechanicks; No Pride, Vanity or Affection: No Fops, Bullies, Drunkards, strolling Whores, or Poxes: No ranting, lewd, expensive Wives:

No stupid, proud Pedants: No importunate, over-bearing, quarrelsome, noisy, roaring, empty, conceited, swearing Companions: No Scoundrels raised from the Dust upon the Merit of their Vices; or Nobility thrown into it on account of their Virtues: No Lords, Fiddlers, Judges or Dancing-masters.

From the moment that the banished Gulliver despairingly sets sail from Houyhnhnmland, his pride, his misanthropy, his madness are apparent. Deluded by his worship of pure reason, he commits the error of the Houyhnhnms in equating human beings with the Yahoos. Captured by a Portuguese crew and forced to return from sullen solitude to humanity, he trembles between fear and hatred. The captain of the ship, Don Pedro de Mendez, like Gulliver himself, shares the nature of the Houyhnhnm and the Yahoo; and like the Gulliver of the first voyage he is tolerant, sympathetic, kindly, patient, and charitable; but Gulliver can no longer recognize these traits in a human being. With the myopic vision of the Houyhnhnms, he perceives only the Yahoo and is repelled by Don Pedro's clothes, food, and odor. Gradually, however, he is nursed back to partial health, and is forced to admit in the very accent of his admired horses, that his benefactor has a 'very good *human* Understanding.' But the Gulliver who writes this book is still under the control of his *idée fixe*, and when we last see him he prefers the smell and conversation of his two horses to the company of his wife and children. This is misanthropy in Timon's manner, not Swift's. In the brilliant and intricately ironic coda with which the book ends, Swift directs his savage, comic gaze straight at Gulliver and his insane pretensions.

My Reconcilement to the *Yahoo*-kind in general might not be so difficult, if they would be content with those Vices and Follies only which Nature hath entitled them to. I am not in the least provoked at the Sight of a Lawyer, a Pickpocket, a Colonel, a Fool, a Lord, a Gamester, a Politician, a Whoremunger, a Physician, an Evidence, a Suborner, an Attorney, a Traytor, or the like: This is all according to the due Course of Things: But when I behold a Lump of Deformity, and Diseases both of Body and Mind, smitten with *Pride*, it immediately breaks all the Measures of my Patience; neither shall I ever be able to comprehend how such an Animal and such a Vice could tally together.

The grim joke is that Gulliver himself is the supreme instance of a creature smitten with pride. His education has somehow failed.

He has voyaged into several remote nations of the world, but the journeys were not long, because of course he has never moved outside the bounds of human nature. The countries he visited, like the Kingdom of Heaven, are all within us. The ultimate danger of these travels was precisely the one that destroyed Gulliver's humanity—the danger that in his explorations he would discover something that he was not strong enough to face. This befell him, and he took refuge in a sick and morbid pride that alienated him from his species and taught him the gratitude of the Pharisee—'Lord, I thank Thee that I am not as other men.'

Swift himself, in his personal conduct, displayed an arrogant pride. But he was never guilty of the angelic, dehumanizing pride of Gulliver, who writes in a letter to his Cousin Sympson:

> I must freely confess, that since my last Return, some corruptions of my *Yahoo* Nature have revived in me by Conversing with a few of your Species, and particularly those of my own Family, by an unavoidable Necessity; else I should never have attempted so absurd a Project as that of reforming the *Yahoo* Race in this Kingdom; but, I have now done with all such visionary Schemes for ever.

Jonathan Swift was stronger and healthier than Lemuel Gulliver. He hated the stupidity and the sinfulness and the folly of mankind. He could not accept the optimistic view of human nature that the philosophers of the Enlightenment proposed. And so he could exclaim to his contemporaries: 'O wicked and perverse generation!' But, until he entered upon the darkness of his last years, he did not abandon his fellow man as hopeless or cease to announce, however indirectly, the dignity and worth of human kind.

R. S. CRANE

*The Rationale of the Fourth Voyage**

I have busied myself off and on for many years with the problem of what Swift was trying to do in the "Voyage to the Country of the Houyhnhnms"; and in spite of numerous failures to solve the problem to more than my temporary satisfaction, I have recently come back to it with renewed hope, fortified by the current upsurge of scholarly writing on the rationale of the fourth Voyage and by the suggestions and criticisms of friends. The problem turns, I think, on three principal questions, and it is with the comparative merits of the different and conflicting answers which these appear to admit of that I shall attempt to deal. The first question has to do with the terms in which the satirical thought of the Voyage is framed; the second with the general method of the Voyage; the third with the form and purpose of its unifying argument.

The most obvious answer to the question of what the satire of the fourth Voyage is in general about is that suggested by the text itself. It would seem from this that the basic terms of reference in the Voyage are psychological and moral in a broadly human and non-sectarian sense. It is in such terms, clearly, that Gulliver narrates his encounter with the Yahoos and the Houyhnhnms and depicts the radical change in his thoughts and emotions about mankind that results from this encounter. But may it not be that there are other concepts lying behind these, of a more particularized

Published for the first time. By permission of the author.

*A paper read at the annual meeting of the Modern Language Association in December, 1955. I have since uncovered a body of historical evidence which tends, I think, to support the thesis about Swift's argument in the fourth Voyage I have developed here; this I hope to publish shortly. [See pp. 402–406 below.] On the general question of Swift's "Platonism," see Jeffrey Hart, "The Idealogue as Artist: Some Notes on 'Gulliver's Travels.'" *Criticism*, II (1960), especially pp. 129–131.

sort, which constitute, in Swift's intention, the real substance and point of the work? That this is the case has been urged upon us in several recent studies, the common thesis of which is that Swift conceived his characters and his story as he did for the sake of enforcing a specifically religious and Christian view of things—either negatively by attacking current doctrines incompatible with the dogma of original sin (this would account for the assimilation of men to the Yahoos) or positively also by insisting on the reality of divine grace and the scheme of redemption (this would explain the commonly felt limitations of the Houyhnhnms and the presence in the narrative of the good Don Pedro).

I find it hard, I must admit, to accept this theory. There is no doubt that Swift could have conceived the fourth Voyage, had he wished, as a theological allegory: the materials for a satirical defence of religion were certainly in his possession. I cannot, however, find any decisive evidence, internal or external, that he actually did so conceive it.

We might expect that if Swift had meant his story to be a contribution to Christian apologetics, there would be some unequivocal hints of this in his correspondence, or that his closest friends, like Pope and Arbuthnot, would have been aware of the fact. But no such testimonies have come to light. We might also expect that in an age like the early eighteenth century, when it was no disgrace to speak out on behalf of religion, a satire that turned primarily on theological issues would make its intention evident in the text itself. But where in the fourth Part of Gulliver are there any clear indices that we ought to think, as we read it, about original sin, divine grace, the necessity of religion, or the heresies of Shaftsbury and the deists? Imagine the "Voyage to the Houyhnhnms" to be a completely anonymous work, and judge then how nearly impossible it would be for a good scholar to prove, by internal evidence, that its writer was a clergyman with strong orthodox convictions, or even a Christian at all.

It is not difficult, of course, knowing who the writer was, to find symbolic equivalents in the details of the story for the terms and doctrines of whatever theological argument our hypothesis presupposes. But of all the passages so used in the various theological readings of the fourth Voyage that I have seen, there are none that do not seem to me capable of other, and usually much simpler, constructions in the moral and psychological terms of Gulliver's own narrative. And it is significant, furthermore, that these readings (along with most of the current non-theological readings) have been based on an assumption about the general method of the Voyage, as a work of literary art, which is at the very least debatable.

The crucial question about Swift's method in the fourth Voyage can be put very simply. Is it primarily an allegorical or symbolic method, or is it not? Must we construe the main figures of the story—the Houyhnhnms and the Yahoos especially—as embodiments, in imaginative forms, of general concepts, or is it sufficient to regard them merely as actors in what the eighteenth century would call a marvelous fable?

The question has nearly always been answered in favor of the first alternative. The fourth Voyage has most commonly been considered to be a work that has to be interpreted, like *Everyman* or *The Pilgrim's Progress*, by finding abstract meanings for its characters in some scheme of moral, psychological, or theological principles.

This may indeed be the right view; but if so, we might expect that critics reading the Voyage as popular allegory would agree more completely than they have done on what the meanings are. The Houyhnhnms, for example, have been equated sometimes with man as he ought to be and sometimes, especially of late, with almost the reverse of that. And the contrast between the Houyhnhnms and the Yahoos has also been given a wide range of differing allegorical interpretations. For one critic, it represents the antithesis between man in the state of nature according to Locke and man in the state of nature according to Hobbes; for another, the discrepancy between beings who have escaped the Fall and beings in whom the evil effects of the Fall are carried to an extreme; for still another, the "war" in Gulliver's self between the rational and animal parts of his nature (as if the Voyage were a body-and-soul debate); and for various other critics, various other things.

It is natural to suspect, therefore, that this diversity of interpretation—to which there seems to be no limit—may be not so much a sign of the richness, or obscurity, of Swift's thought as of the fact that these interpreters have been working on a false assumption about his technique. Why do we have to look for allegory in the fourth Voyage at all? The Voyage can be perfectly well understood as merely what it purports to be; namely, a marvelous or fantastic fable, literally narrated, in which the Houyhnhnms and the Yahoos are not metaphors or symbols standing for general ideas, but two species of concrete beings, the one beyond any known human experience, the other all-too-possible anywhere, whom Gulliver has been thrown with in his travels and has come to venerate and abhor respectively. The moral or thesis of the fable, on this assumption, is brought home to the reader directly through the story itself, which is essentially the story of how Gulliver, seeing the virtues of the Houyhnhnms "in opposite view to human corruptions" and realizing the "entire congruity" between men and the Yahoos, undergoes an extreme revolution in his opinions and feelings about "human kind." And we apprehend and respond to the moral simply by following this story and drawing such inferences from it concerning ourselves as it is calculated to produce in us.

This conception of the general method of the Voyage has just as much antecedent probability, I think, as the more usual conception, and it involves us, besides, in many fewer difficulties of interpretation. It is entirely in harmony, moreover, with either of the two ways of understanding the form and point of Swift's main argument in the Voyage which I shall now go on to discuss.

The question of the satirical point of the fourth Voyage has been made to center, in most recent studies, on the problem of Gulliver's misanthropy and of how far this final state of mind of Swift's hero can be thought to reflect the state of mind of Swift himself. When the issue is put in this way, I am bound to agree with the almost unanimous verdict of contemporary writers on the Voyage and its author that a simple identification of Gulliver's creator with Gulliver is absurdly naïve. I do not think, however, that I am obliged to draw all the consequences from this sensible position that have been drawn from it of late, as to the formula of the satire itself.

For it has been assumed by a growing number of critics that if Swift is not Gulliver (as he certainly is not), then Gulliver must be in error when he reacts to some or all of his experiences as he does, and hence must be designed to strike us, at the end of the Voyage and perhaps before that also, as a comic or ironical figure, who is surely right in recognizing and hating the Yahoo elements in man but just as surely ridiculous, or worse, in seeing only those elements and in admiring so unqualifiedly the rational horses.

This theory, or some variant of it, has been advanced by critics who consider the Voyage to be a satirical defence of Christianity and by critics who do not. And the contention in both cases is that Swift, in constructing the narrative of Gulliver's transformation from a "lover of mankind" into a perfectionist misanthrope, went out of his way to introduce various signs into the story the natural effect of which would be to discredit, for attentive readers, the extreme conclusions drawn by Gulliver himself from his stay in Houyhnhnmland. Such devices have been found in Swift's depiction of the Houyhnhnms, in his characterization of Gulliver, and in his invention and treatment of the episode of Don Pedro.

The Houyhnhnms, it is argued, impress us as both coldly repellent and as funny: how could they then have been intended as proper objects of Gulliver's "love and veneration"? As for Gulliver himself, he is, on the one hand, in his basic excellence of character, a striking rebuttal—we are told—of his own final view of human nature and, on the other hand, in his excesses at the end, when he shuns his family, walks and neighs like a horse, and spends much of his time in his stable, obviously a victim of comic mania. The function of the incident of Don Pedro—with his conspicuously kind treatment of Gulliver and Gulliver's merely sullen toleration of him—is thought to be no less clear. Had Swift meant us to take seriously Gulliver's "antipathy to human kind," wouldn't he have made his rescuer an unmistakable Yahoo? And isn't his emphasis on Don Pedro's virtues a plain indication, therefore, that he wanted us to think of Gulliver, at this final stage, as a person so infatuated with a false or one-sided theory of human nature that he is blind to any facts which contradict it?

Thus has Swift been saved from the old charge of morbid misanthropy at the expense of his hero, who now becomes the vehicle of an argument which does indeed discourage us from thinking over-well of our fellow men but which, in its ultimate point, is more than a little reassuring as to the capacity of at least some human beings for rising far above the Yahoo level.

I owe it to several of my friends that I now see more clearly than I once did the weaknesses of this hypothesis and the possibility of a perhaps more convincing alternative. It is very hard to reconcile it for one thing, with the plain statement of Swift that "the chief end" he proposed, in his writings in general and in *Gulliver* in particular, was "to vex the world rather than divert it." For who is going to be greatly vexed by a satire the grand climax of which—if it was really meant to be taken as many have recently read it—will always provide an alibi for even the most Yahoo-like individual, since all he has to do is to identify himself, complacently, with such exceptions to the general attack as Gulliver and Don Pedro?

But also, and more important, the reasonings employed in support of this current view are by no means as persuasive as they appear to be at first glance. I need to make, I think, only one assumption, which is surely warranted by what we know of Swift's literary habits—namely, that he was capable, in a satire with a straight serious intention, of making light of his subject and characters, perhaps at times too much, in the interest of fantasy and humor, and also of pushing his main point, hyperbolically, as far as it would go, perhaps even farther. But if this is granted, then we are no longer forced to posit an ironical thesis, at the expense of Gulliver, in order to explain why, in the fourth Voyage, the Houyhnhnms and Gulliver are often comic, or why Gulliver's misanthropy is rendered in such extreme terms.

And the other supposed signs of Gulliver's error admit similarly of alternative constructions. The Houyhnhnms are charged with being humanly unsympathetic, and so they are. But what if Swift really wanted his readers to take the same view of their superiority to human corruptions that Gulliver takes? It would surely then have been an artistic error to endow them with the amiable weaknesses of human beings. It is not true, moreover, that they strike us as merely repellent all or even most of the time. Consider only whether we, too, are not very often put sharply on the defensive, along with Gulliver, when his Houyhnhnm "master" marvels how creatures "pretending to reason" can do, without shame, all the evil things Gulliver assures him that men are accustomed to do. The Houyhnhnms are undoubtedly the least satisfactory part of the Voyage, but that is owing in large measure, I think, to the intrinsic difficulty of Swift's task: try to think of any writer who has ever given us wholly convincing and attractive images of perfect excellence in either non-human or human shape. The argument from the deficiencies of the Houyhnhnms is thus not very strong. Nor need we take Gulliver's own admirable disposition as necessarily a sign that he is absurd in looking up to the Houyhnhnms: he had to be a man good enough to be able to recognize and admire "virtues and ideas" superior to his, or his story, as he tells it, would not make sense. And the episode of Don Pedro is likewise susceptible of a non-ironical interpretation. For suppose that what has happened to Gulliver, in Swift's conception of the fable, is not essentially distinct from what Gulliver himself thinks has happened; suppose Swift's point is that Gulliver really has seen for the first time virtue and reason in their fullest living manifestations: we should certainly expect him, on his return, to be so blinded for a while by his vision as to be able at best only to tolerate even the worthiest members of his own species. A worse kind of rescuer than Don Pedro would consequently have been a blunder, since the whole logic of the satirical argument would be spoiled.

These last remarks may suggest what I think that argument in general is. It is an argument broadly moral and psychological rather than specifically Christian in its reference, worked out not allegorically but by means of a marvelous fable, and dependent, for its satirical point, on our taking Gulliver's misanthropy not as an error but as, in substance though not in degree, the natural and proper consequence of the experience he has had. The best analogue to it I can think of is the old argument familiar to all of us—and perhaps also to Swift, though I do not know—in the myth which Socrates relates to Glaucon in the seventh Book of the *Republic*: how the prisoners in the cave sit facing the wall with their backs to the distant light and thus see only the shadows of things, not their reality; how one of them is then taken forcibly up out of the cave and brought face to face with the sun; how, when he has become used to the brightness of this, he congratulates himself on his good fortune and feels sorry for the prisoners still in the cave, thinking that he would rather be anything else in the world than live and think as they do; and how, on being finally taken back to the cave, his eyes are "blinded by the darkness," because he has come in suddenly out of the light, and so, for a time, he tends to "blunder and make a fool of himself," and his companions say that his visit to the upper world has ruined his sight. It is not surprising, says Socrates, if those who have caught a glimpse of the absolute form of the Good are unwilling to return to mundane affairs, if they seem to act foolishly when they do return, and if their minds long to remain among higher things.

The argument of the "Voyage to the Houyhnhnms" is, I suggest, of the same general order as this in its essential form—only transposed into an eighteenth-century key of humor and satiric hyperbole and given a moral instead of an intellectual emphasis. As embodied in the fable of Gulliver, who has seen not the sun but merely the noblest of animals and who reacts to the sight and to his enforced return to mankind even more extravagantly than the prisoner, the argument is well calculated to serve Swift's avowed end of vexing the world by shocking it violently but wittily out of its complacency with itself; and it does this, let me add, in a way that no more compels us to identify Swift with his hero than we are obliged to identify Socrates—or Plato—with the man who blundered and made a fool of himself, for a while, on being brought back to the cave.

W. B. CARNOCHAN

Gulliver: The Satirist on Himself

The most useful insight in new readings of the *Travels* concerns Gulliver. He is a ludicrous—though not laughable—figure at the end of his tale; it is hardly conceivable that Swift did not know what he had done. If Gulliver's behavior has something in it of the inspired fool's madness, it has more of the hack writer's. Therapeutically occupied in venting speculations for the universal benefit of mankind, he is as much a "projector" as anyone in the Laputian academy, as proud, as condescending, as foolish. If Swift holds up for ridicule a character whose gross incomprehension, in Book II, has been supplanted at last by attitudes that his creator (in some moods) shared, we can anticipate the reasons. Again we are faced, now in dramatic form, with Swift's self-critical ways.

Humor of a kind persists: Pope's "heroic" epistle from Mary Gulliver to her husband, which Swift liked enough to incorporate in the *Travels* after the first edition, makes explicit the sexual innuendo of Gulliver's retreat to the stables. At first Lemuel's wife strikes a note of pathos that briefly tempts agreement with those who have turned the book into a discourse on the Christian's familial duties:

From *Lemuel Gulliver's Mirror for Man*, pp. 90–105. Berkeley: University of California Press, 1968. Reprinted by permission of The Regents of the University of California.

WELCOME, thrice welcome to thy native Place!
—What, touch me not? what, shun a Wife's Embrace?
Have I for this thy tedious Absence born,
And wak'd and wish'd whole Nights for thy Return?
(1–4)

Mary Gulliver is the faithful Penelope, her husband the caricature of Ulysses. The elegiac note subsides, however, with a double entendre—" 'Tis said, that thou shouldst cleave unto thy Wife; / Once *thou* didst cleave, and *I* could cleave for Life," (9–10)—and the whole thing turns from pathos to crude allusion:

Not touch me! never Neighbour call'd me Slut!
Was *Flimnap*'s Dame more sweet in *Lilliput*?
I've no red Hair to breathe an odious Fume;
At least thy Consort's cleaner than thy *Groom*.
Why then that dirty Stable-boy thy Care?
What mean those Visits to the *Sorrel Mare*?
(25–30)

As a humorous grotesque, Gulliver solicits very little human feeling. The grotesque averts customary responses by making them irrelevant; it is Swift's defense against self-involvement.

But Gulliver is more than a grotesque. As a self-caricature, he embodies all Swift's doubts about his motives and his literary vocation. Professor Elliott calls the satirist satirized an archetypal theme; his examples are Alceste, Shakespeare's Timon, and Gulliver.[1] Even more accurately, Gulliver is the satirist self-satirized—for his tendency to inclusive statement, for his impossible hopes of reforming the world, for his anger at the ungodly, for his converting imagination, his pride, his dreams of the perfected life. John F. Ross calls it the final comedy of the *Travels*, "that Swift could make an elaborate and subtle joke at the expense of a very important part of himself," but this is bleak comedy of introspection.[2] And at the very last, when feeling cannot any longer be averted by grotesquerie or deflected by irony, the evidence of pain breaks through, as we shall see.

If a principal motive for the caricature of Gulliver is the need to back away from hyperbole—the identification of man and Yahoo—it is only one motive among many. Equally important is

[1] Robert C. Elliott, *The Power of Satire* (Princeton, 1960), pp. 130–222.

[2] John F. Ross, "The Final Comedy of Lemuel Gulliver," *Studies in the Comic*, University of California Publications in English, VIII, No. 2 (Berkeley, 1941), p. 196.

Swift's self-conscious awareness that satire, despite its would-be usefulness, despite any hope the satirist may genuinely entertain, and no matter who its explicit object may be—one man, some men, or all mankind—hardly ever reforms anyone, much less the world: "SATYR *is a sort of* Glass, *wherein Beholders do generally discover every body's Face but their Own.*"[3] The Augustan satirist, committed to social reform, carries a burden that the formalist does not: how is he best to set a glass before the reader, whose response to satiric attack will be to join hands with the satirist or with the Brobdingnagian king and rejoice, vicariously, to see the "Bulk" of men getting what they deserve?[4] Even with the last turn of the knife—"how came you to claim an Exception from all Mankind?"—the heart, it may be, is unmoved. It is any reformer's problem and it defies solution.

But Swift will not give in, any more than he will give in to his knowledge that the congregation ignores the preacher: "No Preacher is listened to, but Time." And, in the same spirit: "How is it possible to expect that Mankind will take *Advice*, when they will not so much as take *Warning?*" Yet, on the very same page of *Thoughts on Various Subjects* where these reflections occur, there is another quite different in kind: "POSITIVENESS," Swift says, is a useful trait for those who would influence others; the preacher or orator—or, no doubt, the satirist in his own way—"will convince others the more, as he appears convinced himself." No matter that the appearance, in this formulation, is as important as the conviction. As Edward Young puts the dilemma, in the preface to *Love of Fame:* "It is much *to be feared,* that misconduct will never be chased out of the world by *Satire*; all therefore that is to be said for it, is, that misconduct will *certainly* be never chased out of the world by Satire, if no Satires are written."

Swift would not have claimed more. He writes Ford (August 14, 1725) about the *Travels:* "they are admirable Things, and will wonderfully mend the World," words that Professor Nichol Smith described as the "top note of exaltation in all [Swift's] writings."[5] But the tone of naive optimism is utterly untypical of Swift except

[3] A *Tale of a Tub* [eds. A. C. Guthkelch and D. Nichol Smith, 2nd. ed., Oxford, 1958], p. 215.

[4] On the "alliance" between satirist and audience, the problems it poses, and "the manner in which [Swift] circumvents" it, cf. Henry W. Sams, "Swift's Satire of the Second Person," *ELH*, XXVI (1959), 36–44.

[5] D. Nichol Smith, "Jonathan Swift: Some Observations," *Essays by Divers Hands, Being the Transactions of the Royal Society of Literature of the United Kingdom,* New Series, XIV (1935), 46.

in ironic moods. Like Gulliver, he plays the confident projector: surely the assertion that *Gulliver's Travels* will wonderfully mend the word is self-satiric. And, later in his life, the irony recurs when Swift thinks of his barren labors for the Irish. In a note, he apologizes for not being home when his friend Orrery came to visit: "You ought to have sent your Servant instead of coming your self to see me: for then I would not have been abroad to have saved what never can be saved; Ireland." The thought of saving Ireland lingers as the impossibility is acknowledged; Swift's frustrated efforts are all summed up.

And, looking back on the failure of his *Travels* to reform the Yahoos, Gulliver also sees that man cannot be saved, while displaying at the same time Swift's urgent need to make the effort anyway. In the letter to Sympson, added to the text for the Faulkner edition (1735), Gulliver chides his cousin for urging that the work be published. "I DO in the next Place complain of my own great Want of Judgment, in being prevailed upon by the Intreaties and false Reasonings of you and some others, very much against mine own Opinion, to suffer my Travels to be published." He lays the blame to Sympson's optimism, which he claims not to have shared: "Pray bring to your Mind how often I desired you to consider, when you insisted on the Motive of *publick Good;* that the *Yahoos* were a Species of Animals utterly incapable of Amendment by Precepts or Examples: And so it hath proved." But the *Travels* were intended for publication from the first, as anyone who has read them knows. Gulliver gives himself away in his next words: "for instead of seeing a full Stop put to all Abuses and Corruptions, at least in this little Island, as I had Reason to expect· Behold, after above six Months Warning, I cannot learn that my Book hath produced one single Effect according to mine Intentions." In baring Gulliver's original hopes, together with his denial that he ever hoped at all and his attempt to put responsibility elsewhere, Swift probes personal wounds. The *Travels* have not wonderfully mended the world; but he did not think they would. Gulliver learns what Swift has long known: that there is not, as the author of the *Tale* puts it, "through all Nature, another so callous and insensible a Member as the *World's Posteriors*."[6]

Still graver doubts contribute to Swift's self-ridicule; once more, "what I do is owing to perfect rage and resentment, and the mortifying sight of slavery, folly, and baseness about me." Gulliver is

[6] A *Tale of a Tub*, p. 48.

moved by those tyrant-passions that Swift, long before, had singled out in the ode to Sancroft: anger, scorn, fear. Scorn is clad in robes of indifference: "I am not in the least provoked at the Sight of a Lawyer, a Pick-pocket, a Colonel, a Fool, a Lord, a Gamester, a Politician, a Whoremunger, a Physician, an Evidence, a Suborner, an Attorney, a Traytor, or the like: This is all according to the due Course of Things." Anger, finally, is unconcealed: "But, when I behold a Lump of Deformity, and Diseases both in Body and Mind, smitten with *Pride*, it immediately breaks all the Measures of my Patience." No more than Swift can Gulliver heed the impossible advice: "Fret not thyself because of the ungodly." And behind scorn and anger, even perhaps at their source, lies acknowledged fear, diminished since Gulliver first peeped from the window of the sea captain's house and drew back in terror, but persistent still: "I am not altogether out of Hopes in some Time to suffer a Neighbour *Yahoo* in my Company, without the Apprehensions I am yet under of his Teeth or his Claws" (IV, xii). When Swift berates his habitual anger, does he realize that fear also plays a part in his antagonism to the world? However that may be, the vision of a society free from the tyranny of passion has made Gulliver a slave, just as the satirist is the victim of his own ideal imaginings. In the satirist's hands, the measuring stick is converted to the flail. In Swift's hands, the flail is used for self-punishment.

The tyranny of the passions impels Gulliver also to a "violent zeal for truth": he is both zealous for truthfulness and insistent that others share his view of things. And all "violent zeal for truth," Swift wrote in the *Thoughts on Religion*, "hath an hundred to one odds to be either petulancy, ambition, or pride." He has the dissenters principally in mind. His own clerical role he conceives as a defensive one: "I look upon myself, in the capacity of a clergyman, to be one appointed by providence for defending a post assigned me, and for gaining over as many enemies as I can." The calm of the established church is guarded by time and custom. The clergyman's role demands no forays onto foreign ground, and if he gains over enemies, he does so more by allurement than by combat hand-to-hand. But the satirist, even as a member of the same army, is an outrider whose business lies beyond the city walls. If he gains an advantage from the mobility of wit, he runs the risk that he will seem as violent for truth as the most passionate exponent of divinity. And Swift saw in himself the enthusiastic strain he distrusted in others. Having explained to Pope that man is not rational but only capable of reason, and having then described the substance of his misanthropy, he ends with a burst of (mock) missionary zeal: "I never will have peace of mind till all honest men are of my Opinion: by Consequence you are to embrace it immediatly and procure that all who deserve my Esteem may do so too. The matter is so clear that it will admit little dispute." Though always hoping for the clarity that admits no dispute and for the security of the *consensus gentium*, he has rejected a traditional definition and a benevolent view of man that was becoming orthodox. He is hard put to keep up his character as defender of the citadel; plainly he is on the attack. When he enjoins Pope to embrace his opinion "immediatly" and set about the business of making converts, he has turned to jest and uneasy recognition of the desire to force his views on others. Gulliver, whose fear and hatred of the English Yahoos go ironically together with his efforts to reform them, is a parody of the man who can have no peace of mind until all honest men embrace his opinion.

If the follies and vices of mankind, in the logic of the *Travels*, can all be attributed to the ruling passion of pride, then Gulliver's one failing that subsumes the rest—his presumption of universal corruption, his overconfident hope of changing things, his passions, and his zeal—is his self-proclaimed moral superiority. Were he really to see himself as incorrigibly a Yahoo, we might forgive him the eccentricity. It is the self-esteem of the projector, critic, and reformer that we resent: "I write for the noblest End, to inform and instruct Mankind, over whom I may, without Breach of Modesty, pretend to some Superiority, from the Advantages I received by conversing so long among the most accomplished *Houyhnhnms*" (IV, xii). Gulliver even tells Cousin Sympson that he no longer shares the frailties of others. Taking strength from the company of his two "degenerate *Houyhnhnms*," he still improves "in some Virtues, without any Mixture of Vice." We recognize, as he cannot, the processes of mind by which ideas "of what is most Perfect, finished, and exalted" lead the visionary from the frontiers of height to those of depth, from insight to blind pride. Gulliver is kin to Swift's other benefactors of mankind—the hack, who tells us he writes "*without Vanity*";[7] or the modest proposer; or Simon

[7] *Ibid.*, p. 47: "when an Author makes his own Elogy, he uses a certain form to declare and insist upon his Title, which is commonly in these or the like words, *I speak without Vanity*; which I think plainly shews it to be a Matter of Right and Justice. Now, I do here once for all declare, that in every Encounter of this Nature, thro' the following Treatise, the Form aforesaid is imply'd; which I mention, to save the Trouble of repeating it on so many Occasions."

Wagstaff, author of the *Compleat Collection of Genteel and Ingenious Conversation,* whose rhetoric is a recognizable though crude instance of Gulliver's self-commendatory style:

> I will venture to say, without Breach of Modesty, that I, who have alone, with this Right Hand, subdued Barbarism, Rudeness, and Rusticity; who have established, and fixed for ever, the whole System of all true Politeness, and Refinement in Conversation; should think my self most inhumanly treated by my Countrymen and would accordingly resent it as the highest Indignity, to be put upon the Level, in point of Fame, in after Ages, with *Charles* XII. late King of *Sweden.*

Wagstaff's desire to subdue conversational "Barbarism, Rudeness, and Rusticity" reminds us more of Mr. Spectator and Swift, and of their hopes for an English academy, than of Gulliver; but in resorting to the same parenthetic and defensive phrase, so obviously false—"without Breach of Modesty"—Gulliver and Wagstaff reveal their common bond.

Their case and that of Swift's other vain projectors is the satirist's also; he too seems to claim superior wit, wisdom, or virtue.[8] Like Horace, he may insist on his right to be left alone by the mob, striking up an alliance with a few like-minded and like-talented men: "I have often endeavoured," Swift writes Pope, "to establish a Friendship among all Men of Genius, and would fain have it done. they are seldom above three or four Cotemporaries and if they could be united would drive the world before them; I think it was so among the Poets in the time of Augustus; but Envy and party and pride have hindred it among us." The self-protective alliance is potentially militant—"if they could be united [they] would drive the world before them." It is an unguarded moment. Samuel Johnson said of Swift and his friends: "From the letters that pass

[8] Alvin Kernan, *The Cankered Muse: Satire of the English Renaissance* (New Haven, 1959), p. 26. Swift is not alone as a satirist whose instincts conflict with his values. Kernan says: "St. Jerome in his satiric letters takes his contemporaries to task for their unchristian behavior, but his own bitter attacks—as he remembers from time to time—violate the fundamental tenet of the Christian religion, charity. Juvenal's satirist adheres to some loose variety of Stoicism, but his fiery indignation stands in direct contrast to the Stoic ideals of passionless calm and stern endurance of misfortune, and he is forced to explain that though Nature, the principle of right reason operating through the universe, forbids his satiric outbursts, indignation insists upon them: 'si natura negat, facit indignatio versum' " (pp. 25–26).

between him and Pope it might be inferred that they, with Arbuthnot and Gay, had engrossed all the understanding and virtue of mankind, that their merits filled the world; or that there was no hope of more."[9] Johnson dislikes Swift and construes the facts harshly; still we know what he is talking about.

The pride of the Juvenalian satirist is more overt, uncompromising. He has no allies; he exploits his self-portrait as the lone hero; he *is* proud not to be like other men. Like Swift in his final *Examiner* (June 7, 1711), he may even seem to resent being a member of the species:

> For my own particular, those little barking Pens which have so constantly pursued me, I take to be of no further Consequence to what I have writ, than the scoffing Slaves of old, placed behind the Chariot, to put the General in Mind of his Mortality; which was but a Thing of Form, and made no Stop or Disturbance in the Show. However, if those perpetual Snarlers against me, had the same Design, I must own they have effectually compassed it; since nothing can well be more mortifying, than to reflect, that I am of the same Species with Creatures capable of uttering so much Scurrility, Dulness, Falshood, and Impertinence, to the Scandal and Disgrace of Human Nature.

The satirist-victim, transformed now to the triumphant warrior, is beyond reach of the crowds. In the grandiose image, however, lies a muted sense of recognition: the image tends to self-parody. Behind the satirist as warrior stands the slave appointed to remind him that he is only a man—"a Thing of Form," perhaps, but the same cautionary reminder as Swift's to Sheridan. In this last of his *Examiner* papers, Swift glances at the extremes to which envy, party, and pride lead men like himself who are at least capable of being rational.

Anyone who calls his critics snarling curs will be accused of snarling back at them; anyone who calls his critics an "odious" and "offensive herd" (as Swift did in the ode to Congreve) will be called odious and offensive in his turn. That is the moral to the hack writer's anecdote of a "*fat unweildy Fellow*," who curses those around him as they watch a mountebank in Leicester Fields: "*Lord! what a filthy Crowd is here; Pray, good People, give way a little, Bless me! what a Devil has rak'd this Rabble together.*" A

[9] Samuel Johnson, "Swift," *Lives of the English Poets*, ed. George Birkbeck Hill (Oxford, 1905), III, 61.

weaver makes the obvious retort: "A *Plague confound you . . . for an over-grown Sloven; and who (in the Devil's name) I wonder, helps to make up the Crowd half so much as your self? . . . Bring your own Guts to a reasonable Compass (and be d—n'd) and then I'll engage we shall have room enough for us all.*"[10] Whoever claims to "some Superiority" over those he wants to inform and instruct will get the same legitimate response: "*Bring your own Guts to a reasonable Compass.*" Of the two theoretical questions we began with—"What is man?" "What is a sane man?"—the second is easier to answer and does not in the long run require philosophic or even psychometric precision. A sane man realizes he is like other men—"how came you to claim an Exception from all Mankind?" Whatever our frailties, the satirist shares them; whatever the essential nature of man, he participates in it.

Though grounded in a sense of his own shortcomings, Swift's self-satire also has another, less intimate aspect. As with the Yahoos, personal impulses have strategic value. By anticipating what the censorious world will say, the satirist tries to disarm it; and Swift's revenge on his Juvenalian side not only implies a defense of Horatian tradition, it also places the *Travels*, once and for all, within the tradition. If Gulliver is Swift's *alazon*, as he has been called,[11] the satirist who stands behind him is the *eiron*, implicating but also guarding himself by self-deprecation.[12] There is no older tactic, though it is practiced here in a way that usually escapes notice and with such underlying intensity that the strain is almost too great. Swift's self-portrait as Gulliver; Horace's as a "fat pig from the herd of Epicurus"; the usual Socratic pose—each disguise demonstrates the ironist's knowledge of his ignorance and frailty. Serious self-criticism leads to ironic self-justification; that is how *Gulliver's Travels* becomes another instance of the satirist's apology for his art.

Such apologies are usually ignored or, as in Swift's case, misunderstood. Commonplaces about the treacherous nature of irony are seldom so well illustrated. Since the *Travels'* first appearance, hostile critics have accused Swift of what is less conditionally true of

[1] A *Tale of a Tub*, p. 46.

[2] James R. Wilson, "Swift's Alazon," *Studia Neophilologica*, XXX (1958), 153–164.

[3] Extremes meet: *eiron* and *alazon* are separate halves of the same personality. But so too, each cancels the other: Swift approaches the mean, which is truth, in self-awareness.

Gulliver. And Swift took the trouble to reply in a poem called "A Panegyric on the Reverend D--n S---t"—if, in fact, this is the "scrub libel" on himself that he composed in the fall of 1730. He describes it in a letter to Lord Bathurst: "I took special care to accuse myself but of one fault of which I am really guilty, and so shall continue as I have done these 16 years till I see cause to reform:—but with the rest of the Satyr I chose to abuse myself with the direct reverse of my character or at least in direct opposition to one part of what you are pleased to give me." There are difficulties in applying this description to "A Panegyric on the Reverend D--n S---t"; but the use of mock-panegyric criticism as a means to self-justification is the sort of Chinese puzzle that pleased Swift, and the poem is probably his. These are the last lines:

> For *Gulliver* divinely shews,
> That *Humankind* are all *Yahoos*.
> Both Envy then and Malice must
> Allow your hatred strictly just;
> Since you alone of all the Race
> Disclaim the *Human Name*, and Face,
> And with the *Virtues* pant to wear
> (May Heav'n Indulgent hear your Pray'r!)
> The *Proof* of your high *Origine*,
> The *Horse's Countenance Divine*.
> While G-, S-, and I,
> Who after you *adoring* fly,
> An humbler Prospect only wait,
> To be your *Asses Colts* of *State*,
> The *Angels* of your awful *Nods*,
> Resembling you as *Angel Gods*.

On the assumption that this oblique defense of his humanity precludes Swift's admiring the Houyhnhnms, it has been used as evidence for the anti-Utopian reading of the *Travels*. If Swift does not "disclaim the *Human Name*, and Face," however, that has nothing to do with the horses. Knowing how very vulnerable he is ("Gulliver divinely shews, / That *Humankind* are all *Yahoos*"), he claims only that he neither wants to be a horse nor pretends to be divine.

And even Gulliver, preposterous though he is, comes to realize that by no act of will can he transform himself. The disaffection that leads him to look for refuge in the stable becomes his pain:

the satirist resents the perceptions that set him apart. Whatever Gulliver pretends, he is not content to converse with his horses; when we see him last (leaving aside the letter to Sympson), he is trying to come to terms with the English Yahoos. He resolves to look often in the mirror—the same mirror that he is holding up for others to see themselves—"and thus if possible habituate my self by Time to tolerate the Sight of a human Creature." He hopes he can overcome his fear and so be able "to suffer a Neighbour *Yahoo* in my Company." In fact, he wants to "make the Society of an *English Yahoo* by any Means not insupportable" (IV, xii). The solitary island he had wanted to find would not have answered his needs; it would have offered no escape from himself. Perhaps Pope thinks of Gulliver, in the *Essay on Man*: "Who most to shun or hate Mankind pretend, / Seek an admirer, or would fix a friend."

Similar in its effect to the moment when he learns of his banishment from Houyhnhnmland, Gulliver's would-be reconciliation is usually slighted, but is of very great importance. It proves his hatred of man is not in Timon's manner and is fatal to the argument of those who distinguish Swift's misanthropy from Gulliver's. Timon's manner, to be sure, varies according to the source. We cannot know whether Swift remembers Lucian's Timon, or Shakespeare's, or even Thomas Shadwell's in his adaptation of Shakespeare (1678), or none of these. But Shadwell had sentimentalized the figure of the man-hater, and it is the traditional Timon in Shakespeare's or Lucian's manner who is evidently made the foil to Swift's and Gulliver's misanthropy.[13] Apemantus says to Shakespeare's protagonist, after their long flyting in Act IV: "live, and love thy misery" (IV.iii.396). Timon nurtures the hatred that destroys but also consoles him. Hating Athens, he has prayed that he might hate all mankind. And in Lucian's *Timon, or the Misanthrope*, the protagonist is comic, but his hatred is not less self-willed. He confers on himself the name by which he wishes to be

[4] Shadwell's main addition to the play was the part of the faithful Evandra. Timon dies pronouncing this valediction to her:

I charge thee live, *Evandra!*
Thou lov'st me not, if thou wilt not obey me;
Thou only! dearest! kind! constant thing on earth,
Farewel. (*The History of Timon of Athens, the Man-hater* [London, 1678], p. 82).

But Evandra is true to her word and stabs herself. Timon's manner, in Shadwell's revision, is in fact to love the individual; but we are not inclined to believe a word of it.

known, *Misanthropos*. Gulliver, who is not in love with misery and death, has no more in common with Lucian's avaricious hermit than with Shakespeare's tormented misanthrope. He wants to make life bearable if he can. He shows some gratitude to the Portuguese sea captain (in whom he recognizes "very good *human* Understanding") and tries to conceal his antipathy to mankind in Mendez' presence; if this antipathy grows stronger as he comes into closer touch with civilization, it yields no satisfaction. Shakespeare's Timon, though he has to concede the virtues of one man (his steward Flavius), resents the challenge to his conviction that all are vile: "How fain would I have hated all mankind!" (IV.iii.506). The remark, characteristic of him, would be uncharacteristic of Gulliver. Neither Swift nor Gulliver, in short, are misanthropes in Timon's manner; and Swift, despite a sharper perception of man's individual worth, shares with Gulliver an unwilling estrangement from men: "O, if the World had but a dozen Arbuthnetts in it I would burn my Travells." If Swift shows his love for the individual, he shows also how few he has found to love. He is no misanthrope by choice; he would burn the *Travels* if he could, but he has not found even a dozen Arbuthnots in the world.

When he makes an exception of his friend, however, he cannot quite let it go at that: "O, if the World had but a dozen Arbuthnetts in it I would burn my Travells but however he is not without Fault." The "Fault," says Swift, is like one that Bede ascribes to the early Irish Christians: "There is a passage in Bede highly commending the Piety and learning of the Irish in that Age, where after abundance of praises he overthrows them all by lamenting that, Alas, they kept Easter at a wrong time of the Year. So our Doctor has every Quality and virtue that can make a man amiable or usefull, but alas he hath a sort of Slouch in his Walk. I pray God protect him. . . ." How came Swift, it is as much as to say, to claim for Arbuthnot the exception from all mankind that Arbuthnot would not claim for himself? And, on the other hand, how came Swift to be obsessed with the communal guilt of mankind, even with Arbuthnot's slouch that compares so badly with the noble and even gait of the Houyhnhnms? "I pray God protect him": this poignant expression of friendship more violent than love is also a recognition of our manifold frailties. The pendulum of the mind still swings to and fro.

Gulliver's Travels, then, anticipates its critics, anticipates and answers them. If the satirist recognizes so well the limitations of his craft, the uncertain value of his motives, and the exaggerations of his rhetoric; if his separation from others is not just a mask but is also his pain; if all this is so, and he still persists in his calling, affronting the benevolent and confirming his own isolation, then the satiric response itself is no wanton indulgence. It is an ugly world that prevails against so many promptings of instinct and of reason.

A. E. DYSON

Swift: The Metamorphosis of Irony

In an age of few or shifting values irony becomes, very often, a tone of urbane amusement; assuming the right to be amused, but offering no very precise positives behind the right. It can degenerate into a mere gesture of superiority, superficially polished and civilized, but too morally irresponsible to be really so. *Eminent Victorians* is an example of such irony which springs to mind. Lytton Strachey uses the tone of Gibbon in order to deflate the Victorians, but divorces the tone from any firm moral viewpoint, and so makes of it a negative and somewhat vicious instrument.

Irony can, also, become a mode of escape, as we have good cause to know in the twentieth century. To laugh at the terrors of life is in some sense to evade them. To laugh at oneself is to become less vulnerable to the scorn or indifference of others. An ironic attitude is, as we should all now agree, complex and unpredictable: fluctuating with mood and situation, and too subtle in its possibilities for any simple definition in terms of moral purpose or a "test of truth" to be generally applicable.

This is not, however, a state of affairs as new, or unusual, as we might be tempted to think. Even in that great age of moral irony,

From *Essays and Studies*, 1958 (1959), pp. 53-67. London. Reprinted by permission of the author and the publisher, *The English Association.*

the eighteenth century, the technique is far from being simple. Irony is, in its very nature, the most ambivalent of modes, constantly changing colour and texture, and occasionally suffering a sea-change into something decidedly rich and strange. In the work of Swift, who will concern us here, we find, at characteristic moments, that the irony takes a leap. It escapes from its supposed or apparent purpose, and does something not only entirely different from what it set out to do, but even diametrically opposite. Nor is this just a matter of lost artistic control or structural weakness. At the moments I have in mind the irony is at its most complex and memorable. It seems, in undergoing its metamorphosis, to bring us nearer to Swift's inner vision of man and the universe. It ceases to be a functional technique serving a moral purpose, and becomes the embodiment of an attitude to life. And just as Alice was forced, on consideration, to accept the metamorphosis of the Duchess's baby into a pig as an improvement ("it would have made a dreadfully ugly child: but it makes rather a handsome pig, I think"), so the readers of Swift will have to agree that the final impact of his irony, however disturbing, is more real, and therefore more worth while, than its continuation as simple moral satire would have been.

But this is to anticipate. We must begin by reminding ourselves that Swift *is* a satirist: and that satire, fiercer than comedy in its moral intentions, measures human conduct not against a norm but against an ideal. The intention is reformative. The satirist holds up for his readers to see a distorted image, and the reader is to be shocked into a realization that the image is his own. Exaggeration of the most extreme kind is central to the shock tactics. The reader must see himself as a monster, in order to learn how far he is from being a saint.

The Augustan age, as Professor Willey has most interestingly shown, was especially adapted to satiric writing. An age which does not really believe in sin, and which imagines that its most rational and enlightened ideals have been actualized as a norm, is bound to be aware also, at times, of a radical gulf between theory and practice.

> . . . if you worship "Nature and Reason," you will be the more afflicted by human unreason; and perhaps only the effort to see man as the world's glory will reveal how far he is really its jest and riddle.

Economic and acquisitive motives were coming more and more into the open as mainsprings of individual and social action; Hobbes's sombre account of human nature in terms of competition and conflict was altogether too plausible on the practical level for the comfort of gentlemen philosophers who rejected it, as a theory, out of hand. The turning of Science, Britannia and The Moderns into idols was bound, in any case, to produce sooner or later some iconoclasm of the Swiftian kind. Satire thrives on moral extremes: and at this period, with Hobbes at hand to provide a view of man which was at once alarmingly possible and entirely opposite to the prevailing one, satire was bound to be very much at home.

It should follow from this, and to some extent really does, that Swift was a moralist, concerned, as he himself puts it, to "wonderfully mend the world," in accordance with the world's most ideal picture of itself. *Gulliver's Travels* is far more complex and elusive, however, than this intention would suggest. It is, indeed, a baffling work: I have been re-reading a number of excellent and stimulating commentaries on Book IV, and find that there are disagreements upon even the most fundamental points of interpretation. Clearly, we cannot arrive at Swift's "true" meaning merely by reversing what he actually says. The illusion that he is establishing important positives with fine, intellectual precision breaks down when we try to state what these positives *are*.

On the surface, at least, the irony does work in ways that can be precisely defined. Swift has a number of techniques which he is skilled in using either singly, or in powerful combination. At one moment he will make outrageously inhuman proposals, with a show of great reasonableness, and an affected certainty that we shall find them acceptable; at another, he will make soundly moral or Christian proposals, which are confidently held up for scorn. Again, we find him offering, with apparent sympathy and pride, an account of our actual doings, but in the presence of a virtuous outsider whose horrified reactions are sufficient index of their true worth. Swift can, notoriously, shift from one technique to another with huge dexterity; setting his readers a problem in mental and moral gymnastics if they are to evade all of his traps. In Book III, for example, the Professors at Balnibarbi are presented as progressive scientists, of a kind whom the Augustan reader would instinctively be prepared to admire. We quickly find that they are devoid of all common sense; and that unless we are to approve of such extravagant projects as "softening marble for pincushions" we have to dissociate ourselves from them entirely. But when we do this, Swift is still ready for us. "In the school of political projectors," says Gulliver, "I was but ill entertained; the Professors appearing in my judgement wholly out of their senses" (a pleasant reassurance, this, that we have done well to come to a similar conclusion some time before). The crowning absurdity is that these "unhappy people were proposing schemes for persuading monarchs to choose favourites upon the score of their wisdom, capacity and virtue . . . of rewarding merit, great abilities and eminent services . . ." and so on. Dissociated from the Professors, we find ourselves, once more, in Swift's snare.

The technique is, of course, one of betrayal. A state of tension, not to say war, exists between Swift and his readers. The very tone in which he writes is turned into a weapon. It is the tone of polite conversation, friendly, and apparently dealing in commonplaces. Naturally our assent is captured, since the polite style, the guarantee of gentlemanly equality, is the last one in which we expect to be attacked or betrayed. But the propositions to which we find ourselves agreeing are in varying degrees monstrous, warped or absurd. The result is the distinctively satiric challenge: why, we have to ask, are we so easily trapped into thinking so? And is this, perhaps, the way we really do think, despite our normal professions to the contrary?

The technique of betrayal is made all the more insidious by Swift's masterly use of misdirection. No conjuror is more adept at making us look the wrong way. His use of the polite style for betrayal is matched by his use of the traveller's tale. The apparently factual and straightforward narrative with which *Gulliver's Travels* opens (the style of *Robinson Crusoe*), precludes suspicion. We readily accept Gulliver as a representative Englishman fallen into the hands of an absurd crew of midgets, and only gradually realize that the midgets, in fact, are ourselves, and Gulliver, in this instance, the outside observer. The same technique is used, I shall argue, in Book IV: though there, the misdirection is even more subtle, and the way to extricate ourselves from a disastrous committal to Gulliver's point of view far more difficult to discover.

So much, then, for the purpose of the irony, and its normal methods. It is, we notice, accomplished, full of surprises, and admirably adapted to the task of shocking the reader for his moral good. For a great part of the time, moreover, it functions as it is intended to. When Swift is satirizing bad lawyers, bad doctors, bad politicians and *id genus omne,* he is driven by a genuine humanity, and by a conviction that people ought not to act in this way, and need not act so. His tone of savage indignation is justified by the content, and relates directly to normal ideals of justice, honesty, kindness.

On looking closely, however, we find that his irony is by no means directed only against things which can be morally changed. Sometimes it is deflected, and turned upon states of mind which might, or might not, be alterable. Consider, for example, the Laputians. These people never, we are told, enjoy a moment's peace of mind, "and their disturbances proceed from causes which very little affect the rest of mortals." They are preoccupied with fears of cosmic disasters, and apprehensions that the world will come to an end. The ironic treatment pre-supposes that Swift is analysing a moral flaw, but it seems doubtful whether such fears can be regarded whclly a matter of culpable weakness, and even more doubtful whether ridicule could hope to effect a cure. The problem exists in a hinterland between the moral and the psychological, between sin and sickness. The Laputians are temperamentally prone to worry: and worry is not usually regarded, except by the most austerely stoical, as simply a moral weakness.

This dubious usage points the way to the real metamorphosis, which occurs when the irony is deflected again, and turned against states of mind, or existence, which cannot be changed at all. The irony intended to "wonderfully mend the world" transmutes itself into a savage exploration of the world's essential unmendability. It is turned against certain limitations, or defects (as Swift sees them), in the human predicament that are, by the nature of things, inevitable. When this happens, Swift seems to generate his fiercest intensity. The restless energy behind the style becomes a masochistic probing of wounds. The experience of reading him is peculiarly disturbing at such moments; and it is then that his tone of savage indignation deepens into that *disgust* which Mr. T. S. Eliot has called his distinctive characteristic.

In the first two books of *Gulliver* alterations of perspective usually precipitate this type of irony. The Lilliputians are ridiculous not only because they are immoral, but because they are small. The life of their court is as meaningless as it is unpleasant: their intrigues and battles a game, which Gulliver can manipulate like a child playing with toys, and as easily grow tired of. Gulliver himself becomes ridiculous when he is placed beside the Brobdingnagians; whose contempt for him, once again, is not wholly, or even primarily, a moral matter. The King, after hearing Gulliver prattling about his "beloved England," comments "how contemptible a thing was human grandeur, which could be mimicked by such diminutive insects," and continues

> Yet I dare engage, these creatures have their titles and distinctions of honour; they contrive little nests and burrows, that they call houses and cities; they make a figure in dress and equipage; they love, they fight, they dispute, they cheat, they betray.

The force, here, is in "mimicked," "diminutive insects," "creatures," "little." The smallness of Gulliver and his kind makes anything they do equally contemptible, their loves as much as their battles, their construction of houses and cities as much as their destructiveness. The survey is Olympian; and the human setting, seen from this height, becomes, irrespective of moral evaluation, a tale of little meaning though the words are strong.

Likewise, the hugeness of the Brobdingnagians makes them potentially horrible. The sight of a huge cancer fills Gulliver with revulsion, as, too, does the sight of giant flies who "would sometimes alight on my victuals, and leave their loathsome excrement or spawn behind."

What do these alterations in perspective suggest? We are made to feel that perhaps all beauty or value is relative, and in the last resort of little worth. To be proud of human achievement is as absurd as to be proud of our sins. The insignificance of men in space suggests an inevitable parallel in time. Perhaps men really *are* no more than ants, playing out their fleeting tragicomedy to an uninterested or scornful void. The irony, now, is an awareness of possible cosmic insignificance. It is exploring a wound which no amount of moral reformation would be able to heal.

In Book IV of *Gulliver* the irony completes its transformation, and is turned upon human nature itself. Swift's intensity and disgust are nowhere more striking than here.[1] This is the classic

[1] That striking *tour-de-force* 'A *Modest Proposal*' springs to mind as an exception. There, too, as Dr. Leavis has argued in his fine essay, the effect

interpretative crux: and Aldous Huxley's remark, that Swift "could never forgive man for being a vertebrate mammal as well as an immortal soul" still seems to me to be the most seminal critical insight that has been offered.

The crux centres, of course, upon what we make of Swift's relationship to Gulliver. How far is Gulliver a satiric device, and how far (if at all), does he come to be a spokesman for Swift himself? The answer seems to me to be by no means clear. If we accept Gulliver as Swift's spokesman, we end in a state of despair. On this showing, it would seem that Swift has openly abandoned his positives, and that when he avows that he has "now done with all such visionary schemes" as trying to reform the Yahoos "for ever," he has passed from ironic exaggeration to sober truth. Few readers will be willing to take this view, especially when they reflect upon the dangers in store for those who identify themselves with Gulliver too readily. And yet, if we reject this, what is the alternative view to be? Swift leads us very skillfully to follow Gulliver step by step. If at some point we depart from his view of himself we have to depart also from the Houyhnhnms: who seem, however, to be an incarnation of Swift's actual positives, and the very standard against which the Yahoos are tried and found wanting. What happens in Book IV is that Gulliver is converted gradually to an admiration of the Houyhnhnms, and then to an acceptance of their judgements upon himself and his kind. The result of this enlightenment is that he comes to realize also the unattainability of such an ideal for himself. He sinks into bitterness and misanthropy, and ends, as a result of his contact with the ideal, far more unpleasant and unconstructive than he was before.

---

is almost wholly negative and destructive. The force of the irony is so savage that it robs its supposed positives of any power of asserting themselves. The ghastly imagery of the market and the slaughter-house ceases to sound like satiric exaggeration, and appals us with the sense of actuality. Man, we feel, really *is* as brutal and sordid as this. Theories that he might be otherwise are merely an added torment, so energetically is his inhumanity realized, so impotent is the theoretic norm in the face of this reality.

A necessary conflict seems, too, to be exposed between our ideals of humanity and rational behaviour, and the actual motives of competition and self-interest which move society. Society can no more really be expected to change for the better than Yahoos can be expected to turn into Houyhnhnms. The law of love is absolutely incompatible with things as they are.

At some stage, it seems, he has taken the wrong turning: but where has the mistake occurred?

The construction of the Book is of great interest. Gulliver first of all comes across the Yahoos, and is instantly repelled by them. "Upon the whole, I never beheld in all my travels so disagreeable an animal, or one against which I naturally conceived so strong an antipathy." Soon after this, he encounters the noble horses, and is equally strongly impressed, this time in their favour. Almost at once, he starts to discover between himself and the Yahoos an appalling resemblance: "my horror and astonishment are not to be described, when I observed, in this abominable animal, a perfect human figure." At this stage, it is the physical resemblance which disturbs him. But later, as he falls under the influence of the Houyhnhnms, he comes also to accept a moral resemblance. And this is at the core of the satire.

The cleverness of Swift's technique is that at first the horses are only sketched in. They are clean, kindly, rational, but apart from seeing them through Gulliver's eyes we learn little in detail about them. Gulliver is first "amazed to see . . . in brute beasts . . . behaviour . . . so orderly and rational, so acute and judicious." But almost at once he finds that they regard *him* as the "brute beast," and with somewhat more justice "For they looked upon it as a prodigy, that a brute animal should discover such marks of a rational creature." From this moment, the Houyhnhnms start to insinuate into Gulliver's mind a vision of himself that becomes increasingly more repellent. They begin by rejecting his claim to be truly rational, speaking of "those appearances of reason" in him, and deciding that he has been taught to "imitate" a "rational creature." When they compare him with the Yahoos, Gulliver at first objects, acknowledging, "some resemblance," but insisting that he cannot account for "their degenerate and brutal nature." The Houyhnhnms will have none of this, however, deciding that if Gulliver does differ, he differs for the worse. "He said, I differed indeed from other Yahoos, being much more cleanly, and not altogether so deformed; but in point of real advantage, he thought I differed for the worse." The reason for this judgement—a reason which Gulliver himself comes to accept—is that his "appearance of reason" is a fraud; and that what seems reason in him is no more than a faculty which makes him *lower* than the Yahoos.

> . . . when a creature pretending to reason, could be capable of such enormities, he dreaded, lest the corruption of that faculty, might be worse than brutality itself. He seemed therefore confident, that instead of reason, we were only possessed of some quality fitted to increase our natural vices.

Up to this point, the reader might feel fairly confident that he sees what is happening. The Houyhnhnms really are ideal, and Gulliver's conversion to their point of view is the lesson we should be learning. The contemptuous view of mankind formed by the Houyhnhnms is the main satiric charge. The view that man *is* a Yahoo and cannot become a Houyhnhnm is satiric exaggeration: near enough to the truth to shake us, but not intended to be taken literally. We shall be "betrayed" if we identify ourselves with Gulliver at the points where the horses scorn him, but safe enough if we accept his conversion at their hands.

This, I fancy, is what many readers are led to feel: and to my mind, in so leading them, Swift sets his most subtle trap of all. The real shock comes in the middle of Chapter VIII, when Gulliver turns, at long last, to give us a more detailed description of the horses. We have already been aware, perhaps, of certain limitations in them: they have a limited vocabulary, limited interests, and an attitude of life that seems wholly functional. But Gulliver has explained all these limitations as virtues, and persuaded us to see them as a sign of grace. No doubt, we feel, these horses *are* noble savages of some kind, and their simplicity a condition and a reward of natural harmony. It remains for the fuller account to show us two further truths about the horses: the first, that they are not human at all, so that their way of life is wholly irrelevant as a human ideal; and the second, that their supposedly rational way of life is so dull and impoverished that we should not wish to emulate them even if we could.

Their society, for instance, is stoic in appearance. They accept such inevitable calamities as death calmly; they eat, sleep and exercise wisely: they believe in universal benevolence as an ideal, and accordingly have no personal ties or attachments. The family is effectually abolished: marriage is arranged by friends as "one of the necessary actions in a reasonable being"; husband and wife like one another, and their children, just as much and as little as they like everyone else. Sex is accepted as normal, but only for the purpose of procreation. Like all other instincts, it is regarded as entirely functional, and has no relevance beyond the begetting of a standard number of offspring. They have no curiosity: their language, their arts and their sciences are purely functional, and restricted to the bare necessities of harmonious social existence. Life is lived "without jealousy, fondness, quarrelling or discontent"; and it is lived in tribal isolation, since they are "cut off from all commerce with other nations."

This impoverished and devitalized society is the one which Gulliver uncritically accepts as an ideal, and on the strength of which he sinks into a most negative and unedifying misanthropy. And yet, so plausibly does Swift offer this as the ideal of Reason and Nature which his own age believed in, so cunningly does he lead us to think that this is the positive against which a satiric account of the Yahoos is functioning, that the trick is hard to detect. Even the fact that Gulliver is in an escapist frame of mind is not immediately apparent, unless we are on the alert.[2] We see at once, it is true, that the Houyhnhnms are not *like* men: that physically Gulliver might be a monkey but is nothing like a horse, and that this physical placing is linked with a moral one. Yet we assume that this placing is only one more satiric technique: and it is with a distinct shock that we realize that it exists at a more fundamenal level than any *moral* amendment on the part of a man could resolve. The Houyhnhnms are literally not human: they are inaccessible to Gulliver not because they are morally superior, but because they are physically non-existent. They are mental abstractions disguised as animals: but they are no more animals, really, than the medieval angels were, and nothing like any human possibility, bad or good.

The horses have, in fact, no passions at all. Their "virtue" is not a triumph over impulse and temptation, but a total immunity from these things—and an immunity which is also, by its very nature, an absence of life and vitality. They have no compulsive sexual impulses, no sensuous pleasures, no capacity for any degree of human love. They have no wishes and fears, and scarcely any ideas. If they are incapable of human bestiality they are even less capable of human glory or sublimity; and it is only because Swift

[2] e.g. ". . . For, in such a solitude as I desired, I could at least enjoy my own thoughts, and reflect with delight on the virtues of those inimitable Houyhnhnms, without any opportunity of degenerating into the vices and corruptions of my own species." (Book IV, Chapter XI.)

prevents us from thinking of humanity as anything other than a real or potential Yahoo that this is not at once immediately apparent.

What is the true force of Book IV, then? Swift seems to my mind, to have posed, in new form, and with appalling consequences, the old riddle of man's place as the microcosm. Instead of relating him to the angels and the beasts, he relates him to the Houyhnhnms and the Yahoos. The Houyhnhnm is as non-bodily and abstract, in its essential nature, as an angel, the Yahoo a beast seen in its most disgusting lights. As for man, represented by Gulliver, he is left in a disastrous microcosmic vacuum. Instead of having his own distinctive place, he has to *be* one or the other of the extremes. Swift drives a wedge between the intellectual and the emotional, makes one good, the other evil, and pushes them further apart, as moral opposites, than any except the most extreme Puritans have usually done. The result is the kind of tormenting and bitter dilemma which always lies in wait for those who do this and, to quote Huxley again (a writer temperamentally very similar to Swift himself), who cannot "forgive man for being a vertebrate mammal as well as an immortal soul." The ideal is unattainable, the vicious alternative inescapable, and both are so unattractive that one is at a loss to decide which one dislikes the more.

Once again, then, the irony intended for moral satire has undergone a metamorphosis: and starting as an attempt to improve man, ends by writing him off as incurable.

But how far did Swift intend this to be so? This is the question which now becomes relevant, and the answer cannot, I think, be a straightforward one. My own feeling is that we are faced with a split between conscious intention and emotional conviction, of a kind which modern criticism has familiarized us with in Milton. Perhaps Swift really did intend a simple moral purpose, and was not consciously betraying his reader into despair. And yet, the unpleasantness of the Yahoos is realized so powerfully, and any supposed alternative is so palpably non-existent, that he must have been to some degree aware of his dilemma. He must have known that men do, for better or worse, have bodily desires, and that the Houyhnhnms were therefore an impossible ideal. He must have known, too, being a man, that Houyhnhnms were both very limited and very unattractive. And in identifying Reason and Nature with them, he must have been aware that he was betraying his own positives and those of his age: leaving the Yahoos in triumphant possession of all the reality and the life, and removing the possibility of any human escape by way of Reason or Nature from their predicament.

As a satire, *Gulliver* can work normally only if we can accept the Houyhnhnms as a desirable human possibility: and this, I do not for a moment believe Swift thought we could. The very energy of the style is masochistic—a tormenting awareness of its own impotence to do, or change, anything. Swift is publicly torturing both himself and the species to which he belongs.[3] The irony, then, intended for moral reformation, has undergone a more or less conscious metamorphosis; and the total effect of Book IV, as Dr. Leavis has insisted, is largely negative.

There are, nevertheless, before this is finally asserted, one or two compensating factors to notice. The first, often surprisingly overlooked, is that Swift cannot really have supposed his readers to be Yahoos, if only because Yahoos could not have responded at all to *Gulliver's Travels*. The deliberate obtuseness with which Gulliver prattles of his "beloved England" will register only with a reader much less obtuse. The reader must not only be betrayed but see that he has been betrayed: and in order for this to happen he must have more intelligence and more moral sense than a Yahoo. Swift knew, in any case, that his readers *were* Augustan gentlemen with ideals of human decency that he had in common with them, and that however much a case against them could be both thought and felt, the ultimate *fact* of Augustan civilization—a fact embodied in his own style as much as anywhere—was not to be denied. *Gulliver's Travels* might leave us, then, with a wholly negative attitude, but the very fact of its being written at all is positive proof that Swift's own total attitude was not negative.

This may seem commonplace: but it leads on to another con-

[3] We might feel, today, that in exploring the dangers of dissociating reason from emotion, and calling the one good, the other bad, Swift really did hit on the central weakness of his age: that Book IV is still valid, in fact, as a satire upon Augustanism itself. The Augustans, at their most characteristic, disapproved of strong emotions as necessarily disruptive, subordinated even those emotions they could not exile to the stern control of "Right Reason," and found no place for "feeling" in their search for "truth." This attitude, we might decide, is doomed to failure by the actual nature of man—and Swift, by driving reason and emotion to opposite poles (with the result that man can live happily by neither) reveals just *how* impossible it is.

sideration, equally important, which most commentators upon *Gulliver* seem oddly afraid of: namely that Swift, writing for gentlemen, intended to give pleasure by what he wrote. When Gulliver says of the Yahoos (his readers), "I wrote for their amendment, and not their approbation," there is a general readiness to accept this at its face value, and to credit Swift with a similar sternness. Sooner or later most writers about *Gulliver* hit upon the word "exuberance," and then pause doubtfully, wondering whether, if Swift is so moral and so misanthropic as we think, such a word can have any place in describing him. Yet "exuberant" he certainly is, even in Book IV of *Gulliver*. The "vive la bagatelle," the flamboyant virtuosity of *A Tale of a Tub* is less central, but it is still to be detected, in the zest with which Gulliver describes bad lawyers, for example, and in the fantastic turns and contortions of the irony. Clearly, Swift enjoyed his control of irony: enjoyed its flexibility, its complex destructiveness, his own easy mastery of it. Clearly, too, he expects his readers to enjoy it. The irony is not *only* a battle, but a game: a civilized game, at that, since irony is by its very nature civilized, presupposing both intelligence, and at least some type of moral awareness. The "war" is a battle of wits: and if one confesses (as the present writer does) to finding *Gulliver* immensely enjoyable, need one think that Swift would really, irony apart, have been surprised or annoyed by such a reaction?

On a final balance, I fancy that we have to compromise: agreeing that *Gulliver* ends by destroying all its supposed positives, but deducing, from the exuberance of the style and the fact that it was written at all, that Swift did not really end in Gulliver's position. He was, at heart, humane, and his savage indignation against cruelty and hypocrisy in the straightforwardly satiric parts reflects a real moral concern. He was, also, iconoclastic, and disillusioned about the ultimate dignity of man at a deep level: and when his irony undergoes the type of metamorphosis that has been discussed here, it is as disturbing and uprooted as any we can find. But he always, at the same time, enjoyed the technique of irony itself, both as an intellectual game, and as a guarantee of at least some civilized reality. Very often, even at the most intense moments, we may feel that pleasure in the intellectual destructiveness of the wit is of more importance to him than the moral purpose, or the misanthropy, that is its supposed *raison d'être*. Irony, by its very nature, instructs by *pleasing:* and to ignore the pleasure, and its civilized implications, is inevitably to oversimplify, and falsify the total effect.

NIGEL DENNIS

Swift and Defoe

Gulliver's Travels . . . begins with the will-power only partly roused and being employed with extreme grace, wit and subtlety; it ends with the will at its most vehement and monstrous, reflecting in this development the author's own march from his old self to his new one. It does not give the impression of having been planned as it stands from the start; on the contrary, it suggests that each part inspired its successor, and that the appetite grew with the feeding—a hunger for greater intensity and more powerful amplification being felt more and more strongly as the work proceeded. A great deal has been written about its originating in the ideas and table-talk of Swift and his London friends, but without questioning the correctness of this ascription, must we not also allow *Robinson Crusoe*, which appeared in 1719, some of the honor of having set it going? We cannot do so with any firmness, unfortunately, but we can certainly use the one book as a point of departure for the other; for the two, seen side by side, form a wonderful pair, representing two sorts of writing, two entirely disparate views of fiction and two superbly opposed authors. To describe *Gulliver's Travels* as Swift's deliberate retort to *Robinson Crusoe* would be unwarranted, but if we amuse ourselves by considering it as such, the result is as informative as it is entertaining. Moreover, we never see Swift more clearly than in relation to Defoe: each demands the presence of the other, in the sense that each side demands the presence of the other if we are to understand a battle, a Parliamentary conflict, a divided nation.

Defoe embodies everything that Swift hates: he is the other half of England that Swift struggled all his life to suppress or ignore and by which he was defeated and driven into isolation. Defoe, with his brickworks and bankruptcies, is the rising small business-

From *Jonathan Swift: A Short Character*, pp. 122–133. New York: The Macmillan Company and London: George Weidenfeld & Nicolson Ltd., 1964.

man whom Swift saw very correctly as the man who would unseat his timocracy of landed gentlemen and substitute an economy of stocks and shares for one of estate and title. He is the Roundhead Dissenter to whom the Whigs run as an ally in their fight with the Tories of the Established Church—and, by turning to him, change what was formerly a private quarrel between Anglican landlords into a lasting division between regicide Puritan merchants and honorable county squires. Swift is the gentleman-author whose chosen home is society and the dignified sphere of the well-educated and well-born; Defoe is the born gander of Grub Street, the father of all that is noisiest and freest in modern journalism. Defoe is liberty in the form in which Swift detested it most: he is the rogue whom Swift loved best to "swinge," and his life is a constant, rapscallionly muddle, bursting with excitements and devoid of all dignity. Where Swift goes in danger of the Tower, Defoe's natural punishment is the pillory: the higher place is reserved for the treasonable gentleman, the lower for the provocative hack. The two men have only three things in common: the first is that they both took service under Harley, Swift as unpaid propagandist and Defoe as paid informer; the second is that they were both passionately in favor of the educating of women; and the third is that both were capable of satire. We expect satire from a Tory like Swift, but we are surprised and interested to find it in an enthusiastic Whig. Yet Defoe's *The Shortest Way with the Dissenters*, the satirical essay for which he was put in the pillory, anticipates exactly in tone and tendency Swift's *Modest Proposal* for dealing with surplus Irishmen: the only real difference between the two essays is that Defoe's makes its plea for the mutilating of Dissenters in rather a blunt way, whereas Swift's plea for eating babies is made with the refinement and gentility that we expect from a clergyman of the better class.

Of the two Defoe is by far the more sympathetic and agreeable man and fits most happily today into the excessively unaustere society that composes our democracy. He is the beginning of the social struggle of which we are the end, and he presses forward into modern times proportionately as Swift fights backwards into the time behind him. When we hold each man's masterpiece in our hands we hold the halves of one apple—the apple of discord that, in its wholeness, represents the England of the early eighteenth century.

Robinson Crusoe has been called aptly "the primary textbook of capitalism"—and who can resist the amusement of reading it as such? What author ever built such a warehouse or drew up a more satisfying inventory? Every page is a merchant's catalogue of hardware, woollens, leather goods and crockery, and from the fields outside the warehouse come the baaing of the good tradesman's flocks and the ripple of the breeze through his stalks of corn. All these goods, together with a snug house fenced and barricaded interminably against burglars, are available to the forceful capitalist, who, by diligent sowing of a little seed, builds his frugal investments into interest-bearing property. And how excitedly we labor with Crusoe, first for mere self-survival, later for a higher rate of interest and greater abundance of possessions! How we share his horrified terror when that most magical of all moments in fiction, the footprint in the sand, tells us brutally that some barbarous intruder threatens not only life but property! And how thankful we are to know that our heroic investor does not stand alone—that his marvels of free enterprise are noted and sanctioned by God Himself! For, certainly, there never was a book in which God's hand was busier—helping in the factory, making sound economical suggestions, keeping an eye on things generally and asking nothing in return but prayers—heart-felt prayers, of course; but who would *not* pray heartily to such a generous Father? No Puritan but Bunyan ever wrote a happier book; no merchant ever looked upon his gains and declared with greater self-satisfaction that the earth was the Lord's and the glory thereof.

At the time *Robinson Crusoe* appeared Swift was reading all the travel books he could find: they were all trash but a perfect antidote to the spleen, he assured Miss Vanhomrigh. Merely to imagine him reading *Robinson Crusoe* is enough to make one laugh, for it is pleasing to picture his contemptuous response to Defoe's unceasing power to declare, in all imaginable matters, his faith in all that Swift despised. Each author, to begin with, sets out upon his "Travels" with the intention of discovering only that which he already knows and erecting in a strange land that which he knows to have been built at home. Defoe turns a primitive island into a commercial enterprise: the only enemy to this sort of civilization is the naked savage—the terrifying cannibal whose primitive appetites threaten disaster to the God-fearing businessman. But Swift's islands are never menaced by barbarism: on the contrary, the only atrocities he finds are those of civilized, cultured persons who have degenerated grossly from the happier, natural state of man and have espoused reason only in order that "the corruption of that faculty might be worse than brutality itself." Where Defoe looks with horror at the naked footprint Swift looks with equal horror at the imprint of the court-shoe, and Gulliver, even after being wounded by savages, would still prefer "to trust myself among those barbarians, than live with European Yahoos." The Dissenting merchant and reformer never doubts that trade and colonization confer civilized benefits upon savage people: it is the Tory churchman who argues, with the modern radical, that colonists are no better than an "execrable crew of butchers" enjoying "a free license . . . to all acts of inhumanity and lust."

Man himself, as he walks the world, drives the two authors to opposite poles. Defoe will have no truck with the naked body; his excitements come from the fabricating of its garments out of the available raw materials and from its foodstuffs and implements. But the High Church Dean despises "the subject of . . . diet, wherewith other travellers fill their books," and where Defoe asks that we admire the fur hat and skin-breeches, Swift keeps pulling off these contemptible disguises and pressing our eyes and noses to the hairy warts and stenches of the flesh below. The Puritan is far too respectable even to mention the functions of the body, but the Dean's book abounds in hogsheads of urine and the voiding of excrement. This is why *Robinson Crusoe* is an essentially materialistic book and yet a wholly unphysical one, whereas *Gulliver's Travels* is only occasionally materialistic and always passionately physical.

The numerous other "opposites" in the two books are all very engaging and highly characteristic of their respective authors. Crusoe is a simple man of Defoe's own class; Gulliver, like Sir William Temple, is a graduate of Emmanuel College, Cambridge. Unlike Defoe's God, the Dean's is much too detached and Olympian to be involved in Gulliver's absurd affairs—and Gulliver himself is much too much an average gentleman to waste a moment in prayer. The Dissenter, once he has built himself a small realm abroad, delights in allowing "liberty of conscience throughout my dominions"; the Dean, however, does not lose the opportunity of requiring the monarch of Brobdingnag to assert that "a man may be allowed to keep poisons in his closet, but not to vend them about for cordials."

But the most entertaining contrast between the books, from a literary point of view, is in each author's declared intention. *Robinson Crusoe* is the work of a journalist; it is essentially what we would call a "documentary," or a blunt unpolished recital of the plain facts—yet it is of this documentary that Defoe says: "My story is a whole collection of wonders." *Gulliver's Travels,* on the other hand, *is* a whole collection of wonders—as much an imaginary creation as *Crusoe* is not and, for the most part, most admirably "turned" and polished. Yet Swift declares of it: "I could perhaps, like others, have astonished thee with strange, improbable tales, but I rather chose to relate plain matter of fact, in the simplest manner and style. . . ." Thus does each author indulge the perfectly excusable pretence that suits his book, the journalist seeking to elevate his facts into fancy, the wit to resolve pure fantasy into facts.

Robinson Crusoe, one may say, never gets off the ground at all: it is rarely touched by the imagination and asks nothing of the intellect. But *Gulliver's Travels* is a work of pure intellect, an act of unceasing invention. Defoe, patiently assembling material facts, needs forty pages of preliminaries to wreck his hero on a desert island; Swift, anxious to leave the factual world behind, carries Gulliver to Lilliput in little more than a page. Defoe, having retailed one fact, merely goes on to retail the next fact; but the chief purpose served by a fact in Swift is to be a spring-board into fantasy. And nothing about *Gulliver's Travels* is more interesting than to study the way in which this fantasy is anchored—to see why, even at its most fantastic moments, it does not lose its ties with the earth. To see how Swift does this, is to see what satire must always do if its angry fantasies are to be brought safely home.

Napoleon, discussing at St. Helena the innovations of the French Revolution, declared himself entirely in favor of the change made by the revolutionary intellectuals to the Metric System of weights and measures. But he pointed out that the mathematicians who arranged this change made a typical academic mistake: by throwing away the old *terms,* they turned weights and measurements into inhuman abstractions. The man who works with a terminology of *hands, feet,* and *ells* in effect bases all his calculations on the parts of his body: even when he speaks in terms of *poles* and *chains,* he is still speaking of what he regards as extensions of his own arms. But once he must calculate in *ares* and *meters,* he must lose his sense of physical conjunction with the world, and the loss of this sensuous tie, Napoleon believed, was precisely the sort of loss that always should be avoided in the modernizing of ancient systems.

In this spasm of light from a dying star we see clearly one of the great strengths of *Gulliver's Travels*—the anchoring of the high-flying mind to the physical body. This is not the book of an abstract "projector" calculating in a world apart; it is a book in which man *is* the measure of all things. We find this first, of course, in the simple matter of relative sizes in Lilliput and Brobdingnag, but it is the actual estimating of these proportions—the terms in which they are assessed—that is so unabstract and gives the book its fleshy solidity. Like Defoe, Swift will often tell us how small or large a thing was by giving its linear measurement; but, unlike Defoe, he prefers to lay a human limb alongside it, to make his comparison, and to press our eyes, noses and ears into the service of his imaginings. In the huge magnifications of Brobdingnag, the purring of a cat is not described in mere adjectival sonorities; instead, it is "like that of a dozen stocking-weavers at work." A gigantic infant's cry is "a squall that you might have heard from London Bridge to Chelsea"; and twenty wasps, "as large as partridges," sweep in at the window "humming louder than the drone of as many bagpipes." The Brobdingnagian queen can "craunch the wing of a lark, bones and all, between her teeth, although it were nine times as large as that of a full-grown turkey," and her table knives are "twice as long as a scythe." Each fly is of the greatness of "a Dunstable lark" and, as it walks, demonstrates its essential monstrousness to the eye of the tiny observer by leaving behind it a loathsome trail of excrement, spawn and "viscous matter." One paring from the Queen's thumbnail serves for the back of a horn comb, bladed with "stumps of the King's beard"; the corn on the toe of a royal maid-of-honor is of "about the bigness of a Kentish pippin"; sliced from its owner and carried home to England, it can be "hollowed into a cup, and set in silver." Waves of overpowering stench and scent are emitted by the naked bodies of those royal maids, and each charming mole that spots the skin stands "broad as a trencher, and hairs hanging from it thicker than packthreads." The thump on the scaffold floor of a murderer's decapitated head is such as to shake the ground for "at least half an English mile," while—most astonishing simile of all—the "veins and arteries [of the trunk] spouted up such a prodigious quantity of blood, and so high in the air, that the great *jet d'eau* at Versailles was not equal for the time it lasted." Reversed in their proportions to fit the world of Lilliput, the similes are more charming than gross, but they always retain their intense, familiar quality—tiny men ploughing through Gulliver's snuff-box "up to the mid-leg in a sort of dust" and sneezing dreadfully as they go; examining letters and diaries in which every character is "almost half as large as the palm of our hands"; discovering a pocket-watch, "which the emperor was very curious to see, and commanded two of his tallest yeomen of the guards to bear it on a pole upon their shoulders, as draymen in England do a barrel of ale." "I have been much pleased," says Gulliver, "with a cook pulling a lark, which was not so large as a common fly; and a young girl threading an invisible needle with invisible silk."

This intense proximity, this use of commonplaces to ground the imagination, has a curious effect. It is not noticed by the reader when he finds it pleasing: he merely smiles at the image without inquiring into the techniques that have made him smile. But when the simile is gross—when excrement and hairy moles replace invisible needles and snuff—he not only sees the technique but begins to wonder what sort of man the author was. Yet it should be plain that the same method is being used throughout and that there is a grand unity of treatment that covers in one way the nicest and nastiest things. For every grossness in Swift there is a corresponding delicacy—a point nicely made by Pope in his well-known lines on Swift. But whichever course, fine or gross, he chooses to take, an intensely personal intimacy lies at the core of it. The grand flights of his imagination are made plausible only by the point from which they take their departure, and this point is always the living human being and his familiar belongings, sensations and habits. Nor is there any limit to the use of this admirable art; it can be applied not only to the coarsest and most delicate things but also to the occasions when genius displays itself by listing details in the simplest way and then turning them, without the least change of expression, to irresistibly human account:

> . . . Their manner of writing is very peculiar, being neither from the left to the right, like the Europeans; nor from the right to the left, like the Arabians; nor from up to down, like the Chinese; but aslant, from one corner of the paper to the other, like ladies in England.

The life we share with Robinson Crusoe has no place for such extraordinary felicities. It is, in the friendliest sense of the words, merely a life of gain, technical security, adventure and everyday ingenuity; it provides neither insight into human behavior nor interest in human thought. *Gulliver's Travels* begins where *Robinson*

Crusoe ends; it inquires and reflects where the other rests content to act and possess. We see Crusoe naked only when he is afraid, but we see Gulliver in all his human weaknesses—in his fear, his vanity, his pride, his shame, his shivering little skin. Neither Gulliver nor Crusoe is of much interest as a principal character, but each is uninteresting for a different reason—Crusoe because his material possessions loom larger than he does, Gulliver because his story would have no solid center if he himself were made as dramatically extraordinary as the situations and persons he meets: in this respect we may compare him to the plain Martin in *A Tale of a Tub.* We ask that Gulliver be a bigger man only for one reason—we cannot forgive him for surrendering to the Houyhnhnms and recognizing in himself and us the beastly image of a Yahoo. And we do not forgive him for this because we shall never forgive Swift for it.

A good way to examine this matter is to compare good-humoredly the conclusions of *Robinson Crusoe* and *Gulliver's Travels.* In both books, the hero is carried safe back to Europe by a kindly ship's captain, a Portuguese in Gulliver's case, an Englishman in Crusoe's. We know the revulsion that the return to the world excites in Gulliver—how he shrinks from the touch of his own wife and children, how repugnant he finds the stench and character of the Yahoo. But we should remember, too, how different the world seems to Defoe's returning castaway. Crusoe finds that the world is good—indeed, that it is overflowing with probity and justice. The twenty-eight years of his absence have been devoted by his honest partners to the preservation and increase of his investments, and the totting up of the grand total, with the occasional pause for an *Ave Maria,* forms a most suitable conclusion to this best of mercantile books. Twelve hundred chests of sugar, 800 rolls of tobacco, thousands of golden Portuguese moidores, large Brazilian plantations worked assiduously by black slaves: it all amounts to "above £5,000 sterling" and a South American estate of "above £1,000 a year." And when we hear the chink of those moidores, do we not exclaim with Crusoe: "It is impossible to express the flutterings of my very heart when I looked over these letters and especially when I found all my wealth about me"? Do we not agree most heartily with him that "the latter end of Job was better than the beginning"? And are we at all surprised to find Job in that *galère*?

This is the happy end we all want—honest men, a banker-God,

and accumulated interest. Defoe never denied it even to the worst of us: once Moll Flanders stopped being a whore and a thief and invested in probity and God, her income rose in due proportion with her piety, cementing the delights of capital to the forgiveness of sins. And because we feel that things *should* turn out like this in a novel—that money is what Job is being so patient about; that money is what Swift loses when Miss Vanhomrigh dies—we are profoundly offended when Gulliver shrinks from touching us, and his author, peeling us down to mere skin and claws, wipes us from his sight as stinking Yahoos. His terrible insult has survived two centuries unimpaired: it hurts us today even more than it hurt its first readers. Many, indeed, protest that no author who really believed in God could find it in his heart to condemn us so unkindly; others, more expert in the study of Swift, have turned the insult by tracing it to a psychological deformation in the author. All of which has one very amusing result—that we regard *Robinson Crusoe,* which is a documentary, as an acceptable piece of fiction, but dismiss *Gulliver's Travels,* which is a pure fiction, as a libellous piece of documentary. Yet this absurd conclusion suits both authors admirably, for Defoe, as has been noted, pretended to be a teller of wonders, while Swift pretended to be a reporter of facts. The journalist set out to please his public; the Dean intended to roast it. Both authors succeeded admirably in their intentions, and both are read still in the spirit in which they wrote. Both would be overjoyed to know it.

II

JOHN LAWLOR

The Evolution of Gulliver's Character

The master-stroke in the design of *Gulliver's Travels* is the characterization of Gulliver himself. If the satirist's problem, in Swift's conception, is to break down the defensive reaction of the reader, it is of the highest importance that Gulliver himself, the observer and reporter, shall win respect for his candour and objectivity. Once we have learnt to trust Gulliver the rest of the way to self-revelation will be made insensibly, even fatally, easy. It is therefore vital that Gulliver's qualifications for his task shall be carefully conveyed. Gulliver's education is happily rounded; he is versed in both arts and sciences, and yet without any suggestion of the paragon. He must be *l'homme moyen*—disinterestedness will win confidence. Secondly, the pattern of his voyaging must be so arranged as to bring about, albeit insensibly, development in his character. These fundamental considerations are well understood by Mr. A. E. Case in his notable treatment of "The Significance of *Gulliver's Travels*." [1] Swift's "intention to deepen the character of his principal figure" is "an integral part of his main design": and Mr. Case traces very well the development from "an amused and superior toleration" to the turning point, in the sixth chapter of the Voyage to Brobdingnag, where Gulliver is "really on the defensive for the first time." [2] Swift's artistry at this point is of

From *Essays and Studies*, 1955 (1956), pp. 69-73. London. Reprinted by permission of the author and the publisher, *The English Association*.

[1] The concluding essay in *Four Essays on "Gulliver's Travels"* (Princeton, 1945).

[2] *Ibid.*, pp. 105, 115 and 116.

the highest order, and it is perhaps doubtful whether Mr. Case does full justice to it. Gulliver begins the seventh chapter with a confession that he has not told the whole truth to the King of Brobdingnag—for the first time he takes the reader into his confidence: his report of European institutions has been edited, out of "that laudable Partiality to my own Country" which he knows the honest reader will share. Mr. Case appears to miss the force of this development in Gulliver, though he notes both the statement of "partiality" and the significant fact that Gulliver later exhibits "only a modified rapture upon his return to England." What has happened is that Swift, through the King of Brobdingnag, has fired his first broadside, the denunciation of the "most pernicious race of little odious vermin that nature ever suffered to crawl upon the surface of the earth." This Gulliver cannot accept: he is bound as the truthful narrator to record it, but the reader need not fear that so fantastic a charge is to be taken seriously. Not only does Gulliver share with the reader his "partiality" for our "noble and most beloved country," as Mr. Case notes, but he goes on to explain that the King's notions are part of "the miserable effects of a confined education." Gulliver the practical man is well to the fore here: the King's ideas are conceived in isolation from the real world—"the manners and customs that most prevail in other nations." The account of Brobdingnagian institutions that follows runs in the same vein: it is all too easy—for example, since in their army everyone serves under his own landlord or elected leader, the fact that they are "perfect enough in their exercises, and under very good discipline" is one "wherein I saw no great merit; for how should it be otherwise . . . ?" Mr. Case is right to speak of Gulliver "on the defensive"; contempt is a well-recognized form of defensive reaction. What has helped to bring about the change is the fact of size. Tolerance in Lilliput, where man is the giant, must give way to increased wariness where a man may be trodden underfoot. Johnson's comment on bigness and littleness is wide of the mark unless we underline "*Once you have thought*" of it.* The decisive transition that Swift accomplishes at this point—the change from Gulliver the neutral observer to Gulliver the apologist for his own country—is prepared for in the commanding simplicity of the King, dwarfing his human interlocutor. So Gulliver is not

* "When once you have thought of big men and little men, it is very easy to do all the rest." [Ed. note.]

harmed by the broadside. What was to devastate passes harmlessly over his head: in the "glass" the King holds up Gulliver disclaims any recognition of himself. The satiric train has been laid and fired—but to no effect: "narrow principles and short views" are all this outburst can illustrate. The King, from this point of view, is that fantastic idealist the satirist, who seeks to castigate our faults by clear appeals to reason: and Gulliver is his unscathed reader, refusing the appeal and explaining its laughable inappositeness.

So we can move on with Gulliver, who remains in this special sense *our* witness. In the celebrated third book, as Mr. Case observes, "he has now become the detached and half-cynical commentator on human life from without. In this voyage alone he is an observer and not an actor." This is the interval before he is drawn in again to active participation: and Mr. Case comments soundly on the opening paragraph of the last book where Gulliver speaks of his having remained at home "in a very happy condition." At the outset of his last voyage he is

> a man who has adjusted himself to a consciousness of the ordinary and even the extraordinary vices and follies of humanity. In this state he does not recognize that the Yahoos have any likeness to man. . . .[8]

It is of the highest importance to remember that Swift is faced with a distinct problem of contrivance. The worst that can be said about humanity has left Gulliver unconvinced. How then to bring home to Gulliver his true predicament? Mere pronouncement will have no decisive effect: that has been tried in Brobdingnag, where the King's implied appeal to Reason had left Gulliver unmoved but wary of fantastic idealism. This time, the assault is to come from within. The *tour-de-force* that Swift contrives is that Gulliver is drawn to love the Houyhnhnm race. Out of his own mouth is man condemned. No longer is it for the satirist to state the law and pronounce sentence for shortcomings. The method is precisely inverted—let man declare his "positives," and then he has involved his own law and judged himself. So it is fitting that the Gulliver who is at last brought to self-recognition is not the untried, superior traveller of the beginning of the work, but the experienced observer.

[8] Case, pp. 117-118.

The point is deepened when we recall his first encounter with the Yahoos and with the Houyhnhnm. Each seems to this experienced traveller a kind of beast: and his aversion from the insufferable Yahoos is only paralleled by the condenscension of his attempt to fondle the noble Houyhnhnm "using the common style and whistle of jockeys." The development of this book is Gulliver's deepening awareness that the Yahoo-kind is his own species: and the pathos that accompanies this progressive realization proceeds all the way from that first act of unwitting effrontery, through the painful clinging to all that prevents complete identification with the Yahoos, his one suit of clothes, to the final realization that even as a servant and disciple there can be no place for him in the land of the Houyhnhnms. It is not always understood why Gulliver must go: his is a supreme loneliness, for, falling infinitely short of the perfection of his masters, he is yet differentiated from the "wild Yahoo" in possessing "some rudiments of reason." This is potentially dangerous, for when "added to the natural pravity of those animals," the consequences are impossible to contemplate. Gulliver's plight is indeed desperate. Swift's satiric genius has penetrated to the final truth that when man falls, he falls below the level of the brute creation. A wild Yahoo is one thing: a Yahoo with "some rudiments of reason" presents incalculable possibilities of harm. This time the mirror has been so contrived that we cannot choose but see ourselves, and turn revolted from what we are.

> When I happened to behold the reflection of my own form in a lake or fountain, I turned away my face in horror and detestation of myself, and I could better endure the sight of a common Yahoo than of my own person.

Mr. Case's treatment fails at this most crucial moment of Gulliver's rejection. "In the end," he writes, "the master dismisses Gulliver with regret and shows no disinclination to his society. In other words, a somewhat above-average Englishman was not altogether unacceptable company for a perfect being." [4] This is at the furthest remove from Gulliver's leave-taking; for

> as I was going to prostrate myself to kiss his hoof, he did me the honour to raise it gently to my mouth. I am not ignorant how

[4] Case, p. 110.

much I have been censured for mentioning this last particular. For my detractors are pleased to think it improbable that so illustrious a person should descend to give so great a mark of distinction to a creature so inferior as I.

We are a world away from that first attempted condescension of Gulliver "using the common style and whistle of jockeys" towards the Houyhnhnm. The reversal of roles perfectly exemplifies the truth towards which Swift has directed us through our guide. The conclusion of the whole endeavour is that pride is an absurdity. "I am not in the least provoked," says Gulliver in the close, "at the sight of a lawyer, a pick-pocket, a colonel, a fool . . . this is all according to the due course of things." There is the vocation of the satirist at an end: how to blame men for what is "all according to the due course of things"? But there is still one task left for intelligence and imagination: let man realize that things are thus with him, so that he will refrain from pride, the crowning absurdity in "a lump of deformity and diseases both in body and mind." We have left the world of corrective satire: nothing is to be done. The citadel of the reader's insentience has been taken not by outward assault, but from within. The defensive blindness has been penetrated. If the beginning of wisdom is to know ourselves, how very far we are from wisdom when normal satire cannot bring us even to identify ourselves! So the radical question is asked and decisively answered. Swift has reached the frontier of satire: man is not to be blamed for what is his natural state. Only let him see himself for what he is.

PAUL FUSSELL, JR.

The Frailty of Lemuel Gulliver

During his four voyages, Gulliver undergoes countless profound intellectual and psychological humiliations, from the cumulative impact of which his morose, self-righteous, self-pitying state of mind at the end of the fourth voyage is an almost predictable result. The man who, devoted now to merely intellectual "systems," finally comes to prefer the company of two young stallions and their groom to the presence of his own human family is a man whose initial conviction of rational self-sufficiency has been gravely injured, and a man who has been left without means for the restoration of his dignity but outrageous expressions of a mad (and, to a humanist, sublimely comical) self-regard.

Although *Gulliver's Travels* is a series of variations on the theme of intellectual and psychological pride, the expression of this theme (as we see when we focus on the physical Gulliver) is accomplished less by direct revelation of Gulliver's mental attitudes than by a characteristically Swiftian employment of particularized physical emblems and correlatives. Throughout his career Swift makes it clear that he is uninterested in merely describing and reacting to the states of mind which he is anatomizing: instead, he thrusts into the reader's face some concrete physical emblem of a corrupted mind or psyche. The squalor of Chloe's mind, for example, finds its emblem in filthy towels; the Æolists express their meager, gaseous intellectual matter by belching through their noses; the spider emits his self-manufactured nastiness from his own behind. And in *Gulliver's Travels*, Swift's method of inventing vivid physical correlatives for moral circumstances results in an important recurring motif of physical injury, damage, pain, and loss. This motif is expressive of extreme physical frailty and vulnerability, of the pathetic likelihood of damage to weak and unassisted things, whether

From Paul Fussell, Jr., "The Frailty of Lemuel Gulliver" in *Essays in Literary History*, edited by Rudolf Kirk and C. F. Main. New Brunswick, N.J.: Rutgers University Press, 1960. Reprinted by permission of the publisher.

minds, eyes, limbs, or even hats and breeches. The physical damage which Gulliver either undergoes or fears becomes, through concrete, muscular rendering, a uniquely naturalistic emblem of the damage wrought by experience on Gulliver's presumably self-sufficient mind. It is this motif of physical injury, damage, and loss that I now wish to explore in an attempt to point to an important theme in *Gulliver's Travels*, and, at the same time, in an attempt to define Swift's most characteristic method of imagination.

From the beginning to the end of his travels (with time out now and then, of course, for standard touristic inquiries), Gulliver generally suffers rather than acts. Crusoe, once cast away, acts, and he acts with great vigor and stubbornness, but Gulliver is the archetypal victim. He anticipates the modern victim-protagonist in the work of Kafka or in the early works of Hemingway, the man whom things are done to. Most obviously, Gulliver is cast away four times, and each time in a more outrageous manner than the last. Even though, as a surgeon, he is more likely than most to dwell obsessively on his own physical injuries, and even though his commitment to the scientific ideals of the Royal Society impels him to deliver his narrative with a comically detailed circumstantiality, he records a really startling number of hurts. In the voyage to Lilliput, for example, his hair is painfully pulled, and his hands and face are blistered by needle-like arrows. During his visit among the people of Brobdingnag, Gulliver is battered so badly that we are tempted to regard him as strangely accident-prone: his flesh is punctured by wheat beards; twice his sides are painfully crushed; he is shaken up and bruised in a box; his nose and forehead are grievously stung by flies the size of larks; he suffers painful contusions from a shower of gigantic hail-stones; he "breaks" his shin on a snailshell; and he is pummeled about the head and body by a linnet's wings.

In the third voyage Gulliver is given a respite: his experiences here are primarily intellectual, and he is permitted for a brief period to behave as curious tourist rather than universal sufferer. But the final voyage, the voyage to the land of the Houyhnhnms, brings Gulliver again into dire physical jeopardy. His last series of physical ordeals begins as his hand is painfully squeezed by a horse. And finally, as he leaves Houyhnhnmland to return to England, he is made to suffer a serious and wholly gratuitous arrow wound on the inside of his left knee ("I shall carry the Mark to my Grave"). Looking back on the whole extent of Gulliver's foreign experiences before his final return to his own country, we are hardly surprised that Gulliver's intellectuals have come unhinged: for years his body has been beaten, dropped, squeezed, lacerated, and punctured. When all is said, his transforming experiences have been as largely physical as intellectual and psychological. So powerfully does Swift reveal Gulliver's purely mental difficulties at the end of the fourth voyage that we tend to forget that Gulliver has also been made to undergo the sorest physical trials: during the four voyages he has been hurt so badly that, although he is normally a taciturn, unemotional, "Roman" kind of person, he has wept three times; so severely has he been injured at various times that at least twenty-four of his total traveling days he has been forced to spend recuperating in bed.

In addition to these actual emblematic injuries which Gulliver endures, he also experiences a large number of narrow escapes, potential injuries, and pathetic fears of physical hurt. In Lilliput, the vulnerability of his eyes is unremittingly insisted upon: an arrow barely misses his left eye, and only his spectacles prevent the loss of both his eyes as he works on the Blefuscan fleet. Furthermore, one of the Lilliputian punishments decreed for Quinbus Flestrin is that his eyes be put out.

And in the voyage to Brobdingnag, Gulliver's experience is one of an almost continuous narrow escape. He almost falls from the hand of the farmer and off the edge of the table. Stumbling over a crust, he falls flat on his face, barely escaping injury. After being held in a child's mouth, he is dropped, and he is saved only by being almost miraculously caught in a woman's apron. He is tossed into a bowl of cream, knocked down but not badly hurt by a shower of falling apples, and clutched dangerously between a spaniel's teeth. He is lucky to escape serious injury during a nasty fall into a mole hill. An agonizing fall of forty feet seems to bode ill for Gulliver, but no—his breeches catch on the point of a pin, and again he is wonderfully saved from destruction. In the same way, during the sojourn at Laputa, Gulliver is afraid of some "hurt" befalling him during the episode of the magician. And likewise in the fourth voyage Gulliver is frequently conscious of potential injury.

But Gulliver, this physically vulnerable ur-Boswell on the Grand Tour, is not the only one in the book who suffers or who fears injury: the creatures he is thrown among also endure strange catastrophes of pain and damage, often peculiarly particularized by Swift. Thus, in Lilliput, two or three of the rope-dancing practitioners break their limbs in falls. A horse, falling part way through Gulliver's handkerchief, strains a shoulder. The grandfather of the Lilliputian monarch, it is reported, as a result of breaking his egg upon the larger end suffered a cut finger. In the same way, the fourth voyage is full of what seem to be gratuitous images of injury and pain: for example, Gulliver carefully tells us that an elderly Houyhnhnm "of Quality" alighted from his Yahoo-drawn sledge "with his Hind-feet forward, having by Accident got a Hurt in his Left Fore-foot."

Nor are all these injuries confined to the bodies of Gulliver and his hosts. Gulliver's clothing and personal property are perpetually suffering damage, and, when they are not actually being damaged, Gulliver is worrying that, at any moment, they may be. Of course, mindful of Crusoe's pathetic situation, we are not surprised that a shipwrecked mariner suffers damage to his clothing and personal effects. But we may be surprised to hear Gulliver go out of his way to call careful attention to the damages and losses he suffers. In the first voyage, for example, Gulliver circumstantially lets us know that his scimitar has rusted, that his hat has been sorely damaged by being hauled through the dust all the way from the sea to the capital, and that his breeches have suffered an embarrassing rent. The boat in which Gulliver escapes to Blefuscu is, we are carefully told, "but little damaged." Once off the islands and, we might suppose, secure from losses and accidents until his next voyage, Gulliver loses one of his tiny souvenir sheep—it is destroyed by a rat aboard ship.

Presumably outfitted anew, Gulliver arrives ashore in Brobdingnag with his effects intact, but the old familiar process of damage and deterioration now begins all over again. Wheat beards rip his clothes; a fall into a bowl of milk utterly spoils Gulliver's suit; his stockings and breeches are soiled when he is thrust into the marrow bone which the queen has been enjoying at dinner; his clothes are again damaged by his tumble into the mole hill; and his suit (what's left of it) is further ruined by being daubed by frog slime and "bemired" with cow dung. Likewise, in the third voyage, our attention is called to the fact that Gulliver's hat has again worn out, and in the fourth voyage we are informed yet again by Gulliver that his clothes are "in a declining Condition."

At times, in fact, Gulliver's clothes and personal effects seem to be Gulliver himself: this is the apparent state of things which fascinates the observing Houyhnhnm before whom Gulliver undresses, and this ironic suggestion of an equation between Gulliver and his clothing, reminding us of the ironic "clothes philosophy" of Section II of *A Tale of a Tub,* Swift exploits to emphasize that damage to Gulliver's naturalistic garments is really damage to the naturalistic Gulliver. The vulnerability of Gulliver's clothing, that is, is a symbol three degrees removed from what it signifies: damage to Gulliver's clothes is symbolic of damage to Gulliver's body, which, in turn, is emblematic of damage to Gulliver's self-esteem.

These incidents of injury and destruction are thus pervasive in Gulliver's travels, as one is reminded by the recurrence, very striking when one is attuned to it, of words such as "hurt," "injury," "damage," "accident," "mischief," "misfortune," and "spoiled." Once his attention is aroused to what is going on physically in *Gulliver's Travels,* the reader senses the oblique appearance of this pervading vulnerability motif even in passages which really focus on something quite different. For example: "His Majesty [the Emperor of Blefuscu] presented me . . . with his Picture at full length, which I put immediately into one of my Gloves, to keep it from being hurt." In *Gulliver's Travels* Swift never allows us to forget that there is a pathetic fragility in his objects, both animate and inanimate.

G. WILSON KNIGHT

The Sensory Structure of the Travels

Gulliver's Travels, however plain and realistic its surface, depends on a symbolic, sensory-physical structure. Books I and II use people either dwarf-like or vast. And the logic within this imaginative structure repays exact attention. Compare with Shakespeare's and Milton's feeling for kingship this description of the King of Lilliput:

> He is taller by almost the breadth of my nail than any of his court, which alone is enough to strike an awe into the beholders. His features are strong and masculine, with an Austrian lip and arched nose, his complexion olive, his countenance erect, his body and limbs well-proportioned, all his motions graceful, and his deportment majestic. (Ch. II.)

And his proclamation:

> Golbasto Momaren Evlame Gurdilo Shefin Mully Ully Gue, most mighty Emperor of Lilliput, delight and terror of the universe, whose dominions extend five thousand *blustrugs* (about twelve miles in circumference) to the extremities of the globe; monarch of all monarchs, taller than the sons of men; whose feet press down to the centre, and whose head strikes against the sun; at whose nod the princes of the earth shake their knees; pleasant as the spring, comfortable as the summer, fruitful as autumn, dreadful as winter . . . (Ch. III.)

These rely for their satiric force on our knowledge of his size. His *pride* is felt to be absurd—compare Pope's hatred of pride—when we remember his pigmy physique. Yet size is only relative. The King of England viewed by a hypothetical creature much

From *The Burning Oracle* (1939), pp. 117-22. London. Reprinted by permission of the author.

larger would appear correspondingly small; but so, for that matter, would the larger person in similar plight—as indeed Gulliver himself does in Book II, where it is clearly stated that the King of England must have suffered similar indignities had he been there. So a sequence of bigger and bigger people can be imagined indefinitely. Swift has therefore, in playing with size, said precisely nothing. But see what has happened. Pride has been condemned, not by the author but by the reader. A new perspective reveals a truth which, once recognized, stands independent of any particular perspective: while, the recognition being our own, knowledge of the trick played on us will not invalidate it. Or we see that pride, so easily dethroned by an unreality, can only be so satirized since it depends on one. It is felt to be fundamentally a make-believe: whereas self-sacrifice, courage, simple good sense, are not: for all qualities in the book inherently praiseworthy do not appear invalidated at all. Something similar happens in Byron's otherwise very different *Don Juan*. The judgements are all the time our own, Swift merely forcing them to daylight recognition. This recognition is not always bitter, and may touch pure humour, comparable with that of Pope in *The Rape of the Lock*: as when, in Book II, after Gulliver's elaborate and proud exhibition of nautical skill in a tank with Glumdalclitch's breath for wind, the girl, it is quietly and unobtrusively observed, hangs the boat on a nail to dry. The humour depends on recognition of a possible context in which any pride may appear funny. Such ludicrous events condition, with Swift, true narrative power and sincerity, his admirable scheme leaving him nothing to do but the barest description of—and this is characteristic—a simple *action*. Having the right nouns ready, he has only to attach the verb. The power of surface simplicity is fed entirely from the symbolism beneath.

Reliance on direct sensory-physical effects is greater in Book II than Book I. Especially interesting is Swift's use of small animals of a supposedly disgusting or absurd sort. The first Brobdingnagian he meets looks on Gulliver as 'a small dangerous animal' that may 'scratch' or 'bite,' such as a 'weasel'; while Gulliver himself fears he may be dashed to the ground as 'any little hateful animal' a man has a mind to destroy. The man's wife screams on seeing him as 'at the sight of a toad or a spider.' When the boy is to be punished for holding him up in air by the legs, Gulliver intercedes, remembering a boy's natural mischievousness towards sparrows, rabbits, kittens, and puppy dogs. To him a cat is now three times the size of an ox. Gulliver's fight with the two rats is satirically heroic and his pride ludicrous: especially when the maid picks up the dead one with a pair of tongs and throws it out of the window. He sleeps in a doll's cradle in a drawer. They consider him a *splacknuck*. Glumdalclitch was once given a lamb which later went to the butcher and she fears the same may happen to Grildrig. He is carried in a 'box' with gimlet holes to let in air. The dwarf, in professional jealousy, drops him into a large bowl of cream, but, being a powerful swimmer, he survives. His legs are also wedged by this dwarf during dinner into a marrow-bone 'where I stuck for some time, and made a very ridiculous figure.' Flies, 'odious insects,' trouble him, and he is admired for cutting them in pieces with his knife. Fierce wasps steal his cake but he shows courage in attack and 'dispatches' four of them. . . . And then there is the monkey catching and squeezing him and taking him on to the roof, feeding him with food from its own mouth, patting him when he will not eat. And all this is built into that explicit statement of the king who sees Gulliver's kind as 'the most pernicious race of little odious vermin that nature ever suffered to crawl upon the face of the earth.'

I apologize for this rather obvious list. But observe its emphasis on actions. Swift follows the Shakespearian tradition of nauseating animals: spiders, toads, monkeys, &c. The experience is similar to that Shakespeare projects into *Othello*. The comparisons aim at outlining sense of both indignity and disgust. The substance is to this extent quite non-rational, and of an immediate and sensory sort, however it may be used to blend with rational thinking. . . .

Sense-reaction may be specifically human: as when Gulliver in Lilliput puts out the fire burning the palace with his own water; in the heavy emphasis on ordure in the same book; and the descriptions of a meal and execution in Book II. The most precise expression of such sensory feeling comes in the exquisitely devised Book IV. Book I is sometimes indecisive: as when the Lilliputians, usually reflecting European weaknesses, are suddenly made to present Utopian ideals of education and justice; and in Book II the King and his people, who stand for reason, justice, and intellectual precision (as in references to neat prose and learning), are also horrible, because large, examples of physical coarseness. The confusion is unavoidable. But Book IV, where none occurs, is the more perfect work. The author has found exact equivalents to his intuition in the Houyhnhnms and Yahoos. The choice of horses may be related to Swift's excretory prepossessions, since the scent of stables is strangely non-abhorrent to man. Consider this passage:

> The first money I layed out was to buy two young stone horses, which I keep in a good stable, and next to them the groom is my greatest favourite; for I feel my spirits revived by the smell he contracts in the stable. (Ch. XI.)

In contrast Gulliver is disgusted by human odours. Horses thus become Swift's highest creatures, the intellectual design being clearly dictated by a sensory, almost poetic, aversion. . . . In the Yahoo physical and intellectual satire are beautifully at one. Gulliver's Houyhnhnm master tells how five of the Yahoos will quarrel violently over enough food for fifty, each wanting all for himself, and only failing to kill each other for want of the human inventions Gulliver has described; how they will dig with their claws for coloured stones, carrying them to their kennels and pining away if they be removed. As for drink, they suck a juicy root that goes to their heads:

> It would make them sometimes hug, and sometimes tear one another; they would howl, and grin, and chatter, and reel, and tumble, and then fall asleep in the dirt. (Ch. VII.)

The physical is one with the moral satire. The hatefulness of the Yahoo form is emphasized together with its comparative uselessness and limitations in strength and speed, and subjection to cold and heat. The concealing by clothes of otherwise 'hardly supportable' human 'deformities' apears to Gulliver's master thoroughly wise. Indeed, the Yahoos hate each other presumably because of their 'odious shape.' The Houyhnhnms

> had very imprudently neglected to cultivate the breed of asses, which were a comely animal, easily kept, more tame and orderly, without any offensive smell, strong enough for labour, although they yield to the other in agility of body; and if their brayings be no agreeable sound, it is far preferable to the horrible howlings of the Yahoos. (Ch. IX.)

Such a passage shows clearly how Swift's famous understatement and lucidity depend mainly on his first finding satirical-symbolic schemes so exactly suited that barest narration releases all the emotional force desired. No first-order writer is independent of sensory symbolisms; and Swift's striking realism and fine use of the active verb measure the madness of his tale.

BONAMY DOBRÉE

Swift and Science, and the Placing of Book III

Le cœur a des raisons que la raison thinks it best to ignore —and it was the logic of the emotions that took Swift in the writing of the *Travels* from Brobdingnag to Houyhnhnmland. The mind's logic would next have dealt with man's intellectual pride— and Swift returned to write Book III and fit it into its proper mental place; but the creative warmth engendered in writing of the giants drove him from the comparative detachment of that episode to the deeper phase of the Yahoos. That was the emotional movement; but it behoves us to look at the object with which Swift presented us, for that is the way he wanted to manipulate our minds, so it is to Laputa that we must go next. This voyage has never been popular, even Arbuthnot was disappointed in it; it seems at first sight too much of a rag-bag of all the left-overs in Swift's satirical armoury; both the scientific references and the political ones are at once too contemporary and too recondite. To the student of Swift it is fascinating, especially since it has been discovered how closely Swift had followed the *Transactions of the Royal Society,* how he had fused the immediately political with the rest, and had spoofed the more solemn asseverations of idealists. The Book has classical, literary, scientific, political, and philosophic sources, all welded together in this amazing fantasia; it is a night-

From *English Literature in the Early Eighteenth Century* (1959), pp. 454-57. Oxford. Reprinted by permission of the Clarendon Press, Oxford University.

mare which the dreamer does not feel to be such. We are wrong to require more unity than a nightmare possesses; we should be thankful that it is so miraculously gay.

Swift's main purpose in this book, apart from his political strokes which refer more especially to England's treatment of Ireland, was to take to a ridiculous logical conclusion the suggestions made by the scientists. It is great fun and is often very funny; how far there is real prevision in it may be matter for doubt. It is true that the Laputans discovered the satellites of Mars more than a century and a half before the scientists of Europe did; but it is also true that a great many things that Swift mocked at as chimerical have come to pass—we do, for example, extract sunshine from cucumbers, though we put it into globules and call it Vitamin C. We make fruits ripen at all seasons of the year. Much of the joke, alas, depends upon our knowing the references; though some are fairly obvious to anybody of average reading. For instance Sprat, in his *History of the Royal Society,* had enunciated his famous dictum that the ideal of prose was to deliver 'so many "Things," almost in an equal number of "Words" '; at the Academy of Projectors this becomes the sages with the 'Scheme for entirely abolishing all Words whatsoever' by carrying round sackfuls of objects. In the same way, all but one or two of his fooleries of this kind are drawn direct from the *Transactions,* though it makes for clarity to note that Swift divided his projectors into the mechanical and the political. But since his political observations do not differ from those in the other books, although they have their particular comic angle and the deadly serious reference to England's treatment of Ireland, what emerges in this book and nowhere else in the *Travels* is his attitude towards science, and, of course, to the old despised pedantries.

It is the ghost of Aristotle in Glubbdubdrib who states the argument against science:

> He said, that new Systems of Nature were but new Fashions, which would vary in every Age; and even those who pretended to demonstrate them from Mathematical Principles, would flourish but a short Period of Time, and be out of Vogue when that was determined.

That, in a sense, is true, as we now realize; but it is also irrelevant. What matters is that man at any given time should have a conception of the universe—of, if you like, the way God's mind works in so far as any particular thing is concerned—on a level with his physical experience. Swift, as far as we know, did not despise science; what he objected to was the self-glorification of the petty virtuoso dissecting flies, and the absurd pretensions of the second-rate scientist to 'explain' the inexplicable. In the ridicule he cast upon the whole Academy, and on the Laputan philosophers, he was proclaiming that none of these things really matter; what does matter is man's realization of his duty to man. The fool in any sphere is meat for the satirist; but Swift, while including the petty strutter, was aiming at something far more fundamental. He was really asking the question, 'What is the proper object of man's most strenuous intellectual attention?'; and since this is a question that should be asked all the time, there is still a freshness about this part of the *Travels* in spite of the very specific references for almost every absurdity with which he amused the readers of his own day.

The third Book may not in itself be very coherent, but it is a necessary gap in the emotional sequence, for in it Swift can use a certain relieving lightness he could not for a moment risk in the last. The satire is sometimes good-humoured chaff, as when he speaks of the 'very common Infirmity of human Nature, inclining us to be more curious and conceited in Matters where we have least Concern, and for which we are least adapted either by Study or Nature,' a theme taken up more fiercely in 'The Beast's Confession' (1732). This Book is necessary again for another reason, namely that our sense of actuality has to be shifted. The first two Books, fantastic as they are, strain our belief beyond the probable, no doubt, but not beyond the possible; there are, after all, pygmies, and there are, or at least have been, giants. In Book IV (already written) we are going to be presented with something it will be very difficult for us to accept; but compared with Book III, the Houyhnhnms and Yahoos are easy to swallow; in Book III Swift might have said as frankly as Lucian did, 'I humbly solicit my readers' incredulity'; and if we can allow our fancy to be held captive in any of those islands even for a minute, we shall be susceptible of being trapped into feeling a sense of reality about the following and most serious part of the whole work.

And there is one further point where the Voyage to Laputa is essential—in the description of the Struldbrugs. Whether their source be classical—especially through the Tithonus myth—or the then recent account of the tribe in 'Casmere' that lives to an advanced and horrible, desireless old age does not matter. The description, and the whole episode, is, of course, valuable in itself; our dreams of a wise old age are illusory, and Swift brings out every atom of the eternal human comedy. But there is more purpose in it than that; for the statement in this part is, 'You want desperately to live,' and in the next part we hear the inexorable voice asking, 'Very well then; under what conditions will you accept life?'

KATHLEEN WILLIAMS

The Shadowy World of the Third Voyage

From Lagado Gulliver makes his way to Glubbdubdrib, where again he is in a world of no-meaning, of delusion and death, darker and more shadowy than Laputa. In the palace of the sorcerer who is governor of the island he has a series of singularly uninformative interviews with the ghosts of the famous dead, and Alexander and Hannibal, who as conquerors and destroyers had little to recommend them to Swift, make particularly trivial replies. We are given a gloomy enough picture of both the ancient and the modern world, and upon this ghostly history follows the most somber episode of all, that of the Struldbrugs of Luggnagg, in which the lesson of Laputa with its naïve hopes, its misplaced ambition, and its eventual sterility is repeated with more open seriousness. A right sense of values, a proper attitude to living, is here suggested not through the handling of contemporary aims and habits of thought but through the figure of man, immortal yet still painfully recognizable, and perhaps owing some of its power and poignancy to Swift's own fear of death and, still more, of decay,

From *Jonathan Swift and the Age of Compromise*, pp. 173-77. Lawrence.

of a lingering old age giving way at last to helpless lunacy. Gulliver, hearing of the immortals, cries out "as in a Rapture," exclaiming upon the wisdom and happiness which they must have achieved. They must, he says, "being born exempt from that universal Calamity of human Nature, have their Minds free and disingaged, without the Weight and Depression of Spirits caused by the continual Apprehension of Death," and he is only too willing to tell his hearers how he would plan his life, if he were a Struldbrug, to bring the greatest possible benefit to himself and his country. In fact, of course, the immortal and aged creatures, though free from the fear of death, are yet as full of fears and wretchedness as any other men: being what we are, we will always find occasion to display those vices which as human beings we will always have, however long we may live. The Struldbrugs certainly do not keep their minds free and disengaged, and for them the prospect of endless life does not conjure up visions of endless improvement in wisdom and virtue. They regard their immortality as a "dreadful Prospect" even as other men regard their death, and indeed they long to die as did the wretched Sibyl in Petronius's *Satyricon*, regarding with great jealousy those of their acquaintance who go "to an Harbour of Rest, to which they themselves never can hope to arrive." Immortal man is still man, limited in his capacity for growth, sinful, fearful, dissatisfied; the somber simplicity of the passage, and indeed of the whole of the visit to Glubbdubdrib, is reminiscent of Johnson's methods rather than of Swift's, and the message is essentially similar. Gulliver, who has dreamed of being a king, a general, or a great lord, and now dreams of being a Struldbrug, has to learn the same lesson as the Prince of Abyssinia: that life is a serious, difficult, and above all a moral undertaking, that whatever excuses we may find for ourselves, however we may dream of the greatness we could have achieved under other conditions, we will realize at last that humanity is always the same, and that there is no escape from our vices and our trivialities. Gulliver says that he grew "heartily ashamed of the pleasing Visions I had formed; and thought no Tyrant could invent a Death into which I would not run with Pleasure from such a Life," and that he would have been willing, if it had not been forbidden by the laws of Luggnagg, to send a couple of Struldbrugs to England to arm the people against that fear of death which is natural to mankind.

So the "Voyage to Laputa," which opens among a people essentially frivolous in its refusal to face the facts of human existence, ends face to face with inescapable reality. Laputa, where the search for the clarity of abstractions involves such confusion in the living world, seems at first merely hilarious and absurd, but as confusion turns to mechanism and destruction this remoteness and unreality becomes not only ludicrous but evil, and the countries about Laputa and Balnibarbi are seen to be places of superstition, sorcery, and tyranny, of ghosts and the corpselike immortals of Luggnagg. The voyage to illusion, the escape from facts, ends in a darker reality than any Gulliver has yet encountered. Gulliver himself, in this book, becomes a part of the world of illusion and distorted values. Already in the earlier voyages the shifting, inconsistent quality which Gulliver shares with all Swift's satiric mouthpieces has been made to contribute to effects of relativity, and to suggest the hold of physical circumstances over mankind. That he is, generally, a different man in Brobdingnag and in Lilliput is made into part of Swift's presentation of human nature. In the "Voyage to Laputa," any still surviving notion that Gulliver is a safe guide through these strange countries is ended. He ceases to have any character and, in effect, vanishes, so that for the most part the satire speaks directly to us; the "mouthpiece" performs no real function. The transparent account of "Tribnia, by the Natives called Langden," where "the Bulk of the People consisted wholly of Discoverers, Witnesses, Informers, Accusers, Prosecutors, Evidences, Swearers," owes nothing to Gulliver, and would be quite inconceivable from what we have known of him before; in the second voyage he had "wished for the Tongue of Demosthenes or Cicero, that might have enabled me to celebrate the Praise of my own dear native Country in a Style equal to its Merits and Felicity." Here he is being frankly used for ironic comment, as his exaggerated enthusiasm shows; in the description of Tribnia, he is not being used at all. From time to time he is given a momentary reality, but of the most perfunctory kind; there is no attempt to endow him even with the one or two dominant characteristics that he is given elsewhere. His approval of projects, or his tendency to dream about impossible situations instead of getting on with the business of living, his dismissal of obviously desirable political reforms as "wild impossible Chimaeras," are, quite openly, mentioned for satiric purposes of a very simple kind. The handling of Gulliver is in fact far less interesting, and his contribution is far slighter, than in any other book, probably because his function had been worked to its limits in the voyages already written, which included the "Voyage to the Houyhnhnms." But whether or not Swift planned it so, Gulliver's virtual lack of function, indeed of existence, in the "Voyage to Laputa" has a certain effectiveness in contributing to the atmosphere of meaningless activity and self-deceit, leading to a shadowy despair. The gradual undermining of the comparatively solid worlds of Lilliput and Brobdingnag was achieved partly through a shift in Gulliver's position; here he merges completely into his surroundings, and serves merely to describe what he sees, so that we cannot take him seriously as an interpreter. When he reappears in Book IV, we are well prepared to find that his function will not be a simple one either of sensible comment on the vagaries of a strange country, or of admiration for a Utopia, for we have accepted him as one of the many figures in the *Travels*, expressing meaning by his relationship to them, and no more exempt than they from satiric treatment. As a completion of the processes begun in Lilliput and Brobdingnag, and as a preparation for the resolution in Houyhnhnm-land, the Laputan voyage performs its task adequately, though without the formal elegance and neatness of the other books.

EDWARD W. ROSENHEIM, JR.

The Satiric Fiction

When the *Travels* is viewed simply as a tale, Gulliver seems a reasonable and convincing protagonist. His restlessness and curiosity lead him to travel; his understandable frailties precipitate many of his dilemmas; his resourcefulness extricates him from them. He is benign enough to invite our sympathy, honest enough so that, once within the make-believe framework of his story, we are never tempted to accuse him of saying "the thing that is not." His deficiencies and rigidities are plausible, and plausible too are

From Edward W. Rosenheim, Jr., *Swift and the Satirist's Art*, pp. 158–160; 166–167. Chicago: The University of Chicago Press, 1963.

the consequences to which they lead within the plot. His character is, indeed, without peculiarity; whether as narrator, hero, or dupe (and he is variously all of these) he must be taken as one of ourselves.

Nor is there anything inconsistent in the satiric use which Swift makes of the character he has created. Gulliver is not a politician, a projector, a profiteer, pedant, lawyer, or lecher; the assaults upon these and other kinds of person and institution are achieved through what Gulliver sees and tells. He is, on the other hand, a travel-writer, an Englishman, a European, a human being, and where he is employed as surrogate-victim it is in one of these roles. Where he is truly a critic—where, that is, he literally offers judgments which essentially coincide with our own—it is at a level appropriate to his rather commonplace faculties; he is disgusted at whatever is grossly repellent, outraged by palpable cruelty or deceit, puzzled or amused by arrant folly. If, in very occasional passages, he displays an uncharacteristic cynicism, it seems engendered by a kind of blandly uncritical acceptance of evil as a fact of life. Thus, for example, his simple-minded astonishment at the political projectors of Lagado, who sought to instil notions of civic virtue into the conduct of government . . . reveals him as a sort of *faux ingénu*. His naïve dismissal of such reformers as mad, that is, expresses the bitter truth that it is hopeless to expect wisdom and honesty in government affairs. Although these sentiments are somewhat at odds with the glowing account of political appointment and preferment which Gulliver has earlier given to the Brobdingnagian king, they are not incompatible with his general character. The belief that governmental corruption is inevitable is a standard one in the doctrinal equipment of the ordinary man. (Indeed, great numbers of Americans today seem to accept, with a complacency equal to Gulliver's, the presumably inalterable venality and guile which operate within that political system they venerate above all others.)

Thus Gulliver in his several roles—as observer and reporter, as master and victim of circumstance—is a thoroughly flexible agent of Swift's many purposes yet preserves that consistency of character which renders him, wherever necessary, credible and sympathetic. With such a character there are few limits to what a writer like Swift can do, and the *Travels* might well have gone on and on (or, for that matter, ceased earlier), leaving its readers with a rich miscellany of literary experiences, now satiric, now comic, now philosophic, untroubled by questions of unity, development, or total significance. This, in effect, is what is provided by such purely episodic but triumphantly satiric works as Lucian's *True History* or *Don Juan* or even, essentially, *Candide*. And it is, I believe, what is provided by the first three voyages of *Gulliver's Travels*. For despite the brilliant symmetry of conceit which links the first two books, it is Gulliver and what happens to him—rather than any unified satiric purpose or procedure, any coherence of imagery or idea, any singleness of philosophic vision—to which alone we look for organic continuity. What happens to Gulliver, moreover, is presented in a series of basically dissociated episodes, some with the magnitude and complexity of his disgrace, danger, and escape from Lilliput, others as short and simple as his Brobdingnagian encounters with the wasps, the monkey, and the rats. Among these episodes there are few relationships of antecedent and consequent. No character—not even the beloved Glumdalclitch—survives beyond one or two phases of Gulliver's adventures. Gulliver is confronted by no persisent problem, engaged in no compelling inquiry or search beyond the desire to return home (and even this plays little part in the second voyage). With the establishment of Gulliver's character and his propensity for travel, we are confronted with the possibilities for incident on whose substance and magnitude Swift's own wishes and talents impose the only limitation. This is, so to speak, a literary system of "occurrences," each to be relished for its own effect and in its own way, deriving credibility and intelligibility, to be sure, from the presence of a single character and the recurrent use of a voyage as the central activity of each book, but possessed of no further organic quality, whether of structure or of purpose.

All this is abruptly, even violently, changed with the voyage to the Houyhnhnms. This book, too, is above all a narrative, a series of happenings, yet happenings which are profound and startling, which are inseparably linked within the wholeness of a single myth, and which involve Gulliver in a sustained process of inquiry and discovery.

The belief or vision which Voyage IV presumably embodies has, quite understandably, commanded enormous attention. In our final chapter we shall attempt to discuss the philosophic ground from which this extraordinary fable proceeds, but at this moment we should recognize that the most obvious—and certainly a very crucial—way in which Book IV differs from its fellows is in the nature of its plot. However we may be tempted to attribute the singularity of the fourth book to the depth, intensity, or strangeness of its ultimate "meaning," we must also note that the "system of occurrences" by which the earlier books proceed has here yielded to an account of a single though complex experience. And that experience, fantastic though its form may be, is at heart one of the most shocking and powerful of which the human mind can conceive, for it is, in effect, a discovery so profound that a man's total view of life is violently and irrevocably altered. . . .

In the final analysis, our scrutiny of the *Travels* as a fictional narrative supplies the minimal unity which embraces the entire book, yet, perhaps paradoxically, forces us to recognize that, beyond this, no unifying artistic formula can be produced. As pure narrative and as philosophic myth, the Voyage to the Houyhnhnms is indeed climactic, but climactic largely by virtue of its contrast to, rather than its development from, the voyages which have preceded it. Against the shifting variety of the first three books, against their appearance of ebullient formlessness, the Fourth Voyage emerges with organic clarity as a magnificent finale. In its orderliness and magnitude, it is unanticipated and independent, and the more powerful for that fact. Yet it casts no retroactive magic over the pages which have preceded it. Their own freedom refuses to be embraced by a single concept of theme or belief, and they resist the boundaries imposed by a single satiric motive or a conventional literary formula. They are informed and sustained by invention; they are the product of a talent which, however varied the uses to which it is put, is unflaggingly and supremely imaginative.

J. MIDDLETON MURRY

Gulliver's Conversion amongst the Houyhnhnms

From these glimpses of the polity of Brobdingnag we may fairly conclude that it represents Swift's vision of a practicable ideal —roughly, an England whose 'glorious Revolution' was not nullified, as Swift believed it had been, by the development of party-faction, court-corruption, a moneyed interest, and the establishment of a standing army. Gulliver does his patriotic best to conceal the

From *Jonathan Swift*, pp. 338–41. New York. Copyright 1955 by J. Middleton Murry. By permission of Noonday Press, a subsidiary of Farrar, Strauss and Giroux; and Jonathan Cape Limited.

political deformities of his own country; but the King examines him severely, and elicits the truth. Indeed, in his long series of leading questions, his Majesty shows a detailed knowledge of the seamy side of English society that would hardly be plausible in a realistic fiction, unless we were to regard Brobdingnag as having emerged from a similar corruption. But the willing suspension of disbelief comes easy enough. The main point to grasp is that the King of Brobdingnag extracts the truth from a reluctant Gulliver, or rather compels him to assent to the truth of his own unflattering deductions from Gulliver's evidence.

When he comes to the land of the Houyhnhnms, Gulliver's attitude changes radically. It takes him a long while to adjust to the new and astonishing society of truly rational beings. He stays longer in Houyhnhnm land than in any other; and he needs to do so. For he has to undergo a mental and spiritual revolution, of which the consequence is that he becomes incapable of saying 'the thing which is not.' Now, it is of his own motion that he tells his master the truth concerning English society. And a crucial factor in his spiritual purgation is his realization that he belongs to the species of the Yahoos. The picture of these repulsive brutes has been resented as a blasphemy on humanity. In one important respect, which shall be considered, it is. But in so far as the qualities of the Yahoo are to be 'cunning, malicious, treacherous and revengeful' and unteachable, it would be hard for a detached observer of the behaviour of the human race during the last fifty years to deny that there is sufficient likeness between mankind and the Yahoos to give us food for thought. At least it would not be wholly unjust to describe mankind, on the evidence of this behaviour, as a race of sophisticated Yahoos. Notably, it is when Gulliver describes the happenings in a European war, that the Houyhnhnm his master experiences 'a disturbance in his mind, to which he was wholly a stranger before.'

Although he hated the *Yahoos* of this country, he no more blamed them for their odious qualities, than he did a *gnnayh* (a bird of prey) for its cruelty, or a sharp stone for cutting his hoof. But when a creature pretending to reason, could be capable of such enormities, he dreaded lest the corruption of that faculty might be worse than brutality itself. He seemed therefore confident, that instead of reason, we were only possessed of some faculty fitted to increase our natural vices.

The possibility which so disturbs the Houyhnhnm is that the faculty which the sophisticated Yahoos possess may be a corruption of 'reason.' But he comes to rest in the confidence that it is a different faculty altogether.

Quite rightly, for it is evident that the 'reason' which the Houyhnhnms possess, and which Gulliver in their society and by force of their example comes partly to acquire, is not the faculty of ratiocination at all. It is the gift of discerning and doing what is good. It is because Swift uses 'reason' in this distinctive sense in Book IV that he could say to Pope that *Gulliver's Travels* was based on the proposition that man is not an *animal rationale* but only *rationis capax.* Capable of 'reason,' in this sense, can only mean capable of developing in oneself a discernment of the good, and a devotion to pursuing it, and simultaneously of developing an incapacity to pursue evil. This is what Swift asserts when Gulliver says of the 'reason' of the Houyhnhnms:

> Neither is reason among them a point problematical as with us, where men can argue with plausibility on both sides of the question; but strikes you with immediate conviction, as it needs must where it is not mingled, obscured or discoloured by passion and interest.

This 'reason' exists, according to Swift, as a mere latent potentiality in humans, and only becomes operative when the mind is free from passion or interest, that is to say, when it is purged of what Santayana calls 'animal egotism.' And this purgation happens to Gulliver in consequence of his discovery that he belongs to the Yahoo species. It is a painful process of self-discovery and self-annihilation. For the only difference between a human such as himself and a Yahoo consists in the addition of the faculty of ratiocination, which, being morally neutral, becomes in the human being merely an instrument in the service of the fundamental animal egotism of the Yahoo. But besides this there is a gleam or germ: the possibility of the emergence of 'reason' when the radical vice of animal egotism is discerned in oneself and overcome. When man has seen himself in the mirror of the Yahoo, he may be purged. Then 'reason,' or the true self, may be liberated from its animal bondage.

It is highly characteristic of Swift that he should represent the society of purged and liberated spirits as a community of horses. The peculiar cast of his mind is nowhere more simply evident. The device not only enables him to avoid the difficulty of representing a community of entirely good human beings, without insipidity, but enables him to make visible, in a concrete and vivid symbol, the almost generic difference between the animal and the spiritual, the enslaved and the liberated man. The element of dullness and monotony which would otherwise be inseparable from an attempt to depict a society of completely virtuous humans becomes in a sense natural when they are horses. We do not expect them to be idiosyncratic; or talkative, trivial or mean. Moreover, since the distinguishing feature of regenerated humans is that they are instinctively and spontaneously good, the use of the 'noblest' animal to represent them is appropriate and effective. On the other hand, it enables Swift to suggest a specious solution to a problem which deeply concerned him: the reconciliation of reason and sex. That solution, in its turn, is intimately connected with what has been justly felt to be excessive savagery of his picture of the Yahoos. This is too important a question to be considered in passing. Here we are concerned solely with what is positive and profound in the parable of Book IV.

The substance of it is that moral goodness, or 'reason,' is a second and better nature, achieved by means of a ruthless self-purgation; but there is a change in kind—a rebirth. Perhaps the most notable of the marks of this change is the one on which Gulliver insists in chapter XII, at the very end of his narrative.

My reconcilement to the *Yahoo*-kind in general might not be so difficult, if they would be content with those vices and follies only which nature hath entitled them to. I am not in the least provoked at the sight of a lawyer, a pickpocket, a colonel, a fool, a lord, a gamester, a politician, a whoremaster, a physician, an evidence, a suborner, an attorney, a traitor or the like; this is all according to the due course of things: but when I behold a lump of deformity, and diseases both in body and mind, smitten with *pride*, it immediately breaks all the measures of my patience; neither shall I ever be able to comprehend how such an animal and such a vice could tally together . . . But the *Houyhnhnms,* who live under the government of reason, are no more proud of the good qualities they possess, than I should be for not wanting a leg or an arm, which no man in his wits would boast of, although he must be miserable without them.

It recalls St. Paul's rebuke to the Corinthians: 'What hast thou that thou didst not receive? Now, if thou didst receive it, why dost thou glory as if thou hadst not received it?' That is the specifically Christian version of the same spiritual truth. Goodness, when really achieved, is known not to have been achieved by our own efforts. Reason, when it is true reason, is not a personal acquisition; it is not a faculty of which it can be said, 'I possess it': it possesses me.

This naturalness of the reason and goodness of the Houyhnhnms is the cause of Gulliver's delay in recognizing it for what it is. 'At first, indeed, I did not feel that natural awe, which the Yahoos, and all other animals, bear towards them; but it grew upon me by degrees.' It is as though Gulliver had at first to grope his way in an unfamiliar dimension, or be gradually initiated into a mystery. But once he is there, his values change. In consequence of the same inward revolution, the impulse to defend his own human society, as he had done before the King of Brobdingnag, abandons him completely before the Houyhnhnms. He is ruthlessly veracious about it. . . .

W. B. C. WATKINS

Sense of Tragedy in Book IV

. . . let us examine more specifically the objections to the *Fourth Voyage*. . . . First, its unreasonableness. Swift's usual satirical method is that of a devastating logic, but in a curious way. He more frequently gives an appearance of logic than actual logic—even logic on the basis of a preposterous major premise. Fundamentally, his reasoning is emotional, however cleverly he may mask it as superb common sense. Digressions are really an essential part of him, because his mind is the sort that kindles to an idea, then

From *Perilous Balance: The Tragic Genius of Swift, Johnson, and Sterne* (1939), pp. 21-23. Princeton. Princeton University Press.

plays about it in flashes of lightning, like Donne with his metaphysical conceits. In the *Fourth Voyage*, unlike the first, he is not being rationally satirical most of the time, because here he is treating not incidental problems of human life, but the very core of his belief—the dichotomy, beast and reason in man. His intense worship of reason combines here with the terrible disillusion of reason to produce a powerful emotional conviction in which common sense has no place.

The Yahoos are a disgusting incarnation of bestiality. They are Hamlet's 'beast that wants discourse of reason.' In the repeated imagery of excrement and filth Swift is not indulging in mere sensationalism; he is employing a poetic device used, among others, by Shakespeare, Spenser, Donne, and Milton. Are his Yahoos really more revolting than the portrayal of Error or the unmasking of Duessa? Is he less justifiable than Donne in such lines as

> Ranke sweaty froth thy Mistresse's brow defiles,
> Like spermatique issue of ripe menstruous boiles?

Are Swift's intentions less commendable than Shakespeare's in having Hamlet describe Gertrude and Claudius

> In the rank sweat of an enseamed bed,
> Stew'd in corruption, honeying and making love
> Over the nasty sty?

They are not, if we consider what despair and loathing of outraged sensitivity caused them.

The Houyhnhnms are not so successful an imaginative creation as the Yahoos, one must admit. A symbol of ideal perfection is more difficult, and Swift became entangled in the method of realistic narrative which he had used so brilliantly with the Lilliputians and Brobdingnagians. His marvellous skill in invention fails to make the horses convincing; they become at times ridiculous in a way which Swift could hardly have intended. But the satirical conception of prostrating man to kiss the hoof of the horse has its points.

It is this partial failure with the Houyhnhnms which blinds us to the magnificently conceived and executed finale to the *Fourth Voyage*, which portrays Gulliver as inconsolable at leaving the Houyhnhnms:

When all was ready, and the day came for my departure, I took leave of my master and lady, and the whole family, my eyes flowing with tears, and my heart quite sunk with grief. . . .

My design was, if possible, to discover some small island uninhabited, yet sufficient by my labour to furnish me with the necessaries of life, which I would have thought a greater happiness than to be first minister in the politest court of Europe; so horrible was the idea I conceived of returning to live in the society and under the government of *Yahoos.*

Finally, after sundry adventures with natives, Gulliver is picked up by a Portuguese ship:

. . . I remained silent and sullen; I was ready to faint at the very smell of him and his men. . . . I would not undress myself, but lay on the bed-clothes, and in half an hour stole out, when I thought the crew was at dinner, and getting to the side of the ship was going to leap into the sea, and swim for my life, rather than continue among *Yahoos*. . . .

As soon as I entered the house, my wife took me in her arms, and kissed me; at which, having not been used to the touch of that odious animal for so many years, I fell in a swoon for almost an hour . . . during the first year, I could not endure my wife or children in my presence, the very smell of them was intolerable. . . .

Gulliver, unable to bear the *smell* of human beings, seeks sanctuary in the ammoniac smells of the stables, with their nostalgic reminiscence of Houyhnhnmland. This last touch, like many in his treatment of the ideal horses, is consciously humorous, but humor of the serious import and macabre tone of Hamlet's

Thrift, thrift, Horatio!

Well said, old mole! Canst work i' th' earth so fast?

A certain convocation of politic worms are e'en at him.

It is the bitter humor of the oversensitive, self-conscious man who can laugh at his own suffering, at his being such an unconscionable time in dying.

If we take this imagery of smells figuratively, it expresses perfectly the heart-breaking despair of a man who has had a vision of perfection from which he awakened to sordid reality. Gulliver's forced exile from Houyhnhnmland represents just that. The ideal makes the real unbearable. The separation of reason and body is, admittedly, too extreme; the relegation of man to the state of Yahoo, which that final identification of man with Yahoo certainly means, is too sweeping. But *Lear* is a sweeping condemnation of 'the poor forked animal'; *Hamlet* demands why such fellows should be allowed to crawl between earth and heaven. This *Fourth Voyage of Gulliver* is not the most perfect but is the most profoundly moving thing Swift wrote. His satire passes over into tragedy.

R. S. CRANE

The Houyhnhnms, the Yahoos, and the History of Ideas

Whatever else may be true of the [Fourth] Voyage, it will doubtless be agreed that one question is kept uppermost in it from the beginning, for both Gulliver and the reader. This is the question of what sort of animal man, as a species, really is; and the point of departure in the argument is the answer to this question which Gulliver brings with him into Houyhnhnmland and which is also, we are reminded more than once, the answer which men in general tend, complacently, to give to it. Neither he nor they have any doubt that only man, among "sensitive" creatures, can be properly called "rational"; all the rest—whether wild or tame, detestable or, like that "most comely and generous" animal, the horse, the reverse of that—being merely "brutes," not "endued with reason." The central issue, in other words, is primarily one of definition: is man, or is he not, correctly defined as a "rational creature"? It is significant that Gulliver's misanthropy at the end is not the result of any increase in his knowledge of human beings in the concrete over what he has had before; it is he after all who expounds to his Houyhnhnm master all those melancholy facts about men's

From "The Houyhnhnms, the Yahoos, and the History of Ideas" by R. S. Crane, in *Reason and the Imagination: Studies in the History of Ideas*, edited by J. A. Mazzeo. New York: Columbia University Press and London: Routledge & Kegan Paul Ltd., 1962. Reprinted by permission of the publishers.

"actions and passions" that play so large a part in their conversations; he has known these facts all along, and has still been able to call himself a "lover of mankind." The thing that changes his love into antipathy is the recognition that is now forced upon him that these facts are wholly incompatible with the formula for man's nature which he has hitherto taken for granted—are compatible, indeed, only with a formula, infinitely more humiliating to human pride, which pushes man nearly if not quite over to the opposite pole of the animal world.

What brings about the recognition is, in the first place, the deeply disturbing spectacle of the Houyhnhnms and the Yahoos. I can find nothing in the text that forces us to look on these two sets of strange creatures in any other light than that in which Gulliver sees them—not, that is, as personified abstractions, but simply as two concrete species of animals: existent species for Gulliver, hypothetical species for us. The contrast he draws between them involves the same pair of antithetical terms (the one positive, the other privative) that he has been accustomed to use in contrasting men and the other animals. The essential character of the Houyhnhnms, he tells us, is that they are creatures "wholly governed by reason"; the essential character of the Yahoos is that "they are the most unteachable of brutes," without "the least tincture of reason." The world of animals in Houyhnhnmland, in other words, is divided by the same basic differences as the world of animals in Europe. Only, of course—and it is the shock of this that prepares Gulliver for his ultimate abandonment of the definition of man he has started with—it is a world in which the normal distribution of species between "rational creatures" and irrational "brutes" is sharply inverted, with horses, whom he can't help admiring, in the natural place of men, and man-like creatures, whom he can't help abhorring, in the natural place of horses.

This is enough in itself to cause Gulliver to view his original formula for his own species, as he says, "in a very different light." But he is pushed much farther in the same misanthropic direction by the questions and comments of his Houyhnhnm master, acting as a kind of Socrates. What thus develops is partly a reduction to absurdity of man's "pretensions to the character of a rational creature" and partly a demonstration of the complete parity in essential nature between men and the Houyhnhnmland Yahoos. There is of course one striking difference—unlike the Yahoos, men are after all possessed of at least a "small proportion," a "small pittance" of reason, some in greater degree than others. But I can see no clear signs in the text that this qualification is intended to set men apart as a third, or intermediate, species for either Gulliver or the reader. For what is basic in the new definition of man as a merely more "civilized" variety of Yahoo is the fundamentally irrational "disposition" which motivates his habitual behaviour; and in relation to that his "capacity for reason" is only an acquired attribute which he is always in danger of losing and of which, as Gulliver says, he makes no other use, generally speaking, than "to improve and multiply those vices" whereof his "brethren [in Houyhnhnmland] had only the share that nature allotted them."

It is clear what a satisfactory historical explanation of this line of argument in the Voyage would have to do. It would have to account for Swift's very patent assumption that there would be a high degree of satirical force, for readers in 1726, in a fable which began with the notion that man is pre-eminently a "rational creature" and then proceeded to turn this notion violently upside down, and which, in doing so, based itself on a division of animal species into the extremes of "rational creatures" and irrational "brutes" and on the paradoxical identification of the former with horses and of the latter with beings closely resembling men. Was there perhaps a body of teaching, not so far brought into the discussion of the Voyage but widely familiar at the time, that could have supplied Swift with the particular scheme of ideas he was exploiting here? I suggest that there was, and also that there is nothing strange in the fact that it has been hitherto overlooked by Swift's critics. For one principal medium through which these ideas could have come to Swift and his readers—the only one, in fact, I know of that could have given him all of them—was a body of writings, mainly in Latin, which students of literature in our day quite naturally shy away from reading: namely, the old-fashioned textbooks in logic that still dominated the teaching of that subject in British universities during the later seventeenth and early eighteenth centuries.

It is impossible not to be impressed, in the first place, by the prominence in these textbooks of the particular definition of man which the Voyage sought to discredit. *Homo est animal rationale*: no one could study elementary logic anywhere in the British Isles in the generation before *Gulliver* without encountering this formula or variations of it (e.g., *Nullus homo est irrationalis*) in his manuals and the lectures he heard. It appears as the standard example of essential definition in the great majority of logics in use during these years at Oxford, Cambridge, and Dublin; and in most of those in which it occurs, it is given without comment or explanation as the obviously correct formula for man's distinctive nature, as if no one would ever question that man is, uniquely and above all, a rational creature. . . .

But the logicians had more to offer Swift than the great authority which they undoubtedly conferred on the definition "rational animal." They could have suggested to him also the basic principle on which the inverted animal world of Houyhnhnmland was constructed, and consequently the disjunction that operated as major premise in his argument about man. Whoever it was, among the Greeks, that first divided the genus "animal" by the differentiae "rational" and "irrational," there is much evidence that this antithesis had become a commonplace in the Greco-Roman schools long before it was taken up by the writer who did more than any one else to determine the context in which the definition *animal rationale* was chiefly familiar to Englishmen of Swift's time. This writer was the Neoplatonist Porphyry of the third century A.D., whose little treatise, the *Isagoge*, or introduction to the categories of Aristotle, became, as is well known, one of the great sources of logical theorizing and teaching from the time of Boethius until well beyond the end of the seventeenth century.

And there was, finally, one other thing in these logics that could have helped to shape Swift's invention in the fourth Voyage. In opposing man as the only species of "rational animal" to the brutes, Porphyry obviously needed a specific instance, parallel to man, of an "irrational" creature; and the instance he chose—there were earlier precedents for the choice—was the horse. The proportion "rational" is to "irrational" as man is to horse occurs more than once in the *Isagoge*; and the juxtaposition, in the same context, of *homo* and *equus* was a frequently recurring cliché in his seventeenth-century followers, as in the passage in Burgersdicius just quoted: other species of brutes were occasionally mentioned, but none of them nearly so often. And any one who studied these books could hardly fail to remember a further point—that the distinguishing "property" of this favorite brute was invariably given as whinnying (*facultas hinniendi*); *equus*, it was said again and again, *est animal hinnibile*.

To most Englishmen of Swift's time who had read logic in their youth—and this would include nearly all generally educated men—these commonplaces of Prophyry's tree, as I may call them for short, were as familiar as the Freudian commonplaces are to generally educated people today, and they were accepted, for the most part, in an even less questioning spirit, so that it might well have occurred to a clever satirist then that he could produce a fine shock to his readers' complacency as human beings by inventing a world in which horses appeared where the logicians had put men and men where they had put horses, and by elaborating, through this, an argument designed to shift the position of man as a species from the *animal rationale* branch of the tree, where he had always been proudly placed, as far as possible over toward the *animal irrationale* branch, with its enormously less flattering connotations.

HENRY W. SAMS

Satire as Betrayal

. . . Swift's frequent use of the device of putative authorship assumes a special significance, for it implies that his exordia may be ironic. From the very outset he holds himself aloof from the reader, commending not himself, but an intermediary buffoon. Many students of Swift have commented on this aspect of Swift's art. Its fundamental importance is everywhere noted. No other device so nearly comprehends within itself the qualities which distinguish the satires of Swift from direct criticism of the sort that one finds, for example, in the speeches of Burke.

In one sense, the effect of putative authorship may have been overestimated, for readers have sometimes assumed that the putative author introduced at the beginning of a work is a consistent character and that he remains the same throughout the work. As a matter of fact, the first function of the putative author is that of establishing a contract with the audience, that is, of the exordium. This function once fulfilled, the putative procedure may be only casually or occasionally remembered. . . . in the *Travels*, Gulliver is at once the author and the protagonist of his narrative. Readers

From ELH, *a Journal of English Literary History*, XXVI (1959), pp. 38-41. Baltimore. Reprinted by permission of The Johns Hopkins University.

are invited to accept a degree of what is called "identification" with him, and some readers, accepting this identification, have been inclined to take the fourth book of the *Travels* at literal face value, as a sermon instead of a satire.

Swift's exordia, his introductory contracts with his readers, are subtile, reassuring, and ambiguous. Their effect is to win approval and confidence even though they withhold the commitment of the controlling intelligence, that is, of Swift's own intelligence. They leave open the possibility that he may re-enter the argument when he finds re-entry expedient, and that he may re-enter as either enemy or friend. . . .

The fourth book of the *Travels* is in many ways the fiercest of Swift's satires. Gulliver slowly realizes that he must acknowledge his kinship with the Yahoos. The ritual farewell to the Houyhnhnm master is a relinquishment of his hope to achieve rationality. The book is usually glossed by a citation of Swift's plaintive letter to Pope, despite the fact that Gulliver apparently, and the Yahoos certainly, are somewhat less than *rationis capax.*

The fourth book is part of the carefully devised fable. It has qualities different from those of a letter to Pope. It has content which cannot be reduced to a simple statement of doctrine. The farewell to the Houyhnhnms is not unrelievedly sententious. Gulliver's parade of sentimentality for the rational is not without its element of incongruity.

The crux of the matter is in the conclusion of the volume, and in the interpretation which one makes of Gulliver's felicity with his English horses. If the perfections of the Houyhnhnms are indeed perfect, and if the people of England are indeed Yahoos, then Swift's final counsel is a counsel of despair. But if the final chapter is read as betraying the doctrine of the Houyhnhnms, the effect is somewhat different.

It should be remembered that upon his return from the Houyhnhnms Gulliver could not endure the presence of other human beings. Their odor offended him. The idea of their caresses nauseated him. Above all he despised in them their sin of pride. Sitting with his commonplace English horses, loathing all human creatures, he said: "I here intreat those who have any Tincture of this absurd Vice, that they will not presume to appear in my Sight."

At this point it seems reasonable to object to Gulliver himself.

Although he inveighs against pride, he displays in his own person the external symptoms by which pride may be recognized. The effect is satiric betrayal.

. . . One of the ancient principles of debate is to induce an opponent to adopt a position which he will later be forced to abandon. In disputation, the moment of victory is the moment at which an adversary is compelled to adjust his premises to the demands of the argument. Aristotle's *Topica* is a description of strategies by which this end may be systematically accomplished. Certain passages of Swift's satire are examples of strategies by which a similar effect can be poetically accomplished.

In Book IV of *Gulliver's Travels* Swift advances a doctrine and wins its acceptance. The doctrine is that of the Houyhnhnms. He then betrays it by his description of Gulliver's final excesses. The reader, convinced on both counts, revises his opinion and is compelled to be aware of the revision. His awareness is satiric effect. The image in the satiric mirror is his own.

C. J. RAWSON

Gulliver and the Gentle Reader

The book ends here, with Gulliver a monomaniac and his last outburst a defiant, and silly, petulance. We are not, I am sure, invited to share his attitudes literally, to accept as valid his fainting at the touch of his wife (IV, xi) and his strange nostalgic preference for his horses. He has become insane or unbalanced, and I have already suggested one reason why, in the whole design of the work, this is appropriate: it makes his rant viable by dissociating Swift from the taint of excess, without really undermining the

From "Gulliver and the Gentle Reader" by C. J. Rawson in *Imagined Worlds: Essays on Some English Novels and Novelists in Honour of John Butt*, edited by M. Mack and I. Gregor. London: Methuen & Co., Ltd., 1968. Reprinted by permission of the publisher.

attack from Swift that the rant stands for. It is Gulliver's manner, not Swift's, which is Timon's manner, as critics are fond of noting, which means that he (like Lucian's or Plutarch's Timon), and not Swift, is the raging recluse. But his are the final words, which produce the taste Swift chose to leave behind: it is no great comfort or compliment to the reader to be assaulted with a mean hysteria that he cannot shrug off because, when all is said, it tells what the whole volume has insisted to be the truth.

It is wrong, I think, to take Gulliver as a novel-character who suffers a tragic alienation, and for whom therefore we feel pity or some kind of contempt, largely because we do not, as I suggested, think of him as a "Character" at all in more than a very attenuated sense: the emphasis is so preponderantly on what can be shown through him (including what he says and thinks) than on his person in its own right, that we are never allowed to accustom ourselves to him as a real personality despite all the rudimentary local color about his early career, family life and professional doings. An aspect of this are Swift's ironic exploitations of the Gulliver-figure, which to the very end flout our most elementary expectations of character consistency: the praise of English colonialism in the last chapter, which startlingly returns to Gulliver's earlier boneheaded manner, is an example. The treatment of Gulliver is essentially *external*, as, according to Wyndham Lewis, satire ought to be. Nor is Gulliver sufficiently independent from Swift: he is not identical with Swift, nor even similar to him, but Swift's presence behind him is always too close to ignore. This is not because Swift approves or disapproves of what Gulliver says at any given time, but because Swift is always saying something *through* it.

Gulliver in his unbalanced state, then, seems less a character than (in a view which has much truth but needs qualifying) a protesting gesture of impotent rage, a satirist's stance of ultimate exasperation. Through him, as through the modest proposer (who once offered sensible and decent suggestions which were ignored), Swift is pointing, in a favorite irony, to the lonely madness of trying to mend the world, a visionary absurdity which, in more than a shallow rhetorical sense, Swift saw as his own. At the time of finishing *Gulliver*, Swift told Pope, in a wry joke, that he wished there were a "Hospital" for the world's despisers. (If Gulliver, incidentally, unlike the proposer, does not preach cannibalism, he does ask for clothes of Yahoo-skin — IV,iii — and uses this material for his boat and sails — IV,x.) But Gulliver does not quite project the noble rage or righteous pride of the outraged satirist. The exasperated petulance of the last speech keeps the quarrel on an altogether less majestic and more intimate footing, where it has, in my view, been all along. Common sense tells us that Swift would not talk like that in his own voice, but we know disturbingly (and there has been no strong competing voice) that this is the voice he chose to leave in our ears.

Still, Gulliver's view is out of touch with a daily reality about which Swift also knew, and which includes the good Portuguese Captain. Gulliver's response to the Captain is plainly unworthy, and we should note that he has not learnt such bad manners (or his later hysterical tone) from the Houyhnhnms' example. But we should also remember that the Captain is a rarity, who appears only briefly; that just before Gulliver meets him the horrible mutiny with which Book IV began is twice remembered (IV,x; IV,xi); that the first men Gulliver meets after leaving Houyhnhnm-land are hostile savages (IV,xi); and that just after the excellent Portuguese sailors there is a hint of the Portuguese Inquisition (IV,xi). The Captain does have a function. As John Traugott says, he emphasizes Gulliver's alienation and "allows Gulliver to make Swift's point that even good Yahoos are Yahoos." But above all perhaps he serves as a reasonable concession to reality (as if Swift were saying there *are* some good men, but the case is unaltered), without which the onslaughts on mankind might be open to a too easy repudiation from the reader. In this respect, he complements the other disarming concessions, the humor and self-irony, the physical comicality of the Houyhnhnms, Gulliver's folly, and the rest.

Even if Swift is making a more moderate attack on mankind than Gulliver, Gulliver's view hovers damagingly over it all; in the same way that, though the book says we are better than the Yahoos, it does not allow us to be too sure of the fact. (The bad smell of the Portuguese Captain, or of Gulliver's wife, are presumably "objective" tokens of physical identity, like the She-Yahoo's sexual desire for Gulliver.) This indirection unsettles the reader, by denying him the solace of definite categories. It forbids the luxury of a well-defined stand, whether of resistance or of assent, and offers none of the comforts of that author-reader complicity on which much satiric rhetoric depends. It is an ironic procedure, mocking, elusive, immensely resourceful and agile, which talks at the reader with a unique quarrelsome intimacy, but which is so hedged with aggressive defenses that it is impossible for him to answer back.

Finally, a word about the Houyhnhnms. It is sometimes said that Swift is satirizing them as absurd or nasty embodiments of extreme rationalism. Apart from the element of humor, discussed earlier, with which they are presented, they are, it is said, conceited and obtuse in disbelieving the existence or the physical viability of the human creature. But, within the logic of the fiction, this disbelief seems natural enough. The Lilliputians also doubted the existence of men of Gulliver's size (I,iv), and Gulliver also needed explaining in Brobdingnag (II,iii). In both these cases the philosophers are characteristically silly, but everybody is intrigued, and we could hardly expect otherwise. Moreover, Gulliver tells Sympson that some human beings have doubted the existence of Houyhnhnms, which, within the terms of the story (if one is really going to take this sort of evidence solemnly), is just as arrogant. More important, the related Houyhnhnm doubt as to the anatomical viability or efficiency of the human shape (apart from being no more smug than some of Gulliver's complacencies *in favor* of mankind) turns to a biting sarcasm at man's, not at the Houyhnhnms', expense when, as we have seen, the Houyhnhnm master supposes that man is not capable of making war (IV,v).

The Houyhnhnms' proposal to castrate some younger Yahoos (IV,ix) has also shocked critics. But again this follows the simple narrative logic: it is no more than humans do to horses. Our shock should be no more than the "noble Resentment" of the Houyhnhnm master when he hears of the custom among us (IV,iv). To the extent that we *are* shocked, Swift seems to me to be meaning mildly to outrage our "healthy" sensibilities, as he does in the hoof-kissing episode. But in any event, the Houyhnhnms get the idea *from* Gulliver's account of what men do to horses, so that either way the force of the fable is not on man's side. The fiction throughout reverses the man-horse relationship: horses are degenerate in England (IV,xii), as men are in Houyhnhnmland. Again, I think man comes out of it badly both ways: the Yahoos of Houyhnhnmland make their obvious point, but the suggestion in reverse seems to be that English horses are poor specimens (though to Gulliver better than men) because they live in a bad human world. At least, a kind of irrational sense of guilt by association is generated. We need not suppose that Swift is endorsing Gulliver's preference of his horses to his family in order to feel offended about it. At many (sometimes indefinable) points on a complex scale of effects, Swift is getting at us.

The Houyhnhnms' expulsion of Gulliver belongs to the same group of objections. It seems to me that some of the sympathy showered on Gulliver by critics comes from a misfocused response to him as a full character in whom we are very involved as a person. The Houyhnhnm master and the sorrel nag are in fact very sorry to lose Gulliver, but the logic of the fable is inexorable: Gulliver is of the Yahoo kind, and his privileged position in Houyhnhnmland was offensive to some, while his rudiments of Reason threaten (not without plausibility, from all we learn of man's use of that faculty) to make him a danger to the state as leader of the wild Yahoos (IV,x). The expulsion of Gulliver is like Gulliver's treatment of Don Pedro: both episodes have been sentimentalized, but they are a harsh reminder that even good Yahoos are Yahoos.

The main charge is that the Houyhnhnms are cold, passionless, inhuman, unattractive to us and therefore an inappropriate positive model. The fact that we may not like them does not mean that Swift is disowning them: it is consistent with his whole style to nettle us with a positive we might find insulting and rebarbative. The older critics who disliked the Houyhnhnms but felt that Swift meant them as a positive were surely nearer the mark than some recent ones who translate their own dislikes into the meaning of the book. But one must agree that the Houyhnhnms, though they are a positive, are not a *model*, there being no question of our being able to imitate them. So far as it has not been grossly exaggerated, their "inhumanity" may well, like their literal *non*-humanity (which tells us that the only really rational animal is not man), be part of the satiric point: this is a matter of "passions."

They are, of course, not totally passionless. They treat Gulliver, in all personal contacts, with mildness, tenderness and friendly dignity (IV,i). Gulliver receives special gentleness and affection from his master, and still warmer tenderness from the sorrel nag (IV,xi). Their language, which has no term for lying or opinion, "expressed the Passions very well," which may mean no more than "emotions" but does mean that they have them (IV,i). In contrast to the Laputans, who have no "Imagination, Fancy and Invention" (III,ii), but like the Brobdingnagians (II,vii), they excel in poetry (IV,ix), though their poems sound as if they might be rather unreadable and are certainly not enraptured effusions.

But their personal lives differ from ours in a kind of lofty tranquillity, and an absence of personal intimacy and emotional entanglement. In some aspects of this, they parallel Utopian Lilliput (I,vi), and when Gulliver is describing such things as their conversational habits ("Where there was no Interruption, Tediousness, Heat, or Difference of Sentiments"), a note of undisguised wishfulness comes into the writing (see the whole passage, IV,x). W. B. Carnochan has shown, in a well-taken point, that such freedom from the "tyrant-passions" corresponds to a genuine longing of Swift himself. I do not wish, and have no ability, to be psychoanalytical. But in a work which, in addition to much routine and sometimes rather self-conscious scatology (however "traditional"), contains the disturbing anatomy of Brobdingnagian ladies, the account of the Struldbrugs, the reeking sexuality of the Yahoos and the She-Yahoo's attempt on Gulliver, the horrible three-year-old Yahoo brat (IV,viii), the smell of Don Pedro and of Gulliver's family and Gulliver's strange relations with his wife, one might well expect to find aspirations for a society which practised eugenics and had an educational system in which personal and family intimacies were reduced to a minimum. Gulliver may be mocked, but the cumulative effect of these things is inescapable, and within the atmosphere of the work itself the longing for a world uncontaminated as far as possible by the vagaries of emotion might seem to us an unattractive, but is surely not a surprising, phenomenon.

But it is more important still to say that the Houyhnhnms are not a statement of what man ought to be so much as a statement of what he is not. Man thinks he is *animal rationale*, and the Houyhnhnms are a demonstration (which might, as we saw, be logically unacceptable, but is imaginatively powerful), for man to compare himself with, of what an *animal rationale* really is. R. S. Crane has shown that in the logic textbooks which commonly purveyed the old definition of man as a rational animal, the beast traditionally and most frequently named as a specific example of the opposite, the non-rational, was the horse. Thus Hudibras, who "was in logic a great critic," would

> undertake to prove by force
> Of argument, a man's no horse.

The choice of horses thus becomes an insulting exercise in "logical" refutation. The Yahoos are certainly an opposite extreme, and real man lies somewhere between them. But it is no simple comforting matter of a golden mean. Man is dramatically closer to the Yahoos in many ways, and with all manner of insistence. While the Houyhnhnms are an insulting impossibility, the Yahoos, though not a reality, are an equally insulting possibility. Swift's strategy of the undermining doubt is nowhere more evident than here, for though we are made to fear the worst, we are not given the comfort of knowing the worst. "The chief end I propose to my self in all my labors is to vex the world rather than divert it": and whatever grains of salt we may choose for our comfort to see in these words, "the world," gentle reader, includes *thee*.

RICARDO QUINTANA

Situation as Satirical Method

Before pressing on in further search of Swift's satiric method, we ought perhaps to establish our larger view. The misinterpretation of Swift is proverbial, but with fewer exceptions than is sometimes realized those who have written about him have fought energetically against the deep-lying prejudices of the sort voiced so deplorably and so brilliantly by Thackeray. It happens that we know a good deal of both the private life of Swift and his public career, and much about his motives, interests, prejudices, and theoretical convictions. Criticism, as distinct from biography, is concerned to find the relationship between the man and the artist, but this it can

From *University of Toronto Quarterly*, XVII (1948), pp. 131-33. Toronto. Reprinted by permission of the author and the publisher.

do with some degree of effectiveness only through a sense of the general problem. How do the writer as man and the writer as artist stand to one another? Where does personality end and impersonality begin?

Satire, as much as and no less than drama and lyric poetry, is a construct. It is precisely devised literary composition, a form of rhetoric. It may proceed, as we have seen, by way of characters whose actions are recorded objectively or who speak as in a play; but even in the absence of such ikons there is still the assumed character of the satirist, which despite a convincingly deceptive egotism is quite as much an imaginative creation as any ikon. Nor, in another and more vital respect, is there any substantial difference between satire on the one hand and drama and lyric poetry on the other. Each of these fashions its own world, not as Swift creates the land of the Houyhnhnms or Shakespeare the island of Prospero, but rather in the sense that *Gulliver's Travels*—all of it—is a world, that *The Tempest*—the play as a totality—is its own, complete universe. This special world is a most complex structure, having a logic of its own which governs feeling and speech. It is at once a way of looking at things, a way of feeling, and a way of speaking.

The writer himself, the man with a human character and practical motives, is present of course, but he stands several levels away from this manner of feeling and speech. The avowed intention of the satirist is to expose folly and evil and to castigate them, and there is no satire worthy of the name which does not in fact establish a moral dichotomy: right over against wrong, rectified vision or virtue against twisted vision, human dignity and freedom against stupidity, blindness, perversity. If the moral sense of some satirists —of Byron, for instance—seems elementary, the moral sense of Swift we recognize as that inherited from the humanist tradition, in which man's freedom was defined in terms of ethical responsibility and in accord with the Christian awareness of human incapacity and failure. The drift of Swift's satiric statements, their intellectual-ethical significance, the practical effects they were designed to achieve are made clear by the history of the age and our knowledge of Swift's character. The impact of his satires is another problem, for their meaning as satiric constructs embraces something which is more than their practical meaning and qualitatively different from it. What this other thing is, is the question, or rather, how to find the terms which will enable us to talk about it without evasion. It is a way of thought and feeling, but only as it is a method—a tone, a style, a manner of execution—can it be described in the language which criticism must come to when it seeks to put close observation in the place of impressionism.

It is essential to sense the fact that the method of Swift is a good deal more than what we often think of as a method. Fundamentally, it is an imaginative point of view, making possible and controlling a kind of translation into terms peculiar to a certain angle of perception. This means that it cannot be exclusively identified with any single procedure or device however characteristic of Swift. Though dramatic construction marks all of his best-known satiric works, it would be a mistake to regard such construction as the gist of the matter. Similarly, we have to resist any temptation to single out Swift's use of allegory or of parody in an effort to isolate his method. All of these devices operate together; they are modes of expression within a single language; they are functions of something larger. What name we find for this enclosing method is not particularly important, since there is no precise term that can do all the necessary work. *Situational satire* will serve.

A satire of Swift's is, we may say, an exhibited situation or series of such situations. Once the situation has been suggested, once its tone, its flavour have been given, it promptly takes command of itself and proceeds to grow and organize by virtue of its own inherent principles. It is a state of affairs within which, as we mistakenly put it, "anything can happen"—mistakenly because everything that does happen is instantly recognized as a part of *this*, a unique situation. Nevertheless, the room for self-improvisation seems limitless, and the comic scale ranges from the hilarious to the grim. It is to be observed that the satirist is himself not involved: he is as much an observer, as much outside all the fuss and nonsense, as we are. (Is it this that we mean when, in speaking of the satires, we comment on the "coldness of Swift"? We know that he was not cold, else we should not be quoting his epitaph as we do.) For the incidents which come to pass no one can be held responsible, any more than for the ideas and emotions which appear. What we have is, literally, an exhibition: everything is shown; everything is at least one degree removed from reality. In short, the situation may be thought of as a kind of chamber within which ideas and emotions are made to move and collide at accelerated speed.

BASIL WILLEY

The Limitations of Satire

Whatever technique the satirist uses (there are many gradations of irony, in Swift, for instance, which I am not to examine here), his effort is always to strip the object satirized of the film of familiarity which normally reconciles us to it, and to make us see it as in itself it really is, as the child saw the unclothed emperor in Hans Andersen's story. This frustration of the 'stock-response' is sometimes achieved in Swift and Voltaire, for example, by a deliberate refusal to see, in some ignoble object which custom has consecrated or made symbolic, anything further than the object itself. Thus Voltaire's Quaker, who for the time being represents Reason, says of a recruiting campaign:

'Our God, who has commanded us to love our enemies, and to suffer without repining, would certainly not permit us to cross the seas, merely because murderers cloth'd in scarlet, and wearing caps two foot high, enlist citizens by a noise made with two little sticks on an ass's skin extended.'

Or Gulliver, when enlightening the King's ignorance on the advantages of gunpowder, explains

'that we often put this powder into large hollow balls of iron, and discharge them by an engine into some city we were besieging, which would rip up the pavements, tear the houses to pieces, burst and throw splinters on every side, dashing out the brains of all who came near.'

Bentham, says Mill, habitually missed the truth that is in received opinions; that at any rate, I suggest, is what the satirist does and

From *Eighteenth-Century Background* (1946), pp. 106-08. New York. Reprinted by permission of Columbia University Press and Chatto and Windus Ltd.

must do. He must, whether deliberately or no, miss precisely those aspects of the ignoble thing which in fact make it endurable to the non-satiric everyday eye: that is to say, he must ignore the *explanation* of the thing satirized—how it came to be, its history. It is a fact of experience that *tout comprendre c'est tout pardonner*, and the satirist *ex officio* cannot pardon, so he must decline to understand all and explain all. Satire is by nature non-constructive, since to construct effectively—to educate, for example, to reform, or to evangelize—one must study actual situations and actual persons in their historical setting, and this kind of study destroys the satiric approach. This is not to say that satire is not or has not been often a most valuable weapon for the moralist. When the 'pardon' I have spoken of means the toleration of avoidable evil, satire has an important function. But 'pardon' is not the only or the inevitable attitude engendered by a historical study of persons and institutions; one may, if one is a moralist, an educator, an apostle or a revolutionary, desire to alter and amend things after having explained them. Satire seems to occur somewhere between acceptance and revolution, and it is not surprising, if this is so, that the early eighteenth century should have been its most high and palmy time. Swift himself, for all his discontent (divine or pathological), was no revolutionary; his satire, as we have suggested, always refers to standards which exist ready-made, and which would become operative without need for subversive change, if only men would not perversely depart from them. To these standards, however, Yahoo man *will* not adhere, and Swift seems at last to throw up the sponge—to abandon hope of ever lessening the disparity between the ideal and the actual. Instead, he barricades himself within his ivory tower of reason, and there 'enjoys' the bitter satisfaction of knowing himself the only wise being in an insane or bestial world, or, at most, of sharing, with a few kindred spirits (Pope or Arbuthnot), his own consciousness of superiority. Other satirists—Cervantes, Fielding, Dickens—have been known to fall in love with their abstractions, and Don Quixote, Joseph Andrews, and Pickwick have emerged full-formed from the satiric shadow-world. But Swift fell more and more out of love with man, and the result—his final tragedy—was the total dissociation of Houyhnhnm from Yahoo. So remote became his ideal that he could not symbolize his disembodied rationals as men at all, but only as horses. Man delighted him not, no, nor woman neither, so he escaped into his satiric fairyland or solaced himself with the strange baby-prattle of the *Journal to Stella.*

F. R. LEAVIS

Swift's Negative Irony

But what in Swift is most important, the disturbing characteristic of his genius, is a peculiar emotional intensity; that which, in *Gulliver,* confronts us in the Struldbrugs and the Yahoos. It is what we find ourselves contemplating when elsewhere we examine his irony. To lay the stress upon an emotional intensity should be matter of commonplace: actually, in routine usage, the accepted word for Swift is 'intellectual.' We are told, for instance, that his is pre-eminently 'intellectual satire' (though we are not told what satire is). For this formula the best reason some commentators can allege is the elaboration of analogies—their 'exact and elaborate propriety'—in *Gulliver.* But a muddled perception can hardly be expected to give a clear account of itself; the stress on Swift's 'intellect' (Mr. Herbert Read alludes to his 'mighty intelligence') registers, it would appear, a confused sense, not only of the mental exercise involved in his irony, but of the habitually critical attitude he maintains towards the world, and of the negative emotions he specializes in.

From 'critical' to 'negative' in this last sentence is, it will be observed, a shift of stress. There are writings of Swift where 'critical' is the more obvious word (and where 'intellectual' may seem correspondingly apt)—notably, the pamphlets or pamphleteering essays in which the irony is instrumental, directed and limited to a given end. The *Argument Against Abolishing Christianity* and the *Modest Proposal,* for instance, are discussible in the terms in which satire is commonly discussed: as the criticism of vice, folly, or other

From *The Common Pursuit* (1952), pp. 74-76, 84-87. London. Reprinted by permission of the author and the publishers, Chatto and Windus Ltd. and George W. Stewart, Inc.

aberration, by some kind of reference to positive standards. But even here, even in the *Argument*, where Swift's ironic intensity undeniably directs itself to the defence of something that he is intensely concerned to defend, the effect is essentially negative. The positive itself appears only negatively—a kind of skeletal presence, rigid enough, but without life or body; a necessary pre-condition, as it were, of directed negation. The intensity is purely destructive.

The point may be enforced by the obvious contrast with Gibbon —except that between Swift's irony and Gibbon's the contrast is so complete that any one point is difficult to isolate. Gibbon's irony, in the fifteenth chapter, may be aimed against, instead of for, Christianity, but contrasted with Swift's it is an assertion of faith. The decorously insistent pattern of Gibbonian prose insinuates a solidarity with the reader (the implied solidarity in Swift is itself ironical—a means to betrayal), establishes an understanding and habituates to certain assumptions. The reader, it is implied, is an eighteenth-century gentleman ('rational,' 'candid,' 'polite,' 'elegant,' 'humane'); eighteen hundred years ago he would have been a pagan gentleman, living by these same standards (those of absolute civilization); by these standards (present everywhere in the stylized prose and adroitly emphasized at key points in such phrases as 'the polite Augustus,' 'the elegant mythology of the Greeks') the Jews and early Christians are seen to have been ignorant fanatics, uncouth and probably dirty. Gibbon as a historian of Christianity had, we know, limitations; but the positive standards by reference to which his irony works represent something impressively realized in eighteenth-century civilization; impressively 'there' too in the grandiose, assured and ordered elegance of his history. (When, on the other hand, Lytton Strachey, with a Gibbonian period or phrase or word, a 'remarkable,' 'oddly,' or 'curious,' assures us that he feels an amused superiority to these Victorian puppets, he succeeds only in conveying his personal conviction that he feels amused and superior.)

Gibbon's irony, then, habituates and reassures, ministering to a kind of judicial certitude or complacency. Swift's is essentially a matter of surprise and negation; its function is to defeat habit, to intimidate and to demoralize. What he assumes in the *Argument* is not so much a common acceptance of Christianity as that the reader will be ashamed to have to recognize how fundamentally unchristian his actual assumptions, motives, and attitudes are. And in general the implication is that it would shame people if they were made to recognize themselves unequivocally. If one had to justify this irony according to the conventional notion of satire, then its satiric efficacy would be to make comfortable non-recognition, the unconsciousness of habit, impossible.

. . . The positives disappear. Even when, as in the Houyhnhnms, they seem to be more substantially present, they disappear under our 'curiosity.' The Houyhnhnms, of course, stand for Reason, Truth and Nature, the Augustan positives, and it was in deadly earnest that Swift appealed to these; but how little at best they were anything solidly realized, comparison with Pope brings out. Swift did his best for the Houyhnhnms, and they may have all the reason, but the Yahoos have all the life. Gulliver's master 'thought Nature and reason were sufficient guides for a reasonable animal,' but nature and reason as Gulliver exhibits them are curiously negative, and the reasonable animals appear to have nothing in them to guide. 'They have no fondness for their colts or foals, but the care they take in educating them proceeds entirely from the dictates of reason.' This freedom from irrational feelings and impulses simplifies other matters too: 'their language doth not abound in variety of words, because their wants and passions are fewer than among us.' And so conversation, in this model society, is simplified: 'nothing passed but what was useful, expressed in the fewest and most significant words . . .' 'Courtship, love, presents, jointures, settlements, have no place in their thoughts, or terms whereby to express them in their language. The young couple meet and are joined, merely because it is the determination of their parents and friends: it is what they see done every day, and they look upon it as one of the necessary actions of a reasonable being.' The injunction of 'temperance, industry, exercise, and cleanliness . . . the lessons enjoined to the young ones of both sexes,' seems unnecessary; except possibly for exercise, the usefulness of which would not, perhaps, be immediately apparent to the reasonable young.

The clean skin of the Houyhnhnms, in short, is stretched over a void; instincts, emotions and life, which complicate the problem of cleanliness and decency, are left for the Yahoos with the dirt and the indecorum. Reason, Truth and Nature serve instead; the Houyhnhnms (who scorn metaphysics) find them adequate. . . .

Swift's negative horror, at its most disturbing, becomes one with his disgust-obsession: he cannot bear to be reminded that under the skin there is blood, mess and entrails; and the skin itself, as we know from *Gulliver*, must not be seen from too close. Hypertrophy of the sense of uncleanness, of the instinct of repulsion, is not uncommon; nor is its association with what accompanies it in Swift. What is uncommon is Swift's genius and the paradoxical vitality with which this self-defeat of life—life turned against itself—is manifested. In the *Tale of a Tub* the defeat is also a triumph; the genius delights in its mastery, in its power to destroy, and negation is felt as self-assertion. It is only when time has confirmed Swift in disappointment and brought him to more intimate contemplation of physical decay that we get the Yahoos and the Struldbrugs.

Here, well on this side of pathology, literary criticism stops. To attempt encroachments would be absurd, and, even if one were qualified, unprofitable. No doubt psychopathology and medicine have an interesting commentary to offer, but their help is not necessary. Swift's genius belongs to literature, and its appreciation to literary criticism.

We have, then, in his writings probably the most remarkable expression of negative feelings and attitudes that literature can offer—the spectacle of creative powers (the paradoxical description seems right) exhibited consistently in negation and rejection. . . .

A great writer—yes; that account still imposes itself as fitting, though his greatness is no matter of moral grandeur or human centrality; our sense of it is merely a sense of great force. And this force, as we feel it, is conditioned by frustration and constriction; the channels of life have been blocked and perverted. That we should be so often invited to regard him as a moralist and an idealist would seem to be mainly a witness to the power of vanity, and the part that vanity can play in literary appreciation: *saeva indignatio* is an indulgence that solicits us all, and the use of literature by readers and critics for the projection of nobly suffering selves is familiar. No doubt, too, it is pleasant to believe that unusual capacity for egotistic animus means unusual distinction of intellect; but, as we have seen, there is no reason to lay stress on intellect in Swift. His work does indeed exhibit an extraordinary play of mind; but it is not great intellectual force that is exhibited in his indifference to the problems raised—in, for instance, the *Voyage to the Houyhnhnms*—by his use of the concept, or the word, 'Nature.' It is not merely that he had an Augustan contempt for metaphysics;

he shared the shallowest complacencies of Augustan common sense: his irony might destroy these, but there is no conscious criticism.

He was, in various ways, curiously unaware—the reverse of clairvoyant. He is distinguished by the intensity of his feelings, not by insight into them, and he certainly does not impress us as a mind in possession of its experience.

We shall not find Swift remarkable for intelligence if we think of Blake.

HERBERT DAVIS

Aspects of Swift's Prose

We know now from Swift's letters to Charles Ford that he took particular interest in Faulkner's third volume, which was to contain *Gulliver's Travels*. He admits that he had been annoyed by the changes introduced in the original edition, owing to the fears of the printer, not so much because of the things omitted as because of certain passages which were added in a style so slovenly that he was unwilling to have them remain in a volume which would be known as his work. Here then are samples of writing which Swift himself felt should be recognizable as something he could never have done. Here are passages which have been printed in some later editions of *Gulliver*, which the critics ought to have suspected from internal evidence of style alone. He had written, for instance, with little attempt to disguise the real object of his attack:

> I told him, that in the Kingdom of *Tribnia*, by the Natives called *Langden*, where I had long sojourned, the Bulk of the People consisted wholly of Discoverers, Witnesses, Informers, Accusers, Prosecutors, Evidences, Swearers; etc.

This is pointed and definite and unhesitating. He continues to charge the politicians in that kingdom with arranging plots to an-

From *Essays on the Eighteenth Century Presented to David Nichol Smith* (1945), pp. 27-32. Oxford. Reprinted by permission of the Clarendon Press, Oxford University.

swer their private advantage and describes the methods of dealing with those who are to be accused. In the first edition, to remove the sting, it is all made hypothetical and carefully packed in soft layers of verbiage:

> I told him, that should I happen to live in a Kingdom where Plots and Conspiracies were either in vogue from the turbulency of the meaner People, or could be turned to the use and service of the higher Rank of them, I first would take care to cherish and encourage the breed of Discoverers, Witnesses, etc.

Once given the clue it is certainly not difficult to detect the padding:

> Men thus qualified and thus empowered might make a most excellent use and advantage of Plots. . . .
>
> This might be done by first agreeing and settling among themselves. . . .
>
> They should be allowed to put what Interpretation they pleased upon them, giving them a Sense not only which has no relation at all to them, but even what is quite contrary to their true Intent and real Meaning; thus for Instance, they may, if they so fancy, interpret a *Sieve* etc.

For Swift rarely follows that loose fashion of coupling his verbs and nouns like this—qualified and empowered, use and advantage, agreeing and settling—and is incapable of such clumsiness as 'not only which has no . . . but even what.'

But the chief changes were made in the Fourth Book, to cushion the blows which Swift had dealt against the profession of the Law and against a First or Chief Minister of State. I do not think we could find anywhere a better proof of the conciseness of Swift than in the fifth and sixth chapters of the Fourth Book of *Gulliver*, if we read what he wrote as printed in Faulkner's edition:

> I said there was a Society of Men among us, bred up from their Youth in the Art of proving by Words multiplied for the Purpose, that *White* is *Black*, and *Black* is *White*, according as they are paid. To this Society all the rest of the People are Slaves.

That is surely Brobdingnagian in style—clear, masculine, and smooth; without multiplying unnecessary words or using various expressions. The attack is direct and unqualified, and therefore dangerous. Again Swift was justified in expecting his critics to recognize that the substituted passage which appears in the early London editions could not have come from his pen, for it is cautious and qualified, and therefore out of key with the context; and its meaning is completely clouded by the multiplication of unnecessary words.

I said that those who made profession of this Science were exceedingly multiplied, being almost equal to the Caterpillars in Number; that they were of diverse Degrees, Distinctions, and Denominations. The Numerousness of those that dedicated themselves to this Profession were such that the fair and justifiable Advantage and Income of the Profession was not sufficient for the decent and handsome Maintenance of Multitudes of those who followed it. Hence it came to pass that it was found needful to supply that by Artifice and Cunning, which could not be procured by just and honest Methods: The better to bring which about, very many Men among us were bred up from their Youth in the Art of proving by Words multiplied for the Purpose that *White* is *Black*, and *Black* is *White*, according as they are paid. The Greatness of these Mens Assurance and the Boldness of their Pretensions gained upon the Opinion of the Vulgar, whom in a Manner they made Slaves of, and got into their Hands much the largest Share of the Practice of their Profession.

The attack in the sixth chapter on the First or Chief Minister of State was not tampered with, but instead the danger was removed by introducing it with an extraordinary piece of patchwork intended to prevent the reader from a malicious interpretation at the expense of any recent British statesman. Again the style is so entirely unlike Swift and the change in tone so sudden that a careful reader could not fail to be suspicious of some tampering with the text. Had Swift been concerned to avoid any possible reference to Harley and Queen Anne, he would not have trusted to such a preposterous sentence of clumsy compliment; nor would he have ruined the whole effect of his satire by assuring his master that he was referring only to former times in Britain and to other courts in Europe now:

where Princes grew indolent and careless of their own Affairs through a constant Love and Pursuit of Pleasure, they made use of such an Administrator, as I had mentioned, under the Title of *first* or *chief Minister of State*, the Description of which, as far as it may be collected not only from their Actions, but from the Letters, Memoirs, and Writings published by themselves, the Truth of which has not yet been disputed, may be allowed to be as follows: . . .

Whether he wrote as Drapier, Bickerstaff, or Gulliver, or as the Dean of St. Patrick's, there were, I believe, certain standards which we may always apply, certain qualities which we can always recognize; for they are the marks of the mind and of the art of Jonathan Swift. And the particular quality of his prose that we have been considering as something both distinctive and remarkable—its conciseness—is also an essential mark of his mind and his art. That explains his greatness and his intensity; it explains also what were the things he could not do. In order to be plain and simple it is necessary to clear the mind of speculation and compromise, and to avoid in art the distortions of height and depth and the deception of colour.

He held that all knowledge is intended for use, not for idle curiosity or the pleasure of speculation. In matters of belief there must be boundaries between the spheres of faith and reason, and limits set to prevent disorder from the revolutionary forces of scepticism and critical inquiry. In matters of ethics he was content with a simple form of dualism, which defines the borders of right and wrong and when applied to political and social matters divides everything into a system of parties, Whigs and Tories, Ancients and Moderns, conformists and nonconformists, the forces of enlightenment and the forces of dullness—and finally a world of friends and enemies. In matters of political and ecclesiastical history he makes astonishing simplifications which provide a series of political parallels endlessly recurring, and of constant validity for all mankind. It is evidently a pattern simplified for common use which sometimes surprises us almost into a belief that it must be true, when it enables him to pack into a concise statement such a telling political generalization as this:

in the course of many Ages they have been troubled with the same Disease, to which the whole Race of Mankind is subject; the Nobility often contending for Power, the People for Liberty, and the King for absolute Dominion.

Like most of his contemporaries he approved of the activities of the scientists in so far as their work could be of practical use in agriculture and manufactures and navigation and medicine. But he feared the quackery and conceit of these investigators and logically was driven to make his attack on all kinds of technical jargon, as the very symbol of that kind of speculation which was in danger of separating its activities from all connexion with the common needs of man, and becoming, as law and theology and medicine had already done, a separate guild whose activities had long been of questionable value to the public, whom they had each in their own way made their ignorant slaves.

And finally, the art of the writer is likewise for use, not for his own pleasure, nor for the pleasure of his readers. It is functional. Therefore the method will vary whether it is for edification in sermons, for moral or political instruction in essays and pamphlets, or whether it is intended to sting and vex the world into a greater concern for political justice or the decencies and proprieties of social life. But it will always be short, clear, and concise, and directed to the immediate purpose. And there is a further requirement: if it is to be effective, it must never be dull. The task of the satirist is attack, and the weapons in his hands must be sharp and keen. His strokes must be brilliant and rapid. He must overcome his antagonist by cunning and surprise. He must lure him on by raillery and irony, and confound him by the brilliant flashing of wit. But above all he must preserve all his strength and force, avoiding unnecessary flourishes. His vision must be clear and his glance unwavering until the bout is over and his opponent is overcome. There is no place here for heroic boasting or laughter, for the wildness of anger and rage, for primitive outbursts of hatred and lust. He cannot cry to the gods to help him or rouse the spirits from the vasty deep. He cannot lift his eyes to the hills for help or wait for the right configuration of the stars to give him confidence. He has nothing but his own skill and his own knowledge of the weakness of his adversaries. His art is confined within very human boundaries, within the limits of his own age and social order and of the common idiom of his time.

BIBLIOGRAPHY

STUDIES OF SWIFT

Ricardo Quintana's *Mind and Art of Jonathan Swift* (1936; reissued 1953) remains the best general introduction to Swift and his work, though it should be supplemented by the same author's more recent *Swift: An Introduction* (1955), and also by Kathleen Williams' *Jonathan Swift and the Age of Compromise* (1958), an appraisal of the body of Swift's work.

Though still in progress, Irvin Ehrenpreis' *Swift: The Man, His Works, and the Age* (vol. I, 1962; vol. II, 1967) promises through its comprehensiveness to be the definitive modern biography. Henry Craik's two-volume *Life of Swift* (1882; rev. ed. 1894) is the best of the nineteenth-century biographies; still useful are Leslie Stephen's *Swift* (1882) and J. Churton Collins' *Jonathan Swift* (1893). The essays in Ehrenpreis' earlier *The Personality of Jonathan Swift* (1958) are biographical and critical in emphasis. J. Middleton Murry's *Jonathan Swift: A Critical Biography* (1954) is often suggestive, but persistently marred by a recklessness of interpretation; more extreme is Phyllis Greenacre's ingeniously earnest *Swift and Carroll: A Psychoanalytic Study of Two Lives* (1955). For an exciting corrective to Murry and Greenacre, see the essay on Swift in Norman O. Brown's *Life Against Death: The Psychoanalytic Meaning of History* (1959). Swift as cleric is studied by R. W. Jackson, *Jonathan Swift: Dean and Pastor* (1939) and—more narrowly, but meticulously—by Louis A. Landa, *Swift and the Church of Ireland* (1954). Swift's public standing is surveyed in Donald Berwick's *The Reputation of Jonathan Swift, 1781–1882* (1941); of related interest is Harold Williams' commentary on "Swift's Early Biographers," in *Pope and His Contemporaries: Essays Presented to George Sherburn* (1949).

Swift's satirical methods are analyzed from varying perspectives by John M. Bullitt, *Jonathan Swift and the Anatomy of Satire* (1953); Martin Price, *Swift's Rhetorical Art: A Study in Structure and Meaning* (1953); and Edward R. Rosenheim, *Swift and the Satirist's Art* (1963). Herbert Davis' *Satire of Jonathan Swift* (1947) consists of three essays on Swift's literary, political, and moral satire (the last exemplified by *Gulliver*). The various guises and points of view assumed by Swift in his writings are given close attention in William B. Ewald's *Masks of Swift* (1954); Chapters 10 and 11 treat Gulliver. C. A. Beaumont's *Swift's Classical Rhetoric* (1961) omits discussion of the *Travels*, but demonstrates Swift's employment of formal rhetorical modes. See also the substantial sections on Swift in Robert C. Elliott, *The Power of Satire* (1960); Martin Price, *To the Palace of Wisdom* (1964); and Ronald Paulson, *The Fictions of Satire* (1967).

The tercentenary of Swift's birth brought forth several collections of miscellaneous essays: *Fair Liberty Was All His Cry*, ed. A. Norman Jeffares

(1967); *Jonathan Swift, 1667–1967*, eds. Roger McHugh and Philip Edwards (1968); and, of particular note, *The World of Jonathan Swift*, ed. Brian Vickers (1968).

The standard bibliography, Louis A. Landa and James E. Tobin, *Jonathan Swift: A List of Critical Studies Published from 1895 to 1945* (1945), has been extended in time by the separate publication of James J. Stathis, A *Bibliography of Swift Studies, 1945–1965* (1967). Complementary to both listings is Milton Voigt's *Swift and the Twentieth Century* (1964), which provides a selective, but vigorously cogent, review and placement of modern scholarship.

STUDIES OF *Gulliver's Travels*

Barroll, J. Leeds. "Gulliver and the Struldbrugs." *PMLA*, LXXIII (March 1958), 43–50. Relates the Struldbrugs to a lengthy literary tradition in which old age, fear of death, and desire for immortality are typical subjects of satire and reflection.

Carnochan, W. B. *Lemuel Gulliver's Mirror for Man*. Berkeley and Los Angeles, 1968. Related essays with emphasis on the *Travels* in relation to modes of Augustan satire.

Case, Arthur E. *Four Essays on "Gulliver's Travels."* Princeton, 1945. The four essays deal with textual matters (defending the authority of the 1727 edition); matters of chronology and geography; personal and political references; and the general significance of the *Travels*.

Clubb, Merrel D. "The Criticism of Gulliver's 'Voyage to the Houyhnhnms,' 1726–1914." *Stanford Studies in Language and Literature* (1941), 203–232. A revealing survey of responses to Book IV, and of the images of Swift that accompanied them.

Dircks, Richard J. "Gulliver's Tragic Rationalism." *Criticism*, II (Spring 1960), 134–149. Gulliver in Book IV exemplifies the excesses of eighteenth-century rationalism.

Eddy, W. A. *Gulliver's Travels; A Critical Study*. Princeton, 1923. Though by no means exhaustive in its listings or treatment, this early study gives many of Swift's sources and indicates somewhat his manner of adapting them.

Ehrenpreis, Irvin. "The Meaning of Gulliver's Last Voyage." *A Review of English Literature*, III (July 1962), 18–38. Swift's satire, in pressing the reader to reassess his definition of man, relates back to seventeenth-century efforts to define the nature of man.

Elliott, Robert C. "Gulliver as Literary Artist." *A Journal of English Literary History*, XIX (March 1952), 49–63. This close analysis of point of view tests the premise that the *Travels* are the memoirs of a misanthropic sea captain, and implicitly raises the problem of whether the book can, in fact, be read as a novel.

Fink, Z. S. "Political Theory in *Gulliver's Travels*." *A Journal of English Literary History*, XIV (September 1947), 151–161. On Swift's political theory and its background (cf. A. E. Case, above).

Frye, Roland M. "Swift's Yahoos and the Christian Symbols for Sin." *Journal of the History of Ideas*, XV (April 1954), 201–217. The description of the Yahoos includes many of the physical traits associated with sin and depravity by religious writers of the sixteenth and seventeenth centuries.

Halewood, William H. and Marvin Levich. "Houyhnhnm Est Animal Rationale." *Journal of the History of Ideas*, XXVI (1965), 273–278. The Houyhnhnms represent "perfect and essential" man and therefore the sole "realistic" norm for evaluating human behavior.

Kallich, Martin. "Three Ways of Looking at a Horse: Jonathan Swift's 'Voyage to the Houyhnhnms' Again." *Criticism*, II (Spring 1960), 107–124. How the Houyhnhnms appear to a modern, to Gulliver, and—conjecturally—to Swift.

Kelling, Harold D. "*Gulliver's Travels:* A Comedy of Humours." *University of Toronto Quarterly*, XXI (July 1952), 362–375. Explores the ironic effects of Gulliver's partial point of view.

Moore, John B. "The Role of Gulliver." *Modern Philology*, XXV (May 1928), 469–480. An early but still useful exposition of Gulliver's character and its development through the four voyages.

Nicolson, Marjorie and Nora Mohler. "The Scientific Background of Swift's *Voyage to Laputa*." *Annals of Science*, II (July 1937), 299–334; reprinted in Nicolson, *Science and Imagination*, Ithaca, 1956. A detailed study of Swift's use of the *Transactions* of the Royal Society for his satire on science.

———. "Swift's 'Flying Island' in the *Voyage to Laputa*." *Annals of Science*, II (October 1937), 405–430. Swift's sources and his use of them.

Reichert, John F. "Plato, Swift, and the Houyhnhnms." *Philological Quarterly*, XLVII (April 1968), 179–192. A detailed comparison of *The Republic* and Book IV of the *Travels*.

Ross, John F. "The Final Comedy of Lemuel Gulliver." *Studies in the Comic*, University of California Publications in English, 1941, VIII, No. 2, 175–196. One of the earliest of modern studies to argue that Swift did not share Gulliver's final misanthropic view of man.

Sherburn, George. "Errors Concerning the Houyhnhnms." *Modern Philology*, LVI (November 1958), 92–97. An important counter statement to recent interpretations of Book IV which stress the limitations of the Houyhnhnms.

Stone, Edward. "Swift and the Horses: Misanthropy or Comedy?" *Modern Language Quarterly,* X (September 1949), 367–376. Book IV is essentially comic in vision, not misanthropic.

Suits, Conrad. "The Role of the Horses in 'A Voyage to the Houyhnhnms.'" *University of Toronto Quarterly,* XXXIV (January 1965), 118–132. Gulliver is entirely sane; mankind, not the Houyhnhnms, is the object of satire.

Sutherland, John H. "A Reconsideration of Gulliver's Third Voyage." *Studies in Philology,* LIV (January 1957), 45–52. Book III has an inner unity and also is integral to the total pattern of the *Travels.*

Taylor, Aline Mackenzie. "Sights and Monsters and Gulliver's *Voyage to Brobdingnag.*" *Tulane Studies in English,* VII (1957), 28–82. Important for what it suggests of Swift's use of contemporary material—in this instance, eighteenth-century equivalents of the freak show.

Taylor, Dick. "Gulliver's Pleasing Visions: Self-Deception as a Major Theme in *Gulliver's Travels.*" *Tulane Studies in English,* XII (1962), 7–61. A detailing of Gulliver's capacity for self-deception.

Tilton, John W. "*Gulliver's Travels* as a Work of Art." *Bucknell Review,* VIII (December 1959), 246–259. Affirms the *Travels* on three accounts: its structure is coherent, its point of view consistent, and its hero psychologically convincing.

Traugott, John. "A Voyage to Nowhere with Thomas More and Jonathan Swift: *Utopia* and *The Voyage to the Houyhnhnms.*" *The Sewanee Review,* LXIX (Autumn 1961), 534–565. To the extent that they ironically apprehended their Utopias, Swift and More could inhabit their "city of the mind" and yet participate in its corrupt counterpart.

Tuveson, Ernest. "Swift: The Dean as Satirist." *University of Toronto Quarterly,* XXII (July 1953), 368–375. Considering his religious commitment, Swift could not have offered the Houyhnhnms as his ideal.

Tyne, James L. "Gulliver's Maker and Gullibility." *Criticism,* VII (Spring 1965), 151–167. Relates the gullibility motif of the *Travels* to Swift's use of the same motif in his poetry.

Wedel, T. O. "On the Philosophical Background of *Gulliver's Travels.*" *Studies in Philology,* XXIII (October 1926), 434–450. The religious and philosophical context governing the *Travels.*

Williams, Harold. *The Text of Gulliver's Travels.* Cambridge, England,

1952. Written to justify the authority of the 1735 text (cf. A. E. Case above), this brief study brings together valuable information on the writing, publication, and revision of the *Travels*.

Williams, Kathleen. "Gulliver's Voyage to the Houyhnhnms." A *Journal of English Literary History*, XVIII (December 1951), 275–286. The Houyhnhnms represent an extreme impossible to emulate, and thus are an unlikely model for man.

Wilson, James R. "Swift's Alazon." *Studia Neophilologica*, XXX (1958), 153–164. Gulliver as imposter.

NORTON CRITICAL EDITIONS

AQUINAS *St. Thomas Aquinas on Politics and Ethics* translated and edited by Paul E. Sigmund
AUSTEN *Emma* edited by Stephen M. Parrish
AUSTEN *Pride and Prejudice* edited by Donald J. Gray
Beowulf (the Donaldson translation) edited by Joseph F. Tuso
BLAKE *Blake's Poetry and Designs* selected and edited by Mary Lynn Johnson and John E. Grant
BOCCACCIO *The Decameron* selected, translated, and edited by Mark Musa and Peter E. Bondanella
BRONTË, CHARLOTTE *Jane Eyre* edited by Richard J. Dunn *Second Edition*
BRONTË, EMILY *Wuthering Heights* edited by William M. Sale, Jr., and Richard Dunn *Third Edition*
BROWNING, ROBERT *Browning's Poetry* selected and edited by James F. Loucks
BYRON *Byron's Poetry* selected and edited by Frank D. McConnell
CARROLL *Alice in Wonderland* edited by Donald J. Gray *Second Edition*
CERVANTES *Don Quixote* (the Ormsby translation, revised) edited by Joseph R. Jones and Kenneth Douglas
CHAUCER *The Canterbury Tales: Nine Tales and the General Prologue* edited by V. A. Kolve and Glending Olson
CHEKHOV *Anton Chekhov's Plays* translated and edited by Eugene K. Bristow
CHEKHOV *Anton Chekhov's Short Stories* selected and edited by Ralph E. Matlaw
CHOPIN *The Awakening* edited by Margaret Culley
CLEMENS *Adventures of Huckleberry Finn* edited by Sculley Bradley, Richmond Croom Beatty, E. Hudson Long, and Thomas Cooley *Second Edition*
CLEMENS *A Connecticut Yankee in King Arthur's Court* edited by Allison R. Ensor
CLEMENS *Pudd'nhead Wilson and Those Extraordinary Twins* edited by Sidney E. Berger
CONRAD *Heart of Darkness* edited by Robert Kimbrough *Third Edition*
CONRAD *Lord Jim* edited by Thomas C. Moser
CONRAD *The Nigger of the "Narcissus"* edited by Robert Kimbrough
CRANE *Maggie: A Girl of the Streets* edited by Thomas A. Gullason
CRANE *The Red Badge of Courage* edited by Sculley Bradley, Richmond Croom Beatty, E. Hudson Long, and Donald Pizer *Second Edition*
DARWIN *Darwin* selected and edited by Philip Appleman *Second Edition*
DEFOE *A Journal of the Plague Year* edited by Paula R. Backscheider
DEFOE *Moll Flanders* edited by Edward Kelly
DEFOE *Robinson Crusoe* edited by Michael Shinagel
DICKENS *Bleak House* edited by George Ford and Sylvère Monod
DICKENS *David Copperfield* edited by Jerome H. Buckley
DICKENS *Hard Times* edited by George Ford and Sylvère Monod *Second Edition*
DONNE *John Donne's Poetry* selected and edited by Arthur L. Clements *Second Edition*
DOSTOEVSKY *The Brothers Karamazov* (the Garnett translation) edited by Ralph E. Matlaw
DOSTOEVSKY *Crime and Punishment* (the Coulson translation) edited by George Gibian *Third Edition*
DOSTOEVSKY *Notes from Underground* translated and edited by Michael R. Katz
DREISER *Sister Carrie* edited by Donald Pizer *Second Edition*
Eight Modern Plays edited by Anthony Caputi
ELIOT *Middlemarch* edited by Bert G. Hornback
ERASMUS *The Praise of Folly and Other Writings* translated and edited by Robert M. Adams
FAULKNER *The Sound and the Fury* edited by David Minter

FIELDING *Joseph Andrews with Shamela and Related Writings* edited by Homer Goldberg
FIELDING *Tom Jones* edited by Sheridan Baker
FLAUBERT *Madame Bovary* edited with a substantially new translation by Paul de Man
FRANKLIN *Benjamin Franklin's Autobiography* edited by J. A. Leo Lemay and P. M. Zall
GOETHE *Faust* translated by Walter Arndt, edited by Cyrus Hamlin
GOGOL *Dead Souls* (the Reavey translation) edited by George Gibian
HARDY *Far from the Madding Crowd* edited by Robert C. Schweik
HARDY *Jude the Obscure* edited by Norman Page
HARDY *The Mayor of Casterbridge* edited by James K. Robinson
HARDY *The Return of the Native* edited by James Gindin
HARDY *Tess of the d'Urbervilles* edited by Scott Elledge *Third Edition*
HAWTHORNE *The Blithedale Romance* edited by Seymour Gross and Rosalie Murphy
HAWTHORNE *The House of the Seven Gables* edited by Seymour Gross
HAWTHORNE *Nathaniel Hawthorne's Tales* edited by James McIntosh
HAWTHORNE *The Scarlet Letter* edited by Seymour Gross, Sculley Bradley, Richmond Croom Beatty, and E. Hudson Long *Third Edition*
HERBERT *George Herbert and the Seventeenth-Century Religious Poets* selected and edited by Mario A. DiCesare
HERODOTUS *The Histories* translated and selected by Walter E. Blanco, edited by Walter E. Blanco and Jennifer Roberts
HOMER *The Odyssey* translated and edited by Albert Cook
HOWELLS *The Rise of Silas Lapham* edited by Don L. Cook
IBSEN *The Wild Duck* translated and edited by Dounia B. Christiani
JAMES *The Ambassadors* edited by S. P. Rosenbaum
JAMES *The American* edited by James W. Tuttleton
JAMES *The Portrait of a Lady* edited by Robert D. Bamberg
JAMES *Tales of Henry James* edited by Christof Wegelin
JAMES *The Turn of the Screw* edited by Robert Kimbrough
JAMES *The Wings of the Dove* edited by J. Donald Crowley and Richard A. Hocks
JOHNSON *Ben Johnson and the Cavalier Poets* selected and edited by Hugh Maclean
JOHNSON *Ben Johnson's Plays and Masques* selected and edited by Robert M. Adams
MACHIAVELLI *The Prince* translated and edited by Robert M. Adams *Second Edition*
MALTHUS *An Essay on the Principle of Population* edited by Philip Appleman
MARX *The Communist Manifesto* edited by Frederic L. Bender
MELVILLE *The Confidence-Man* edited by Hershel Parker
MELVILLE *Moby-Dick* edited by Harrison Hayford and Hershel Parker
MEREDITH *The Egoist* edited by Robert M. Adams
Middle English Lyrics selected and edited by Maxwell S. Luria and Richard L. Hoffman
MILL *On Liberty* edited by David Spitz
MILTON *Paradise Lost* edited by Scott Elledge
Modern Irish Drama edited by John P. Harrington
MORE *Utopia* translated and edited by Robert M. Adams *Second Edition*
NEWMAN *Apologia Pro Vita Sua* edited by David J. DeLaura
NORRIS *McTeague* edited by Donald Pizer
Restoration and Eighteenth-Century Comedy edited by Scott McMillan
RICH *Adrienne Rich's Poetry* edited by Barbara Charlesworth Gelpi and Albert Gelpi
ROUSSEAU *Rousseau's Political Writings* edited by Alan Ritter and translated by Julia Conaway Bondanella

ST. PAUL *The Writings of St. Paul* edited by Wayne A. Meeks
SHAKESPEARE *Hamlet* edited by Cyrus Hoy *Second Edition*
SHAKESPEARE *Henry IV, Part I* edited by James L. Sanderson *Second Edition*
SHAW *Bernard Shaw's Plays* edited by Warren Sylvester Smith
SHELLEY *Shelley's Poetry and Prose* selected and edited by Donald H. Reiman and Sharon B. Power
SMOLLETT *Humphry Clinker* edited by James L. Thorson
SOPHOCLES *Oedipus Tyrannus* translated and edited by Luci Berkowitz and Theodore F. Brunner
SPENSER *Edmund Spenser's Poetry* selected and edited by Hugh Maclean *Second Edition*
STENDHAL *Red and Black* translated and edited by Robert M. Adams
STERNE *Tristram Shandy* edited by Howard Anderson
SWIFT *Gulliver's Travels* edited by Robert A. Greenberg *Second Edition*
SWIFT *The Writings of Jonathon Swift* edited by Robert A. Greenberg and William B. Piper
TENNYSON *In Memoriam* edited by Robert H. Ross
TENNYSON *Tennyson's Poetry* selected and edited by Robert W. Hill, Jr.
THOREAU *Walden and Resistance to Civil Government* edited by William Rossi *Second Edition*
TOLSTOY *Anna Karenina* (the Maude translation) edited by George Gibian
TOLSTOY *Tolstoy's Short Fiction* edited and with revised translations by Michael R. Katz
TOLSTOY *War and Peace* (the Maude translation) edited by George Gibian
TOOMER *Cane* edited by Darwin T. Turner
TURGENEV *Fathers and Sons* edited and with a thoroughly revised translation by Ralph E. Matlaw *Second Edition*
VOLTAIRE *Candide* translated and edited by Robert M. Adams *Second Edition*
WATSON *The Double Helix: A Personal Account of the Discovery of the Structure of DNA* edited by Gunther S. Stent
WHARTON *The House of Mirth* edited by Elizabeth Ammons
WHITMAN *Leaves of Grass* edited by Sculley Bradley and Harold W. Blodgett
WILDE *The Picture of Dorian Gray* edited by Donald L. Lawler
WOLLSTONECRAFT *A Vindication of the Rights of Woman* edited by Carol H. Poston *Second Edition*
WORDSWORTH *The Prelude: 1799, 1805, 1850* edited by Jonathan Wordsworth, M. H. Abrams, and Stephen Gill